The Prime M

William Henry Giles Kingston

Alpha Editions

This edition published in 2024

ISBN 9789362095879

Design and Setting By
Alpha Editions
www.alphaedis.com
Email - info@alphaedis.com

As per information held with us this book is in Public Domain.
This book is a reproduction of an important historical work.
Alpha Editions uses the best technology to reproduce historical work
in the same manner it was first published to preserve its original nature.
Any marks or number seen are left intentionally to preserve.

Contents

"The Prime Minister" .... - 1 -

Volume One—Chapter One. .... - 5 -

Volume One—Chapter Two. .... - 17 -

Volume One—Chapter Three. .... - 32 -

Volume One—Chapter Four. .... - 45 -

Volume One—Chapter Five. .... - 56 -

Volume One—Chapter Six. .... - 71 -

Volume One—Chapter Seven. .... - 83 -

Volume One—Chapter Eight. .... - 93 -

Volume One—Chapter Nine. .... - 105 -

Volume One—Chapter Ten. .... - 119 -

Volume One—Chapter Eleven. .... - 131 -

Volume One—Chapter Twelve. .... - 145 -

Volume Two—Chapter One. .... - 159 -

Volume Two—Chapter Two. .... - 171 -

Volume Two—Chapter Three. .... - 187 -

Volume Two—Chapter Four. .... - 201 -

Volume Two—Chapter Five. .... - 211 -

Volume Two—Chapter Six. .... - 219 -

Volume Two—Chapter Seven. .... - 223 -

Volume Two—Chapter Eight. .... - 229 -

Volume Two—Chapter Nine. .... - 237 -

Volume Two—Chapter Ten. .... - 243 -

Volume Two—Chapter Eleven. .... - 249 -

Volume Two—Chapter Twelve. .... - 257 -

Volume Two—Chapter Thirteen. .... - 265 -

Volume Two—Chapter Fourteen. .... - 270 -

Volume Two—Chapter Fifteen. .... - 275 -

Volume Two—Chapter Sixteen. .... - 284 -

Volume Two—Chapter Seventeen. .... - 291 -

Volume Two—Chapter Eighteen. .... - 300 -

Volume Two—Chapter Nineteen. .... - 311 -

Volume Two—Chapter Twenty. .... - 317 -

Volume Two—Chapter Twenty One. .... - 321 -

Volume Three—Chapter One. .... - 329 -

Volume Three—Chapter Two. .... - 335 -

Volume Three—Chapter Three. .... - 344 -

Volume Three—Chapter Four. .... - 356 -

Volume Three—Chapter Five. .... - 362 -

Volume Three—Chapter Six. .... - 370 -

Volume Three—Chapter Seven.	- 379 -
Volume Three—Chapter Eight.	- 392 -
Volume Three—Chapter Nine.	- 400 -
Volume Three—Chapter Ten.	- 409 -
Volume Three—Chapter Eleven.	- 418 -
Volume Three—Chapter Twelve.	- 424 -
Volume Three—Chapter Thirteen.	- 433 -
Volume Three—Chapter Fourteen.	- 438 -
Volume Three—Chapter Fifteen.	- 447 -
Volume Three—Chapter Sixteen.	- 457 -
Volume Three—Chapter Seventeen.	- 472 -
Volume Three—Chapter Eighteen.	- 480 -
Volume Three—Chapter Nineteen.	- 491 -
Volume Three—Chapter Twenty.	- 500 -
Volume Three—Chapter Twenty One.	- 507 -
Volume Three—Chapter Twenty Two.	- 511 -

"The Prime Minister"

Having resolved to employ myself, during a prolonged residence in Portugal, in writing some work of fiction on that country, it struck me that the Times of the Marquis of Pombal would afford a good subject, untouched, as it is, by any other author. For a considerable time I delayed commencing my undertaking, almost in despair of finding the necessary materials. I wrote frequently to Lisbon to procure information, and mentioned my purpose to several Portuguese friends, who, at length, put at my disposal all the documents they possess relating to the private history of their families. From them I have composed the following work.

I enjoyed, also, free access to the public Library at Oporto, a magnificent establishment, containing many thousand volumes, in all languages. Nor must I omit to mention the courteous attention I received from Senhor Gandra, the chief Librarian, in aiding me in my search for the works I required. Here I found several valuable volumes, in French and Italian, relating to the administration of the Marquis of Pombal, and the intrigues of the Jesuits; and some, in Portuguese, giving an account of the earthquake.

The Library is established in a large building, formerly the Convent of S. Lazaro, the principal room vying in size and elegance with any of which the first cities in Europe can boast. There are, also, numerous other apartments, occupying the entire floor of the edifice, now crowded with books, which it will take many years to arrange.

My history commences in the summer of 1755, the year of the great earthquake of Lisbon, some time before which period, the weak, bigoted, and profligate King John the Fifth of Portugal, after allowing his country to sink into a state bordering on ruin, had finished his pernicious reign, and worthless life, being succeeded by his son, Joseph the First.

Though in the character of Joseph there appears to have been, in some respects, but a slight improvement over that of his father, he was certainly less superstitious; while he possessed the valuable quality of appreciating the talents of others, which caused him to select as his adviser, Sebastiaö Joseph de Carvalho, afterwards created Marquis of Pombal, one of the most energetic men his country has ever produced. Carvalho was now at the head of the administration, and had begun that system of reform, (which ended but with his fall from power,) although he had not then succeeded in gaining that implicit confidence of his sovereign which he afterwards possessed. For the particulars of the history and state of the country antecedent to the time I speak of, I refer my readers to the introduction to the "Memoirs of Pombal," lately published, written by the Secretary to the Marquis of Saldanha, Mr Smith, though in many points I differ from that gentleman in the view he takes of the great Minister's character and actions.

The Marquis of Saldanha is a descendant of Pombal; and his Secretary has naturally been biassed in favour of his patron's ancestor. The only book he appears to have consulted, besides the documents in the State Paper Office, is that above-mentioned, which I have before me, in Portuguese, though written originally in French, by an admirer of the Minister. Mr Smith's work did not reach me at Oporto, until my own manuscript had been forwarded to England; which circumstance I mention, to exonerate myself from any appearance of ingratitude in speaking thus of a person of whose labours I might be supposed to have taken advantage. When any similarity appears, we have drawn from the same source.

To excuse the barbarous executions of some of the first nobility in Portugal, Mr Smith says, that some of equal cruelty have taken place in France and Germany. To show that the complaints made by the victims of the Minister's iron policy, who crowded the prisons, were unjust, he cites a memoir, in manuscript, written in prison, by the unfortunate Marquis d'Alorna, who, he says, makes querulous complaints of not having his linen changed sufficiently often, though he had frequent intercourse with his family.

I have perused an exact copy of the MS. Mr Smith has seen, if not the identical one. In it, the unhappy Marquis speaks indignantly of the dark, narrow, and damp cell which was his abode in the Junguiera prison for many years, he being scarcely supplied with the common necessaries of life, while the Marchioness was confined in some other equally wretched place, separated from her children, who were distributed in different convents. The husband states that he received one letter from his wife, written with her left hand, she having lost the use of her right side from a rheumatic complaint, brought on by the dampness of her lodging. A year or so afterwards another reached him, written by holding the pen in her mouth, she having then lost the use of both her hands. This was the sort of free intercourse the Minister allowed, and, it must be remembered, neither were found guilty of any crime. The Marquis mentions the history of many of his fellow-prisoners, several of whom died in prison; and, he states, after some years' confinement, by means of bribes, they were able to obtain some communication with their friends from without. In the body of the work will be found many details from the MSS. I have spoken of.

Mr Smith does not inform his readers, when mentioning the outbreak at Oporto, in consequence of the formation of the obnoxious Wine Company, that not only the wine-sellers rose up in arms, but that the wine-growers, who, it was pretended, were to be benefited, marched into Oporto, and demanded its abolition; nor that, when the troops arrived from Lisbon to quell the revolt, the city was given up to their unbridled license, the chief magistrate and sixteen principal citizens having been executed, while the prisons were crowded with others.

Once established, with its blood-stained charter, a post in the Company was considered one of the most valuable rewards the Minister could bestow for services performed for him, his own immense fortune having been acquired, indirectly, through that very Company. Mr Smith affirms that the wealth to which the Minister's eldest son succeeded was left him by various members of his family; but, as his family were universally known to be poor, such it is difficult to believe was the case. Mr Beckford, in his Diary in Portugal, laughs at the young Count, for having endeavoured, during the whole course of a morning visit, to persuade him that his father had never attempted to amass a fortune. Pombal, on retiring from office, left the treasury rich; but that is no proof that he had not taken care to supply his own chests by any means which he considered justifiable. One can scarcely wonder at his acting as was so generally the custom.

The aim of these Memoirs of Pombal is to throw a halo of glory over his life and actions, of which he was undeserving. The Minister is compared in them, as he was fond of comparing himself, to Sully. I do not make these observations unjustly to depreciate this work; but that I may not be accused of unfairly portraying a man whose really great qualities I duly appreciate; nor have I described him as performing one action that is not well authenticated. I am not a greater friend to the system of the Jesuits than is Mr Smith; but do not wish to abuse them for the sake of exhibiting the Minister in brighter colours.

Pombal, like Napoleon, was never prevented from doing what he considered necessary to forward his own views either political or private, by any laws, human or divine. His motto was, *Quid volo quid jubeo.*

March, 1845.

Volume One—Chapter One.

Joyous and sparkling waves were leaping up from the deep blue expanse of the vast Atlantic, as if to welcome a gallant vessel, which glided rapidly onward in all the pride of beauty. Her broad spread of white canvass, extended alow and aloft, shining brightly in the sunbeams; she looked like a graceful swan, a being of life and instinct, floating on the waste of waters, her head turned towards the coast of fair Lusitania; her bourne, from which she was as yet far distant, being the majestic Tagus. A fresh summer breeze filled her swelling sails, now favouring her like friendship in prosperity, but which would, probably, when the sun sank beneath the ocean, fall away, as friends too often do from those whose sun has set in adversity. A broad white flag emblazoned with the arms of Portugal, floating from her peak, and the long pendants which fluttered from her mastheads, showed that she belonged to the royal navy of that country; and, by the number of guns she carried, she appeared to be a well-armed vessel of her class; but the abundance of gilding and bright paint with which she was in every part decorated, betokened her to be intended more for show or pleasure, than for the rough work of actual service. She was a ship very similar to what we now call a corvette, having a single battery of long heavy guns, and a high-raised deck at the aftermost part, on which was placed an armament of small brass pieces and swivel-guns, with a few pieces of the same calibre on her topgallant-forecastle; so that, although her purposes might in general have been peaceful, she was, if properly manoeuvred, fully able to make a stout resistance against any vessel under the class of a large frigate.

Several persons were walking the deck, one of whom, by the air of undisputed authority which sat well upon him, as he paced the starboard side, was evidently the commander; and near him appeared a young and handsome man in the costume of a civilian; while the rest of the party, who kept respectfully on the opposite side of the ship, were composed of the lieutenants and other officers belonging to her.

The young man had for some time been standing on the break of the poop, leaning over the rail, and eagerly looking out in the direction towards which the ship was bending her course; his thoughts, perhaps, far outstripping his own tardy progress, and rejoicing in the happiness of again meeting parents, kindred, or friends; or it may have been, that some feelings yet more tender occupied his bosom. He was aroused from his reveries, whatever might have been their tenour, by a no very gentle touch on the back; and, turning round, he beheld the captain of the ship. "What, my young friend!" said the latter, in a clear, cheerful tone of voice, "not yet tired of gazing on the dark blue line of the horizon, as if you expected to see the shores of Lusitania leap out of the water by magic, and would fain not miss the first view of our loved home? Well! well! Such is youth, always eager and enthusiastic, fancying itself near its object, though as yet far distant, and, like a young puppy, or a baby, unable to measure distances, till, by constant practice, and by many a fall, it has learned to discover the true situations of objects."

The speaker was a man who had somewhat passed the meridian of life, his hair already turning grey, and his good-natured, well-formed features considerably furrowed and bronzed by exposure to hot climes and stormy weather.

"What, Senhor Pinto, shall we not see the land to-day?" inquired the youth, in a tone of disappointment. "I thought we were close to it, and have been looking out for it all the morning."

"So I have observed," answered the Captain, "but was unwilling to break down unnecessarily all those castles in the air which I saw you so busily occupied in building; however, I must now tell you that, from the thick weather and fogs which have for so many days attended us, we are rather out of our reckoning; and it was early this morning we discovered, by an observation, that we are yet considerably to the northward of our latitude."

"How tantalising!" returned the youth. "I had hoped that by this hour to-morrow we should have been safely moored in the Tagus."

"Hope! Ah, 'tis a feeling in which youth may sometimes indulge with advantage, as it oft carries him through difficulties and disappointments, on his first setting out on the voyage of life, which might otherwise have made him turn back into harbour; but it often, too, proves a sad *ignis fatuus*, and, like a false light to the mariner, leads him on to quicksands and rocks, where it leaves him in the lurch. Now, an old sailor like myself is not to be deceived; and it is long since I gave up hoping; consequently, I am never led astray by such false lights. I find the surest way of being contented is, never to expect anything, and I then can never be disappointed, but receive as a Godsend, and be thankful for, each piece of luck that falls in my way. That is what I call philosophy."

"But, my dear sir!" returned the other, with animation, "you thus stifle one of the most noble, the most glorious principles of our nature, the very mainspring of our actions, without which we should weakly yield to the first blast of misfortune which assailed us; it supports the lover in his long absence from his mistress, the prisoner in his dungeon, the mother watching o'er her child, the sick man on his bed of suffering: 'twas hope which a kind Heaven bestowed on man when sin and death were introduced into the world, to prevent his sinking into abject dejection. Take all else from me, but teach me not to cease to hope."

"Nay, nay, my dear Don Luis, you misunderstand me; I would not deprive you of that which you so warmly cherish on any account," returned Captain Pinto; "I wish merely to warn you that the object of your hopes may be like one of those beautiful islands we used to hear of, covered with glittering temples and palaces of crystal, but with which no cruiser ever came up, though some have sailed half round the globe, thinking each day they must drop an anchor in one of their tempting harbours. I've seen such sights in my time, but I never altered my course for them, and never intend to do so."

"Ah, you can never, then, have experienced the glowing, eager sensation of hope almost accomplished," exclaimed Don Luis earnestly, "when a few more days or hours will place the longed-for object within your power."

"Pardon me, but I have though," interrupted Captain Pinto; "but that was years ago, and I then found that the picture I had conjured up always far surpassed the reality. You forget that I too was once young, and experienced all the sensations in which you now rejoice; but it is age which has taught me how fallacious they are, and I can no more be deceived by them. Now, I dare say you, in your heart, think me a sullen old fellow, who delights in conjuring up in the horizon dark clouds, to overcast the bright blue sky under which you bask; but you must remember I am an old seaman, who have spent the best half of a century on the troubled ocean in all seas and climes, and that, like a good master, I would teach you to be prepared for the tempests and rough seas you must encounter, and to avoid the hidden rocks and sandbanks which lie in your course."

"Thanks, thanks, my good sir; I understand your motives," answered Don Luis; "but I confess that I would rather you should not now darken my horizon with either false or real clouds: it is too temptingly bright and beautiful not to wish it so to remain."

"Well, I will give you no more lessons to-day," answered Captain Pinto; "you have had as much as you can bear at one time; for I fear that you are no very apt scholar. But to show you the advantage of not hoping and fretting yourself to death for what there is little chance of obtaining, here am I, upwards of fifty, a hale hearty fellow, though I have only just now got the command of this little toy of a nutshell, with which I am as contented as if I was captain of a line-of-battle ship, and think myself very fortunate to have her; for if that great man Sebastiaö Jozé de Carvalho had not become one of the King's ministers, I should still have been an humble second lieutenant, and might have continued so to the end of my days. How, indeed, could I expect to rise in times of peace, with no friends at Court, no money to bribe, and though I am noble," the old man drew himself up proudly as he spoke,—"for otherwise I should not presume to be on such intimate terms with you, Senhor Don Luis,—yet, I am not, I confess, of the Puritano families, who have hitherto monopolised everything, but Carvalho is biassed by no such considerations; he is no friend to the Puritanos; he selects men for their merit alone, and some of that he may, I flatter myself, have discovered in me; at all events, I may boast he knew I would serve my country faithfully."

"Of that I have no doubt, my friend," answered Don Luis, who had been listening to the old officer's long speech with some impatience, which, however, he endeavoured to conceal. "But can you tell me *how* soon we shall reach the Tagus?"

"Ah, there again, ever anxious for the morrow? Ha, ha! there is some greater magnetic attraction drawing your soul towards Lisbon, beyond the mere natural wish of embracing your parents, brothers, sisters, uncles, aunts, a whole host of cousins, and other relations and friends; for people don't mind deferring that pleasure for a few days. Come, come, there is some fair lady in the case. I know it. Confess, confess I have hit it. Donna Theresa d'Alorna, for instance; the beauty of Portugal; the pride of the province; the toast of Lisbon; at whose feet kneel daily all the gay and gallant youths of the country to do homage to her charms? 'Tis said that even the king himself has become captive to her beauty, though that is only whispered; but the lady is scornful, it seems, and treats all alike with cruelty and disdain. There is no calculating the mischief she has committed: half-a-score of duels have been fought about her; one youth drowned himself in the Tagus, but was fished up before he was quite dead, the water having cooled his love; another was going to hang himself, but prudently informed a venerable aunt of his intention, who prevented him; and a third put a pistol to his head, but the weapon, like his skull, having no contents, he escaped destruction. I do not know what you will do when you have gazed on her charms; but I trust that if she treats you as she has other admirers, you will bring some of your hope into play, and seek a kinder mistress."

While Captain Pinto was speaking, the countenance of the youth alternately betrayed anxiety, fear, and anger; but as no expression had been uttered at which he could possibly cavil, he was obliged to listen in silence to a discourse, every word of which was, to his sensitive feelings, like vinegar poured on a wound. His torturer kept his eye fixed on him all the time, watching each movement of his features as a skilful surgeon feels the pulse of his patient during a painful operation. "Yes, your unconquerable hope will stand you in good stead," he proceeded to say. "And yet the love of Donna Theresa were, by all accounts, a proud thing to boast of—more valued from the difficulty of obtaining it."

"How know you that I love her?" exclaimed Don Luis, suddenly: "I thought that secret hidden within my own bosom."

"Think you that you could have sailed so many days with me, Jozé Pinto, and I not discover the inmost secrets of your soul? Why, every scrap of paper with which the cabin has been strewed, covered with rhymes, has had her name inscribed on it; in your dreams, as you swung in your cot, even during the fiercest gale, you spoke but of her. I have heard it whispered in the calm night breeze which brought back your sighs, and I'll wager 'tis graven indelibly on every mast of my ship."

"You treat me severely, Captain Pinto," answered Don Luis. "Although I may in my sleep have uttered that name so dear to me, which I have always held sacred, for I will not deny my affection; and though I may have written it on some paper which has escaped from my portfolio, yet I have not converted your masts into shrines sacred to love: they are not honoured by being marked with that name."

"Well, then, I will confess I was but trying you," answered Captain Pinto; "I will acquit you of ever allowing even a scrap of paper with Donna Theresa's name on it to escape from your portfolio, or of ever having uttered it, to my knowledge, in your dreams, for I am not addicted to remaining awake when once I turn into my cot; indeed I knew not the lady of your affections till this minute, when I, by hazard, mentioned her name, and you owned your secret, though I long ago discovered your heart was not as free as I could wish it; but, seriously speaking, my young friend, I would have you think earnestly of what I have said, though my words sounded jokingly, and it may prove a valuable lesson to you. I will not breathe a word against Donna Theresa in particular; but remember numbers surround her, offering up daily incense of sighs and flattery, so that it were madness to confide too much in her constancy, or that of any woman so situated, and two years work great changes in the feelings of all. Come now, try to suppose her heartless and inconstant: 'tis better than being too sanguine; and I should grieve to see your heart breaking through disappointed love."

"To believe her heartless is impossible," exclaimed Don Luis. "Though, on my word, you seem anxious to shake my confidence in her sex in general."

"O, no," answered the Captain, laughing, or rather, it might be said, chuckling: "some are perfect angels—till you know them."

Don Luis did not answer, though he could scarce avoid being angry with his friend for his preventive cauterisation, although the wound did not smart the less severely for its being well intended; and at that moment some necessary duty of the ship called Captain Pinto from his side, who, as he left him, muttered, "Poor youth, poor youth, if he persist in trusting to the love of such an one as Donna Theresa, he will be sadly disappointed!" Don Luis was left to pursue undisturbed the no very pleasant meditations to which his late conversation had given rise.

That our readers may no longer be in suspense as to whence the ship we have described came, we may inform them that she was a man-of-war, belonging to the crown of Portugal, though fitted up as a yacht; that she was now returning from the shores of England, whither she had conveyed an ambassador from His Most Faithful Majesty to the Court of London, and that the young Don Luis d'Almeida, who had, for some time past, been travelling in that country, after having made the tour of Europe, had taken advantage of the opportunity of returning in her to his native land.

The father of Don Luis, the Conde d'Almeida, was a noble of the purest blood, and one of the most ancient families of Portugal; but their fortune had been much reduced through the improvidence of some of the latter possessors of the title, their honour preventing them from employing any of those unjust, or at best doubtful means which others of their rank did not scruple to use to increase their wealth, and their pride forbidding them to engage in any mercantile speculations, a prejudice less general in the present day than at that time, and one above which even the Conde d'Almeida could not be expected to rise.

The Count had several brothers, who died childless; the youngest, and by far the most talented, having during the former reign been banished, for some political crime it was said, when the ship which conveyed the young and audacious advocate of civil and religious liberty was, with all her crew, overwhelmed by the waves, "a just punishment, doubtless, for his daring and impiety," observed the pious King John's confessor, when the news was brought home: there was also one sister, who had married the Marquis d'Alorna, and, dying young, left her only child without a mother's fostering care and protection, the lovely Donna Theresa, who had, as we have seen, won the early affections of her cousin, Don Luis.

The Count, a man of an enlightened mind, had devoted himself to the education of his only son, who had imbibed from him all his sentiments of honour and virtue, with the same true pride of ancestry which made him incapable of committing any deed derogatory to the dignity of his lofty birth. Such was the young noble we have introduced to our readers, firm in principle, enthusiastic in temperament, eager in pursuit of his aims, with a candour and want of suspicion in his manner which appeared to arise from ignorance of the world, but was rather the result of the secluded and strict system of education he had undergone, which had kept him unacquainted with the vices of society till his principles had been formed to guard against them, nor had it prevented him from acquiring a clear insight into the characters of men, when once he began his career amongst them. The plan pursued in his education we deem, in most cases, to be a very dangerous one, when a young mind is plunged unprepared to combat with the follies and vices of the world; but he, fortunately, at once became disgusted with them, and learned to dread their glittering temptations, as the mariner does the light sparkling froth which, on the calm blue sea, plays over the hidden sandbank. In person he was of good height, and well-formed; of the most polished and graceful address; his bright dark eye sparkling with animation, or flashing with anger; his voice of rich and clear melody, so that under no disguise could he have appeared otherwise than a gentleman.

Captain Pinto has already, in a few words, given as much of his own history as we are acquainted with, and though his personal appearance had not the stamp of nobility impressed on it, his features betokened a kind disposition, (for we are great physiognomists,) notwithstanding that he had lately given utterance to some observations which sounded rather sour and morose; but he had spoken with the best intentions, thinking that some advice was necessary to check the too ardent hopes of his young friend, and having his reasons perhaps for supposing he might be deceived. But it is high time that we should return to our narrative.

The sails were now trimmed to meet a slight variation in the wind, which blew less steadily than in the morning, and that duty being completed, the captain resumed his walk by the side of Don Luis, whose feelings of annoyance had by this time completely subsided; indeed, to his generous disposition, it was impossible to continue angry any length of time, with one who evidently took a warm interest in his welfare. "Now, my young friend," observed the worthy commander, after taking several turns in silence, "you will soon be convinced of the advantage of being prepared for disappointment," at the same time pointing to some small dark clouds rising right ahead from the horizon. "Look at those black heralds of strife and tumult, not of the puny strife of men, but of the majestic rage and fury of the elements. A few minutes ago you were felicitating yourself in the fond anticipations of meeting those dear to you before to-morrow has closed, or at the furthest on the following day, and with the fair fresh breeze and smooth sea we were enjoying, you had every reason for your hopes; and now behold how suddenly they may be blasted; for if an old seaman's prognostications are not false, we shall have before long a stiff gale directly in our teeth, and then, farewell to our friends in Lisbon for a week at the shortest calculation! That is no gentle summer gale brewing away to the south-east. See how quickly the clouds gather, and what a thick heavy bank they form, resting like a high land on the sea."

"I should be ungrateful if I were to grumble at the prospect of remaining a week or so longer under your kind care," returned Don Luis; "but I confess that I did hope to arrive in a much shorter period at Lisbon."

"I know you did, I know you did," said the Captain. "Very natural it was for you to do so; and I should think that, long ere this, you must have become heartily tired of the society of an old fellow like myself,—though I have seen something to talk about in my ramblings through the world."

Don Luis, with sincerity, protested that he had passed the time on board most agreeably.

"Well, I trust you have not found me wanting in hospitality, at all events," continued the old officer, "though you have full right to complain of our long voyage; but let me tell you, we have had, for this time of the year, most unusual weather; first, the heavy gales we experienced; then the thick heavy fogs, which hung like funereal palls over the face of the deep; next the smooth sea and sudden favourable breeze, which seems, however, inclined to play us a jade's trick, and leave us in the lurch; and now those threatening clouds away there to the south-east. That is not the quarter from whence gales generally spring up off this coast; but if those clouds don't hold a very large capful of wind, I am very much mistaken. During the whole course of my life I never met such unnatural weather, and I don't like the look of it. Depend on it there's something strange going to happen, though I would not say so to the crew, or to the women, if we had any on board, and thank Heaven we have not."

The officer who had charge of the navigation of the ship, who in the English service is called the master, more correctly denominated by the Portuguese the pilot, at that moment came up to the captain, taking off his hat respectfully, as he pointed out the dark clouds in the horizon. "We shall have a gale before long, Senhor Captain," said the veteran, who was a fine specimen of the sailor of times long, alas! passed by in the annals of Portugal, during her palmy days of naval supremacy. "'Twill be a breeze which will make us look sharp after our sticks. Shall we begin to get in some of our light canvass; for I like not the look of the weather. There is a storm out there, muttering ugly threats, from which 'twere wiser to take warning."

"You are right, Senhor Nunez," answered the Captain. "Those are signs of a gale, or we have been to sea for a century between us to very little purpose; but there is no immediate necessity to shorten sail, so we may as well not lose the advantage of the breeze, while it lasts, to make as much way good in our voyage as we can; for we shall probably, before long, be blown far enough from our course to weary us with beating up to our port once more."

"As you think fit, Senhor, but it will be down on us without much further warning," observed the pilot, as he kept his glance towards the south-east.

The officers continued walking the deck, but their conversation was short and disjointed; their eyes constantly glancing round the horizon in search of further signs of the coming storm; yet, notwithstanding the prognostications of the commander and the pilot, the breeze held tolerably steady, only shifting now and then half a point or so, which required a corresponding attention in trimming sails, so as not to deviate from their course.

"Ah, Captain Pinto," exclaimed Don Luis, with a smile on his lips, "I trust that this once, at least, my hopes rather than your forebodings may be realised; see, the breeze is still our friend, nor does it seem inclined to desert us, and perhaps, after all our fears, yonder mass may prove but a fog bank, through which we may quickly cleave our way."

"Still sanguine, and expecting better fortune than will probably fall to our lot? But, although your hopes are bright, I am not to be deceived by any treacherous appearances. Even while you have been speaking the breeze has fallen; look over the side, and observe the ship makes much less way through the water than she did a few minutes ago; and see her wake, for how short a distance does the foamy line extend ere the waves obliterate all signs of it! Mark me, the breeze, like hollow friends, will soon desert us. Ah! said I not true? The words have scarcely passed my lips ere my predictions are fulfilled."

As he spoke, the sails gave one loud flap against the mast, though they again bulged out as the last effort of the dying breeze once more filled them. In a moment the commander was all life and animation. "In all studding sails, Senhor Alvez," he shouted to his first lieutenant. "They are like officious friends, and do us more harm than benefit."

"All hands, shorten sail," was echoed through the ship, as the sailors sprung with alacrity on deck.

"Be quick, my men, be quick! There's no time to lose!—Man your downhauls!—Let fly your gear!" shouted the Captain, through his speaking-trumpet; and in a minute the light, airy canvass, before extended like wings on each side of the larger sails, was taken into the tops, or hauled down on deck. "Hand the royals, Senhor Alvez," cried the commander again. "Furl topgallant-sails, and down with the royal and topgallant-yards!" he quickly added. "We may as well relieve the craft of all top-hamper: she'll dance all the lighter for it."

These orders were quickly accomplished by a ready and active crew, who sprung aloft with all the activity, and somewhat of the chattering, of monkeys; for, in those times, the strict discipline and regularity of the present day were not observed in any service, and silence was not considered a necessary part of duty. Scarcely had the men returned on deck, when they were again ordered aloft, although it had now fallen a complete calm, the vessel rolling on the long smooth swell which seemed to rise without any impelling power, like the breathing of some vast giant in his sleep. The sun, now sinking rapidly in the ocean, still shone with dazzling brightness, from a dark blue sky yet unclouded in that part of the heavens in which his course lay. The sails flapped lazily against the masts, with a dull sound like a distant cannonade, the timbers creaked, and the water splashed, as she slowly rolled from side to side, the bubbles of foam sparkling brightly around the black and shining wales.

"Hand the courses—brail up the mizen!" suddenly shouted the Captain; for in those days the last-mentioned sail was carried,—a large unwieldy latteen-sail, with a long heavy yard, requiring a strong force of the crew to hand, instead of that which we now call a spanker. After much hauling and labour, the order was accomplished. "Close reef and furl the topsails!" he added; "we will show naked sticks to yonder blast, and may then laugh at its efforts! There is no use running the chance of having our canvass blown out of the bolt-ropes."

In a few minutes the towering pillar of canvass had disappeared; and the ship, under bare poles, rocked like a cradle on the ocean, without advancing an inch in her course; the helm, too, having lost all its guiding power, her head moved slowly about, as if uncertain of its way. The atmosphere, which in the morning had been so brisk and light, became loaded and oppressive to the feelings; but as yet no breath even of the adverse blast was felt. A thick haze was collecting round the disk of the sun, which had now assumed an angry, fiery hue,—its size many times increased from its ordinary appearance; and, as it sank into the ocean, the fierce glowing blaze of the western sky, tinged with its light the borders of the approaching mass of clouds.

"Seldom have I seen the sun set in so hot a passion," observed the Captain to Don Luis. "He does it in kindness, however, to warn us that we shall be wishing for his light again before he can possibly appear to aid us."

Onward came the frowning mass of clouds, with their light, fiery *avant couriers*; and, as the shades of night were fast throwing a dark mantle over the ocean, suddenly, without a moment's warning, a fierce squall struck the ship, turning her head rapidly round, the water hissing and foaming about her bows. For a few moments again all was calm,—the angry breath, which had blown, seeming but some sudden ebullition of the spirit of the tempest, and to have passed in forgetfulness away. Yet treachery lurked beneath that tranquil air. Down came the blast with no second notice—strong and furious—driving onward before it the light and buoyant corvette. Away she flew over the milk-white ocean, like a sea-bird in search of its finny prey, now dipping her head into the trough of the fast-rising sea, then again ascending, and shaking it, to free herself from the sheets of spray which dashed around her.

"You see, my friend," said Captain Pinto, touching Don Luis on the arm, "that my forebodings, as you called them, have turned out truer than your hopes. A few hours ago you were looking out ahead for land, and now how things have changed! There lies the land right over the taffrail, or a little on the larboard-quarter; for this gale has come from the south east, and here are we doomed to beat about, like the Flying Dutchman, before our port, without a chance of reaching it. But patience! it is a fine wind for outward-bound ships, and we must be content to be the sufferers." He then beckoned the pilot to his side. "What say you, Senhor Nunez, shall we heave the ship to? There is no use running away from our course."

"We may heave to the ship, if we like," replied the old seaman; "but I much doubt if we have any canvass on board to keep her there: she would bear it if we made sail; though I suspect the wind would soon take it in for us. If I might advise, we will run on before it while it lasts; for I do not think, by the way it came on, it will hold long; and then there will be less risk of damaging the ship."

"Let it be so, Senhor Nunez," answered the Captain. "Such, also, is my opinion. A gale like this is not to be played with, if one would keep one's gear in condition."

The waves were not as yet running very high, but were short and broken, tossing up their thin foam-covered crests with sudden, quick, and angry jerks, seeming to excite each other to fury as they vied in their maddening leaps. The sky had become of one dark hue, the thick mist flying rapidly over it; and the sea, when perceived under the frothy sheet which covered it, had assumed a cold, leaden colour. It would have been a sad and dreary prospect to the seamen, with their long night-watch before them, had not custom reconciled them to their hard lot, and caused them to be insensible to the dangers they encountered. Everything was made snug on board; and, steady men being placed at the wheel, the captain, followed by Don Luis, retired unconcernedly to his cabin, desiring to be called, if any change took place. Such was the state of affairs, as the almost impenetrable shades of night fell over the face of the ocean, while onward dashed the ship into the dark unknown expanse, like a man plunging, by his own intent, into the unexplored future of another world.

Volume One—Chapter Two.

It was yet some hours before dawn. The gale had rather increased than lessened in fury, the corvette, with all her canvass closely furled, was driving impetuously before it, the wind whistled and howled through the rigging; the waves, now rising in mountainous billows, dashed high in wild confusion, and, rolling towards her, seemed, with savage intent, about to overwhelm her; but, proudly holding her course, she rushed through them unharmed. At intervals, too, flashes of lightning darted from the overcharged clouds, lighting up the scene again to leave the mighty void in greater obscurity than before.

At a moment when the heavens had emitted a flash longer continued and brighter than usual, a loud cry from the look-out men ahead was heard. "A sail ahead! Starboard! hard-a-starboard! or we shall be into her!" was passed along the decks with startling rapidity, and there was scarce time for the vessel to answer the helm, before the lofty masts and spars of a ship were seen towering to the sky, so close on board them, that the corvette seemed to graze her yards, as they flew by her like lightning. The stranger seemed, by the glance they had of her, to be a large ship, hove to on the starboard tack, under a close reefed main-topsail.

The old pilot, who had just come on deck to relieve the second lieutenant from his watch, gazed earnestly towards the void in which she had disappeared, as if he would penetrate its thick curtain of darkness, and shook his head as he observed, "I like not thus to meet a bark such as that we have just passed. She is an omen of death and destruction to some who float on these seas; and if she was built in any known port, I am very much mistaken."

"What, Senhor Nunez! do you not take her for a real ship?" asked the second lieutenant. "For my own part, by her appearance, I had no doubt of it, and I felt my heart beat all the lighter when we were clear of her; now, if she were a phantom, as you seem to say, we should have gone clean through without any damage."

"That comes of trusting to your new-fangled philosophy, instead of putting faith in the signs Heaven sends us to warn us of danger," answered the pilot. "Not that I mean to say there was anything holy in yonder bark; but Heaven often permits evil spirits to work out its own purposes, for which she may perhaps be allowed to wander on this stormy ocean. I have not doubled the Cape for the last fifty years without seeing such sights as would make your hair stand on end, and your heart sink within you."

"Well, well, I will not now dispute the point with you," responded the young officer, "you are an older man by many years than I am, and of course have seen many more wonderful things; but we will discuss the subject some day when I can manage to keep my eyes open, which I can now scarcely do; however, ought I not, before I turn in, to let the captain know what we have seen?"

"Do as you like; but it will be rousing him up to little purpose," said the old man. "The chances are, that the next time we see her, she will be right ahead, with all her canvass set, coming down upon us."

The lieutenant was just descending to the main-deck, when at that instant a cry of surprise from one of the young midshipmen arrested him, and the stranger was perceived dashing after them, as she emerged from the obscurity, her white canvass gleaming brightly, as it reflected the flashes of lightning. He hastened down to call the captain, who, at the first summons, rushed on deck, where he was soon joined by his young passenger.

"I did not expect to see yonder stranger where he now is," said the pilot, as, the captain joining him on the poop, he pointed out the phantom-looking ship; "and, for the life of me, I cannot make him out; but I think no good of him. He is more likely to be a foe than a friend to any mortal cruisers."

"Whether he be friend or foe, he seems at all events in a great hurry to speak us," exclaimed the Captain; "but methinks his speaking-trumpets will not be of much avail in a hurricane like this; why, the spirit of the storm laughs all human efforts to naught; and I should have thought he could scarcely have distinguished our bare poles through this inky darkness."

"Those on board her don't require any night glasses to see their prey," said the old Pilot, gloomily; "they scent it from afar, as the vulture does a carcass."

"Whether he can see us or not, here he comes," shouted the Captain. "Beat to quarters—we will be prepared for him. Topmen, ready aloft. We will make sail, if necessary," he added, turning to Senhor Nunez; "but he is, probably, one of our fire-eating friends, an Englishman, who will never let a ship on the high seas escape their scrutiny, in the hopes of finding an enemy worth engaging."

"I don't think he belongs to any nation that carries a flag," answered Senhor Nunez, piously crossing himself, "and I have been vowing two wax candles to our Lady of Belem, to be bought out of my arrears of pay, if she will shield us from all the powers of darkness."

"Our blessed Lady protect us from such!" said the Captain; "but I think we shall have none but mortal enemies to contend with in yonder ship."

The men, in the meantime, went steadily to their quarters; and now that there was considerable danger to be incurred, their tongues were kept in silence, their ears ready to catch any orders that might follow, though they fully shared in the old pilot's ideas as to the supernatural character of the ship in sight.

"Let every alternate gun be run out on the starboard side, Senhor Alvez," said the Captain; "we cannot fight our entire battery in a sea like this; and a few well-handled guns will do more work than a whole broadside ill served; but I do not surmise we shall be brought to that pass. She will scarcely wish to fight us, and I have no intention of attacking her till I know what she is."

This disposition of the crew took some little time to make, as there was danger, as well as difficulty, in putting the guns in fighting order. "Keep her edging away to the south," he added, to the quarter-master, who was conning the ship; "we will endeavour to keep our friend on the starboard side."

The order was scarcely given, when the stranger, ranging up on the starboard quarter, a voice from her forecastle hailed them; but the loud roaring of the blast, and dashing of the waves, drowned all distinctions of sounds, and before Captain Pinto, seizing his speaking-trumpet, had time to answer, a shot from her bow gun whistled over their heads, followed by six or eight others, as she ranged alongside; but, flying high, they did little damage.

"Ah! our friend has taken the tone of his temper to-night from the weather, and is rather inclined for strife; but we will show him, whoever he is, that he has caught a Tartar. Fire! my men, fire!" cried the Captain, "and aim low; he deserves some punishment for not making more polite inquiries respecting our health before he began the engagement, as a gentleman should do." The order was obeyed with alacrity, two or three of the shot seeming to take effect on the hull of their adversary: for, by the bright flashes of the guns, some white spots were perceptible on her bulwarks, which might have convinced others less determinately superstitious, of her substantial nature.

"Topmen aloft, and make sail!" shouted the Captain, through his speaking-trumpet; "we will fight this daring stranger to every advantage; for it will not do to allow him to haul across our bows, as he seems to have some intention of doing, even at great risk to himself. At all events, he is not a person to be trifled with."

The fore and main-topsails, closely-reefed, were now let fall, and, with great exertion, extended to their yard-arms; the two ships being thus on an equality of sailing, continued to run side by side, exchanging every now and then strong and noisy proofs of their vicinity, by an irregular discharge of their guns, as they could be brought to bear in the heavy sea that was running, and as they gained a momentary glance of each other. It was fearful thus fighting amid darkness on the raging ocean, which, of itself, afforded dangers sufficient to encounter; yet 'twas a scene which made the heart of Don Luis throb with wild excitement, such as he had never before experienced—the howling of the tempest, the muttered growls of the thunder, the roar of the guns, their bright flashes, and the forked lightning, which played around the masts of the ships, as if to remind them that they were liable to destruction from a far greater Power than that of which their own mortal efforts were capable. As yet the guns of the enemy had done no more damage than cutting some of the running rigging; but it was impossible to say what mischief those of the corvette had inflicted in retaliation, though, from the pertinacity of her opponent, it was supposed to have been but slight.

"If yonder ship does not carry the devil and a whole host of his imps on board, she must be an Englishman," said the old Pilot, coming up to the captain's side; "for no other mortals would have dreamed of engaging in a night like this, and she must fancy that she has got alongside a Frenchman: there's no doubt of it."

"I know not of what nation he is, though I am pretty certain of his mortal qualities," answered the Captain. "But if he is an Englishman, I wish we could find some way of letting him know we are friends, for he will not leave us till he has either sunk us or blown us out of the water, if we cannot manage to treat him in the same way."

"Where is the enemy? Where is the skulking foe?" was echoed along the decks by some of the crew; for since the last discharge of her guns their opponent had disappeared in the impenetrable darkness which surrounded them, increased by a thick mist, which came driving past; while others exclaimed, "Holy Virgin, that was no mortal bark! Ah, she has vanished as suddenly as she appeared! May the saints protect us, and gain us forgiveness for our sins; for we have been fighting with the powers of darkness?"

"That fellow is no Englishman, or he would not for a moment have lost sight of us, if he thought us an enemy," cried the Captain. "No, no, I know those haughty islanders too well. He is some Frenchman, perhaps, who, from the few guns we used, mistakes us for a smaller vessel of the foe, and will be down again upon us directly. We must fight our whole broadside, Senhor Alvez, at every risk, to undeceive him as to our size; and we will take care that he does not run away from us, whoever he may be."

"If we were to sail on till doomsday we should never come up with him, were he to seek to avoid us," muttered the old Pilot, as he gazed earnestly towards the spot where the ship was last seen.

The first lieutenant descended to the main-deck, to see the orders executed: the guns were then loaded and run out, a most perilous undertaking; for the sea rushed through the open ports each roll the ship made, flooding the decks, almost filling the guns, wetting the ammunition, and extinguishing the matches. The seamen, frequently up to their knees in water, were exposed to the danger of the guns breaking loose, an accident which did indeed occur more than once; but, encouraged by their officers, they perseveringly retained their stations. Once, indeed, the dangers and horrors of the terrific scene overcame the courage of some, and they showed symptoms of abandoning themselves to despair, calling on the Virgin and all the saints to aid them; but the gallant Captain Pinto, followed by Don Luis and some of the other officers, rushed among them, so earnestly encouraging them to do their duty, both by words and gestures, that they promised to fight to the last gasp, and sink with their colours flying.

Don Luis returned with the captain to the poop, offering to take charge of some of the small brass guns and swivels, should they come to closer quarters.

During this state of doubt and uncertainty, every instant seemed an hour; for no one could tell when they might again be engaged, or what might be the issue of the combat with an adversary which was equal to, if not larger than their own vessel. As the thick mist we have spoken of flew past them, the dim outline of the foe was again distinguished by some of the keenest eyes on board, still in the same relative position in which they had last seen her, and by her movements she evidently had them in sight, but seemed disinclined to renew the engagement.

"Give him a shot for the honour of Portugal," shouted the Captain. "We will convince him that we, at all events, are perfectly ready to fight."

The order was immediately obeyed; but the stranger took not the slightest notice of the challenge.

"We will near him, to discover, if possible, who he is. Port your helm a little. That will do, we shall soon edge down to him."

A few minutes, however, convinced him that the enemy had no intention of meeting at nearer quarters; for, no sooner did she perceive the aim of the Portuguese, than she altered her course in the same degree that they had done; and it may easily be understood that, in so high a sea and strong a wind, it was very difficult, except by the consent of both parties, to approach each other without imminent danger to her who should most deviate from her course.

Hours passed on, the mysterious and phantom-looking bark still hovering in the same direction; and thus, like two wild horses scouring along the plains of Tartary, did the two ships continue, now dashing with fierce impetuosity into the boiling cauldron, then rising again, and springing forward, in their mad career, over the very summits of the froth-crested billows. Had not the crew of the corvette had clear proofs that the stranger was, like their own craft, composed of substantial timber, and her guns served by mortal hands, they would have been more convinced than ever that she was one of those phantom barks which were believed to scour the ocean in heavy gales, as a warning to the mariner of approaching destruction; and even the less superstitious might have fancied her, by some optical delusion, the reflection of their own ship upon the dark mist which surrounded them, so regularly did she imitate all their movements. Thus the night wore on, the men almost sinking with fatigue at their guns; for they were obliged to be every moment on the watch to prevent their being overturned; nor could they venture to secure them, lest the enemy should bear down upon them, and find them unprepared to meet her.

"I see the aim of him who commands yonder ship," exclaimed Captain Pinto, after examining the stranger attentively through his glass. "He hopes to weary us out, and then to run us on board; but we will be even with him: or perhaps he is wisely waiting to discover whether we are friends or foes before he expends any more powder and shot. Secure the guns and close the ports, Senhor Alvez, and let the men take some rest. He is not likely to wish to attack us again before daylight, and we must take care to be up before him; or, if he tries to near us before then, we must pay him the same compliment that he just now did us, and get out of his way."

The men were glad enough to secure the guns; but it was a time of too much anxiety and excitement for any to quit the deck, where they remained, filling each other's ears with marvellous legends of mysterious barks which their friends, in like situations, had beheld, and which had melted away like thin mist when the first grey tints of morn appeared. At length the wished-for dawn began gradually to dissipate the terrific obscurity of the night, and all doubts as to the reality of the stranger bark were removed by perceiving her still broad on their beam under her two closely-reefed topsails. The wild confusion which reigned supreme on the waste of waters was rather magnified by the dim uncertain light of morning: the waves, with foaming crests, leaping madly around, the thick misty clouds flying rapidly along, one lawyer, as it were, above the other, through which not a ray of the sun's beams could escape to cheer the voyagers—all was cold, dreary, and threatening. The gale, too, which had given promise of falling during the latter hours of the night, now again, as if recovering strength with the returning day, increased with such sudden fury, that, before any warning was given, the main-topsail was blown clear off the bolt-ropes, rent into a thousand shreds, with a loud report like a near clap of thunder, and, flying over the fore-topsail-yard, was carried far out of sight ahead.

"Get a new main-topsail on deck," shouted the Commander, in momentary expectation of seeing the fore-topsail share the same fate; "we must not be without our wings with yonder stranger in our neighbourhood," he added, turning to Don Luis. "These are the variations of a sea-life, my young friend,—a day of sunshine and calm, and two of clouds and tempest."

"Away aloft, and bend the new sail," cried the Captain, after a minute's silence. "The enemy keeps steadily on her course, as if there were no such beings as ourselves in existence."

By the time that the fresh topsail was got aloft, and bent to the yard by the willing seamen, broad daylight was on the world of waters.

"Hoist our colours, and let him know who we are," exclaimed the Captain; but when the flag of Portugal blew wildly from the peak, no answering signal was made by the stranger, though, being not a mile distant, he must clearly have perceived it.

"He suspects those are not our true colours," observed the first Lieutenant.

"Whether he does or does not, see he is edging down towards us again, to make us out more clearly," said Captain Pinto. "Beat to quarters; should he prove no friend, which I much doubt, we will be prepared for him." As he spoke, a small ball was seen to ascend to the peak of the stranger, and the blue banner of Morocco, with its crescent emblem, flew out in a broad sheet to the blast. "Ah, I know the rascal now," continued the Captain, "he is a Salee rover, the greatest miscreant that ever sailed the ocean—with a crew that will not fight except they fancy themselves secure of conquering, and then show very little of a victor's mercy. Slavery or death is the only fate those they capture must expect at their hands."

While Captain Pinto was speaking, the two ships were drawing near each other. The Salee rovers of those days were strongly armed ships, fitted out by the piratical states of Algiers, Tripoli, Tunis, and the town of Salee, and other places on the north coast of Africa, their crews composed of robbers, murderers, and malefactors of every description, chiefly the refuse of the Levant, and of every nation under the sun, though calling themselves Turks. Their hands were against every man, and every man's hand was against them; they revelled in blood and slaughter, and mercy or any tender feelings of our nature was a stranger to their hearts. As they seldom fought, except in the hopes of booty, they were feared by all the mercantile navies in the world (for their depredations extended far beyond the straits of Gibraltar); and all the European governments succumbed, in the most extraordinary way, to their tyrannical power, actually paying tribute to be free from their impositions.

All hands on board regarded anxiously the approaching pirate, though with less apprehension now that they knew with whom they had to contend.

"I knew all along that the devil had something to do with that vessel," cried the old Pilot, in rather an exulting tone. "If ever demons inhabit human forms, they dwell in those wretches who compose her crew; and let us thank the saints that we have a good ship and plenty of guns to defend ourselves, or we should not see another day."

"He thinks that we are no Portuguese, but one of the cruisers of Naples, or perhaps of his holiness the Pope," said the first Lieutenant, "or he would not show so daring a front to us."

"No, no!" answered Captain Pinto, with some bitterness in his tone; "he knows well enough that this is a Portuguese ship; but he does not know that old Jozé Pinto commands her, or perhaps he would moderate that flaunting air. Once on a time no nation dared insult the flag of Portugal on the high seas; but that time has long passed away, and now all think they may venture to do so with impunity: however, my friends, let us show that we still retain the spirit of our fathers. Give them a shot, to convince the picarooning villains that we are awake from our morning nap. Do you, Senhor Albuquerque," he said, turning to a young officer who was standing near him, "exercise your skill in gunnery on yonder pirate: a young eye and eager hand may throw a shot when a more practised man may miss his aim." The young officer flew eagerly to obey his chief, and scarcely had the match been applied to the touch-hole before the effect of the shot was seen, as some white splinters were observed to glance from the bulwarks of their adversary.

"Viva!" was shouted by all the crew in chorus.

"A few more shots like that would curb the vile infidel's pride," cried the old Pilot; but he had scarce finished his sentence, when a bright flame issued from the side of the stranger, and a crashing shower of shot passed over them, slightly wounding some of the smaller spars; one, however, swept the deck, killing one and severely injuring another of the crew.

"Chance more than skill directed those shots," cried the Captain, to encourage the crew, whose rage was immediately excited by the death of their comrade. "Ah! see they show their true character, and are sheering off to avoid the punishment they know is their due. Let them feel we are not to be insulted with impunity. Fire!"

At the word, the guns of the corvette were discharged with considerable effect on the very hull of the rover, who was evidently, for the time, satisfied with fighting, as he immediately put his helm to port, and at great risk, the seas breaking over his sides, sheered off from his determined opponent. We have already explained the various dangers incurred while fighting the guns in that heavy sea, it being much to the credit of the crew that they could do so at all; and it was thus some time before they could again discharge them, when the enemy had gained a considerable distance, the shot falling harmlessly into the water. In truth, at such a time, it was the object of neither ship to engage, as victory could have been of no advantage to either; for it was utterly impossible to have boarded the prize by means of boats; and if the two ships had run alongside of each other, it was probable, if not certain, that both would have sunk in the deadly embrace: a prolonged combat would also have proved the destruction of both. They therefore, by mutual consent, again kept on their course, eyeing each other with hatred and suspicion.

The crew of the corvette were again ordered to secure their guns, when they set about performing the ordinary duties of the ship; the look-out men in the tops keeping a watchful eye on every movement of the corsair, whose very disregard of them seemed to betoken treachery; the only signal her crew made that they were conscious of the presence of a hostile bark being that their pirate banner yet blew out to the blast as a defiance. Thus for the whole day did the Portuguese ship and her foe drive before the furious and unrelaxing gale, the officers and crew in watches throwing themselves beneath the shelter of the poop-deck to snatch a few minutes' repose, no one being willing to go below even for an instant.

The Moor appeared to carry as many guns, if not more than the corvette, being perhaps also of greater tonnage; and the probabilities were, that she had by far the strongest crew, as it was the custom of the Salee rovers to crowd their decks with men, their usual mode of fighting being to run their enemy on board, when, rushing like a host of furies on the devoted ship, their numbers generally carried the day; however, under the present circumstances, that mode could be of no avail, and he therefore very wisely avoided coming to closer quarters.

Sleep visited not the eyes of Don Luis, and scarcely would he allow himself time to snatch a mouthful of food, so excited had he become by the late skirmish, and the wild scene of confusion round him, no one more earnestly eyeing the enemy, as he prayed for the abatement of the gale, to have some chance of punishing the daring pirate for his presumption in thus insulting the flag of his country. "Though the proud days of chivalry have passed away," he exclaimed to himself, "I will prove that I am no carpet knight, but worthy of the gallant warriors from whom I am descended, whose lances were ever foremost in fight and tourney. Here is an unlooked-for opportunity of distinguishing myself, which will not, I trust, be torn from me; and I will seize some trophy from yonder lawless stranger to lay at the feet of my beloved Theresa, when how proudly will she welcome me, as I return among a band of warriors, after a hard won victory, instead of from a voyage without danger, and from a land of peace and security, as she expects!"

Such thoughts very naturally passed through a young and enthusiastic mind, but which, uttered aloud, would, to the generality of people, have appeared to arise from Quixotic folly; and it must be confessed, that his servant Pedro did not in the least participate in his master's romantic feelings, though ever ready to share his fortunes. He, all the time, most earnestly prayed that the devil would run away with the stranger, or that he would go to the bottom before he had time to send any more cannon balls on board the corvette. As for bearing a trophy to his lady loves—for Pedro owned to two, one in his native village, and another in Lisbon—it never entered his head; for he well knew they would much prefer a piece of gay coloured calico to a bit of bunting, which they could not convert into a petticoat. Pedro was certainly not a romantic lover. It was curious, yet so it was, that the warnings of his friend, Captain Pinto, never once occurred to Don Luis; nor did the recollection for a moment cross his mind, that, instead of victory and a speedy return to his native land, a long painful slavery, or a sudden death, might be his lot.

Not a gleam of sunshine broke through the thick mass of clouds during the whole course of the day, which passed on without any variation till the fast increasing gloom announced the return of night with all its horrors; for, in the southern latitudes, in which they were, the sun scarcely sinks, before darkness overspreads the world; and thus in a short time they again lost sight of the enemy in a dense curtain of mist, which added to the obscurity. The captain, therefore, called a council of war to consider the best plan to pursue, being unwilling to miss the foe, and anxious at the same time not to run farther out of their course than they could help, should the gale subside, as it had lately given some promise of doing.

The officers were collected round their commander, the old pilot strenuously giving it as his opinion, that, as soon as the gale moderated, they should haul their wind, and leave their phantom opponent to pursue, uninterrupted, her demon-directed course; persisting that she would lead them through stormy seas and tempests half round the world before she disappeared. The greater number, also, were of opinion that they ought to haul their wind, or lay the ship to, when their deliberations on the subject were quickly settled by a warning cry from the men in the tops; and, at the moment when most considered the enemy yet at some distance, he was perceived on their starboard quarter, looming through the obscurity. The crew needed no order to fly to their guns, or the officers to their respective posts; and scarcely had her lofty masts appeared ranging up alongside, before a broad sheet of flame issued from her ports, and a shower of shot passed over them.

"Fire, my men! fire low!" shouted the gallant Commander; and the shot seemed to tell well upon the hull of the stranger. The guns were again hauled in, loaded and fired with great rapidity, before their adversary had time to give them a second broadside; the seeing which much animated the men.

"Well done, my gallant fellows!" cried the Captain; "remember that you are Portuguese and good Catholics, and that yonder ship contains a crew of vile infidels. Our colours are still flying at our peak, and there they shall fly till I am knocked overboard; so all you have to do is to fire away as hard as you can, and by the blessing of the Holy Virgin we shall be the conquerors." This short, pithy speech much animated the crew; who, putting firm confidence in the courage and sagacity of their leader, renewed their efforts with redoubled vigour. "See, Don Luis," added the Captain, "the infidel is near enough to feel our swivels and light guns, and if you will undertake to command them, they may do some service." Don Luis sprang gladly to obey the captain's order, followed by Pedro; who, now that he could not avoid fighting, exerted himself as well as the bravest, working the guns with considerable effect.

The firing on both sides had now become warm; the enemy being in earnest, and evidently eager, on some account or other, to bring the contest to a speedy close. Their guns were discharged as rapidly as they could be loaded, doing much execution on board the corvette, striking down several men on the main-deck, and one on the poop, close to Don Luis, though each shot was returned with equal vigour. The flashes of the guns clearly showed the enemies to each other, for they were now running along not a quarter of a cable's length apart; the Portuguese aiming always at the hull of their opponent, with the determination of sinking her, if possible; while she fired in the hopes of cutting away their spars and rigging, and crippling their masts; that, unable to escape, she might be able to take possession of them at leisure: the only objects the rovers sought in victory being booty and prisoners.

A truly awful scene was that night-engagement, as the two small barks, on that vast wild waste, surrounded with all the majestic horrors of ocean strife, filled with human beings regardless of Heaven's wrath, strove, with all the animosity of demons, to hurl each other to destruction, nor thinking of their own fate.

The infidel had wrongly calculated on an easy victory, when he attacked a ship commanded by so hardy and brave a seaman as Jozé Pinto; for his crew, confiding in his courage and seamanship, fought as well as any seamen in the world—as the Portuguese always will do when well led—and, after an hour's engagement, the effect of their efforts became perceptible, in the slackened fire of the enemy. Both the wind and sea had now much fallen; and, as the storm broke, flashes of lightning darted from the clouds—for a moment casting a lurid glare on the hostile ships and the foaming cauldron between them—again leaving a more fearful gloom on the scene. "Where is the infidel, where is the infidel?" was again shouted by the crew, after a bright flash had dazzled their eyes, and she had for the last minute ceased firing. "She's gone, she's gone!" The officers looked eagerly out—no one could see the pirate ship—but they dreaded some treachery: the guns, therefore, were loaded and run out; the crew waiting in breathless expectation to catch sight of her, when she was again perceived coming up close on their quarter, with the intent, it seemed, to range up alongside; yet nothing but madness or desperation could have instigated them to the act, for certain destruction threatened both, if she should attempt to board; for, once joined, the sea must overwhelm them both.

"Boarders, come aft," shouted the Captain: "starboard the helm." The manoeuvre caused the rover to miss his aim, and as he threw his grapnels, they fell into the water. "Steady, again," the Captain cried; but the rover was not to be deceived a second time; for, with determined daring, putting his helm also to starboard, he ranged alongside, and locked his yard-arms in a deadly embrace with those of the Portuguese. A loud shriek of horror arose from many, even of the brave, on board. "Silence, men, silence!" cried Captain Pinto: "aloft, and cut away: be prepared to repel boarders." The men sprang to the rigging as ordered: all knew that their lives depended on their activity. A loud crashing noise was heard as the stout spars tore and wrenched each other from the ropes which held them, falling in splinters from aloft; but as yet the hulls of the ships had not touched, the sea in foaming torrents dashing up between them, and inundating the decks of both. What we have been describing took place in a few seconds.

"Fire!" shouted the Captain; and the balls were seen to tear up the sides of the rover, who appeared to be incapable of answering the discharge.

Still onward dashed the ships, their spars and rigging yet locked together, the wild sea threatening each moment to claim them as its prize; when, as for an instant their hulls ground together, a form was seen to spring from the shrouds of the pirate ship on to the deck of the Christian. "Faithless tyrants, I am no longer your slave!" he exclaimed, as he hurled his gleaming sabre among the people he had just quitted: "I may now die among my countrymen." The words were scarce heard amid the tumult, or the action seen; and, as he fell, the cutlass of a seaman brought him bleeding to the deck, where he lay, trampled on and disregarded, amid some of the Portuguese who had been struck down. At the same moment, the glare of the forked lightning exhibited a hundred swarthy turbaned figures on the nettings and lower rigging of the Rover, and, like a rush of fierce vultures on their prey, with loud yells, the foremost threw themselves on the deck of the corvette, when the upper works of the two ships again separated.

"Onward, my men, onward!" shouted Captain Pinto, rushing forward to repel them at the head of a party of his best seamen, with Don Luis by his side, who, at the first fierce onset, warded off a blow which might have proved fatal to the gallant chief. But the pirates fought with all the ferocity of despair and fanaticism, for they neither expected nor asked for mercy; their only hope was in victory. Yet, notwithstanding the desperate resistance they made, they could not withstand the superior numbers of the Portuguese: loudly rung their fierce war cries; their sharp sabres flashed brightly as they strove for life, every moment expecting to be reinforced by their friends, who waited but the returning roll, when the upper works of the ships should again meet, to rush on board; the flashes from the muskets of the marines, and the pistols of the seamen, between the gleams of lightning, alone exhibiting the combatants to each other, all the lights on board having been extinguished to prevent the enemy from taking aim. Again they rallied, the Portuguese giving way. A gigantic Moor, who had fallen as they first leapt on board, now extricating himself, attacked Don Luis with such desperate fury, that, although he defended himself with courage and coolness, he would have been overthrown, had not Pedro contrived to get a cut at the Moor's arm, which brought him bleeding to the deck. The brave captain once more calling upon his men, pressed the Moors hard: inch by inch they were cut down, or forced back, till they were driven over the nettings into the dark yawning gulf below, or ground by the sides of the ships. But this short success had cost the Portuguese dear, and even their chief felt that they could with difficulty contend against the swarm of desperate miscreants, who were ready at the moment to throw themselves headlong among them, nor had the people aloft yet succeeded, in spite of all their efforts, in clearing the rigging.

Again the nettings of the two ships touched, and, uttering loud yells, crowds of the foemen hurled themselves from their posts in the rigging with their gleaming sabres in hand; but it was to destruction;

for at that instant a tremendous sea rushed up between the two ships, tearing away all the fastenings which held them aloft.

The Rover made one roll to starboard; a vivid flash of lightning threw a momentary lurid glare over her, as her crew were seen to spring the larboard rigging, every lineament of their dark features distorted with the wildest rage and despair: those livid, demoniacal countenances were long fixed in the memory of all who saw them. The wild frothy sea leaped high between the two barks, but the pirate rose not again: a piercing shriek of agony was the last sound heard ascending in the night air, high above the loud roaring of the tempest. For one instant only were the masts and spars of the Salee rover seen ere the dark waves rolled triumphantly over the spot where she had been.

The Portuguese gazed with horror, for from such a fate, too, had they narrowly escaped through Heaven's mercy. Continuous flashes of lightning darted from the clouds, exhibiting, far astern, the outstretched arms and despairing features of the sinking wretches; but they were pirates, accursed by Heaven and man, and deserved no aid, could any have been afforded them, and the victors bounded on proudly in their course.

Volume One—Chapter Three.

Scarcely had the lawless career of the Salee rover thus awfully terminated, as we have narrated at the end of our last chapter, than the spirit of the storm, as if satisfied with the sacrifice offered to him, began to relax his fury. The heavy clouds cleared gradually away, and the bright stars (those cheering beacons to the mariner) were seen glimmering from the clear dark blue sky: the wind, too, shifted to the southward of east, and the sea fell considerably, so that the repairs of the corvette could be carried on with much less danger and difficulty than at first. The damages she had sustained in her long encounter with the corsair, were of less consequence than might have been expected, considering the size and power of the enemy; and the seamen attributed their victory to their fervent prayers to the Virgin, and all the saints, and to the vows of offerings at their shrines.

This was, however, no time for thought—activity and energy of action were now demanded; every officer and man was employed; the captain urging them to their work; for till the standing rigging could be secured, their masts, which had fortunately escaped injury, might any moment have gone overboard. A few only of the shrouds were found to have been cut away, which being put to rights in the best way they could effect, and a fresh running rigging rove, a reef was shaken out of each of the three topsails, and the ship brought to the wind, with her head towards the shore. Boldly did she buffet the billows, like a gallant hunter straining every nerve to clear the heavy ground of a fresh ploughed field.

During the greater part of the time, Don Luis remained on the poop, giving such assistance as he was able; but, on an occasion like the present, a landsman can be but of little use, and on the first moment of cessation from toil, the Captain joined him, exclaiming, "Ah, my young friend, Heaven be praised that you have escaped uninjured; for, had you suffered in the engagement, I should have blamed myself for treating you with sad want of hospitality on the ocean. But you have now added to the wonders of your travels a sea adventure worth talking about; and do not forget to mention a brave youth who saved his captain's life; at all events, Jozé Pinto will not be ungrateful, if he ever has the opportunity of showing his gratitude."

"It is I who have to thank you for preserving my life, and the lives of all on board, by your bravery and conduct, Captain Pinto," returned Don Luis, "and proud I am to have fought by your side."

"Talk not of it, my friend; for this is no time to stand bandying compliments," answered the Captain. "Ah, Senhor Nunez," he added, turning to the pilot, who was just then passing them. "Were you at last convinced that we had mortal foes to contend with?"

"I know not, senhor," answered the old man; "they fought like devils, at all events, and till I see some of them make the sign of the cross, I shall still believe them evil spirits."

"They are all long ere this in the world of spirits," said Captain Pinto; "for none, I think, can have escaped among all the wild crew."

While he was speaking, a party of seamen were seen ascending the poop, dragging up between them a man, who by the dim light of a lantern held before him, appeared to be severely wounded in the shoulder. His dress consisted of the Moorish jacket and trousers; his head was bound by a white turban, now torn, disordered, and wet with blood; his features were swarthy and haggard, and his figure tall and well knit. He looked round with a wild confused stare, as if scarce recovered from the effects of some stunning blow, evidently endeavouring to collect his scattered thoughts, in order to speak.

"Whom have you brought hither?" asked the Captain of the seamen; "I thought not a pirate had escaped."

"This, by the blessing of the Virgin, is the only one on board," answered one of the men, "and he would not have been here now, had not Senhor Alvez ordered us to bring him to you, instead of throwing him overboard, with the rest of the cursed wretches, as we were about to do. We found him scarcely breathing under two of our slain comrades, and some say he must be the man they saw leap on board the moment the ships ran foul of each other, who they thought had long ago gone with his brother infidels to the bottomless pit."

The first lieutenant at the same time came up to corroborate the statement, and to give in an account of the loss they had sustained, six men having been killed, and a considerable number wounded by sabre cuts while repelling the boarders.

"Let some one bind the wounds of that man, Senhor Alvez. Carry him below, but secure his feet, that in the frenzy to which these people are liable, he commit no mischief," said the Captain. "I will examine him to-morrow at leisure, when he is fully certain to prove worthy of hanging;" but, as he was speaking, consciousness returned to the mind of the stranger; for at that moment, uttering a few words, he made a gesture of supplication. The captain looked at him earnestly, as the light of the lantern fell upon his features; again the same gesture was repeated, when he once more sunk into a state of insensibility. Whatever it was, it seemed to have a magic effect on Captain Pinto, as scrutinising him closely, he said, as if to himself, "'Tis strange, and yet it must be so;" then exclaimed aloud, "bear him carefully to my cabin, for, though an infidel, he is a human being like ourselves, and now hapless, and in our power, he is no longer an enemy; let the surgeon attend to him, the moment he has seen to the more serious wounds of our own people. Gentlemen, I take this stranger under my protection; for I have reason to suspect that he is not what he seems. Don Luis, I request your company in my cabin," saying which, the captain, accompanied by Don Luis, followed the seamen, who, surprised at the change of orders, bore the wounded stranger to the cabin, where he was carefully placed on a couch, and his host, with his own hands, commenced, in the most tender way, to examine his wounds till the surgeon made his appearance, when that officer pronounced them not dangerous, if immediately attended to. Restoratives being applied, he at length gave signs of returning animation, and sitting up, gazed wildly at the people who stood around him; but the captain would allow none to question him till he had been supplied with dry clothes, and every comfort that could be thought of. All were then desired to quit the cabin, the Captain requesting Don Luis to retire to his own berth till he summoned him, then approached the captive, and taking his hand, "My brother," he said, "can I do ought else to relieve you? Speak, I need but to know your wishes, to follow them to the utmost of my power; I ask not now your name, or whence you come, for speaking will fatigue you."

"Thanks, my brother, thanks," returned the stranger, "you follow the greatest of all precepts, charity to the distressed. More I ask not; but I would give you some account of myself, that you may report it to those whose curiosity may be excited. You see before you a Christian gentleman and a Portuguese, though 'tis long, long since I saw my beloved country. Know me by the name of Senhor Mendez, no willing companion, believe me, of the vile pirates you sent to destruction."

"My suspicions were not wrong then," said the Captain, drawing still nearer, and gazing earnestly at him; "and, if I mistake not, I have seen those features before, though when or where I cannot recall to mind."

The wounded man smiled faintly, "You have seen them before, Captain Pinto," he said; "but years have passed since then, and time, in the thousand changes it has been making, has not spared them, nor do I think that my nearest friends could recognise him who is before you: we have grown from youth to age since we last met."

"I am at fault then," answered the Captain; "nor can I guess when I knew you."

"It is as well that you should remain in ignorance for the present, my friend," answered the stranger. "I know that I can fully trust you; but remember that there are some secrets which are dangerous to the possessor, and I would not make you incur peril on my account if possible."

"I will ask no further, my brother," said the Captain; "rest and sleep are absolutely necessary for you, therefore I must insist on your speaking no more," saying which he placed his guest back on the couch, and summoned Don Luis to join him in a repast which he ordered to be brought in, the first food they had found time to taste for hours, so that both were ready to do full justice to it.

While they were at table, the light of the lamp falling strongly on the countenance of Don Luis, drew the attention of the stranger towards him. "Ah!" he exclaimed, "whom have you near you, Captain Pinto? If fever does not disturb my brain, I think that he whom I see before me is an Almeida. Speak, youth! Do not you belong to that family?"

Don Luis started on hearing himself addressed. "I am an Almeida," he answered. "The only son of the Count of Almeida."

"I knew that I could not be mistaken," said the prisoner, half to himself. "By what an extraordinary fate do I meet you!—but I am wandering. Stir not from where you are; I would gaze upon those features I once knew so well. Yet no! 'tis a spirit I see before me,—a form long since sunk to the grave! Ah, it stirs not! vain illusion! I see the flag of Portugal, of my own loved country. Never more shall I fight beneath that banner. The ship fills; the raging ocean is around me, and I must die amid these vile pirates. Blood flows fast—red, red blood—'tis that of my country's foes; Heaven protect me!" For some minutes the stranger was silent, and appeared to have sunk into slumber.

The captain made a sign to Don Luis not to answer, when he perceived that the wounded man was already beginning to ramble in his speech, when the surgeon, having made the rounds of his other patients, returned; and feeling his pulse, advised that he should be left alone and in quiet.

Having finished their repast, the captain beckoned Don Luis to accompany him on deck, where they found that, during the short time they had been absent, a great improvement in the weather had taken place. The clouds had entirely disappeared, leaving the sky pure and deeply blue, sparkling with myriads of stars: the sea, though still running, was regular, shining, as far as the eye could reach, with bright flashes of phosphorescent light, which rose and fell with the yet foaming waves, the ship seeming to float amid hillocks running with molten gold like lava down the sides of a volcano; a steady breeze also was blowing, which enabled them to steer a direct course for Lisbon.

The dead were collected together, and placed beneath the poop-deck, covered by the flag for which they had so bravely fought, there to await till the following morning the last religious duties which could be paid them, ere they were committed to the sailors' grave—the boundless deep. Several had fallen; some killed by the cannon-shot of the Rover, and others in the desperate struggle when the pirates rushed on board, among whom one officer only was numbered, the brave young Albuquerque, who the surgeon came to announce had just then breathed his last, from several desperate sabre wounds he had received in the conflict. He was the officer who fired the first successful shot at the rover's ship; and, elated with the praise he received from his commander, he was among the first to oppose the enemies, cutlass in hand, when they boarded. He was now brought on deck, wrapped in his bloodstained sheets, his once bright eye closed for ever; his features, lately playful with animation, now ghastly and fixed, as the pale light of the seamen's lanterns fell on them. He had always been a favourite with his commander, who bent mournfully over him, as he was placed beside his more humble shipmates. "Alas! poor youth," said Captain Pinto; "do thus end all thy bright hopes and aspirations? Yet why should I grieve?—Thy days, though few, have been joyous; and thou hast been removed ere sorrows and disappointments had crowded round thee (as too surely they would have done, except thy lot far differed from that of other mortals). Farewell, brave youth! Many a tear will be shed for thy fate in the home of thy fathers; and gladly would I have died instead of thee: for there are few to mourn for old Jozé Pinto." Having given vent to his feelings, he covered the pallid features of the dead youth with a flag, and joined Don Luis, who stood near, watching this gentle trait in the character of the seemingly rough and hardy seaman.

The most important repairs in the ship had been now accomplished; the decks required no washing, for the heavy seas which had broken over them during the terrific engagement, had performed that office; and the watch being set, she had assumed somewhat of her ordinary appearance. Gladly did every one who could be spared from duty throw themselves into their hammocks to seek repose, Don Luis dreaming that he still beheld the agonised features of the drowning pirates; and Pedro, that he was hewing away at the head of the Moor who had attacked his master, but which, notwithstanding all his efforts, kept grinning at him with horrid grimaces.

The first pale streaks of morn called everybody into activity; for there was still much to be done before the ship could be restored to order.

The melancholy duty of committing the slain to the deep was performed just as the sun rose bright and warm above the waves; and many an honest tear was shed by the comrades of those who were never more to bask beneath his genial rays; while many a vow was made to have masses offered up for the repose of their souls.

The weather, as if to make amends to the voyagers for the ill-treatment they had experienced, continued serene and favourable, and the corvette bounded lightly over the now bright and laughing waters. The horrors and dangers they had undergone fading gradually from their memories, as events scarcely appertaining to themselves; for so are we constituted: the most acute pains, the greatest trials of nerve, which in anticipation we have dreaded, when past, are thought of with indifference; and the recollection of pleasure is, alas! still more evanescent. It is crime alone, a stinging conscience, which is the only lasting torment, and the remembrance of good deeds the only true durable happiness, for of that none can rob us.

For many hours during the day after the engagement with the Salee rover, Senhor Mendez continued in a state of unconsciousness; nor towards the evening, when he appeared to revive, would Captain Pinto, by the surgeon's advice, allow him to enter into conversation,—the extraordinary manner of his preservation, and the interest the captain took in him, causing many surmises on board. Don Luis was also anxious to learn somewhat of the stranger; but as his friend was not communicative, he did not think right to question him on the subject.

Two days had thus passed by, when, as the captain and his young friend were seated in the cabin, the stranger awoke from a sound slumber, and, raising himself on his couch, looked around. "I have deeply to thank you, Captain Pinto, for your care of a wounded prisoner," he said, "who has caused you, I fear, much trouble, and who may cause you much more; but perhaps you already know more than I would have revealed; for, tell me, did I not ramble wildly in my speech the other night, when overcome by fever?"

Captain Pinto assured him that he had in no way committed himself by anything he had said.

"I rejoice to hear it, for your sake, and for that of the youth I see by your side; for though I would not deceive you, and feel assured that I might confide in both, I would not willingly entrust you with a secret which might prove dangerous to the possessor."

"In what you say follow your own counsel," answered the Captain; "for I would not wish to influence you, though you may put as full confidence in the discretion of Don Luis d'Almeida, as in mine; and be assured that we shall be ever ready to aid you to the utmost of our power."

"His name is, I trust, a guarantee for his honour," returned Senhor Mendez; "and though I have weighty reasons for concealing the early part of my history, I will narrate, in as brief a way as possible, some of the latter events of my life, which will account for my being on board the Salee rover which your gallantry sent to destruction; though far rather would I have sunk unknown amid those drowning wretches, whose dying shrieks yet ring in my ear, than risk the safety of one to whom I am so deeply indebted. You see before you a man who has, throughout life, been constantly on the point of attaining, as he supposed, wealth and happiness; when, ere the cup reached his lips, it has been rudely torn from his grasp, and he has been hurled back to poverty and wretchedness; yet ever, when least expected, fortune has again shed her deceitful smile upon him. I was yet young, when, after passing through many vicissitudes of fortune, I arrived, poor and unknown, on the shores of India; but I yet retained more than wealth can purchase, the great ingredient, the first principle of success, an unbroken spirit, full of hope and confidence. I had learned, I thought, that wealth was the only certain road to power, and that with power alone could I attain my ends; for I had deep and bitter wrongs to avenge, and wealth, therefore, I determined to obtain by every means consistent with my honour. Though many of the rank in which I was born, would have looked upon mercantile pursuits as wholly derogatory to their dignity, nameless and unknown, I laughed at such prejudices; and soon finding means to bring my talents into notice, I obtained an employment in which I was eminently successful; when one high in power, who had always borne me a deadly enmity, arrived in Goa, and would, I felt confident, recognise me through all the disguises I might assume. I well knew that, were I discovered, the civil and ecclesiastical power would be brought into play against me, and the Inquisition, with all its diabolical tortures, stared me in the face. I fled to China, from which country I was obliged once more to migrate to the newly-acquired possessions of the British in India, where my intimate knowledge of the customs and language of the natives, aiding my own perseverance, enabled me to acquire, at length, the fortune I sought. I transmitted it by degrees to England, and having wound up my affairs, I set sail for that country, intending from thence to make any further arrangements I might deem advisable; but I was not destined to reach it. The ship which bore me was wrecked on the coast of Africa, and I, with the few who escaped death, was made prisoner by a tribe of savages, who retaliated on us a few of the cruelties their countrymen have experienced from those of our colour. For upwards of a year I remained in captivity, when I contrived to get on board a vessel, trading on the coast for gold-dust and ivory, and bound for Cadiz. We had a prosperous run, and expected in two or three days to have reached our destination, when a large vessel bore down upon us, crowded with men. Resistance was hopeless, and flight impossible; and as she ran alongside, to our horror, we recognised the costume of the implacable enemies of Spain, the Algerines. The cargo being taken out of the vessel, she was sunk, the lives of the crew being spared for the sake of their value as slaves, for which purpose they were carried to Algiers, and there sold. Any fate appearing to me preferable to that which they were doomed to suffer, I embraced the offer the captain of the rover made me of joining his ship, and assuming the turban, in the secret hope of being ultimately able, by these means, to make my escape. Whether he suspected me, I know not; but he was certainly very unwilling to lose the services I was able to afford him through my knowledge of various languages, and a strict watch was kept on my movements, so that upwards of another long year passed away without my being able to effect my purpose. The scenes of horror and outrage I was doomed to witness, seemed to me as a punishment for my sins; but, fortunately, we never fell in with a Portuguese vessel, so that I was guiltless of spilling the blood of any of my countrymen, till the chief of the pirate crew, mistaking your ship, in the night of the gale, for a merchantman, determined to give chase, in hopes of finding you an easy conquest.

"Great, indeed, was my grief, when, on the following morning, we discovered that you were a man-of-war and a Portuguese; for, notwithstanding all my persuasions to the contrary, he insisted on attacking you, declaring, that as you were probably short of hands, you would fall an easy prey, and that he required a new ship as a consort to his own. Having once made up his mind, nothing would deter him from his purpose; and my expostulations causing my faith to be suspected, the other officers insisted that I should be placed in the most exposed situation when we boarded, which proved, however, the salvation of my life. Once or twice my spirits were revived by the hope that we had missed you; but at length the rovers resolved to cripple you, if possible, to prevent your escaping, though they found that they had encountered a far more determined antagonist than they expected. When, however, some proposed drawing off, or waiting till the sea went down, to run you on board, it was discovered that two shots had entered between wind and water, and that the ship was filling fast. Their only hope of preservation was now to run you on board, although at imminent risk of destruction to both; but as there was no other alternative, the purpose was immediately put into execution, and had not the ships separated so providentially for you at the moment they did, it is probable either the pirates would have become the masters, or both would have sunk together."

"No, no, Senhor Mendez, the vile infidels should never have become masters of this ship while I lived," suddenly exclaimed Captain Pinto: "say, rather, we should all have been food for fish, had not the rover, by the favour of the saints, sunk when she did: but I beg your pardon for interrupting you."

"I have little more to add," returned Senhor Mendez, "except to express my joy at finding, on my recovery, that you were the victors. I must beg, too, that even what I have now mentioned regarding myself may not pass your lips; for surmises, with the slightest clue, may lead to inquiries, and my secret be discovered."

Both his auditors assured him that what he had said should be inviolable. "Thanks, sirs, thanks," he answered. "I have exerted myself to give this sketch of my adventures, to remove any suspicions you might have entertained regarding me, the thought of which I could not endure, and now weariness overpowers me;" saying which, he sunk back, and appeared to slumber.

It was not until the sixth day after the engagement, that the lofty ridges of the rock of Lisbon, tinged with the ruddy beams of the rising sun, greeted the anxious eyes of the voyagers, rising like a welcome beacon out of the blue and shining ocean. The morning was pure and lovely, such as the fair clime of Portugal can often boast; the very air sparkling with animation. The gentle breeze came in irregular breaths off the land, laden with the odour of aromatic herbs and flowers, so grateful to the senses of those who have inhaled nought but saline particles during a protracted voyage. They had made the land rather to the north of the rock, which was looked upon as a very good land-fall by the old pilot; for it must be recollected that we are writing of nearly a hundred years ago, since which time navigation has made great strides in improvement; and, as they coasted along, Don Luis eagerly watched each village and point they passed, while Pedro greeted, no less delighted, and with much more violent gesticulation, each spot of his beloved Portugal, as the seamen pointed it out to him.

"Ah! at length your hopes may, perhaps, be realised," said the Captain, as he came on deck, smilingly addressing Don Luis; "but you see how fallacious they before proved, and while you expected to have landed a week ago, we have only just passed the spot where we then were; and, in the meantime, have narrowly escaped destruction by the two great dangers of the sea—the tempest and the fight. Thus you will find it through life, and remember the history of Senhor Mendez: he seemed to have given it to strengthen my advice; but observe, I do not thus bid you despair: on the contrary, I wish to prevent your falling into despondency, by teaching you to be prepared for the difficulties I know you must encounter, and by showing you that you may surmount them. Here were we hurried away from our haven as rapidly as a man may be from the high path of rectitude into the dark gulf of crime, and it has cost us almost as much exertion to return; but yet, at length, our haven is nigh, and we have every prospect of attaining it."

"Believe me, captain, I am grateful for the interest you take in my welfare," answered Don Luis, "and will endeavour to profit by your warning and counsels, which are of double value, as I feel that I required them."

"Be assured that I am not fond of giving advice to those who I know will disregard it," answered the Captain; and, seeing that his friend was about to speak, he added, "remember, I will not exchange with you the current coin given for advice, when both are empty and valueless; so we will say no more on the subject."

"As you wish, my friend," answered Don Luis. "Then what think you of your prisoner, or rather guest, Senhor Mendez?"

"That he is rapidly recovering from his wounds," said the Captain.

"Yes, he daily gains strength," said Don Luis: "but I mean as to who he is."

"That he is one who seeks to remain unknown," responded Captain Pinto. "Do not ask me further respecting him; for I cannot satisfy you, though he has made me acquainted with his history. He will pass for a Portuguese born in the colonies, and I shall thus be able to afford him assistance while he remains in Lisbon; and as few even on board have seen his countenance, and as I shall land him as a wounded man, there is no danger of his being recognised."

While this conversation was going forward, the ship was slowly running down the coast; and as we have ourselves sailed over the same ground, we are able accurately to describe it. On the low flat ground which stretches away to the north of the rock of Lisbon, they could clearly perceive with their glasses the domes and towers of the Escurial of Portugal, the immense palace and convent of Mafra, built by that pious debauchee, John the Fifth. This vast edifice is of a quadrangular form, showing a front towards the sea some seven hundred feet in length, with a lofty portico in the centre, which leads to the church. It seems, by its extent, rather calculated for a fortress, in which to quarter all the troops in the kingdom, than a refuge for humble monks, or a calm retirement for royalty. A suburb, as it were, of houses and cottages has sprung up around it.

They next passed under the serrated ridges of the rock of Lisbon towering towards the heavens, embosomed among which lies the beautiful and romantic vale of Cintra, rising, like an oasis in the wilderness, from the arid and scorched plains surrounding Lisbon. From the sea few of its beauties can be perceived, the only conspicuous object being the cork convent of Nossa Senhora da Penha, perched like an eyrie amid the most lofty cliffs, the first name being given to it from its being lined with cork to shield the monks from damp, as great part of it is hewn out of the solid rock. One small gap in the mountain alone allows the voyager a glimpse of the paradise within, filled with cork, orange, citron, olive, and numerous other trees and sweet-scented shrubs. Having doubled the cape, from beneath whose caverned rock the deep murmur of the sea was heard, they passed across the bay of Cascaes, with its low sterile cliffs, and a fresh sea breeze setting in, they entered the majestic Tagus by the northern passage, with a small island to the right entirely covered by a circular castle of white stone, built to protect the mouth of the river, called the Bugio fort. The scene was highly animating to those who had spent day after day without meeting, on the dreary expanse of waters, a friendly bark to cheer their sight, as they beheld numberless vessels, of all classes, sailing up the river with the fresh sea breeze, and boats of every description darting here and there over the sparkling waves. There was the lofty Indiaman, or richly-laden Brazilian ship, (for at that time Portugal monopolised the entire carrying trade to her colonies,) surrounded by a hundred boats which had come out to welcome relations and friends from their long voyage, or to inquire for those who remained behind, or might perhaps never return. Then there was the heavy-sailing English merchant brig, characteristic of her nation, possessing more bottom than speed, and proving to the world that the first maritime people could build the ugliest vessels, not surpassed in that respect by the tub-like, yellow-sided Dutchman, laden with cheeses in the shape of cannon balls. Among them were seen, in strong contrast, the graceful, high-pointed lateen sails of the Portuguese Rasca, used chiefly in the coasting trade; and the native schooner, or Hiate, with hulls not destitute of beauty, but rigged with masts raking at different angles, and their gaffs peaked at unequal heights; and also the curious Lisbon fishing-boat, shaped like a bean-pod, curving up at stem and stern, with a short rounded deck at each end, and a single high lateen sail. Then there were sloops, schooners, etc, etc, but all made way for the royal cruiser, as she proudly sailed up the stream, lowering their flags as she passed them in mark of respect. Passing close to the white tower of Belem and its gothic church at the westernmost part of Lisbon, they at length dropped their anchor opposite to that picturesquely-beautiful city, which rises on many hills from the shores of the wide-flowing Tagus, the white buildings glittering in the sun, crowned by the dark frowning castle, surrounded by suburbs intermixed with gardens filled with the richly-tinted orange-trees; but it was in those days very inferior in point of size and beauty to what it is now, and, alas! on entering it, its outward promise was found to be sadly deceptive; the streets were narrow, ill ventilated, and badly constructed, with a degree of dirt far surpassing that of any other European city; the extraordinary healthiness of the climate, and the heavy rains, aided by the canine scavengers which swarmed in it, and contributed to carry off the impurities, alone preventing it from being yearly visited by the plague, which the inhabitants took no other means to avoid. Amid this collection of dirt were, however, to be found numerous fine palaces, rich convents for both sexes, highly adorned churches of elegant architecture, and various other public buildings surpassed by few cities of the time. The river is here several miles in breadth; and on the opposite shore, which is composed of rugged cliffs, once stood old Lisbon, (Note), the ancient capital of Lusitania; while, looking up the stream, it has, from its wide extent, the appearance of a magnificent lake, which diminishes considerably the apparent height of its banks.

As it is not our intention to give a topographical description of Lisbon, we will return to the more interesting subject, we doubt not, of our narrative. No sooner were the sails furled, and the anchor had touched the ground, than, as the gallant bark rode securely on the smooth surface of the Tagus, she was surrounded by hundreds of boats, filled with eager and questioning passengers, and such shouts, cries, and vociferations, filled the air, that it was difficult to hear an order given or a reply made.

While Don Luis was waiting till the captain was prepared to accompany him on shore, and gazed admiringly on the beautiful panorama around him, his heart beat quick with the joyful anticipation of at length meeting her on whom, during his absence, all his thoughts had centred. He pictured to himself her delighted surprise at his unexpected return, and the rich blush which would suffuse her lovely cheeks, as, overcoming the natural bashfulness of love, forgetful of the formal etiquette of society, of everything, in her joy of seeing him, she would throw herself into his arms. Then he thought of the thousand questions she would ask of his adventures, and the answers he should make; of the animated glances of her bright eyes, as he described the storm and night-engagement with the rover, with the share he had taken in the strife; how she would tremble with agitation, as he recounted the dangers he had undergone, and how doubly dear he should be to her heart after all his escapes. Not once did his good friend Pinto's warnings and forebodings occur to him; not once did he think of the history of Senhor Mendez. How, indeed, could any dark or dismal thoughts intrude, surrounded by a scene of such loveliness, with that pure blue sky, and that clear sparkling atmosphere! All appeared to him of rosy hue, nor did he remember how false and treacherous was the outward appearance of the very city at which he gazed—a fit emblem of the fair promises of the world, full of foulness and deceit.

His thoughts were quickly broken in upon by the captain summoning him to the boat, which conveyed them on shore; and once more with joy did he press his native soil, as, attended by Pedro, he hastened to his father's house, while Captain Pinto repaired to the Admiralty, to report the arrival of his ship.

Note. Ourique, opposite Lisbon, the birth-place of Portuguese monarchy.

Volume One—Chapter Four.

We must now quit the free, boundless, ever-varying ocean, on which we delight to dwell, with its exciting incidents of the chase, the tempest, and the fight, for the confined space of a crowded city.

The palace of the Marquis d'Alorna was situated near the centre of Lisbon, on the rise of a hill, at a short distance from the river; and although the approach to it was through what we should now consider narrow, dirty streets, it was an edifice of some consideration, constructed of fine hewn stone, with a handsome entrance, through which a carriage might drive to the foot of a broad flight of steps, leading to that part of the mansion inhabited by the family, the lower part being appropriated for stables, and for the use of the inferior order of domestics, and where also the family coaches stood in conspicuous array. But it is to the upper story of the building, where, in Portugal, are frequently situated the most agreeable rooms of the house, that we would introduce our readers. It was a large apartment, a broad balcony in front, with a heavy, highly-carved balustrade of stone-work, from which was seen a fine view of the Tagus, blue and sparkling in the bright sunshine, and covered with white dancing sails, wending their course in every direction. The interior decorations of the room were rich, but not according to the most approved taste of the present day. Over the windows hung curtains of yellow damask, which cast a glare anything but becoming to the complexions of the inmates, and the ceiling was decorated with a fresco painting of some allegorical subject, most difficult to determine. The walls were covered with tapestry, representing a scene in Arcadia, it might be presumed, from a number of fair ladies figuring in the landscape in the fanciful costume of shepherdesses, with crooks in their hands adorned with flowers and ribbons, who ought to have been tending several flocks of sheep scattered far and wide; but their attention was diverted from these pastoral duties by listening to the passionate addresses of sundry youths, in bag wigs and swords, who were kneeling at their feet in all the most approved attitudes of devotion. A surprising number of waterfalls, temples, bridges, and romantic cottages, fit abodes for love, peace, contentment, and little children, filled up the interesting picture. In a small alcove on one side was an altar, on which stood an image of the Virgin and Child; the mother dressed in robes of blue and gold stripes, trimmed with pink, and a crown of silver and precious stones on her head, the whole figure surrounded by bright wreaths of artificial flowers; but it appeared a pity, since so much expense had been lavished on her decoration, that the same pious hand had not afforded even the slightest garment to shelter from the inclemency of the weather the little smiling cherub in her arms. The floor was of highly polished chestnut, not covered by any carpet, except a narrow strip below a row of high-backed chairs, of dark carved mahogany, placed against the walls. Several doors opened from the room, affording a long vista beyond, of other apartments, to the opposite windows of the palace, through which might pass the refreshing breeze from the river.

But it is time that we should describe the occupants of the chamber; for there were several of the gentler sex seated in a circle near the open window, some on low chairs or stools, the others having placed themselves on the ground in the eastern fashion, with their work before them.

The lady who seemed of most consequence in the party was reclining with her back to the side of the window, so as to command a view of the world without, and, at the same time, to see and hear what was going forward in the room. She was young—very young; by her appearance scarcely counting eighteen summers of life, and beautiful as the pure sky of her native clime; but already on that high and pure brow had thought, care, or passion, cast a faint, scarce perceptible sign, which came and passed away like a thin fleeting cloud. The bright hue of health and spirits was on her oval cheeks, and there was a sparkling lustre in her full dark eye, which, at times, however, wanted, alas! that soft gentle expression so much more requisite to the eye of ebon hue than to any other: but who could quarrel with the faultless features of her exquisitely chiselled countenance? Her figure was scarcely of the average middle height, but it was beautifully formed, every limb rounded to perfection; indeed it was rather full than otherwise, relieved by her swan-like throat, and the fine fall of her shoulders.

She was sumptuously dressed in richly flowered silks; her hair, of raven hue, drawn from off her forehead, and slightly powdered, was arranged in many curls, and fastened at the summit with pins of gold. She had been occupied, or rather pretended to be occupied, in working with silk on canvass, the fashionable employment of ladies in those days; but the work appeared to be proceeding but slowly, as the small part only of a design was seen, and it was now thrown, with various bright coloured balls, at her feet. The rest of the party were rather more industriously employed in the like sort of occupation, though the gay peals of light laughter which rose from the circle, showed that they were not very earnest about it; their incentive to merriment appearing to proceed from a personage not the least remarkable of the group, seated opposite to the lovely being we have described. Her features were of jetty black, of that intense ugliness rarely seen in youth, at all events but in the negro race; and although she was scarcely more than three feet high, her head was as large as that of a full-grown person, with round shining eyes, a good-natured, contented smile ever playing round her full ruddy lips, which disclosed a full proportion of immense pearly teeth, the grotesqueness of her features increased, evidently by design, by a costly costume of every hue: her hair, too, according to the fashion, being dressed in a high peak, was decorated also with ribbons of the most glaring colours. The little lady did not, however, appear at all conscious of the absurdity of her appearance; but, on the contrary, seemed to consider herself habited in a most becoming costume, receiving all the compliments which were jokingly paid her, as her due. When she spoke, the tones of her voice were as deep as those of a full-grown person, and when she became excited in conversation, there was a degree of harshness about them far from agreeable.

"Well, my sweet mistress," said this curious-looking being, rising as if about to take her leave, "I must tear myself away from your enchanting presence, to return to the high personages who sent me, with the joyful news of the prospect of your quick return to health; but, ere I go, I must acquit me of my mission, and deliver this holy relic, with which I was charged, as a sovereign remedy against all human ills." Saying which, she produced a small silver casket, from a large bag which she carried in the shape of a reticule, adding, "Know that it contains part of the precious remains of the most holy Saint Anthony, being his true and veritable little finger, presented to her majesty by the pious father Malagrida, who certified the many miracles it had worked in the various parts of the world to which he had borne it. You will find therein that which will cure you of your malady in the space of a few hours, if you keep it in your own possession," she whispered, with a significant expression, as she delivered the case into the hands of the young beauty.

"Express my gratitude to her majesty for her bounteous kindness in remembering me," answered the young lady, "and say I have a firm and pious trust in the efficacy of her holy remedy. In truth, it is well able to cure me of all the malady with which I am afflicted," she added, laughing. "But, remember, Donna Florinda, that is not to be a part of the message you are to deliver."

"Oh no," answered the jet-coloured little lady; "trust to my discretion—I thought as much when I brought the casket, which, however, I will leave, as you may require it; though those sparkling eyes, and the rich colour on those lovely cheeks, betoken little sign of disease."

"My illness was one imposed on me by my honoured father, at the instigation of his lady wife, to prevent my attendance at Court," answered the young lady; her eye flashing angrily as she spoke. "Thank Heaven! I shall soon be my own mistress, nor will I yield again to their unjust commands."

"Spoken like a girl of spirit," said the Dwarf. "I like those who will never submit to tyranny; and be assured that his majesty will much applaud your determination, for all the Court mourn the absence of its brightest ornament. But I must not stay chattering here, or it will be supposed I am lost, and then there will be a hue and cry all over Lisbon in search of me; for I am much too valuable a person not to be a prize to any who could carry me off."

"You would indeed be a treasure, Donna Florinda, to the happy person who possessed you, but their majesties esteem you far too much to part with you willingly," returned the lovely girl, laughing.

"Methinks they do, and I have no intention of quitting them. I know when I am well off.—Now, again, my sweetest friend, adieu." Saying which, Donna Florinda sprang up, imprinting a kiss on each cheek of the beautiful girl, who received the salute, as a thing of course, and then curtseying with an air intended to be very dignified, she turned to quit the apartment.

"Run, maidens, run," exclaimed the young lady. "Run and attend Donna Florinda to her chair. Haste all of you, and pay her proper respect." The maids, accustomed to the imperious orders of their young mistress, threw down their work, and followed Donna Florinda, for so their majesties of Portugal had been pleased to call their black favourite; and no sooner was the room cleared, than with eager hands the young lady opened the casket which had been sent her. It contained, doubtless, the little finger of Saint Anthony, but it contained also a small fold of paper, which she hurriedly abstracted, placing the casket aside, as a thing she valued not.

Agitation was visible on her countenance, as with trembling fingers she tore open the note. "Enchanting, beautiful girl," it ran, "too often have I gazed enraptured on those matchless charms to resist longer their enslaving power. Though the barriers of custom and bigotry intervene to keep us asunder, yet would I break through all obstacles to win one smile of acquiescence to my ardent wishes from those bright eyes! and ah! believe that this heart, which has never felt till now one pang of love, though surrounded by the fairest, the most lovely in the land, has at length been punished for its obduracy; nor can I experience one moment of peace till I know that this has been accepted by her for whom it is intended, and that she will deign to send some answer favourable to my hopes. From one who would, were it possible, lay a crown at the feet of the most captivating of her sex." No signature was attached to the epistle; but, as the lady's eyes glanced hurriedly over it, her breathing grew quick, a blush mantled on her neck and cheek, though remaining but a moment ere a pallor succeeded, as she placed it in her bosom, on hearing the return of her attendants along the corridor leading to her apartment. Her principal attendant gazed at her earnestly, with an expression of concern.

"Surely, Senhora, you are now really ill indeed; and I fear St. Anthony's finger has been of slight benefit. Let me run and procure you some of the restorative medicine I am ordered to take."

"No, no, there is no necessity for it," answered the young lady; "I merely slightly pricked my finger as Donna Florinda left the room, and the pain was acute, and made me feel faint; but it has passed away and left no mark. I shall be well again directly."

As she spoke her former colour returned to her cheeks, but the smile which had sat on her lips was not so easily recovered; and though she attempted to talk with animation, her gaiety was forced and unnatural. Before many minutes had passed, another visitor was announced as the Marchioness of Tavora, at which name the attendants stood up respectfully, the young lady advancing herself to the door of the apartment to receive her guest. The lady who now entered was of majestic deportment, with firmness and dignity in every movement, at the same time that there was much feminine beauty in her features; for, although they had much passed their prime, they yet retained a large portion of those charms for which she had once been celebrated, without any of the disfiguring marks of old age. She gazed with a look of affection, as she addressed the young lady, who conducted her respectfully to a chair, and placed herself on a lower seat at her feet.

"I have come, my sweet daughter, as an ambassadress from my son, the heir of his father's wealth and titles, earnestly to press his suit," began the Marchioness; "you know how fondly he loves you, and all the necessary preliminaries having been arranged between the Marquis of Tavora and your father, your consent is alone wanting to fix the day on which he may be made happy. Say, then, that you will not defer the day, and let me be the bearer of the joyful tidings to my boy."

"I am highly flattered by the honour you do me, Senhora Marqueza," answered the young lady, "and by the preference your son shows me; but I do not feel myself worthy of his love without giving mine in return, and I would rather not wed yet."

"Do I hear aright?" exclaimed the Marqueza, with surprise, and a degree of anger in her tone. "Can you, whom I already look upon in the light of a daughter, dream of disobedience to your father's commands, and refuse my son's proffered alliance? Such a thing is impossible. Have you not constantly given me reason to suppose that you would throw no difficulty in the way,—then why this sudden and unaccountable change of opinion? But I know that these words do not express your feelings: they were uttered more from a freak of maiden bashfulness, than from any confirmed determination. To such folly, however, you must not yield. Think well again before you give your final answer; for of such as that you before uttered I cannot be the bearer."

The young lady remained silent for some minutes; a pallid hue again overspread her features, and she gasped for breath, as if some intense feelings were passing through her bosom; but the Marchioness, occupied with her own thoughts, did not, apparently, observe her. At length, by a strenuous effort recovering her composure, she looked up. "If such is the will of my father, that I should wed, I will follow it," she said; "my hand, when he shall claim it, is at your son's command; and I must crave your pardon that I at first refused the proffered honour."

"My sweet daughter, you have made me most happy," exclaimed the Marchioness, folding her in an affectionate embrace. "My beloved son, on whom you know every sentiment of my heart is placed, will hasten to throw himself at your feet; but say, my fair child, when you will crown his joy, by bestowing that hand he prizes so much?"

"I would petition for a short delay," returned the lovely girl; "let the day be in November next: he will not have long to wait; and it is but short time to prepare to quit a home where I have spent the few happy days of my life, and for the future, alas! oh, may Heaven protect me!" The last part of the sentence was uttered rather to herself than aloud, nor did the Marchioness attend to the words.

"I will not, at present, urge you to fix an earlier time, though I would have wished it sooner; but perhaps my son may have more influence," said the Marqueza, smiling. "I must now go to relieve his mind of the anxiety which oppresses it, and before long, expect your loving bridegroom here." Saying which, the Marchioness of Tavora arose, and, embracing the young lady, she quitted the apartment with the same stately dignity with which she had entered, attended, with the utmost respect, by the retinue of maidens who waited on their young mistress.

We scarce dare describe the thoughts of the bride elect, of that young and lovely creature who seemed formed for virtue and happiness alone. She hastened to the open window to seek fresher air, for that in the room oppressed her, she thought, and stood gazing, with dilated eye, on the pure blue, calm sky, so contrasted with the agitation of her bosom. "Alas! for what am I prepared?" she exclaimed; "what a dark gulf do I see yawning beneath my feet, which no human power can aid me to overleap. Could I summon courage, I might yet escape; but then how blank and desolate would my heart become! No! I could part with happiness, rank, wealth, all the world esteems; but I cannot yield up love. Ah, why should I tremble or hesitate? Have not others done the same? and without risk, how can power and greatness be obtained? And yet, oh, heavens! I wish it had been otherwise."

Thus giving utterance to broken and disjointed sentences, in a tone often of despair and grief, her small delicate hands clasped together, she continued at the window for some minutes. Again she was silent, when what sounded more like an hysterical laugh than one of joy broke from her lips. "It were destruction to turn back now," she cried; "and, my young lord marquis, I am your most humble bride. Begone, from henceforth, all vain foolish fears and regrets, which gaiety will easily dissipate." She turned quickly round with a smiling countenance, for she heard a footstep approaching, thinking it was one of her female attendants; but she started suddenly at seeing, instead, the tall figure of a young and handsome cavalier, advancing rapidly towards her with the intention, it appeared by his gestures, of saluting her on the cheek without waiting for permission, had she not drawn back with an expression of anger in her countenance, and, throwing herself into a chair, coldly held out her hand. The movement had the effect, as by magic, of arresting the young man in his headlong career. He gazed at her for some time, without uttering a syllable, with a steady, mournful, and surprised look. "Can it be possible that I am so changed, during an absence but of two years, that you know me not?" he at length exclaimed. "I cannot, dare not, believe that Donna Theresa would thus cruelly have behaved, had she known me."

"Oh, I know you perfectly, my good cousin," answered the young lady; "nor do I perceive that you are in the slightest degree changed from the boisterous, forward youth you were when you set out on your travels, if I may judge by the unceremonious way in which you forced yourself into my private apartments."

The young cavalier gazed at her with amazement, while a look of pain, or we may say rather of agony, crossed his handsome features. "Do I hear aright," he exclaimed passionately, "or am I in some horrid dream? Yet methought all was reality till I entered here; but now I cannot, dare not believe my senses."

"You appear to me to be perfectly awake, Don Luis; nor do I wish you on any account to believe otherwise. Look round this room; the tapestry, the hangings, the furniture are the same; nor am I very much altered in appearance since the time you quitted Portugal. Your own extravagant expectations are alone not realised." She spoke in a tone half of banter and half serious,—"Come, come, my good cousin, lay aside, for Heaven's sake, that tragic air, more suited to the stage than to private society, and tell me to what cause I am indebted for this sudden visit from one I thought was basking in the sunny smiles of the fair beauties of England."

"Can you, Theresa, can you ask such a question?" exclaimed the young Cavalier, (in whom our readers may recognise Don Luis d'Almeida,) with grief and tenderness in his tone. "Does not your heart tell you that you were the first person I should fly to see on my return to my native land—that you were the magnet which has drawn me hither?"

"You do me too much honour," answered Donna Theresa, coldly; "but I should have supposed your filial affections would have prompted you first to throw yourself at your father's feet before you took the trouble of paying your respects to your numerous cousins, however intimate you may have been with them in your boyish days."

"Your words are but cold, heartless mockery to my feelings," answered Don Luis, vehemently. "Have you so soon forgotten our mutual vows of love and constancy, which Heaven recorded to stand as indelible witnesses against either who should be guilty of perfidy? Have you forgotten our troth, plighted in the sight of God, which none but ourselves can annul, with his just curse on the one who causes it to be broken? Were all my vows and protestations of love and attachment looked upon as mere empty words, which the passing breath of summer might blow away? Have a few months of absence served to wither what was once so fair and lovely? No, no, it is impossible! Say, did you never love me? Was I deceived from the first? Was my love considered but as a plaything to amuse, till some more glittering toy presented itself to attract your attention?"

"You overwhelm me with the rapidity and multiplicity of your questions, Senhor," answered Donna Theresa; "I can scarcely comprehend your long speech about love and constancy, and your violence frightens me. However, I will make due allowance for the uncouth manners you have acquired among the islanders, in whose territories you have been travelling, and will try to answer you to the best of my abilities. I certainly do recollect that, in our childish days, we were foolish enough to make some absurd promise to each other, which I no more hold as binding than any other act made by infants; besides, I have received absolution for any such deeds on my part, though I do remember you made a great many strange oaths and protestations, which I now consider highly improper; therefore, pray let me ask you, Senhor, by what authority you put these questions, not very complimentary, in truth, to me?"

"Great Heavens! can you expect me to remain calmly before you, while I listen to such words? You ask me by what authority I thus speak. By your own expressions when we parted; by your last fond embrace; by my own ardent, devoted love, which has not for one moment, by thought or deed, proved disloyal; your vows, protestations, tears, and sighs,—they, they give me authority to speak."

"Holy Mary, you frighten me with your vehemence!" exclaimed the young lady, raising her hands to hide her countenance; "I thought you had more wisdom than thus to make yourself appear ridiculous. Have I not before said, that people, when they grow up, are not to be answerable for all the folly and nonsense they may have committed in their childish days; then why insist on what no girl of sense can allow?"

"Say no more, Donna Theresa, say no more," cried Don Luis; "I were dull indeed not to comprehend your meaning. You have drawn aside the veil which shrouded my eyes; for I had thought that an inconstant and treacherous heart could not dwell within a form so lovely, so graceful as yours; but now, alas! what a hideous spectacle is laid bare to my sight! Donna Theresa, you have much to answer for to your sex. You have been the first to shake my faith in the innate purity and virtue of woman; for I supposed all who were so beauteous in form, must possess natures equally fair and adorable; but from henceforth, for your sake, can I place confidence in no one."

"Senhor, you are growing insolent," exclaimed the lady, rising from her seat, with an angry spot on her lovely brow; "you presume too much on our relationship and childish friendship, when you dare utter expressions like these, which no cavalier should venture to make use of before a lady."

Don Luis drew a step nearer, as if not understanding her last observation. "It is impossible that I am really awake!" he exclaimed, with deep passion. "A few fleeting months could not so alter Donna Theresa's tender, loving nature, as to make her, with cold, callous indifference, inflict so cruel, so bitter a wound on a heart which has thus faithfully adored her. No no, I wrong her, I foully wrong her! I wrong her gentle sex itself to suppose it possible. I see how it has been—I have, during my absence, been maligned; my character has been traduced, she has been taught to consider me false and faithless; a wretch unworthy of a thought; but I will discover the slanderer, and though I follow him through the world, I will punish him for his baseness. Speak, Theresa, speak! say it is so, and relieve my heart from the overpowering weight which is sinking it to despair; for then may I quickly clear my fame, and regain the priceless jewel I have lost!"

What woman's heart could withstand such an appeal? not Donna Theresa's, surely. Indeed, it would have been more fortunate for herself and her family had it been of a less tender nature. She appeared moved, as, with a slight falter in her voice, scarcely perceptible to any but a lover's ears, she exclaimed, "On no one, but on my own head, rests the blame; and on me let your anger fall. I have wronged you, Luis; I would have spared you this, but the time is passed for reparation, and my actions are not in my own power; yet we are no longer children, that I should mourn for the past, or that you should do aught unbecoming a man. Pardon me, Luis, for my heartless treatment; but I will no longer tamper with your generous feelings: my hand is pledged to another!"

Don Luis started as if an electric shock had struck him. "All is finished, then," he exclaimed, "and my fondly-cherished hopes are blasted! I will not reproach you, lady—I will not question you further. May he who has gained your hand not find that he also is betrayed." He stopped, and gazed a moment at her countenance. "Oh! pardon, pardon me for such words," he cried: "no, I will not, even in my thoughts, condemn you. For your sake I would have died; and, with my life, I will still protect you against all who may wrong you. Theresa, you know not what agony you have caused."

"Spare me, Luis, spare me," exclaimed his cousin. "I have told you that I have no longer power over my own destinies, and therefore words are thrown away. It were better for both that this interview should end; and, when we next meet, let us forget the past. Farewell."

Don Luis started at that word, casting one long earnest gaze at her, full of reproach and grief, which he could not repress. "Farewell, Theresa; may the happiness I do not expect to find be your lot!" he cried, in a voice broken with agitation, and rushed from the apartment.

Donna Theresa stood for a minute motionless, gazing in the direction her young cousin had gone, while bitterly did her conscience condemn her; but she was too proud, too firm in her resolve, to allow it to conquer. For good or for evil her course was taken, and she had determined nought should deter her from following it; yet the intensity of her feelings almost overcame her, and it was some time before she could recover herself, as she stood at the open window eagerly inhaling the fresh air, till the return of her attendants. They had judiciously kept away; for, it must be known, that in no part of the civilised world are Abigails more discreet than in Portugal; and, when they saw a handsome young cavalier rushing up stairs, whom most of them remembered as the playmate, and latterly the ardent admirer of their mistress, judging from their own feelings on such an occasion, they naturally concluded the cousins would wish for a short time, to enjoy, uninterrupted, each other's society. With most commendable consideration, therefore, they lingered on their return; or, at all events, did not approach nearer than the keyhole of some of the doors leading into the apartment, where they became highly-interested spectators of the drama enacting within; so that Don Luis gained, unawares, several warm advocates in his cause; for all joined in deprecating their mistress's cruel treatment of so handsome a cavalier, each one feeling that she could not have found it in her heart to be so obdurate.

Volume One—Chapter Five.

It has just occurred to us, that our readers will begin to suppose we design to make Don Luis d'Almeida our hero; but we must disclaim intending to introduce any such character; though, were we writing a romance, instead of compiling a history of the times of the great Marquis, he might, very properly, be considered in that light; indeed, we take great interest in his fate, for we cannot help sympathising with the sorrows of one, whom the blind archer has treated so cruelly; and we therefore omit many incidents mentioned in the voluminous manuscripts before us, in order to describe his proceedings, which, retrograding a little, we will now relate, from the time he landed with Captain Pinto from the corvette. His first impulse was to hasten to the palace of his father, the Conde d'Almeida; both longing to throw himself at the feet of a parent he revered, and knowing that he should there learn where Donna Theresa was residing. In his first hope he was disappointed; for, on entering his father's hall, a solemn silence reigned around, and everything wore a deserted and melancholy air. Instead of the grey-headed porter, and the group of liveried menials, water-carriers, idlers, and beggars, the maimed, and the blind, who usually throng the entrance of every noble's house in Lisbon, his feet aroused three or four hideous specimens of the canine race, who had thought fit to make it their abode during the heat of the day, till they should sally forth at night to join their brethren, and enact the part of scavengers to the city.

Pedro's loud vociferations, after sundry interrogations from some one above to inquire their business at the palace, at length brought down an old domestic, who no sooner caught sight of the person he thought was a stranger, than, in his agitation, letting his keys drop on the stone pavement, he rushed forward, with outstretched arms, to fold his young master in an embrace which lasted some minutes, now tapping him on one side, now on the other; but Don Luis took it as a matter of course, returning it with equal cordiality, till Pedro came in for a slighter share of the old man's welcomes. He was next obliged to go through the same ceremony with an old lady, whom the chirrupping voice of the old major domo called down. Her grey locks were partly concealed by a neat white handkerchief, fastened over her head, while another covered her shoulders, below which appeared a gown of a staid, sombre colour, a large black rosary and crucifix hanging down to her waist. To his eager inquiries for the Count, his father, he could for some time elicit no other answer than various broken exclamations.

"Oh, holy Virgin! oh, Jesu Maria! these are bad times, dangerous times," and they looked round cautiously to see that no one was within hearing. "There is now one in Portugal who is each day becoming a greater favourite of our lord the king, and who can do anything in the country, who rules the holy Church, who rules the people, and who seeks to rule the fidalgos also. Oh, he's a great man, doubtless, but he's much to be feared. Well, senhor, it was only the other day that your father's friend, Senhor Alfonzo Botelho, was arrested, we know not on what account, and thrown into prison, and when the Senhor Conde, your father, was exerting himself to the utmost for his liberation, and applied to Senhor Sebastiaö Jozé de Carvalho, the privy counsellor to the king, it was hinted to him that he might share the same fate if he interfered."

"What say you?" exclaimed Don Luis. "Have any dared to throw my honoured father into prison?"

"Heaven deliver us from a like calamity," answered the old couple. "Oh no, senhor, it is not so bad as that; but when the Senhor Conde came home, he ordered his carriage and his horses, and the escudeiro, and the other servants to be prepared, and set off the next day for the Quinta."

"This is indeed bad news you give me," answered Don Luis. "And I must hasten away to-morrow to join my father: I have therefore no time to lose in Lisbon. First, can you tell me if my fair cousin, Donna Theresa d'Alorna, is residing in the city, or is she in the country?"

"Oh, senhor, the Senhora Donna Theresa is at present at the house of the marquis, her father; but, alas! she is much changed from what she was; for she never comes here now to spend the day; though, to be sure, she has more to occupy her than formerly, for it is said she has become a great favourite of the queen, and is constantly at Court; and that is not a good place for young ladies, who are much better-employed staying at home, and learning to work and to embroider."

"The dissipations of a Court will have no power to alter Donna Theresa's heart," exclaimed the lover. "But now, my good Lucas and Senhora Anna, I must hasten away, though I will soon return; for I have much to learn and much to tell you."

"But you cannot think, senhor, of leaving the house without taking something to eat," exclaimed the old lady: "you would die of hunger, and you always used to have a very good appetite."

"All, senhor, do stay," added old Lucas, "and we will soon cook you up something to please you."

"I am not hungry, I assure you, my good friends," answered Don Luis; "and I cannot remain, but I will leave Pedro to recount all the wonders he has seen, and the dangers he has escaped;" saying which, he hurried off in the fond hope of finding his mistress fair and loving as ever. How grievously he was disappointed we have seen; and he then remembered Captain Pinto's warning and advice.

On rushing from the apartment of his false and fickle mistress, Don Luis scarcely knew whither he was wandering. All his bright hopes and aspirations were crushed and blighted at the moment he expected to find them realised. A weight was on his heart, from which he felt none could relieve him, and he believed that from henceforth the world for him could have no happiness in store; but yet he recollected that he was a man, and he resolved not to sink tamely under his cruel fate.

Now we opine that romance writers would have made their heroes act very differently; they would either have thrown themselves, in despair, into the Tagus, or flown to weary the live-long hours in deploring their hapless lot, with groans and sighs, beneath the mournful shade of some solitary grove; but Don Luis was of a very different character. In the first place, he was too brave, and too much in his senses, to quit the world; and he had been taught, and believed, that he had no right to give up existence till summoned by a higher Power than his own will. Nor is suicide a crime at all common with his countrymen: they live under too bright a sky, and breathe too pure and elastic an atmosphere, to wish to change them for the gloomy, narrow tomb. Had he been of that disposition which delights to brood over grief in solitude, there were no shady groves in the neighbourhood of Lisbon whither he could repair to indulge his propensity, if we except a few orange and olive plantations, where he would most certainly have been accompanied by a rabble of little boys, to wonder what he could be about, probably mistaking him for some actor rehearsing his part in a tragedy. To return home was almost as bad; for he knew that he should be assailed by the importunate, though kind, questions of his old domestics; and though he had many relations and friends in the city who would be glad to see him, he could not bring himself to call upon them.

Inaction, in the present state of his feelings, was dreadful to him, yet, as he mechanically bent his steps towards his home, he found himself there before he had made up his mind what course to pursue. He was encountered on the steps by Lucas, who observing his young master's agitated countenance, comprehended at once that all was not as he wished. "These are sad times, senhor, sad times," said the old man, "and I fear you found Donna Theresa changed with them; but don't fret, senhor; come up stairs, and tell Anna all about it, and she will be able to give you the best comfort; for she nursed you when you were a little baby, and knows how to treat you."

The major domo's garrulous tongue reminded Don Luis that such was the very thing he wished to avoid, and he was about to rush out of the house, when another sentence of the old man's made him remain, "Oh! senhor, I forgot to tell you, that Ignacio d'Ozorio is here; he came with a message from your most reverend cousin, the holy Father Jacinto da Costa, to the Senhor Conde, to say that he wished to see him on urgent business, not being aware that he had quitted Lisbon; and when he heard that you had arrived, he said he would remain to see you, and that, perhaps, you would visit Father Jacinto instead of the Count."

"I will speak to Father Ignacio," said Don Luis; "where is he?"

"He awaits you in the drawing-room, senhor."

"Welcome back to Portugal, my son," said the Jesuit, in that calm, bland voice, so universal among the members of his order. "I came here, expecting to find your respected parent, but, as he is absent, I feel confident my superior will be glad to see you."

"I trust that my reverend cousin, Father Jacinto, is not unwell?" said Don Luis.

"His health does not fail him, nor his mind, though the latter is sorely vexed by the attacks which are daily made against our order, and which require all his energy and talents to combat; but on that subject he will speak to you."

"I will gladly accompany you, and am ready this instant to set out," returned Don Luis.

"You know not, my son, the changes which have taken place during your absence; for it is now dangerous to be seen holding conversation with one of our order, so hated are we by the secretary of state, Sebastiaö Jozé de Carvalho. I will precede you, and announce your coming."

After the Jesuit had departed, Anna and Lucas did their utmost to detain Don Luis till he had eaten of the repast they had prepared; but declaring that he had no appetite, to pacify them, he begged them to reserve it till his return, and with hurried steps set out towards the convent of which his cousin was the principal.

He had a considerable distance to traverse, through many narrow dirty streets, up and down hill, till he reached the convent, situated in the upper part of the city. It was a plain and solid building of stone, suited to the unostentatious tastes and habits of its founders, whose great care is, to avoid show or pretensions of any sort. He was received at the entrance by one of the lay members of the order, who informed him that the principal was at that moment engaged with a stranger, and requesting him to wait for a short time, till he should be at liberty to receive him, and conducting him, through several passages and corridors, to a small apartment appropriated to the guest who might visit any of the fathers, he there left him. If primitive simplicity, and want of all outward decoration, were marks of peculiar sanctity, this room might vie with any in holiness; for, except a few high-backed chairs, of some dark wood, and a table of the same colour, with writing materials, furniture there was none, the walls being simply whitewashed, and the ceiling of chestnut, a wood much used in Portugal, particularly in monastic buildings.

Don Luis, being left alone, paced the room with hurried steps, half repenting that he had thus exposed himself—he knew not for how long a time—to the company of his own bitter and agitated thoughts. There was not an object within to draw off his attention; neither, at that moment, would a picture of Titian's, nor a statue from the hands of Praxiteles, have had sufficient charms to attract his observation. But at length he reached an open window, which looked into a garden filled with orange-trees loaded with their delicate-tinted flowers and rich fruit, round the roots of which the gardener had just allowed to flow a rill of water; and the grateful trees were exhaling their delicious odours, in return, as it were, for the benefit bestowed, scenting the air far and wide. So balmy was the air, so soothing the scent, that even his sad thoughts yielded to the soft influence of kind Nature's gifts,— a calmness stealing imperceptibly over his soul, and changing the whole current of his thoughts. "How delightful would it be," he fancied, "to rest, in a quiet seclusion like this, from all the cares and troubles of the world, free from the anxieties and disappointments of love, the fever of ambition, the intrigues of the Court, the scenes of strife which rage beyond its walls! Yet!—No, no," he exclaimed, after his thoughts had been quiescent for some time, "man was not formed for such a life. How could I endure the seclusion and monotony of the cloister, the fasts and penances, the routine of worship, the separation from the gentler part of creation, false and fickle though they be?" he added bitterly. "No, I am not formed for a life of seclusion and indolence."

How often he might have changed his opinion during the course of the ensuing minutes, it is impossible to say, when the brother who conducted him into the apartment again appeared, to inform him that the principal was waiting to receive him. As he was passing through a long corridor, a person hastened by him, whose features a gleam of the evening sun lighted strongly up; but his conductor, taking no notice of the stranger, hurried him on till they reached the door of a chamber at the further end of the passage, knocking at which, a voice desired them to enter; and the brother, making a low reverence, retired. No sooner did the occupant of the room, in which the young noble found himself, perceive him, than, with a bland and cordial manner, he rose from his seat, and advanced to welcome him.

He was a man every way worthy of observation: his figure was tall and erect, the height of his appearance increased by the close-fitting, dark robes of his order, although he had already passed the meridian of life, and age had sprinkled a few grey streaks amid his dark hair. His forehead was clear, pale, and lofty, his cheeks were sallow and sunk in, with scarcely any colour on his thin lips, which, when not speaking, he kept firmly closed. His nose was aquiline, delicate, and transparent; but his eyes were the most remarkable features of his countenance, though they were sunk far in his head, of a grey tint, and of no considerable size; but it was their expression, and the bright searching glances they threw around, full of intelligence, which made persons addressing him feel that he could read every thought passing in their minds; and few but acknowledged to themselves that they stood in the presence of a superior being. His voice, too, was melodious, though powerful and manly; his enunciation rapid and clear, with a perfect command of language. Such was the man whose unseen subtle influence was felt by all ranks and conditions of people. But there was another greater than he, though scarce his superior in mind or ambition, but with greater boldness of execution, to whom, for a time, the force of circumstances gave the predominance,—an opportunity which he failed not to use to hurl his antagonist to destruction.

"Welcome, my son," he said, in a low, clear voice, as he led Don Luis to a chair opposite his own. "Welcome, my young relation, to the land of your nativity, though you come at a time of much anxiety and trouble. I had sent to your father to advise him of certain circumstances which have come to my knowledge, against which it is both his interest and mine to guard in our respective estates. When shall you see your father?"

"I propose to set out for the Quinta to-morrow," answered Don Luis.

"What! before you have seen your fair cousin, Donna Theresa d'Alorna?" returned the Jesuit. "But why do I ask?—you have seen her already, and the blow has fallen which I feared awaited you. I was aware of your love for Donna Theresa, and that she at one time returned it, for your interests have ever been dear to me, Luis; but I have since discovered that she no longer regards you with affection; and I now know that her hand is irrevocably engaged to another. Had I known of your arrival, I would have saved you the bitter feelings of learning the truth from her own lips; for well do I know how ill in youth we can bear disappointment, which, in our more advanced age, when our passions are cooled and our judgment is matured, we consider but of little moment."

"Nor age, nor philosophy could blunt the feelings of one who has loved as I have done," answered Don Luis, vehemently. "I dreamed not that you divined my love for my cousin Theresa; but since you know it, (for otherwise I should not venture to speak to you on such a subject,) tell me, Father, have I no hopes? Has she not been forced to accept the hand of another? If so, at all hazards, I will rescue her from destruction. None shall dare to tear her unwillingly from me."

"I can give you no hopes," answered the Priest, gravely. "She is engaged of her own freewill: nor can she ever be yours; but I speak, I know, to one of too superior an understanding to mourn for what he will soon learn to consider at its true value, a glittering, a tempting, but an empty bauble. What matters the loss of the love of a sex ever false and uncertain?"

"Say not so!" exclaimed Don Luis, interrupting him; "say not she is false—say not her sex is false! I alone am to blame for my own wretchedness. I set my hopes of happiness on a cast, and have miserably failed; and now what more have I to expect or wish for, than a speedy end to my woes on the field of battle, or amid the ocean tempest?"

The Priest smiled, as he answered calmly, "Is love, then, the only object of man's life? Are there not a hundred other occupations for the mind? Is not ambition alone sufficient to employ his thoughts? Will not power satisfy him? Does fame bring no satisfaction? Has wealth, and all that wealth can give, no allurements? Say not, then, because you have suffered this first check in the prosperous current of your existence, that life has nought else in store for you. The antidotes which I propose are sufficient to make you soon smile at your present feelings as the effect of a youthful folly."

"You cannot convince my heart," answered the young man. "But should I seek for consolation by the remedies you advise, at what can ambition in this country aim? How can power be obtained? or how can I, with honour, seek for wealth?"

The Priest, smiling, again said, "You speak as one who knows not the world. I mean not the outward, material world, the common machinery which moves the every-day actions of men: any coarse, ordinary being, with a little cunning and observation, may gain sufficient knowledge of that to accumulate wealth, and to guide his way free from danger amid the throngs of his fellows. But I speak of the minds and passions, the inward and intricate workings of the souls of men; of that accurate knowledge of the past, and keen observation of the present, by which we can foresee the future, thus to be able to determine exactly how mankind will act in masses or as individuals, and stoically to look upon the world as a vast chess-board, and its inhabitants as the chess-men, whom we move without any volition of their own, as a player free from any part or feeling with the senseless blocks; as well as to learn how to gain a command over ourselves, and thus to soar above the passions, the frailties, the vanities, and the folly of the common herd. Such is the true knowledge of the world to which a philosophical mind and dauntless soul may attain; and in such, my young friend, would I instruct you."

Don Luis remained silent with astonishment, while the priest keenly marked the effect of his words. "Is this the man," he thought, "whom I have regarded as the humble priest and confessor—the meekly-pious minister of our holy faith? But how and where can this knowledge be attained?" he said, looking up; "what means have I of learning the lore you speak of?"

"Have I not said that I would instruct you?" said the Priest. "Within the quiet precincts of these walls you may learn the first rudiments, and within the pale of our order you may become a master in the science."

"What! can you advise me to give up my title, my name, and fortune, and to assume the gown of a priest?" exclaimed Don Luis, hurriedly. "I expected not such advice from you."

"I advise you to do nothing rashly," returned the Jesuit, calmly. "But yet, let me ask you, what are rank and name but empty sounds, though often encumbrances to their possessors? And for your fortune, I grieve to say, for your father's sake, that has greatly diminished of late, so that, in truth, I ask you to give up but little, and offer you in return power and knowledge—the true science of the knowledge of mankind, for with us alone does it exist. Do I say exists? Alas! I ought rather to say existed; for, with some rare exceptions, how few are initiated into its mysteries! Their dull, sensual minds are incapable of comprehending them; and they have thus failed, miserably failed, in all the ends for which our order was instituted, by men as superior to those of the present day as light to darkness. What a comprehensive, what a noble and glorious conception was that of our great founder, and his immediate successors, who even jet more improved and systematised his plans;—but of that I will speak anon. I now speak openly to you, my young cousin, more so than I would to any other not in our order; but I know that I may trust to your honour not to divulge what I may say. I have liked you from your earliest youth. I have watched anxiously over you, and I have seen in you qualities which I would wish to cultivate, to conduct you to high destinies; and I frankly confess that I seek to join you to our company, as one fully able to elevate it again to its former standard of power."

Few men can entirely withstand the influence of compliments addressed to their mental superiority, and Don Luis was thus insensibly attracted to listen to the conversation of the Father. "I fear that you would find I did not answer your expectations," he at length said; "for I feel that I am but dull of comprehension, nor can I even understand to what the knowledge you speak of could lead."

"Is not knowledge confessed by all philosophers to be power? and for what are all men striving through life but for power?" responded the Jesuit. "For what purpose do kings make war but to increase their power? and yet their utmost aim is to rule over the sinews, the bones, the bodies of men, to extend their sway over the senseless earth which they call their own. But how far, how immeasurably superior is the power at which we aim!—we would rule over the minds of men—we would bend their insane passions to our own will, and would make them, by those means, the tools to work out our glorious projects. Hear me, then, and learn the sublime idea of our founder, which, had he and his immediate followers been succeeded by men equal to themselves, would long ere this have been realised. His aim—how superior to the ambition and vaunted glory of any conqueror who has spread desolation over the fair face of the globe!—was to join all the kingdoms of the earth under one sceptre, and that sceptre swayed by our hands; ay, by the humble friars of the order of the mystical Jesus; and yet, far different would it be from the power to which the Pontiff of Rome can ever hope to attain. Ah! you think such aims cannot be accomplished; yet, look around at every Court in Europe, and see how nearly we had once succeeded. Scarce a sovereign whose mind was not under our direction; and were it not for the dull, stultish understandings of those who have been admitted into our order, our success might have been complete. But they, alas! are beings so completely overwhelmed with the gross, sensual passions of our nature, as to be utterly unable to comprehend the pure, esoterical principles of our faith; and ignorantly interpreting, without a key to the mysteries, the words they find in that volume, never written to meet the eye of the vulgar, they fail in all the great aims of our existence as an order. In this country they have still more greatly erred, and, instead of securing friends, they have raised up enemies. The whole body of the priesthood is against us; but their united efforts we might despise, had we not a deadly foe in the person of Sebastiaö Jozé de Carvalho, the minister of the king, whose dauntless courage, boundless ambition, and the unscrupulous means he employs, make him more to be feared than any who have ever yet appeared in arms against us. So dull are those who are sent to work with me, that I cannot make them comprehend the means by which alone they can stem the torrent, or rather, turn it aside; nor is it in the power of one man to do so; yet have I done much, and even alone, will I boldly strive for the glorious principle of our constitution."— His eye dilated, and he unconsciously rose from his chair, as with increased energy, he continued—"and if I fail, and am hurled, as I most assuredly shall be, to destruction, I shall have the consolation of knowing that I have played for a glorious stake."

"Your words overpower me with astonishment," exclaimed Don Luis. "I did not suppose such ideas could have been conceived by the heart of man, much less by the members of an order whose quiet and unobtrusive manners are their marked distinction."

"Trust not ever to such deceitful appearances as the outward manners of a man," answered the Father; "a general, who would succeed against the foe, must not show his position and strength. Luis, I have thus spoken openly to you, far more so than to any who have not passed the threshold of our order; for I would win you to enter; and I know that I may trust to your judgment and honour; and were it not strictly forbidden, I should not fear to confide to you all the mysteries of our admirable institution. Ah!" he exclaimed, as his eye brightened, and a proud smile lighted up his majestic features, "an institution based on such firm, such true principles of philosophy, must live, though, for a time, it may sink beneath persecution—though, for a time, through the ignorance and obtuseness of members incapable of comprehending its tenets alone, its aims may be perverted, and its power diminished, yet the true word, the principle of its existence, will never be lost; and when the world least expects it, when people are unprepared to oppose it, will it spring up with power and lustre far surpassing what it ever before attained. In countries the most liberal and enlightened will it possess the greatest influence, by means of that very education of which they boast—ay, even in that country from which you have just returned, whose Church, through the absurd folly and neglect of its own ministers, has become a mere cipher in the state, without a shadow of authority over the people; yet does the true principle exist among a few sagacious men, who will cherish it as the lapidary does a precious jewel, whose value, when yet uncut, is unestimated by the common eye. The day will arrive when all those who acknowledge the symbol of the cross will again be joined under one ruling power,—the glorious aim of our order. You deem me enthusiastic and visionary in my hopes, because you know not the secret means by which we work. You know not how we become acquainted with the intricate operations of the minds of all with whom we come in contact, of all classes and religions. We learn the passions, the frailties, the foibles of every one; and thus many, unknown even to themselves, are our tools, and while they fancy that they are obeying the rules of their own sect, are but working out our ends. The end with us sanctities the means, and thus, to attain our objects, we consider every disguise, every fraud, allowable. Know, also, that though our open and avowed members are numerous, yet they fall far short of the real strength of our body; for we have among the priests of each of the various sects of the religion of the cross our secret brethren, who are strenuously working for the great cause. Ah, you start! but the idea is not new; and such was practised before that religion became known to the world; and in that very country which boasts of possessing what is called the blessing of religious liberty do we most strenuously work the whole force of that intricate machinery, which was for years forming, before it was brought to perfection; and thus shall we be able to laugh to scorn the puny efforts of those who dare to oppose us; for even now, in the seats of learning, in every university of the kingdom I speak of, are the seeds sown which will, sooner or later, bring their fruit to perfection. And it is among the young and pliant minds, while they fancy themselves most secure, that we most easily work our way. But the great assistants to our cause are the softer sex; for, by their gentle influence are others won over to aid us, and we therefore spare no means to gain them. We work upon their vanity; the tendency of their natures to adoration; the feeling that they must lean for support on others, to make them place their trust in us; and when such means fail, we win their love: their passions make them subservient to us, and they become our slaves for ever.

But such license has been much abused by the baser members of our order, who cannot comprehend that it is over the minds alone of their flock that authority is given them, to gain which any means may be pardoned."

There is no bait which has more alluring attractions than the idea of possessing illimitable power over the minds of our fellow men; yet Don Luis was not caught by it. And, although the Father was enthusiastic in his hopes, he did not exaggerate the influence which his sect possessed throughout the world; as for his predictions with respect to Britain, at this day their great stronghold, we must examine well the principles professed openly by a large body of the members of the Established Church, encouraged by many of the highest rank in it, and admired by the greater number of the young aspirants for the clerical profession, and then let us judge whether they were well founded or not. But we wish not here to discuss the subject, and have given merely the opinion of one high in his order, as we have found it written, whose mind was raised far above the vulgar aims of his associates.

Don Luis heard with unmitigated astonishment the doctrines which the Father so boldly advanced; although, from the various societies in which he mixed during his travels, particularly in Paris, where those principles of false philosophy were generally discussed, which led to the atrocities of the revolution, he was not quite so much startled as most men of his rank in Portugal would have been; yet he was of too generous, too unambitious a disposition to be thus tempted to grasp the mysterious and potent sceptre presented to him.

"Father," he answered, gravely, after some minutes' silence, "my ambition aims not at such power as you describe; and, methinks, few but those who have from their youth been educated in your order, could be brought to train their minds to forward a system which has, to the uninitiated, too much the appearance of treachery towards their fellow men; for as such I feel it, though, to you I speak with no disrespect, and am grateful for the confidence you repose in me, which, be assured, I will not betray; but I must endeavour to seek some other field for my exertions than the one you offer."

The Jesuit looked at him sternly; it seemed, that an almost imperceptible smile—it might have been a sneer—played round his mouth. "I did not anticipate such an answer from you, Luis," he said, "but thought you would take a more comprehensive and philosophical view of the principles I have explained to you; yet, my wish being alone to convince your understanding, I will not further press the subject, though I feel assured you will, before long, learn to change your opinion. However, for the present, my good cousin, I trust your mind will be sufficiently employed on the reflections to which our conversation has given rise, to make you forget the treachery and deceit of Donna Theresa—qualities which, you seem to insinuate, belong exclusively to our order. Now, let me tell you, that, in communication with the world, all men use deceit; that it is impossible to succeed without it; and that truth, as society is constituted, is utterly incompatible with its customs. Indeed, the latter quality exists but in one science, and that is in geometry: all else is false or unsatisfactory. Talk, therefore, no more of deceit and treachery, for the world, our very existence, is full of it, and you cannot avoid the common lot." The Priest smiled, perhaps at his own reasoning, and continued—"Now, my dear cousin, think of what I have said, and when you return to Lisbon, we will speak further on these matters. In the meantime, you must be the bearer of important information to your father, which I have gained from an indubitable source. Learn, then, that Carvalho is using every effort to crush our order,—so strong a barrier to his ambition,—and, knowing that the nobles are our firm upholders, he intends to weaken their influence in the state, by bringing accusations of all sorts against them; when he will imprison, banish, or execute all whom he fears. I have reason to think that he, at present, suspects there is a plot hatching against him; but he allows it to proceed, anxious to get as many as possible drawn into it, and, amongst them, your father. Advise him, therefore, to remain quietly at his Quinta; neither answering, nor, if possible, receiving, any communications made to him, till he hears further from me; and when you return to Lisbon, avoid intimacy with any one, for you cannot discern friends from foes in these times. And now, my son, farewell: I expect another visitor, and must not detain you."

"Farewell, most reverend Father," answered Don Luis, rising at the hint, and respectfully kissing the hand held out to him. "I shall not easily forget your conversation; and your advice I will bear to my father."

The tinkle of a bell summoned a lay brother, who escorted Don Luis from the apartment, the Superior following the young man's retiring form with his piercing glance. "He will yet be mine," he uttered, half aloud. "He is wary and timid, and will not take the bait at the first sight; but it is too bright and dazzling not to attract him at last, and he will play round it till he is caught."

The door again opened, and another visitor entered, the Superior rising and embracing him with every mark of respect; and, having led him to the seat he had himself occupied, took one of humbler dimensions, while he seemed prepared to listen attentively to the words which might fall from the lips of his friend. He was a man far advanced in life, of a tall and gaunt figure; his gown, of the fashion of the Jesuits, fitting ill around him. His hair, only partially grizzled, though shorn at the top, he wore (unusually for a priest) in long straggling locks, probably in affectation, to increase the wildness of his extraordinary countenance, which was furrowed and bronzed by exposure to the weather and burning climes. His features were coarse, and thoroughly unintellectual; but his eyes gave expression to the whole physiognomy: they were large, round, dark, and lustrous, with a certain turn in them which caused those who beheld him to suppose that they were glancing in different directions. Every lineament proclaimed the fanatical enthusiast, which the style and substance of his oratory fully confirmed.

Such was the appearance of the holy Father Malagrida, for he whom we have described was that celebrated personage. "Pax vobiscum, holy Father," he began, in a low, deep voice, though with rather a nasal sound. "The spirit of the Blessed Virgin ordered me, in a dream, to come to you, to consult you regarding the best means of preserving the honour and glory of our order inviolate at this critical juncture; yet think not that it was a common dream which prompted me, but a beatific vision of the fair daughter of Saint Anne, in the form she wore before she knew that she was to be the joyful mother of the King of men."

"You are favoured with partiality by Heaven, Father Malagrida," answered the Superior; "and happy are you to rejoice in so great a blessing, while I am left to grope my way in darkness, without any such signs of Heaven's approbation."

"My prayers to Heaven, my fastings and castigations, my long and arduous voyages, with all the perils of the sea and land, have not been thrown away; and as a reward for my pious exertions, it has been given me to see visions, and to prophesy events, even before the saints above know them; ay, to speak in strange tongues the words of truth, even in such strange tongues that none can understand them."

"You are doubtlessly highly favoured," answered his wary companion; "but methinks a little less outward demonstration of zeal, at the present moment, would have been more advisable, and you would yet have retained your post as confessor to the queen, and enjoyed the lofty satisfaction of leading her gentle soul to eternal salvation."

"Ah! that is the subject about which I would speak," answered Malagrida: "most foully have I been thrust out of my office, and I would revenge myself, or I would say it is the duty of our order to punish that heretical, iron-hearted man, Sebastiaö Carvalho, who has been the cause of all the injuries inflicted on us."

"You speak words of wisdom, my brother," returned the crafty Jesuit; "but how would you accomplish the noble end you have in view, so greatly to the advantage of our holy religion, and the safety of our order?"

"I would stir up the people against him, as one hateful in the sight of Heaven; I would call down the thunder of Rome upon his head; and I would work upon the fears and piety of the king to recall those who have for so long possessed the precious care of his soul, ere he delivers it into the power of the prince of darkness in the person of his minister."

"But should the king refuse to hear you, and still follow the evil suggestions of Carvalho?" asked the other.

"Then will I make him tremble on his throne!" exclaimed Malagrida. "The nobles and the people shall rise against his unholy power, and his death shall teach monarchs that our order is not to be trampled on with impunity."

"Truly, my brother, the spirit of inspiration is on you," said the Superior, casting a keen glance towards him. "And nowhere can our order find a more zealous advocate."

"For that was I born; for that have I fought; and for that will I die!" exclaimed Malagrida with enthusiasm. "Such is the spirit which should animate all our order, and we should triumph, in the name of our Lord, against all opposition which frail man can offer."

We need not detail the whole of the conversation, which proceeded for a considerable time in the above style: the cool, calculating policy of Father da Costa strongly contrasted with the wild enthusiasm of Malagrida, upon which he worked, while the latter, at the same time, through the ravings of madness, showed a shrewdness and sagacity in worldly matters, where the interests of his order were concerned, which did credit to the school in which he had been educated. When Malagrida had retired—"Stubborn madman that you are," muttered the Superior, "you are yet a necessary and useful tool in the hands of those who know how to wield you, though alone you are like a scythed war-chariot, dragged on by wild horses without a guiding hand, carrying havoc and destruction wherever it appears."

Volume One—Chapter Six.

At the time of which we write, the streets of Lisbon were, perhaps, the most rugged, the most ill-lighted, the worst paved, and the most filthy, of any city in Christendom. It is true lanterns were placed before the shrines of the saints, at nearly every corner of the streets; but the glasses of some had been sacrilegiously broken, and the pale lights which glimmered from the rest served but to make more palpable the obscurity of the other part of the way; indeed, it was considered often a service of danger, by the wealthy citizen, to venture out without a torch-bearer and several armed men to protect him from the bands of marauders, who were constantly prowling about, and hesitated at no kind of atrocity. Assassination and robbery were of nightly occurrence; seldom, indeed, was the latter committed without murder; the system of the ruffians being first to plunge their daggers into the bosoms of their intended victims, and then to rifle them. Thus, although private revenge often prompted the deed, as the murdered man was always found stripped of his valuables, he was supposed to have fallen as a chance offering to Siva, and no further notice was taken of the affair; the faint cry of *Acad el rey*! (Note) as the cold steel entered his unguarded bosom, was heard ringing through the night air, and the trembling citizens, fearful of being subpoenaed as witnesses, or accused of the deed, would keep close their doors, and leave the unfortunate wretch to perish unaided, when timely succour might have saved him, should the dagger, by chance, have ineffectually accomplished its work.

But few years ago, we remember returning at early dawn from a party, when we encountered several persons, and two guards, standing round a man on the ground weltering in blood yet flowing warm from a deep wound in his side. A convulsive shudder passed through his frame, yet no one attempted to aid him, the guards keeping every one off with their bayonets, saying it was their duty to allow none to touch him till the officers of justice had arrived to inquire into the case. The man was then past recovery; but had aid been afforded him when first discovered, he might probably have been saved; yet, surrounded by his fellow creatures, he was allowed to bleed to death without a saving hand held forth. If we recollect rightly, he had been an officer in the Miguelite army, and had committed several atrocious acts; but had he been a friend, the same would have occurred. But to return to earlier times. It was then also the practice of the dissolute and idle young fidalgos to range the city with bacchanalian songs, injuring and insulting all they met; often on the slightest resistance, spilling blood, and committing, indeed, every sort of excess, besides amusing themselves, in their milder moods, with those practical jokes at one time fashionable in England, and probably imitated from them. In his youth, it was said that Sebastiaö Carvalho had been a leader in one of the most daring of these bands, when, to make his gigantic height more conspicuous, he dressed himself with a white hat and shoes, driving all rival parties before him. Being thus perfectly acquainted with all the mysteries of the system, he had determined, now that he had succeeded to power, to put down all disorders of the sort. Such was the state of Lisbon in 1755, and, as far as cleanliness was concerned, it was not much improved in 1830; but since then, under the beneficial influence of a liberal and more enlightened government, vast improvements have taken place; drains have been formed; it is paved and well lighted, and as well patrolled as any city in Europe, though not more so than the second city of the kingdom, Oporto, through any part of which a person may walk at night without the slightest fear of robbery, owing to a highly efficient municipal guard.

Though there were doubtless many more important personages who figured at that period, we must not lose sight of our friend Don Luis. It was nearly dark when he issued from the portals of the Jesuits' College, and, the distance to his own residence being considerable, night had completely set in by the time he reached the lower part of the city, when it occurred to him that it would have been more prudent to have ordered Pedro to attend him. But his mind was too much engrossed by the conversation he had held with Father da Costa, to think much of the danger he ran; and as one strong poison will often prove an antidote to another, so had the new ideas opened to his view banished for a time the recollection of his own griefs and disappointments. He hurried on as fast as the badness of the way would permit, through streets extremely narrow; the houses being lofty, with many stories, their fronts adorned with various figures carved in stone, and the upper floors projecting beyond the lower, little light was afforded to the passenger, from the sky, even when clear and spangled with stars, as it was at the present time. He had already reached the street leading to that in which his father's house was situated, without meeting any interruption, when, having just passed a shrine dedicated to Saint Anthony placed at a corner house, a small lamp burning in front of it, shedding forth its pale light, like a sad epitome of the glorious illumination that pious man spread among his much loved Lusitanians, his eyes, now directed on the ground, to pick his way clear of the immundicities which strewed the way, and now in front, in a vain endeavour to pierce the gloom, he fancied that he saw on the white stone wall of a house close to him, which the rays of the lamp reached, the shadow of a man, with arm uplifted, in the attitude of one about to strike. His nerves were fortunately well strung, his courage undaunted, and his frame well knit and active to obey his will; but not a moment was there for thought, and as the threatening apparition caught his eye, quick as lightning he sprang round, ere a dagger, gleaming brightly, had time to descend, and, seizing the hand which grasped it, wrenched the weapon from the power of the cloaked assassin, who stood behind, and dealing him a heavy blow on the face with the handle, laid him prostrate on the ground. The ruffian was, however, not without support; for, at the same moment, a man sprang across the street with dagger in hand, ready to avenge his comrade. But Don Luis was not to be taken thus at advantage; for, retreating a step, his own sword was prepared to receive the wretch on its point. The latter, however, throwing himself back in time, fled a few paces, and gave a shrill whistle, which was answered at several points, and three men rushed forward with threatening attitudes and unsheathed weapons. Don Luis was fortunate in his ground, having a wall with a projecting buttress behind him, and an uneven pavement in front, the lamp of Saint Anthony affording sufficient light to see objects around with tolerable distinctness. He was, notwithstanding, obliged to exert his utmost activity and skill to keep his assailants at bay, being happily a good swordsman, an accomplishment even then considered a necessary part of a gentleman's education. The clash of steel rang loudly through the silence of night, but none put their heads out of their windows to inquire the cause; and, Luis disdaining to give the usual cry for assistance, was well nigh exhausted with his exertions, when, most opportunely, a person, passing a neighbouring street, was attracted by the noise, and appeared so suddenly on the scene of action, that the bravoes had scarce time to turn and defend themselves.

"Fight on, gallant sir, for the honour of gentlemen!" shouted a clear, manly voice. "Help here! *Acad el rey*! help, ye lazy citizens, to drive away a set of cowardly rascals, who dare not face us man to man! No matter, we might call till doomsday, and no one could come; so here is at you, sir villains;" saying which, Captain Pinto, for he was the speaker, redoubled his efforts to repel the marauders.

"Thanks for your aid, thanks, Captain Pinto," cried Don Luis, recognising his voice; "I have but short breathing time to speak."

"Ah, my young friend, Don Luis, is it you?" answered the Captain. "Back, ye villains, back!"

"Don Luis!" exclaimed one of the men, with an oath. "We have made a mistake."

"No, no," shouted another,—"cut them both down—they must not escape."

At that instant, a broad glare of red light burst on the scene of action, proceeding from several torches borne by a party who were turning the corner of the street.

"Fly," cried the ruffians, "fly! or we shall be captured."

"You shall not get off so easily," cried the Captain. "We will teach you not to attack gentlemen in this way in future." The men attempted to escape; but Don Luis and his friend held them in check on one side; while, on the other, the party with the torches, led on by a person who seemed of distinction, rapidly approached. Making, however, a desperate effort, they rushed past them, and were lost in the obscurity, except one, through whose arm, Captain Pinto's sword entered, and brought him to the ground.

The chief of the new comers, taking a torch from the hand of one of his attendants, ordered them, in an authoritative tone, to seize the disturbers of the public peace, and advanced towards the Captain and Don Luis, on whom they were on the point of laying hold.

"Ah!" he exclaimed, "my good friend, Captain Pinto!—not yet tired of fighting? I trust you are not injured,—and your companion?" he added, holding the torch nearer Don Luis's countenance.

"Don Luis d'Almeida, my fellow voyager," answered the Captain.

"Ah, the son of an excellent father," observed the stranger; "I hope he, too, is safe?"

"Many thanks to your Excellency, we are both uninjured," returned Captain Pinto. "And my young friend, who was the first attacked, fought as bravely as he did before the enemy."

"I am glad to hear it," said the stranger. "Brave men are more scarce than cowards. Carry those men off to prison," he added, turning to his followers, who secured the two ruffians who had been unable to escape. "The affair must be looked into to-morrow. You, gentlemen, I will accompany to your houses, for these streets are unfortunately not fit to be walked by honest men, without guards and lights; but such things shall be amended before long."

The stranger was a man of almost gigantic stature, and, as he strode rapidly to the scene of conflict, his movements exhibited strength and activity; the suit of dark cloth in which he was dressed, such as is now worn exclusively at Court, setting off to advantage his muscular and well knit figure. There was also a confident air of authority in his words and actions, which betokened one who felt that he had a right to command. "Come now, gentlemen, we will proceed," he said; and ordering the torch-bearers to advance, the party moved forward, the guards bringing up the rear with the prisoners, who no sooner saw into whose power they had fallen than they quietly submitted to their fate. Don Luis was at a loss to conceive who the tall stranger could be, and as he found himself walking on the opposite side of him to his friend, he had no opportunity of asking.

"All, Senhor Don Luis," he said, "you have lately been travelling, I understand from Captain Pinto, in a country where such disorders as these do not occur, and where a man may walk the streets at night, or journey from one end of the kingdom to the other, without fear of losing either his purse or his life."

"Scarcely so, senhor," answered Don Luis, "robberies are constantly occurring even in the public streets; but the English have, in general, an abhorrence of shedding blood, except that of their enemies."

"Ah, that arises from their not being able to purchase absolution at as cheap a rate as do our countrymen," interrupted the stranger, with a sarcastic laugh; "aided, perhaps, by a wholesome fear of detection, the best preventive of crime. However, continue: it gives me pleasure to hear accounts of England, a country I much admired, during my short residence there; although, not having time to acquire the harsh language of its inhabitants, I had some difficulty in becoming acquainted with its internal arrangements. At all events, a person may travel on the public roads without arms, or without fear of being robbed as here."

"Pardon me, senhor, such is not the case," answered Don Luis. "The roads are constantly infested by men on horseback, who levy contributions, even in the very neighbourhood of the capital, on the unarmed traveller."

"Ah! I am glad to hear we are not so very much less civilised than our old friends and allies, who are apt to boast themselves so much our superiors," returned the stranger. "We have now arrived at your house, senhor, and I will not detain you; but as I have many questions to ask respecting England, I should wish to see you to-morrow morning at eight o'clock, and till then, adeos."

"I regret that I cannot do myself that honour, senhor," answered Don Luis; "for I intend to set forward at daybreak to visit my father, who is in the country."

"I should advise you to defer your journey to a later hour," said the stranger, in rather an angry tone. "I shall esteem your doing so a favour," he added, more mildly, as if correcting himself. "You also forget that you will be obliged to appear at the examinations of the ruffians who attacked you. For the present, I will leave Captain Pinto with you, who will perhaps accompany you in the morning. Adeos, Senhor Pinto, till the morning, when I shall see you with your young friend." Saying which, the stranger moved on, without waiting for an answer, leaving the Captain respectfully bowing, and Don Luis much amazed, at the door of the palace, at which one of the guards had loudly knocked.

After sundry careful interrogations from within, the door was unbarred and opened. "Who is that man, who seems of so much authority here?" eagerly demanded Don Luis of his friend, as they were admitted into the hall by old Lucas.

"No other than Sebastiaö Jozé de Carvalho," answered the Captain; one of the ministers of the king, "who does more work in a day than the other two in a month, and has more brains in his head and courage in his heart than all the fidalgos in Portugal put together. You will do well to follow his request; for he is not fond of having his wishes neglected."

"In one respect I will, in requesting you to take up your abode here," said Don Luis, as they mounted the steps, preceded by the old steward. "Of the rest we will consider; but I like not his authoritative tone."

"Well, I will set you the example of obedience, by accepting your hospitality instead of returning on board my ship; and I trust you will follow my advice for the rest."

Old Lucas now ushered them into a large apartment hung round with paintings, and adorned with crimson hangings, much faded and moth-eaten, it must be confessed; indeed, all the furniture wore an air rather of past than present splendour, except on a table in the centre, where was laid out a repast, which, considering it was intended for a single person, exhibited a profusion of eatables, affording considerable satisfaction to the worthy captain, though, as may be supposed, poor Don Luis felt but little inclination for the good things set before him. Much to the chagrin of the old domestic, who stood near, pressing him to taste of the various dishes, and praising their qualities, he could scarcely touch them. The old man, looking with a melancholy glance at his young master, shook his head, thinking that some serious illness must have attacked him. "Ah! this comes of going to sea, and wandering in strange countries among heretics," he thought; "but his native air and proper food will soon restore him to health. Come, senhor, a little of this marmalade will do you good; it is of your old nurse's making, and you used to be very fond of it once upon a time."

"Thank you, my good Lucas, I have already finished supper; but I hope another day to do more justice to Senhora Anna's cookery. For the present, leave us; for I have much to say to Captain Pinto."

The old man unwillingly quitted the room, with many a lingering glance behind. "Ah! he is sadly changed from what he once was, poor young gentleman! Oh dear, oh dear!" he ejaculated, as he slowly retired.

The hardy sailor, however, made ample amends to the viands for his host's want of appetite. "Come, Luis," he said, "tell me how fared you with Donna Theresa? Ah! I had better not ask; your countenance tells your tale."

"Your warnings were but too just, and I have been miserably deceived," answered the young man.

"Do not make yourself unhappy; you will recover sooner than you expect," said the Captain. "Remember our voyage: dark clouds and storms for the greater part of the time; and yet the sun burst out brightly, and we arrived safe in port at last. Take my word for it, everything happens for the best, and you may some day rejoice that you have undergone what you now consider so great a misfortune."

"You have already prophesied too truly for me now to contradict you," said Don Luis; "but it is difficult to persuade a man that a bitter draught is pleasant to the taste."

"I do not say that it is pleasant, but, with returning health, he will be glad he took it," said the Captain, laughing. "Come, come, this is our first evening on shore after a long voyage, and we must not be sad—so here's a health to the fair ladies of Portugal, and I am sure there are plenty of them, so that, if one is not kind, there are others who will be so. That is a sailor's maxim, and I should advise you to adopt it; 'twill save many a heart-ache."

"Oh! do not talk on the subject," exclaimed Don Luis, not relishing his friend's principles; "I am not of so callous a nature."

"Well, we'll change the subject; and, while I am giving advice, let me strongly urge you to call to-morrow on the minister. He is a man not to be trifled with; and though he is a firm friend to those who please him, he is a relentless enemy to any who venture to oppose his objects."

"But why should I fear him, I have no favours to ask, and he has no means of injuring me?" said Don Luis.

"Do not confide in that," answered the Captain. "If you displease him, he will find means of avenging himself when you least expect it. He never yet forgave an offence. Though he is my patron and friend, and a man with many qualities I admire, I know his faults, and they are terrible ones. Pity is an utter stranger to his bosom, and the life of man he looks upon as a thing of nought, to be disposed of at his pleasure. While other men tremble with fear, his nerves are only the better strung. I remember him when he married Donna Theresa Noronha, the niece of the Conde dos Arcos, and a relation of the proud Duke of Aveiro. Her relations all protested against the match, stigmatising him as a low-born profligate, unworthy of their alliance; but he laughed, and bore her off in spite of them, though they have vowed vengeance on him ever since. But we shall see which will ultimately conquer; and, mark me, every step he takes to power is one nearer to their destruction."

"You describe a person whose friendship I would rather shun than seek," said Don Luis.

"There you think wrong," said the Captain, laughing. "He is just the person you ought to make your friend; for he can be of more Service to you than any one else; while, if you fail to win his regard, and make him your enemy, you will find him a most dangerous one. At all events, call on him with me to-morrow."

"Though fear of his enmity does not influence me, I will follow your advice, my good friend, and accompany you, which I am also hound to do after the service he rendered me to-night."

"It matters but little what your motives are, so that you follow his wishes," returned the Captain.

We need not follow further the conversation of the two friends, which lasted till a late hour, when at length, having arranged to call, early the following morning, on the minister, they separated to their respective rooms, Don Luis with his heart yet heavy, and his head in a whirl of confusion, from the various and important occurrences he had met with since his landing in the morning; indeed, it was with difficulty he could persuade himself that he had passed only a few short hours on the shores of Portugal, so great a change had taken place in all his thoughts and feelings. At the present period of his career, Carvalho made no attempt to vie in outward show with the rich and luxurious fidalgos of Lisbon, his mansion being small, and his domestic arrangements unostentatious; the guard at the door, who presented arms as Captain Pinto and his young friend entered the hall, being the only sign that a person of consequence resided there.

On giving their names, a servant, without delay, ushered the two gentlemen up stairs into a small ante-room, where he left them for a moment, and immediately returned, saying that his master would receive them, when, throwing open a side door, he made a sign to them to enter, and Don Luis found himself in the presence of his acquaintance of the previous evening.

Carvalho, habited in his morning gown, was pacing the chamber, which he evidently used as his dressing-room, while a secretary, at a desk near the window, was busily occupied in writing according to his dictation; the last few sentences he spoke being heard by his guests before he appeared to remember their presence. He then suddenly turned, having assured himself that his instructions were fully understood, and received them with that frank and courteous politeness for which the Portuguese are so justly esteemed, and in which he particularly excelled; placing them on seats opposite to the one into which he threw himself, in such a position that he might every now and then turn and give directions to his secretary.

"I am glad to find that your foreign travel has given you habits of punctuality and early rising," he observed; "customs I wish the young men of your rank would more generally follow."

"I was anxious to thank your Excellency for the aid you afforded me last night," returned Don Luis; "and I therefore seized the earliest moment to pay my respects."

"Ah! that reminds me that you need not be detained in Lisbon to appear as a witness against the ruffians. They did not intend to take your life, it appears, but mistook you for another person; however, a few weeks' imprisonment will benefit them; and I conclude that you do not intend to remain long away from Court. The king looks with a jealous eye on those who absent themselves, wishing to see himself, as he ought to be, surrounded by his nobles, who seem often to forget that they but hold their rank from him, and that, at his pleasure, they may again become mere commoners."

"My movements will depend entirely on my father's will," answered Don Luis; "and, after my long absence, he will probably desire me to remain with him."

"Your father is a man I much esteem," said the Minister; "and regret that some slight he conceives himself to have received should have driven him from Court; for I cannot suppose that he is tainted with disloyalty to our sovereign, which is more than I can say for some of the haughty fidalgos of the land, whose pride, by heavens! soars so high, that they seem to consider themselves his superiors; let them beware, or it shall be brought low enough."

The manner of the speaker for a moment became excited; but he quickly resumed his usual calm demeanour, as he continued—"Offer my compliments to your father, and say I must request he will not detain you long away, for I feel confident that his majesty will wish to give you some employment suitable to your rank, and the high talents I know you to possess."

Don Luis, surprised at the compliment, for he could not conceive how the minister knew anything about him, could only bow in return; nor was he particularly pleased with its authoritative tone, as coming from a man whom he had been taught to consider, on account of his birth, but of little consequence; particularly when he heard threats uttered against the class to which he belonged. The Minister, eyeing the young man narrowly, to observe the effect of his observations, then addressed a few sentences to Captain Pinto, during which time Don Luis, happening to look in the direction of the secretary, observed that his glance was fixed on him; but it was immediately withdrawn, the latter person applying himself studiously to his occupation; it was, however, sufficient to attract Don Luis's attention more especially to his countenance, which he could not help fancying that he had seen somewhere before, and at no great distance of time. It was not probable that he had met him abroad, so that it could have been only on the previous day;—perhaps he had passed him in the street—for he possessed only an undefined, dreamy sort of recollection of the countenance;—when, on a sudden, it struck him that those expressive eyes and features were the same he had for a moment seen in the corridor of the Jesuits' College. Yet it was extraordinary that a person employed by one who was a professed enemy of that order should have been found holding communication with them, and he felt confident that the secretary had either been playing false to his master, or deceiving in some way the holy fathers. However, he wisely, for the present, kept his counsel: determining, as in duty bound, to take the first opportunity of mentioning his suspicions to his cousin, Father da Costa, between whom and the Minister he knew there was no cordiality. He had just arrived at this conclusion, when Carvalho again turned to him, making many minute inquiries about his travels in England, which showed him, notwithstanding his declarations to the contrary, to be well acquainted with the laws and customs of that country. "Ambassadors," he observed, "have less chance than any other strangers of learning the true state of a country; it is the interest of everybody round them to blind their eyes; and if they attempt to move about incognito, and alone, they are considered as spies, and every action is watched. In despotic countries, such as Austria, and I hear also in Russia, the matter is much worse; and I have heard of the whole country, by the borders of a road, being populated, and villages built, on the occasion of the visit of some distinguished personage, which vanished when he had passed by; though he went away with the impression that it was one of the most fertile and populous countries in the world."

The Minister smiled at his own story, as, in duty bound, did his guests, and Don Luis began to doubt that he could possibly possess the violent and sanguinary temper which was reported: he made many more inquiries, and seemed much pleased with the answers Don Luis gave; then, in the most bland, and courteous manner, informed him and Captain Pinto, that he would no longer detain them, begging the former to call upon him on his return to Lisbon. As they rose to depart, Don Luis caught the eye of the secretary again turned towards him, with a sort of inquiring glance, but he had no opportunity of observing further, as he was obliged to follow the captain from the room.

As they were crossing a corridor, and about to descend the stairs, a young girl passed them, with light ringlets falling over her shoulders, and laughing blue eyes. In no way abashed at sight of the strangers, she bowed gracefully, and bounded on. "Who can that fair creature be who passed us?" asked Don Luis.

"The eldest daughter of the Minister by his present wife, Donna Leonora, Countess Daùn, whom he married during the time he was envoy at the Court of Austria;" answered Captain Pinto; "she shows her mother's Saxon blood."

"Yes, and her high birth," said Don Luis: "she is very beautiful."

"Very," was the Captain's laconic reply.

"You appear to have pleased Senhor Carvalho," observed Captain Pinto, as they walked homeward; "I should advise you to profit by the advantage."

"Why so? he will probably soon forget me," said Don Luis.

"Indeed he will not. He takes an interest in your welfare, from a youthful friendship for some member of your family, who is no more, and from whom he received some deep obligation, which he would repay to you; and now you understand why he desired to see you."

Note. Hear the king!—a cry for help.

Volume One—Chapter Seven.

The Portuguese, with much *naïveté*, relate a story which is told against them, that Noah, a few years ago, paid a visit to this our planet, on which he once on a time played so conspicuous a part; but that, as he travelled from country to country, and kingdom to kingdom, his fond anticipations of reviving the early recollections of his living days were far from being gratified; for not a spot of earth which his rather numerous progeny now inhabit could he recognise, so many changes had all undergone, and nowhere did he find himself comfortably at home till he arrived on the shores of Lusitania. How did his heart beat with tender remembrances, as he travelled through the country! "Ah!" he exclaimed, enraptured, "this is indeed the land I love; the self-same as I left it: the same system of agriculture, the same style of architecture, the identical roads, not a stone removed, a few more ruts, to be sure, caused by passing time, like the wrinkles in a friend's face; the same manners, and the same customs. Ah! beloved Portugal, constant and unchangeable; here will I take up my abode." Saying which, the venerable patriarch pitched his tent, where he sojourned during his stay on earth; and the inhabitants, in hope of being honoured by another visit, still adhere to the same system.

Now, although there can be no doubt that the above is a very witty story, we can assure our readers that it is not perfectly correct in all respects, inasmuch as there are fine churches, though it is difficult to determine the order of their architecture; and there are palaces and castles, which we do not in history find there were when Noah dwelt upon earth; but we do very strongly suspect that the roads, if there were any, could not have been worse. Also, with respect to inns, or houses of public entertainment, they cannot be very much improved since his time; for anything more execrably bad than they generally are, in any country within a week's sail of England, can scarcely be conceived; and we have good reason to suppose that they have not very much altered since the days of the Marquis of Pombal.

In describing, therefore, a Portuguese country inn of a hundred years ago, the picture of one of the present day will fully answer our purpose, even of that to which we are about to conduct our readers, which yet exists with few marks of change about it. It stands on the northern edge of a wild sandy common, broken into irregular hillocks, partially sprinkled with gum-cistus, gentian, the flowering heath, and other low shrubs and plants, while, in the far distance, is perceived the long dark line of a pine-forest. The ground on the other side of the inn is cultivated, though very imperfectly; and here and there a few mean cottages may be seen, with heaps of dirt in front, and pools of mud, in which the favoured pigs of the inhabitants delight to wallow. The inn is a long low building, the bush hung out on a pole in front being the sign that all are welcome to enter, as was once the custom in England. The walls are of rough stone, having a row of windows, with red shutters, rather battered, and destitute of glass, on the upper story; but the only opening on the ground floor is the large entrance door, which leads at once into a spacious stable, strewed with straw, and with no very great attention to cleanliness; a manger, running round it, without any divisions for stalls; so that the animals therein may, at will, amuse themselves by kicking at each other, free from those unsocial restraints which English civilisation has introduced; very like a certain class of liberals, who would do away with wholesome laws, much for the same sensible object. This is decidedly the best part of the building, as much attention being paid to the comfort of the animals as to that of their owners; though, by a partition of rough deal boards, an apartment is separated from it to the right, which serves the purpose of kitchen, parlour, and bedroom, to the greater part of the family and guests. On a low hearth, on one side of it, a wood fire blazes, the smoke escaping through the doors and windows, as it best can; and on the walls, near the fire-place, are hung a few large and very ordinary kitchen utensils, the other parts being adorned with horse furniture, rows of onions, dried fish, and other provisions of the coarsest sort. A rough deal table and benches run close to the wall the whole length of the apartment; and there is a shorter one on the opposite side, near the fire. The floor is of clay, perfectly black, and beaten hard, but worn into irregular undulations and holes where most trodden on. We are now describing the past and the present, and probably the future, for many years to come, though we cannot pierce the gloom of the dark abyss of time; but as our business is rather with the past, we prefer adhering to that tense. The further end of the room opened into a sort of stable-yard, from which freely entered at all times several long-legged, thin white swine, with a youthful progeny of grunters, who were allowed to satisfy their inquisitive natures, if not their appetites, by poking their snouts into every pan or utensil they met with in their peregrinations, receiving now and then a gentle rebuke, administered with the bottom of a frying-pan, by the nimble-handed damsel who officiated as chief of the culinary department, accompanied by a no very complimentary epithet, at which they grunted forth their disapprobation, and continued the same proceedings. Besides the pigs, numerous fowls appeared to be welcome visitors, being allowed to establish their roost on the rafters of the roof, in one corner, and to hop about and pick up what escaped the vigilance of the yet more favoured animals. Nor must we forget, having begun with the dumb species, instead of the nobler part of creation, to mention two or three dogs, whose appearance was far from prepossessing, as they stalked about among the guests, in eager expectation of the morsels thrown to them, or of the crumbs which fell from the table. They were of a dirty yellow colour, their heads something like that of a fox, but with bodies lean and gaunt as a wolf, to which race they appeared to belong. Such is the large dog of the country; but there is every gradation of shape, size, and colour, down to the smallest turnspit, to give any specific name to which would be impossible. Having described the dogs, we must now mention the agile Griskenissa, the youthful queen of those regions. She was a laughing-mouthed damsel, her lips rather thick and full, disclosing the most pearly teeth, her nose *retroussé*, between a pair of large sparkling black eyes, and her figure rather more fully developed, particularly about the bust, than would accord with the Venus de Medicis. A rich bloom brightened the nut-brown tint of her not very delicate complexion, whose dark hue was increased by her occupations over the fire. Her hair was drawn back, fastened in a knot behind, and covered with a coloured handkerchief, a white one being thrown over her shoulders. The sleeves and skirt of her gown being tucked up, exhibited a pair of stout arms and legs of the same build, destitute of stockings or shoes. The noise of her tongue was, as Captain Rolando, in the "Honeymoon," describes most unjustly that of her sex in general, like the clatter of a mill; the more she moved about, the faster it went, the grist being the questions and jokes of her guests, to which she failed not to give some sharp repartee. She was aided in the actual work of cooking by an old crone, who, now bending over the fire, was engaged in stirring a mess of broth simmering in a large pot, while a little boy, clothed in the smallest quantity of raiment which could possibly cover his body, was employed in bringing wood to feed the flame. The master of the house generally walked about with his hands in his pockets, a cigarito in his mouth, and his cap set rakingly on one side, by far too fine a gentleman to attend to the wants of his guests, though occasionally, to those of higher degree, he would condescend to make a low bow as they departed, provided they paid well, and shared with him a bottle or so of his best wine.

The sun had some time set, the apartment being thrown into obscurity, except near the blaze of the fire, and at the further end of the long table, where, round a brass lamp of that elegant shape used by the Romans, and still to be seen in Italy, were seated the landlord and four or five of his guests, deeply immersed in some game of cards, their countenances exhibiting all the eager passions of men who had large sums at stake. Indeed, several gold and silver pieces were seen to change hands, to the evident rage of the losers; though, from the dress and appearance of the men, one would not have expected to find them possessed of so large an amount. Their costume was soiled, and patched with divers shades of cloth: it consisted of short braided jackets, and red waistcoats, loose trowsers and long gaiters, with a red sash round the waist, in which was stuck, without any attempt at concealment, a long knife, in a sheath, towards whose hilt the hand seemed to have a natural tendency to move. On their heads they wore round, low-crowned hats of black felt, with rather broad brims, which, pulled a little forward, effectually concealed the features.

At the smaller table, near the fire, were several other people, discussing in silence their suppers of cabbage broth, inattentive to what was going forward at the other end of the room. Two hours of the night had passed away, the card party yet eagerly proceeding in their game, with slight variations of fortune, when the clatter of horses' hoofs was heard, and the boy was loudly summoned to hold a lantern while the animals were stalled and fed; and, soon afterwards, two men, wrapped in large riding cloaks, entered, and glancing at the guests near the fire, advanced towards the end of the long table. The gamblers, looking up for a moment, received them as friends; but their interest in the game was far too intense to permit their attention to be withdrawn for a longer period; the others looking patiently on, till one of the former sprang from his seat, exclaiming, "By St. Anthony, I play no more: curses on the game; I've lost my last testoon, and owe more to boot. How to pay my debts I know not."

One of the new comers, fixing his eyes on him, smiled significantly. "What, Salvador," he said, "know you not how a man of spirit may best recruit his exhausted finances? Banish all fears, I will soon put you in the way of it."

"Thanks, senhor, I have trod it before," answered Salvador; "but I like not the sight of the gibbet in the distance."

"Fool!" muttered the other; "no man of courage is frightened at such a phantom."

What further might have been said was cut short by another of the party dashing the cards to the ground, and trampling on them almost with screams, in his fury at having become the loser of all his wealth, darting fierce scowls at those who were the gainers, particularly the landlord, who had managed to pay himself well for the time occupied in the game, and who, now calling to the boy, ordered him to pick up the scattered pack.

The game now terminated; and the party, having again resumed their seats, made many inquiries of their newly-arrived friends. "We little expected to see you here so soon," said the Landlord; "what made you leave Lisbon so suddenly?"

"A cursed mistake we committed last night, when two of our friends fell into the hands of justice. We had been engaged by the Conde de San Vincente, who gives us plenty of employment, to get rid of a rival of his in the affections of a certain lady; and, after following our man for some way, who we knew would make no resistance, and, feeling quite sure of him, just as Miguel was about to give him his quietus, out he whips his rapier, and uses it so manfully, after knocking down Miguel, that he kept us at bay till a friend came to his assistance; but we should have got the better of them both, when, who should pass by but the devil, in the shape of Sebastiaö Jozé de Carvalho himself, who forthwith seized on Miguel and Baltar, whom he has clapped into prison; and we, thinking Lisbon may be too hot for us, came off here; for he is not apt to let any escape whom he may wish to find."

"Ah! San Vincente is a man I like to serve," said another. "His very cowardice is a recommendation, as he first pays one well to commit a deed he dare not do himself, and then double to keep it concealed."

"Yes, if it were not for the hatred of the proud fidalgos for each other, we honest, humble men should not be able to exist."

"Ay, thank the saints, they give us work enough to keep our hands in practice, though scarce enough to let us live like gentlemen," cried another.

"Forsooth, the profession has fallen into much disrepute lately, since pretenders to it offer their services to commit a murder for a couple of crowns. Such shabby villains ought to be scouted from society," exclaimed a fourth. "When a man does undertake to do a piece of work, let it be for something, or he is acting dishonestly towards others, besides being guilty of a meanness of which any gentleman ought to be ashamed."

"Silence, Senhores, silence!" exclaimed the Landlord, looking round; "your conversation is becoming of a nature not fit for common ears: and see, some persons at the other table are opening theirs to listen."

"Never fear," answered one of the last comers; "we are not ashamed of our profession, as long as it is exercised with credit."

"That may be," said the Landlord; "but you must remember the respectability of my house. I might lose my customers, if it were known I had the honour of your friendship. No offence to you at the same time."

"Well, well, Senhor Bernardo; say no more on the subject," said the other, laughing. "Ah! see, here comes your daughter with our supper; both dainty morsels, I doubt not."

"Of the latter you may taste at will, but with my Rosa I should advise you not to attempt to make free; for she uses but scant ceremony towards those who offend her," answered the Landlord.

"Not I! I never offended a pretty girl in my life. Hey, my bright Rosa?" said the guest, chucking her under the chin as she placed a dish of rice and stewed fowls on the table; but in return for the liberty, he received a sound box on the ear; and she tripped off, laughing, before he could catch her to renew the offence.

"Carramba! but your daughter does hit hard," exclaimed the man; "though let us see if her cookery will make amends for her cruelty."

As Rosa, having placed another dish on the table, was again hastening away, she encountered from a personage who just then entered the room a fresh attack of the same sort, but, it must be confessed, with scarce the same obduracy; for "Oh, Senhor Frade!" and a loud giggle, was the only answer she gave to the salute, which sounded through the apartment.

"Pax vobiscum!" exclaimed the person who had committed this atrocity, as he advanced out of the obscurity towards the group among whom he espied the landlord, well knowing that there would the best cheer be found. As the light fell on him, he exhibited a broad, sinewy figure; and throwing back his cowl, his shorn crown and coarse brown robes, with satchel by his side, proclaimed him to belong to the mendicant order of the Capuchins, his well-filled cheeks showing how assiduously he pursued his avocation. His bullet-shaped head was encircled by a rim of coarse red hair, to which colour his features assimilated; a broad snubby nose, and a pair of blear, though keen, roving eyes, made up the man. He was welcomed by all the party, with whom he appeared to be on the most intimate terms.

"Now, for the love of the saints, my pretty Rosa," he exclaimed, as he took his seat at the post of honour near the master, "bring me something to eat, for I am almost dead with hunger and thirst;— anything will serve; a stewed pullet or so, or some broiled pork and lemon; you know that I am not particular as to the things of the appetite;—and hark you, my Rosa dear, if you can find the remains of a bottle or so of old wine, bring it, in the name of the Virgin; for I am thirsty and tired."

The holy Father's request was not disregarded, and he was soon busily employed in discussing the viands set before him, failing not to do ample justice to Rosa's cookery, during which time he would not answer a word to the numerous questions put to him; but, having finished, and wiped his mouth on the sleeve of his gown, giving a last pull at his bottle of wine, his tongue was loosened, and all the party bent their heads forward to listen to what he had to communicate; the subject of the conversation being such as to oblige them to speak in tones not loud enough to be heard beyond their immediate circle.

"What news do you bring us, Senhor Padre?" asked one of those who had lost at cards. "Have we a chance of picking up a little booty? for we are very low in the world."

"Ah, my son, always thinking of lucre and worldly gain," answered the Friar, laughing, "but I am in an amiable humour, and will not tantalise you long."

"Well, Padre, no delay; out with your news," exclaimed several of the party, bending still closer round him, with eager expression of countenance.

"Know then, my sons, that there is a chance of some work to-morrow morning which may fill our empty pockets; but recollect, we all share alike; I am not to employ my wits, and to wear myself into a phantom to gain all the information, and then to allow my convent to be deprived of the just profits."

"Never fear, Senhor Padre, your convent shall not suffer in the division," said the Innkeeper; "but come, let us hear your news."

"'Tis this, then. As I passed through the village of Santa Cruz, I learned that the noble Senhor Gonçalo Christovaö and his family are staying at the Quinta of the Conde de Villarey, on their way to Lisbon, and their mules and litters are to be in readiness to start to-morrow morning at daybreak, they having the intention of breakfasting here. So there's a double chance for you, Senhor Estalajadeiro. You first get well paid in an honest way for the stewed cats and tough old cocks you furnish them; and then our friends here will reap the harvest that remains, no slight one, if I mistake not; for there are, besides Senhor Christovaö and and his fair daughter, Donna Clara, so I learned, three maid-servants, all of whom, depend on it, will be decked out in their gold ornaments, though they will make some slight fuss in delivering them; and then there are the escudeiro and three other servants, who will run away on the first show of a blunderbuss, as will, probably, the whole troop of muleteers who accompany them."

"Bravo, most holy friar! you deserve our warmest thanks for your services to us," exclaimed one of the party; "and where would you advise us to wait till our friends pass?"

"Has not your own sense pointed that out to you?" answered the Friar. "At the edge of the moor where the pine grove commences, I should advise you to watch, and you can then have a clear view over the common on one side, while you must place a scout to see that no one approaches on the other."

"Admirable generalship!" exclaimed he who had before spoken. "Were it not for your shaven crown, you would make us a capital leader, if you had courage enough to face the danger."

"Courage!" cried the Friar, casting an angry look at the speaker. "Because I do not bluster and bully, you think I have not courage. I have done, and would do, many a deed you dare not!"

"Ah, friar, you boast already, do you? Remember, what are you, but the jackal to our prey? I'll venture you would turn pale at the sight of a few drops of blood."

"Fool, 'tis you will turn pale at sight of your own blood!" exclaimed the Friar, springing up, and drawing from a sheath under his gown, a long sharp stiletto, which he plunged with a steady hand into the fleshy part of the shoulder of the man who had spoken. "Now remember not to taunt me again; and recollect your life was in my power; an inch more of the steel would have silenced your tongue for ever."

"Peace, Senhores, peace!" exclaimed the Landlord, seizing the arm of the friar, who without effort shook him off. "Remember the credit of my house; and if you wish to shed blood, let it be outside my doors."

"Do not fear, my friend," answered the Friar coolly; "'Tis but a slight lesson I gave to Senhor Jozé here, to speak more respectfully to one of my cloth in future. Come, man, I can cure as well as kill;" saying which, he bound up the arm of the wounded man, who, like a cowed hound, submitted without another word.

"Bravo, Frade, bravo! you are a fine fellow, and shall have all you wish," cried the rest of the respectable assemblage.

"Well then, my friends," said the Friar, "to convince you that if I am a jackal, I am a lion also, I will lead you in person to this adventure; but then remember I must have the lion's share also."

"Agreed! agreed!" exclaimed the party. "With so holy a guide we must be successful."

"The plan is then arranged, senhores," said the Landlord; "and now to bed. Remember you must rise betimes to be in readiness for the work, as it will not do to be observed quitting my respectable house on such an errand after the sun is up."

The party now broke up, some stealing off to make their couches in the stable, others in different corners of the room; while the landlord, dismissing his daughter and the rest of his household to their places of repose, drew a seat near the fire, where he and the friar remained for some time in earnest conversation. The latter then rolling himself up in his gown, and pulling his cowl over his head, fell fast asleep on the bench, the host retiring to an upper room which he inhabited.

We have, as yet, described only the lower part of the house; but it possessed also an upper story intended for the accommodation of any guests of higher rank who might honour it with their presence. The greater part was occupied by one large chamber, surrounded by small recesses, in which were placed beds of most execrable hardness, invented, one might suppose, to counteract any tendency to effeminacy which the climate might have caused. As if in mockery, over the beds were thrown gaily worked cover lids, beneath which, alas! by the uninitiated traveller, neither peace nor quiet was to be found, as swarms of fierce inhabitants of two rival races were ever ready, like the Lilliputians on that renowned voyager Captain Lemuel Gulliver, to avenge on the body of the intruder any inroad made on their territory. Curtains were hung across some of the recesses intended for the guests of most consideration, and a rough table and benches were placed down the room, the windows, as we have before said, being destitute of glass, and the walls of aught but the rough mortar. Such were the only accommodations afforded even to the highest ranks; but the inns received little patronage from any, for, in the first place, no one moved about more than was absolutely necessary, and, when they were obliged to make a journey, the house of any gentleman on the road was always hospitably open to them, as is the case at the present day.

The cold grey light of the early morn had just broken upon the world, when a party of horsemen sallied out of the inn, mounted on most sorry-looking animals, the small horses, or rather ponies of the country, but whose nimble and surefooted paces belied the estimation one formed of their qualities at the first glance. The men wore their large broad cloaks, one side of which being thrown over the shoulder, and almost over the head, completely concealed their features, while the rest hung down, covering their own bodies, and a great part of those of their horses.

The robes of the friar were not perceived among them; but there was a most suspicious-looking figure who took the lead, with a broad slouched hat on his head, fastened tightly down with a handkerchief under his chin, and from beneath it appeared a rim of closely-cut red hair, and a ruddy face with a pair of twinkling eyes, the rest of the form, which was evidently of no slender mould, being enveloped, like the others, in a broad cloak. Their ponies carried them at a pace between a canter and a quick shamble over the heath we have described, in the direction of Lisbon, towards the long line of dark forest which was seen in the far distance from the higher ground on which the inn stood.

The master of the inn remained at the door, watching them till they could be no longer distinguished from the shrubs and clumps of heath which sprinkled the ground. "May the devil prosper them!" he exclaimed, "for were it not for such gentry, my very good friends, I might e'en shut up my house and go begging or robbing like them." Having thus given vent to his thoughts, he retired within to say his prayers, and to calculate the probable amount of his share in the profits of the expedition.

Volume One—Chapter Eight.

The glowing sun of that lovely clime was already high in the heavens, in which not a cloud or vapour was to be seen; the air came soft and pure over the heath, laden with balsamic odours; and a blue, sparkling, transparent haze played over the ground, giving the promise of a scorching day. The notable daughter of the landlord stood at the door of the inn, her fingers busily employed in spinning from the distaff stuck in her waist, while she sang, at the top of her voice, an air, which, at the end of each verse, fell into a low cadence, and amused herself, by looking along the road in each direction, for the approach of travellers. At length, a cloud of dust rising in the north, greeted her eyes; and as it gradually drew nearer, she heard the jingling of bells sound faintly through the air, the most pleasing music to the ears of a Portuguese innkeeper, when she perceived that it was caused by several litters, sumpter mules, and a party of horsemen. She hastened in to give the joyful intelligence to the rest of the family, who, with her father, quickly assembled at the door to welcome the travellers, whoever they might be; for, as there was no other inn for several leagues on either side of them, there could be no doubt that they would there stop to bait their animals, and refresh themselves.

The Landlord muttered to himself, with an oath—"They are very numerous, and, if they choose to fight, my friends will have the worst of it.—Patience! I shall make my profits, at all events. Ah, honesty and a regular business is the best policy;" with this consoling reflection, he waited the arrival of the party.

An arriero, or muleteer, came running on in front, to announce that the illustrious fidalgo, Gonçalo Christovaö, was approaching; and soon afterwards, a dignified and venerable gentleman, on a stout horse, rode up, accompanied by a grave-looking personage, in the dress of a Benedictine monk, and followed by two servants, who, throwing themselves from their mules, respectfully assisted him and his companion to dismount, when they stood ready to receive the first litter which arrived.

We have often, on entering a church or palace in Italy, been directed to some picture, kept closely veiled from the vulgar eye; and, as the curtain was drawn aside, have been delighted, by viewing the lovely portrait of a Madonna or Venus from the pencil of Rafaelle or Titian; and far more, as the dignified cavalier drew aside the curtains of the litter, would the eyes of our readers have been enraptured, by the vision of bright and rare beauty which was disclosed; for surely, not even those great masters of the sublime art could, in their most blissful moments, have conceived or executed aught more perfect.

"Oh, Jesus Maria, how lovely!" exclaimed the laughing Rosa, paying an unaffected tribute of admiration to nature's choicest work; and clapping her hands with delight, as the Portuguese peasantry invariably do, when they behold anything that causes admiration or surprise, she ran forward to offer her services.

The lovely vision we have mentioned was, as the acute reader may have supposed, a young lady; and, as she descended from the litter, leaning on the gentleman's arm, her figure was perceived to be rather above the ordinary height of her countrywomen, but slender, and most gracefully formed; her face, as we have said, was beautiful, and very fair, with light brown ringlets escaping from under the blue hood of her travelling dress. In those days, the fashion of wearing bonnets had not been introduced even among the highest ranks; the hood or veil, thrown over the head, being considered sufficient protection; and certainly, a more elegant covering than the head-dresses worn in France or England at the same period. Indeed, an out-of-doors dress was scarcely required, as ladies seldom appeared abroad, except in their carriages or chairs: even in the present day, were they to take more exercise than they are in the habit of doing, their youthful promise of beauty would not be so sadly unrealised, as it too frequently is. As soon as the young lady had alighted, and had been ushered into the inn, the other litters drew up, from the first of which descended a respectable-looking old dame, with spectacles on nose, a parrot on a stand, two bird-cages, and a sleek, long-haired Angola cat. From the appearance of the old lady, she was the *Ama*, the nurse, or governess to the fair girl. A damsel followed her out of the litter, with sundry packages and baskets of eatables. Two other waiting women got out of the third litter, short, dark, and black-eyed girls; while the fourth was empty, probably, for the accommodation of the master. Five or six baggage-mules, and two mounted men-servants, brought up the rear, besides a number of drivers belonging to the litters and mules, who kept up with the cavalcade on foot.

As his distinguished guests retired into the house, the landlord, bowing most obsequiously, ushered them (alas! through the stable and kitchen), up a sadly narrow and dirty flight of steps, to the room we have described before, where the servants spread a repast they had brought with them, the landlord being perfectly content with supplying the muleteers and their animals with food.

Rosa could scarcely keep her eyes from the young lady, as she bustled round her, offering to perform any service in her power; and when, at length, she had contrived to separate her from the rest of her party, looking down on the ground as she spoke, she whispered "Do not be afraid, senhora, whatever sort of people you may meet on the road, for I am sure they would not harm any one so lovely."

"What do you mean, my good girl?" asked the lady, in a sweet tone. "We are not likely to meet any one to harm us, for they say the roads are perfectly free from robbers."

"Oh no, senhora, Heaven deliver us from robbers; I do not speak of them," answered Rosa, in a hesitating manner, "but there are all sorts of odd people about, and I thought I would put you on your guard, that is all. I am sure they will not harm her," she uttered, as she turned away with a tear in her eye.

The young lady was not at all alarmed by the hints the good-natured girl threw out; indeed, she so little attended to them, that she forgot all about them a minute afterwards.

The travellers, after remaining nearly two hours at the inn, their horses and mules being refreshed, again proceeded on their way, the host redoubling the obsequiousness of his bows as they departed, and wishing them, with much apparent earnestness, a successful journey. The track, for it did not deserve the name of a road, lay over the uncultivated moor we have before spoken of; the hollows and hillocks they were obliged to cross or to circumvent, much prolonging the distance, the utmost pace the litters could advance being scarce a league an hour; a great contrast to the present railroad speed of other countries. This slow progress was very fatiguing, increased by the fine dust, dried by the summer heats, which rose in thick clouds at every step the animals took; there was also scarce a breath of air, the fervent rays of the sun shining with uninterrupted force on their heads.

Senhor Christovaö and the grave friar rode on in front, out of hearing of the rest of the party; the latter evidently endeavouring to press some matter of importance on the consideration of the gentleman. "Depend on it, senhor, the peaceful serenity of a monastic life is the most happy lot a female can enjoy in this vale of tears; there, free from the cares and disappointments which her sisters in adversity are doomed to suffer, she spends her days in prayers and thanksgivings, in anxious expectation of the arrival of her heavenly Bridegroom."

"Your arguments are very powerful, Senhor Padre," returned his companion; "but yet I feel some compunction in depriving my daughter, against her will, of the innocent pleasures which accord with her age and sex."

"Such ideas are but the instigations of the evil one, jealous that an immortal soul should be lost to him for ever," answered the Priest. "Trust not to any feelings which war against the spirit on the side of the flesh. No human mind can conceive the dark machinations which the father of sin employs to drag forth a chosen child from the bosom of our holy Church, except we, who in our avocations study his works, and are prepared to repel him with the arms of our faith."

"You doubtless speak words of truth and wisdom," said the gentleman; "nor would I hesitate to allow my daughter to follow the bent of her inclinations, did she feel any calling for the life of the cloister; but she knows not what is to be her fate, or the reason of our going to Lisbon, for I have never yet ventured to inform her of my intentions."

"Let that be my care," returned the Priest, frowning darkly. "I will prepare her gentle soul for the happy change. But have you never, then, informed her of her mother's dying wish, delivered to me after she had received extreme unction at my hands, that her daughter should be dedicated to the service of the Church?"

"I confess, Father, that I have hesitated to speak to her on the subject, fearful of throwing a gloom over the bright and elastic spirits of her youth," returned Senhor Christovaö.

"Know you not, that the sooner the wings of a young bird are clipped, the less will it wish to fly; and therein have you done wrong; but clearly do I perceive the work of Satan again, in this seeking to ruin your soul, and that of your daughter. Ah! he is even now riding near you, plotting deeds of darkness. Get thee gone, thou spirit of evil!" he exclaimed with vehemence, making the sign of the cross. "Avaunt thee, Sathanas! Fear him no longer, my son; he has flown off to the regions of iniquity, from whence he came."

"With you by my side, I fear not the evil spirit," answered the Fidalgo, though the expression of his countenance belied his words; "and I will take the earliest opportunity of putting your directions into execution, though I knew not that my wife had expressed a wish that her daughter should enter a convent. During her last illness, you informed me she often prayed that I would permit her child to assume the veil, rather than I should compel her to wed against her inclination. This I consented to do, trusting she would nor wish to rebel against my will in the choice of a husband: as yet, her heart is free, and I have arranged that she shall marry, though yet she knows not of it, the young Conde de San Vincente, one of the oldest Puritano families, and one of the most wealthy; so that he is in every way unexceptionable. He is also a great friend of my son, who is very anxious for the match; and he tells me that the count is longing to see his intended bride. I therefore trust I shall have no difficulty on the subject, and that Clara, who has always been a dutiful child, will make no objections."

"With all these arrangements I was perfectly acquainted," said the Priest, in a calm tone; "but suppose she objects to marry the young count, will you not then follow her mother's wishes? or, I may say more—for, know that your wife devoted her daughter to the Church, and the quiet of her soul depends on the fulfilment of her vows."

"Father, you press me hard," exclaimed the Fidalgo, in a tone of voice which showed that his feelings were galled; and his ghostly confessor saw that he might be going too far. "I seek to do what is best for the honour of my family, for my daughter's happiness, and for the repose of the soul of my departed wife; what more would you have me do?"

"It is enough," returned the Priest; "you promise, then, that if your daughter, Donna Clara, refuses to obey your wish that she should marry the Conde de San Vincente, she shall assume the veil, with the portion that you would bestow on her if she wedded; for, remember, if you do not, it is at the peril of your own soul, of her's, and of that of your departed wife."

"I promise so to do, holy Father, if thus her sainted mother vowed her to the Church," exclaimed the Fidalgo; "but I know that my sweet child will not for a moment dream of disobeying my wishes."

"I seek alone the good of her precious soul," returned the Priest; and for some time they rode on in silence.

During this discussion, the fair subject of it, little suspecting that her fate was being thus summarily settled, was thinking alone of the amusements she was to meet with in the capital, to which this was her first visit, her life having been spent in the quiet seclusion of her father's quinta, at a short distance from the city of Oporto, whose pointed walls could be seen from the windows of the mansion. All before her was unknown, and she had painted it bright and beautiful; for her soul was pure, and her mind contented and happy; nor had all the specious reasonings of the intriguing monk, who acted as her father confessor, been able to sully the one, or cast a gloom over the other; for God has benignantly afforded a sacred shield to some of the fair beings of his creation, whose own weakness and loveliness would expose them to the attacks of the darkly designing and wicked, who, though they see not, yet feel its power, and wonder at their own defeat.

Senhor Gonçalo Christovaö was the head of one of the oldest and purest noble families of Portugal, their motto being, "Kings descend from us;" not one of his ancestors having intermarried with any other family, unless they could show an equally pure escutcheon. Though of the highest class of fidalgos, he disdained to accept any title, which he saw often bestowed on men whom he looked down upon on account of their birth, priding himself far more on the antiquity of his own descent. This system was, at that time, strictly adhered to by a certain number of families, claiming the high distinction of being called Puritanos, or those of pure race, they being the highest class of fidalgos. The Fidalguia rank above the Nobres, and are entirely independent of all titles: they are divided into a great number of classes, according to the quarterings on their shields, each considering it a disgrace to marry out of their own pale.

The Nobres rank with the English esquire, being simply gentlemen who carry arms, though they often rise to rank and influence, from which, indeed, no class of the present day are debarred; but, until the time of Pombal, the Fidalguia had exclusively retained among themselves every post of power and authority, wreaking their vengeance on any who ventured to interfere with what they considered their privileges.

This short digression is necessary to explain the position in society held by Gonçalo Christovaö, for so he delighted to be spoken of. After riding for some time in silence by the side of the priest, he guided his horse close to his daughter's litter, remorse and sorrow combating in his heart with the superstition and bigotry the friar had endeavoured to instil into it; but when he was about to speak on the subject he intended, his courage again failed him, and he smiled as he gazed on his lovely child, and inquired how she bore the fatigues of the journey.

Two weary hours passed away in crossing the moor, before the party reached the borders of one of those large pine-forests, with which the face of Portugal is so thickly sprinkled. The trees grew so closely together that it was impossible to see far amongst them; and a high bank rose on one side of the pathway, which led through a deep dell, with a sparkling rivulet running at the bottom of it. It was a shady and cool spot; but after having just quitted the bright sunshine, a certain gloomy air appeared to hang over it, and for the first time the warning of the maid at the inn occurred to the mind of the fair Clara. "Oh! my father, what a dark forest this seems!" she exclaimed; "are not robbers sometimes met with in these places? I know not why, but I do not feel so happy as I did before, and cannot help wishing you had more people to guard you."

"Fear not, my sweet child," answered the Fidalgo; "we muster too strong to dread an attack from any band of robbers we are likely to encounter; and if any should dare to molest us, they shall pay dearly for it."

The words were scarcely uttered, when several musket-shots were heard, as if discharged from among the trees; and one of the servants fell from his mule,—the blood streaming from a wound in his side; and the animal of one of the other men reared, and rolled over, with his rider, to the ground. Donna Clara trembling with agitation, gazed anxiously at her father, who, drawing his sword, looked around, fearful lest any other shots from the unseen assassins might injure his child.

Confusion and dismay took possession of all the individuals of the cavalcade; the women in the litters screamed loudly and long, and the men stood aghast, not knowing which way to turn to meet their treacherous foe.

"Lift your fellow from the ground, and push on in close order," cried Gonçalo Christovaö; "we must not remain here to be murdered. Look well to your arms, and miss not your aim, if any of the villains show themselves."

But, alas! the order was useless; for, before the party could advance many paces, another volley was discharged among them, bringing down one of the hindmost litters, containing the maid-servants, whose shrieks and cries of terror utterly confounded the men, who stood paralysed, without attempting to offer assistance; and, at the same instant, eight horsemen, with pistols in their hands, dashed from among the trees towards the fidalgo and the litter of Donna Clara.

"Do not attempt to fire!" exclaimed one who appeared to be the leader of the band, "or you will repent it. You are in our power, and we might, if we had chosen, have killed every one of you; but, provided you make no resistance, we do not wish to shed blood, and are sorry for having hurt the servant. Deliver your money and jewels quietly, and you shall pass on: if you refuse, we shall possess ourselves of them without ceremony."

"Wretches! how dare you thus speak to me?" demanded the Fidalgo, indignantly. "Retire instantly, and allow my people to pass without molestation, or I will order them to fire."

"Hark! to the fidalgo—he is vapouring!" cried one of the band.

"If you dare to resist, you shall be the first victim, Senhor Fidalgo!" exclaimed he who had first spoken. "And remember your daughter—her fate be on your own head!"

The priest rode fiercely towards them, exclaiming, "Begone, wretches! or dread the anathema of the Church on your souls!"

"Hark to the priest—he's preaching!" cried one with a broad-brimmed hat drawn over his eyes, laughing. "Pooh, pooh, Senhor Padre, we are not afraid of mother Church; so do not waste your breath: we can get a priest to curse you in return, you know."

The brow of Gonçalo Christovaö grew dark with anger. "Vile miscreants!" he exclaimed, "you shall not intimidate us. Forward, my men!"

The servants who were near their master prepared to obey; but the muleteers seemed no way inclined to fight.

"Ah! is it so?" exclaimed the captain of the banditti. "Fire on the fools!"

Several shots were discharged; but, fortunately, none of the party were injured; and the robbers, drawing their swords, rushed on with loud oaths, but were met with steady courage by the fidalgo and his two attendants—he parrying, with great skill, every blow aimed at him, till his servants were both disarmed, but his arm growing weary, at length, of wielding his blade, a sudden blow wrenched it from his grasp, and he was thrown with violence to the ground. The priest, in the meantime, remained by Donna Clara's litter, though he looked fully willing, had he possessed a sword, to have joined in the fray; while the muleteers stood trembling by, without attempting to interfere.

"You would have acted more wisely to have saved us this trouble," exclaimed the leader of the robbers, as they prepared to bind the hands of the servants,—several of them dragging the priest from his mule, and treating him in the same way; the muleteers falling down on their knees, and crying for mercy, expecting every moment to have their throats cut. The fidalgo remained stunned on the ground; and, when the robber approached the first litter, to see whom it contained, Donna Clara, overcome with terror at seeing her father, as she supposed, dead, had fainted. The ruffian gazed with astonishment not unmixed with admiration, at the fair girl, now with her eyes closed, as pale as death itself; and for a moment he fancied that some shot must have struck her,—awe preventing him from even daring to touch her, till her gentle breathing convinced him that she lived; but his courage soon returned. "Quick, now, my men!" he cried. "Look into the pockets of these gentlemen, and put gags into the mouths of those senhoras, who are screaming loud enough to be heard across the forest, if they do not choose to be silent, and to deliver up their trinkets quietly. The baggage-mules must accompany us, till we can examine their burdens at our leisure."

The banditti lost not a moment in obeying these orders, though they found considerable difficulty in executing some of them; particularly in gagging the maid-servants, who fought most desperately, before they would deliver up each separate article of their ornaments. The more booty the robbers acquired, the more their avarice increased.

Donna Clara had now partially recovered; and, looking wildly around,—"Oh! my father, my father!" she exclaimed, "where are you?"

At the sound of her voice, a new idea seemed to strike the robber leader. "Ah! methinks this fair lady would fetch a high ransom," he exclaimed. "Come, senhora, you must condescend to make use of a less easy conveyance. Do not be alarmed, your father is not seriously hurt," he added, in rather a softer tone; "and if you will quietly accompany us, no harm shall befall him."

"Go with you! oh, whither?" cried the young lady, in a tone of horror. "Oh, allow us to pursue our journey, and my father will reward you."

"We trust not to the promises of a fidalgo, but take care ourselves to secure the rewards we require," answered the robber. "Come, lady, no more delay. You must leave your litter, for it cannot pass between the trees where our path lies." Saying which, he rudely seized the arm of the lovely girl, who had not attempted to move till he touched her, when she instinctively drew back; but she was as a dove in the talons of a vulture; and, dragging her forward, he compelled her to descend to the ground.

Trembling with terror, she gazed around, when she beheld the form of her parent, and, breaking from the bandit, threw herself, with a shriek, by his side, raising his head, and endeavouring to recall him to life. As, regarding none around her, she hung over the inanimate form of her parent, chafing his temples, kissing his pale cheek, and using every effort to recover him which her affection dictated, even the hardened ruffians paused ere they attempted to drag her from his side; but the love of gain triumphed over all the better feelings latent in their bosoms, which her beauty had for the moment elicited, and he who appeared to be the captain was again approaching her, when the fidalgo gave signs of returning animation, and, opening his eyes, gazed anxiously at his daughter. She uttered a cry of joy, on discovering that life yet remained, giving expression to her feelings by tender endearments; but the ruffian was not to be deterred from his purpose a second time, and, seizing her arm, attempted to tear her away. With slender efforts she endeavoured to resist the outrage, clinging still closer to her father. "If you have the feelings of men, you cannot be so cruel as to compel me to leave my father thus," she exclaimed. "Oh, wait, at least, till I see him in safety."

"Come, come, this is absurd folly, and waste of much precious time," cried several of the band in impatient tones.

"Give the old gentleman a shake, which will soon bring him to himself; and let him understand, that if he does not ransom his daughter in the course of three days, he will not see her again," said he with the slouched hat.

In vain the fair girl pleaded for pity, as two of the robbers held her in their grasp, while the others raised her father, who was now sufficiently recovered to comprehend his situation. He of the slouched hat again made his proposal, with threats of vengeance if it was not acceded to.

"Hear me!" cried the Fidalgo, in a tone of rage and agony. "You dare not commit the base outrage you propose, or the vengeance of every honest man in Portugal will follow and destroy you; but yet, if without further delay you set my daughter at liberty, I most solemnly promise you any sum you may venture to demand. Do you consent?"

"No, no, senhor," answered the leader: "we have risked our necks, and must be paid with good security; nor do we consider the empty word even of a fidalgo sufficient. You must send us the money, or you know the alternative, while we retain your daughter in our power."

"Wretches, no! 'tis impossible I should consent!" exclaimed Gonçalo Christovaö. "I would rather stab my daughter to the heart, and then plunge the dagger into my own breast, than trust you."

"As you like, senhor; but we do not intend to give you the choice. Here, tie this noble fidalgo to a tree, with his servants round him, and the priest to offer him consolation, and perhaps by the time some traveller comes by, he may have thought better on the subject," said the leader.

"You dare not do it, villains!" exclaimed the Fidalgo, his agony increased to the highest pitch. "Release my child, or the vengeance of Heaven will fall on your heads."

"Gag him, gag him!" cried several of the band, as they dragged him towards a tree to bind him to it.

"If you are less than demons, hear me!" he again exclaimed, as he put aside indignantly the rough hands near his face. "Let my daughter and her attendants go free, and she shall forward the ransom, while I remain with you."

"Oh no, senhor!" answered the Captain; "you are doubtless a very valuable and important person; but that would not at all answer our purpose. You would cause us much more trouble to keep; and if, by any chance, the ransom did not arrive, we could, after all, only kill you in revenge, while your fair daughter would make a charming wife to some of us. You understand, senhor! 'Twill lower your pride a little, when you see one of us kennel dogs, as you call us, your son-in-law. Think of that. These are our terms; and we do not alter them. Again, I say, we must have done with this folly. Collect all the party, and curses on them, while I hold the lady."

The banditti, according to their leader's order, now set to work in earnest, binding the fidalgo, the priest, and the servants to trees at some little distance from each other. They then treated the muleteers in the same way, who deplored, with tears, the loss of their animals; but when it came to the females' turn, one of them contriving to get the gag out of her mouth, set up a scream loud enough to be heard at the distance of a mile, to which she continued to give reiterated utterance, struggling so bravely, that it was some time before that implement to which it is said women have so great an aversion, could be replaced.

"Do not attempt to escape, Senhor Fidalgo," said one of the robbers, as approaching Gonçalo Christovaö, and drawing his long knife, he flourished it in the air. "Remember we could just as easily have cut your throat as let you live, and thank the saints that it is not our interest to do so. Some one will doubtless set you free before night approaches, otherwise you may find the wolves rather troublesome— adeos."

Donna Clara, too much overwhelmed with terror and agitation even to utter a faint scream, remained a passive spectator of the scene, scarcely comprehending the extent of her danger; nor was it till the captain of the banditti lifted her on his horse, that she seemed to return to consciousness, and even then she appeared less alarmed for her own safety than for that of her father.

The robbers, having effectually rifled every one of the travellers, even making the muleteers deliver up the few coins they possessed, collected their booty, and driving the baggage-mules together, took a pathway which appeared leading out of the main track across the forest. The captain remained the last, to see that nothing was left behind; when, bearing Donna Clara before him on his saddle, deaf to her prayers and entreaties, and regardless of her father's agonised glances, he turned his horse's head to follow his companions.

Volume One—Chapter Nine.

There are some feelings of the heart so intense that language possesses no words of sufficient force to describe them; and such was the passion which wrung the bosom of the proud fidalgo, when he saw his daughter, a being he loved, a part of himself, carried off by wretches so base and low that he looked upon them as formed of different materials from himself. It was far worse suffering than the martyr at the stake is doomed to bear; and rather would he have beheld his child torn by the wild beasts of the forest, than thus exposed to the lawless violence of such men. The agony of his fury deprived him almost of sensation, and of life itself; but the robber chief heeded him not, further than giving utterance to a scoffing laugh, and bestowing a glance of triumph and derision, over his shoulder, as he was disappearing among the trees; when, at the same moment, one of the band, who had been kept as a scout at some distance along the road, was seen galloping to the spot at a furious rate; and, as he perceived the captain, "Fly!" he cried, "fly! danger is near. A party of horsemen are close upon my heels." At these words the robber, plunging his long spurs into his horse's flanks, urged him between the thick-growing trees, followed by the scout, into the depths of the forest, where they were completely concealed from view.

The faint cries which, in her terror and despair, Donna Clara uttered, were yet heard, when a horseman approached, urging on his steed at the utmost speed, and the heart of the father heat again with the anxious hope of succour for his child; for, even as he flew along, his appearance bespoke him a cavalier of rank, being also followed by four servants at a short distance in the rear. He reined in his steed when he came near the spot where Gonçalo Christovaö was bound, and was about to dismount.

"Think not of me, senhor," exclaimed the Fidalgo. "But hasten through that path to the right, and rescue my daughter from the hands of ruffians who have borne her off."

At that moment a faint cry was heard through the forest, nor needed the cavalier other inducement to dash forward in the direction from which it proceeded, pointing with his hand, as he rode towards the trees, to the party who remained bound, to indicate them to his servants, one of whom, as he came up, leaped from his horse, and busied himself in releasing them, while the rest galloped after their master into the forest. No sooner did the fidalgo find himself at liberty, than seizing a sword which had been left on the ground, he rushed off in the direction his daughter had been carried, followed by his faithful escudeiro, who was the next person released from his bonds. The rest of the servants and the priest were soon set at liberty, as were some of the muleteers, the former hurrying off to join their master, entirely forgetting, in their haste, to release the women; but, fortunately for them, the muleteers had either more gallantry, or were less anxious to enter into danger. The priest also stalked off in the same direction, muttering dark curses on the heads of the robbers. When released by the muleteers, the old nurse was in an almost insensible state, from terror at the danger of her young charge; but the youthful females, even before their arms were set at liberty, made most significant gestures to have their mouths cleared of the handkerchiefs so unceremoniously thrust into them, which operation was no sooner performed, than, as the renowned Baron Munchausen's horn, when brought near the fire, gave forth the tones frozen up during the winter, so did they give vent, as if to make amends for their compulsory silence, to the most piercing shrieks, one trying to outvie the other in their loudness and number, so that it might have been supposed they were undergoing some fresh attack from the robbers, instead of being released by their friends. The old nurse threw herself on the ground, giving way to her terror in tears. "Oh my child! my dear child!" she cried; "they have torn her away, and I shall never see her more."

We must now follow the course of the young cavalier, who had arrived so opportunely on the scene of action; indeed, were we not writing a true history instead of a romance, we might be supposed to have brought him in merely for dramatic effect; but we can assure our readers, that in this, as in every other instance, we are adhering closely to the very voluminous, though rather illegible manuscripts, from which, with infinite labour, we are culling the present volumes. Perhaps, also, more interest may be taken in his adventures, when it is learnt that he was no other than Don Luis d'Almeida, on his way from Lisbon to his father's quinta, near Coimbra, accompanied by Pedro and some other attendants. As, with considerable risk, he galloped between the trees, he did not even turn his head to see if his servants were following, so eager was he to rescue the daughter of the venerable-looking person he had observed bound. As may be supposed, from the intricacy of the thickets and the closeness of the trees, very slow progress could be made by people encumbered in any way as the robbers were, and thus scarce three minutes had passed before Don Luis perceived them a short distance in advance, they being unconscious, from not hearing his horse's hoofs on the soft grass, that they were pursued. He was thus enabled to approach close to them before he was discovered, when, seeing only one man, the whole band reined in their horses, the hindermost wheeling with the intention of cutting him down, their leader ordering them not to fire, lest the report of their arms should show where they were: but the first who attempted to attack him paid dearly for his temerity; for, drawing a pistol from his holster, he discharged it, and the ruffian fell from his horse. This success somewhat checked the ardour of the rest in closing with him, and at the same time drew the attention of his servants to the spot. Fortunately for him, too, the robbers, having fired their guns, had forgotten to reload them, and before they could do so, his attendants were seen urging on their horses through the trees. The banditti, upon this, drew back together to reload their pieces; but Don Luis, seeing the advantage this would give them, drew his sword, and rushed on the foremost, his valour excited by catching sight of the light robes of the lady among them, the trees growing thickly around preventing more than one attacking him at a time. The captain of the band now approached, still holding the fainting form of Donna Clara in his grasp. "Fire, you fools!" he cried. "Never mind if you hit Damiaö. It cannot be helped; for we shall be cut down in detail, if we get not rid of yon daring madman. Fire!"

Two of his party obeyed; but their aim was uncertain, and the balls struck the trees near them.

"Fire again!" shouted the Captain; and another of his men having loaded his piece, discharged it; but it was for the destruction of a friend; for the ball striking Damiaö's horse, the animal fell, and Don Luis, dealing a blow on the ruffian's head before he could recover himself, rode furiously at the captor of the lady. His three followers at the same time coming up, gave full occupation to the remainder of the band, who were, however, still superior in numbers; and though their courage was somewhat lessened by the loss of their companions, yet the hopes of keeping possession of their booty induced them, led on by him with the slouched hat, to continue the combat. The bandit chief, encumbered as he was by his fair prize, would have been completely unable to defend himself from Don Luis's furious attack, had he not interposed her as his shield; but the young cavalier was not thus to be baffled; for, changing suddenly his sword to his bridle hand, and leaning forward, he so dexterously clasped the lovely girl round the waist, that the robber, completely taken by surprise, relinquished his hold, and beheld her securely seated in front of her rescuer before he had time to draw a weapon for his defence; when Don Luis, again changing his sword to his right hand, dealt him a blow on the shoulder, that completely disabled him from further resistance. A shot from the pistol of Pedro had likewise severely wounded him with the slouched hat; and the shouts of Gonçalo Christovaö, and his attendants, being now heard, the banditti lost courage, and, turning their horses, galloped after their wounded leader, leaving Don Luis master of the field, with all the booty, except the jewels and money they carried about them. With the fair charge he held in his arms, it was impossible for him to attempt to follow; nor did he think fit to risk the lives of his attendants in a pursuit, which, considering that the robbers were probably well acquainted with the country, would no doubt prove fruitless.

As, his faithful Pedro holding his horse, he gently lifted Donna Clara to the ground, he now, for the first time, observed her extreme beauty; and, though he had fancied his heart seared to all female attractions, he could not help acknowledging that he had never seen one so lovely as the fair girl to whom he had just afforded such essential service. "Fear not, lady," he said, in a tone modulated by his feelings; "you are free from all danger, and your father, also, is unharmed. See, here he comes to assure you of his safety."

As he spoke, the fidalgo arrived on the spot, and Don Luis's heart beat quick with new, undefined sensations, as Donna Clara, forgetting all her terrors and danger on seeing her father in safety, sprang forward, and fell weeping on his neck, while he folded her in a tender embrace. For some minutes neither could find words to give utterance to their feelings of joy, which were too deep, too tender, indeed, for mere words; the father standing gazing on the lovely countenance of his daughter, as she reclined in his arms, while she looked up with an inquiring glance to assure herself that she was not deceived. At length, the Fidalgo addressed Don Luis with that dignified air which marks the man of true nobility.

"Senhor, you have bestowed an inestimable benefit on me," he said: "let me not longer remain in ignorance of the name of one to whom I would endeavour to offer that earnest gratitude which, however, no words can express."

"Oh! do not speak of gratitude, senhor," answered Don Luis: "it is I who have to rejoice in my happiness at having been of service to one so fair and lovely as your daughter. My name is Don Luis d'Almeida."

"Ah! the son of one whose reputation I well know," answered the Fidalgo. "And truly delighted I am to hear by whom so great a weight of gratitude has been imposed. My name, also, you may probably have heard; it is Gonçalo Christovaö."

"A name so illustrious I could not fail to have heard, senhor," answered Don Luis; "and my satisfaction is doubled at knowing to whom I have been of service." The fidalgo bowed in return for the compliment, at which he was well pleased; nor did it fail to increase his estimation for the person who paid it.

"But pardon me, Don Luis," he said; "we ought no longer to remain here; for those wretches are capable of any treachery, and may return to fire on us at a distance."

"You observe rightly, senhor; we will no longer delay here," answered Don Luis; and, offering his support to Donna Clara on one side, while her father aided her on the other,—she, expressing her thanks to her gallant deliverer much more by looks than words,—they conducted her towards the spot where the litters had been left; the patient mules having stood quiet during the whole time of the affray.

The muleteers, with shouts of pleasure, collected their scattered beasts, whom they had never expected to see again, and busily employed themselves in putting the litters and baggage to rights. Leaving the body of the slain robber as food for the wolves, the servants dragged forward his companion who had been wounded, one of them, more humane than the rest, attempting to stop the blood flowing from a deep wound in his shoulder, but in vain; yet the man, though he felt himself to be dying, would give no information respecting the rest of the banditti. They were close to the road, when they encountered the priest; and the wounded robber, seeing a person in the clerical dress, earnestly entreated that the consolations of religion might be administered to him. At a sign from the priest, he was therefore placed on the bank, facing the road, and the servants retiring, the holy man knelt down by his side, to hear the confession of his sins, before which he could offer none of the satisfactory comforts of absolution; but the detail occupied a considerable time; for his peccadillos were, alas! of no slight magnitude, nor of little interest, it would seem, by the look of earnest attention which overspread the countenance of his listener. The robber threw many a dark imputation on the characters of some of high rank and influence in the realm, by whose instigation he had committed various atrocities, yet unconfessed and unabsolved. "Now, Father," said the dying man, "absolve me from these sins which press most heavily on me, and I will afterwards make confession of the remainder."

"Not so, my son," answered the Priest; "you must make a clear discharge of your conscience; for I may not afford absolution to a heart yet loaded with iniquity."

"Oh! Father, I am dying, and feel that I am a miserable sinner!" ejaculated the man, with a feeble voice; "but there is a deed I swore not to reveal to any one, and I may not break my oath. Oh! grant me, then, absolution, ere I die."

"That may not be," answered the Priest; "oaths made to sinners like ourselves, for a wicked purpose, can be annulled by a minister of religion, as the only way of making retribution for the crime."

"It was a deed of blood, Father, but I sought not to do it of my own accord; another instigated me to it by bribes which my poverty could not resist, and I swore never to reveal it."

"I have said such oaths are valueless!" exclaimed the Priest eagerly. "Come, haste, for your last moments are approaching, when you will be consigned to the terrible flames of purgatory, for thousands and thousands of years, without a mass said for the repose of your soul, if you do not go at once to the ever-burning and bottomless pit, among infidels and heretics."

The hair of the man stood on end with horror, at the picture of torment offered to his imagination; his eyeballs rolled wildly, as with clenched hands he for an instant sat upright on the ground, and seemed as if about to rise altogether.

"I will confess, I will confess!" he cried, "though I break my oath. 'Twas the young Conde de San Vincente who hired me by a large bribe to do the deed. There was a lady whose affections he sought to gain, but her husband was—Oh, Father, where are you? I am cold—very cold!" cried the man.

"Who was the husband?—you slew him?" asked the Priest, stooping down over the dying wretch.

"He was the—" but ere he could pronounce the name which hung quivering on his lips, he uttered a loud shriek, and, with a convulsive shudder, fell back a lifeless corpse. The priest, however, had heard enough for his purpose; and uttering, or pretending to utter, a prayer over the body, he rose from the ground, and some of the servants coming up, one of them threw a cloak over the distorted features of the dead man.

While the scene of horror we have described was enacting, Don Luis had been actively employed in restoring order to the scattered cavalcade; his first care being to place Donna Clara in her litter, in which her old gouvernante accompanied her. The fidalgo was too much injured and fatigued to remount his horse, and therefore took his seat in his litter; the two wounded men-servants being placed in the third, while the females mounted the mules of the former; one of the mules of the fourth litter having been wounded, they were unable to support a burden.

These various arrangements having been made; the fidalgo, with many expressions of gratitude, would have bid farewell to his deliverer; but Don Luis, fearful that the brigands might again return, insisted on escorting him and his daughter to Leiria, the nearest town on the road to Lisbon, where, if thought advisable, a guard might be procured. "I should be performing but half my devoir as a knight, if I were to quit you in the middle of the forest," said Don Luis; "a few hours' delay can be of slight consequence to me, and I may happily be of some further service to you."

"I cannot refuse your courteous offer, senhor," answered the Fidalgo, pointing to his daughter. "For my daughter's sake, it is most acceptable, as I yet tremble for her safety."

Further delay being unnecessary, the party was again put in motion, Don Luis now riding by the side of the fidalgo's litter, and ever and anon, notwithstanding his previous intentions to the contrary, approaching that of Donna Clara, to inquire if she had recovered from her alarm, and to assure her that she had no further cause for fear; an assurance in which, proceeding from the lips of so handsome a cavalier, and uttered in a tone of respectful courtesy, she could not fail to put implicit confidence. Notwithstanding his words, however, he kept a constant and watchful glance on every side, having also given private instructions to his own people, and to those of Gonçalo Christovaö to have their arms in readiness for any sudden attack. By insensible degrees he was led to enter more into conversation with his fair companion, and, as he spoke, his words became animated with a new spirit; all thoughts of the past being banished from his mind, while the roses again returned to her cheeks before blanched by fear, her soft eyes beaming with a strange and undefined happiness.

While Don Luis rode on to address the fidalgo, the old Nurse began to comment on his appearance. "What a handsome young cavalier is that," she said; "so brave too,—why, the servants say he killed ten of the brigands with his own hand! What a noble countenance he has! with such sparkling black eyes! and how many polite inquiries he made after our health! Oh! mine is sore shaken by the fright.—Is he not handsome?"

"Do you think so, good nurse?" answered Donna Clara unconsciously. "I did not look.—He is very brave and very good, I am sure."

"That he is; and so gallant, too," said the Nurse. "How few young gentlemen would take the trouble to turn back to protect us. What a pity he is married!"

"Married!" exclaimed Donna Clara; and there was a sinking at her heart, and she felt her cheek again grow pale, she knew not why.

"If he is not married, he soon is to be, to his cousin Donna Theresa d'Alorna. The moment I heard his name I remembered that I had learned all about it from Senhora Anna, his father's housekeeper, whose birth-place is near Oporto, and who came back to see her kindred some time ago."

While the old lady was thus running on, the subject of her conversation again rode to the side of the litter; for it was extraordinary how incumbent on him he considered it to make frequent inquiries respecting the young lady's health. Now, many people will ask if Don Luis had thus suddenly forgotten Donna Theresa and all his griefs; and though we cannot, with perfect certainty, answer that question, yet we have strong reasons to suspect that, for the time, he thought very little about either one or the other; nor had he, indeed, from the moment when he dashed his spurs into his horse's flanks, as he rode forward to rescue Donna Clara from the power of the brigands, and, as now he rode by her side, gazing on her lovely countenance, and regarding her as one who confided in him for protection, he knew not how it was that all nature seemed suddenly to have assumed a brighter garb, and the weight to have been lifted from his heart. We must, however, beg no one to suppose we mean to insinuate, either that he had fallen in love with the lady, or that she had fallen in love with him, at first sight; because all people of mature judgment agree that, if such is possible, it can occur alone to very silly young people; and that the descriptions of such folly are to be found only in the most absurd and extravagant romances. Of course, therefore, in a grave history, like the present work, we should not venture even to hint at such a thing; and, with regard to his affection for his cousin, it must be remembered that she had treated him with great cruelty and deceit; and that young hearts, however their possessors may fancy them seared and blighted, are of a very elastic and reviving nature, requiring but the warm sun and genial showers of spring to restore their freshness and bloom.

However that may be, when Don Luis again rode up to the side of the litter, his thoughts dwelt on no other subject than its fair occupant, and he felt a slight sensation of disappointment, as, instead of leaning forward to hear what he had to communicate, she reclined back in her seat. "I fear Donna Clara is fatigued with all she has undergone," he observed.

"Yes, senhor," she answered, with a half averted eye, "I have, indeed, yet scarcely recovered from terror, though I know it is foolish to be further alarmed; but—" and she hesitated to proceed.

"Do you know, Senhor Don Luis," exclaimed the old Nurse, eager to speak, and at the same time to relieve the embarrassment of her charge, "that I have heard a great deal of you, and seem to know you perfectly well, though I never saw you before. Ah! senhor, I have heard, too, of your fair cousin, Donna Theresa, and am surprised she is not with you; for I thought you were to have been married before this."

At Donna Theresa's name a cloud passed across the cavalier's brow.

"You must have been misinformed, senhora," he answered gravely. "My cousin is engaged to the Marquis of Tavora."

"Oh! I beg your pardon, senhor," said the old Nurse; "I hope I have not offended by the question; but I hear that she is a very lovely young lady."

"Oh no, no, you have not offended," said Don Luis, as he rode from the side of the litter, to avoid showing the blush which burned on his cheek at hearing an affair so lightly alluded to, which he had fancied unknown to the world. Very different was the effect of his words on Donna Clara; for though she felt that, whether he was single, engaged, or married, ought to be a matter of complete indifference to her, yet a certain uneasy sensation seemed removed from her breast, and she again leaned forward to speak, when she found he was no longer by her side.

More than an hour elapsed before Don Luis again approached the litter, during which period the young lady unconsciously allowed a number of new sensations, which had never before been known to her, to take possession of her heart; and she welcomed his return with a smile whose sweetness might have softened the bosom of a stoic,— and certainly her gallant deliverer was not one. For the remainder of the journey he did not leave the side of her litter for more than a few minutes at a time, always gladly again returning to it; and, although they had emerged some time before from the dark forest of pines, and were traversing a comparatively thickly-peopled country, so that all fear of the brigands was banished, yet he insisted on accompanying the party to the end of their day's journey. As the travellers wound round the base of a hill, the bright rays of the evening sun were throwing a ruddy hue on the topmost turrets of the once proud castle of Leiria; which, standing on the summit of an eminence, situated to the north of that most ancient town, now burst on their view, enclosed in an amphitheatre of hills, surrounding a smiling, well-cultivated valley. A road winding round the foot of the hill conducted them, through the narrow streets of the town, to the house of a fidalgo, who, though absent, had requested Gonçalo Christovaö to take up his abode there.

Don Luis spent the evening in the society of the fidalgo and his daughter; nor did he lose the ground he had gained in the estimation of either; though the priest regarded him with frowning looks, keeping a lynx-eyed watch on every expression of his countenance, and on each word he uttered: the whole party, however, overcome with fatigue, were glad to retire at an early hour to rest.

The sun had already risen above the walls of the town on the following morning, before Don Luis thought of ordering his horses, and he then considered it but an act of common courtesy to wait till he had seen one of Donna Clara's attendants, to inquire how their lady had borne the fatigues of the journey, and at last, when a black-eyed soubrette tripped down stairs, she kept the handsome stranger in conversation with abundance of questions in return, hoping that he neither had suffered in any way, and finishing by assuring him that her young mistress would be quite offended, she felt sure, if he departed without allowing her again to thank him in person for his gallantry. These observations, we must remark, were entirely the damsel's own ideas; for, of course, Donna Clara would not have dreamed of delaying Don Luis in his journey on her account; but so thought not the soubrette, and she was merely acting towards her mistress as she would have wished others to do towards herself; for it is remarkable what quick perceptions her class possess on such matters. He therefore could not be so ungallant as to refuse her request, and then he bethought him also that he ought to pay his respects to Gonçalo Christovaö, who had not yet issued from his sleeping apartment. He had for some time been pacing the drawing-room with rather impatient steps, when, on facing the door, it opened, and Donna

Clara appeared, enveloped in the full and graceful drapery of her travelling dress, a slight pallor on her delicate cheeks, her eyes soft and liquid, and with a slight degree of bashfulness in her manner as she advanced into the room. There seems to be always a brighter halo of freshness and purity, circling round a young and innocent girl when she first greets the early morn with her smile of gladness, before the glowing sun of noon-day has cast his scorching beams upon her head to dim the seraph-like lustre of her beauty. So lovely, indeed, did Donna Clara appear to the eyes of Don Luis, that for a moment, as the blood rushed quickly from his heart, he stopped, unconsciously, to gaze with admiration involuntary; but, recovering his usual manner, he approached her with graceful courtesy, to inquire if she had suffered from the terror and fatigue of the previous day. She answered, in tones of silvery softness, a sweet smile beaming on her lips, and, as she spoke, his eyes wandered over her features, imprinting every lineament indelibly on the tablets of his memory. Though he knew it not, neither age, grief, nor madness itself, could efface that image of beauty he had drawn. Years might pass away, his own eyes might grow dim, that lovely form might fade, but there it would remain, unchangeable, cherished, and adored!

Though old age has stolen on us, it has made us neither sullen nor morose, and we can yet find pleasure in recurring to the fresh days of our youth, when a lovely face had power to make an impression on our hearts; and we can thus vividly picture to ourselves many of those, seen perhaps but once, suddenly bursting on our view, like a picture of Titian's, never to be forgotten; and it is from those we describe the fair creatures we would introduce to our readers. Now and again we have met the same, we have fancied, in the person of a younger sister, or a daughter, or perhaps of no kindred except that of sentiments and disposition, which always give a similar expression to the countenance. Sometimes, too, we have met the self-same being, changed, alas! from the creature of angelic loveliness we once knew;— the roses have fled her cheeks, the sylph-like form is no longer there; we hear no more her soft silvery voice; but soon some old familiar expression, some reference to past days, conjures up the former image in all its glowing tints of loveliness, and we deem our youth again returned, and once more do her joyous laughter and the sweet notes of her voice ring, like fairy music, in our ears. 'Tis for this reason that we esteem painting the first, the most divine of the arts; for, with regard to music, the hand or the voice may fail; with poetry, the language may alter or be lost, and the words bring no meaning to the senses; but painting has survived the destruction of kingdoms, the dispersion of nations, a people whose language and very name would have passed away, but that the productions of this art remain to tell their history. Who has not gazed with rapture on some lovely, almost speaking, portrait of one absent, or perhaps lost to us for ever? As we have stood before it, we have seemed to hold converse with it; the eyes have appeared to burn with the mysterious light of intellect, and the lips to move; and we have answered to the words we in fancy heard! Can poetry or music work this magic effect? No; they have their own charms—and oh! how powerful our soul confesses! but we have seen paintings which combine all, which have poetry in every line, and music in every tint.

We are fond, we confess, of making digressions, either when travelling through beautiful scenery, or in conversation, to sketch the views, and to cull the flowers to be found on each side of our path, which, however pleasant to ourselves, who know what is before us, is a bad system to pursue, we own, when our readers are anxious to proceed with our history, and we must therefore apologise to them for our wanderings, and promise in future to keep as much as possible in the direct path.

We must again request our readers to understand, that we do not affirm that Don Luis was in love with Donna Clara; but that we merely wish to explain clearly that he was not at all likely to forget her, which circumstance may be of consequence to remember for the elucidation of the subsequent part of this narrative; to hasten on with which, we need not give the conversation which took place between them, because, also, though highly interesting to themselves, it may not be so to our readers.

At length, however, Donna Clara appeared to be seized with a fit of timidity, wherefore we do not know; for Don Luis was most respectful, and he intended to appear as reserved and cold as he was fully convinced he felt; and we can only guess, therefore, that it was at the time he was employed in making that mental portrait we have described, in which process his eyes were necessarily fixed on her fair features. Now his eyes had a melancholy, tender glance, owing to his late unhappiness; and we have observed that, from the pitying nature of the female heart, such always make the strongest impression on it; and it is a fact for which we will vouch, that, precisely at the same time, she was making the same use of her eyes, in drawing on her mind, though in a slightly different way; for, while his were fixed while he spoke, with a steady gaze, her glances were but for a moment, ever and anon, lifted to his countenance, and again quickly thrown on the ground, as a miniature painter does in the practice of his art. Now, the young people were taking each other's miniatures in the most artistical way, though they were not aware of it; nor was the operation quite finished (for they found much pleasure in prolonging it) when Gonçalo Christovaö entered the room to relieve his daughter from the slight embarrassment she was beginning to feel. The morning meal was then placed on the table; and, during the time necessarily employed in discussing it, they threw in a few finishing touches, before omitted, which certainly made the portraits very perfect—fully equal to those from the pencil of Rochard, who so frequently, while preserving an exact likeness, improves on the beauty of the originals; though it was impossible such should be the case with the miniature Don Luis carried away of Donna Clara, however much she might have flattered him.

Breakfast in those days was composed of different materials from what it is at present in England, tea being used by very few in the morning except as a medicine, light wine and water being drunk instead, with a little bread, the noon-day meal and the supper being the only substantial repasts.

During the course of conversation, Donna Clara mentioned a serious loss which had occurred to her of a small case of jewels. "I prized them highly, not for their intrinsic value, but that they were my beloved mother's; nor have I even ever lifted them from the box since she last placed them there."

Don Luis, of course, as a man of gallantry, vowed that he would use every exertion to recover them, though he could scarcely tell how he should set about the task. Donna Clara, we need not say, thanked him, with many blushes, for his kind intentions; at the same time more minutely describing her lost treasure, for she could not resist a sort of presentiment that he would recover it.

The morning meal having been discussed in the way we have described, and a very pleasant way Don Luis thought it, though it had not a fattening effect on him certainly, for he quite forgot to eat anything, the litters were ordered to the door, and he had the honour of leading the young lady to her seat, in doing which he was quite surprised to discover a slight trembling of her hand, as unavoidably he gently pressed it, though nothing of the sort occurred with Senhora Gertrudes, the old nurse, as most gallantly he placed her opposite to her mistress, by which slight attention he completely won that most respectable old lady's heart. He then offered his arm to the fidalgo, who gave him a warm embrace at parting, making him promise to visit him soon at Lisbon. He then observed that the curtain of Donna Clara's litter was loose, so he flew to secure it, for which service he received a rich reward in a sweet smile and a few words of thanks; they, of course, required a suitable answer, and thus he lingered by her side until the whole cavalcade were waiting his last bow, to be put in motion. He delayed them some time before he discovered such to be the case, and was aroused only by hearing the fidalgo's voice inquiring of the muleteers why they did not proceed, and their answering that they were ready. Donna Clara then bent her head, and waved her hand, Gonçalo Christovaö bowed, and all his attendants took off their hats, which salutation being returned by Don Luis, the whole party moved forward; but he did not quit his position till the last faint tinkle of the mules' bells had died away. He might have stood there longer, as Pedro, who had been making his private comments on what he observed, thought very probable; but knowing that it was high time his master should be in the saddle, he brought his horse close to him, making the animal rear a little, while he held the stirrup, a very significant gesture for him to mount. Looking round, and seeing all his party prepared, he threw himself on his horse, courteously returning the bows made by the bystanders, and set forward to retrace his steps of the previous day. Having now introduced two very interesting young people to each other, we will leave them to pursue their journeys in different directions, while we turn to other scenes and fresh characters, for none of which, however, have we so much regard as for those we have just quitted.

Volume One—Chapter Ten.

In looking over the many various and bulky documents before us, from which we are compiling this history, we see an account of a personage who played a conspicuous part in the scenes we are about to describe. Dom Joseph Mascarenhas and Lancastre, Duke of Aveiro, was descended from Dom George, a natural son of John the Second, King of Portugal, called the Perfect. He was hereditary grand master of the house of the King of Portugal, president of the court of the palace, and one of the high lords of the kingdom. He was not born to this high rank, owing it more to a caprice of fortune than to any good qualities he possessed. His elder brother, the Marquis of Gouvea, having fallen in love with the wife of a fidalgo of the first order, and won her affection in return, which was discovered by the husband; as the only way of enjoying their criminal passion, he fled with her to a foreign country. Such, according to the laws of Portugal, is considered a capital crime, and punished by perpetual banishment, which sentence being carried into effect against the marquis, his younger brother succeeded to his title and estates. An uncle of the Gouveas, Father Gaspar de Incarnaçaö, one of the many priests by whom the old king, John the Fifth, was surrounded, being soon after nominated Prime Minister, through his interest, the dukedom of Aveiro, which had previously become extinct, was bestowed on Dom Joseph. During the reign of that imbecile and fanatical sovereign, he had enjoyed considerable influence at Court, when he had made a deadly and personal enemy of Sebastiaö Jozé de Carvalho, then a young and daring adventurer, without power or influence, who had presumed to lift his eyes towards a lady of his family, whose affections his handsome figure and gallant manners had won. The duke, highly indignant at the daring presumption of one whom he designated as a low-born plebeian, strenuously opposed the match, threatening vengeance on the head of the lover if he presumed to persevere, at the same time insulting him with every term of opprobrium. But the man who was destined to curb and break the haughty spirits of the whole body of a potent nobility, was not likely to be deterred from his purpose by the threats of a single family; and, in spite of all their care, he bore the lady off from the seclusion in which they had immured her to keep her out of his way. In consequence of this insult to the honour of his family, the duke had sworn the most deadly vengeance against Carvalho, taking every means to thwart his aspiring aims; and thus did the blackest hatred rankle in the breasts of both, each seeking the first opportunity to destroy the other. His duchess, by whom he had one son, the Marquis of Gouvea, yet a child, was sister to the Marchioness of Tavora, but devoid of her pride and ambition, and devoted entirely to her domestic duties.

The duke, at the time of which we write, had retired, during the heat of the summer, to his country-house of Azeitaö, on the borders of the Tagus, at some distance from Lisbon. A hot and sultry day was near drawing to a close, the setting sun just tingeing the topmost boughs of a grove of shining leaved orange-trees, beneath whose shade the master of the domain had for some time past been pacing, in no very enviable mood, it would seem, from the fierce and discontented expression which sat upon his brow, and the violent action in which he was indulging. His outward appearance certainly did not betoken his lofty birth and ancient lineage, except that the haughty and imperious air he wore showed that he was accustomed to have his commands implicitly obeyed; his figure being low, and destitute of symmetry and grace. "Curses on the man who has dared to come between me and my plans," he exclaimed, as he struck his clenched hand against his brow. "Trusting in the confidence the king has foolishly reposed in him, he has dared, not only to treat me, the chief noble in the realm, as an equal, forsooth, but with marked insult and disdain, to exhibit his hatred and jealousy of my rank; but he shall not continue so to do much longer, all powerful as he deems himself. Would that the assassin's knife could reach his bosom! but the fools are afraid of his giant strength and figure, and declare that no steel can harm him. Oh, that heaven or hell would send me aid to work out my vengeance!—I would give half my wealth to see him dead at my feet!"

"What wouldst thou, my son?" said a voice, in a deep and hollow tone. He started, with horror on his countenance. His thoughts, his conscience told him, had been evil, and he was one over whom superstition and bigotry held full sway; for a moment, therefore, he expected to see the father of sin in a bodily presence rising up before him. He looked up, and beheld a dark figure of gigantic height, it seemed, amid the thickening shadows of the trees. A cold sweat stood on his brow. Had his dark thoughts then conjured up a spirit of evil? With noiseless steps the figure approached over the soft mossy ground, and, instead of the unwelcome visitor he had expected, he saw the Father Malagrida standing before him. He breathed more freely, and felt his courage revive in the presence of so righteous a man, whose sign alone was sufficient to keep at bay the whole infernal host.

"What would you, my son?" repeated the Father. "Some half-uttered sentences fell on my ear, and I observed your violent action. Tell me, my son, what thoughts oppress your bosom, and I will pour balm into it."

"Father, you cannot aid me," said the Duke; "it is beyond your province."

"There is nothing beyond my province, there is nothing I cannot foresee," exclaimed the Jesuit, in a deep tone. "Think you I see with the mortal eyes men see with, or judge with the judgment of the vulgar? No, my son, my spirit is elevated above the world. The vision of prophecy illumines my mind, and where men of common souls, unenlightened by Divine grace, grope on in the dark, like blind moles, all before me is clear and light. Speak not, then. I know your thoughts, and you need not fear to indulge in them; for they are righteous and sanctified. You would seek to inflict a just punishment on the evil doer—you would chastise him who has elevated himself, by aid of the spirit of darkness, to a post of power, in order that he may heap damnation on his own head by afflicting with cruelties and insults those chosen of the Lord as his servants."

"Father, you have divined my thoughts," exclaimed the Duke. "I was, at the moment you arrived, considering by what means I could bring down punishment on the head of that man, Sebastiaö Jozé de Carvalho, equally the foe of the fidalgos and of religion."

"All means are allowable when the end proposed is holy," answered the Jesuit. "And what more righteous object than the punishment of the wicked? Be assured, my son, that Heaven will avenge itself in due time on the destroyer of its servants, and blessed will those be who are chosen as the instruments to work out its inscrutable ends. Hear me, Duke of Aveiro! The Lord of Heaven has chosen me, as he did the most holy prophet Balaam of olden time, whose deep learning taught him to understand the language of the beasts of the field; and to me he has given in charge to deliver his messages to the kings and potentates who rule the world. Thus does he declare that he who is exalted shall be brought low, and that he who will protect his servants shall be exalted even to sit on the regal throne."

The Duke started. "Is such the message Heaven deigns to send to me?" he exclaimed, as he gazed with a look of doubt and astonishment at the speaker.

"Ah, thou confidest not in my sayings," exclaimed Malagrida; "thou doubtest that I speak the words of inspiration. Beware, Duke of Aveiro, beware of the temptations of Satan!"

"Holy Father, I believe your words," answered the Duke, trembling.

"Rememberest thou not, then, that in thy veins flows the royal blood of Portugal? then why not mount that throne when he who now reigns has departed? Say! ought he to rule a Catholic people, who cherishes the persecutor of our holy religion, who confides in one who would destroy the bulwarks of the Church, who has driven its most devoted servants from his presence? No, my son, I will answer for you, no. Such a man ought not to live, and blessed is he who does the work of Heaven in destroying him."

The Duke stood gazing on the Jesuit as one whose senses are bewildered by the sudden communication either of joyful or disastrous intelligence. Had he ever before indulged in thoughts such as these words conjured up? Yes, he had; but, as he thought, he trembled; but now all his fears were banished, and those imaginings which he had before fancied were the instigations of the evil one, he was now told, were the inspirations of the Divine will. Neither the Duke nor Malagrida had moved since they first met; the tall gaunt figure of the priest appearing of still greater height from a bright gleam of sunshine, which, piercing through the foliage, fell upon his head, as he waved his arms wildly round while he spoke; the former now standing in the deep shade beneath the thickly growing orange-trees, which extended in a long avenue, the ground beneath being striped with lines of the brightest gold and black. Now, some may suppose that Malagrida was an impersonification of the evil one, come to tempt the unfortunate Duke to his destruction; but such was not the case. He had from his earliest day's been an enthusiast, with an eager mind, weakened by the exercises of superstition, and now insanity was making rapid progress over it, though he still retained a considerable spice of that species of cunning which often accompanies madness, pointing out the best means of attaining what was most advantageous to him. He thus, while he fancied that he was giving utterance to the inspirations of Heaven, was perfectly well aware that he was making a tool of the weak and bigoted Duke, not discovering that he was himself influenced by another his superior, but who, in his estimation, was vastly his inferior in talent and holiness. Respecting the latter quality he might not have far erred.

He stood gazing down on his noble dupe for several minutes. "Come," he said, "my son, whose brow I may some day see graced by a regal diadem, let us walk beneath this shady grove, and talk further on this subject. Should Heaven not alter its intention of placing you on the throne of these realms, you will not forget the interests of the Church, and of one of its most devoted servants, who has been the privileged and true prophet of your elevation."

"No, holy Father, trust to my gratitude," answered the Duke. "The Church, under my protection, shall flourish in full power; and you shall ever remain the guardian of my conscience, and my spiritual adviser."

"Such is well, my son," answered the Jesuit; "and, ere long, your good intentions will be rewarded. In the meantime, be prepared for the events which are at hand, and be not dismayed by the difficulties in your path. He who would succeed must suffer all things, and dare all things; nor fear but that the Church will grant absolution, even unto the shedding the blood of the wicked."

"I understand your words, Father," answered the Duke, in an agitated and hollow tone. "The matter you speak of is of deep importance, and requires mature consideration; yet would I hazard all to destroy that upstart Carvalho, who so insolently lords it over us nobles, by birth his masters."

Thus conversing, the Duke and Malagrida continued pacing the orange grove till the quick coming shades of darkness made it no longer safe to speak aloud on such dangerous subjects, lest any, unperceived, might approach and overhear them.

As the name of the Father Malagrida was at one time known over a great part of the Catholic world, by some lauded as a saint and prophet, by others scorned as an impudent hypocrite and impostor, we may be excused for giving a slight sketch of his history.

Gabriel Malagrida, an Italian, was born in 1689, at Mercajo, in the Milanese, and was thus, at the time we have introduced him, upwards of sixty years old. At an early age he migrated to Portugal, then the paradise of priests and religious adventurers of all classes, but particularly of the Jesuits, who possessed the supreme control over the consciences of the royal family and the chief nobility; and into that order he was there, after the usual probation, admitted. His peculiar talents were soon discovered, and he was despatched as a missionary to South America. Over the whole of that part under the dominion of Portugal he travelled barefooted and alone; his only sustenance the wild roots and herbs, which he dug with his own hands; his body being covered with the marks imprinted on it by the teeth and claws of the wild beasts he encountered. Having escaped the glories of martyrdom, such a life fully entitled him to the character of a saint of the very first order, which, on his recall by his superior, he took every opportunity to improve; adding to it that of a prophet and worker of miracles, thousands being ready to swear to the fulfilment of the predictions he had uttered, and to the miracles he had wrought. King John the Fifth, of pious memory, who ever preferred the society of bigots, flatterers, buffoons, and fools, to the cares of government, for which he probably felt a consciousness of total incapacity, leaving his kingdom to rapid decay, while he was slowly toiling to merit heaven and gain forgiveness for rather numerous peccadillos, which private memoirs hint he had some difficulty in giving up, had distinguished Malagrida by marked partiality, and had performed what were called exercises under his direction. He had, likewise, been a favourite with the queen, Mary Anne of Austria; and, on his return from South America, the present king, Joseph, then Prince of Brazil, had gone out to meet him, and throwing himself at his feet, had implored his blessing. It is, indeed, scarcely possible, in the present day, to conceive a Court so completely debased by superstition, so overrun by herds of slothful, ignorant, or designing priests, as was that of Lisbon; from whose worse than Augean filth it was Carvalho's Herculean undertaking, in some degree, to cleanse it for the time. Malagrida having thus retained almost supreme power over the consciences of the chief persons in the realm for a long series of years, his hatred was rancorous and deadly against the man who had deprived him of it; and the Minister had occasion for the utmost watchfulness and talent to guard himself against the secret machinations and the public attacks with which he and the rest of his order attempted to destroy him.

When Carvalho first returned to Portugal, after his embassy to the Court of London, he had paid every respect to the Jesuits, particularly to Father Moreira, the confessor to the Prince of Brazil, in order, by his aid, to gain the confidence of the heir to the throne; but no sooner did he find his power secure, than he threw off the mask and proclaimed himself the enemy of the whole order, whom he declared the chief cause of the ignorance and bigotry of the people.

It is not surprising, therefore, that they should regard with fear and hatred a man so opposed to all their principles of government; and, accordingly, they used every means in their power to instigate the people against him, thundering anathemas on his head from their pulpits, and spreading tracts, loaded with abuse, among all circles. No one equalled Malagrida in the measures he took, or the daring he exhibited; but, though years first rolled on, the bitter and relentless vengeance of the Minister ultimately overtook him.

Such was the man we left with the Duke of Aveiro: their conference was yet unfinished, when, having taken another turn, they had reached the further end of the avenue, which led to a small grotto of stonework, surrounded by a thicket of low shrubs. Malagrida laid his arm on the shoulder of the Duke, exclaiming, with deep energy, "Nought but the death of the persecutor of its servants will satisfy the vengeance of Heaven."

A hollow voice echoed, "the vengeance of Heaven!" and, at the same time a noise was heard in the shrubbery. Both the monk and the noble started—perhaps neither had quite deceived themselves as to their secret aims.

"Avaunt thee, Sathanas, if thou art the spirit of evil," exclaimed Malagrida.

The Duke trembled with agitation. The rustling noise was again heard. "Ah! 'tis some villain spy," he cried, drawing his sword and rushing towards the spot. "His death shall secure his silence."

Being now persuaded that it was a mortal enemy he had to encounter, his boldness returned, and, without hesitation, he sprung into the thicket; but all was silent: the gloom preventing his seeing many feet before him. He beat about for a considerable time, plunging his sword into every bush that appeared darker than the others; but to no purpose, for the sound was not repeated. Malagrida watched on the outside, but no one appeared.

"It was a deception of the evil one, to turn us from our path," he cried. "Come forth, my son, and fear not. That was no mortal voice we heard, and with me you need fear no spirit of darkness."

The Duke at length came out of the shrubbery, his dress torn and disordered, and his voice yet trembling with alarm. "Surely some one must have been hidden there," he said: "yet, if there was, he must have escaped, and will report our words to one who is not likely to forget them."

"Fear not; no mortal could have remained undiscovered," answered the Jesuit; "and of nought else need you be afraid."

"Since you affirm it, Father, I am convinced also that the noise was caused by no mortal being," said the Duke; "but we ought no longer to remain here. I like not this threatening gloom. Let us return to the more open ground: the air here is oppressive and damp, and aids to conjure up doubts and fears to my mind."

"Again, I say, fear not; but remember my words—both dare and do," returned Malagrida. "It is now time that I should depart."

"First come, then, to the house, holy Father, and take some refreshment and rest," said the Duke.

"My body requires neither food nor rest when I am about a great work," answered the Priest. "It is advisable, also, that I should be observed by none of your retainers. Return, then, to your house, and forget not what I have said. I will tarry in this spot to see if the evil one shall again venture to make his presence known, and if he comes not before long, secretly, as I came, will I again depart. Farewell, my son."

The Duke, however, was unwilling to leave the side of the holy man, with the prospect of a long dark avenue before him, which he must traverse alone, exposed to the assaults of the spirits of evil; but Malagrida signed him to depart, waving his arms wildly round, and then, turning towards the grotto, disappeared in the gloom.

He waited not a moment longer, but with quick steps hurried towards his house, his heart beating with apprehension; and, as he went, he fancied that he heard voices on every side gibbering and muttering threats and curses against him, till his terror made him break into a run; nor did he stop till he arrived at the door of his mansion. Pale and breathless with the exertion, his brow covered with perspiration, he rushed into the room where his duchess was sitting, not perceiving her, and threw himself into a seat. She looked up, alarmed, marking his disordered appearance.

"What is the matter with my lord?" she said, as she approached him, and took his hand.

The contact of a human being, and one for whom he possessed as much affection as he was capable of feeling for any, revived his spirits. "Oh! nothing, nothing!" he answered. "A freak made me run faster than I have run since I was a boy."

"I rejoice to hear it; for I feared you were ill, or that something had alarmed you," returned the Duchess.

"Oh no! I am well—perfectly well," exclaimed the Duke, bursting into a wild laugh. "Ha! ha! What think you of the title of Queen, fair lady? Would it not be a proud thing to be a king, to trample on the neck of that insolent plebeian Carvalho, who now lords it so boldly?"

"He is a bad man, my lord," answered the Duchess, meekly; "and Heaven will punish him."

"Bad! he is the incarnation of the evil one," cried the Duke, stamping his foot. "But you answer not my question. Would you not be a queen, and see your Marquezinho a prince? Ha! then you might be proud indeed!"

"I seek not for more than I possess," answered the lady. "Oh! my lord, indulge not in such dangerous thoughts: they can but bring destruction on your head. That you do think of them I know too well; for I have of late heard you muttering them in your sleep."

"Then go to bed, and dream of them yourself, fair lady: you will find them pleasant and enticing," said the Duke, again laughing.

"It is early, my lord, and the sun has but just set," answered the Duchess.

"Oh, I forgot—I forgot!" exclaimed her husband. "No matter, you must keep country hours. It is good for the health: so to bed—to bed, and dream of a royal crown."

"'Tis a dream, my lord, which has cost many a one his head," said the Duchess, sadly.

The Duke started, and his pallor again returned. "What folly is this?" he exclaimed, angrily. "I spoke but in jest.—Now, obey me, and to bed!"

The duchess turned a look of grief towards her haughty lord; but, accustomed to obey his imperious commands, she retired to her room.

"That woman is not to be trusted," muttered the Duke, when left alone. "She has neither ambition nor courage. It was folly to speak to her on the subject."

We constantly observe that weak and vain men have some parasite attached to them, who plays on the former quality by flattering the latter for his own individual interests, at the same time despising and often destroying the very person who supports him, like the noxious weed the tree to which it clings; and such an one had the Duke of Aveiro, in the person of his secretary, master of the household, and chief butler, Captain Policarpio d'Azevedo; for in all those capacities did that worthy gentleman serve him, besides holding a commission in the army. The duke now summoned his confidant, ordering supper to be brought, and having disencumbered himself of his morning costume, and dressed in a light gown, he seated himself at table. Captain Policarpio soon appeared, bearing a dish, which he placed before his master; and then took his station behind his chair, while a troop of other servants followed, with the remainder of the repast, who were ordered forthwith to retire. It may seem strange, but it is a notorious fact, that at the time of which we speak, and even until very lately, commissions in the army were procured by the nobles for their domestics, as a reward for services often of a very doubtful nature. Many of the principal fidalgos retained in their household three or four of these gentry holding the rank of captain, who waited on them at their meals, dressed in their uniforms, and often decked with the Order of Christ; and it was not till the army was remodelled by Lord Beresford, that the abuse was finally abolished. It may be supposed that an army so organised could not be in a very efficient state, or possessed of officers with a very high tone of feeling among them. It also showed the arrogant dispositions of the fidalgos, who thus attempted to assume even more than the state of princes.

"You have now served me faithfully for some years, Policarpio, and it is time your services were more amply rewarded," began the Duke.

"Oh, your Excellency is too kind, too generous; for when you are served for love, why speak of reward?—the satisfaction of following so good a master is in itself sufficient payment," answered the Escudeiro, sidling round, so as to come in sight of his lord.

"Because it is my pleasure to repay those who serve me faithfully and well as you have done," answered the Duke. "It may soon, too, be in my power to reward you far more than I have yet done; for when the master rises, so will those who follow him. Mark that, Policarpio!"

"How can my lord rise higher than he is at present?" said the flatterer, surprised at the question, and eager to learn to what it might further tend. "Is not my lord already one of the greatest men in the kingdom, both in rank and wealth?"

"I was so, truly, under the reign of our late pious king; but things have changed, and a vile upstart has dared to insult my honour; but the day will come, and soon, too, when I may have my full revenge, and he who now triumphs in power shall writhe beneath my feet."

"May my lord have success in all his wishes, and enjoy full revenge on all his enemies!" answered the Escudeiro.

"Wishes are but of little avail, without action," observed the Noble; "and much must be accomplished before my hopes are fulfilled."

"Whatever need be done, I will undertake to serve you, my lord," answered Captain Policarpio, bowing, and laying his hand to his heart.

"Ah, my friend, you are a man in whom I can place implicit confidence," said the Duke; "and I know that you would rejoice in my prosperity. What think you, then, if the crown of Portugal were placed on my brow? Would not then my friends have cause to esteem themselves fortunate?"

"Those are already fortunate who serve your Excellency; and no one is more calculated to adorn a throne," answered the subtle follower,—his own ambition taking fire on the instant at thoughts of his master's aggrandisement, in the advantages of which he might well expect to participate. "And well do I feel assured that you will not neglect those who have hitherto obeyed you faithfully. Do but point out the means to attain your aims, and no scruples, no obstacles shall deter me from prosecuting them."

"Well, well, we will talk of that anon, my worthy servant," answered the Duke. "It is but lately Heaven has thought fit to inspire my heart with such mighty aims; nor have I yet been able to form any plans; but this alone I know, that while that enemy to our holy religion, Sebastiaõ Jozé de Carvalho exists, all will be fruitless; and he who would do me service will strike a poniard to his heart. In this will he commit no sin, as I have been assured by Heaven itself, in the sacred person of one of its most devoted ministers."

"I should fear nothing to serve my master," said Policarpio. "But how can the death of the Minister alone place your Excellency on the throne?"

"Hark, you!" whispered the Duke, drawing his servant close to him. "The king himself may die. He is weak and sickly; or he may be killed while hunting; he may be thrown from his horse, or a shot may strike him.—Ha! dost thou understand me?"

The attendant nodded, a smile of satisfaction passing over his features. "I comprehend, I comprehend; nor will your Excellency's hint be thrown away."

Much more, to the same effect as the above, the Duke spoke, a mixture of blasphemy, folly, and daring, to which his worthy servant listened with profound humility and attention, fully determined to take advantage of the knowledge he had gained; if successful, to follow the fortunes of his master, or to betray him, if he saw a probability of his plans failing: and thus are traitors nearly always served.

However, we must confess that we take no interest in these personages, or their conversation; nor do we believe that it would either instruct or amuse our readers—which is our only aim in writing—were we to detail it: we therefore refrain from doing so. Indeed, would the truth of history allow us, we would gladly consign all bad characters to the shades of oblivion, and describe such only as had high and noble motives for their actions; but, alas! as the world is constituted, did we do so, we should be most justly accused of compiling an extravagant and absurd romance, without either truth for the groundwork, or nature in the colouring; thus neglecting what we conceive are the great rules to be observed by those who would paint an historical picture of days gone by. We are, therefore, compelled to introduce such a man as the Duke of Aveiro, in whom we have sought, but sought in vain, to discover some redeeming qualities; but he appears to have possessed but few friends, even among his own class, and those of his own political opinions; as he is described by all as a man singularly ignorant and grossly superstitious; of a vindictive and savage disposition, and arrogant and haughty to all who approached him. We wished to have drawn him otherwise; but we found it impossible so to do and adhere to truth. This we mention, that our readers may not suppose we have caricatured in his person a Portuguese nobleman of the past century, who could thus weakly yield to the instigations of a designing madman like Malagrida, and believe in his blasphemous prophecies; but we can assure them that we have faithfully translated the very language of that person, avoiding even much that might shock the ear of the present generation.

The insane ambition of the Duke being once kindled with the hopes of promised success, every thought of his mind was occupied with projects, equally replete with wickedness and folly, to compass his end; nor did he from that time forth again know one moment of tranquillity or happiness. Leaving his duchess and young son at Azeitaö, he, a few days afterwards, set off for Lisbon, with a nephew, who constantly resided in his house, accompanied by his constant attendant, Captain Policarpio, and followed by a train of servants.

Volume One—Chapter Eleven.

We invariably feel much satisfaction, when, in turning over the pages of the manuscripts before us, we come to the name of Don Luis d'Almeida, albeit he played no very conspicuous part in the events of the times; yet we take pleasure in following his course, and we also feel tolerably certain that we are about to read of some interesting adventure.

We left him, followed by his train, riding through the narrow and winding street of Leiria, towards the gate by which he had entered the previous evening. As he wound down the rugged pathway, after passing the gates, he cast a last look at the battered moss-grown walls, and ruined towers of that ancient town, now for ever associated in his mind with the fair young being from whom he had there parted, and then, putting spurs to his horse, he galloped on, at the great risk of breaking his neck, his followers in vain endeavouring to keep him in view. His luggage also would certainly have been left to the mercy of the brigands, had he not fortunately recollected that such might be its fate; so he wisely drew in his rein, and allowed his horse to proceed at its own pace till his party should come up with him.

He could not discover the reason, but so it was, that, although proceeding towards his home, he did not enjoy his morning ride half so much as that of the last evening. It could not be because a certain young lady was travelling south while he was going north; for he thought, and fancied that he thought very wisely, that he could not take any interest in one, although he acknowledged her to be very lovely, whom he had neither seen nor heard of twenty hours before. He concluded that it was because he disliked solitude, and he had now no one with whom to converse; but, for some reason or other, he did not think half so much of the infidelity and treachery of Donna Theresa; and when he did think of the subject, he began rather to pity her, and to congratulate himself on having escaped from the toils of a heartless coquette. It was some time, however, before the last happy idea occurred to him, for at first his feelings towards her were rather bitter; then he was angry with himself for indulging in them, and then very miserable, and then, as if by magic, appeared the portrait he had Daguerreo-typed in the morning, of Donna Clara in her travelling mantle of blue silk.

But we shall never carry Don Luis to his home, and back again to Lisbon, if we do not proceed at a faster rate. To account for his having four persons in his train, we must explain that, besides Pedro, one other only was his own servant, the third was a native of Galicia, of that hardy race called Gallegos, who come with willing hands, light, honest hearts, and empty pockets, to make their fortune in Portugal; and the one in question was returning to enjoy the fruits of his labour with his family, in respectable independence in his native land, now mounted on a stout mule, with his pockets well lined with gold. He had easily obtained permission to accompany Don Luis thus far, having once served in his father's house. The other man was a tenant of the count's, whom legal business had called to Lisbon. Pedro, whose heart was light and free, amused himself from morning till night by singing, in high glee at returning once more to his home to relate all the wonders he had seen in his travels.

After waiting a couple of hours at a small village on the road to bait their animals and recruit themselves, it was late in the day before they entered the forest in which the attack on Gonçalo Christovaö had been made, and the party began to look around, in expectation of a fresh encounter with the banditti, although that kind of gentry were not fond of meeting with those from whom little booty, and abundance of hard blows, were to be expected. However, as they neared the scene of the encounter, even Don Luis began to think it would have been wiser to have procured a guard, or waited for a larger party of travellers, lest the banditti, observing their small number, might, to revenge themselves for their defeat, pick them off from an ambush at a distance. Pedro no longer sang his merry songs, his fellow said all the prayers he could remember, the Gallego vowed a candle to Saint Jago de Compostella, and the farmer a pig to the priest, if they escaped the danger. The muleteers who had charge of the baggage, though they had seen nothing of the fray, caught the contagion of fear, giving but scanty promise of fighting if brought to the trial. The body of the robber was no longer there, but at a little distance from the spot where he had been left, lay his hat, and part of his dress, torn and bloody, telling plainly that Christian sepulture he would never now enjoy; for limb by limb had the body been borne off by the savage inhabitants of the forest. Don Luis stopped a moment involuntarily on the spot, shuddering at the wretch's fate; but Pedro, being in no romantic humour, hinted to his master that all the time they were affording an opportunity to the comrades of the deceased to take better aim, and begged him to move forward without delay, declaring that he saw the muzzle of a gun projecting from among the thick-growing leaves beyond the bank.

Accordingly they proceeded down the hill, and crossed the stream, the rest keeping close to Don Luis, and splashing him not a little in their hurry to get across, looking anxiously behind them, to see if the brigands were in their rear, and expecting every moment to hear the sharp click of the locks of their carbines, with the ringing report of their discharge, each hoping that he should not be the one picked off. When they mounted the opposite hill, and had arrived on the open heath, the hearts of all the party beat more freely, and as they got beyond musket range of the wood they laughed at their previous terrors, no longer feeling inclined to scold their master for the coolness he had shown, or the slow pace at which he had chosen to ride.

The sun had just sunk as they reached the inn where Gonçalo Christovaö and his family had rested the day before, at the door of which the buxom Rosa was standing, busily employed in spinning, and looking out for a stray traveller; and of course her delight was proportionably great, when she found that so large a party, with so graceful a cavalier, were about to honour the house with their presence.

The horses and mules were stalled, and Don Luis was shown upstairs, while Pedro set himself to work to aid Rosa in preparing his master's supper, during which operation he exerted his utmost powers of pleasing to ingratiate himself in her favour. But she was either out of humour at something, or offended by his addresses, for she returned his attentions with scanty courtesy, appearing anxious to get rid of his presence; that, however, was not so easy a matter, as he had never been remarkable for either bashfulness or modesty: at all events, if he ever had possessed those qualities, he had most effectually eased himself of them during his travels. Do all he could—praise her beauty, her figure, or her voice as she sang at her employment over the fire—Rosa was not in the mood to be won by any of his fascinations, and insisted on carrying up some of the dishes herself; perhaps it was from her very natural wish to see more of his master, as she had not every day the opportunity of admiring so handsome a guest.

As she was preparing the table, Don Luis could not help observing a handsome ring, with a sparkling diamond, on her little finger, an unusual ornament for a person of her class, though with her gala costume she might have worn ear-rings and several gold chains. He made no remark till she went down stairs and returned again, when, in a playful manner, he admired the jewel. "Sim senhor, it is very pretty," she answered, rather confused, and busied herself in putting the dishes in order.

"What kind friend gave you so pretty an ornament?" said Don Luis; "I fear you run a great risk of dimming its lustre."

At that moment a noise, which sounded very like a growl, though it might have been a groan, proceeded from one of the recesses in the room, across which a curtain was drawn.

"What noise is that?" exclaimed Don Luis, "Have you any sick person in the house?"

"'Tis an unfortunate frade, a very holy man, who was taken ill here last night," answered the damsel. Another growl interrupted her observations. "I'll run and bring you up an omelette, senhor," she said quickly, as she escaped out of the room.

Pedro gave his master a nod, as much as to say, "I do not exactly believe her," when, running towards the curtains, he poked his head between the in, and then took the liberty of drawing them aside, so as to let the light fall into the recess, where a pair of ferrety eyes were seen glaring forth, with no very amicable expression, on the intruder, while a ruddy countenance, with a red rim of hair under a black skull cap, appeared above the bed clothes.

"In the name of all the saints, let down the curtain, and allow a sick man to rest in peace," exclaimed a gruff voice. "The light hurts my eyes, and prevents me from sleeping."

"Your pardon, senhor," answered Don Luis, politely. "My servant's curiosity has made him commit a solecism in good manners, for which pray excuse him."

"Well, let him draw the curtain, and leave me to repose," returned the voice, ending the sentence with what sounded very like an oath, too profane to proceed from such reverend lips.

Pedro did as he was ordered; but not until he had taken another glance, to assure himself that he had before seen that pair of eyes at no very distant period, though he did not express his opinion aloud to his master, nor could he venture to do so by signs; for he felt a moral conviction, that they were still glaring on him through some opening in the drapery, an idea which, as may be supposed, made him feel anything but at his ease. He determined, however, to keep a narrow watch on the inmate of the recess, and on the movements of several other doubtful-looking personages whom he had seen about the inn; yet he was puzzled how to prevent them from guessing that his suspicions were aroused; for he knew that every word he uttered in the room would be overheard; and, if he whispered to his master, it would make the matter still worse; therefore, like a prudent statesman, he determined to wait the course of events.

By the time he had arrived at this determination, Rosa returned, and began to clear away the dishes, when he observed that she no longer wore the ring on her finger; yet he forebore to make any further observation on the subject. He waited till he was preparing his master's couch for the night, when he seized the opportunity to make him comprehend his suspicions, by pointing significantly towards the recess, in which the sick friar lay, then, putting his head on the pillow, and shaking it, and drawing his finger across his throat, and again shaking his head; by which signs, Don Luis understood him to say, "If you do go to sleep, you will have your throat cut;" no very pleasing prospect for a person so overcome by weariness, that he could scarcely keep his eyes open. Pedro, however, merely meant to advise him not to go to sleep till his return; and he then hurried out to hint his doubts, if possible, to the rest of the party, and to desire them to come up stairs immediately, where they could roll themselves up in their cloaks, in the corners of the room, begging them on no account to separate.

Don Luis, having also his suspicions aroused, observed, as he looked round the room, that his luggage, with his holsters, had been piled up close to the recess in which the friar slept. It might, certainly, have been placed there by accident; but, for caution's sake, as he walked about the room, he very quietly removed his weapons, and hung them up close to his bed, carefully examining the primings of his pistols. Pedro soon returned with the rest of the party, and, having assisted in undressing his master, who threw himself on the bed, he rolled himself up on the ground close to him, while the other men followed his example in another corner, from whence, in a few minutes, loud snores proceeding, gave notice of their being wrapt in sleep. A small lamp, burning in the centre of the room, gave a dim and uncertain light, throwing long shadows from the tables and chairs, and exhibiting a troop of mice, like tiny phantoms, playing on the floor, and picking up the crumbs from the evening repast. Having gazed at these objects for some time, till they grew still more confused, Don Luis could no longer resist the inclination he felt to close his eyes, persuading himself that, after all, there was no cause for fear.

Two or three hours passed quietly away, when, on a sudden, he was awoke by an exclamation from Pedro; and, starting up, he beheld him grasping tightly the legs of a man, whom he recognised as the invalid friar; who, with uplifted arm, was on the point of plunging a long knife into poor Pedro, having already possessed himself of the holsters, when Don Luis sprang up, and seized him firmly.

"Spare my life, senhor," he said with the greatest coolness; "I was not going to take yours; but merely to carry your weapons out of harm's way; for I do not like to see such murderous things in the hands of youths."

While he was speaking, Pedro had contrived to rise and seize his other arm.

"How dare you tell me so abominable a falsehood?" exclaimed Don Luis.—"Wretch! you are in my power, and deserve to die."

"I am in your power at this moment, I very well know," answered the Friar; "but, if you were to kill me, you would not benefit yourselves. I should therefore advise you to allow me to return quietly to bed, and I shall be grateful; if not, a cry from me would bring a whole party of men, who have sworn to avenge themselves on you, and who would make small ceremony in cutting all your throats, and burying you before morning."

"I grant you your life, then, in trust that you will show your gratitude," said Don Luis.

"Was a Capuchin friar ever ungrateful?" exclaimed their prisoner. "Well, then, I should advise you to barricade the door, load your arms, call your servants, and declare, if any body tries to enter, you will shoot me. Now, having given you my advice, let me go quietly to bed again, for I really am ill, and undertook only to withdraw your pistols, lest you should hurt anybody with them."

"Well, Senhor Frade," answered Don Luis, laughing, "you certainly are a most cool and impudent gentleman; but I will trust to you, when we have secured the door; in the meantime, you must consent to sit quiet for awhile, with your arms tied behind you, in this chair."

"Take care what you are about, senhores. You hurt my arm, which I sprained badly the other day, or you would not have caught me so easily," observed the Friar.

"Oh!" thought Pedro, as he saw that the friar's arm was bandaged up and bloody, "Well, well, holy Father, you must sit quiet then," he added, aloud, then called to his fellow-servant: "Come here, Bento, and take the liberty of shooting the friar through the head, if he attempts to call out, while I assist our master in securing the fortress. I'll be answerable for your getting absolution."

The friar was therefore obliged to sit down, while Bento stood over him; Don Luis, and the rest of the party, with as little noise as possible, placing the tables and chairs against the door, though such a barricade would offer but slight resistance, should any strong force be used outside. They then examined the room well, to see that no one else was hidden there, and to discover if there were any other outlets, by which they might be surprised.

In the course of the search, as Pedro was looking into the cell of the friar, he discovered a broad-brimmed hat, thrown under the foot of the bed, so he brought it out, and placed it on that reverend person's head, nodding most approvingly, as if to an old acquaintance; then threw it back to whence he had taken it.

"You may now retire to your couch, Senhor Frade," said Don Luis.— "We will no longer disturb the tranquillity of your slumbers; and, on condition that you do your best to aid us, you shall not suffer."

"I promise you, on the honour of a friar, that if I can help it, no harm shall happen to you; and in return, you must promise me, on the honour of a fidalgo, that you will never mention to any human being that you have seen me here, or allow your people to do so, whatever your suspicions may be; for I have repented of certain little peccadillos I have committed, and intend to lead a new life."

"If you adhere to the conditions, I promise not to betray you," said Don Luis.

"Very well; and now, in mercy's sake, don't keep me up in the cold any longer," said the Friar.

"Permit me first, senhor, to deprive you of that delicate little penknife," said Pedro, taking the friar's dagger from his hands, "and now, pray retire to your couch."

The friar was not long in doing as he was ordered; and, as if to convince them of the purity of his conscience, he was soon fast asleep, as might be supposed from his loud snores.

Not long afterwards, some one was heard pressing against the door. "Curses on the lazy friar," muttered a voice outside, in a low growl, yet loud enough to be heard through the crevices of the walls,—"He's snoring away like a hog, without thinking of his promise to us."

"Open the door, and steal softly in," said another voice. "You can easily get possession of their arms, when we can rush in to bind them, and then it will be time enough to bind the estalajadeiro, and the rest of the household, though I suspect Senhora Rosa will give us some little trouble; however, we can let her loose the first, to release the rest, when we are far off with the booty."

"A very good plan, doubtless; but I am not going to run the chance of being shot by that hot-headed youngster. What can have become of the frade? Hark! the lazy brute is still snoring on, forgetful of our interests."

"Will nothing waken him?" said another voice. "Try the door again."

Another attempt was now made to open the door without noise. Don Luis and his servants stood prepared, with pistols in hand, to defend themselves, while Pedro kept his eye on the snoring friar, who, the more the people outside spoke, made the louder nasal music to drown their voices. After the door had been several times gently shaken, and the wooden fastening turned in several ways to no purpose—

"Carramba!" exclaimed one of the voices. "They have secured the door inside, and, unless that houndish friar will wake up, we shall be foiled completely. Curses on the fool! There he snores away. This delay will never do; we must dash open the door, and cut all their throats."

"By Saint Anthony, nothing would give me greater satisfaction," said another. "I long to revenge myself for the loss that youth caused us yesterday, and see, Heaven has delivered him into our hands!"

"So do I; but the estalajadeiro declared he would have no murder, nor any of the horses taken, which might be traced to give his house a bad name; and that nobody should know he had a hand in it."

"That is very well; but I should like to know what we are to do then?" asked another.

"There is only one way left: dash the door off its hinges, tie the young fidalgo and his servants to the beds, and walk off with whatever we may find convenient."

"Agreed, agreed!" said two or three voices. "Your plan is a good one, Rodrigo. Call the others up stairs. Remember, we all rush in together; and do not forget to give the friar a good beating, as if by mistake, to punish him for his stupidity. We would dash his brains out if he were not useful."

The Friar snored louder than ever. Several feet were heard ascending the stair; then there was a sudden rush, and the ill-secured door was dashed off its hinges with a loud noise, falling inside, when a dozen or more dark forms were seen attempting to scramble over the tables and chairs.

Don Luis fired his pistol, unwisely, perhaps—one ought to try negotiation before going to war—and the ball took effect on some one in the rear; then changing his sword to the right hand, he rushed forward to meet the first who should enter, while his servants discharged their pistols at the aperture, now crowded with human beings.

"Murder! murder!" shouted the Friar, leaping up in his bed, as if just awoke from sleep; but Pedro kept his eye upon him.

"Carramba! fire in on them, or we shall have more holes in our ribs than the doctors can cure."

"Hold!" shouted the Friar: "if you do, you will kill me, you fools!"

The robbers heeded him not, throwing a volley into the room; but no one fell. At the same time, a shrill female voice was heard crying out, "Murder! murder!"

"On, comrades! We must not be baulked by this foolery!" and before the smoke cleared away, making a desperate rush, they leaped over all obstacles into the room, the headmost attacking Don Luis with great fury; but they were not good swordsmen, and for several passes he easily kept them at bay. Numbers, however, must soon have overpowered him, those behind again loading their muskets, when he received succour from a quarter he little expected.

"I will keep my promise, and soon clear the room of these rascals, while you go and aid your master," cried the Friar to Pedro. "By all that is sacred, I will."

Before Pedro had time to answer, he sprang up, seizing a thick oak stick from the head of the bed, and rushed towards the robbers, flourishing it over his head, and exclaiming, "I will pay you for your kind intentions towards me, my masters."

This sudden reinforcement made the parties more equal; for Pedro, seeing that the friar really intended to aid them, was able to assist his master. Down came the friar's stick on the head of the foremost robbers, and blow after blow descended with more execution than the swords of Don Luis and his party.

"The friar has turned traitor," shouted several voices. "Cut him down, cut him down!"

"Hold, hold, ye fools!" cried the Friar, in return. "Back, back, or it will be the worse for you!"

At that instant the innkeeper seemed aroused from his slumbers; for his voice, also, was heard exclaiming, "Back, back, ye cursed idiots! What! would you have my house looked upon as a den of thieves for this night's work? Back, back! or by the Holy Virgin some of you will not live to repent it!"

He seemed to be enforcing his orders by blows; for a scuffle was heard outside, above which arose the shrill tones of a woman's voice, the robbers appearing to be giving way.

The man with whom Don Luis was chiefly engaged glared fiercely on him. "You killed my brother yesterday, and I will be revenged on you," he exclaimed. "I know you, Don Luis d'Almeida: you foiled me before; but we shall meet again ere long, when this blade shall drink your life's blood:" saying which, with curses on his companions for their cowardice, he bounded down the stairs after them, leaving Don Luis and his attendants masters of the room; while the innkeeper and the friar were seen on the top of the stairs, the latter still flourishing his cudgel, and vehemently abusing the banditti in no measured terms. The voices of the robbers were heard outside, in high and fierce dispute, the sounds gradually dying away as they gained a greater distance from the house.

The innkeeper, followed by the friar, then entered the apartment, making many apologies for the outrage. "I hope, senhor, you will not bring ruin on an unfortunate man, by mentioning the occurrences of the night," he said, in a supplicating tone. "You see, senhor, I am entirely in the power of those gentlemen, and could not avoid what happened; therefore, as none of your party are hurt, and you have wounded two of the banditti, I trust that this punishment will satisfy you."

"Oh yes, yes; I know that Don Luis will be generous, and act like a true fidalgo," interrupted the Friar. "You see that I kept my word; so in future remember you may trust to a friar's promise: and now, by your leave, cavalheros, I will go to bed again, for the night air does not agree with me, and my shoulder is painful." Saying which, he composedly walked to his recess, and covered himself up with the clothes.

"I ought to make no terms with you," said Don Luis; "yet, having no wish to ruin you, I shall not complain, if you will undertake that we receive no further annoyance."

"Oh yes, senhor, yes; on my word of honour as a gentleman, you shall be unmolested," returned the Innkeeper, putting his hand to his heart, and bowing low.

"The fidalgo will do as we beg him, I know," cried the Friar, from his dormitory; "so go away, and leave him to finish the night in peace."

"You will not blame me, senhor, for what has occurred. Well, senhor, I am happy again, so, if your servants will help me, I will put up the door, and leave you to repose."

Though Don Luis was not to be deceived by the humble demeanour of the innkeeper, or the cool impudence of the friar, his only prudent plan was to pretend to believe them. He therefore waited till order was restored in the room, and the innkeeper had bowed himself away, when, loading his pistols carefully, he threw himself on his bed to wait for daylight. Pedro, however, still suspecting treachery, did not trust to a word that had been said; but, as soon as he saw that his master was again asleep, drawing a chair to the table, he sat himself down with his pistols before him, and a flask of wine, which, standing quietly in a corner, had escaped destruction. "Now, Senhor Frade," he thought, "if you play me false—and I cannot say I trust you—I will have a pop at you with one pistol, while the other shall bring down the first man who attempts to come in at the door." The other servants, though very much frightened at first, dropped off, one by one, to sleep; but he, conquering his drowsiness, kept his eye on the friar, every instant expecting to see the banditti rush into the room. He earnestly longed for day, to quit the place; and, at length, his wishes were gratified by seeing a pale stream of light gleaming through the ill-closing shutters, when, as it grew brighter and brighter, he hurried to open them, and to let in the fresh morning air, rousing his master and the rest of the party.

The Friar sat up in his bed and nodded familiarly to him. "If you had trusted to me you might have spent a pleasanter night, Senhor Pedro," said he: "I hope, however, you enjoyed your vigils. Good morning, Don Luis: you remember your promise."

"I do not intend to betray you," answered Don Luis; "but you must do me another service. Some jewels were stolen from a young lady who travelled this way yesterday, and I must insist on their being given to me, that I may restore them to their owner; now, I doubt not that you are able to procure them for me. Will you undertake to do so?"

The Friar thought for a minute. "If I undertake to procure the jewels, what am I to expect in return?" he asked.

"You well know that you deserve nothing, and that I am too lenient in allowing you to escape unpunished," answered Don Luis; "but I will give an hundred milreas to the person who brings them to my father's house in the course of a week."

"The bargain is struck," answered the Friar. "And now, senhor, adeos: I shall always retain a high respect for you."

"I cannot exactly return the compliment," said Don Luis; "but I shall always remember you, as the most daring, impudent scoundrel I have ever met."

"Va com Deos. Get along with you; you are joking, fidalgo," returned the Friar, laughing. "I am but a poor mendicant servant of heaven, and be assured I shall not forget you in my prayers."

Don Luis did not answer him; but, followed by Pedro and his other attendants, bearing the luggage, he repaired to the stable, where their beasts were saddled, and they were soon ready to depart.

The landlord made his appearance, followed by Rosa, with tears in her eyes: "You will not be cruel, senhor, and make a complaint about what happened last night," she said; "for if you do, you will ruin us all, and we shall be sent to prison, or turned into the road to starve."

"I have already said I would make no complaint," answered Don Luis; "and, Senhor Estalajadeiro, I must discharge my bill to you."

"Oh, senhor, I cannot think of such a thing after the inconveniences you have endured," answered the landlord, bowing; "yet, senhor, I am a poor man with a family. It is but a trifle, four milreas in all, for which I shall be thankful."

"Very well, here is the amount," said Don Luis, giving him the money; "and I should advise you to be more careful in future what guests you entertain." Saying which, he leapt into his saddle, and, with his attendants, resumed his journey towards his home, the landlord bowing most humbly till they were out of sight.

Pedro, eager to let his tongue have full play, took the liberty of an old servant, and rode up to the side of his master, whose horse's head he allowed to be just a little in advance, as a mark of respect. "Those people at the inn are very great rascals, senhor," he began.

"There can be but little doubt of it," returned his master.

"Ah, senhor, and the greatest of all is the friar. Do you know, senhor, he was one of those who attacked Gonçalo Christovaö, yesterday? I marked his slouched hat, his ferret eyes, and the cut on his shoulder, which he declares is a bruise: now I saw plenty of blood about it, and blood does not flow from a bruise in that way."

"I suspected as much," said Don Luis; "but were I to make a complaint against him, no notice, probably, would be taken of it; for his robes will protect a friar as long as he is guilty of no heretical opinions, even though he may have committed murder, and the other people would take an early opportunity to revenge themselves, while I should not benefit society."

"You were quite right, senhor, in what you did," answered Pedro; "I wish merely to observe, that we must not trust to any of them; for, depend upon it, both the friar and the landlord are in league with the robbers; though, for some reason or other, it did not suit them to cut our throats, as the rest wished to do. I hope that, none of them are on the watch to pick us off as we ride along; and if it pleases you, senhor, had we not better push on as quick as we can through this grove? These trees afford such close shelter to lurking foes, who may shoot every one of us without our being able to get near them."

Notwithstanding Pedro's apprehensions, they passed the grove in safety, and again emerged into a more open country, partly cultivated, though in a very careless way, with a few miserable hamlets and cottages scattered here and there; and round the fields near them were trained vines, propped up some four or five feet from the ground, from which the thin common wine used by the poor people is made.

Towards the close of a long day's journey, during which they had twice rested their horses, Don Luis and his followers arrived in front of a handsome gateway, over the top of which the arms of the Almeidas were placed, beautifully carved in stone. He gazed at them with pride for an instant, while Pedro dismounted to open the gates; and, as he entered a long avenue of cork-trees, his heart beat with the fond anticipation of again being pressed in the arms of a father who fondly loved him, and for whom he, in return, felt the most devoted affection and respect.

The sun shone brightly through the trees on the broad open space in front of the house, in the centre of which a bright jet of water sparkled high in the air, throwing on all sides its glittering drops, as it descended again into a large circular tank swarming with fish of gold and silver scales. A flight of broad stone steps, with heavy balustrades, led up to the entrance door of the house, which was, as is usually the case, of a single story, the ground floor being used only for servants' rooms and offices. It was a long low building, with two wings, the centre part receding and forming a court in front between them. Over the entrance were again seen the arms of the family, delicately carved, on a large stone shield; and in many parts of the building were either small shields or devices taken from it; but, besides these ornaments, the house had few lordly pretensions. Just as they arrived in front of the mansion, a servant belonging to the premises caught sight of them, and shouting at the top of his voice, as he ran forward to meet them, "The young Count, Don Luis, our Morgado, is arrived," seized his young master's hand, and covered it with kisses. The noise brought out the heads both of male and female servants from various windows, who, when they saw who had arrived, popped them in again, and hastened down, each anxious to be the first to welcome their young lord; so that, by the time he reached the steps, a number had collected to offer their congratulations. At the same moment, a venerable and dignified-looking person appeared at the door, whom Don Luis no sooner saw, than, leaping from his horse, he sprang up the steps, regardless of all the smiling faces on each side, and threw himself, half kneeling, into his arms. His father, for it was the old Count, embraced him affectionately. "My son, my son," he exclaimed, "your return restores light and joy to my heart; nor have you, Luis, disappointed my fond expectations. I am proud, very proud of you." What words could be more gratifying to a son's ears? and Luis was a son to appreciate them.

After the first greetings with his father were over, he turned to the old domestics, who, with smiling countenances, stood around, anxious to show their pleasure; nor was their zeal feigned, for there is in Portugal that kindly communication kept up between master and servant which causes the latter to take a warm interest in all connected with the welfare of his superior. Suffice it to say, that sincere were the rejoicings throughout the household at the return of their young lord; nor was Pedro forgotten, as he took very good care to assure himself.

Volume One—Chapter Twelve.

Here we have arrived at the last chapter of our first volume, without having advanced any way in our story; but it is, we conceive, an error on the right side, as the chief interest will be found in the two following ones, without any fear of our materials being exhausted.

We have also placed ourselves in a dilemma; for while we are anxious to describe certain events which befell Don Luis, our gallantry would lead us to follow the fair Donna Clara on her journey to Lisbon; for, although far advanced, as we are, down the vale of years, and invulnerable to the soft blandishments of the sex, that feeling, or sentiment, still retains its influence over us, owing to our having been educated before the civilisation of our countrymen was refined by their intercourse with the Indians of North America, or the intellectual inhabitants of Australia—before, indeed, the days of modern chivalry.

It is remarkable that, although Senhora Gertrudes exerted herself to the utmost to amuse her young lady, Donna Clara found her journey from Leiria to Lisbon very long and tedious; and it more than once occurred to her, how far more agreeable it would have been had Don Luis d'Almeida been travelling in the same instead of in a contrary direction; but she did not utter her thoughts to her old nurse—indeed, she scarcely acknowledged them to herself. The weather, too, had become dark and gloomy, and the horses of a small body of cavalry, whom her father had procured as an escort for part of the way, created a dust and disturbance, the men looking much more like banditti than soldiers, so that she was very glad when the towers of Lisbon, and the broad flowing Tagus, appeared in sight. When the travellers were within a short distance of the city, a party of cavaliers were seen approaching, who drew in their reins as they came close to the fidalgo; one of the foremost leaping from his horse, and advancing towards him. He was a young man of graceful and refined exterior, dressed rather in the extreme of fashion, with an abundance of lace to his ruffles and shirt, his waistcoat richly flowered, and jewels glittering on the handle of his sword; his countenance, also, bore strong marks of dissipation, and there was a wild, careless manner in his whole air.

"Welcome to Lisbon, my honoured father; and my fair sister, I trust she has not suffered from the journey. I have brought my friend, San

Vincente, out to meet you," he added, introducing a young man, whose dark handsome countenance was disfigured by a lowering brow, and a furtive glance of the eye. Both gentlemen bowed low and often.

"I am most happy in having so early an opportunity to make the personal acquaintance of one of whom I have heard so much, and with whom I hope shortly to be yet more intimate." The count bowed lower still at the compliment, and the priest, who rode near his patron, eyed him narrowly.

"We received notice of your approach but at a late hour, and instantly mounted our horses to ride forward to meet you," said the young Fidalgo. "Excuse me, I will now go and address my sister;" and he rode up to the side of her litter. "Ah, my pretty Clara, blooming and fresh as ever!" he said, after the first greetings were over. "I am delighted to see you drawn out of the seclusion of that horrid place, Oporto, to enjoy the gaieties of the capital, where you will soon get rid of that bashful timidity which sits so ill upon you. Ah! I have a friend whom I must introduce to you, the Conde de San Vincente; see, he is riding by the side of our father. You have often heard of him, of course?"

"I have heard his name mentioned," answered his sister; "but little else respecting him."

"You will know more of him soon, then. He is an excellent fellow, and a particular acquaintance of mine; rather proud and haughty towards the scum of the earth, the lower orders, and not of a very forgiving temper if insulted; but those are qualities ladies seldom find fault with. I will bring him up to you presently, to pay his respects."

"Oh no, no, do not inconvenience the count. You will have another opportunity of introducing your friend," said Donna Clara.

"What a timid little bird you are," answered the young Fidalgo, laughing. "Now, I dare say your heart is fluttering with agitation. Why, the count is dying to see you, I have so praised you to him; and as soon as he can escape from the side of our father, he will come to throw himself at your feet."

He soon afterwards rode on and joined his father and the count, when, having contrived to bring their conversation to a close, he returned with the latter to the side of his sister's litter. Clara cast a hurried glance at the countenance of her brother's friend, and with that quick perception with which some women are fortunately endued, in that one moment she read more of his character than her brother had discovered during the whole course of his acquaintance; not that she could dream of the dark crimes and vices of which he was capable; such was impossible to her pure mind; but she saw something there which she did not like, she knew not what, and she returned a cold bow to the many flourishes of his hat, and chosen phrases of compliment with which the count honoured her.

Though rather piqued at her indifference, he was not in the least abashed; but kept his place on one side, while her brother rode on the other, endeavouring, though in vain, to win her attention by flattery to her beauty and by stories of the day, till they arrived in front of the palace of the Marchioness of Corcunda, a relation of Gonçalo Christovaö, where he had been invited to take up his abode during his stay in Lisbon. The count threw himself from his horse, and offered to hand Clara from her litter, an attention she could not, without marked rudeness, refuse; but as her hand touched his, a shudder passed through her frame, such as, it is said and believed, the victim feels in the presence of his destroyer; and she turned aside her head, to avoid the glance of those dark baneful eyes, which she felt an undefined consciousness were capable of withering her young pure happiness, her very existence itself.

Again bowing coldly to him, she withdrew her hand, when he was obliged to take his leave, while she flew to join her father, who with great ceremony conducted her upstairs, and introduced her to the old marchioness, who, surrounded by a number of old women, more hideous, if possible, than the witches in Macbeth, was standing ready to receive her guests at the entrance of the ante-room leading to the state apartment, a mark of very great distinction. She was a lady well advanced in years, of most grave and formal aspect; every motion of her body, and every thought of her mind, being regulated by what she considered the strict rules of etiquette. Her dress, like her mind, was composed of the stiffest materials, her gown being of a thick rich silk, capable of standing alone without the wearer, making a loud rustling as she moved forward and curtsied to Clara, whom, timid and blushing, her father presented to her; when the old lady bestowed a kiss (rather savoury of snuff, it must be owned) on each side of her face. "You are a very pretty young lady," she said, staring at her; "so was I once; but the world since then has changed with me, as it will with you. I am glad to see you, Gonçalo Christovaö," she added, though her looks belied her words; for it appeared impossible that any feelings of gladness could exist beneath that rigid aspect. "Remember, you are to make my house, and all it contains, entirely your own during your residence here: a daughter of yours will not be guilty of any of those levities in which young ladies of the present day are too apt to indulge; and I hear that you have brought your most excellent confessor with you, who will instil into her mind those principles of decorum and religion so essential in the conduct of a young lady." The marchioness having delivered this oration, led the way to her room of state, her attendants drawing aside to allow her and her guests to pass, and then followed in line, and arranged themselves on each side of the apartment.

The conversation was continued in the same stiff and formal strain, so that poor Clara was delighted when she was allowed to retire to the rooms appropriated to her use, where Senhora Gertrudes was ready to receive her, not at all more pleased than her young lady with the attendants of the marchioness.

Although, during the excitement of the journey, Clara had borne up against the effects of the terror she had endured, when she attempted to rise on the morning after her arrival, she fell back on her couch weak and feverish, and a severe illness seized her, which for many days confined her to her room; during which time numerous were the inquiries made at the door of the palace, the fame of her beauty having spread among the nobles of the city, all eager to see the new ornament which they hoped was to be added to the Court.

The most constant visitor was the Conde de San Vincente, for his fiery passions had been at once captivated by her tranquil beauty; the very indifference she had exhibited towards him serving to increase the flame, so that, looking on her as his affianced bride, he vowed the most deadly vengeance against any who should venture to come between him and the consummation of his hopes. He had sufficient tact carefully to conceal his character from her father, as he had, indeed, the darker shades from her brother, who would not otherwise have continued on the same intimate terms with him, though, it is to be feared, from the low state of morals at that time in society, he would not have treated him with the scorn and hatred he deserved.

Unremitting, therefore, in his attentions to the fidalgo, making promises of large settlements, and a handsome establishment, he completely won him to forward his wishes; indeed, in those times, few fathers ever thought of asking their daughters' consent in forming for them a connexion in which the whole happiness of their future life was concerned; and the young ladies, having few opportunities allowed them of choosing for themselves, generally yielded to their fate without a murmur; too often afterwards indemnifying themselves at the expense of their husband's honour.

In the meantime poor Clara remained in happy ignorance of the fate awaiting her; though the hints carelessly thrown out by her brother had for the time alarmed her; but she persuaded herself that he had but spoken in joke, and thought no more on the subject; her only remaining doubts being occasioned by her not having been informed of the reason for her visit to Lisbon. She was occasionally visited by the old marchioness, whose conversation was very far from contributing to enliven her, being chiefly long homilies for the regulation of her religious and moral conduct, and warnings against the sins which the pomps and vanities of the world would lead her to commit. Then she would launch out into praise of the advantages to be derived from a life of seclusion from the temptations of the world, ending with deep regrets that she herself in her youth had not rather assumed the veil, than subjected herself to the unhappiness she had endured; though it may be observed that she had never thought so till she had lost all taste for the pleasures she reprobated, and had contrived for a long course of years to yield very freely to the temptations she spoke of, without very seriously damaging her reputation; the marquis, her husband, having been of a very kind and indulgent disposition, and she having discovered certain peccadillos of his, which enabled her to keep a constant check over him, and prevented him from inquiring too minutely into what she chose to do.

The chief cause of her present style of conversation was, that the Padre Alfonzo, who had determined, for reasons of his own, that his fair young penitent should assume the veil, and was now employing every means he thought likely to aid his purpose, had for that reason assiduously paid his court to the marchioness from the moment of his arrival, and easily gained her over to his views, pointing out the advantages which Clara would find, both in a spiritual and moral point of view, in a monastic life, and the misery she would endure if united to a man of so bad a character as he hinted that of the count to be. He also assured the old lady that it would much contribute to gain pardon from heaven for her own trespasses, if she were the means of offering so acceptable a sacrifice to the Church; and the last argument completely gained his point.

Gonçalo Christovaö was at first very much alarmed at his daughter's illness, but being assured by the physicians that there was no danger to be apprehended, he with resignation awaited her recovery. It must be observed, that though, in this instance, the doctors were perfectly right, they knew very little of the subject, their chief specific being that of Doctor Sangrado, and a judicious administering of mummy powder, and various drugs long since banished from every pharmacopeia in civilised Europe. Fortunately they came to the determination that Clara did not require bleeding, and thus, under the care of kind nature, she was allowed to recover without their interference, and all praised the physicians who had wrought so speedy a cure. Her father, having made up his mind that she should become the bride of his estimable young friend, the Conde San Vincente, determined, as soon as he considered she was sufficiently recovered to bear conversation, to open the subject to her. Now, he was, as we have said, a very amiable man, and an affectionate father; but he was one of those people who, according to circumstances, may be either praised for their firmness or blamed for their obstinacy; if he had once taken an idea into his head, he was very fond of retaining it, from the difficulty he had in getting it there. Of his own accord, and by the advice of his son, he had determined that his daughter should espouse the Conde San Vincente, while his confessor, in whose judgment he put implicit confidence, had persuaded him, by dint of much argument, that if she would not marry according to his will, she must inevitably assume the veil. Besides the quality which his enemies would have called obstinacy, he possessed another, which the same persons would have designated as a passionate temper, though his admirers might look upon it as a just indignation: it had rarely been aroused, principally from his having always enjoyed his own way, no one attempting to oppose his will, so that he was not even aware of it himself, imagining that he was of the mildest disposition possible. When he entered his daughter's apartment, he found her risen from her bed, and seated on a sofa near the open window, enjoying the fresh air, the only remedy which she required to restore her to perfect health. He took her hand as he seated himself by her side. He began much in the way fathers always must begin when they have the same sort of subject to communicate, particularly when they have some floating suspicions that it may not afford entire satisfaction to their hearers, and that they must be prepared for a slight opposition to their will, as his confessor had warned him might now be the case. He talked a great deal about his love and affection, and his care for her interests and happiness, in answer to which his daughter looked into his face, and thanked him with a sweet beaming smile, and an assurance of her confidence in his love. Then he talked of the necessity of leaving as large a fortune as possible to his son, whose expenses were, he confessed, considerable, that he might maintain the family honour and dignity, in which she most readily acquiesced. He next approached the main point. He observed that young ladies must form matrimonial connexions suitable to their family and station, and that nothing was more disgraceful or wrong than for a person of pure and noble blood to wed with one who could not boast an equal number of quarterings on their escutcheons. Clara said she had always heard such was the case, and believed it fully; then she looked down on the ground, wondering what was next to come. The Fidalgo went on to observe, that there were very few unmarried men of his acquaintance whom he should consider as a suitable match for his daughter, that many of pure blood were poor, and that he would, on no account, expose her to the miseries of poverty; and that there were several aged bachelors and widowers who were most unexceptionable, but that there were objections to her marrying an old man, especially if not very wealthy. She again thanked him, and agreed in some part of the observations. It did occur to her for an instant, and she longed to say so, that she thought she had met with one who might perhaps please him, but her modesty restrained her, so she blushed at her own thoughts, and fixed her eyes more intently on the ground. He had now arrived at the delicate point, and he began to speak quicker, as if to get over it; for he saw his daughter turning paler every instant, and he could not bear to watch her, so he averted his eyes while he spoke. He said that he had looked round among all his acquaintance, in which search her brother had materially aided him, to find a suitable husband for her, as he considered that she ought now to marry; that, after infinite trouble, he had succeeded in selecting one in every way her equal in blood, being of the highest Fidalguia, and of title and large property, so that she must consider herself as a very fortunate girl. Poor Clara now trembled violently, but her father did not, or would not, observe her agitation. He continued, that her intended husband was a particular friend of her brothel, who much wished the match to take place; that he was the young Conde San Vincente; and that he had engaged his word as a fidalgo that she should marry him and no one else: therefore, that she must be prepared to receive him on the following day as her future husband. At this communication Clara turned deadly pale, and trembled so violently, that she almost fell from her seat. Her worst suspicions were realised: that dreaded man must be her husband! She shuddered at the thought; for her confessor had taken care to instil into her mind his opinion of the count, more by dark insinuations than by any direct accusation; for the former he knew would have far greater effect, while the latter might be refuted, and might injure himself. There was a spirit in the bosom of that young girl which she knew not of, both firm and enduring, enabling her to resist tyranny with determination; but she first made use of the feminine weapons most natural to her age and habits.

"Oh, my father, I love you, and have always sought to obey your wishes; but do not now require of me what I cannot do,—cause me not now to act in disobedience to your commands. Oh! alter that decision, which it would break my heart to obey. It is impossible that I should love the count, and you would not make me wed one for whom I can never feel affection?"

The fidalgo looked at her with amazement. He had never supposed it possible that she should offer any resistance to his wishes, though they might not at first please her. It is just probable that, had she not mentally daguerreo-typed that likeness of Don Luis at Leiria, she might not have thought of opposing the commands of her father, who, however, never made any such calculation; nor had the said Don Luis even occurred to his recollection, as he knew him to be the son of a poor noble, whose property was much involved.

"What is this nonsense I hear about love and affection? What objections can you have to the count? He is young, handsome, and rich, as you know; and as you have scarcely seen him, it is not possible that you can dislike him; so that you will soon learn to love him as much as is necessary; and what further would you wish? Come, come, Clara, I have always been an indulgent father to you,—do not let me now find you a disobedient child, in the most important affair of your life. Am not I the fittest person to choose a husband for you? and tell me, how could you, who can know nothing of the world, select one for yourself? Such an idea would be unmaidenly and highly incorrect, and one in which no young lady would dream of indulging; and I have pledged my word to the count, therefore you must marry him."

Clara did not see the clearness of her father's reasoning. "I would do all to please you," she again answered; "I would die, and, oh! willingly, for your sake; but this I cannot do."

"Clara, beware you do not make me utter such words as I thought never to speak to you. My honour is dearer to me than my life: it is dearer even than my child's life or happiness; and my honour is pledged to the count. It must be so."

"Oh, my father, I must die, then, if I obey you!" returned the fair girl, faintly.

The fidalgo's heart was softened, and, for the moment, he repented of his pledge; but it must be redeemed, if the count demanded it.

"Clara, there is an alternative, but one that I wish you not to choose. Your mother, on her death-bed, made it her dying request that you should rather take the veil than marry against your will. I have vowed to fulfil her wish. I give you, therefore, your choice. Within a month you must wed the Count San Vincente, or give up the world and all its pleasures, and dwell for the remainder of your life in the gloomy precincts of a convent. But I know my pretty Clara will recover from her fit of bashful fears, and long before that time the count will have won the love you speak of."

"Oh no, no!" exclaimed Clara, with energy. "Let me far rather enter a convent. I will at once so decide; and let me not be exposed to the dark glances of the count, which alone fill me with terror."

"Clara, you will excite my just anger," returned the Fidalgo, in a tone which very plainly showed his anger was excited already. "I will not now hear your decision. At the end of the month we will again speak on the subject; till then I will not allude to it. I insist on your receiving the count, in the meantime, and shall inform him that he must not expect your answer till that period has elapsed."

Clara burst into tears; but her father was angry, and they did not influence him. He was, as we have said, not accustomed to be opposed. Seeing that she continued weeping (it was at her father's unkindness, so unusual in him, towards her), his feelings were moved, which made him only still more angry; so he rose to quit her, in order to avoid the sight. "Clara, this is but increasing your folly. I must now quit you, and remember to-morrow to wear at least a serene countenance to receive the count." He stooped down, as was his wont, to kiss her brow, when she threw herself on his neck, and wept hysterically; but he placed her again on the seat, and left the room, muttering, "It must be thus," and ordered Senhora Gertrudes to attend her mistress.

The proud fidalgo was not the most happy man in Lisbon that night. As he met Senhora Gertrudes, he told her to advise her young mistress to think of marrying, instead of entering a convent, which general directions the old lady was very well able to obey.

"What is it the fidalgo has been telling me, that my child wishes to go into a convent? Why, she never before uttered such an idea to me! Would she have all that beautiful fair hair cut off, and hide that lovely face within the gloomy walls of a nunnery? I should die to see my child so lost to the world."

"Oh no, no, I do not wish to go into a nunnery, my good ama," returned Clara, as soon as she had recovered sufficiently to speak; "but I do not wish to marry."

"Not wish to marry! Ha, ha! that's what many young ladies say, but don't mean, minha alma! You would be very happy to marry, if the right person offered. Now, suppose that handsome young Don Luis d'Almeida proposed to you. Would not he please you, my child?"

"Oh, but he is not the person selected for me, my good nurse," answered Clara, blushing as she spoke.

"Who is it, then, my love?—speak, pray," cried the nurse anxiously.

"It is that dark Count San Vincente, my brother's friend," answered the young lady.

"Oh, he is not half so handsome as Don Luis; so I am not surprised at your not liking him; and he did not even deign to speak to me, when he came out to meet us on our coming here. Don Luis will suit you much better, and I will tell the fidalgo so. Come, now, dry your eyes, and you shall be happy."

We fear, Senhora Gertrudes, you were not fulfilling your master's intentions by your last impolitic observations.

"But, alas! my kind nurse, my father has pledged his word to the count, and cannot retract," answered Clara.

"I don't understand anything about pledging words; but I will not have my child made unhappy, to please that rude count. So do not fear, my soul. I will persuade your father, or I will frighten the count. I will do something or other; but you shall neither marry him nor go into a convent. Now, go to bed again, my love, and to-morrow you will be quite well and happy."

As soon as it was reported that Donna Clara was sufficiently recovered to receive visitors, numbers crowded to the door of the marchioness's palace, eager to ascertain, in person, whether the beauty was over praised, which, it was generally supposed, would adorn the Court. Among the first who came to make her acquaintance, whom she received in her own apartment, was Donna Theresa d'Alorna, the betrothed of the young Marquis of Tavora; for, although their families were in no way related, that intimacy had been kept up between them which existed generally amongst the Fidalguia, and was so necessary for their own preservation as an order, against all other classes. As Donna Theresa was announced, a slight blush tinged the fair cheek of Donna Clara; for she could not avoid coupling her name with that of Don Luis, till she recollected that he had himself contradicted the report her nurse had heard; and she rose to receive her visitor with that elegant courtesy so natural to her. The young ladies saluted each other on the cheek before they spoke, when Clara led her guest to a seat.

"I have been longing to come and see you, since I heard of your arrival," Donna Theresa began. "And no sooner was I told that you could receive me, than I flew hither."

Clara thanked her for her politeness.

"They told me you were very beautiful," she continued; "and, for a wonder, report has not exaggerated your perfections. Oh! you will commit immense havoc in the Court. You have but to appear, to conquer!"

Clara smiled, and assured her she was too complimentary.

"Oh, not half enough so!" she answered; "but it is said you are already given away; that the bargain is struck, the arrangements made; and that the Conde San Vincente is the happy man. However, I now see you are a great deal too good for him. You cannot have seen him very often, I suppose?"

"I have seen him but twice," answered Clara.

"Oh, how fortunate you were!" answered Donna Theresa, laughing. "Few have so many opportunities of judging of their future lords and masters. Then, for a second wonder, the report is correct, and you are betrothed to the count?"

"Oh, I trust in Heaven not," said Clara, sorrowfully: "I could never love the count."

"Very likely not," returned her visitor, laughing. "It is a question seldom asked of us poor girls till we arrive at the altar, with a lie on our tongues. But your father wishes for the match?"

Clara bowed assent.

"Oh, then, I fear, poor bird, you are entrapped; but you need not be unhappy alone, for you have plenty of sisters in affliction;" and a shade passed over the lovely countenance of Donna Theresa.

"But is it possible to marry a man one cannot love?" asked Clara, with emphasis on her words.

"Possible! why yes, such is but a trifle, which thousands do every day," answered her guest, laughing at her simplicity. "It is a trifle not worth thinking about. We poor women are doomed to have husbands of some sort; such is our unavoidable lot, and we must submit to it; but for my part, I prefer having one I do not love; for he will give me much less trouble in managing, and I shall be able to enjoy as much liberty as I can desire. Now I should advise you to follow my example."

Clara shook her head; she was shocked at what she heard.

"Ah, I see you have a great deal of rustic simplicity to cure yourself of, before you can properly appreciate the pleasures of a city life; but after you have married the count, I shall find you wonderfully improved."

"I can never marry the count: I shall enter a convent rather," said Clara.

"Oh, horror of horrors! I know not why such places were invented, except as a punishment for our sins, or by some sour, crusty old fathers, to frighten their daughters into obedience to their tyrannical commands. I have heard some extraordinary stories about two or three convents in the old king's time, which I will tell you; for they may amuse you, though I do not think they would encourage a modest young lady to enter one, as they are not much improved since then."

We do not give the stories; for we must observe, that the minds of young ladies in those days were less refined than at the present time; and that they assumed far more freedom in their language, particularly those who had been educated like Donna Theresa; though the recital, to which Clara's pure ears were unaccustomed, made the blushes rise on her cheeks. It is only necessary to say, that several convents were entirely suppressed by Pombal, on account of their scandalous excesses and immoralities, which had become a disgrace to civilisation and Christianity.

Donna Theresa's conversation had, however, the effect of making Clara feel that she ought rather to undergo any misery than assume the veil; and, that her only course was to obey her father's commands; an opinion, her new friend did her utmost to foster. She became also accustomed to the count's expression of features, which had, at first, alarmed her; for he exerted himself to please her, and her brother lost no opportunity of praising his generous qualities. The count had also contrived to gain over the old marchioness, by a variety of artifices, which he well knew how to practise, and the confessor, for some unexplained reason, had not again spoken to Clara on the subject of her taking the veil; so that she was left, poor girl! with the old nurse, as the only friend in whom she could confide, or who seemed to take a real interest in her welfare. Yet, simple virtue, and purity of thought, will often strengthen the weak to counteract all the wiles and plots of the subtle intriguer, though confident in his strength and talent. Thus affairs continued; her month of probation was nearly drawing to a close, and, in a few days, she must consent to receive the count as her husband, or assume the veil; all she had heard increased her dislike to the latter alternative, and everybody around her endeavoured to persuade her, that the other was a very happy lot.

The count had, by some means or other, discovered the cause of the delay; and that she was hesitating about accepting him, not from his having any rival in her affections, whom he might chastise, as he vowed he would, if he discovered one; but, because she felt so great an antipathy to him, that she fancied she should prefer a life of seclusion in a convent, to wedding him with rank, wealth, and liberty. This was not very complimentary to him, nor was he pleased by it; but he was not a man who foolishly gave vent to his feelings in outward show, though he vowed an oath, deep and bitter, that, once master of that bright jewel, he would wring her young heart for its present obduracy, till she should repent ever having dared, for an instant, to oppose his lordly will.

He persuaded the marchioness that gaiety was most likely to restore her young friend to her usual state of spirits and health; and, perhaps, the old lady was not sorry to discover a plausible excuse for opening her palace once more to the gay world. Her father and brother wisely judged that if they could give her a taste for the amusements of society, she was less likely to wish to quit it. There was also to be a Beja Mao, literally a kissing hands, or drawing-room, at the Court, when she was to be introduced to the royal family, so that there was little time afforded her for thought or meditation; indeed, very little would have turned the scale, and made her accept the count at once; but she sought to put off the day, which she knew must seal her misery, till the end of the period allowed her.

The only person who appeared to be an indifferent spectator of what was taking place, was the father confessor, Padre Alfonzo: he merely kept his gaze fixed on her, with an ominous frown on his brow, whenever the count was engaged in conversation with her; and his was, perhaps, the only eye beneath which the glance of the young noble cowered.

A few days before the end of the month, the confessor encountered the fidalgo alone: it was towards the close of the evening, as he was pacing a long gallery of the palace, hung with the grim portraits of some of his ancestors, who were those likewise of the marchioness.

"Your daughter appears inclined to obey your wishes," said the Priest. "But if not, you remember your vow to our holy Church; and let your heart be steeled, and your honour unsullied, as was that of your noble predecessors. Let me feel confident that your wife's dying request may be fulfilled, and again swear, that as long as the count urges his suit to your daughter, she shall accept him, or become the bride of Heaven."

"Father, I have already said so, and I again swear, that she shall marry the man I choose, or assume the veil," exclaimed the Fidalgo.

"I am satisfied," said the Priest.

End of the First Volume.

Volume Two—Chapter One.

In painting a true picture of times and events, we must introduce among our figures the wealthy and great, the wicked, the wretched, and the indigent, or we should present no true likeness of the world as it exists; we must also beg leave to bring forward a personage who was certainly not wealthy or great; who vowed that he was not wicked, for he performed his duty to God and man; who was not wretched, for he was singing all day long; while he declared that he could not be indigent, for he possessed abundance to supply all his wants, though, fortunately for himself, they were very few.

This personage was a cobbler. Now, it is a curious fact, which no one will venture to dispute, that, from the time of the cobbler who tacked the bits of Ali Baba's brother together, as mentioned in the authentic history of the Forty Thieves—with which we trust all our readers are acquainted—to the days of the celebrated cobbler who lived in a stall, "which served him for parlour, and kitchen, and hall," cobblers have borne a strong similarity to each other, with distinctive qualities separating them from other men, as can be proved by the above and numerous other instances, both in all countries and all ages.

In England, a tailor is looked upon, not only as inferior to other men, but actually to be of no more consideration than the ninth part of a man: now, in Portugal, the same unjust sort of prejudice exists against shoemakers; consequently, cobblers are considered utterly below all notice.

Our cobbler, however, did not care one iota for the opinions of people, whom, in his sleeve, he despised and ridiculed: "For," said he, when he had collected a small knot of attentive listeners, "if, in England, as I hear, they laugh at a tailor, and esteem a cobbler, and here they honour a tailor and despise a cobbler; while in France, for what I know to the contrary, they may admire both, and not think much of a hat-maker; and if, in this country, no man will carry a load, while our next door neighbours come on purpose so to do, I should very much like to know who is in the right, and who in the wrong, and which trade is really derogatory to the dignity of man? Mark another absurdity—how different nations and people despise each other, when one may not be at all superior to the other. When Jerusalem was a city of the Jews, I should like to know who would have dared walk into it and scoff at a man because he was a Jew? Here every one reviles that people. If a Turk comes here, he is stared at as a savage and a heathen; and if a Christian goes to Turkey, he is called an unbeliever and a barbarian—now which is right, and which is wrong? Why should I, therefore, put myself out of my way to follow any other trade than the one I like? I choose to be a cobbler: it suits my taste. I can talk, sing, or meditate at pleasure, while I mend shoes. What fools men are! The statesman thinks no one so wise as himself; the lawyer considers the soldier only fit food for powder; while the latter despises the peaceable merchant; the merchant looks upon all in trade as beneath him; and he who deals in silks thinks himself infinitely superior to the vendor of leather; while they all join in despising the cobbler. What fools, what fools men are! Why, I laugh at them," he would say, as he wound up his discourse, at the same time indulging in a low, quiet chuckle. These observations very much edified and pleased his auditors, who, being of about the same rank in society as he appeared, felt that such sentiments were their own; adding, on their parts, that all distinction of classes was a most unjust arrangement. They would then begin to discuss among themselves, whether they were not as well able to govern the state as those who actually held the reins. When they got to this point the cobbler laughed at them. He was fond of laughing at people who talked nonsense. He thus laughed, in turn, at the greater part of the world.

While we have been giving this long account of the character and sayings of the cobbler, we entirely overlooked the main points to be described; namely, his outward appearance, and when and where he lived. Our readers, we dare say, expect to hear that he was an odd, little, crooked old fellow, with a dirty face and unshorn locks; but we can assure them history informs us, on the contrary, that he was once young—nor was he now old; that he was well-made, and when he drew himself up, his height was respectable; that when his work was done, and he had shaved and washed, his face was as clean as that of any of his very numerous acquaintance. From this description, it may be deduced, that his appearance was in his favour; his colour was dark, his eyes were piercing and jetty black, as was his hair, and that he had fine teeth, and a long nose, rather hooked. Some, indeed, hinted that he was a Jew; but, being a strong athletic fellow, with his long sharp leather-knife by his side, none dared call him so to his face; besides, he was constant at his devotions, and a regular attendant at all religious ceremonies; none more devoutly kneeling and crossing themselves when the mysterious and sublime Host passed by, borne under a rich canopy, in the hands of a venerable priest, accompanied by monks and choristers chanting forth hymns of praise, and preceded by some pious person tinkling a bell, to give notice of its approach, that all, uncovered, might bend in adoration.

No one knew exactly whence he came; but, a short time previous to the events we have related in the former part of this history, he made his appearance one morning with his stock in trade on his back, and established himself in a deep recess in the wall of a large house, directly facing the entrance to the palace of the Duke of Aveiro. He set down his stool, threw a bundle of leather on one side, the implements of his craft on the other, with a few old shoes, put his lapstone on his knees, and began working away as if he had lived there all his life.

He soon made friends with the servants of the palace: he mended the footmen's shoes, charging them less, and doing the work better, than any one else could have done; and next, one by one, the women brought out their slippers or sandals; and for each he had a smile and a compliment, or a piece of wit, in readiness: sometimes a moral reflection, if the beauties of the dame he addressed had become faded by years, and if he had observed her kissing with greater fervour the little images of saints brought round from the churches, or more constant in her attendance at mass than others. If the lady was young, with sparkling black eyes, he knew exactly how to bestow his praise, and, at all events, their feet were a sure subject for compliment. Considering the small sums he charged, they could not but wait to pay him with a little chat, while he was putting the last stitch or so into his work; for, come when they would, so it was that a few minutes' work always remained to be completed; and, as they did not complain, he did not correct his fault, being thus enabled, in a quiet, confidential way, to learn all that was going forward in the establishment. What he learned will be detailed in the course of this history.

We have said that he had taken up his abode in a recess in the wall of a house opposite the palace; but we do not wish to describe the house as facing the palace, for it looked into a street running at right angles to it; the recess being part of a doorway in the garden-wall, now stopped up. This house was inhabited by a very rich merchant and his family, most exemplary Catholics, who set a lesson of piety to the community by their regular observance of all the ordinances of the Church, and by their fastings and alms: yet, notwithstanding this, people dared to point the finger of scorn at them, stigmatising them as Jews and heretics, and longing to show their zeal for religion by offering them up in that grateful sacrifice to the benign power, the most holy Auto da Fè—thus to become sharers in their hoarded riches. Whatever were their own private notions regarding the established faith, they certainly suffered under the inabilities of the New Christians, as those were called who had Jewish or even Moorish blood in their veins, the term having origin from the following cause.

At an early period in Lusitanian history, we find that the Jews had collected in great numbers in Portugal, and down to the reign of John the First they had their synagogues and rabbins; indeed, in no country in Europe did they enjoy greater prosperity, their wealth adding much to the power of the kingdom.

In Spain, also, they had acquired considerable influence, till the reign of Ferdinand and Isabella, when those pious sovereigns having driven the Moors from their dominions, conceived that their duty to Heaven ordained that they should depopulate the other half of the cities in Spain, by banishing the Jews also. This idea, fostered by the avarice of some and the bigotry of others, was put into execution, and great numbers of the unfortunate refugees were received by John the Second on condition of their paying a certain tribute, and quitting the kingdom within a limited period, he undertaking to provide them with vessels to transport them wherever they desired to proceed. The king's state of health prevented him from seeing his orders put into execution, while the captains and seamen of the vessels treated those who had embarked in the most barbarous manner; keeping them at sea till they had entirely consumed their own provisions, and then compelling them to buy of them at exorbitant rates; so that those who remained in Portugal, fearful of the like treatment, allowed the prescribed time to elapse, and thus forfeited their liberty. Such was the situation of the Jews when Emanuel began his reign, and generously restored them to liberty, for which extraordinary benevolence they offered him, in gratitude, a large sum of money; but he refused it, in the hopes of gaining their affections by kind treatment, and converting them to Christianity. At length, however, bigotry, and envy at their increasing wealth, caused a loud clamour to be raised against them, and Emanuel was induced, contrary to his own judgment, by the representations of his counsellors, and the interference of the Spanish sovereigns, to order all, both Jews and Moors, who refused to embrace the Christian faith, to quit his dominions. A day was fixed for their departure, after which all who remained in the country were to lose their liberty; but, as it approached, the king, greatly afflicted at the thoughts of driving so many of his subjects into banishment, devised a scheme which was eventually of great benefit to the kingdom. He ordered all the children of the Jews, under fourteen years of age, to be forcibly taken from their parents, that they might be educated in the

Christian faith, thus gaining converts to the Church at the expense of all the laws of justice and humanity.

"What a moving spectacle was this to behold!" exclaims the reverend Father Ozorio. "Children torn from the agonised embraces of their screaming mothers, or dragged from the necks of their affectionate brothers and sisters, from whom they were to be for ever separated, while the fathers sternly gazed, and cursed the perpetrators of deeds they had no power to avenge! The city of Lisbon was filled with cries and lamentations; even the spectators could not refrain from tears. Parents, in the excess of their frenzy, were seen to lay violent hands on themselves; many, rather than submit to the severity of the decree, hurling their infants into wells and pits. Never was such tribulation heard in Israel since the days of Herod the Tetrarch!"

No vessels had been provided for their transport, as had been promised, and thus, when the day for their departure had passed, they again forfeited their liberty. Thus harassed, they at length, to recover their children and their liberty, affected to become Christians, the king giving them every encouragement, so that the greater number lived contentedly in the Portuguese dominions.

Though thus professing the religion of the country, it could not be supposed that they could regard it with any fond affection, and consequently their faith was ever looked upon with suspicion by the rest of the inhabitants, particularly by those who envied their industry and wealth: that hell-invented tribunal of the Inquisition taking every means, on the slightest pretext, to subject them to its tyrannical power. Many embraced the earliest opportunity of escaping to Holland, England, and other free countries, where they could enjoy uninterruptedly the exercise of their faith. Those that remained still continued to intermarry among themselves, and, it was supposed, not without considerable reason, to exercise in private the rites they were forbidden to perform in public. Whatever, therefore, was their profession of faith, none gave them credit for their belief in the holy Catholic Church, but bestowed on them the distinctive appellation of New Christians, which they retained at the time of which we are now speaking.

The Marquis of Pombal, with that liberal policy which marked many of his actions, finally abolished all such distinctions; but before he had succeeded in doing so, King Joseph took it into his most sagacious head, that, for the benefit of religion, there ought to be some sign placed on all those with Jewish blood in their veins. He consequently ordered a decree to be promulgated that all such should wear white hats.

The Minister remonstrated, but in vain. Finding reason ineffectual, he pretended compliance, and presented himself to the king with the edict, at the same time drawing out from under his cloak two white hats. On the king inquiring the meaning of the joke—"Oh!" replied Pombal, "I come prepared to obey your majesty's edict, with one hat for you and another for myself," thus hinting the well-known fact, that the royal family itself was not entirely free from the imaginary stain; the family of the Minister also, it was said, having sprung from the stock of Abraham, as are a vast many others. The king laughed, and gave up the point.

On the death of Joseph, and the banishment of his Minister, when bigotry and priestcraft regained their supremacy, the New Christians were again subject to persecutions, and it is only under the present free constitution that all difference has been finally, and, we trust, for ever, abolished.

But we have wandered from our subject, and have, by nearly a century, forestalled events. Our readers will exclaim, What has this long account of the Jews, and King Joseph and his Minister, with the white hats, got to do with the cobbler and his stall? *Spera hum poco*— (which is to say, in Portuguese, "Stop a little," a very favourite expression before all their actions, whereby they often lose the right time)—we shall presently see; for if it has nothing to do with the cobbler, it has with the family under whose walls he plied his trade, for they were New Christians; many indeed affirmed that they still adhered to the faith of their forefathers, and there were various stories current respecting the performance of their ancient rites. It was said, that when strangers were admitted to the house, there was one room, of considerable dimensions, always kept closed, which was supposed to be dedicated to the purposes of a synagogue. The vulgar believed that, at the Feast of the Passover, they immolated a Christian child yet unweaned; the origin of which idea was, of course, the sacrifice of the Paschal lamb; and there were various other stories, equally absurd and revolting, having less foundation in truth. However, Senhor Matteos de Menezes and his family had escaped the power of the Inquisition: it might have been by timely donations of no inconsiderable amount to holy Mother Church, so that even the Grand Inquisitor himself could not doubt the completeness of their conversion, and the purity of their faith.

Having given a full description of the locality of the cobbler's stall, we may now go on spinning the thread of our history; and if some of our readers complain that we have turned our mystic spindle too slowly, we must beg their pardon, and assure them that we are about to progress at a rapid rate, with scenes of the most thrilling interest, such as will cause their eyes to ache ere they can lay down the book.

The cobbler was one day seated in his stall, hard at work, hammering a new heel on to a shoe, at the same time thinking of the number of fools there were in the world, and yet how few were aware that they belonged to that class of creation; for, as we observed, our cobbler was a philosopher in his way, and had he been born in the higher ranks of society, he would have been a noted wit and satirist, laughing at the follies and scourging the vices of his equals. But he found the follies of the poor too slight, or too sad, to laugh at, and their vices more the fault of institutions than their own, and beyond correction. Next, he thought of the state of the nation. He saw a priesthood wallowing in sloth, corrupted, bigoted, and abandoned to every vice; a nobility haughty, ignorant, vicious, and tyrannical; a king weak, superstitious, and profligate; a people sunk in apathy, and the grossest superstition, without courage or intelligence to assert their rights. And he pitied them; but he knew there was one man in the realm able and willing to overthrow the power of the first, to crush the arrogant pride of the second, to rule the king, to enlighten the people, and to give justice to all; and he had long determined to aid his designs; for the cobbler had more power than the world supposed, and he thanked Heaven he did not belong to any of these classes. These thoughts had just passed through his mind, when he heard a tramping of steeds, and looking up, he beheld a cavalcade approaching, at the head of which rode the Duke of Aveiro, accompanied by his handsome young nephew on one side, while on the other was his equerry, Captain Policarpio, in earnest conversation with him, heedless of the people who thronged the streets, the horses bespattering them with mud and dirt, the attendants, also, taking a pleasure in causing confusion and annoyance to all whom they passed. A youth, with a basket of oranges on his head, was offering them for sale, when one of the domestics adroitly managed to make his horse sidle against him. The vendor of fruit, with a cry of terror, endeavoured to escape, when his foot slipped, and letting go his basket, the contents rolled out on the ground, over which the others trampled, with loud laughter at the disaster, none deigning to make the slightest amends to the youth. Some of the passers by stopped to assist him, for he was sobbing piteously at his loss, but dared not complain.

Our cobbler saw the occurrence. "Take care, my masters," as he watched the arrogant noble who had just reached his palace gates; "take care, or you will discover, when too late to remedy your faults, that your days of prosperity have passed away." No sooner did the duke enter the lofty gateway of his palace, than the major-domo rushed down stairs to hold his stirrup while he alighted, his young kinsman throwing himself from his steed, without waiting for assistance, and the attendants bustling about and creating more noise and confusion than was at all necessary.

"Why has the duke so suddenly returned to the city?" thought the Cobbler. "I must watch and learn, for 'tis about no good, I am certain."

It has just occurred to us, that we have never given our cobbler's name. By diligent search through the vast pile of manuscripts before us, we have discovered the important piece of information that he was called Antonio, generally with O *Memendab*, or the Mender, added thereto. No dignified title, certainly! but he was contented with it, and so must we be; for we cannot anywhere discover what was his other name, if he ever had one, which we deem problematical.

Several days passed before Antonio became much wiser as to the cause of the duke's movements than on the first day of his arrival, though he narrowly watched all his outgoings, and incomings, and also most diligently questioned the servants who stepped across the street to have five minutes' chat with him. The duke had just driven out, when one of the lackeys, rejoicing in the name of Jozé, was sauntering about the hall, and having nothing to do, bethought him that he would honour the cobbler with his society.

"Good day, Senhor Jozé," said the Cobbler, as he saw him approach; "you have pleasant times of it, with nothing to do, and plenty to eat, while I must hammer, hammer, and stitch, stitch, all day long, to earn a few *vintems* to supply my food."

"You are right, Senhor Antonio, you are right," answered Jozé, as he leaned, with his hands in his pockets, a toothpick in his mouth, and his legs crossed, against the wall; "we have a tolerable life of it; for, except that the duke sits inside, while we stand outside, what difference is there between us? and when the people take off their hats, it is as much to our fine coats as to him. Then we eat the same food, and drink the same wines as he does, only a good deal more of each than he can, in which we have the advantage of him, and as for knowledge, between ourselves, there is not much difference either."

"Ah! the duke is a good master, and blessed with good servants," returned Antonio.

"Why, as to his servants, I must not speak, as I am one of them," answered Jozé, pulling out his ruffles; "but his Excellency himself—whom God preserve—would be all the better if he did not beat us so confoundedly when he is angered; but that is a trifle—it is his privilege, and we must be content."

"You are right, Senhor Jozé, there is no use quarrelling with one's lot. What would be the advantage to him of being a duke, if he might not do what pleases him?" said the Cobbler, plying his awl as if he thought much more of mending the old shoe on his lap, than of the words he was speaking. "He appears to be fonder of taking carriage exercise than he was?"

"Oh! he is driving about all day," said Jozé, "first to one place, then to another; now to pay his respects to his majesty, then to some fidalgo he never before thought of visiting. It is said that this change has been worked by the influence of the pious saint, the holy Father Malagrida, who tells him, that to be at enmity with his fellow-men is sinful and wicked, and that he must reform his life, and be in charity with all. To prove his sincerity, the last time it was my turn to go out, we drove to the palace of the Marquis of Tavora, to whom he has not spoken for years; but he craved forgiveness for some insult he had committed towards him, and when they parted, they embraced in the most affectionate way, the duke kissing the hand of the marchioness most lovingly. Oh, it was quite pathetic to see them!"

"Oh, it must have been," returned Antonio; "and you say he has renewed his friendship with several other nobles?"

"Oh yes, there was the Count d'Atouquia, who had never spoken to him since he ran his brother through the body one night in a street brawl, and now they are hand and glove: then he has written to the Count d'Almeida, before whom he used to carry himself so haughtily, though the count thought himself just as great a man as our lord. Then he paid a visit of ceremony to the Senhor Silva, whom he has constantly passed in the streets as if he was some commoner or plebeian; and he dined yesterday with the Marquis d'Alorna, with whom he was on bad terms formerly. We do not know what to make of it; and I should not think of speaking on the subject to any one but a friend like you; but, to tell you the truth, our opinion is, that there is some marriage about to take place between the young viscount, our lord's nephew, and some lady of one of these noble families, or perhaps his son is to be betrothed to one of them."

"I have no doubt you have exactly hit off the truth," said the Cobbler, nodding his head sagaciously; "but I would advise you not to talk about your lord's affairs to people in general: to a friend like me it is different; for you know the less said the soonest mended; but I am as close as cobbler's wax," and he kneaded a lump of that composition in his fingers.

"Ah! I know you are, or I should not be so great a fool as to talk to you as I do," said Jozé, sagaciously. "By-the-bye, have you heard of the marriage about to take place between the young Marquis of Tavora, who is a great friend of our young viscount, and the daughter of the Count d'Alorna?"

"Not I," answered Antonio; "I hear nothing except what my friends like to tell me as I sit at my work," and he strenuously stitched away at the shoe on his lap.

As soon as the evening arrived, Antonio packed up his tools, and placed them within the hall of Senhor Menezes' house, where it was his custom to leave them, by permission of the servants, with whom it seemed he was acquainted, though they seldom came out to talk to him. He then, looking to see that no one observed him, repaired, after taking many turnings, as was his wont, to his lodgings, which, considering his apparent poverty, were far more respectable than could have been expected. He there, throwing off his working suit with an air of disdain, and washing his hands and face, attired himself in the garments of a man of fashion, when, buckling a sword to his side, and throwing a cloak over his shoulders, he again sallied forth in such guise, that no one could have recognised in him the humble cobbler of the morning. He now appeared a well-grown man of some thirty-five or forty years of age, with large dark whiskers, and full black eyes, as he walked along with an independent air, and perhaps a slight swagger in his gait, as if he enjoyed his emancipation from his daily toil. He again looked cautiously around, throwing the right side of his cloak over his left shoulder, and hastily traversing several streets up and down hill, he arrived before a mansion, at the door of which a sentinel was stationed. He gave some name to the porter, who immediately allowed him to pass, another servant showing him into an anteroom on the top of the first flight of steps. "Wait here a few minutes, senhor, and my master will speak with you," said the domestic, as he withdrew with the quiet step of one accustomed to attend on people high in office.

"I have information that may be of great value," thought Antonio to himself, as he paced up and down the ill-furnished room; "but the reward may be proportionably great; and I would far rather confide in him than in any of the miserable wretches who have crawled till now about the Court, and have seized the high offices of state, their pride overflowing with the thoughts of their bastard descent from some profligate prince or mitred abbot of a few centuries back, since which time they have had but little fresh blood to improve the stream." He thought this, as we have said; for he was not one to give utterance to what was passing in his mind: a door opened, and a man of dignified carriage and lofty stature stood before him, in whose presence even Antonio shrunk into insignificance.

It was the Minister Carvalho. "Ah! my faithful Antonio, you are ever punctual to your time," he began. "Had I twenty such strenuous supporters, Portugal would quickly again lift up her head among the kingdoms of Europe." Antonio bowed, in acknowledgment of the compliment, which he valued exactly at what it was worth. "But tell me, my friend, what information have you collected lately?" added the Minister, speaking quickly.

"I have seen much, and guessed more, please your Excellency," answered Antonio. "In the first place, the duke returned suddenly to Lisbon, and has since then renewed his acquaintance with various families with whom he was formerly at enmity. Now, a man does not do so unless he is about to repent of his sins, or, far more probably, unless he is about some mischief. Then, Senhor Policarpio has been running about in all directions, like his master, making friends with those whom he never before deigned to address; though he is insolent enough to many over whom he dares to tyrannise. The duke also constantly receives visits from that mad Jesuit Malagrida, a professed enemy of your Excellency, and from many others openly disaffected to your government; but I have brought here a list of all those who have visited the duke; and here is another, containing the names of those with whom he has had communication at other places, as far as I can learn." Saying which, he handed two papers to the Minister, adding, "With these your Excellency will be able to form a better opinion than I can venture to offer."

"Ah!" exclaimed the Minister, taking the papers eagerly, and running his eye over their contents. "Beware, my lord duke, or you will soon, methinks, be in my power; and we shall then see if you dare to scorn the lowly commoner. I see his aims," he continued, half speaking to himself. "He hopes to gain our sovereign's ear, and then, with an army of parasites, to hurl me to destruction; but I am prepared for his machinations, and ere long he shall feel so. I must break the pride of these arrogant fidalgos, or they will lord it over the king himself,—

base wretches, whose whole being is composed of avarice and the most sordid selfishness, without valour, honour, or patriotism,—who care not for the fate of their country, so that they can undisturbedly enjoy their own luxuries. Ah, miscreants! I will overwhelm you when you little expect it!" Suddenly stopping in his soliloquy, he seemed to recollect that another person was present, and turning to Antonio, he again addressed him. "The information you bring me is valuable, my friend; but there is much yet to be learned. Continue constant to your purpose, and you shall be rewarded highly: in the meantime, take this purse. You have earned it well."

Antonio stretched not out his hand to clutch the gold, as many would have done; but, unconsciously drawing himself up, he replied, "No, senhor; pardon me, I seek not such reward. Freely, and of my own accord, I have served you, and no gold would repay me for the days of watching and drudgery I have for this purpose undergone. Because the blood of Abraham flows in my veins, think not that I must needs be avaricious. When I was in want of money, you gave it me; if I require more, I will ask it; but such is not the recompense I seek. When the time comes, I will demand my reward, and it will be such alone as you in justice will be bound to grant."

Carvalho gazed at the speaker earnestly. "You have a soul above your class, and deserve a higher destiny," he said.

"I may not be what I appear to the world, nor seek I a higher destiny than is my lot," returned Antonio. "If I have your Excellency's permission, I will depart."

"You are at liberty; I will detain you no longer," said Carvalho. "Adeos, my friend."

Antonio bowed low to the Minister, who retired to his inner chamber; while, as he found his way, unquestioned into the street, he whispered to himself, "He will serve my purpose."

Volume Two—Chapter Two.

We find ourselves so constantly recurring to Don Luis d'Almeida, that we begin to fear our readers, particularly the fairer portion of them, will soon get heartily tired of hearing so much about him; and, therefore, to please them, we would, were we composing a mere story from our own brain, effectually get rid of him, by carrying him into a dark forest at midnight, amid a storm of thunder and lightning, when a hundred brigands should rush upon him from their lurking places, and plunge their daggers into his bosom; but that, by so doing, we should infringe the plan on which we have determined, to adhere strictly to the truth of history. We do not, however, feel ourselves called upon to describe minutely the events of each day, and we will, therefore, pass over rather more than a week, which he had spent in his father's society, when, towards the evening, he was seated, in a listless humour, with a book in his hand, on a stone terrace, overlooking a garden, stretched out below it. But his eyes seemed to glance much less frequently at the pages before him, than at the pure blue sky, or the bright parterres of flowers, the sparkling fountains, the primly cut box trees, and the long straight walks; though, even then, it seemed that his eye was less occupied than his mental vision. But we need not inquire what were his thoughts; perhaps, they were of the scenes he had witnessed in his travels; perhaps of Theresa's falsehood; and there is a possibility of their having been of the fair portrait he had so quickly taken of Donna Clara.—A servant suddenly recalled him to the present moment, by informing him that a holy friar, waiting at the gate, begged earnestly to see him on some matter of importance.

"I will speak to him," he exclaimed, rising; and, throwing down his book, he took his way towards the gate. He there perceived a figure in the monastic habit, walking slowly up and down, and, turning his head with a cautious look in every direction; and, as the person approached, he was not long in distinguishing the features of the friar who had played so very suspicious a part at the inn.

"Ah, my young friend," exclaimed that worthy personage, with the greatest effrontery; "I have not, you see, forgotten either you, or your requests. It struck me, that you very much wished to possess the jewels you spoke of, so, from the strong desire I felt to serve you, I exerted myself diligently to procure them for you. I hope that you have not forgotten your part of the contract; for, though I should myself require no reward, yet I was obliged to pay various sums to the persons who held the property."

"I perfectly appreciate your feelings, reverend Father," returned Don Luis. "Nor have I forgotten my promise. Where are the jewels?"

"I have not been able to bring them with me, my son, for weighty reasons; but where are the hundred milreas? for though that sum is not a quarter of their real value, the gentlemen who had appropriated them have a predilection for hard cash."

Don Luis had good reasons for suspecting that the friar was deceiving him, as he answered, "The money shall be forthcoming when you show me the jewels; but, under the circumstances of the case, you can scarcely expect me to pay you beforehand."

"Why, I confess that you have seen me in rather suspicious company, senhor; but yet it is cruel to doubt the honesty of an humble friar. To convince you of my sincerity, I have brought this ring, which I believe belonged to the young lady you said had been robbed by those rascally banditti."

Don Luis took the ring which the friar offered. "This, Senhor Frade, is but a small portion of the trinkets I expected. It was for the recovery of the casket I promised you the reward."

"I am aware of that, senhor; but I wish to show you that, though you doubt me, I put every confidence in your honour; and, if you were not so impatient, I would deliver the proposal which I came here to make. In the first place, I beg you will keep that ring, as an earnest of my sincerity; and, if you will trust me with the money, I will return with the casket; but if not, the only way by which you can recover it, is to follow my directions."

Don Luis considered a moment; but there was such a roguish glance in the twinkle of the friar's eye, that he thought it would be folly to trust him, and that he should probably neither see the casket nor his money again, though he would willingly have risked a far larger sum for the sake of recovering the jewels. Yet he wished first to hear what the friar had to propose.

"I see how it is," said the Friar, laughing. "You think me a rogue in grain, so there is no use concealing the matter; but I am not offended, I assure you. Other people have thought me so too, who knew me better than you do, till they found out their mistake, as you will some day: however, if you had trusted me, you might have saved yourself considerable trouble."

"Well, well, Father," interrupted Don Luis, getting rather impatient at all this circumlocution, "let me hear your proposition, and then I shall be able to determine how to act."

"You must know, then, my young friend, that this precious casket, which you are so anxious to gain, is in the possession of a very holy and pious man, an aged hermit, whose food is the roots of the earth, or the nuts from the trees, and his drink the pure water from the brook," began the Friar, speaking very slowly, and eyeing Don Luis, with a laughing glance. "And thus it befell, that this holy man became possessed of the casket. You know a hill, which stands about two leagues from hence, on the summit of which is a chapel dedicated to our Lady of the Rock?"

"Yes, yes," answered Don Luis, rather impatiently, and vexed at the friar's evident intention of putting his temper to the proof, "I have often been there in my boyhood; but pray proceed with your story, if you intend it to lead to anything satisfactory."

"Of course I do, my young friend," answered the Friar. "I was going to tell you where the holy man resides, when you interrupted me. You must know, then, that beneath the hill on which the chapel stands, there is a cave, which has of late years been cleared from the rubbish which formerly blocked it up, and has been converted into a very tolerable habitation for the summer months, during which period this holy man is constantly there to be found, as he is at present, or was when I was there last, attending to the duties of the sacred edifice above. His great sanctity, his prayers, and fastings, have on many occasions been found to be of the greatest service, both in replenishing his pockets, and in restoring those to health who have consulted him; but his great forte is in saying masses for the souls of the departed, which have double the efficacy of those of any other religious person, as he constantly affirms, and no one can disprove, nor does any one dream of disputing the word of so holy a man. I am now, senhor, approaching the point which is of more consequence to you. You must know that the comrades of the men, whom, as I am told, you killed in the forest, when they attacked the fidalgo Gonçalo Christovaö, were tolerably well aware that they had a considerable share of unrepented crimes on their consciences; and that, consequently, their stay in purgatory would be of rather long duration, unless great exertions were made to get them clear of it. Now, most of them having a fellow-feeling for their unfortunate friends, turned it in their minds how they could best contrive to shorten their residence in that very unpleasant abode; and, at last, it was agreed that they should engage the holy man I speak of, and of whom they had all heard, to say as many masses as half the booty they had taken would supply, at the lowest possible rate; for which purpose, they laid aside the very casket you are in search of. Now, it chanced that I was paying a visit to this holy man, who, I am proud to say, is a friend of mine; and he showed me the casket, begging me to estimate its value, that he might know how many masses he ought to say. I no sooner beheld it, than I at once recollected your request; so I told him that, though in Lisbon it might be sold for a larger sum, yet he would here be very fortunate if he succeeded in receiving a hundred milreas for it, particularly as I suspected it was stolen property; for which sum he might say fully sufficient masses to get the souls of the departed rogues quietly domesticated in the realms of Paradise. He agreed with me, that, if it did not, it must be their own fault, for being so desperately wicked, so that there could be no help for them. I then told him, that if he would let me have the casket, I would return with the money for it; but it is very extraordinary, senhor, that he objected to do so,—not, of course, that he could have any doubts about my honesty, but that the happiness of the souls in purgatory would be at stake, if, by any chance, it was lost. I had no arguments to offer to his objections, so I was obliged to give up the point; and I hastened here to inform you of the discovery I had made, that I might either return with the money, or allow you to go and fetch the casket yourself. If you still persist in so unjustly distrusting me, senhor, if you will visit our Lady of the Rock early to-morrow morning, you will there find the holy man performing mass. Wait till it is over, and the people have departed,— for the fame of his sanctity has collected many worshippers there,— follow him to his cave, without speaking; when, if you produce the money, he will restore the casket to you; then, without staying to inquire further, return home. If, however, you will allow me to advise you as a friend, add twenty milreas or so to the amount, to increase the number of masses; for you must remember that it was by your hand the men fell, though I do not mean to say that it was not their own fault; but it will be charity well bestowed, as I fear they were wretched sinners, and, do all we can, they must remain in purgatory a long time."

Don Luis listened to this long story with considerable doubts as to the truth of the greater part of it, yet it was so in accordance with the ideas and customs of the times, that he could not altogether discredit it; he therefore answered, "I must thank you, Senhor Frade, for the trouble you have taken in my service; and I beg you to inform your holy friend that I will repair to his hermitage to-morrow morning, and will take the amount agreed on to release the jewels."

"Then you will not trust me with the money, senhor?" said the Friar, smiling. "Patience—I am not easily offended, and take it all in good part; but do not forget the additional twenty milreas; and if you happen to have a little spare cash about you to bestow on an humble and indigent servant of the Church, I shall be thankful, and will not forget you in my prayers; for I have come a long distance to serve you, and have put more trust in your honour than you seem inclined to place in mine."

"I will pay you for the ring, Senhor Frade," said Don Luis, who could not help being amused at the imperturbable impudence of the friar; "though you seem to forget certain incidents which occurred at the inn, on my journey here,—not to mention others on the previous day."

"Now, now, you ought not to rake up old grievances," answered the Friar. "It is not charitable; and charity is the first of Christian virtues, you well know. Besides, you cannot deny that I have served you faithfully."

"I will not refuse you," said Don Luis, bestowing all the silver he had about him, "you argue so logically to gain your point. I trust that you will not play me false."

"Confide in the honour of a Capuchin," said the Friar, putting his hand to his heart. "May we meet again under happier auspices than those by which we became acquainted; and, believe me, I am grateful for your bounty. Adeos, senhor! It is growing dark, and I have a long way to go before I rest; but an humble friar has nought to fear."

"Farewell, my friend!" said Don Luis. "I certainly have met none like you."

"Oh, you flatter—you flatter," was the answer. "Do not, however, forget your friend. Diogo Lopez is my name,—an humble one at present; but it may become some day well-known to the world. Adeos, adeos, senhor!"

Don Luis, without further parley, re-entered the Quinta, and, for some minutes, he fancied that he could hear the quiet chuckle of the friar echoing in his ears.

Early the next morning he ordered his horse, telling Pedro whither he was going; and, putting his pistols in his holsters, with his sword by his side,—for in those days nobody ever thought of riding, forth unarmed,—he set off for the chapel of our Lady of the Rock,—not forgetting the hundred milreas to redeem the casket, to which he added twenty more, to be expended for the benefit of the souls of those miserable men to whose deaths he had certainly contributed, though he in no way blamed himself on that account. It must be remembered that he had been brought up in a strict belief of the religion of his country; nor had he in any way learned to doubt the main points of that faith in which all those dear to him confided; so that he had full confidence in the efficacy of prayer for the souls of departed sinners; nor do we wish to dispute the point with those who profess the same creed.

The road he was obliged to take, scarcely deserving the name of one, was so broken, and cut up into deep ruts, and covered with loose stones, that nearly an hour elapsed before he reached the foot of the little rocky hill on which the chapel stood. There, perceiving a lad sitting on the top of a wall, "whistling for want of thought," and without any occupation, he called to him, and bade him hold his horse, with the promise of a reward, while he climbed up the winding rugged path to the top of the rock. It was an isolated height, rising far above all the neighbouring hills,—thus commanding an extensive view on every side. The little chapel was built on the highest point, with a rude stone cross in front, and surmounted by five tall pine trees, their taper stems bent by the blasts to which they were exposed, without a branch below their broad, ever-verdant heads. The chapel was a rough building, of merely two gable ends, and a small porch in front, facing the west; but the view fully repaid the trouble of mounting the hill, even had he come without an object. To the south, over an undulating country, covered with fields and pine-groves, he could distinguish his father's house and estates; on the west, in the furthest point in the horizon, was to be seen a thin bright line of blue, indicating the presence of the boundless ocean; while on the north appeared the heights of Coimbra, covered with its colleges, monasteries, and churches, below which ran the placid stream of the Mondego, on whose willow-covered banks once wept, with tears of anguish, the lovely and ill-fated Ines de Castro, for ever celebrated in the immortal song of Camoens. On the east, again, over a wide sea of pine-forest, which, indeed, extended on every side of the rock, rose hill upon hill, and mountain upon mountain, till the furthest ridges were lost in a blue haze.

Don Luis entered the chapel, which was, as the friar told him it would be, filled with country people, some beating their breasts, others kissing the ground, and licking up the dust, and the rest rapt in an ecstasy of devotion; while the little altar glittered with lighted tapers. The walls of the edifice were hung with offerings from the pious;

among which were seen, carved in wax, what were intended to be representations of the arms, legs, feet, or hands of the human body, those members having been cured by the miraculous interposition of our Lady of the Rock, and the prayers of the holy hermit; these falling to her share, while he appropriated whatever was offered in the shape of money, observing, that such could be of no possible use to our Lady, who was supplied with all she could require. There were also pictures of her appearance in the bodily form, to comfort and assure her devout worshippers. A priest, whose features Luis could not distinguish, further than that he was an aged man, with a long flowing white beard over his breast, clothed in his vestments, was performing the ceremony of mass. It was, however, nearly completed; so, having knelt down, and offered up a short prayer, he again retired, to wait till the people had departed, in order to follow the priest to his cave, as he had agreed. While he was standing and gazing at the lovely view, he heard a groaning near him, and, turning round, he beheld a sight which might have caused a smile on his lips, had he not rather pitied the unfortunate sufferers. There were two old women, who appeared to have started together in a race, on their unprotected knees, in which they were endeavouring to make a certain number of circuits round the chapel, each strenuously trying to get as close to the walls as possible, to save her distance. A strong, sturdy-looking fellow soon after came out, and commenced the same penance; but he very soon distanced his aged competitors for absolution, quickly performing his rounds, at the same time vehemently beating his breast. Perhaps his knees were hardened by habitual kneeling in devotion; but Luis observed a most suspicious thickness about them, which might have been caused by their recent swelling, or he might have taken the precaution to pad them, suspecting to what his sins would condemn him. He, however, gained the credit of zealous penitence.

Before this ceremony was quite completed, the rest of the congregation came out of the chapel, and among them was a man whom Don Luis caught eyeing him very narrowly, but, the moment the man saw that he was observed, he disappeared hastily down the hill. Don Luis, therefore, concluded that he was merely astonished at seeing a gentleman there at that early hour of the morning. He had some time longer to wait before all the people had quitted the hill, when, as he was still admiring the view before him, he heard a slight noise, and his name whispered, and, on turning round, he saw the priest who had officiated at the chapel descending the rock by a steep path on the opposite side to that which his congregation had taken. Luis directly followed him, when he saw a signal for him to do so; but so quickly did the venerable person descend, that he could scarcely keep him in view without danger of breaking his neck, from his ignorance of the stepping-stones in the side of the hill, with which his guide, from his unhesitating pace, seemed perfectly familiar. He had proceeded about three-quarters of the way, and had yet some of the most precipitous part of the descent to make, when he perceived the priest, who had reached the bottom, after looking cautiously around, proceed a few paces at the base of the rock, and, again repeating his signal, disappear beneath an overhanging cliff. As soon as Luis had likewise reached the bottom, he followed the same course; when, as he was passing under the cliff, he again heard his name called by a voice which seemed to proceed from the bowels of the earth, and, looking earnestly in that direction, perceived a small cavity in the side of the rock, but so shrouded by brushwood, that he might easily have passed it several times had it not been particularly called to his notice.

"Enter, my son, and fear not," said the voice: "nought but what is holy is here to be found."

Luis, putting aside the boughs which grew across the entrance, and stooping low to avoid striking his head against the rugged arch which formed it, entered the cave; but, on first leaving the bright glare of sunshine, his eyes were so oppressed by the darkness, that he could not venture to advance, until suddenly a small flickering light appeared before him, sufficient, however, to show him that he stood in a naturally vaulted chamber, or rather passage, in which he might stand perfectly upright, of some twelve feet in width, but of a length it was impossible to determine, the sides of the jagged and unhewn rock, and the floor, being covered with soft fine sand. In vain did his sight seek to pierce beyond the twinkling light, but it served to guide his footsteps, when it seemed to be in motion, and approaching him. He now saw the venerable figure of the hermit standing a short way up the cave, with snowy beard, the hair round his shaven crown and his eyebrows being of the same silvery hue. In his hand was a small taper, which he held before him.

"What seekest thou of me, my son?" he uttered, in the same low tones Luis had before heard. "If it is aught which my prayers can be of service to gain for thee, they shall, without intermission, be offered up."

"In this case your prayers are not required, most reverend hermit," returned Don Luis. "I understand that you have in your possession a casket of jewels which you are willing to deliver to me for a certain recompense."

"It is the truth, my son. I have a casket, about which I was yesterday speaking to that most holy and devout brother, the friar Diogo Lopez, a man in whom the gifts of Divine grace shine most conspicuously, my most particular and esteemed friend, yet one whose fair fame the tongue of calumny has dared to slander; who has been accused of consorting with robbers and evil-doers, even to sharing in the profits of their mal-practices. Oft has he come to me, with tears in his eyes, mourning his hard fate; and, in the hopes of gaining the favour of Heaven to clear his fame, has he flagellated his back with the cord of repentance, till the blood has flowed in torrents to the ground. Oh! brother Diogo is truly a righteous man!"

"Your pardon, Father! I came to inquire for a casket of jewels, and not to discuss the character of Frè Diogo; about which the less said in his praise the smaller will be the chance of his actions contradicting your words," answered Luis.

"You are severe, my son, you are severe on brother Diogo. But about the jewels; now you recall the circumstance to my mind, I do recollect that he told me that a young and estimable friend of his was anxious to obtain them; and that he was to come here this morning, with a hundred and fifty milreas, which he was willing to give for them, besides thirty more which he was anxious to offer for masses to be said for the souls of certain unfortunate men who were killed a few days ago."

"You are under a slight error with regard to the amount of the sum I promised your respectable friend; but the hundred milreas I will give when you deliver the casket, and I will, beyond that, offer twenty more to be expended in masses."

"That is acting like a true fidalgo," answered the Hermit; "and I feel assured that the souls of the brigands will be highly obliged to you. Of course, I must have been mistaken with regard to the additional fifty milreas; but age has somewhat impaired my memory, and I cannot doubt the word of so honourable a gentleman. As you may, perhaps, be anxious to gain possession of these same jewels, if you will follow me to the head of the cave, you will find the casket on a little stone altar; there deposit the money, with any further trifling donation you, in your generosity, may be inclined to offer, take up the casket, and depart in peace. With the casket you will find a sealed packet, to whom directed I know not, never having been instructed in the profane art of reading a written hand; my breviary, and the lives of the saints, having occupied my whole attention. It was found within the casket; but being of no value to those who found it there, they honestly gave it to me, and I restore it to you. Follow me, my son."

Having thus spoken, the hermit proceeded up the cave for several yards, when he suddenly stopped and placed the taper in a socket on the little altar he spoke of; but by the time Luis had reached the spot he had disappeared. Luis looked around in every direction, but it was impossible to pierce the surrounding gloom, the faint rays of the taper not extending to the sides of the cavern, by which he concluded it must have considerably increased in size; so that the holy man was yet watching him at no great distance, though himself invisible. The taper cast its light on the surface of the altar, and on a small stone cross, rudely carved, which surmounted it, a few rays alone throwing a faint gleam on the roof above, from which hung down long and transparent stalactites, the floor being here moist and slippery; indeed, a light murmuring sound gave notice that a spring ran through this part of the cavern. Two small steps conducted him to the altar, when he found that the hermit had not deceived him, for there were the casket and the packet. He opened the former, and letting the light of the candle fall on the interior, it displayed a glittering collection of various trinkets, such as were then worn by ladies; closing the case, he placed it securely about his person, and then examined the superscription on the packet. It was in a delicate female handwriting, and directed thus:—"To Gonçalo Christovaö." Luis secured that also carefully in his bosom; and then, placing on the spot from which he had taken them three separate parcels of money,—two of the amount promised, and another of ten milreas intended for the hermit himself, the very great holiness of whose character he could not, however, help doubting,—he was about to take the taper from the altar, with the intention of finding his way to the month of the cave.—"Hold! impious man!" exclaimed the voice of the Hermit; though, from what quarter it came it was impossible to tell. "Take thy sacrilegious hands from off that candle, which must remain till I have counted thy gifts. Retire the way by which you came."

Don Luis, though not particularly well pleased at this address, thought it would be of no avail either to answer or to disobey the order; and accordingly endeavoured so to direct his course as to reach the entrance of the cavern, hoping soon to see the light of day streaming in from the opening in the rock. Holding his sword in its scabbard before him, to prevent himself from running suddenly against the side of the cave, should he miss the right course, he slowly groped his way onward, but had not advanced far when he found the value of his precaution by its striking against the rock. He looked round, intending to take a fresh departure from the light, when he found that it had been extinguished, and that he was in utter darkness. He now felt convinced that some trick was being played off against him, at the bottom of which he strongly suspected was the holy Frè Diogo; though, had robbery been intended, it might have been committed at once, without delivering the casket or packet. It must be confessed that he was in a very disagreeable position; shut up in a dark cavern, and, for aught he could tell to the contrary, surrounded by robbers, or, at the best, in the power of some daring impostors. He was inclined, as well he might be, to be very angry; but he knew that losing his temper would not at all aid him to get out of the trap; besides, utter darkness, such as surrounded him, has generally a very soothing effect on the mind. The ground on which he stood was still hard and damp, so that he knew he could not yet have reached the passage by which he entered, and for some moments he could not resolve to proceed, fearful of becoming more confused, and of perhaps falling into some deep cavity, through which the water he heard must find its way. He determined, however, if violence was intended, not to be taken without a stroke for life; silently, therefore, drawing his sword, he grasped it firmly in his right hand, while with the scabbard he felt around on his left side. He fancied that he could hear the breathing of some one near him, but, as he swept his sword round, it met nought but the empty air. Now Luis was, as he had often proved, possessed of as much of that quality called courage as most men; but there are many who will face danger without shrinking in open daylight, and when they see and know the strength of their foe, who would feel very uncomfortable when shut up in the dark, and not at all knowing what to expect, which was exactly his case at present. His patience, also, was quickly worn out. "I beg, most holy hermit, that you will not consider me like a mole, with eyes to see, or claws to work my way out of this cave; but, as I am anxious to return home, that you will throw a light upon my path to enable me to do so," he exclaimed, with some degree of anger in his tone.

"Turn, then, to the left as you face the rock, and you will soon see the bright light which shines on all men alike, the light of day;" said a voice at some little distance.

"If he does, he will plunge into the deep hole through which the stream flows; his feet are close to it already," answered another voice.

"Then he is not where I thought he was," said the first; "but let him turn to the right then, and he will be free."

"I beg you will finish this mummery," exclaimed Don Luis, "and show me the way out of this place."

"Beware that you utter no blasphemy," said the voice. "Now, look more earnestly, and you will behold the light before you."

At that moment a small flame burst forth, towards which he immediately advanced, and found himself treading on the soft sand in the narrow passage. The light was again extinguished, but in its stead he saw, at some distance, the sunshine gleaming through the mouth of the cavern. Glad to escape from the place, he was hurrying towards it, when a loud noise resounded through the rocky vault, and he found himself again in complete darkness, and could distinctly hear a suppressed chuckle of laughter.

This was trying his patience too much. "Whether saint or devil," he exclaimed, "let me go free from your abode."

"Blaspheme not, my son," answered the voice; "but your temper shall no longer be tried; only, remember in future to cast no reflections on the character of my esteemed friend, the holy Frè Diogo;" and a loud peal of laughter resounded through the vault, whose echoes had no sooner died away, than a door he had not before perceived was thrown open, and the sunshine again streamed in, when he saw, standing on one side, the venerable form of the hermit.

"Farewell, my son," said the latter personage. "My devotions have been sadly disturbed by sounds of unwonted merriment, in which the spirits of darkness have indulged, even as they did in the hermitage of the most holy Saint Anthony. Ah! I see you were prepared to combat with the weapons of carnal warfare; but those avail not against the inhabitants of the infernal regions. 'Twas with his crosier and breviary, not to mention the pair of red-hot tongs, that the great saint put to flight the Prince of Darkness; and such are the weapons with which I fight. I will detain you no longer: again, farewell, my son. Your shortest way home is to mount the path by which you came here, and to descend on the other side of the hill. Above all things, do not speak ill of the holy Frè Diogo."

"Farewell, most holy hermit," answered Luis; "though, I suspect, if you allow such proceedings in your hermitage, its character for sanctity will be somewhat damaged."

"No fear of that, my son," said the venerable personage; "there is no character in the world so quickly gained, or so easily maintained, as that of sanctity, which is the reason so many people assume it who have lost all claim to any other. Remember that, my son, for I have full cause to know the truth of what I say. Now Heaven speed you, for you are a good youth!"

With these words, the hermit retired into the recesses of the cave, and Luis issued into the open air. As advised, he climbed up the hill by the steep path he had descended, which he found far less difficulty in doing; and crossing to the other side, he was happy to perceive his horse quietly grazing in a field below, somewhat impeded in the operation by the bit in his mouth, while the boy had gone to sleep by his side, wondering when the fidalgo would return.

Luis roused the boy, and gave him a piece of silver, probably a larger amount than he had ever before possessed, while he threw the reins over his horse's neck and prepared to mount. The lad's eyes glistened with delight, and in a moment he appeared to be brisk and intelligent enough. "A thousand thanks, for your charity to a poor lad, senhor," he said; "and I have something to tell you. Some time after you were gone away, while I was lying down on the grass, thinking of going to sleep, some strange men came up to your horse, and, without saying a word, took your pistols out of the holsters, threw out the priming, and returned them quickly back again. They looked so fierce, that I was afraid to say anything; so I snored away, pretending to be fast asleep, and the men directly afterwards went away; but I forgot all about it till you gave me the piece of silver."

Luis immediately examined his pistols, and found that they had been tampered with; then, carefully reloading them, and giving the boy another piece of money for his information, he mounted his horse, and regained the road, and had just done so when he saw a horseman galloping along to meet him, in whom he was by no means sorry to recognise his servant Pedro.

"Oh, senhor!" exclaimed the honest fellow, when he came up to him, "I am delighted to see you safe and sound; for my mind misgave me, ever since you told me you were going to meet an acquaintance of that rascally friar;—Heaven forgive me if I wrong him;—so at last I determined to take a horse and follow you; but now I have found you, it is all right, and I hope you will forgive me my fears for your safety."

While Pedro was speaking, their path was leading them a little way round the base of the hill; and before his master had time to answer, several men sprung out from behind some large rocks, which lay scattered around, and seizing their bridles, attempted to drag them from their horses. Pedro, who was armed only with a thick stick, laid about him most manfully, keeping the robbers, for such they appeared to be, at bay; and Don Luis drew a pistol from his holster, threatening to shoot the man nearest him; but the fellow only laughed, daring him to fire, which he immediately did, and the man dropped. Upon this, the others, undaunted, rushed on him with loud cries of vengeance, and before he could draw his sword or use his other pistol, they grasped him by the arms, dragging him from his horse to the ground. Pedro fought on some time longer, proving that a good oak stick in the hand is better than a sword by the side, and had very nearly succeeded in rescuing his master, when the robbers, fearing that such would be the case, made a rush on him all together, and pinioned his arms behind him.

The report of Don Luis's pistol had, at this juncture of affairs, called another actor on the scene, whom Pedro, at all events, did not expect to find in the character of a friend. This personage was no other than the worthy Frè Diogo, who was seen rushing down the hill, flourishing a cudgel very similar to the one he had used with such effect in their service at the inn, and shouting at the top of his voice, "Off, off you rascals! Is this the way you dare to treat my friends?"

He was quickly on the spot, dealing his blows with no gentle force on every side, soon emancipating Pedro from thraldom, and driving off those who held Don Luis. "How dare you, ye villains, attack a friend of mine, who came to visit me, with my word pledged for his security?" he cried. "I hope, senhor, you are not injured. Well, then, it does not matter, and I see you have punished one of them. Pick up that fellow, and away with you; for I see he's more frightened than hurt."

The men sulkily obeyed, raising their fallen comrade, who proved to be only stunned, the pistol ball having merely grazed his head.

So quickly had these incidents occurred, that Don Luis had scarcely time to speak before he found himself again at liberty; and when he turned to thank his deliverer, he could not help being amused at his appearance. The dark robes, the rim of carroty hair, and the red eyes were there; but above the eyes were a pair of thick, bushy, white eyebrows. "The venerable hermit!" he exclaimed.

"What, senhor, have you found me out?" said Frè Diogo, laughing. "Well, don't betray me, or you will injure my character for sanctity, and 'tis the last thing I have now to depend on."

"I should be ungrateful for the service you have just now afforded me," answered Don Luis. "Though, for your own sake, my friend, I wish it were more justly established."

"Oh! that is a trifle, senhor,—I mean, the service I have done you," said the Friar. "What do you stand gaping there for, you rogues? Off with you," he shouted to the robbers, who still stood at some little distance, while Luis and his servant mounted their horses.

"Come, Senhor Frade, pay us for our work, then," answered one of the men. "We came to rob this young fidalgo by your orders, and we won't, go back empty-handed."

"Oh, you villains! you will ruin my character if you talk thus;—that was to be if the young fidalgo was not charitable; but he has won my heart; and remember, the man who injures him is my enemy. However, here is more than you deserve," and he flung them the ten milreas Luis had left for the hermit, on which each of the men made him a low bow, and hurried away. Nothing abashed, he again turned to Don Luis. "You see, senhor, the truth of the saying exemplified, that charity brings its own reward. Now, if you had not been charitable, I confess the temptation to rob you was very great; but when I found the amount of your offering, I repented, and, as you see, came to rescue you. If you have a trifle about you, you can repay me at once;—well, never mind, if you have not; another time will do;—but don't say a Capuchin is ungrateful, that's all. Now, farewell, senhor; we shall meet again, I doubt not. You will not betray me, I know; and I am sure Senhor Pedro there will not, for he is an honest fellow; and if he does, I shall break his head some time or other. You had better make the best of your way home, and not encounter those men, as they have not the same feelings of honour that I have. Now, don't answer;—I know what you would say, that I am a rogue in grain; but it cannot be helped... Adeos, senhor."

Without waiting for an answer to this specimen of consummate impudence, which, indeed, Don Luis would have had some difficulty in making, he again began to mount the hill, indulging in a loud chuckle as he went. Don Luis and Pedro, however, followed his advice, though they could not admire his principles.

"That friar seems to be a very great rogue, senhor," said Pedro, as they rode home.

"Not much greater, I suspect, than many others," answered his master; "only he certainly does not take much pains to conceal it."

We must apologise to our readers for occupying so much of their time with this rather unromantic adventure of Don Luis's, and hope that his character will not have been injured in their estimation by it.

He remained some weeks longer under his father's roof, without any very important event occurring to him; and, in the mean time, we must beg leave to fly back again to Lisbon.

Volume Two—Chapter Three.

We find it chronicled in history, that, either on the 10th or 20th of October, for the figures are nearly obliterated in the manuscript before us, AD 1754, their Majesties of Portugal held a Beja Mao, or what is in England styled a drawing-room, at which all the first fidalgos and nobles of the land were expected to attend. The palace the royal family then inhabited was very different to the one in which their august successors now reside; not one stone of the former remaining upon another to mark the spot where that proud building stood, every vestige having been obliterated by that relentless and fell destroyer the earthquake, and by the devouring flames it caused. It was situated more in the centre of the city, in no way to be compared as a structure to the present edifice, which, were it but finished, would be remarkable for its grandeur and beauty; but, alas! it stands a monument of high aims and vast ideas, but of feeble and unenergetic execution. But we are talking of the old palace, which was, however, a considerable building of highly-wrought stone work, the interior being richly decorated with painted ceilings and walls, with gilt mouldings, costly hangings of crimson damask and brocade, tables of silver inlaid with jewels, besides tapestry and silks in profusion, and many other valuable articles too numerous to describe.

Although so late in the year, the heats of summer were not abated; and though for many weeks past the sun had constantly been obscured by dark and unaccountable vapours, it at times broke forth with even greater force than usual, as it did on the morning of which we speak, upon the heads of a vast throng collected in front of the palace, to witness the nobles alighting from their carriages of state. And, truly, the carriages of that day in Portugal were very remarkable vehicles, such as would most certainly collect a crowd, were they to make their reappearance in any country in Christendom. They were huge lumbering affairs, the arms of their noble owners being emblazoned on every part, painted in the brightest and most glaring colours; but, as nothing superior had ever been seen in the country, the people thought them very magnificent, and the more they were covered with paint and gold, the warmer were the praises bestowed upon them; indeed, it may strongly be suspected, that if a modern equipage, with its simple elegance and strength alone to recommend it, had appeared, it would have been scouted as not worthy of notice, so generally are true merit and beauty disregarded by the undiscriminating eye of the vulgar.

Those being the days when bag-wigs and swords were in general use, the courtiers did not afford so much amusement to the spectators as they do in front of St. James's Palace; the Portuguese Court having, with more taste, changed according to the fashion of the times, not requiring all loyal subjects, who are anxious to pay their respects to their sovereign, to make themselves ridiculous, by appearing habited in the antiquated and ill-fashioned suits of their grandfathers. There would be some sense in masquerading, if every gentleman were obliged to dress in the rich and elegant costume of the age of Henry the Eighth, or Elizabeth; and it would also have the beneficial effect of keeping away a vast number of penniless plebeians, who, on the day of each drawing-room and levée, crowd the royal antechambers, to the great injury of the ladies' dresses and the amusement of the nobles and officers. But we are describing Portugal, and ought not to be talking of England, and its many amusing follies and prejudices.

A guard of honour was drawn up in front of the palace; but their presence was scarcely required to keep the peace, for there was no shouting or disturbance of any sort. The young nobles were more reputably employed than usual, being decked in their gala attire, attending on their sovereigns,—the chief use for which they were created, though they seem to forget it; while the people, untaught by the patriotism of demagogues, to exhibit the liberty and independence of man on every public occasion, by causing annoyance to the other half of the community, as has been so successfully done in the present century, remained quiet spectators of the scene.

We must now proceed to the interior of the palace, which was crowded with the usual number of guards, pages, and attendants of various descriptions. Two of the ministers of the crown had already arrived, and paid their respects; the foreign ambassadors followed, taking their allotted places in the handsome saloon in which the Court was held, where also stood the different members of the royal family, arranged on each side of the sovereigns. The King had just attained his fortieth year, and was of good height, and that free carriage, which a consciousness of rank and power rarely fails to bestow; but his features were far from handsome, with no approach to intellectuality about them, though there was just that degree of acuteness and firmness which taught him to select and protect the only man in his realm capable of rescuing the country from complete destruction. The Queen had but few personal charms to boast of, being destitute also of those soft feminine graces which are so often found to make ample amends for the more evanescent quality of beauty. A haughty expression sat on her lips; her thin and erect figure was rather above the middle height, the inclination she made as her subjects passed before her being stiff and formal. Near the King stood the Infante Dom Pedro, silent, grave, and stern, his features dark and unprepossessing, a true index of his character, which was bigoted, fierce, irascible, and sanguinary. Though in no way attached to his sister-in-law, the Queen, he cordially joined with her in her hatred of the Minister Carvalho, against whom he never ceased his machinations; and though his plots were discovered and defeated by the vigilance of the latter, it was more owing to his brother's clemency and goodness of heart, than to any forbearance on the part of his enemy, that he escaped the condign punishment he so well merited at their hands. Near the Queen stood the young Infanta Donna Maria, a princess equally prepossessing in appearance and manner, her eyes beaming with mildness and intelligence, and a sweet smile wreathing itself round lips which were never known to utter aught but words of gentleness. She truly dwelt in the hearts and affections of the people over whom she was destined to rule; and while to the rest of the royal family, lip-service, with the cold and formal bow, alone was paid, as the courtiers drew near her, the eye brightened, and the heart beat with those warm feelings of love and respect which are ever felt by the true and loyal subjects of her august descendant and namesake, of Portugal, and by all who surround the throne of the young and beloved Queen of Britain.

A drawing-room at the Portuguese Court, although formal and ceremonious, was not quite so tedious an affair as that to which the sovereign of England is obliged to submit; for none but nobles being admitted to that honour, fewer people were present. It was also the custom of the King and Queen to make some observations to those who came to pay their respects, a practice which would greatly relieve the monotony of the almost interminable line of bowing figures, who pass, like characters in a raree-show, before their Majesties of England.

The King was standing, as we have said, surrounded by the royal family, and the immediate attendants at the palace, the more public part of the ceremony not having yet commenced.

"Where is Senhor Carvalho?" he said, looking round; "he ought, methinks, to have been here before now; for it is not like him to exhibit any want of respect to our person. Can any one say why he comes not?"

"We have not seen him, please your Majesty," said one of Carvalho's colleagues in office; "though, doubtless, some affairs of your Majesty's detain him, for no business of his own could make a loyal subject forget his duty to his King; yet 'tis said that Senhor Carvalho spends his leisure time in a way some might consider derogatory to the high office he holds," he added, ever ready to throw a slur on the character of one he both hated and feared. Those words cost him dear.

"Ah! Senhor Carvalho is, doubtless, a most loyal subject, and devoted minister; but it is the interest of all political adventurers to appear so," chimed in the Queen; "and if his zeal were to be judged by his own protestations, he would assuredly be a paragon of perfection. But methinks your Majesty might find, among the pure, high-born fidalgos, some equally as zealous and able as this low pretender."

"No, no," answered the King, hastily. "Sebastiaö Carvalho is no pretender, but has truly at heart the weal of my kingdom, with a mind to conceive, and a soul to execute, great purposes; and where is there a man in Portugal to be compared to him, either in mental or personal qualities."

"In talents he is not deficient, as he has proved, by working himself into power, and of brute strength he possesses enough, certainly," observed a noble lord in waiting, who was privileged to say what he chose; "for I well remember, in one of his drunken fits, some years ago (I would rather not say how many) he broke my head, and nearly let out life itself, by what he called a gentle tap with his sword. As for talents, they were not discernible at College, at all events, except by the quantity of wine he could drink, and the daring impudence of his bearing among his superiors."

"Those are qualities in which plebeians most excel," added another; "but in loyalty and devotion to a generous sovereign, who can equal the noble fidalgos of the land? It is the one sentiment in which all combine."

"Perhaps he has first to pay his devotions at the shrine of his lady love," observed the Queen, with a sneer; "yet we women might excuse him if his gallantry surpassed his loyalty."

The King, never very ready with answers in conversation, found no words to defend his Minister, to whose powerful mind his own had already learned to yield, though he, as yet, neither loved him, nor put implicit trust in him: his power, therefore, was held but by a frail tenure, which the breath of malice might easily have destroyed. A few idle or bitter words frequently weaken that influence which it has been the toil of years in a statesman's life to gain; and such an opportunity as this, the numerous enemies of the rising Minister who surrounded the throne, were certain not to lose.

The courtiers now began to assemble, but the Minister came not.

Having taken a glance at the interior of the palace, we must return again to the streets in the neighbourhood, now thronged with carriages pressing forward to the one centre of attraction.

Our friend, Antonio, the cobbler, had given himself a holiday: not that he was going to Court, though, as he observed, many a less honest man, with a finer coat, might be there; but he was anxious to learn the opinions of people on affairs in general, and he knew that he should be able to pick up a good deal of information in the crowd, among whom he walked, dressed in his gala suit, unrecognised by any as Antonio O Remendao.

He was proceeding along a narrow street, at a short distance from the palace, when he saw approaching, the proud Duke of Aveiro, in his coach, which monopolised the greater part of the way, and slowly proceeded, at a state pace, in accordance with his dignity. A carriage, driven rapidly along, was endeavouring to pass the duke's conveyance; but his coachman, by swerving first on one side and then on the other, prevented it so doing.

"Make way there! make way for his Excellency Senhor Sebastiaö Jozé de Carvalho," shouted the driver of the hindermost carriage; but the other heeded not his words. "Make way there! make way; my master is late to present himself at Court, where his duty calls him, in which he will be impeded by no one," again cried the Minister's coachman.

"Heed not the base-born churl," exclaimed the Duke, from his carriage window. "Does he dare to insult me by presuming to pass my coach?"

The duke's anger increased as the Minister's coachman persisted in the attempt. "Keep in your proper station, wretch," he cried, forgetful of his own dignity, "or by Heavens I will slay you on the spot."

At that moment the carriages had reached a wider space in the street, where Antonio stood, so that the Minister's carriage was enabled to pass the duke's: as it did so, Carvalho looked from the window. "I wish not to insult you, my lord duke," he said; "but the driver of my carriage has my orders to hasten towards the palace, nor will I be disobeyed; regardless of the rank of those I may pass, my duty to my sovereign is above all other considerations." The last words were scarce heard as he drove by, while the the Duke shook his hand with fury.

The Cobbler laughed quietly to himself, as he beheld the scene. "What fools men are!" he muttered. "Now, that noble duke is enraged because a man who is in a hurry passes him while he is not; but he had better take care, and not enrage the Minister in return, or he will be like the man who put his head into the lion's mouth, and forgot to take it out again."

"Ah! does this bold plebeian dare to insult me to my very face?" exclaimed the Duke, as he watched the Minister's carriage; "but, ere long, I will be revenged, and nought but his blood shall wipe out the remembrance of his audacity. He dreams not of the punishment that awaits him. Ah! he shall be the first victim when I attain to power."

"Did your Excellency mark the look of proud derision he cast as he succeeded in passing your coach?" observed the sycophantish Captain Policarpio, who sat opposite to his master, and was ever ready to inflame his anger against those by whose downfall alone he had any hopes of succeeding in his ambitious projects.

"I marked it well, and shall not forget it till he mounts the scaffold," returned the Duke, grinding his teeth with fury. "Boastful as he now is, he will then be humble enough."

By the side of the Duke was his young nephew, to whom he had not ventured to breathe any of his aspiring hopes, well knowing, that neither by habits nor temper was he formed to aid in their accomplishment. The youth now looked up with an expression somewhat of surprise and pain on his countenance, and endeavoured to counteract the influence of Captain Policarpio's observations. "Senhor Carvalho had doubtless good reason for hurrying on to present himself before his Majesty," he said. "Methinks, too, Senhor Policarpio must be mistaken when he supposed that the Minister could have intentionally insulted my uncle."

"There was no mistaking his proud glance, boy," returned the Duke. "You know not the daring impudence of the man; his sole delight is to show his contempt of that rank to which he can never by right belong."

"Yet the King, whom we are all bound to reverence, places confidence in him; and he has already shown good example of his abilities," observed the young Viscount.

"The King is easily deceived by those who choose to flatter him," answered the Duke; "but his flattery shall avail him but little. Ah! we are at the palace, and that daring plebeian has arrived before us. We shall see with what a sneering and bold glance he will front us in the presence chamber, if he escapes his weak master's anger at his dilatory appearance. Let him gaze as he will, every glance shall be repaid by a drop of his life's blood."

While the Duke was thus venting his rage, the Minister, regardless of the anger he excited, drove rapidly on past all the other carriages, and descending at the gate of the palace, hastened to the audience chamber, to kiss the hand of the sovereign, to whose welfare he was devoted.

As he approached, the King's ear was yet ringing with the tones of the insidious voices of those who had been striving to blast his reputation; but the eyes of his slanderers, as if conscious that he knew their vile intent, sank abashed before his steady and confident gaze.

"Senhor Carvalho is late in paying his respects to us," began the King, as the Minister bent his knee before him.

"I trust that your Majesty will pardon me, your most faithful servant, when you learn that I was more deeply engaged in your Majesty's affairs, and the welfare of the state, than those who would poison your gracious ears with lying tales against my credit;" and drawing up his commanding figure, which towered above the crowd of courtiers, his eagle glance ranged over the frowning countenances of those who stood around. "But I know that your Majesty is too wise and generous to believe them, while I can prove my devotion to your service. I have detected, and for the present counteracted, a conspiracy to deprive your Majesty of your sovereign rights, and to bring your mind under subjection of your most subtle foes, the Jesuits. While many, who would endeavour to injure me in your estimation are passing their nights in sleep or dissipation, I have been consuming the midnight oil in your service, snatching, at intervals, a few hours of hurried rest. The details of my researches I will lay before your Majesty at some future period, and, till then, I trust in your goodness not to condemn me."

"We fully trust to your zeal, my friend, and know you to be a most loving and faithful servant," answered the King, banishing, in a moment, all the dark suspicions which had arisen in his mind. "Say no more on the subject at present; but, when this ceremony is over, we will consult in private on the affair. See, numbers are pressing forward to pay their duty to us."

"But not one whose heart beats with fonder devotion for your Majesty," answered the Minister, again bending his knee, and kissing the hand of the King, held out to him, when he retired to his allotted station. The Queen and Dom Pedro looked angrily at him, but dared not utter their feelings; the courtiers glanced at each other, when they were not observed, and shrugged their shoulders, seeing that for the present it was in vain to attempt to injure him with the King; but vowing not to lose another opportunity of renewing their attacks against one whom they had just reason to fear. Carvalho spoke a few words, in whispers, to his colleagues, whose eyes sunk on the ground as he proceeded; and, indeed, no one of that assembly of the proudest and most noble in the land seemed as much at their ease as before he entered, except the King himself, who, on the contrary, uttered his expressions of courtesy to those who came to pay their respects, with greater ease and fluency. One of the first was the Marquis of Marialva, one of the most justly-esteemed nobles of the Court, who ever retained the affection of the King, though he did not escape the jealousy of the Minister, who was, however, never able to injure him. "Do what you will with the others," the King used to say; "but let alone my marquis." He now entered, with a free and graceful manner, for which he was remarkable, and affectionately kissed the hand of his royal friend.

"Ah, my good marquis, we missed you much from our hunting party yesterday," said the King. "We much required your active arm to slay the beast, who gored one of our best dogs before he was slain."

"I had sprained my left arm, and could not guide my horse, or I should not have missed the honour of accompanying your Majesty," returned Marialva.

"We know; we heard of your accident, and are glad to find that you are so far recovered; and, as we have a favour to ask, let us know when you are perfectly strong. We wish to show the English Minister that we have some nobles of our Court—and of no mean rank either—who are fully equal to the feats of agility and strength of which his countrymen boast. Our father—to whose soul God be merciful!—sent to the English Court an ambassador, who was, we heard, the tallest among all the corps diplomatique, and not the least able, we suspect; so that we may vie with those islanders both in strength and size."

The Marquis smiled, as he answered, "I will gladly obey your Majesty in anything you may command, and hope in a few days sufficiently to recover my strength to do so."

A few persons of less note followed, when a disturbance, most unusual at Court, occurred, and a voice, as if in angry discussion, was heard, when the Duke of Aveiro was seen advancing in a hurried and disordered manner. A fierce fire burnt in his eye, and a frown deeply furrowed his brow, while his hand wandered unconsciously to the hilt of his sword; but, as he came close to the King, the presence of majesty restored him slightly to order; yet his carriage was far from having that respectful manner which he was bound to preserve: his step was irregular, and he yet snorted with rage, as, in a careless and indifferent way, he stooped to kiss the hand of his sovereign.

"What has caused my lord duke to be so angry this morning?" said the King. "He seems to forget that he is in the royal palace."

"I forget not where I am, for I have too much to remind me of it," answered the Duke, haughtily. "I have been insulted grossly—insulted by one of the ministers in whom your Majesty pleases to confide, in a way to which no noble can submit."

"Who is the culprit, my lord duke? It seems you have taken a lesson from him," said the King.

"He stands behind your Majesty, even now, I doubt not, plotting mischief in his fertile brain against your throne and the Church—Senhor Carvalho is the man!" answered the Duke.

The Minister cast a withering glance at him.

"The punishment due to my crime is not to be found mentioned in the laws of the realm," he said. "I therefore submit myself to your Majesty's clemency. The offence was in passing my lord duke, in my eagerness to show my respect to my sovereign."

"Is that the whole of the offence, Senhor Duke?" said the King, half smiling. "It is at once pardoned, and we must request your Excellency to move out of the way in future, when any of our officers wish to pass you, in discharge of their duty;" and the King turned aside his head.

"The whole of the offence!" muttered the Duke of Aveiro, as he moved on one side. "For half such an one many a man has, ere now, died."

The highest fidalgos, their ladies and daughters, now followed in rapid succession; among them came the Marquis and Marchioness of Tavora, who had lately been acting the part of viceroys in India, and were, perhaps, but little pleased at being obliged to take a secondary place on the present occasion. They presented their eldest son, shortly to be united to the lovely daughter of the Marquis d'Alorna. Both the sovereigns looked coldly on them as they passed, uttering merely the most common-place observations.

"We have not seen you at Court for some time, my lord marquis," said the King; "but we hope, in future, your own private affairs will not keep you from us. We will not now detain you."

It was observed, that when the young marquis bent to kiss the King's hand, Joseph turned aside his head, with a frown, nor dared to meet the eye of the young man, who, after paying the same compliment to the Queen, moved on one side. His betrothed bride, to whom he was to be united in a few days, followed directly after, led forward by her father, till she reached the presence chamber, when, with a slight agitation in her manner, visible only to the eye of a keen observer, she advanced towards the King, and, as she knelt to kiss his hand, he whispered in her ear—"Fear not, dearest, this must be so; but our love alters not." The unhappy girl blushed, and, as she rose, her eye caught that of the King, bent on her in admiration, when hers fell to the ground, nor did she dare to encounter the angry and fierce glances the Queen cast on her. Her father was received with marked attention, which, unsuspicious of harm, he took as due to his extraordinary merits. Next came the Count of Atouquia, a young noble of unprepossessing appearance, and his countess, a lady much admired by the King.

Trembling with alarm at a scene so strange and dazzling, the fair Donna Clara was now led forward by the aged Marchioness de Corcunda, who had repaired to Court expressly to introduce her. As the beautiful and delicate young being knelt before him, the King smiled with surprise and pleasure, and raising her, bade her take courage, inquiring her name of the old marchioness. "She is, indeed, a bright jewel to adorn our Court, where we hope constantly to see her; and we doubt not many of our gallant fidalgos will enter the lists to win her smiles."

"Her hand is already sought by one of the first fidalgos, your Majesty; but the young lady has a strong desire to become the bride of our holy Church," answered the Marchioness.

The King looked annoyed, and an expression in no way respectful to the Church was on his lips; but he checked his anger, contenting himself merely with saying—

"The Church shows great discernment in choosing so fair a bride; but it is putting too great a temptation in the way of sinners to commit sacrilege, by making them seek to rob it of its prize."

Donna Clara heard these words of compliment, to which her ear was so unaccustomed, that it increased her blushes, adding to the lustre of her beauty, nor knew she which way to turn her eyes, till the marchioness having paid her respects to the Queen, took her arm, and led her through the admiring crowd. The Queen frowned on the lovely girl, and coldly returned her salutation; for she feared, in each new beauty, another rival in her lord's affections. Gonçalo Christovaö followed directly after.

"We have much pleasure in seeing you at Lisbon, senhor," said the King; "but we shall find fault with you, if you allow your daughter to quit the world. We hope you will cause her to alter her intention."

"Your Majesty's pleasure is my law," said the fidalgo, bowing and moving on, fearful of trusting his tongue with further words.

Scarcely a person of any rank or note passed, to whom the King did not address some words; and nearly all had passed by, when a handsome cavalier approached, and, gracefully kneeling, kissed his hand.

"We do not remember to have seen your countenance before, young sir," said the King, pleased with his appearance; "though we shall have much pleasure in seeing it in future. We did not catch your name."

"Luis d'Almeida," answered the young fidalgo. "I have but a short time ago returned from abroad, or I should earlier have paid my respects to your Majesty."

"We are happy to see you, Don Luis," answered the King. "Your father we have not seen for some time; we trust he is in health."

"It is the want of it alone which prevents his paying his respects to your Majesty. Weighed down by years and heavy misfortunes, he scarcely hopes again to visit Lisbon."

"He sends a worthy representative in his son," answered the King, graciously; "and if you feel inclined to remain, we may give you some office in our Court."

"Your Majesty's kindness overpowers me; but my father's state of health claims all my attention, nor could I be long absent from him; therefore, if your Majesty will permit me, I must decline your goodness with the deepest respect," said Don Luis.

"In that please yourself, and give our regards to your father, when you return," said the King, as Don Luis moved on to give place to those who were following him.

At length the tedious ceremony, one of the many penalties royalty is obliged to pay in return for the obeisance of the crowd, was over, and the courtiers, except those in immediate attendance on the sovereigns, were at liberty to go whither they willed. Don Luis, although amid a glittering crowd of the young and gay, felt sad and dispirited; and he had already reached one of the outer rooms on his way to quit the palace, when a page overtook him, and informed him, that Senhor Carvalho requested to see him; and begging him to follow, led the way through various rooms, to a small closet, next to the King's private council chamber. Here he found the Minister, pacing up and down, with a bundle of papers in his hand, prepared to attend when the King should summon him: he stopped in his walk, as he saw Don Luis, and held out his hand kindly to him—

"Ah, my young friend," he said, "I am glad to find that you followed my advice, and returned to Court as soon as you were able to leave your father; and now I hope it is from no want of affection to our sovereign, that you rejected his proffered kindness, as I spoke to him in your favour some time ago, and he promised to befriend you; for I would always distinguish those who have enlightened their understanding by foreign travel, from the ignorant and profligate young fidalgos, who are alike useless to themselves, and dangerous to a state."

"Your Excellency is flattering me at the expense of the Fidalguia of Portugal," answered Luis, his sense of the respect due to his class hurt by the Ministers expressions.

"I speak but the truth of them, young sir," answered the Minister, "and am right in making you an exception; but in truth, I would, for another reason, be of service to any of your family, and regretted much, when the King made his gracious offer, that you did not accept it."

"I have again to thank your Excellency for the interest you take in my welfare; but I should not even have returned to Lisbon so soon, were I not obliged to attend the marriage of my cousin, Donna Theresa d'Alorna, with the young Marquis of Tavora."

"I forgot your connexion with that family; but beware of the Tavoras. They are haughty, ambitious, and proud; and though I fear them not myself, I would not trust those I regard with their friendship."

A page now came to inform the Minister that the King was in readiness to receive him.

"Farewell, Don Luis, and remember my offers and advice," he said, as he turned to follow the page to the presence of the King.

As Luis was leaving the palace, he felt his arm seized in no gentle grasp, and turning round, to his great satisfaction he found his friend Captain Pinto by his side.

"Ah, what! Don Luis turned courtier!" exclaimed the latter. "Well, it is one of the characters of life a gentleman ought to play, though I cannot say it is much to my taste. I cannot stand all the buckram and bowing a man has to go through, though I played my part pretty well to-day, and received all sorts of compliments for sinking the Rover; besides which, I expect to get something about as substantial, in the shape of a cross of some order or other, which, the chances are, I see the next day worn by the escudeiro of my Lord Marquis of Marialva or Tavora. But no matter! it will be intended as an honour, and I may boast how I won it, which few others can do: however, here have I been running on about my own affairs, and quite forgetting to ask you about yours. Tell me first, when did you come to Lisbon, for I have been inquiring for you, and heard that you were not even expected."

"I arrived only yesterday, and remain but till my cousin Theresa's marriage takes place."

"Ah! a sore subject that, I fear; but if you are the man I take you for, you will soon recover from that trifling wound; but I will not talk about it. I was wishing to see you, to deliver a message from Senhor Mendez, who desires to have some conversation with you. He has not yet recovered from his injuries, and begs you will visit him."

"I will gladly do so, if you tell me where I may find him," said Luis.

"I will take you with me to-night, for I do not venture to visit him by day, for reasons I will explain some time to you," answered Captain Pinto.

"I cannot go till late; for I have a visit to pay at the palace of the Marchioness of Corcunda, to deliver some jewels I recovered from some robbers in an extraordinary way to a young lady, who will be anxious to hear of their safety," said Don Luis.

"What! another young lady in the case? I thought you had foresworn womankind for ever," said Captain Pinto, laughing.

"I have seen Donna Clara but once, and am only performing an act of common courtesy," said Don Luis.

"Is she very lovely?" asked his friend. "She is perfection," answered Don Luis. "That fully accounts for it," said the Captain. "I thought it would be so. Eternal wretchedness—no comfort but in the grave! Ha! ha!"

Volume Two—Chapter Four.

When Don Luis reached the palace of the Marchioness of Corcunda, where he had learned that Donna Clara and her father were residing, he saw light streaming from all the windows, and sounds of revelry met his ear. He paused for a moment, doubtful whether he should enter the scene of festivity; but, being still habited in his full dress of the morning, he felt that he was in a proper costume, having also a modest consciousness that he should not be unwelcome to the lady of the mansion, nor, he trusted, to Donna Clara. He therefore boldly approached the door, working his way through a crowd of lackeys, chairmen, and linkboys, and ascended a flight of steps leading to the habitable part of the mansion, following a gay and laughing party of the young and happy. The anterooms were already crowded with company, and in one of them a servant pointed out the marchioness standing ready to receive her guests. As he advanced towards her, people stared at him as one whom their eyes were not accustomed to meet; but none of the fair or young frowned, or seemed displeased at his appearance. Bowing gracefully, he mentioned his name, and expressed his anxiety to pay his respects to Gonçalo Christovaö and his daughter.

"Oh, I have heard of your exploit and gallantry, Senhor Don Luis,— and I know that Gonçalo Christovaö will be equally anxious again to thank you for the service you rendered his daughter. You will find him on the way to the ball-room," said the old Marchioness, coldly.

"And Donna Clara?" said Luis, hesitating.

"Her father will inform you," answered the Marchioness, in the same tone as before.

What these words could mean Luis could not tell, though they seemed to forebode that he would not be as welcome as he hoped; but he could not inquire further, as he had received a strong hint to proceed; bowing, therefore, to the old lady, he looked eagerly among the crowd for Gonçalo Christovaö, to have his doubts removed, but he could nowhere perceive him.

While stopped in his progress by the crowd, a voice, which had once sounded like the sweetest melody to his ear, arrested his attention, and sent a strange thrill, more of pain than pleasure, through his frame; when he beheld before him his cousin Theresa, leaning on the arm of a youth, whose eyes were bent on her as if enchanted with her beauty. He at once recognised the young Marquis of Tavora, whom he recollected in his boyhood; and though, at first, a pang of angry jealousy shot across his bosom, he at once banished the feeling as unworthy of himself, knowing that though, during his absence, the marquis had proved his successful rival, it was owing more to Donna Theresa's ambition and vanity than to any unfair advantage he had taken. Notwithstanding all the affectionate attentions of her betrothed husband, Donna Theresa's manner seemed cold and indifferent, and she returned but short replies to his observations; and when she smiled, to Don Luis her smile appeared forced and unnatural. He gazed at the young pair with grief at his heart.

"Alas!" he thought, "that I should have wasted my best feelings on one so incapable of those tender affections which form the chief jewels of the sex. Oh! woman, woman! lovely and angelic as thou appearest, if thy heart has become cold and callous by contact with the world, how valueless, how empty thou art! Unhappy youth!—she loves him not;—I see it in that forced smile, that cold eye,—and yet he seems not to have discovered it—I pity him!"

Such thoughts, very natural to a rejected lover, and very soothing to his vanity, passing through his mind, he was unwilling to address her, and would have passed unnoticed, when her eye caught his regarding her. For a single moment a blush passed across her features, but the next, holding out her hand, with a smile, she led the young marquis towards him; and, to avoid being guilty of marked rudeness, he was obliged to kiss the fair hand she offered.

"What! you seemed to have forgotten me, my good cousin," she said, in a gay tone, "though I hear you intend honouring me by your presence at my marriage. Ah, you do not remember Don Luis of Tavora. Permit me to introduce my most loving cousin, who has travelled all over the world, I believe; or, at least, to England, and other barbarous countries, where the sun shines only once in the year, and then half the day is obscured by a thick fog, while for six months the ground is covered with snow. Oh, dreadful! I would get rid of such a country altogether: it makes me shiver to think of it, even in this warm room. You have no idea, senhor marquis, how my cousin blinked his eyes when he first came back to clear skies and sunshine, so accustomed had he been to live in the dark."

While Donna Theresa was thus speaking, the gentlemen exchanged the usual compliments.

"Ah, I am glad to see he has not forgotten how to bow properly, or, I rather suspect, he has picked up the art since his return. I protest that, the first day he came back, he had no notion of bending his body, like the English, who, I hear, are either born with one joint only, and that is in their necks, or else they become stiffened from their forgetting to use them. Now, you are going to defend your friends, but don't attempt it; I hate them, with their stiff pride and supercilious airs, thinking every people their inferiors who do not possess such good roads and fine horses as themselves. There was one man who came here, an English lord, I forget his dreadful name, but it pained my mouth to attempt to pronounce it, who compared everything he saw with his own country; and, because our habits and manners differed from those to which he was accustomed, he must needs consider ours far less civilised, and took no trouble to conceal his opinion."

"Though at first rather distant in manner, I was received by many with great cordiality and kindness, and saw much to admire in their manners and institutions," answered Luis, wishing to protect the character of his friends.

"I know nothing about their institutions," exclaimed Donna Theresa, in a pettish tone, "but I know their impertinent superciliousness will make them enemies wherever they go—so talk no more about them. By-the-bye, I hear you have been vying in your exploits with that renowned hero Don Quixote, and rescuing distressed damsels from the power of brigands by the strength of your single arm, and with the aid of your faithful squire Pedro. Everybody in Lisbon is prepared to look upon you as a complete Knight Errant. I heard all about it from Donna Clara herself, who speaks warmly in praise of your gallantry, I assure you; and if she does not think you are perfection itself, she thinks you very near it. I believe if anything could make her angry, it would have been my abusing you to her, but, instead of that, it almost made her cry."

"Where is Donna Clara?" exclaimed Luis, interrupting her eagerly: "I have a packet to deliver to her."

"You will find her in the ball-room, the admired of all beholders, and of none more so than of the Conde San Vincente, of whose lynx-eyed jealousy beware; and now, as I see that you are anxious to deliver your message, I will not detain you. Farewell, Luis!" she spoke in a softer tone.

"I wronged her," muttered Luis, as he hastened to the ball-room. "Her heart is not turned to stone. Such dwells not in the female breast."

As his eye distinguished Donna Clara at the further end of the room, he endeavoured to regulate his pace as etiquette required; but his eagerness impelled him on till he had arrived close to her, when it occurred to him that in his hurry he had not considered how he should address her. She had, however, perceived him, when a richer hue mounted to her cheeks, and her eyes beamed with a brighter light, as she timidly held out her hand. Their eyes met, it was but for a moment; but they there read more than Plato, Aristotle, or all the ancient philosophers ever wrote—at all events what they prized far more. He took that delicate hand, and pressed it with ardour to his lips, and it seemed to inspire him with abundance to say, but yet she was the first to speak.

"Oh! Don Luis, I have been wishing to meet you, to thank you again for your bravery and goodness in rescuing my father and me from the robbers, and for protecting us on our way back. I have often thought of it since—" When Clara had got thus far, she stopped, and wished she had expressed herself differently; besides, she did not know to what it might lead.

Don Luis then thought it high time to speak, to relieve her embarrassment, expressing his happiness at again meeting her, with many inquiries respecting her health, to which she made suitable answers, when he continued—"I have been fortunate in recovering the casket of jewels, the loss of which so much concerned you, and I came hither this evening on purpose to deliver it, not expecting to find a ball going forward."

"How kind, how thoughtful of you!" she exclaimed, repaying him with a sweet smile. "Do not deliver them now, but come to-morrow morning early, when I am sure my father will join with me in thanking you for all your attention to us, if you will take care of them a little longer."

"I would not willingly part with aught belonging to Donna Clara;" and Luis bowed, as many other gentlemen were bowing to ladies near him. But there was a look which accompanied that bow, unseen by any but the lady to whom it was made, which caused her heart to beat quicker than usual. Now Luis, when he entered the room, had most certainly not intended to tell Clara that he loved her, nor had he yet done so, because he was not aware of it himself, but he quickly found it out in the course of their conversation, besides discovering that he was not indifferent to her; a circumstance adding considerably to his boldness in speaking.

It may seem extraordinary to some of our readers that Don Luis should have carried on so interesting a conversation with Clara, unheard by any persons who surrounded them; but such was the fact, for lovers quickly learn to lower their voices and restrain their actions, as we have always heard: indeed, a friend of ours, a miserable younger son, once made an arrangement with a young lady of fortune sufficient for them both, to elope with him, while her unconscious mamma was sitting on the other side of the room. The young lady was severely punished for her fault, by the just indignation of her friends, who refused to have any intercourse with her till, by the death of several relations of her husband's, a coronet was placed on her brow, when their hearts relented towards her, and they thought she had acted very wisely. The moral of this anecdote is, that chaperones must not be too confident because they keep the young ladies near them.

Luis claimed Donna Clara's hand, and led her forth to dance: they then wandered together through several rooms, where they fancied that they were unobserved. The temptation was very great, and he yielded to it. His words were few and low; but Clara's ears were quick, and she heard every one of them; for they were such as she would not have lost for worlds. She longed to ask him to repeat them again, but as she could not do that, she told him they made her very happy; for, at that moment, poor girl, she forgot all but the present. She looked up, and beheld the dark eye of the Count glaring at her from among the crowd. In an instant her joy was turned to anguish; and like a thunderbolt, the recollection of her father's stern decree, and of some dreadful words the friar had once spoken to her, rushed upon her mind.

Luis saw the sudden change in her countenance; but, knowing not the cause, supposed that an illness had seized her, when, forgetful of all his former caution, he exclaimed, "Speak, my beloved, are you ill?"

His agitation was marked by the Count, though his words reached no other ears but hers.

"Oh no, no! Leave me, in mercy," she answered, her voice trembling with alarm: "I am not ill, but I have acted very wrong; I ought to have told you at once of the lot to which I am destined; but oh! believe me, I forgot it in the joy of seeing you. See, the fierce glance of the Count San Vincente is cast on me. Oh! pardon me, that I must now tell you so, I am condemned to wed that dark man, or to assume the veil."

A chill weight pressed on Luis's heart. "Was the bright fabric he had just raised up but a vain illusion?" he asked himself.

Donna Clara was the first to recover herself; she continued, speaking more calmly: "Go now, and confide in me. Yesterday I might have been compelled to accept the Count; but now no earthly power shall make me wed him. The confidence of your love will give me strength to resist all the temptations, and to despise all the threats which are held out to cause me to do that which I knew was wrong, and against which my heart revolted. Come to-morrow, for my father has ever been kind, and he may relent. Tell him openly of our love, and I will beseech him not to sacrifice me to the Count: to you, surely, he can have no objection, and, for very gratitude for what you have done for him, he cannot refuse you."

The last few sentences were spoken while Luis was conducting her to her seat. Unperceived by either, the Count had followed them at a distance, where he stood watching them among the crowd. Clara looked up into her young lover's face, and smiled. "Fear not, Luis, we may yet be happy," she said; but scarcely had she uttered the words, when, as if by some fascination she could not resist, she again beheld from afar the basilisk eyes of the Count glaring on her; but though their glance did not wither her, it at once recalled all her fears and forebodings, and brought clearly to her remembrance her father's words. Her gentle heart sank within her: she could not allow Luis to leave her with hopes which she felt too truly must inevitably be blighted. "Luis," she said, "I cannot deceive myself, and I must not deceive you. My doom, I fear, is sealed. My father, I remember, told me, though I scarce noted his words, that his honour was pledged to the Count, that if I did not wed him, I should become the bride of Heaven, for that such was my mother's dying wish. That I will not wed him, I have assured you, and I know you trust me; the rest is in the hands of Heaven, and in Heaven alone can I confide. Oh! Luis, once again I pray you to leave me. Farewell! for we ought not to meet again."

Luis saw by her looks that his remaining would agitate and pain her more. "At your bidding, beloved one, I leave you now. I will see your father to-morrow, and urge my claim; he cannot be so cruel as thus barbarously to sacrifice you. Farewell!" Saying which, with grief in his tone and look, he tore himself from her side, and hastily threading his way through the crowd of guests, he rushed from the palace.

Clara remained unconscious of all that was passing around, till the Count and her brother approached her. "Who was the gentleman with whom you have been dancing?" said the latter. "He seemed an intimate acquaintance."

The tones of her brother's voice aroused her.

"Don Luis d'Almeida; to whom your gratitude is due for rescuing your father and sister from the power of brigands," answered Clara, with greater firmness than she could have supposed herself to possess; but her womanly pride was roused at the tone of the question, and at the presence of the Count.

"He seemed to presume, then, too much on the service he was so fortunate to perform, for the Count tells me he was engaged in long and earnest conversation with you, which he does not approve, and would have interrupted, had not the etiquette of society prevented him."

"The Count was employed in a truly noble occupation," answered Clara, her gentle spirit excited beyond endurance at the unauthorised interference of the Count and her brother: "nor do I know by what right he claims the privilege of directing my conduct."

"By that of being your affianced husband, my fair sister; and as his friend, I must guard his interests as well as yours," said her brother. "He requests your hand for the next dance, and will then better urge his own claims." Upon this the Count advanced, assuming the softest smile, and in the blandest voice made his request.

Clara shrunk from him, as she answered, "I can dance no more; and I beg the Conde San Vincente will not deceive himself by supposing that any claims he can urge will afford me otherwise than pain."

"Is this, then, madam, the answer I may expect to-morrow—for which I have waited patiently a whole month?" exclaimed the Count, fiercely.

"Such is the only one I can ever be induced to give," returned Clara, with firmness. "Though, had not the Conde San Vincente drawn the answer from me now, I should have preferred giving it through my father."

The Count's brow lowered, and again that ominous glance shot from his eyes. "I give you till to-morrow to alter your determination, madam," he whispered, between his closed teeth; "for I was led to expect a very different answer; when, if I find that a rival has influenced it, as you have given me just cause to suspect, remember that his heart's blood shall pay for his audacity. I will not lose so fair a prize without wreaking my vengeance on him who has ventured to deprive me of it."

Clara turned pale at these words, which her brother could not hear; and though they increased her horror and hatred of the speaker, she smothered the feeling for the moment, for the sake of one who, from the contrast, was every instant becoming dearer to her. "Oh, no," she answered, "you have no rival but the Church, which claims me, if I become not your bride; yet, as a man, a noble, and a Christian, do not urge your claim. I can never love you; but surely that is not a crime: and I will never wed where I cannot love, for that would indeed be crime. Then spare me, for my fate is in your power."

The Count smiled darkly, as he spoke. "You know that I love you, lady, and my love is not a weak, puny passion, to be thrown aside at pleasure; nor will I yield it to any power but the Church, against which even I cannot strive; so do not persuade yourself, that I am, like a boy, to be gained over, by prayers or tears, to do what I should most assuredly repent of. For the present, I yield to your wishes, and leave you; but to-morrow I shall return, and claim the fulfilment of your father's promise." The Count, on this, bowed profoundly, and joined her brother, who was standing at some little distance, and to whom he expressed his conviction that he possessed a rival in his sister's affections in the person of Don Luis d'Almeida, when they together left the palace.

Poor Clara watched their departure with anxiety. What fears does love conjure up in a woman's breast! She knew her brother's fiery temper, and dreaded the Count's vindictive disposition. They might encounter Don Luis; they would quarrel, and he would fall a victim to their anger. She longed to be able to seek Don Luis, and to warn him of his danger; or to have some trusty messenger whom she could send to assist him; but she felt that she was helpless, and so completely did her agitation overcome her, that she was obliged to fly to her own chamber, to give way to her feelings in tears. The old marchioness was excessively angry when she found that the Count had quitted the party, and she could nowhere see Donna Clara. The fidalgo, who had been deeply engaged in a game of cards, knew nothing of his daughter; and when, at last, it was discovered that she had retired to her chamber, which no persuasions could induce her to leave, the old lady grew more sour than ever, and vowed she would never again be guilty of the folly and wickedness of giving a party to please any human beings, as other old ladies have often since done, when their *soirées* have not gone off as well as they expected. Balls in those days, in Portugal, were very solemn affairs, the stately and sedate cotillon being the only dance allowed, people endeavouring, by outward gravity and decorum, to make amends for universal license and depravity of morals; hoops, bag-wigs, and swords, not increasing any inclination for saltatory amusements. How far better is the graceful and animating waltz, the inspiriting galop, and the conversational quadrille, of the present day, with the really correct behaviour so general in society.

Now, we dare say, some of our readers will accuse us of having again fallen into the errors of romance writers, in describing Donna Clara's hasty acknowledgment of her love for Don Luis; and, in our defence, we affirm, in the first place, that such was the fact—which ought to be sufficient. And that none may deem her unmaidenly, it must be remembered that she had naturally thought of him every day since they first met, that she had contrasted him with the Count, for whom she had from the first felt a dislike, and that Don Luis proved he had thought of her and her wishes, by recovering her mother's jewels; besides, he was a very handsome, noble person, and her equal in birth; but, above all, he told her he loved her, and she believed him. Why should she not? More than a month had passed since they first met; and though they had not since personally encountered each other, they had, every day and hour, in spirit; for their love was of that pure essence which neither time nor space can divide, which, born in heaven, outlives decay, and against which neither the powers of the earth, nor the spirits of darkness, can prevail; that heavenly spark which, in an instant kindled, burns brightly for eternity! Love at first sight! We pity the heart-withered worldlings who deem this impossible; who, because the furnace of society has seared and hardened their feelings, laugh and sneer at all the refined and tender sentiments which gentle nature implanted in the bosom of man; though such they truly cannot experience, yet the young and innocent may, and we know, are often thus blessed. We say blessed, for a few moments of such pure ecstasy are of incomparably far greater value than a whole life of apathetic indifference. Those who require confirmation of the truth of our history, we must remind, that Lisbon is considerably to the south of the latitude of Verona, for we firmly believe that a certain William Shakespeare never drew a character not true to life. Now, he tells how, in Verona, the young and ardent Romeo and Juliet loved, and loved so truly, that they died for love; and yet their love in one instant sprung to life, and flourished bright and lovely to the end. Before concluding, we may quote some words spoken by Juliet on their second meeting, and then we think Clara will not be accused of precipitancy:—

Juliet.

"Three words, dear Romeo, and good night, indeed.
If that thy bent of love be honourable,
Thy purpose marriage, send me word to-morrow,
By one that I'll procure to come to thee,
Where, and what time, thou wilt perform the rite;
And all my fortunes at thy foot I'll lay,
And follow thee, my lord, throughout the world."

Volume Two—Chapter Five.

How bright and fair are the hopes of youth, like the early flowers of spring; but how soon, alas! do they, too, wither and decay, beneath the first scorching blast of summer. Poor Donna Clara awoke, the morning after the events we have described in the previous chapter, with a weight at her young heart such as she had never before experienced. A short month ago, the world promised naught but happiness, and now every feeling of joy lay crushed and blighted. Old Gertrudes attended her loved mistress with looks of sorrow, while the business of the toilette was proceeding; and no sooner had she dismissed her Abigails, than she urged her to confide to her bosom all the causes of her grief. She was in no way restrained in her abuse of the Count, describing his character very much in its true light; but her observations, far from relieving Clara's mind, only increased her fears for the safety of Don Luis.

When the old lady heard that her fate was to be settled that very day, her tears flowed fast, as she embraced her affectionately: "I will not have my child torn from me to be shut up in a convent, where I cannot attend on her," she exclaimed. "I don't believe my mistress, your lady mother, who has gone to heaven, ever wished you to go into one at all. I never heard her say so, and there's nobody but the Senhor Confessor who ever did; so I see no reason why you should be forced to do what you do not like. If you were to marry some young fidalgo whom you loved, it would be very different, and all natural; because I might then accompany and take care of you; but this I am determined shall not be, let that stern friar say and do what he will. I don't care for him; for I know more about him than he is aware of, clever as he thinks himself."

The old lady had got thus far in her tirade, when a knocking was heard at the door, and the deep voice of Father Alfonzo demanded admittance, which Clara could not refuse. He entered with a slow step, and a solemn look; and after seating himself by the side of the fair girl, ordered Senhor a Gertrudes to withdraw. She looked as if she would very much like to disobey; but there was no help for it. "I have matter of importance to communicate to my young penitent, which no ears but hers must hear;" so the old nurse, casting a warning glance towards Donna Clara, quitted the room.

"My daughter," began the Friar, "this day you are to make your selection, either to wed the Count or to assume the veil. Now, I would not bias your choice; but I consider it my duty to inform you of certain things which have come to my knowledge, which will have great effect on your future happiness,—but on one condition, that you reveal them to no one; this swear to me, and I will speak them."

Clara took the oath as the Friar directed; for why should she refuse to do that which her confessor asked?

"Know, then, my daughter, that the man whom your father and brother desire you towed is a dark and blood-stained murderer!" and the friar poured into the ear of the gentle girl a tale of horror, which made her cheek grow pale, and her frame tremble with fear. "But remember," he continued, "that you have sworn to reveal this tale to no one, not even to your parent, or dearest friend."

"I will not forget my oath; for my lips could not even utter the dreadful tale," cried the agitated girl.

"'Tis well, then: you renounce all intention of wedding this Count?" said the Friar.

"Oh yes, yes, I would die sooner!" returned Clara.

"You have a far happier alternative in store for you, my daughter," said the Friar: "a life of sanctity and devotion; in which you will be free from the cares and troubles of the world; and in the daily communion of pious and humble women, whose every action is guided by religious and learned priests, you will soon forget all the frivolities and vanities of the society you quit."

"I will submit to the will of Heaven," answered the gentle Clara, in a faint voice.

"Such a temper is highly commendable, my daughter," returned the Friar. "You must prepare to enter, in a few days, the holy retreat selected for you, while, in the mean time, I will make arrangements with the Lady Abbess for your reception. I now go to seek your father, to communicate your pious determination."

"Oh no, let me speak to my father," cried Clara, eagerly. "I would rather that he should hear from my lips that I cannot wed the Count: he may—" and she hesitated, recollecting herself.

"As you will," said the Friar, looking at her suspiciously; "but remember your oath, and dread the punishment of Heaven."

A dreadful doubt crossed her mind: had the Friar any sinister motive for deceiving her?

The Friar rose without again addressing her, and quitted her chamber. He sought the fidalgo, and, notwithstanding Clara's request, he informed him of her determination. "Your daughter seems bent on disobeying your wishes, senhor," he said. "Though I have exerted my humble endeavours to persuade her to follow them, and have placed the character of the young Count in as favourable a point of view as possible, she has a foolish and invincible repugnance to him; however, perhaps a father's persuasions may have more effect than mine; but should you not succeed, be firm, and remember your oath, or dread the vengeance of Heaven!" and the Friar turned aside his head, to hide the dark smile which lighted up his features.

The fidalgo parted from his confessor, and hastened to his daughter's chamber. Clara had sunk on her knees before the little altar and crucifix on one side of her room, to seek aid from Heaven to support that misery which it seemed cruel man had conspired to cause. She rose as she heard her father's footsteps approaching: she had not wept, her grief was too bitter, too hopeless, for tears to give relief; and with apparent calmness she met him as he entered. But already had the blight fallen on that fair brow; the soft lustre of her eyes had been extinguished; the rose had fled her cheeks, and no more did the accustomed smile dwell on those sweet lips. The fidalgo could not fail to see the change; but he made no remark: his thoughts were busy with the arrangement on which he had determined. He loved his daughter much, but his pride was dearer to him than aught else, and for that must every consideration be sacrificed: all peace on earth, all hopes of heaven, must bow before that cursed, blood-stained idol of his soul!

"Clara," he said, as he led her to a seat, "this day the Count will come to receive the answer to his suit. He loves you, my child, for he has often assured me of it. He appears, in every way, such a husband as I should desire for you; and I feel perfectly satisfied with the selection I have made: you will, therefore, I trust, offer no further opposition to my wishes, though Father Alfonzo tells me you have yet some maidenly scruples about accepting one whom you fancy you cannot love."

"I must not for a moment longer allow you to remain in uncertainty, my father," cried Donna Clara. "I cannot wed the Count. I dreaded him at first, though, by your desire, I sought to conquer my repugnance; but now—oh! spare me, my father, spare me! retract your stern decree—I never can be his!"

"Is such your firm resolve, Clara?" asked her father. "Remember the alternative."

"It is, my father; for you know him not!" she exclaimed, as she cast herself kneeling at his feet, while she clasped his hand and gazed into his countenance. "But you will not be so cruel, so unlike yourself, as to compel me to embrace a life for which I have no calling. Father, oh hear me! I love another, fondly, devotedly,—one whom you cannot disapprove,—one who merits your esteem and gratitude. I knew it not before, or I would have told you; I knew not that he loved me; but now that I feel assured of his love, I would not wed another to gain the crown of Portugal! Frown not thus on your child, my father; I have not loved unworthily; he is noble, brave, and good,—he will himself come to urge his suit."

"Who is the person who has dared to win my daughter's affections without my permission?" exclaimed the Fidalgo, interrupting her. "Speak, child!"

"Don Luis d'Almeida," answered Clara, firmly.

"Clara, you have deceived me," said her father. "Has this conduct been worthy of a high-born maiden, to receive the addresses of one, whoever he may be, without your father's permission? But the crime will bring its own punishment. Yet how can it be so? You could have seen him but once, and how know you that he loves you?"

"I saw him again, here, on the evening when he came to tell me that he had recovered the casket with my mother's jewels; and he promised to return this morning to deliver them," said Clara.

"I will receive him, and thank him for his courtesy," returned the Fidalgo, coldly. "I have nothing for which to blame him; and, under other circumstances, I might have consented to his suit, though his poverty is an objection. But it is now too late; my honour is pledged to the Count, and I must fulfil my contract, provided he is worthy of you; nor has he given me any cause to suppose to the contrary."

A gleam of hope shot across the bosom of his daughter, as she exclaimed, "Oh! my father, he is,"—but, like the dark thunder cloud, the remembrance of her oath again rushed on her mind, and obscured the feeling.

At that moment one of her attendants entered, to announce that the Count was waiting below.

"Once more, Clara, I ask you, will you receive the Count?" demanded the Fidalgo, sternly.

"Father, I cannot!" gasped forth his unhappy child. "At least, spare me the horror of meeting him. In everything else I will obey you, but in this I cannot. I will sacrifice all my hopes in life to save your honour; I will give up the world, and the happiness I thought to find in it. I will quit life itself, and oh, gladly! but I cannot wed the Count."

"Clara, you have chosen your lot," exclaimed the Fidalgo, raising her, and placing her on a seat, when he moved towards the door. "I will dismiss the Count at your desire, but I have one only course to pursue, which you have already consented to follow. Prepare to quit me for ever!"

With these words the proud fidalgo left his gentle daughter.

The Conde San Vincente was furious when he heard from Gonçalo Christovaö that his suit was finally rejected, and he demanded that the fidalgo should fulfil his promise in consigning his daughter to a convent, rather than that any other should gain the prize which was not to be his. He concealed, however, the fierce rage which burnt within his bosom at the disappointment of his wishes, and with a show of haughty courtesy took his leave of the fidalgo.

Clara anxiously waited all day, in the hopes of hearing that Don Luis had called, and of receiving the casket he had promised to bring. She knew it was wrong to wish it; but she trusted that Gertrudes would contrive to enable her to meet him; but the day passed away, and she heard not of him, nor could her nurse gain her any information.

We cannot dwell on her grief and wretchedness. Poor girl! she was but one of the many victims to pride, bigotry, and designing hypocrisy. Several days passed away, the friar visiting her constantly, and dwelling strongly on her mother's dying vow, when she had devoted her to the Church; so that, heart-broken and despairing, she agreed to obey her father's commands.

Yet, young and innocent as she was, and free from all sort of guile herself, there was something in the manner and the conversation of the friar which raised horrid doubts in her mind as to the purity of his motives. He did not shock her ear by a word which could be repeated to his discredit; he did not propose aught unbecoming her maiden modesty to listen to, but he insinuated that a conventual life was not of that ascetic nature she had supposed; that pleasures, of which custom forbade the enjoyment in society, might be tasted within the precincts of those seemingly gloomy walls; and that the fair brides of

Heaven were not entirely secluded from all intercourse with lovers of a more earthly mould.

Though she could not understand his discourse, for a virtuous and youthful mind cannot comprehend the extent of villainy of which man is capable, yet how gladly would she have escaped from the life to which she was doomed! But she had promised her father to enter it, and he insisted on her fulfilling that promise; for he believed the Count upright and honourable; yet a word from her would convince him of the contrary—would show him that he had been vilely imposed on; and, by his own acknowledgment, he would yield to her wishes, and she might be happy with the man she loved: but that word her oath forbade her to pronounce. She knew the Count to be a murderer and a dark ruffian, but she could not breathe this knowledge into mortal ear, though her own happiness or life depended on it: hers was indeed a cruel fate.

Her father kept much aloof from her; for he could not bear to meet the eye of his child. He, too, looked pale and wretched; for there was a worm at his heart gnawing at his more tender affections, which his pride endeavoured in vain to crush. Her brother never came near her; he chose to be offended at her rejection of his friend, and when the old marchioness saw her, she scolded her half the time for refusing the Count, and the rest she spent in praising the holiness and pure joys of a conventual existence. Poor Gertrudes was most completely at fault: she had trusted too much to her sagacity and acuteness, and had been foiled at every point; so she spent the day and the greater part of the night in weeping by the side of her young mistress.

At length the day arrived on which Clara was to quit her father's care, and to take up her abode within the walls of the convent.

The convent selected for her was that of Santa Clara, her patron saint, the abbess of which was a relative of Father Alfonzo, a woman of noble family, and many connexions among the high dignitaries of the Church, by whose exertions she had been raised to her present dignity, more than by any peculiar claims to sanctity which she could boast of. In early youth she had been very beautiful; indeed she yet retained many of her former attractions, still having a right to claim the privilege of being considered young. She had assumed the veil from conviction certainly, but it was from the conviction that it would free her from the restraint and formality of a home governed by an austere father, and a bigoted, tyrannical mother; it was also a sure way to save a fame against which the breath of scandal had dared to whisper. Nor was she disappointed in the liberty she expected to enjoy; a devoted admirer she possessed before she entered, having no occasion to die of grief at her loss.

Such was the Mother superior to whose spiritual direction a young and innocent girl was to be confided. Accompanied by the father confessor and the old marchioness, Clara was driven to the convent. On one side of the building stood the church, an edifice of magnificent proportions, elegant architecture, and richly ornamented. The convent itself formed the corner of a square; the high walls of the garden belonging to it making up the remainder.

In front of the great entrance was a courtyard, into which the carriage drove; when, the gates being thrown open, the almost fainting girl was led within her prison walls, and conducted to the community room, where the Mother superior and several of the professed nuns were waiting to receive their new sister, of whose coming they had been forewarned. They received the old marchioness and her young charge with every sign of respect, conducting them to seats, and placing themselves in a row before them, while Father Alfonzo carried on a rapid conversation with the sisters, answering a variety of questions regarding the events which were occurring in the city; any fresh piece of scandal, or witty story, affording great amusement to the assembled party.

At length, the more immediate object of the visit was referred to. "I fear me that our new sister and namesake of our holy patroness is alarmed at finding herself among so many strangers," said the Abbess; "but we will soon teach her to forget the vanities of the world she is about to quit, in the contemplation of the sacred mysteries of our religion." A faint smile crossed the features of the Abbess as she spoke.

Poor Clara was too full of grief to answer, her struggling tears choking her utterance; but she felt that she was sacrificing herself at the shrine of filial obedience, and she endeavoured to find composure in the thought. She had recovered sufficiently to bid farewell with tolerable propriety to the old marchioness, who, after some further conversation, retired, accompanied by the friar, and she was left alone with those who were destined to be her future companions while life lasted, a period which she prayed and felt might be short. The sisters crowded round her, and assured her that she would be very happy, endeavouring by every means in their power to cheer her drooping spirits; but their efforts were ineffectual, for there was that sickness at her heart which death alone could end. They led her unresistingly over the building, showing her their cells, which were fitted up with more taste and luxury than could have been expected; then to the novices' apartments, where she was to take up her residence, till, at the end of the year, her profession was made, and she had assumed the black veil, the sign of her irrevocable vow. As they approached that part of the building, ringing peals of laughter broke on her ear, and she was welcomed by a crowd of young and smiling faces, who seemed little oppressed by gloom or despondency. After being introduced to them, she was conducted through the chapel and choir, and from thence to partake of some refreshment in the refectory; but she turned aside her head with loathing at the very thought of food; and the sisters, seeing that their endeavours to amuse her were vain, showed her the apartment allotted to her as a postulant of the order, and left her to her own reflections.

With her, religion was more of the spirit and principle, than of doctrine, or from education; and she ever flew to her Creator, to offer up thanksgivings for blessings, and for strength to bear afflictions, though till now she had scarce known them.

The evening sun was streaming through the open casement, throwing a bright refulgence around her seraphic countenance, as, with her hands clasped, she knelt before the altar which adorned her chamber, pouring out her soul in prayer, and beseeching forgiveness for her transgressions.

According to the custom of the order, it was some weeks before the new postulant was required to keep strictly the rules of the noviciate; during which time she was expected to become familiarised to the routine of the day, the different forms to be observed, and the duties of the choir; but everything was carefully avoided that could in any way annoy the young novice, or give her cause to be disgusted with her future life. The character of the innocent Clara was at once read by the Lady Abbess; indeed, Father Alfonzo had described it to her as he understood it, so that the secrets of the prison-house were with vigilant care excluded from her view.

Now Heaven forgive us, if we have the slightest thought of easting unjust odium on institutions now happily banished from the greater part of Europe, nor can we do aught but praise that admirable society of the Soeurs de Charité, founded on those great principles which the impersonification of Love and Charity taught to mankind,—a society worthy to have been planned in the gentle breast of woman, the very essence of all that is lovely and tender in human nature,—like an angel of light to a spirit of darkness, when contrasted with the foul and terrible Inquisition,—and blessed must they be who belong to it.

Volume Two—Chapter Six.

We have just discovered that we have been committing a very grave error during the previous part of this work, in writing very long chapters, but it is one which we have resolved forthwith to avoid, and can fortunately do so far more easily than most others into which we are apt to fall. We always ourselves object to long chapters, because subjects and events are too much confused by being run together in them, and as we suspect that most of our fair readers dislike them, we would not willingly tire out their patience.

When Don Luis quitted the palace of the Marchioness of Corcunda, he hastened homeward, his heart throbbing with deeper and more ardent love than he had ever felt for Donna Theresa, but far more full, also, of anxious doubts and fears.

On entering the house, he found Captain Pinto awaiting his return. His friend gazed at him for a moment, and then broke forth into a fit of laughter. Now, Captain Pinto was a very amiable, kind-hearted man; but, as Burke observes, that as we constantly dwell on the misfortunes and miseries of our fellow-creatures, we must consequently take a pleasure in contemplating them, so he seemed to find much amusement in the forlorn appearance of the young fidalgo.

"What! has another fair lady been unkind? have Cupid's shafts again struck the wrong object?" he exclaimed, as Luis threw himself into a seat. "Come, rouse up, my friend; 'tis the fortune of war we are all exposed to, so you must try once more, and the third will be the successful shot, depend on it. I dare say this fair Dulcinea del Toboso, whom your lance so gallantly rescued from the power of the brigands, was, after all, not worthy of your devoted affections. You saw her but once, I think; and I will answer for it no woman has power in that time to cause a man a moment's uneasiness, if he will but think of her calmly and dispassionately."

"In mercy cease your bantering, my good friend," exclaimed Luis; "you mistake altogether the case. I love, and, I am proud to say, am beloved in return by the most charming of her sex; but she has been betrothed, against her will, to another, or the alternative is offered her of entering a convent; and I fear her father is a man of that inflexible temper, that nothing will make him alter his determination."

"What! the thrice-told tale again?" said the Captain, still smiling: "it sounds badly. If she is to marry somebody else, 'tis plain you cannot have her; and if she is to be shut up in a convent, she is equally lost to a man of your honour."

"But I cannot, I will not allow her to be sacrificed," exclaimed Luis, vehemently. "Can you not advise me, my friend?"

"I never even heard of the lady till to-day," answered Captain Pinto, "so I cannot pretend to say; but, from my knowledge of women in general, dear charming creatures as they are, I should advise you to fall in love with somebody else, and I dare say the lady will soon recover also from her fit: they generally do."

"You know not what love is, when you speak thus," cried Luis. "I see that you are in no humour to enter into my feelings, so I will not trouble you with them. I must wait till to-morrow to see her father, and beseech him to favour my suit."

"The wisest plan you can pursue; and if your fortune is larger than your rival's, the chances are that you are successful; if not, I can give you but small hopes. He, of course, is an affectionate father, and considers his daughter's happiness—of which he must be a better judge than she can possibly be—depends upon the settlement each candidate has to offer. However, in the mean time, come with me to pay our promised visit to Senhor Mendez, as he will be expecting us."

In those days people met in society at a very early hour, considerably before the present dinner-time in England, so that the night was not far advanced when Luis and his friend again left the house, having, fortunately, taken the precaution of ordering Pedro to accompany them with a torch, and well armed in case of being attacked. Just as the door was carefully closed behind them by old Lucas, Luis observed some dark figures, wrapped in cloaks, standing on the opposite side of the street; but, supposing them to be casual passers by, he took no further notice of them, nor did they make any advance towards his party. We have before described the disordered state of the streets in Lisbon; for, though there were some military police, they committed more robberies than they prevented, stopping every single passenger to beg of him, and, if they were refused, they seldom failed to take what they required by force. Our friends, however, promised, by their appearance, to make too strong a resistance, to tempt either their attacks, or those of the professional marauders who were abroad; though had they encountered any party of the young nobles who delighted to perambulate the streets in search of adventures, they might have been insulted, to draw them into a conflict; their chief danger, therefore, was from the unsavoury showers which fell, at very frequent intervals, from the windows of the houses, and from the troops of fierce gaunt dogs who howled at them, as, in passing, they disturbed them from their loathsome repast. Rats, also, of enormous size, would constantly cross their path, seemingly in good fellowship with the dogs, and perfectly fearless of the human beings: woe to the unfortunate wretch who should fall, faint or wounded, on the ground!—he would instantly fall a prey to these savage vermin.

The way to the house where they expected to find Senhor Mendez was long, and, as may, from the above description, be supposed, by no means agreeable; nor were they able to hold much conversation, from the necessity both of picking their path, and of keeping on the watch against any sudden attack either from man or beast.

"I must warn you," said Captain Pinto, as they approached the house, "that our friend is still suffering from illness: his wounds were more severe than we suspected, and I much fear his days on earth are numbered."

There were many questions, much unbarring and drawing of bolts, before the people inside the house would open the door to Captain Pinto's summons; for the Portuguese will allow a person to run the chance of being murdered, or to stand shivering in a shower of rain, till they can assure themselves of his name and quality, as we have found to our cost. At length an old lady appeared, with a maid-servant behind her, holding a candle, and, after they had entered, again carefully closed the door. She shook her head, in answer to the captain's inquiries for her guest. "He is very bad, very bad, indeed," she said. "I fear he must soon be sacramentado, or he will depart without the consolations of religion."

When a person is given over by the doctors, a priest is summoned from the nearest church, who comes bearing the holy sacrament under a canopy, accompanied by choristers, and a person ringing a bell, who loudly chant at the door of the room in which the person is dying, or supposed to be so; the very noise and ceremony, however, frequently contributing to extinguish the flickering spark of life. The old lady, desiring Pedro to sit down in the passage to chew the cud of reflection till her return, in which he seemed much inclined to draw her young attendant to aid him, led the captain and Luis upstairs, and, opening a door, announced their arrival to her invalid guest.

Senhor Mendez raised himself from his couch, and gazed anxiously at Luis, as he entered. "This is kind of you, though what I expected you would do, my young friend," he said, faintly, "when you were told of my illness. Words of thanks to you, Captain Pinto, are valueless, when compared to what I owe you."

Don Luis expressed his sincere regret at finding him yet so far from recovered. He smiled faintly as he answered, "I fear it is the nearest approach I shall make to recovery in this world, yet the great hope of reviving in a far purer existence sustains my oft drooping spirits; but I fain would tarry longer here, for I have much to do which I would not willingly leave undone. Captain Pinto is my executor, it may, perchance, be but of a pauper's fortune, and at present I owe everything to him. He, like the good Samaritan whom the priests tell us of, has sheltered and fed the houseless and poverty-stricken wanderer. Remember my words, Don Luis, for they are not spoken idly. Truly does he follow the first great rule of charity; and, though it has become a principle of his existence, I am not the less thankful to him."

"Do not speak thus of me, my friend," interrupted the generous sailor. "I am but acting towards you as you would have done by me."

Luis, with much hesitation, begged to be allowed to afford his aid, if possible.

"I feel confident that you would," returned Senhor Mendez. "But Captain Pinto acts the part of a brother towards me, and what is of nearer kindred? so that I cannot deprive him of the privilege he claims."

Their conversation was long and interesting. The sick man made minute inquiries respecting the Count d'Almeida, and seemed grieved on hearing that he would not return to Lisbon. He advised Luis to cultivate the friendship of the Minister, and spoke with a tone of satisfaction, on hearing that he had offered to befriend him. He warned him not to fall into the vices of the fidalgos, and to shun their bigotry, and overbearing, illiberal conduct. Indeed, he showed himself to be a person far in advance of the generality of his countrymen with regard to his opinions. He informed Luis, also, that he was in daily expectation of receiving accounts from England of the safety of the fortune he had transmitted there from India. The conversation seemed to have revived him; and when Luis, having promised again to call on him, quitted him with the captain, they both felt stronger hopes of his recovery than when they first entered.

Volume Two—Chapter Seven.

We must now follow the Count San Vincente, and his gay and thoughtless friend, whom the former hurried away from the palace of the Marchioness of Corcunda.

"This conduct of your sister's will drive me mad, Gonçalo!" exclaimed the Count, as soon as they were in the street. "Her coldness I could have borne; but to see her receiving, with satisfaction, the addresses of another, is unbearable; but I will punish the youth who has had the temerity to rival me. Let us follow him; he is, probably, alone; and, armed but with his dress-sword, we can make short work of the affair."

"I do not understand you. I cannot seek a quarrel with Don Luis; for he has been of infinite service to my father and sister."

"Boyish scruples!" interrupted the Count, fiercely. "Let us set upon him at once, as men, and punish him for his audacity, in addressing your sister without your permission."

"Can a friend of mine make such a proposition to me?" exclaimed Gonçalo. "We must have mistaken each other strangely. I have been wild and careless, but I have not become a midnight assassin."

"Your pardon,—I was but joking," said the Count. "I thought we might fall in with this Don Luis, and enjoy a little small-sword play; for I confess I have a longing to pink him; but you may stand aloof, and see fair play."

"I have already said, I feel no inclination to force into a quarrel one who has never offended me: if he seeks it, I shall be ready for him. I must, therefore, decline accompanying you."

"Well, well, I will give up my point. He is not likely to be successful with your sister; so it little matters; though at first I felt annoyed, I confess, at his presumption. Come along with me, for I expect some friends at supper, who will help us to pass the night gaily; and we may then sally forth in search of adventures."

They were now near the count's palace; and Gonçalo making no opposition to his proposal, the former led him in, where they found a large party of dissipated young men awaiting their arrival. The count excusing himself for a few minutes, left his friend among them, while he repaired to his own chamber; there casting off the gayer part of his costume, he threw a cloak over his person, and selected a stouter sword than the one he laid aside, which he concealed beneath it. He then again issued into the street; and, walking rapidly along a narrow lane, he knocked at the door of a low, shabby house, but a short distance from his own princely palace.

"Who is there?" said a voice. "'Tis late, and all honest people ought to be in bed."

The Count gave a cant watchword in reply. "'Tis I."

A laugh was the answer; and, the door being unbolted, the dark figure of the bravo we described at the inn on the road to Coimbra presented itself.

"You are welcome, Senhor Conde," said the ruffian, as the count entered, and he bolted the door behind him. "'Tis long since I have had the honour of seeing your Excellency. Have you any work for me?"

This was said in a low, miserable room, into which the count descended, by two or three steps, directly from the street. The floor was of clay, beaten hard; the walls unplastered, and the roof seeming as if inclined to fall in from above. There was a recess, with a wretched pallet-bed in it, and another of the same sort was outside. In one corner, an old woman was seated on a low stool, cooking some mess, odoriferous of garlic, over a small clay stove, lighted with charcoal; but she rose not, nor gave any sign of intelligence at the appearance of a stranger. The count looked towards her, without answering the question.

"Do not fear her," said the man, observing his doubt; "she is only my mother, and she is so deaf that she cannot hear a word, and so foolish that she could not understand it if she did. Do you require anything of me, senhor?" he again asked.

"I should not seek you without a cause," said the Count. "Do you know Don Luis d'Almeida?—though why do I ask?—you ought to know every gentleman, in case your services are required against them, or by them."

The man looked at him, as much as to say, "My services may be required against you some day; and I would as willingly plunge my dagger into your bosom, but that I should lose an employer. Know him?" he exclaimed. "Curses on him! I know him well, and would—"

Then, recollecting that by showing any personal interest, he might lower the value of the service he well knew he was expected to perform, he added, "Yes, senhor, I know his person, I believe. What do you wish to have done respecting him? Remember, the times are bad; for the Minister has apprehended and hung some of my friends lately; so the price of any such work as you fidalgos require of us poor men is rising."

"This is work which will give you little trouble, but it must be done quickly," said the Count. "Go, take two or three of your companions; select whom you please; but my name must not be known. Watch the palace of the Conde d'Almeida, and you will meet Don Luis, either entering or coming out; for I just now parted from him. Strike him the moment you see him; and take care your dagger does not fail in its work. Inform me when your work is done, and I promise you thirty crowns for yourself, and ten for each of your companions. Will that satisfy you?"

"It is but little, your Excellency, considering the danger I run; for all the work falls upon my shoulders."

"Well, I will add ten more, provided it is done to-night," said the Count. "I can no longer delay. Beware you fail me not!"

With these words the count took his departure, perfectly satisfied with the arrangement he had made, and joined his companions at their revels, though, during the feast, he waited, with an anxious look, to hear tidings of the deed having been performed. The young Gonçalo, unsuspicious of the dark vengeance his friend meditated against Luis, and which he would have been the first to prevent, was the gayest of the party, rallying the master of the feast on his gloom and taciturnity, ascribing it entirely to the ill-success with which his advances had been received by his sister.

After leaving the abode of Senhor Mendez, Luis and his friend, who had promised to remain with him, accompanied by Pedro, as their body-guard, made the best of their way towards home, running the gauntlet of the many dangers to be encountered, without suffering from any of them. As they were within sight of the palace, Luis again observed several figures in the same position as before; and this time he pointed them out to Captain Pinto.

"We will keep out of their way," said his friend, "and we can then give them no cause to insult us; for, depend upon it, they are there for no good purpose, probably on the watch to rob or murder some unfortunate wretch. I am very happy to fight at times, but have no fancy for these night brawls."

As he spoke, the group moved towards them, and a figure, emerging from among them, advanced close to them, evidently endeavouring to distinguish their features.

"Don Luis d'Almeida, a friend wishes to speak with you," said the person.

"You must seek him elsewhere, my friend," answered the Captain, preventing Luis from speaking. "Pardon us, we are in a hurry, and would pass on."

The man appeared satisfied, and rejoined his companions, who were about to move away, when they observed our friends stop at the door of the palace, where the captain gave a loud summons. The strangers held a moment's consultation together, and were about again to advance towards them, when the captain, drawing his sword, ordered them to keep their distance; and while they hesitated, old Lucas, more agile than usual, had opened the door, allowing his master and his companions to enter, when the robbers, for such they appeared, retired.

The incident gave a subject of conversation to the friends before they retired to their beds, and the captain was the first to discover the real clue to the proceedings of the strangers. "You say the Conde San Vincente is a suitor of Donna Clara's, and that he observed you speaking to her at the palace of the Marchioness de Corcunda this evening; then, depend upon it, he was either among those gentlemen, or had deputed them to attack you, which they would most undoubtedly have done, had you been alone. I have heard of some of his deeds, and his character is better known than he is aware of."

"Now you give me the idea," said Luis, "I feel confident that I have before heard the voice of that man who spoke to us;—yes, he is one of the brigands who robbed Gonçalo Christovaö in the forest, and afterwards attacked me at the inn, when he swore to avenge the loss of a brother, of whose just death I was the instrument."

"Then I must most earnestly entreat you not to venture out alone, or you are certain to fall a victim either to his revenge, or to that of the count, who has, very probably, employed him to murder you. Do not think that it will exhibit want of courage to take every precaution, for so daring have these ruffians become, that scarcely a night passes without some dreadful murder, and I should deeply grieve to find you among the number of sufferers; therefore, as an old friend, I must make you promise to run no greater risk than you can possibly avoid."

Luis promised faithfully to follow the gallant sailor's advice; and it was fortunate for him that he did so, for in vain did the assassin, Rodrigo, watch night after night to find him alone. The following morning, he repaired, at an early hour, to call on Gonçalo Christovaö, his heart beating with doubts and fears as to the success of his petition. He carried the casket of jewels to restore to Donna Clara, but, on searching for the letter to her father, he could nowhere discover it. After turning over every article of his baggage, aided by Pedro, he was at last obliged to set forward without it, trusting, however, to have frequent opportunities of delivering it. The fidalgo received him with stately politeness, pouring forth torrents of expressions of gratitude for the service he had afforded him; but when Luis mentioned the chief object of his visit, he at first looked confounded with astonishment, assuring him that he had never before heard of a young noble venturing to win a young lady's affections without having first applied to the father for leave to do so; such conduct was excusable only in low-born plebeians, whose marriages were of no importance; that he had, however, no objections to him, except from his want of fortune, which was an insurmountable one; that his daughter could never wed without his leave, and that she was engaged to another gentleman.

This answer, though very polite, was a most discouraging one, as most of our readers will agree; but, at the same time, there was that buoyant nature in the composition of Luis, which made him hope where others would have despaired, though he certainly could not see very clearly on what grounds to found those hopes; indeed, he was obliged to acknowledge to himself that they arose far more from the feelings, than from the judgment.

The fidalgo made a great many more very polite speeches, assuring him that his house, and everything he possessed, was at his service, except his daughter; that he would forgive his falling in love with her, provided he made no further attempts to see her, and that the trouble he had taken to recover the casket, raised him, if possible, even higher in his opinion than before; indeed, there was nobody he more admired in the world; but that he must banish all thoughts of Clara from his mind. We only quote a part of the substance of the harangue, which was very long, and filled with the most courteous and elegant flourishes; indeed, it is extraordinary how very polite people are when they feel confident that they are saying the most disagreeable things in the world.

Luis listened in silence, and answered only by bows, evading carefully every promise the fidalgo endeavoured to draw from him, not to see

Clara again, determining to win her, if he possibly could; for the feelings of what is now, in ridicule, called romantic chivalry, which animated him, rebelled against the thoughts of her being compelled to marry a man she hated; and he was persuaded that every principle of honour and duty called on him to prevent the sacrifice, at every risk to himself, and even in direct opposition to the unjust commands of her proud father.

The fidalgo positively refused the earnest request of Luis, to be permitted to see Clara, even to take a last farewell; nor would he undertake to bear any message to her: indeed, as our readers already know, she was led to suppose that he had not called, nor did even Senhora Gertrudes discover the truth.

At length he was obliged to rise to take his departure, when the fidalgo redoubled his politeness, again thanking him for the casket of jewels, bowing him *out*, not only out of the room, but down stairs, through the hall, and into the very street, so that he had no opportunity of sending to inform Senhora Gertrudes that he was there, which he had some thoughts of doing.

Don Luis made many endeavours to see Donna Clara, or to communicate with her, but they were all alike fruitless, the fidalgo, the marchioness, and the priest, keeping so very strict a watch; though, had it not been for the latter, he would probably have been successful. At length he wrote a letter, which he had every hope would reach her, couched in the most respectful terms, but every line breathing the tenderest and most devoted affection. Day after day he waited for an answer, but it came not; the priest had been too vigilant: his was the only eye which saw the letter, and it served him as a copy for the next he had occasion to write.

Volume Two—Chapter Eight.

More than a week passed away; it was now within three days of the end of October, when Luis had repaired to a neighbouring church, to hear morning mass, and was kneeling on one side of the aisle, attending to the ceremonies going forward; he heard his name pronounced close to him, by a female, in the attitude of devotion, shrouded in the black mantelha, or hooded cloak, then worn by even the very highest classes, at mass. The female turned her head as he looked round, when he recognised the features of Senhora Gertrudes, which gave him more satisfaction than if they had been those of the fairest lady in the land, her young mistress excepted. The old lady sidled up to him, when she whispered, looking, we cannot help acknowledging, as if she was deeply engaged in her devotions all the time—

"Oh, Senhor Don Luis, I am so glad to see you! for I have been trying everywhere to meet you, without success; for that horrid Padre Alfonzo kept so strict a watch on me, that I could not venture to your house. Oh, senhor! they have stolen away my dear child, and they have carried her to a convent, where they have shut her up, and will never let her out again; the cruel, wicked wretches! All the world has conspired against us; and even my old master, whom, till now, I always looked upon as an angel, has grown as bad as the rest, and now I have only got you to depend on. There is my young lady breaking her heart about you, and no one whom she cares about to comfort her."

This news electrified Don Luis. "To what convent has Donna Clara been conveyed?" he exclaimed, eagerly. "'Twill be a consolation to know where she is."

"To that of Santa Clara, senhor," answered Senhora Gertrudes; "and if you will write a short little note to her, I know it will be a consolation to her. There can be no harm in a little note, I'm sure; and I will take care that she receives it."

Luis agreed with her that there could be no possible impropriety in his writing, and promised to do so.

"There is to be mass again here to-morrow, when I will meet you, senhor, and I will carry your note, for I shall be able to gain permission, I hope, to visit my dear young mistress. She will not be obliged to take her first vows for some time to come, and after that there will be a whole year before she can profess; so that, in the mean time, something may happen to release her; so do not be cast down, senhor, as I told her, sweet child, to comfort her, though Heaven alone knows what chance she has of happiness."

The service being concluded, Luis and the old nurse parted, he hastening home to employ himself in composing an epistle to Clara, which, instead of being the very little note the good Gertrudes recommended, swelled by degrees into several sheets, as the thoughts crowded on his mind, though, after all, they resolved themselves into two or three points,—his devotion, his wretchedness, and his hopes; for it was not his nature to despair; besides, he felt assured that his love was returned, and, with that proud consciousness, how could he cease to cherish hope?

We deem that man unworthy of a woman's affection whom the consciousness of possessing it does not raise above all fears, and give hopes of ultimately conquering all difficulties in his path. Such was the effect on the mind of Luis, and he determined that nothing should dispirit him till the fatal veil had, like the dark tomb, separated her from him for ever; then he felt that to him death would indeed be welcome.

He had just concluded his letter, forgetful of how the hours had flown by; his dinner had remained almost untasted; the grateful siesta was not thought of, and the shades of evening had already closed in the day, when Captain Pinto entered his room to remind him that they had on that night agreed to visit Senhor Mendez.

It must be recollected that those were not the days (at all events, in Portugal) of double hot-pressed glossy Bath paper, over which the pen glides with the rapidity of the skate on the virgin ice, which will account for the time he occupied in the employment; besides, he felt a pleasure in prolonging it to the utmost; yet, he was as delighted on completing it as we shall be when we write finis to this compilation, though he was not perfectly satisfied with it, and thought he could have written a better, as will probably be our feeling also.

As before, they were accompanied by Pedro with a torch, and were happy at finding their friend slightly recovered, though still unable to quit his couch. Senhor Mendez turned the conversation on points in which he considered that he could offer advice to Luis. He warned him particularly to beware of the Jesuits, whom he designated as crafty and deceitful men, ambitious alone of increasing the power of their order at the expense of their fellow-creatures, whom, in furtherance of this aim, they kept bound in the chains of ignorance and superstition; and that they were, so far, more dangerous than the other monastic orders, from their very superiority of education and intellect, and from their freedom from those gross vices which stained the character of the rest.

The advice, perhaps, might have been of service to Luis, for he had purposed, on the following day, to pay a visit to his cousin Father Jacinto, whom he had not seen since his return to Lisbon. Senhor Mendez then drew him to speak of himself, and of his love for Donna Clara, his eye flashing with indignation, when he heard of the chief reasons her father had deigned to advance for rejecting his offer.

"O pride and ambition!" he cried, "what banes are they to social intercourse! So this haughty patrician would rather consign his child to splendid misery in the arms of a man she abhors, leading her too probably to vice and disgrace, or would immure her within the profane walls of a convent, than see her wedded to one she loves, because his fortune does not equal what he, in his vanity, considers necessary to support her in grandeur equal to her rank. Mark me," he continued, "do not for a moment suppose that I would advocate unequal alliances, where the family on one side would despise the other, such can seldom fail of bringing misery to both; but I do say, where Heaven has joined two hearts in one, parents draw an awful responsibility on their own heads in venturing to separate them."

We must not longer delay, by giving the further observations Senhor Mendez made, as we have subjects to relate which will afford far more interest to our readers; and we might also run the risk of having our book banished from the library as a work full of pestiferous and dangerous tenets, which would cause us infinite pain, conscious, as we feel ourselves, of the rectitude of our intentions in transcribing what we find before us.

The course Luis and his friend took homeward led them near the residence of the Conde San Vincente, in which neighbourhood they were, Pedro being in advance with the torch, when they encountered a party who woke the night air with their bacchanalian songs, and seemed little inclined either to move out of their way, or to allow them to pass. The torch was immediately knocked out of the grasp of Pedro, who forthwith dealt the perpetrator of the act a severe blow with a cudgel he carried.

"Wretched villain!" exclaimed a young man, by the tone of his voice evidently suffering from the effects of wine, "how dare you to lift your hand against a fidalgo? you shall die the death for your audacity," and, drawing his sword, he was about to run Pedro through the body, had not the captain and Luis, unsheathing their weapons, also sprung forward to rescue him.

"A skirmish, a skirmish!" cried several voices, and the whole of the opposite party rushed forward to attack them.

"Nought but the blood of my foe can wash out the insult I have received," exclaimed the young man, who had been the cause of the fray, setting furiously on Luis, in the blindness of intoxication, not observing to whom he was opposed.

"Ah, you have a sword, too, as well as a stick; then, I conclude you are a gentleman, and fit to engage with—no matter—here's at you!" He, however, was a good swordsman, nor could Luis disarm him, as he wished to do, seeing his state, pressed closely, as he was also by his companions, the Captain and Pedro being abundantly occupied in keeping the rest at bay.

The young man, as we have said, rushed upon Luis, utterly regardless of his own person, becoming, every pass in which he was foiled, more and more daring; and still firmly retaining his sword. At length, Luis grew weary of his attacks, and, perhaps, less cautious not to injure him, when the young man, endeavouring to rush in on him, the former could not draw back in time, his sword passing through his side, and, with a sharp cry, he fell to the ground. The rage of his companions seemed increased by the accident, when Captain Pinto, seeing what had occurred, shouted out—"Beware, cavaliers, this may afford amusement to you, but I am a peaceable man, and do not like fighting, so take warning from the fate of your companion, and draw off, or by heavens, I will run two or three of you through the body, to heighten your pleasure."

This warning, uttered in a determined voice, seemed to have some effect on the obfuscated intellects of the party of debauchees, particularly as the speaker had disarmed two of them, who fell back for support among their companions, by whom, in mistake, they were very nearly run through the body. A few slight scratches had been received by the assailants, which appeared to satisfy them with fighting, and they were retreating, forgetful of their wounded friend, when Luis sprung forward to aid him. What was his horror, when, on Pedro recovering his torch, which had remained burning on the ground, and bringing it to the spot, he beheld in the features of his fallen antagonist those of the young Gonçalo, the brother of Clara.

He was senseless, Luis trusted, more from the fall, or from intoxication, than from the effects of his wound; for he still breathed heavily, although blood flowed freely from his side. As he was about to raise him, some of his companions appeared to have recollected his disaster; and returning, without apparently noticing Luis and his friends, they lifted him amongst them from the ground, and, with staggering steps, bore him along, not uttering a word during the time, till they were nearly out of sight.

Luis was in doubts whether he ought not to follow, to see that more attention was paid to the wounded man, than his friends were likely to be able, in their present state, to afford; but the captain recommended him not to interfere, observing, that as they had sense enough left to carry him out of the road, they would send for the nearest barber to bind up his side, which was all that a clean sword wound required.

"Oh, but he is the brother of my Clara, and may die from the wound he has received," exclaimed Luis.

"That alters the case," said the Captain, and they set forward to overtake the bearers of the wounded man; but though they walked quickly along, by the time they came up with the party whom they fancied were carrying him, he was not to be seen among them. To their inquiries, the people assured them that they must be mistaken, as they had themselves but just turned down from another street, and had heard no sounds of the fray. They then followed another group, whose voices they heard a little in advance; but with like want of success, the people holding silence directly they approached.

"He has, perhaps, been conveyed to the palace of the Conde San Vincente," exclaimed Luis; so they hurried down the street towards it; for it was, as we have said, close at hand; but no one appeared in the neighbourhood, and when, at length, they knocked at the door, after a long time it was opened, and a surly porter declared that no one had been there all that evening, nor had his master left his home since the morning, and had now been in bed for some hours. This might, or might not, have been true; but Luis had no other resource than to return with his friend homeward, dispirited, and full of regret at the accident, wishing that he rather had been the victim; for, should Gonçalo die, he would be looked upon as his murderer, and another barrier, far more insuperable than the former, would be placed against any prospect of his union with Clara. The best consolation the kind-hearted sailor could offer, was, in endeavouring to persuade him, that the wound the young fidalgo had received was probably slight, and that he would recover in a few days; that Luis was in no way to blame, the encounter on his side being perfectly unsought, and that the sufferer and his friends must view it in the same light; indeed, he used every argument that most people would have done in a like case, to soothe the mind of his young friend, though they were of little avail; and it was almost daylight when Luis fell asleep, with his hopes at a lower ebb than he had ever before found them.

With increased anxiety, he repaired, on the following morning, to the church where he was to meet Senhora Gertrudes; and, true to her appointment, he found her kneeling at the same spot, where he had encountered her on the previous day. Notwithstanding the recent unfortunate occurrence, he had resolved to send the letter he had written to Clara; for when his hand had penned it, that was yet unstained with her brother's blood, as his heart was still guiltless of any intention of shedding it.

The old nurse, however, was unconscious of anything that had occurred. "Oh, senhor," she said, "I am so glad that you have not been prevented from coming; for I have got leave to visit my young mistress this very morning, and though she loves me dearly, I am sure that I shall be a more welcome visitor if I carry your little note. Where is it, senhor? Stay,—that nobody may see you deliver it, have the kindness to return me my pocket-handkerchief, which I will drop." Upon which, she adroitly drew the article she mentioned from her pocket, and let it fall by the side of Don Luis, who, stooping down, restored it to her with the letter, which he had conveyed under it.

As she felt the size of the packet, she whispered, "I am afraid, senhor, this is much larger than the little note I promised to carry; but, never mind, I dare say that you have a great deal to say to my young lady, which she will like to hear; and I don't think a long note can do more harm than a short one, so be assured she shall have it. Poor dear, I would do anything to please her."

Luis was longing, all the time the old lady was speaking, to put in a word to inquire for the young Gonçalo. To his question, she answered, that the young master's habits were so very irregular, that no one remarked upon his remaining away for a night; that she had not seen him that morning, nor did she think that he had returned home on the previous evening; but that, just as she was leaving the palace, she was surprised to meet, at that unusually early hour, his friend the Conde San Vincente, (whom she took the opportunity to abuse,) just entering the hall; that she thought he might have come to speak to the younger Gonçalo, or, perhaps, to his father.

Luis then told her, under the promise of the strictest secrecy, that he had unintentionally, and, indeed, against his utmost endeavours, wounded the young fidalgo on the previous evening; that he had been carried off by his party, and he knew not where he had been conveyed. Luis then assured her that his heart was wrung with anguish at what he had done, and besought her, if her mistress heard of the accident, to place his conduct in its proper light, as he had no doubt that occasion would be taken to vilify him, if possible, in her opinion; particularly if, as he suspected, the Conde San Vincente was engaged in the affair.

"Ah, senhor, I am sure it was entirely Gonçalo's fault, who is led into all sorts of mischief by that horrid count," said Gertrudes. "I knew he would some day or other suffer for his folly; and I will take care my young lady does not believe anything to your disparagement."

"In mercy do, my good senhora, or she will be taught to look upon me with horror instead of love," said Luis. "You know not the pangs, the wretchedness, I have suffered, at the thoughts of this fresh misfortune."

"Oh yes, senhor, I can feel for you, I assure you," whispered the old Nurse. "You forget I too was once young and pretty, and had my admirers also, particularly one who was handsome, and constant, and loving; so I married him at last, and some happy years I spent, till he went to sea, and I never heard of him more; but I have ever since felt a kindred feeling for young lovers, and doubly so when my sweet mistress is one of the parties."

Luis felt his heart much relieved by her promises, and just then bethought him of a present he had prepared for her, so requesting her again to drop her handkerchief, he begged her to accept what he offered her, which, considering it was a pair of handsome filigree gold earrings, he had not much hesitation in doing, and seemed mightily pleased at the attention.

While the greater part of the above conversation was going forward, they had risen from their knees, and were standing hid from general view behind one of the pillars of the church, the loud chanting of the service preventing the tones of their voices being heard by any but themselves. The same scene we have described is constantly practised for far more doubtful purposes.

Senhora Gertrudes promising to bring Luis either a verbal or written answer to his letter within a few days, they separated, little dreaming of the accumulated horrors those days were to bring forth. Though his conversation with the old nurse had somewhat restored peace to his mind, by affording him yet a gleam of hope, Luis felt his spirits, like the air, heavy and gloomy. As he walked slowly homeward, the unaccountable and unusual gloom, which, like a funereal pall, had for many preceding days hung over the city, seemed increased in density.

Volume Two—Chapter Nine.

On the morning of the 1st of November, 1755, the murky gloom, which had for so long hung over the city, appeared to have settled down in a dense fog, a phenomenon so unusual, that many turned to their neighbours, and asked if something dreadful was not about to occur, until the sun broke forth, bright and beautiful, dispelling the darkness, and banishing their fears: not a breath of wind disturbed the soft atmosphere, which had more the genial warmth of summer than that late period of the year usually afforded; not a cloud dimmed the pure serenity of the sky; and everybody rejoiced that, at length, the ill-omened clouds had vanished. It was the day of a festival, dedicated in the Romish Calendar to all the Saints; and numerous parties of citizens and mechanics, released from their usual occupations, might be seen hastening through all parts of the city, dressed in their holiday suits, twanging their light guitars, to enjoy themselves in the free air of the country. Happy were they who thus early quitted that doomed city.

It was the day Donna Theresa d'Alorna had fixed on for her marriage, why, none could tell; but so she willed it; and the ceremony was to take place at an unusually early hour, in the chapel belonging to her father's palace, the high dignitary of the Church who officiated on the important occasion being required to perform some other indispensable duty at a later hour. Captain Pinto had been spending some days with Luis, and, early in the morning, parted from him to visit Senhor Mendez, whom, on the previous evening, he had left with an increase in his indisposition. Soon afterwards, Luis, ordering Pedro to attend him, rode forward to the palace of the Count d'Alorna, to be in readiness to attend the ceremony about to be performed. It was one he would willingly have avoided; for, though he retained no love for his beautiful cousin, he could not help feeling many regrets that one on whom he had once set his affections, should be given away to a person for whom he knew she could feel scarce the slightest regard. The count received him with cordiality, introducing him to the numerous members of the Tavora family, who were there assembled to do honour to the marriage of the heir to the rank and dignities of the head of their haughty house.

The marchioness, Donna Leonora, we have already mentioned, a lady yet retaining many marks of her past beauty. She was of a proud and imperious temper, dividing her thoughts between aims for the yet further aggrandisement of her family, and what she considered her religious duties; indeed, by her active and intriguing disposition, she was calculated to succeed in undertakings which others of her sex would have considered impracticable; obstacles only serving with her to increase the ardour of her pursuit.

The marquis, her husband, was a man of dignified and noble carriage, but very different from her in disposition, being of an amiable and gentle temper, yielding his opinion, alas! too much to her guidance. Their second son, Don Jozé, a youth yet scarcely nineteen, was celebrated as much for the beauty of his person, as for the elegance of his manner, and for his honourable and noble disposition; and he at once gained the good opinion of Luis, which afterwards ripened into sincere friendship.

We do not intend to describe the ceremony, which, in the Romish Church, is of short duration. Not a tear was shed by the bride as her father gave her away, but there was a tremulous motion on her lips, and her eye bore a distracted and pained impression, which it wrung Luis's heart to see; and no sooner had he performed the duties required of him, than, without waiting for the feast prepared for the guests, he hastened from the palace, and mounting his horse, desired Pedro to return home, while he endeavoured to dissipate his melancholy feelings by exercise.

He was, at first, doubtful which way to turn his horse's head; but there was an attraction he could not resist, to wander beneath the walls which confined her on whom all his affections had centred; though she might be concealed from his view, yet he remembered a long line of grated windows, through which he had, at times, seen many a young and lovely face gazing on the bright world without, like a bird from its cage, as if longing for liberty; and some latent hope there was in his breast that Clara, too, might be tempted by the beauty of the morning to endeavour to inhale the free air of heaven from her prison windows, the nearest approach to liberty she was doomed to enjoy.

The moment this idea occurred to him, he urged on his steed as fast as he could venture to proceed over the ill-paved and rugged streets, till he arrived near the Convent of Santa Clara; he then, slackening his pace, rode under its lofty walls, gazing up anxiously at each window as he passed, but she whom he sought appeared not. Twice had he passed, and he began to despair of seeing her, fearful also that his remaining there might attract observation and suspicion on himself, when, like a bright light in the black obscurity of the midnight sky, at one of the hitherto dark windows, towards which his eyes were turned, appeared a female form.

A lover's sight was not to be deceived: his heart beat with rapture, as he beheld his beloved Clara; nor was she slow, as her glance fell on the street beneath, in recognising him who had not been absent from her thoughts since they parted. She dared not speak, even could her voice have been heard; but her gaze convinced him that his presence caused her no displeasure. Neither could tear themselves away from the spot they occupied; yet, alas! it was the nearest interview they could hope to enjoy. For some minutes they remained regarding each other with looks of fond affection, when, on a sudden, the docile animal Luis rode snorted and neighed loudly, and then trembled violently. A deep low noise was heard, like carriage wheels passing at a distance; it increased, as if a thousand chariots were rushing by, shaking the earth by their impetuous course. Clara uttered a shriek of terror; for she beheld her lover's steed dash furiously onward, to escape from the dreaded approach of impending ruin. The ill-omened sounds increased. His rider in vain checked him with the rein—the animal uttered a cry of agony, and rearing high in the air, as if struck by a shot in the chest, fell backward with him to the ground. Luis, now in front of the principal entrance to the convent, was uninjured; and, disengaging himself, from his fallen steed, which, rising, galloped madly away, he turned towards the gateway of the building. Again that dread-inspiring convulsion wrenched the solid ground. Shrieks and cries of terror rose on every side. The great gates were thrown open, and crowds of nuns were seen issuing forth, in the wildest confusion and despair, flying they knew not whither, the hopes of self-preservation urging them onward, thoughtless of all they left behind; and from the door of the adjacent church, a like panic-struck mass were rushing forward—men, women, and children—the wealthy and the poor—the noble and the beggar—ladies in their silken robes, and priests in their sacerdotal vestments, in one confused concourse, all trying to pass each other; the aged and the feeble overthrown and trampled on by the young and vigorous. But the implacable spirit of destruction made no distinction between age or sex, strength or weakness; none could withstand the vast masses of masonry which came hurtling on their heads; some few escaped unscathed amid the tremendous shower, but every moment fresh hundreds lay crushed beneath the superincumbent ruins. But Luis, where was he amid the wild uproar and confusion? One only object, one thought filled his imagination. Clara, his own beloved, was within those tottering walls! Could he save her? Not an instant's idea of self-preservation crossed his mind. He flew, as he rose from the ground, towards the gate. His eye ranged over the affrighted countenances of the recluses, but she was not among them. It was impossible she could have reached the entrance in time. He endeavoured to urge his way among them, to enter the house of destruction, but none stayed him to ask whither he went. He cried forth Clara's name, but no one could understand or answer him. A fair girl came flying past him, shrieking with fear: a vast stone fell from the gateway, and, in an instant, that lovely form lay, crushed beneath it, a shapeless mass. He stayed not in his course; but, as he rushed on, "Oh God!" he cried, "such might be Clara's fate!" His bosom seemed bursting with his dreadful feelings: he shrieked, but his voice appeared choked, and without strength. The Father Confessor passed, followed by the Lady Abbess, for whom he stayed not, though, with cries, she implored him to aid her; yet both escaped, and thanked Heaven their righteousness had saved them, while two innocent girls shared the destiny of the former. Luis looked not behind him at their fate; far more terrible dangers were before him, and she whom he sought was in the midst of them! Words cannot paint the horrors which surrounded him; and with far greater rapidity did he rush onward than the time we must take to describe his progress. He, at length, broke his way past the affrighted females, and terror-stricken monks, who impeded his course; but the strength with which his eagerness to proceed inspired him, was even greater than that which their fear gave to the latter; and, triumphing over all obstacles, he reached a large quadrangle, on the right of which appeared a broad staircase, which he knew must lead in the direction where Clara had been. Was she there now? He stayed not to reckon chances. Love gave him the instinct of the Indian to traverse the trackless desert: he hesitated not a moment to consider the path he was to take; for all his thoughts and energies were concentrated on one point, to discover the spot where Clara was to be found. He flew up the stone steps, which yet stood firm, though broad fissures appeared in the walls on each side; he traversed, with the speed of the frighted deer, a long corridor, leaping over many a chasm already formed in the floor, the ceiling, at every step, falling in on him from above; the ends of the stout beams bending down, threatening instant destruction, as their supports, giving way, were leaning towards the street. His breathing was nearly stopped by the exertion, and by the clouds of dust which surrounded him, and which also obscured his sight; yet on he rushed, when, in an instant, his energies were paralysed; the blood forsook his heart; a female form lay before him—oh, Heavens! was it Clara? He stooped down. No, no, that mangled shape could not be hers. A deep wound was in the temple, the fair hair was clotted with blood—he dared not give another glance. No, no, it could not have been her—those, surely, were the robes of a nun. He fled onward; he felt confident that he must have reached the neighbourhood of the window beneath which he had remained gazing at her. Another corridor led him to the right; a door stood open—he rushed in—the roof had given way, but he leaped over the intervening rubbish. Within a deep recess of solid masonry was a window, but he saw no one there. It could not be his judgment which guided him; for, at that awful time, 'twere vain to suppose human judgment could be exercised, or could avail aught. Yet some power drew him on—that inscrutable, that magnetic influence which attracts two souls together—that all-pervading instinct of love!

He paused not till he reached the window. His hopes had not deceived him. Sunk on the ground, her fair head resting against the stone window-seat, he beheld the beloved object of his search. He raised her up—he clasped her in his arms. "Oh, Luis! is he safe?" she whispered, as her head sunk on his shoulder, unconscious of all that had occurred—of the fearful destruction which was going forward. Her last thought had been of him, as she saw him borne away by his maddened steed;—she heard not the wild cries which rose from below, or the shrieks which echoed through the building, or the voice of a friend, calling on her to fly. Her love had preserved her; and they were together, as yet unharmed; and Luis felt (if thought or feeling could be possible at such a moment) that no power could divide them. The same fate awaited them both, but instant destruction seemed to threaten them. If the walls stood, within the recess they might be safe; but already were those shaken to their foundations— another shock, and they must inevitably fall. Such was his rapid idea, as he was raising Clara. Again he turned to fly with her to seek for safety; but where was safety to be found, when the earth itself was lifted, like the ocean's billows, from its level? Still there was happiness and confidence at his heart. Though so many examples were before his eyes, he imagined not the fate which might be theirs. Onward he bore her, by the way he had come, along the broad corridor. For some time his course was unimpeded, till, at length, a vast chasm yawned before him: the whole wall had fallen down, crushing all beneath it. Once more he turned, with his precious burden, still unconscious, in his arms: more than human strength and energy seemed afforded him. Another corridor presented itself, the floor yet affording a passage, though crowded with fragments of the roof. As he flew along it, he observed a stair on one side: that might lead to some egress. He descended rapidly, though scarce a gleam of light was there to guide his steps. When he reached the bottom, he found a passage, narrow and vaulted, leading off on each side. He took that to the left, where the light appeared; but, as he approached it, a strongly-barred window was seen. Near him, a door was left open, at the top of a second narrow and winding stair. Whither that would lead there was no time to consider; but retreat was hopeless by the way he had come, and his only hope of saving the life of the dear being he bore was in onward progress. He descended the steps: to what secret chambers had they conducted him? Another door was before him—it gave way to his touch, and he found that they had reached a low, narrow, and vaulted passage. That it led to the open air he felt assured, from the greater degree of light before him; but the dust prevented his seeing many feet beyond where they were. He hastened on, when again a terrific sound was heard, like the loud echoes of cannon in a mountain gorge—the earth shook beneath his feet—a stunning crash was more felt than heard, as if the globe had been hurled in contact with another body—the strong walls on each side seemed giving way—huge masses of the building, falling on all sides, blocked up all egress in front,—behind, all was darkness! Nature could endure no more: his legs refused to support him, and he sank with his precious burden to the ground; yet consciousness did not forsake him, and he preserved her from injury, bending over her yet inanimate form, that he might shield her to the last, and that his head should be the first to receive the blow which he felt assured must fall. The second violent shock was over, yet crash after crash continued to be heard, as each massive wall and lofty tower, which man in his pride had fancied would last for ever, were overturned like pasteboard fabrics raised by childhood's hands. A third time was the loud thunder beneath the earth heard—the ground shook, and the few remaining walls of the convent were cast down, and that vast fabric, which, a few minutes before, had stood firm and entire, was now one shapeless mass of ruins, with hundreds of human beings buried beneath it. The anguish of death came over Luis: Clara—his own Clara, lay, without breathing, in his arms. Her pulse had ceased to beat, animation had fled, and he welcomed destruction as a boon from Heaven. Each instant the end of all things seemed about to arrive; the shrieks of despair, which had before wrung on his ears, were hushed; the thundering crashes of the falling buildings were no longer heard; and the more terror-inspiring muttered roar beneath the earth had ceased; but foul exhalations arose, and poisoned the air, already filled with suffocating dust; and darkness, impenetrable and oppressive, surrounded the lovers.

Volume Two—Chapter Ten.

Were we to indulge, while describing scenes like the present, in the light jest, or stroke of satire, we should deem ourselves equally capable of laughing at the anguish and wretchedness to which, in our course through life, we have too frequently been witness; our readers must, therefore, pardon us, if, on this occasion, contrary to their wish, we lay aside that inclination we have hitherto experienced, to satirise the follies and wickedness of our fellow-men. It will be our duty to revert to the events which occurred to the principal personages mentioned in this history.

We left the bridal party at the palace of the Marquis d'Alorna. They were assembled in a handsome saloon, which looked towards the street, while all were paying their compliments to the lovely Donna Theresa, and their congratulations to the young marquis, on his happiness at possessing so fair a bride, when a train of carriages was heard passing.

"It is the King and the royal family, on their road to Belem," said the Conde d'Atouquia. "They were to go there this morning."

"I would they were never to return!" muttered the Duke of Aveiro. "It would be no great loss to us."

"Hush! duke," said the Count, who had just sufficient sense to know that silence will often stand in the place of wisdom. "All here know not their own interests. 'Twill be better not to speak on that subject awhile."

When the lovely bride heard the King mentioned, a pallor overspread her countenance.

"Are you ill, my Theresa," inquired her young husband, affectionately.

"Oh no, 'twas a sudden pain, but I am well again," she answered, recovering, and endeavouring to smile. She could not say it was the dreadful struggle between conscience and inclination which agitated her.

The guests had just taken their seats at a sumptuous breakfast, prepared for the occasion, the bridegroom being placed at the head of the table, when that strange sound of chariot-wheels was heard.

"'Tis the King, for some cause, returning home again," exclaimed one. ("'Tis the King of Terrors, riding on the whirlwind of destruction," he might, more properly, have said.)

"No, 'tis a sudden blast, or the roaring of the breakers against the rocks of St. Julian," answered another.

"Mother of Heaven! see, the glasses tremble!" cried several.

At that moment the noise increased. "An earthquake! an earthquake!" shrieked the guests, rushing from their seats towards the window.

The building shook, but scarce a stone fell. "'Twill be over soon," exclaimed the Marquis of Tavora, preserving his presence of mind. "There is more danger in the street than here."

The wildest dismay was visible in the countenances of all, yet none sought to fly, but rushed together towards the recesses of the windows, fancying that numbers might cause security.

"Fear not, my friends," said the Marquis d'Alorna, "this palace is strong, and has resisted many an earthquake. It will alone affect the fragile houses of the plebeians. See! numbers are already in ruins; what clouds of dust rise from them! The shock has passed, and we are safe!"

Scarcely had he uttered the words, when again that sullen roaring beneath the earth was heard. There was no time for flight, they stood paralysed with horror. Donna Theresa showed the fewest signs of fear, as she gazed forth on the city, great part of which lay spread at their feet: she sought not for support, while the other ladies present clung to the arms of those nearest them, except the elder Marchioness of Tavora, who, drawing forth a crucifix from her bosom, called on all around her to pray to the holy Virgin for safety; but, during those moments, the only words any could utter were, "Misericordia! misericordia!"

The wildest cries of agony and fear arose from below, where row beyond row of the thickly crowded streets swayed backwards and forwards, like the agitated waves of the ocean, when the first blast of the hurricane is felt; while the thick clouds of dust which ascended from the falling masses seemed like the foam flying before the tempest.

A strong wind now blew with terrific violence, and, as here and there a view could be obtained of the city, one scene of havoc and destruction presented itself: not a church, or convent, scarce a house, was standing below them, except in the immediate neighbourhood, on the side of the hill; and many of the houses even there were tottering to their base, the people hurrying through the streets, they knew not whither, seeking for safety, and often hurrying to destruction. Numbers had fled to a broad quay, newly built of solid marble, where they deemed themselves in perfect safety; when, as if by magic, it suddenly sank, the water rushing into the vast chasm it had formed, drawing within its vortex, like a whirlpool, numbers of boats and small vessels, crowded with unfortunate wretches, who fancied that it was from the earth alone they had cause to fear. Directly after this dreadful catastrophe had occurred, a vast wave was seen rising on the river, hitherto so calm and shining, and rushing with impetuous force towards the devoted city. The vessels were torn from their moorings, and hurled one against the other. On came the mountain-billow, breaking over the lower part of the city, and sweeping off thousands who had fled to the remaining quays for safety, returning once more to throw back its prey of mangled corpses, amid broken planks and rafters of the ruined houses.

In silent dismay, the festal party stood yet free themselves from harm, though they beheld some of the domestics, who, being on the ground-floor, had rushed from the palace down the street in front, crushed beneath the houses, which fell as they attempted to proceed. The Marquis d'Alorna urged his friends to remain, for several had determined to attempt to escape from the city, the whole of which they expected every instant to behold overwhelmed, when, seeing the fate of their servants, they yielded to his persuasions. Scarcely had they returned to the window, when, with the same dreadful omens, a third shock was felt, though by them but slightly; and, as if struck by a magician's wand, every remaining wall and tower in the vast arena below, which had before escaped, was thrown prostrate, the waves again returning, and rushing high over the ruins, quickly flowing back to their proper boundaries; but not a minute intervened before another mighty billow followed, and another, and another, until every one felt persuaded the city must be submerged.

The mighty throes of nature appeared at length calmed—the roaring noise had ceased; but the wailing of the bereaved inhabitants, and the shrieks and groans of the dying, filled the air. Two elements had already conspired to the destruction of that once opulent and crowded city; but even yet the spirit of destruction was not satisfied, and scarcely had the survivors begun to recover from their first unnerving panic, when a new foe appeared, and flames rose from every fallen shrine and monastery, and from many of the houses yet standing. So paralysed had become the energies of all, that no one attempted to stop the rapid progress of the devouring element. It at first commenced in different spots, like so many watch-fires lighted by an army encamped on the plain, but, by degrees, it extended on every side, till the greater part of the city was enveloped in one vast conflagration.

"Whither can we fly for safety?" cried several of the party, gazing at each other with horror on their countenances. "At all events, let us quit this devoted city," all exclaimed. "But is there a road yet left free?" asked some.

"We must not remain here to be burned alive, having escaped the other dangers," said the young Marquis of Tavora. "My Theresa, I swear to bear you safe, or die with you." The bride hesitated, but her husband insisted on supporting her. "Now, senhores, I will set the example, if you will follow; and we may find some of our country-houses uninjured." His opinion was considered the best to follow by the majority.

"I will order my horses and carriage from my palace," said the Duke of Aveiro; but, when he looked towards his palace, he beheld it one heap of ruins: the proud residence of the Tavoras had shared the same fate, as had those of many other persons present.

The palace of the King, which he and all the royal family had, a few minutes before, so providentially quitted, was overwhelmed in the common destruction; and the Opera-house, a solid and magnificent building, a short time before only finished, had shared the same fate, the side walls remaining alone standing. But this was no time for vain regrets: self-preservation was the first thought of all. The advice of the young marquis was followed, and each of the gentlemen aiding in supporting the ladies, they issued forth from the palace, already deserted by the greater number of the servants, the remainder following them, without leaving one to protect the rich and costly furniture, or even thinking of closing the doors behind them.

The party proceeded onward, keeping as much as possible the higher ground, which had escaped the convulsions which shook the valleys, expecting every moment some fresh outbreak. They had not gone far, when they encountered a fierce-looking band of the vilest rabble of the city, who eyed the rich dresses and the glittering jewels of the ladies, as if longing to possess themselves of them, and stopping, attempted to surround the party, with threatening gestures; but the fidalgos, drawing their swords, cleared a passage through them, receiving only loud jeers and curses as they passed onward. In one place they were obliged to descend the hill for some short distance, where the road was blocked up by the fallen houses, which, as the only course left to them, they must surmount. The scenes which met the eye, it were scarcely possible for ordinary language to describe; men, women, and children, lay, dead or dying, crushed and mangled in every way it were possible to conceive; some of the latter yet crying out, but in vain, for assistance:—their lot might be that of all the party, if they stayed. The only one of the proud fidalgos who really felt for their sufferings, was the young Jozé da Tavora, and he vowed to return and aid them, if possible, when he had conducted his sisters and the rest of his family to a place of safety.

After great labour, they escaped clear of the ruins, and reached some of the highest ground, from whence they could look back on the hapless city. Far as the eye could reach on each side, extending along the banks of the river, was one universal scene of destruction. The greater number of the superb and beautiful churches, the richly endowed monasteries, the public buildings, the palaces, and the dwelling-houses, had, in the course of a few minutes, been either levelled with the ground, or their skeleton walls alone left standing, burying beneath their ruins, as was afterwards ascertained, twenty thousand of the inhabitants. In every direction, also, bright flames arose, wreathing themselves round many buildings which had withstood the shocks; thick clouds of smoke, like twisting pillars, ascending to support the dark canopy which overhung the fatal spot. The river itself presented an almost equally forlorn spectacle; ships were driven wildly in all directions, some dashing against each other, and their crews unable to separate them; others had been dashed to pieces on the opposite shore; some had sunk, some had been carried far up the banks, and were now left dry among the ruined buildings, while the water was covered with wrecks of vessels, beams of timber, and floating bodies. Boats, too, of all shapes and sizes, were floating about, many having been turned keel uppermost by the vast waves. A large concourse of the houseless wretches, whom the catastrophe had driven forth, were now collected on the brow of the hill, bewailing, with groans and tears, their wretched fate: their whole property destroyed, many half clothed, and without a farthing left to purchase the necessaries of life, even if they were to be found; but where was food to be procured for that multitude? Thousands must perish of starvation before it could be distributed.

As the bridal party, after resting from their fatigues on the brow of the hill, were about to proceed to the Quinta belonging to one of their number, where they purposed erecting tents in the open ground, several horsemen were seen approaching. The crowd made way for them; for among the foremost rode the King, and by his side was the towering form of his Minister, Carvalho. No sooner did the former behold Donna Theresa, than his eye lighted up with satisfaction, and, for the moment, forgetful of his city destroyed, and the wretchedness of his people, he threw himself from his horse, which an attendant held, and advanced towards her. While he congratulated her, and those around, on having escaped from destruction, and her husband on his happiness, the Minister, who had also dismounted, stood impatiently by. At last the King recollected himself, and advanced to the brow of the hill. He started back at the view he beheld: he wrung his hands with despair.

"Alas, alas!" he cried, "my beautiful Lisbon! where art thou? It is hopeless to attempt restoring it. Alas! what shall I do?"

"Bury the dead, and take care of the living," answered the Minister, promptly. "'Tis all that can be done."

"Carvalho, you are truly fit to govern my people," exclaimed the King, embracing him.

"Will your Majesty give me full powers to act as I judge fit, without let or hindrance of any sort, and I will undertake to restore order, to supply food, and to rebuild the city."

"Do all that you will; I place implicit confidence in your judgment, and promise to sanction all the measures you pursue."

"It is all I ask," said Carvalho. "I beg your Majesty will return to Belem, to rest after the fatigues you have undergone, and be assured I will not fail in my duty."

The King, taking his Minister's advice, rode back to Belem, while Carvalho, throwing himself into his carriage, which had driven up, immediately commenced issuing orders for the regulation of the inhabitants who had been driven from their homes, and, sending messengers in all directions, to desire the farmers at a distance to bring food to the neighbourhood of the city for their use. Every one obeyed him with alacrity; for, on a great emergency, the mob are ever ready to be ruled by any one who can exhibit confidence in himself. But we are forestalling events, and must return to follow the adventures on that dreadful day of several friends in whom we are deeply interested.

Volume Two—Chapter Eleven.

We left our good friend Captain Pinto, having just parted from Luis, hurrying off on a visit of charity to the stranger Senhor Mendez. He found him, contrary to his expectations, considerably recovered; the slight attack he had suffered on the previous night, which had alarmed his attendant, having passed off, though he was still unable to leave his couch. Seating himself by his side, the gallant sailor detailed to him various circumstances which had happened in the world since he had last seen him, when their conversation turned upon matters of yet greater interest, and so engrossed were they in their subject, that they did not attend to the first dread signals of approaching confusion. Soon again, the noise grew louder, the house shook, and the upper story, with a loud crash, fell in, destroying several unfortunate beings who were residing there.

"'Tis an earthquake!" exclaimed Captain Pinto. "I thought something was about to happen, though it passed my power of calculation to tell what."

"Then fly, my friend, and save yourself," cried Senhor Mendez; "for the whole house must inevitably fall, and will crush you in the ruins."

"I will see what chance there is first of carrying you on my back," answered the sailor, coolly walking to the window, and looking into the street, from whence the most piercing shrieks proceeded. "'Twill be wiser to stay where we are; for 'tis raining rather large stones from the house-tops, and numbers of poor wretches, who have fled thither, he crushed beneath them."

"'Tis a great hazard, but much greater is incurred by remaining here; so, I beseech you, fly, and leave me," reiterated Senhor Mendez.

"This is no time for jesting," said the Captain, "or I might suppose you were inclined to be merry. What! do you ask me to leave a brother in danger, when I might save him? No, my friend, I will perish with you, if such is to be our lot,—we are neither of us children to fear death,—or I will preserve your life."

Saying which, the captain returned to the side of his friend's couch, and drew the head of it within an alcove formed in the wall. "We shall here be far safer than in the street; for the greater part of the house may fall around without injuring us."

In vain Senhor Mendez urged his friend to fly: he persisted in remaining by his side, till he found that words were of no avail. "I will go with you, then," he said. "I have yet strength sufficient to walk to some open space, where the danger will be less." But the captain was resolute; for he well knew that the sick man could not hurry along at the speed which was requisite, nor climb over the impediments they were certain to encounter.

Three or four minutes passed away in a state of dreadful uncertainty, the gallant sailor sitting calmly down, firmly resolved to await the result. Then came the second and most violent shock: the back part of the house was heard to fall, the shrieks and cries were redoubled, crash after crash succeeded; but still the friends were safe, and the captain firmly kept his post. The third shock, which followed some minutes afterwards, was less violent, though a greater number of buildings, shaken by the former ones, were overturned by it.

The front wall of the house was seen to bulge outward. "Farewell, my friend," ejaculated Senhor Mendez, seeing what was about to occur. Down fell the wall into the street, while clouds of dust obscured their sight; but the upper rafters of the ceiling still bound the sides of the building together. Both the friends expected instant destruction; minute after minute passed away, but the wall beneath which they were stood firm; till at length, the air becoming more clear, and the shocks scarcely perceptible, they had the satisfaction of wringing each other's hands as a mark of joy at their mutual preservation, and returning thanks to the great Being who had saved them.

It was in the same way the elegant and beautiful wife of the Minister, the Countess Daun, was preserved. She had not yet risen from her bed when the first shock was felt; but, springing up, she rushed to where her youngest child was sleeping, and with admirable presence of mind and resolution, stood the whole time that the work of destruction was proceeding, within a broad doorway, the front wall of the house being precipitated outward, and the roof falling in and crushing the bed on which she had been sleeping. The rest of the building stood, and she had the happiness, when the convulsions had subsided, of finding her other children unharmed, though she knew not the fate of their father, who had, at an early hour, left his home.

But to return to Captain Pinto. After remaining for a considerable time with his friend in their perilous situation, and perceiving no further shocks, he determined to endeavour to carry him to a place of greater safety. Wrapping him up, therefore, in some clothes which had fortunately escaped, he bore him to the door, standing open, and from thence down the broken steps, and over heaps of ruins, by the back of the house, (for the front was completely blocked up,) and across a small courtyard, where he was obliged to set him down to rest. The wall had been thrown down, exhibiting a street, in a less ruinous state, leading up a steep hill, at the top of which was an open space, surrounded by buildings, which, being only of one story, had resisted the shocks. Thither the captain now led his friend, who insisted on walking, which, with some difficulty, he was able to do, although he sunk down exhausted when he reached the place, where were now assembled a vast concourse of affrighted wretches, with tears and cries mourning the loss of relations and friends,—mothers in tones of misery inquiring for their children, husbands for their wives, sons for their parents and sisters. Here all ranks and conditions were indiscriminately mingled; the proud noble and the loathsome beggar; high dignitaries of the Church in their purple robes; priests who had fled from the altars in their sacerdotal vestments, while celebrating mass; officers and soldiers with their arms thrown aside; nuns and friars in their monastic habits; ladies half-dressed, many without even shoes to protect their feet. Some were rushing to the square, others were flying away, in hopes of finding greater security elsewhere. The greater number were on their knees, offering up broken prayers and cries to Heaven, beating their breasts, with terror in their countenances, and ejaculating, "Mercy! mercy!" Some held clasped in their hands before them crucifixes and images of the saints, which they ever and anon kissed with the most fervent devotion. Some had crawled thither with their limbs broken and their bodies bruised, and were lying, writhing with pain, on the ground, crying out in vain for a drop of water to quench their thirst, many only half clothed, their only consolation, when some of the pious would bring them a cross or an image to kiss, which, with their last gasp, they would press to their lips.

An aged priest was moving among the crowd, with crucifix in hand, exhorting the people to repentance, and endeavouring to offer them every consolation in his power. "Repent, my children; for the wrath of Heaven has descended on you for your sins!" he cried, with tears in his eyes. "You have given yourselves up to every description of wickedness and folly, when you thought none from heaven could see you, and now behold the consequence! Repent, ere it is too late; repent, ere complete destruction comes on you, and your name is erased from the face of the earth! Call loudly on the blessed Virgin; beseech her to intercede for you, and she will hear you; for she loves you as her own children; her heart is tender and compassionate, and she, with sighs and tears, will petition her Son to spare you."

The people flocked around the venerable man, earnestly entreating his benediction; and happy did those deem themselves who could touch even the hem of his garment.

While Captain Pinto was kneeling by the side of his friend, and supporting his head, a person dripping with water rushed by, gazing anxiously into the faces of all he passed. He turned again, and seeing the captain, came up to him. "Oh, senhor, I am wretched and miserable; for I can nowhere find my young master, and know not what has become of him," exclaimed Pedro, for he was the speaker. "I have been hurrying all over the city in search of him, and fear much he must have been destroyed. Alas, alas! I am the only one saved out of the house, which has fallen to the ground. Poor Anna and Lucas are both gone. When we rushed out together, I was a little before them, when the front wall fell and crushed them both—alas, alas!"

"Stay for me," said the Captain. "Assist me to support Senhor Mendez to some place of security, and I will then accompany you to search for your master."

"Care not for me, my friend; but go at once, and search for the youth," said Senhor Mendez. "Perhaps even now he is yet alive, beneath some stone, and you may be in time to save him."

"I will not quit you till you are placed in safety," answered Captain Pinto; and with the aid of Pedro supporting his friend, they conveyed him through the less ruinous parts of the city towards the house of an acquaintance who possessed a large garden in the outskirts. Their road was beset with danger, from the blocks of stone which continued falling every instant from the tottering walls of the buildings; sometimes they were obliged to climb over the ruins, from whence they could hear the groans of the dying and mangled beings who lay buried beneath, but whom it was impossible to attempt to rescue; here, among the masses of stone, limbs were seen protruding,—there the lower part of the body crushed, while the person was yet alive, hopelessly striving to extricate himself; others, more happy, already lay dead, with huge stones on their breasts: but wherever they passed, cries, and shrieks, and groans assailed their ears.

As they proceeded, Pedro gave an account of his adventures. "Oh, senhor, I thought the end of the world was come," he said, "and I never expected to see anybody I knew again when first this dreadful earthquake came on. I scarcely know what happened till I found myself in the Square of Saint Paul's, and the church, and all the buildings round, tumbling about in all directions, and many of the stones almost touching me as they fell; so, not liking that situation, I clambered over the ruins of the church, which had just fallen, crushing hundreds of people beneath it, and reached the broad quay by the river's side, where I thought I should be safer that anywhere else; but I had not been there more than two minutes when a second shock came on, and I was thrown with my face flat on the ground, and had just risen again, when I heard a general cry that the sea was coming in on us. I looked towards the river, and though there was no wind blowing, I beheld an immense wave, rising like a mountain, of its own accord, come foaming and roaring towards the shore. I cast not another look at it, but ran for my life, regardless of the falling stones in the streets; but the water came faster than I could fly, and had I not caught hold of a beam of timber projecting from some ruins, I should have been swept away, as many other unfortunate people were; for the river immediately returned again to its proper level. Thinking there was as much danger from the sea as from the land, I returned back, by the way I came, to the Square of Saint Paul's; but, when I had remained there a minute or so, another shock cast down a great number of buildings which had escaped, and the water rushed even there, so I gave up all hopes of being saved. The water, however, again retired, when I bethought me of my master; for, I confess, before that, my only idea was of taking care of myself. I had been running about in every direction, but could meet nobody even who knew him, till I found you on the top of the hill, where I hoped he too might have gone."

By the time Pedro had concluded his narration, they reached the house of the friend of whom the captain had spoken; and though that had not fallen, the family had deserted it, and were assembled in an open space in the garden, with numerous friends, who had hastened there for safety. They charitably received Senhor Mendez among them, promising to do their best to assist him, when Captain Pinto, without even waiting to take any refreshment, hurried back, followed by Pedro, in search of Luis.

On their way, through the captain's forethought, they procured two iron bars, to aid them in digging among the ruins, should they, by any chance, discover a clue to where he was last seen, though they entertained but slight hopes of discovering him, either dead or alive, had he not escaped uninjured. The horrors and destruction which they witnessed on their way have never been surpassed, if even equalled, during the annals of the world. In many places, also, the buildings had caught fire, and were blazing up furiously on all sides, so that they were obliged to make wide circuits to avoid them. The only clue which Pedro could afford, was that, when his master had parted from him, he had taken a direction by which he must pass by the Convent of Santa Clara, and the captain being in the secret of his friend's feelings, concluded that he might very possibly have remained in the neighbourhood, in the faint hopes of seeing his mistress. Though the chance of discovering him was truly desperate, they determined to persevere; and, not being aware of the entire destruction of that convent, they thought that they might possibly hear something of him from some persons in the neighbourhood, as he would be remarked from being on horseback. After great labour they approached the place; but they looked in vain for the convent—not a wall was standing. As they were crossing a street which led to the square in which it had stood, Pedro's eye was attracted by a dark object beneath the fallen wall of a house; he hastened towards it, and, to his horror, recognised the horse his master had ridden. He wrung his hands in despair, as Captain Pinto came up, pointing to the dead steed, whose head lay crushed by a stone. The captain understood the sign, and joined Pedro in endeavouring to turn over the masses of masonry which thickly covered the ground; the latter, narrowly examining the saddle, to assure himself that he not been mistaken regarding the horse, shook his head mournfully when he found that his fears were too correct. For a long time they plied their task in silence, except when the captain gave some necessary order, expecting every moment to discover the crushed remains of him they sought; for they could scarce indulge a hope that he could by any miracle have escaped. With great labour, and at imminent risk, they cleared away the stones in every direction round the dead horse, the yet standing walls threatening every instant to destroy them, large blocks continually falling with loud crashes near them; but their toil was in vain; and at length, overcome with fatigue, they were compelled, in despair, to desist. Selecting a safe spot, at a distance from the tottering walls, they seated themselves on a mound of ruins, to consult on the next measure to be taken, while they recovered strength to proceed.

They had scarcely been seated there a minute, watching the groups who stood gazing in mute despair, or rushed about with frantic gestures deploring their loss, among the former being a few of the late inmates of the convent, when a person rushed by, his head, sprinkled with white hairs, being uncovered, his dress disordered, with hands outstretched, and eyes wildly gazing on every side. "My child, my child!" he cried, in piercing accents; "has any one beheld my child? I have been deprived of my son, and if now my daughter is torn from me, I am childless!" No one heeded him, for hundreds were uttering the same cries. At a short distance, a woman followed him, with loud shrieks. "My mistress, my young mistress! has any one seen her?

Where have they hid her? where, where?" she was exclaiming, and then gave way again to screams and tears.

Pedro regarded them earnestly. "That is the fidalgo Gonçalo Christovaö. I know him, the father of Donna Clara; and that old woman is her nurse. Depend upon it, senhor, they are in search of the young lady. Alas, alas! I fear that it will be as hopeless as that for my master; but, with your leave, senhor, we will follow them; for I know that if Don Luis was alive, he would be searching for her also."

The captain agreed to the proposal, and hastened after the fidalgo, who no sooner perceived the group of nuns, than he rushed up to them, wildly inquiring among them for his beloved daughter. The captain and Pedro came up with him at the same time: not one of the nuns would venture to speak. With tears he besought them to answer him; explaining, with broken exclamations, that he was the father of a lady belonging to their convent. At length one of the sisterhood, pointing to the ruins, exclaimed, "Alas, senhor, we are the only survivors of the two hundred inhabitants of the convent; the rest lie buried beneath yon shattered walls!"

The hapless father heard no more. Had he not forced his daughter to enter that retreat, she might have been safe; and with a loud cry he fell backwards, and would have sunk to the ground, had not Captain Pinto and Pedro been at hand to support him.

Poor Senhora Gertrudes redoubled her cries, and wrung her hands in despair, as she seated herself on the ground near her master. Regardless of whatever else might happen, and calling on all the saints to restore her young mistress, she would, every now and then, seeing that the fidalgo was unable to comprehend her, reproach him for being the cause of her unhappiness; then she would abuse the convent for falling, and the nuns for leaving her lady behind. Captain Pinto was in a dilemma how to act; he was anxious to search for his friend, at the same time that he was unwilling to leave the fidalgo in his present state, and not a drop of water was to be found to assist in recovering him.

The unhappy father giving no signs of returning animation, the captain grew weary of watching one with whom he was not even acquainted, when his aid was so much more required by others: placing him, therefore, in a situation as far removed as possible from danger, he at length brought the old nurse sufficiently to reason, to induce her to watch by the side of her master, while he, and Pedro, continued their search for Luis. His purpose was first to visit, if possible, the palace of the Conde d'Almeida, in case Luis should have thought of returning homeward, and not hearing of him in that neighbourhood, to work his way to the outskirts of the city, and to make inquiries for him at every place where he found people collected, among whom he could discover any of his acquaintance, intending either to return himself, or to despatch some one with assistance to Gonçalo Christovaö.

Volume Two—Chapter Twelve.

It would be impossible to describe, and difficult even to conceive, a scene in which a greater assemblage of crime, wretchedness, and filth was to be found, than that which, at the time we write of, was offered by the prison of Lisbon.

In a courtyard, where the prisoners were allowed to take whatever fresh air descended within the precincts of that abode of wretchedness, were now collected a number of unfortunate beings, on the countenance of every one of whom might be traced the marks of fierce ungovernable passions, sullen and vindictive humours, a low cunning which had overreached itself, and was longing again for freedom to indemnify itself for its fault. Some were endeavouring to warm themselves in the narrow strip of sunshine which found its way into the courtyard; others were staking all they possessed, a few coppers, perhaps, at games of dice, their eagerness as great as that of the man who is hazarding his thousands; some were carrying on a silent game at cards, the loser, by the motion of his hand towards the place where his dagger used to be, proving the use he would have made of it had he been armed. There were also various other games going forward; but by far the greater number of the inmates of the prison were sitting down, staring with apathetic looks on the ground, and thinking of past, or planning fresh, deeds of wickedness; and though there was every variety of cast of features, and, apparently, many different nations—blacks, mulattos, and Europeans, the same expression and squalor universally prevailed.

On one side of the yard, next the street, was a large hall, with vaulted roof, and strongly-barred windows, at which were posted as many as could clamber up, of men, women, and even children, imploring compassion of the passers by, and fishing up whatever, in their charity, they bestowed, in small baskets, or old hats, at the end of a string fastened to a stick. Here no distinction of age or sex was preserved; men hardened in crime, and young children cast in with their wretched mothers; beardless youths, and girls scarce verging on womanhood; murderers who boasted of their deeds of blood, and miserable beings whom poverty and hunger had tempted to steal a loaf, were thrown together, and scarcely supplied with food sufficient to sustain life: execrations, laughter, screams, and wild songs of desperation, mingling in horrid discord throughout this den of abomination.

In one corner of the yard were seated two men, whose dress had once been superior to that of their surrounding companions, but was now torn, disordered, and dirty in the extreme; their looks betokening them, at a glance, to be villains hardened in crime, exhibiting every mark of the common ruffian.

"I am growing weary of this cursed confinement, and am determined to submit to it no longer," said one.

"Very likely, so am I," returned his companion; "for though we have plenty of good company, and meet many old friends, I like to be master of my own conduct. But how do you purpose escaping, Miguel? Count on me as a staunch supporter; for I shall be happy to get out also, if I knew but the way."

"I have means which will not fail, though I have waited lingering in prison till now, in hopes that others would exert themselves in my favour to procure my liberation; but I see there's no use trusting further to them," returned the other. "I shall send to the count, and let him know, if he does not get me set free before many days are over, I shall give a history of some of our transactions, which will go a good way to blast his character, proud as he is, and secure as he deems himself."

"It's very well talking about it, but do not suppose that any of the haughty nobles would care what such poor wretches as we said against one of their number, even though they might guess we told the truth," responded the other.

"I would soon take means to make him care; and if not, I would give him a lesson with that dagger he has so often paid me to use against others," exclaimed Miguel, grinding his teeth with rage at the thought of having been treacherously treated. "If we can once get out, we will join some of our old friends, and we shall soon be able to lift up our heads in the world again."

"Since this Minister, Carvalho, has taken it into his head to interfere in the affairs of the city, it is easier to get into a prison than to get out of it again," observed the other.

"Fear not, we will manage to escape in spite of him," said Miguel.

Scarcely had he uttered those words, when the dogs beneath the prison walls set up a piteous howl, which was followed by a low, rumbling noise—the walls of the prison shook. All started on their feet, consternation and dismay depicted on every countenance;—a thundering crash was heard, as the side of the vaulted chamber was seen to fall outward, carrying with it the unfortunate wretches who were assembled in the windows.

Regardless of their cries, the remainder of the prisoners made a rush over the fallen ruins; "Hurra for the earthquake! liberty, liberty!" they shouted, some, with wanton barbarity, seizing the muskets of the guards stationed in front of the prison, and dashing out their brains, before they had time to defend themselves.

With wild cries and imprecations, the savage band hurried on, regardless of the dreadful convulsions of nature, attacking, in their blind fury, the affrighted inhabitants, who were flying from their falling houses. They halted not in their mad career till they reached an open space, from whence they could look back on their late abode; and as the second shock came on, when they beheld the prison hurled prostrate to the ground, they uttered wild yells of delight, pointing with gestures of derision towards the spot; in the intoxication of liberty, dancing and singing like a troop of demons.

What was it to them, that every instant thousands were suffering the most agonising deaths?—what cared they that a flourishing city was being destroyed?—they had gained their liberty! "Viva, viva to the earthquake! the loss of others is our gain. Viva to havoc and confusion! all is now our prey.—The rich man's wealth is left unprotected,—Death has parted the miser from his gold,—all is now ours!" and on they rushed. Some of their number were killed by the falling ruins, but what cared they for their loss? it was soon supplied by crowds of accursed wretches like themselves, hardened by years of crime, and excited by thoughts of indiscriminate plunder. They met a man flying with bags of gold. "What ho! Dare you to take our property, fool?" and he was hurled lifeless to the ground. The third shock came—but while others were falling on their knees, with prayers for mercy, they shouted and blasphemed; the wilder the havoc, the greater would be their booty;—what cared they for aught else? Away they rushed through the streets—none dared oppose them. They seized upon arms, which some soldiers had thrown aside. "Hurra, hurra! the city is ours! who is lord now?" they cried.

Hapless were those whom they encountered flying with their wealth; but such paltry booty would not satisfy them. "The shrines of the churches are unguarded; for the earthquake has spared some for us." The candles burnt on the altars, rich gems decorated the figure of the Virgin,—they tore away the glittering jewels,—they seized upon the golden cups and salvers of the Holy Sacrament. An aged priest had knelt in prayer, during the awful visitation, happy to die in the sanctuary of his God. With horror he beheld the sacrilegious deed, and cursed the impious wretches in the name of Him he served. "What, old dotard, darest thou interfere with our pursuits? Knowest thou not that all now is ours?" And, on the steps of the altar, where he stood, they dashed out the old man's brains, and laughed, that no one could bear witness of the deed. They entered the palace of a wealthy noble; for the doors were open—no one was there to guard his property. They wandered through the sumptuous chambers; they found jewels in the chamber of his countess; in another room, a box of gold lay open. The foremost seized on the spoil; the others fought to obtain it—knives were drawn, and blood was spilt; but the wounded scarce stopped to staunch their wounds, so eager were they to grasp the rich plate, which lay scattered about. Nothing could satisfy them: their avarice was excited, and they thought of nought else but gaining wealth.

"To the Mint, to the Mint!" they cried,—"that will be unguarded." Away they hurried, each eager to outstrip the other; but when they arrived there, they found the building entire, and the doors closed; though the soldiers who had been stationed there had fled from their posts. They attempted to force the gates; but though his men had quitted him, their officer, a gallant youth, the son of a distinguished noble, had disdained to fly. Fearless of the savage band, he appeared at a window, and ordered them to depart. They still persisted in attempting to force an entrance, when, collecting the loaded muskets of his men, he, with admirable coolness, successively discharged them, killing several of the foremost ruffians. The rest were disheartened.

"There is abundance of booty to be found elsewhere, without fighting for it," shouted some, and immediately took to flight; others followed, and the bravery of one man, scarce numbering eighteen summers, preserved the building from pillage. His name we know not. Throughout the awful scene he had stood undaunted, every instant expecting the building to fall and crush him, or the earth to open and swallow him up, with the sea breaking from its confines, and rushing towards him on one side, yet refused to quit his post. Surely the sentinels at the gates of Pompeii, when the fiery shower fell on them, were not a greater example of heroic courage and military discipline.

Onward hurried the band of marauders. The house of a wealthy banker was before them. Here they might revel amid his chests of gold. They loaded themselves with plunder, till they could carry no more; but their depredations would be discovered. The earthquake had not committed sufficient ravages to satisfy them; they must increase the destruction and confusion. Some houses were already in flames; they seized on torches, and, like the intoxicated Macedonians in Persepolis of old, they rushed through the city, setting fire to every mansion they plundered in their course.

They passed the royal palace. "The King it was who imprisoned us," they cried; "we will be revenged on him." A great part of the edifice had already fallen; but that did not satisfy them; they ransacked the remainder, though, at the risk of their lives, throwing away what they had before collected, for the sake of what they now found; and then applying their torches in every direction, quitted it exultingly, as they beheld the flames burst forth with relentless fury. Away they sped again, to commit further havoc. No one thought of offering any resistance; so paralysed were the energies of all men, that while their houses and property were being consumed, they looked on, without attempting to interfere. At length the savage horde appeared satiated with plunder, and other yet more brutal passions excited them to fresh deeds of violence. Hapless, alas! were the unfortunate beings who fell into their power: they laughed at the tears and prayers of their victims—wealth could not bribe them; the whole of the city was at their disposal—fear could not intimidate them; they thought not of the morrow, and that day they were lords of all. High rank, youth or beauty, were but greater incentives to their fury—many a grey-haired sire, and gallant husband or brother, fell beneath their blood-stained knives, in striving to protect those they held dearest to them on earth. Not greater atrocities were ever committed in a town taken by assault, and given up to the indiscriminate license of an infuriated soldiery, than did those vile monsters of humanity perpetrate during that and the following days.

At length, having loaded themselves with spoil, four of the ruffians separated from their companions, and slunk away together: they had been the most active and choice in seizing on the booty, leaving to others the work of spilling blood to gratify their savage dispositions. Two of them were the wretches we introduced in the commencement of this chapter, the others had joined them during the day, in their course through the city, and with one of them also we have already as intimate an acquaintance as we could wish.

"Hist, Miguel, hist!" said one, fearful that their companions should hear them. "Where dost purpose to hide thy wealth? It will never do to place it where others may come and seize it."

"Fear not for that, man, there are plenty of places where none will think of hunting; the earthquake has stood our friend in this case, as in many others," said Miguel.

"Say then, Miguel, where wouldest advise to hide it—under the ruins of some church or other?"

"No, fool, no; the churches were too full of gold, and numbers will soon go to dig for it," answered his companion. "That would never do. Hark thee, Baltar! There are plenty of vaults under the monasteries and convents, where no one will think of going. Who will take the trouble to dig out the lazy monks or nuns? So come along; we have no time to lose, and then we may set to work and gain more."

Away they hurried, the other two men following. They examined several places, but none seemed to satisfy them. They saw that they were observed, and, drawing their knives, they waited till the others came up.

"What! think you to rob us of our property?" they exclaimed, with dreadful curses, flying at them with the fury of savage beasts. They plunged their knives into the breast of the foremost, who, with a shriek, sunk dead among the ruins; but the other was prepared for them, and, instead of flying, he stood on the defensive.

"This is folly, to kill each other, when we have so much better employment for our time," exclaimed the man who was the assassin employed by Count San Vincente, and he held out his hand towards those who had just slaughtered his friend.

They laughed. "You are a brave fellow," said Miguel; "so come along. We will hide our booty together."

They examined several other spots, without finding one sufficiently secure for their purpose; at last they reached a vast heap of ruins: not a wall was standing of what had once been an extensive building.

"Ah! this will suit us; and there is no one to observe us!" they exclaimed.

They looked cautiously around, and then, clambering over the remains of a garden-wall, they wandered among beautiful shrubs and flowering plants, which hid from their view the scene of havoc which surrounded them. Those had stood while the proud fabrics raised by the hands of men had fallen. In the centre were round tanks, which had in the morning thrown up glittering jets to cool the air; but the water had deserted them, and the gold and silver fish lay dead at the bottom. A little farther on, the plants were crushed by the fallen stones; and here and there might be seen some female form, killed by the same terrific shower, in a vain endeavour to escape; or, perhaps, at the moment of the shock, employed in tending those very plants which now bloomed sweetly near her. From others the breath had scarcely departed; and the ruffians even fancied that they heard faint sighs proceeding from some; but, uttering brutal jests, they passed on among the ruins. They looked about in every direction, to discover some place convenient for their purpose; and, after climbing over some of the ruins which had fallen the furthest outward, Miguel, who was in advance, came to a spot where, descending a short distance among the vast piles of masonry, he observed the top of a small arched door. He endeavoured to open it, but his single strength was not sufficient.

"Here is the very place to suit us!" he exclaimed, calling his friends to his assistance. "None will ever think of looking here. Now remember, comrades, we swear by the holy Virgin never to reveal the spot to any one, or to rob each other."

"Agreed, agreed!" said the other two.

"Now let us see into what place this door opens; for if we stay talking about it, the city will be half burnt down before we have time to collect our share of the booty which Providence has bestowed."

The three ruffians having come to this resolution, set to work with energy to clear away the stones and mortar which blocked up the entrance to the vault,—a task which, after some labour, and considerable risk of being crushed by the crumbling walls, they at length accomplished. But they had now a new difficulty to overcome; for it was discovered that the door opened against them, having evidently led into an outer chamber, in which they were standing. They, in despair of opening the door, which resisted all their efforts, were about to relinquish the attempt, when an iron bar, which had fallen from some window, caught Miguel's eye, and, searching about, they discovered several others. Thus armed, they renewed their attacks; and, although the door was strong, it could not resist their joint efforts, when once they had managed to insinuate the ends of the bars within a crevice in the wall. On entering beneath the arch, they found themselves in a low, vaulted passage, which appeared to lead off in two different directions; but, after proceeding a short distance in the dark, the foremost stumbled over a heap of stones, which had, probably, fallen from above; and, having no light to guide them, nor means at hand for procuring one, they were fearful of going further. Returning, therefore, to the mouth of the vault, they examined it narrowly on every side, and succeeded in discovering a place in which they considered their treasure would be secure, and could be removed without labour at any time. This was a small recess in the wall,—for what purpose formed, it was difficult to say, unless it could be one of those living tombs in which common report affirms the unhappy victims of monastic tyranny who had broken their vows, or divulged any of the secrets of their order, were at times immured. Having convinced themselves that they could not fix on a better place, they deposited all their treasure within it, in three separate parcels, piling up stones in front, so as completely to conceal the entrance; and then, closing the door, and throwing rubbish in front of it, to secure it further, they hurried off in search of fresh booty.

Volume Two—Chapter Thirteen.

It is a very common saying, that there is honour among thieves; in which, from the information we have collected on the subject, we perfectly agree, provided they are convinced it is their interest to maintain it; but, at the same time, they will ever be very unwilling to place more confidence in each other than they know is absolutely necessary. So thought Senhor Rodrigo, the most noted villain and professional bravo of Lisbon, and so think we, perhaps, of a certain portion of mankind, who are not professional cut-throats, and would be furious if they were not considered men of perfect honour. As soon, therefore, as the bravo saw his two companions busily engaged in plundering, and after he had contrived to fill his own pockets with gold, and had secured as much plate as he could conceal about his person, he hastily returned to the place of concealment they had selected, from whence he intended taking out his own share of the booty, and hiding it with what he had last acquired, in a spot known only to himself. He had cleared away the stones in front of the door, and was about to open it, when he heard his own name called from above, and, looking up, he saw Miguel and Baltar descending towards him with threatening gestures.

"What, Senhor Rodrigo, is this the faith you swore to keep with us? But we are even with you, you see."

"I came but to hide this further booty I have collected; so banish your fears, my friends," he answered.

While he was speaking, having advanced a little way towards them, the door was suddenly forced open, and a man appeared before them, bearing in his arms a female form. The robbers started, as if they had beheld an apparition from the grave; for the gloomy appearance of the spot was increased by being contrasted with the bright glare which the burning houses and churches in the neighbourhood cast on the surrounding ruins. It was some seconds before their courage returned; for, daring and savage as they were, anything which they fancied supernatural had greater power over their minds than either fear of the wrath of Heaven or of their fellow-men.

"Thank Heaven, loved one, we are at length freed from that dreadful vault. Speak, my Clara—speak, to assure me that you have truly recovered!" exclaimed Don Luis; for he it was who, with Donna

Clara, had thus, by the unintentional agency of the robbers, been restored to liberty.

When the robbers entered the vault for the first time, he had been remaining for some hours in a state of stupor, hanging over Clara, who was in one of those deep swoons which, in some instances, have been prolonged for several days. The first rush of fresh air completely restored his senses, as it aided to revive her; but his dismay may be conceived, when, unperceived by them,—for the ruffians passed close to him,—he discovered, by their conversation, their desperate characters. Summoning all his presence of mind to his aid, he remained perfectly quiet, trusting that the men would quickly retire, and allow him to escape with his precious burden in safety. He felt her pulse: it already beat more strongly, and he prayed Heaven to restore her completely. Anxiously he waited till the robbers had secured their treasure, when, what was his horror to hear them close the door behind them! He trusted, however, to be able to force open the door, towards which, bearing Clara in his arms, he groped his way, aided by glimmering streams of light, which found an entrance through various crevices in the door, affording to his eyes, so long accustomed to darkness, sufficient assistance to enable him to reach it. He was driven then to the most maddening despair, when he found that all his strength was not sufficient to open it. He called loudly for assistance; but no one heard him, till at length, in hopeless agony, he seated himself on the ground, with Clara in his arms, under the dreadful anticipation of a lingering and painful death;—though it was not for himself he felt, it was for the loved being he supported; and it was more with regret than joy that he found her gradually reviving. After some time, she uttered a few incoherent words, as one just awaking from sleep; but she was again silent, evidently with the impression that she was labouring under some dreadful dream; and Luis felt that it would be cruelty to assure her of the truth: he was fearful of making even the slightest movement, lest it should recall her to consciousness; and he now mourned that she had not rather died at the first shock of the earthquake, than suffered the tortures she must now too probably undergo.

The return of Rodrigo, and alone, gave him renewed hopes of escape, which were quickly disappointed, when he found that the robber had desisted from opening the door, and was, besides, joined by his companions. During the dispute of the ruffians, Luis, finding that the door yielded to his pressure, forced it open; and, trusting that they would be too eagerly occupied in their own quarrel to pay attention to him, with tottering steps he bore Clara from the vault. The fresh air revived his strength; he looked with horrified amazement at the scene of destruction around him, lit up, as we have said, by the blazing houses; but this was no time for thinking; so, without further delay, he commenced climbing the ruins on the opposite side to that where the ruffians stood. He had already reached the summit of the mound, and was able to look on every side, to decide in which direction he should attempt to escape, when the robbers recovered from their surprise.

"What ho! a spy on our secrets!" exclaimed Rodrigo, climbing after him. "Know that no one passes through this city without paying tribute to us, so deliver up the burden you carry, fair sir."

On hearing these alarming demands, Luis, removing Clara to his left side, and supporting her with his arm, drew his sword, prepared to defend her to the last. As he stood thus on the summit of the pile of ruins, a few shattered walls of the neighbouring church still remaining at a little distance, the red glare of the burning houses casting a bright reflection on one side of his figure, he offered a fine subject for the painter.

As Rodrigo approached him, now that every feature of his countenance was so clearly visible, he recognised in him the Count San Vincente's enemy, whom he had been hired to murder, and the fidalgo who had slain his brother in the forest, and deprived him of his booty.

"Ah! senhor, we at length meet again, where there are none to interfere and save you," he exclaimed, attempting to reach the spot where Luis stood; but the latter kept him at bay with his sword, and the ruffian having no other arms than his knife, was afraid of closing with him till his companions came to his assistance.

Luis saw that to speak to them would be useless, and that he must depend entirely upon his own courage and firmness, and had he had but one assailant to contend with, he might have been successful in defending himself, and the being dearer to him than life; but while Rodrigo was attacking him in front, the other two robbers, climbing up the ruins, suddenly seized him from behind, and the dagger of the former had almost reached his bosom, when the ruffian's arm was arrested by a person who had sprung up to the spot without being perceived by any of the party.

"What, ye villains! were ye about to murder my friend, Don Luis, while he was protecting a lady, too?" exclaimed a loud voice; and Rodrigo, turning fiercely on the new comer, beheld Frè Lopez.

"What demon brings you here, when you are not wanted?" cried the robber, turning on him fiercely, while his companions still held Luis, who in vain endeavoured to break from them.

"Don Luis's good demon, I suppose," answered the Friar. "You forget that your figures can be clearly seen from the street; so, as I chanced to be passing, and observed some fighting going forward, I came to see what it was about. Ah! as I live, that is the very lady who gave us so much trouble in the forest! Hark you, Rodrigo—" Saying which, the Friar drew the robber aside. Their conference was but of short duration, yet it seemed perfectly satisfactory to both; when the Friar addressed Luis, who still remained completely in the power of the other two: "I regret to say, senhor, that though I have been the means of saving your life, I can do nothing further for you; and you must consent to this gentleman's terms, though you may think them rather hard."

"Gladly. Any sum he fixes on I will endeavour to pay," answered Luis; "and you, senhor, who have already done me so great a service, will, I trust, aid me in conveying this lady to a place of safety."

"You are mistaken, senhor," interrupted the miscreant, with a laugh of derision. "I give the Padre your life; but I am to have the lady for my share; so yield her up without further delay."

"Never! I will die first!" exclaimed Luis; but, at that instant, by a signal from Rodrigo, one of the men who held him threw a handkerchief over his head, and dragged him backwards, while the principal ruffian forced Clara from his arms. She was by this time sufficiently recovered to comprehend fully all the horrors of her situation; but the wretch heeded not her cries for mercy as he bore her away, while Luis exerted all his energies to free himself from the others; but they, throwing themselves on him, held him down securely, though with considerable difficulty. His struggles exhausted their patience.

"Give him a taste of the steel!" muttered Miguel; "that will keep him quiet enough."

"Hold!" said the Friar, who stood by, a quiet spectator, without attempting to interfere; "Rodrigo will soon be at a sufficient distance, and then you may set the young fidalgo at liberty. In the mean time, senhor," he added, turning to Luis, "I would advise you to be quiet; your exertions only fatigue, without benefitting yourself in the slightest degree."

"Either destroy me at once, or let me fly to save that lady," exclaimed Luis, in a tone of agony.

"It is not wise to seek death before your time," returned the Friar; "and as for saving the lady, who is already a long way from this, I have not the power to do it. Had I not arrived at the moment I did, the lady would have been in the same condition she now is, and you would have been dead; so you, at all events, have to thank me for your life."

Luis scarcely heard what was said; indeed, so intense were his feelings, that they deprived him of utterance and power of thought, except the all-engrossing one of Clara's fate. Had he been aware of the lawless license practising in the city, his agony would, if possible, have been yet more intense.

"When are we to let this young fidalgo go?" muttered Miguel; "I cannot stay here all night watching him; and I must have some security that he does not betray to any one a spot where we have hid a few trifles we found scattered about the streets."

"I will answer for his honour," returned the Friar; "but stay a little, stay a little, you are in too great a hurry, man."

Though Luis had recognised in his preserver his quondam acquaintance, Frè Lopez, by his tone of voice and his expressions, he certainly could not have done so by his outward appearance; for he had now laid aside all pretensions to a holy character in his costume. On his head he wore a three-cornered hat, and a full wig, with side curls and pigtail; his waistcoat, of flowered silk, was of great length; and his coat and breeches of large proportions, the pockets being now filled, almost to bursting, with a variety of little articles, such as trinkets and gold pieces, which he also, probably, had picked up about the streets; a sword by his side, completed his very unclerical costume. He had seated himself near Luis and his captors, and amused himself for some time in addressing, now one, and now the other; though, from the former, he could seldom elicit an answer.

Volume Two—Chapter Fourteen.

We fear that our readers will begin to suppose that we are romancing, when we describe so many hair-breadth escapes and unexpected interferences, which preserved the lives of the principal characters mentioned in this work; but we can assure them, that some equally wonderful befall us every day of our lives, though we are not aware of the circumstance at the time. The simple case of a man meeting a friend in the street who twitches his button off while he is inquiring after his wife and family, may be equally providential with our examples, though not so romantic; for, had he gone on, he would have been crushed by the falling chimney, or drowned when the bridge gave way. Of course, when we are writing the adventures of people who are continually getting into danger, it must be expected that they will escape somehow or other; and we suspect that most of our readers would find great fault if we allowed them to do so in a common-place, every day sort of way; we shall therefore, as we have before declared it our intention, adhere strictly to what we find in the documents before us.

We left the unfortunate fidalgo in front of the ruins of the Convent of Santa Clara, lying in a swoon, caused by the supposition of his daughter's death, and watched by her nurse, who continued sobbing and wringing her hands in the bitterest grief.

Night came on, though it was scarcely perceptible on account of the bright fires which blazed in every part of the city, and still they continued in the same position; nor did Captain Pinto, according to his promise, return.

"Oh, Santa Maria Jozé! my sweet mistress!" cried poor Gertrudes; "you are torn from us for ever, in your youth and beauty! alas! alas! and here am I, a worthless old woman, alive and well, mourning for your loss!" and again she wrung her hands in despair.

On a sudden her master sat upright, and looked wildly around, unable, at first, to comprehend what had happened; but the sights which met his view soon convinced him of the dreadful reality. His heart was indeed bowed with grief, his pride fallen—his only son was slain, his fair daughter lost to him for ever! Yet, though convinced of her fate, he could not tear himself from the spot—and whither could he go? It was impossible for him to venture through the ruined streets, amid burning houses and falling walls. He had just arrived at a complete perception of his misfortunes, when a shriek struck his ear. A father's senses were not to be deceived—it was his daughter's voice! He rose to his feet as a man rushed by, bearing a female form in his arms. There was no deception—that cry for aid was Clara's—that shape was hers. He in vain endeavoured to arrest the man in his flight—he attempted to pursue—but his strength failed him. He called on him, in accents of despair, to restore his child; but the ruffian heeded him not, and the fidalgo sank exhausted on the ground. Old Gertrudes, also, had striven to follow; but, weak from fatigue and long fasting, she had not taken many steps before her strength failed her; and, uttering cries for assistance, she fell near her master.

Though the group of homeless and helpless nuns still remained where they had first collected, they were in too apathetic a state to offer any assistance. No one thought of impeding the vile ravisher in his course, for, alas! such scenes had already become but too common, and the whole city was now filled with shrieks and piteous cries for mercy, unheeded by the savage miscreants who had become the undisputed lords of all.

Captain Pinto's search for his friend proved, of course, as unsuccessful as at first, till at length he recollected the state in which he had left the bereaved father of his friend's mistress, when, with great difficulty procuring some food, notwithstanding all the dangers to be encountered, he set forward to carry him assistance, accompanied by Pedro and another man, whom he engaged for the purpose.

The ruins of the convent being on the outskirts of the conflagration, he was able, by making a long circuit, to approach it with less risk than he had before encountered; but, when he arrived there, it was some time before he could discover the object of his search, now utterly unable to assist himself. The two servants, therefore, supporting the fidalgo between them, and the old nurse being somewhat revived by some of the food the Captain had brought, which she contrived to eat between her sobs and exclamations of grief, he led the way towards the palace of the Marchioness of Corcunda, which was in the uninjured part of the city. As the party were leaving the fatal spot, a man, with a drawn sword in his hand, rushed up to them with frantic gestures, and the noble sailor's satisfaction may be conceived when he discovered his friend Luis. Pedro, in his joy and hurry to embrace his master, almost let the fidalgo fall to the ground; although Luis offered, it must be confessed, but a poor subject for congratulation. From the broken exclamations of Senhora Gertrudes, the Captain had understood that she fancied she had seen her young mistress, but he was unprepared for the excited vehemence of Luis.

"Fly with me to overtake the monster!" he exclaimed, without waiting to receive his friend's congratulations on his safety. "Which way did he bear her? Have none of you seen her? speak!"

"Of whom do you speak, my friend?" asked Captain Pinto; "for I have but just arrived here."

"Of Clara, of my own Clara!" ejaculated the unhappy lover; "she has been torn from me in the moment of preservation, and conveyed I know not whither; but, as you love me, aid me to recover her. Does no one know which way she was carried?"

The old nurse now recognised Luis. "Does the senhor ask for my young mistress?" she exclaimed. "I knew it was her, I knew it was her, and a savage has carried her away."

"Speak, woman, speak!" exclaimed Luis, with agitation. "Which way did he go?"

"Alack! senhor, I scarcely know; we have moved since then—but let me see: yes, it was there—that was the way;" and she pointed in the direction of a street, on each side of which the houses were burning furiously, the walls every instant falling with loud crashes, and throwing showers of sparks into the air.

As old Gertrudes pointed to the street, Luis, heedless of the dangers, was about to break away from his friends towards it, but the Captain held him back. "It is impossible that she could have been carried amid that fiery strait, or that you could enter it without instant destruction. Hear reason, my friend; it is now some time since she could have passed here, and since then she must have been conveyed to a considerable distance, where it will be utterly impossible, unaided, to discover her. I know her danger is great, but I cannot believe there breathes the hellish monster who would injure her. It is far more probable that she has been carried off by some designing ruffians, for the sake of receiving a reward for restoring her; or, if not, be assured that Heaven will, by some unexpected means, protect her innocence. I cannot believe it possible that any harm can happen to her. Assist me now in conveying her father to a place of safety; you see his helpless state, and you will be performing an act gratifying to her. To-morrow we will collect some friends and attendants, and having procured authority from the Minister, we will search for her in every direction, examining every one we meet, and I trust that success will crown our efforts."

With such like persuasions Captain Pinto strove to calm his friend's mind, although he well knew how fallacious the hopes he endeavoured to excite would too probably prove; but he felt that any deceit was excusable to prevent him risking his life in a search which he knew must be futile; and also, not being in love himself, his judgment was cool, and he was very unwilling to accompany him, from the conviction of the uselessness of the attempt. Pedro, also, though a very brave fellow, and very much attached to his master, was not quite a hero, and, as he had already seen horrors enough to make him wish to avoid further danger, he joined in attempting to dissuade him from pursuing his search on that night, when, at length, the Captain cut the matter short by seizing his arm and attempting to drag him along. "Come, my friend," he said, "you have frequently been guided by my advice; be so now, and accompany me whither I will conduct you."

"What! and leave my mistress to her fate? Never! I go alone, if no one will accompany me!" exclaimed Luis; and breaking suddenly from Captain Pinto, he rushed in the direction Gertrudes indicated that the ruffian who bore away Clara had taken. Pedro, who was supporting the fidalgo, was compelled to place his burden on the ground before he could pursue his master; nor could the Captain even attempt to overtake him with any hope of success. Don Luis had already disappeared down a street, the houses rocking and burning on each side, when Pedro reached the commencement. At that instant, a lofty building, not fifty yards before him, fell with a loud crash, completely blocking up the street, and sending up showers of sparks and flame, like the bursting forth of a volcano.

Pedro stood aghast, trembling at his own narrow escape, and at the too probable fate of his master, with whom all communication was now hopelessly cut off. The Captain now coming up, said, in an agitated voice, as he led him back to where the fidalgo had been left,—"We can be of more service to the living than to the dead. We will see this old man in safety, and then return to search for your master."

This was, indeed, the only thing now to be done, and after many difficulties and much labour they reached the palace of the Marchioness of Corcunda. The door was open, and the mansion deserted, though it appeared not to have been pillaged, and after searching in every direction, it was discovered that the inmates had taken refuge in the garden, where they were collected beneath some orange trees; still uttering lamentations for what had occurred, which were increased when they heard the account Gertrudes detailed to them of the loss of Clara, and on seeing the state the fidalgo was in. The ladies were collected together in the centre, and their female attendants and men servants around them, all wringing their hands and sobbing, not one of them thinking of raising any covering to shelter themselves, or bringing out benches or chairs to sleep on. The Captain, however, with a sailor's activity, set to work to make such arrangements as were practicable, for the comfort of the ladies and of the unfortunate fidalgo, who, as yet, gave few signs of being conscious of what was going forward. The servants worked but slowly, and were afraid of entering the house, although they did not hesitate to obey the Captain, who, it must be remembered, was a perfect stranger among them; but, on occasions of danger and difficulty, the man of courage and talent will always command obedience. Overcome with fatigue, the gallant Captain and the faithful Pedro, after snatching a short rest, again set out in search of Don Luis.

Volume Two—Chapter Fifteen.

Twice had the sun risen over the city of desolation since the dreadful catastrophe of the 1st of November; and the flames yet raged in every part. Nearly twenty thousand persons, it was supposed, had been destroyed by the earthquake; and the greater number of the remaining citizens had quitted the fatal spot, and were encamped in the open fields in the neighbourhood; some with scarcely clothes to cover them, and without food to supply the cravings of hunger. Here all classes and orders of people were promiscuously mingled; respectable citizens reduced to abject poverty by the entire destruction of their property; the hapless virgins dedicated to the service of Heaven, driven from their sanctuaries among the most lawless and abandoned of mankind. Servants and their former masters; ladies, accustomed to gentle nurture, among mechanics, soldiers and porters; the virtuous and the profligate, the rich and the poor, the noble and the beggar, in the same wretched condition. The whole fabric of society was completely disorganised; murders, robberies, and all species of crimes were committed with the most flagrant daring; and naught was heard but groans and cries of distress. Slight shocks still continued to be felt at intervals of every half-hour; famine also had visited them; and, to add to their disasters, the effluvia arising from the vast number of dead bodies which choked up the streets, threatened them with a pestilence; so that hundreds of those who were able had already taken their departure to other towns; and the city would have been completely deserted, had not Sebastiaö Jozé de Carvalho, now created Prime Minister, exerted his utmost power to prevent so unfortunate an event to the kingdom.

It was now that he exhibited, in the greatest degree, that energetic character, and those extraordinary abilities which distinguished him among his countrymen. Having received full powers from the King to act as he judged expedient, both day and night he drove from place to place in his carriage, to observe what was most necessary to be done,—it serving him for his bureau, his couch, and his parlour; the only food he took on the first day being a basin of broth, which the Countess Daun, his wife, brought him with her own hands. His first care was to cut off all communication between the burning part of the city and that which remained entire; for to extinguish the conflagration was beyond his power, or the means of man to accomplish; his next was to despatch messengers into all the surrounding districts, to collect provisions for the houseless inhabitants; and his third was to send round to all the parochial clergy and heads of yet existing convents, to urge them to impress on their congregations and inferiors, as a duty both grateful to Heaven, and called for by man, to bury the dead without delay.

This last order had at first, owing to the paralysation of their energies, with which terror and misery had affected all men, been but negligently obeyed; and the streets were yet, in some places, actually blocked up with the dead, particularly in front of the churches, where they lay piled in heaps, mangled in every shocking way; some burned to cinders or scorched by the flames, and others torn almost to pieces by the savage dogs and vermin. Such sights were, indeed, dreadful to behold, but the eyes of those who had ventured into this arena of devastation and confusion had already become familiarised with them. Some of the noblest in the land had, with philanthropic boldness, wandered amid the ruins, to bear succour to those who might yet providentially remain alive beneath them; and among the first of those charitable persons, who set so bright an example to their fellow-men, was Don John of Bragança, a cousin of the King's, and brother of the Duke of Lafoens, well-known about that time, in France and England, as the Duke of Bragança. It was reported that, in his presence, a young damsel was dug out of a cellar, in perfect health, on the sixth day, and it was fully believed by the pious that she was, as she affirmed, saved from destruction by clasping a figure of Saint Anthony, which was found in her embrace.

But to return to the day we first spoke of. From all the yet existing churches, mournful processions issued, headed by priests or friars, and accompanied by parties of seculars carrying biers, who perambulated the streets, and bore the bodies of the wretched victims, either to the water's edge, from whence they were conveyed to the centre of the Tagus, and sunk with weights; or else to large receptacles prepared in the neighbourhood of the city, when quick-lime was thrown in on them. But, though these toiled all day, little progress appeared yet to have been made in the sad work, so great was the number of the dead.

They were not the only people seen among the ruins; for the ruffian banditti continued their depredations, unawed by the summary punishment of two or three of their number, who had been seized in the fact, and hung, by the Minister's orders, without further trial. But there was one who belonged to neither of those classes, who had been seen, night and day, constantly wandering in every direction, gazing at every female corpse he passed, and eagerly eyeing every person he encountered, fearless of danger from the burning edifices, and disregarding the menaces of the vile wretches he often interrupted in their lawless pursuits. His countenance was worn and haggard, and his dress disordered and soiled, though, from his air and general appearance, he evidently belonged to the Fidalguia. He was closely followed by another person, who, although pale and wearied, did not exhibit the same signs of mental prostration and wretchedness, and was, from his costume and manner, apparently the servant of the first. The day was nearly spent, but still he wandered on, uncertain which way to direct his steps. He stopped to question each person he met; but all considered him as one whose brain had been turned by the horrors of the times, and, disregarding him, hurried by. On he wandered, his search proving, too clearly, as fruitless as at first, till he observed a naval officer, followed by a party of men in uniform, at a little distance: he hurried towards them.

"Have you discovered any traces of her?—have you any chance of finding her?" he eagerly exclaimed, addressing the officer.

"Alas! my dear Luis, no," answered Captain Pinto. "I have as yet been unsuccessful; but the Minister, to whom I recounted your sad tale, has sent for a person who will to-morrow accompany you in your search, and will be of more aid than all the soldiers of the kingdom. He declares that, if these atrocities, which have disgraced humanity since the fatal day, do not cease, he will inflict such severe chastisement on all malefactors as will effectually terrify others from continuing the like excesses. In the mean time, come and take some rest, or you will to no purpose wear out both body and mind with fatigue."

"I cannot rest until I have recovered her; or, if she is lost to me for ever, death will bring me the only tranquillity I can hope for," answered Luis, in a tone of deep melancholy.

Pedro, who had soon discovered and followed his master through all dangers with constant faithfulness, heard this declaration with dismay, and joined the Captain in endeavouring to persuade him to quit his hopeless search for a time, to recruit his strength; but it was not till darkness came on, the first that had shrouded the city for the last three days, for the flames were now subsiding, that he consented to return to the palace of the Marchioness of Corcunda, to snatch a few hours' troubled rest.

Captain Pinto was obliged to leave him, to perform certain duties he had undertaken by the Minister's desire, in watching the banks of the river, to prevent the escape of robbers with their booty in that direction.

On the following morning, the carriage of the Minister was beset by numerous persons complaining of the fresh and atrocious outrages which had been committed during the past night.

On hearing the cases, he directly wrote the following decree, in the name of the King:—

"It having been represented to me, that, in the city of Lisbon and its neighbourhood, since the first of the month, many atrocious and sacrilegious robberies have been committed,—churches have been profaned, houses have been broken open, and people, even when endeavouring to save themselves from the falling edifices, have been assaulted with violence in the streets, to the great scandal, not only of Christian piety, but even of humanity,—and considering that like crimes, by their turpitude, make the perpetrators unworthy of the advantage of the usual process of trial, and indispensably require a prompt and severe chastisement, which may put an end to so horrible a scandal,—I decree, that all persons who have been, or shall be, apprehended for the above-said crimes, shall be tried by the simple verbal process by which the deed may be proved, and that those who are found guilty of those crimes, shall be forthwith forwarded, with the said verbal processes, to the Chief Regidor of the House of Punishment, who shall name, without delay, those Judges whom he is accustomed to name in like cases, that they may, without loss of time, also pass judgment on all the aforesaid processes verbal, so that those judgments passed by them shall be put into execution on the very day on which they are passed, and all without embargo of any laws, decrees, edicts, and ordinances whatever to the contrary, because these are passed for this particular purpose, they still retaining their vigour. The same Chief Regidor having thus understood, let him carry it into execution.—Belem, 4th November, 1755."

Then the Minister despatched orders to the magistrates of every barrier of the city, to erect as lofty gibbets as they possibly could; another decree ordering that the condemned should be immediately hung up, and there left to rot in the sun; and before many days had passed, two hundred persons graced the gibbets; and though probably a few innocent ones may have been among them, the greater number were doubtless a good riddance from society; and, as the Minister observed, violent diseases require violent remedies. This proved the truth of the saying; for the atrocities were at length put a stop to for a time. One man in chains may inspire a youthful Turpins romantic ardour; but we suspect two hundred ghastly corpses would have sickened even Jack Sheppard of his lofty ambition.

We find ourselves anticipating the course of events. As soon as the Minister had ordered the erection of the gibbets, he bethought him it might be as well to assemble some troops to guard them, lest, as the rogues and vagabonds were pretty numerous, they should take it into their heads to hang thereon the honest men instead. Soldiers were, therefore, marched from all directions, so as to form a complete cordon round Lisbon, allowing none to enter or go out without a pass from the chief of police.

It was next thought advisable, since the aforesaid rogues and vagabonds could scarcely be expected to be so convinced of the enormities of their crimes, as to come and offer themselves voluntarily for punishment; and that as they could not possibly be hung without being first caught, any more than a hare can be cooked when still ranging her native fields, that bodies of police should be selected, under fit and proper officers, to apprehend the villains. Some were chosen among the military; but, as the soldiers, it was suspected, might be too apt rather to imitate than suppress the excesses, the greater number were respectable citizens, who were glad to volunteer under good leaders, among whom our friend Captain Pinto was the first chosen.

Even before the morning broke, Luis had again commenced his search for Clara, which proved fruitless as before. On meeting his friend, however, he accompanied him to visit the Minister, to whom he was about to make some reports.

"I have not forgotten you, my young friend," said Carvalho, as soon as he saw Luis. "Though all require my care, yours is a peculiar case, and here is one who will be of more assistance to you than any other I can afford;" and he called a man to his side, to whom he gave some directions, and motioned towards Luis, when he added, "Farewell, and may success attend you!" and again turned to the public business in which he was engaged. That with Captain Pinto was soon despatched, when, accompanied by Luis and the person the Minister had introduced to him, he returned to the city.

Not to keep our readers in suspense as to who this personage was, we may as well intimate that he was our acquaintance, the *ci-devant* cobbler, Antonio; though at present he bore none of the signs of his trade about him, but rather had the appearance of a quiet notary, or sedate shopkeeper.

"I will do my best to serve you, senhor," he said; "but I fear much we shall not discover the young lady. In ordinary times I might have been successful; but now I cannot set about the work in the way I would have done."

Luis, at Antonio's desire, gave him an exact description of Clara, (though perhaps he painted her with the pencil and colours lovers are apt to use,) and then of the ruffian who had carried her off, and of whom, for the same reason, it may be supposed, he did not speak in the most flattering terms; but his hearer, who seemed inclined to smile at the narration, made due allowances for both; and by the time the party had reached the ruined part of the city, he had made himself fully master of all the circumstances of the case. He then, turning to Captain Pinto, begged him to separate from them for a time, appointing to meet him at a certain hour, if he was successful in the first steps he intended to pursue.

Accompanied by Luis and Pedro, who would not leave him, he then plunged into the most intricate and narrow lanes of the city, climbing over ruins, among which were seen the mangled and burnt bodies of the wretched inhabitants, scaring, as they proceeded, the gorged dogs from their horrid feast. Now and then only they met a human being; for none, except for the purposes of concealment, had ventured where, even in better days, few were willing to wander unprotected. Antonio spoke to each one he passed, but all shook their heads in answer; yet, not discouraged by his want of success at first, he pursued the same plan, though the appearance of his acquaintances, it must be confessed, did certainly not afford Luis a very high opinion of his character, for a more villainous set of cut-throats it had never been his lot to encounter, although they were habited in the richest and most costly garments; but these were so evidently part of the spoils they had collected, and sat so ill upon them, that they only increased the ferocity and wildness of their countenances. Once or twice they met persons with whom he held rather longer conferences, and he appeared by degrees to be gaining some information which was satisfactory. At length, as they were turning the corner of a street, they came suddenly on a person who endeavoured to escape them, by hurrying, at some risk, among the smoking ruins, the moment he saw them approaching; but Antonio was too quick for him, and running after him, caught him by the arm. The person made no further resistance; but, on the contrary, as soon as he saw who was his pursuer, he embraced him cordially, seeming to feel much pleasure at the rencontre, accompanying him quietly as he walked on, followed at a little distance by Luis and Pedro.

"Do you know, senhor, that I have seen the figure of that man before," said the latter to his master. "I caught a glimpse of his countenance, and as I am a sinner, and hope to be saved, it is no other than the hermit of Nossa Senhora da Pedra, and the holy padre Frè Lopez."

"Thank Heaven," ejaculated Luis, "that we have met him. It must be him, and he is the only man who will be able to assist me;" and he was hurrying to overtake Antonio and his companion, when the latter, giving him a parting embrace, hastened off in a different direction.

"Who was that person?" inquired Luis, as he joined Antonio.

"A very great vagabond, senhor, but yet not near so great a villain as many who profess to be virtuous. I have known him for a long time, and if he could but resist temptation, he would be an honest man; and I would trust my life in his power, provided it was not his interest to take it."

"If he is the man I supposed, he saved mine three days ago," returned Luis. "Is he not called Frè Diogo Lopez?"

"That is one of his names, to which he has as great a right as to the coat he now wears; but he is no friar, senhor; no, no, he is too honest for that; but if he is tempted to commit any piece of villainy, he assumes the character, as most appropriate for the purpose, he says. He once entered a monastery as a lay brother, where he learned all the habits and customs of the monks; but they did not accord with the ideas of morality he then entertained, so after a couple of years he quitted them, and has ever since wandered about the country in various disguises, as suits his purpose; but if the holy Inquisition get hold of him, I fear he will not be able to escape their clutches."

"But has he given you any information that may be of service to us?" interrupted Luis eagerly.

"That is to be proved," said Antonio calmly; "I know the man from whose power the Frade saved your life, and who carried the lady off; a greater villain there does not exist in Lisbon. I have learned so much from our friend, though the difficulty will be to find this Rodrigo; and the chances are that he will adorn one of the newly-raised gibbets before long. I hope, however, to have an interview with him before that time; and then the sooner he is hung, the sooner will there be one villain less in the world."

"Is this the only clue you have been able to discover?" said Luis, dejectedly. "I fear that it will be of little service."

"Fear not, senhor," answered Antonio: "in the first place, you have the satisfaction of knowing that the lady was not killed by the falling houses, when Rodrigo carried her off; and, in the second, I have reason to suppose that it was not for his own sake he committed the outrage."

"Thank Heaven for that!" ejaculated Luis.

"In the mean time, our friend the Frade is making inquiries which may assist us," continued Antonio. "And we will now, by your leave, find Captain Pinto, to whom I wish to make some reports."

They accordingly proceeded in search of the Captain.

When Don Luis and his companions arrived at the spot where they had agreed to meet Captain Pinto, which was at an open place called the Caes Sodrè, near the royal arsenal, they found the people under his command with several prisoners in their custody.

Antonio examined the countenance of each, but he did not recognise any one till he came to a man lying bound on the ground, his clothes torn and bloody, with two of the guards standing near him, badly wounded. "Ah!" he exclaimed, "Senhor Rodrigo, you know me, I think?"

"Yes," answered the ruffian; "I am not likely to forget you."

Luis looked on with anxiety, for he beheld the ruffian who had carried off Clara; but Antonio, desiring to be left alone with the man, knelt down by his side, while Captain Pinto detailed to Luis the circumstances of his capture. His last act had been in character with his former life. The guards were passing a house from which loud cries were heard to proceed, and on entering it an old man was found weltering in his blood on the floor, and a woman was struggling in the grasp of the ruffian, whose shrieks prevented his hearing their entrance. Before they could seize him, however, he had plunged his knife into her bosom; and then turning on them, had wounded two in his attempt to escape; but at last, after a desperate resistance, he was captured.

Luis shuddered as he heard the account. "Has my beloved Clara been in the power of a wretch like this?" he thought.

Antonio held some minutes' conversation with the bravo. "For what purpose did you carry off the lady?" he said, after some time.

"To serve another, the greater my folly," was the answer.

"And she is there still?" inquired Antonio.

"Yes, if he has not removed her.—Go, I would have my revenge on him. He has deceived me twice, and you may gain the ransom I expected—and then I shall die happy."

Before night the corpse of the noted bravo, Rodrigo, was seen hanging from the highest gibbet at the gates of Lisbon.

Volume Two—Chapter Sixteen.

We have observed, in the course of our very desultory custom of reading, that most novelists delight in endeavouring to make their readers suppose, somewhere about the middle of their second volume, that their hero, or heroine, in whose fate by that time they may have begun to feel some interest, has been engulfed beneath the raging waves, or dashed to pieces from falling off a lofty, sea-worn cliff, or murdered by banditti in a forest, or blown up in a castle, or has made his or her exit from this terrestrial scene in some equally romantic way; for we cannot fill our page with further instances. Now, we confess that, after a little experience, we were never deceived by such ingenious devices. In the first place, very few writers have the hardihood to kill their heroes or heroines at all, for the reason, that few readers approve of the principle; and, in the second, they would not think of doing so till the end of the third volume, as they would find considerable difficulty in continuing their story without them. For our own part, rather than commit so atrocious an act, we would alter the truth of history, and defer the dreadful catastrophe to the final scene.

Having made this preamble, we must return to the ruins of the Santa Clara Convent, at the moment the bravo Rodrigo had torn Clara from the arms of Don Luis, after their almost miraculous escape from destruction. She had just recovered sufficient consciousness to know that she was separated from him, and had no power to liberate herself. In vain she called on Luis to save her, as the ruffian bore her away. He carried her quickly across the ruins, passing close to the spot where her unhappy father then was; and when he saw himself pursued, not knowing by whom, he dashed down the nearest turning with his fair prize, regardless of her cries and prayers for mercy. His progress in that direction was soon impeded by the burning buildings, when he was obliged to turn back part of the way, and make a circuit through the northern part of the city in the direction of Belem, towards which he proceeded on the very opposite side. No one regarded him as he passed: they were either wretches like himself, or unhappy beings who had, that day, perchance, lost all they loved on earth, and heeded not aught but their own misfortunes; besides, alas! such spectacles had become too common to attract the notice of any: no one attempted to rescue her from the ruffian's power. At length, weary from his exertions, for the road he was obliged to follow was long, steep, and intricate, Rodrigo stopped to rest. Even over the most savage bosoms lovely innocence will always be able to exert a softening influence, and we believe that there is no man born of womankind so hardened as not to feel its power. Clara, though she thought not this, for terror had deprived her of all power of thinking, took this opportunity, by a natural instinct, to entreat her captor to restore her to her father, promising him a high reward for so doing.

"So you said once before, lady, when I had you in my power; but I shall not be again disappointed, depend on it," answered the robber. "However, don't be alarmed, for your lover, as I guess him to be, is, as far as I know, still alive, no thanks to my intentions, though; and I am going to take you to one who will treat you well, and pay me highly for my trouble and loss of time, so there is nothing after all to cry about."

"But my father will pay you any sum you demand," quickly responded Clara, thinking she had made some impression on the man's feelings.

"No, no," he answered, "he would not have shut you up in a convent if he cared much about you; besides, for what I know, he may be killed, as thousands were to-day; now my employer was alive a few hours since, and I intend this time to make sure of my reward."

The thoughts of her father's death stopped Clara's further utterance, and the bravo, again lifting her in his arms, bore her onward. He now again turned through some partially ruined streets, several fierce bands passing him who uttered horrid jests, and seemed inclined to dispute possession of his prize; but his fierce threats of vengeance made them desist, for his character was well-known to all.

Full two hours had passed ere he finally stopped before the door of a low house, which appeared uninjured; for while the lofty temples and the proud palaces of the great had been overwhelmed in ruin, the humble shed of the mechanic had escaped.

He forced open the door, and entered without hesitation. An old woman was seated on the floor, trembling and weeping with alarm: a small oil lamp burning near her gave just sufficient light to show the wretched state of the apartment.

He placed Clara on one of the two only chairs the room afforded, and then fastened the door behind him. "Come, rouse up, mother, and stop your tears, the earthquake will do no further harm. Here is a lady I have brought you to attend upon, and remember you must treat her properly."

"Take her away—I want no ladies here!" muttered the old hag, without looking up.

"Hark you, mother! I expect to be well paid for my trouble, and you shall have plenty of gold if I return her safe to her friends. My taste is not for such delicate fish as this."

"Am I to have plenty of gold?" said the old woman, eagerly. "Yes, yes, then I will do all you require."

"That is well," answered Rodrigo. "Treat her kindly, and give her food, if she can eat such as we poor people have; and take care she does not escape, or we shall lose our reward—remember that."

"Ay, ay, we are to have gold, are we? then I will take care she does not get away," returned the hag, glancing at her with her baneful eyes.

"I have said, no harm shall happen to you, lady, so cease crying," said the bravo, turning to Clara; and, whispering a few words in his mother's ear, he quitted the house, locking the door behind him, and taking away the key.

The old woman followed her son's directions, without addressing a word to her prisoner; but, weak and faint as Clara was, she could not, as may be supposed, partake of the fare placed before her. Her witch-like hostess then supported her to a rough couch in a corner of the room, on which, more in a state of fainting than sleeping, she forgot, for a time, the horrors of her situation, though her brain yet retained a confused impression of the terrific sounds and dreadful scenes she had encountered.

It was daylight before the bravo returned, bringing a basket of delicate provisions already cooked and prepared with care, which he placed on the table, without addressing Clara, and withdrew in haste, merely nodding to his mother as he passed out, again locking the door behind him. A few hours' rest had partially restored Clara's strength, and enabled her to take a little refreshment; but to all her questions the old woman was as uncommunicative as her son, pretending entire deafness, to escape being troubled with further ones. Her manner was, however, sufficiently respectful, and she was attentive to her prisoner's wants; but her behaviour was actuated, evidently, more by the hopes of gain than by any feminine or kindly feeling. As she moved about the room, at her work, muttering curses, she would every now and then cast suspicious glances towards the fair girl; but whenever a slight shock of the earthquake was felt, she would fall down on her knees and kiss and fondle the image of a saint, the only ornament the room possessed: as soon, however, as it had passed away, she would again rise and pursue her former occupations. On these occasions, Clara could not avoid trembling with alarm, as she saw the fragile building vibrating with the shock, expecting every instant to be overwhelmed in its ruins; but the earthquake providentially did no further damage than cause pieces of mortar to fall from the ceiling, or the walls, till at last she learned no longer to dread it.

Clara had remained many hours in a dreadful state of doubt and uncertainty, not only as to her own future fate, but as to that of Luis, whom she had last beheld in the power of the ruffians; and of her father, for she could not tell if he had escaped the destruction, which appeared to her universal, though she was unconscious of the horrors of the commencement; when the door of the room was opened from without, and a tall figure entered, wrapped in a large cloak, so as completely to conceal his person, a black mask covering his features. He bowed respectfully towards her as he entered, and then advanced close to where she was seated, her lovely head bent down, and her face hidden in her hands.

"Lady!" said the stranger, "I have been deputed hither by one who adores you to distraction, and who has heard with deep concern of the violence which has been offered to you; but he has taken measures to prevent the return of the ruffian who brought you here, and if you will accept of my escort, I will conduct you to a place of greater security."

Clara started at the first sound of that voice, which made her tremble with fear, for the tones seemed familiar; but then she thought she must have been mistaken, yet she mistrusted the speaker.

"I can trust myself with no one who requires a mask to conceal his features," she answered; "yet let me know to whom I am indebted for assistance, and I may be grateful."

"Circumstances prevent my declaring myself, lady, at present," returned the stranger; "but confide in my honour, and I will escort you from this wretched hovel to an abode, which, though unworthy to receive you, is yet equal to any the city, in its present ruined state, can afford."

"Pardon me, senhor, that I hesitate," said Clara; "for I dare not confide in one unknown; but if you will carry the information to my father that I am here, I shall be deeply grateful."

The stranger listened to this answer with signs of impatience.

"I would do what you wish, fair lady, but I grieve to say your father, if, as I believe, you are the daughter of Gonçalo Christovaö, fell a victim to the destroying earthquake."

"Oh! say you do not speak the truth; you surely must have been mistaken," she exclaimed; "my father cannot be among the dead!"

"It is but too true, lady," was the answer; "and I fear you have few or no friends who have escaped it."

On hearing this sad assertion, Clara bent down her head and sobbed violently, while the stranger stood by, beholding her in silence for some minutes, when she suddenly looked up. "I pray Heaven you may have been deceived in the account you give," she said; "but if not, as you are a man, and, as I believe, from your air, of gentle birth, I entreat you to discover one who has already risked his life to save mine, and in whom I may place entire confidence—Don Luis d'Almeida. Go, senhor, inform him that I am here, and he will strive to show his gratitude to you."

Clara, in the innocence of her heart, referred naturally to the person on whom all her thoughts and feelings centred; but her words seemed to give anything but satisfaction to her hearer. He stamped vehemently on the ground, as he answered, between his closed teeth,—"Know you not, lady, that you speak of one who is the murderer of your brother? and he, surely, is not a fit guardian for you."

She was no longer deceived in the speaker's voice. She rose calmly from her seat:—"Count San Vincente," she said, "the disguise you wear cannot conceal you from me; nor do I believe your words; for I feel firm in the conviction that Don Luis could not have slain my brother. I knew not even that he was reported to have been killed; nor do I believe, from your assertion, that such is the case. Now, leave me, senhor; for I know full well you dare not venture to use violence towards a noble maiden. Find means to inform my friends of my situation, and I will not breathe my suspicions; if not, dread the consequences of this outrage."

"You mistake, fair lady; I am not the person you suppose," answered the stranger; "and though I am unwilling to use threats to compel you to do what I would wish you to perform of your own accord, you must remember that you are completely in my power, and that I fear not the vengeance of your friends; for none will know that you were not lost in the ruins of the convent, till he who seeks to wed you thinks fit to produce you as his bride. Will you now consent to accompany me?"

"Never!" answered Clara, firmly; "I would rather trust myself to the common ruffian who brought me hither, than to one who is capable of deceit and treachery so vile to gain his wishes. Hear me! Whatever betide, I will never become the bride of the Conde San Vincente, and him I know that I see before me!"

"You will gain little by your resolution, lady, which, like women in general, you will be glad to break on the first occasion," answered the stranger. "I leave you now to reflect on my words; and remember, that even if Don Luis survives, which I know not he does, you cannot wed him who has slain your brother; and that such is the case, is well-known by all. Farewell, lady; I trust that, by to-morrow, you will have considered the subject more calmly, when I will again visit you." Saying which, the stranger, bowing low, quitted the cottage, without even deigning to regard the old woman; but Clara was confirmed in her persuasion that he was a principal person concerned in the outrage offered to her, by hearing him again lock the door and withdraw the key, as the keeper of her prison.

For the remainder of the day she was unmolested by further visits; but if she even attempted to approach the window, the old beldame followed her closely, to prevent her, in case she should make any signal for assistance to those passing by; a chance not likely to occur, seeing that the cottage stood in a lane but little frequented at any time, and one end of it being now completely blocked up with ruins.

On the morning of the second day, a knock was heard at the door, to which the old woman went directly, when a hand was thrust in with a basket of provisions, as before, and immediately withdrawn. About two hours afterwards, the tall masked stranger returned, again bowing profoundly, as he advanced towards Clara.

"Lady, I trust that a night's rest has enabled you to perceive your true condition more clearly than you did yesterday," he began. "Pardon me that I appear importunate; but though, as I before assured you, I should be unwilling to force your inclinations, yet I must insist on your accompanying me, without resistance, from this wretched hovel, which is not fit to be honoured: by your presence."

"Neither my opinion of my gaoler, nor my feelings, have changed since yesterday," replied Clara; "nor is the treatment I have received at all likely to alter them; and, as I have before declared, I will not quit this house, unless in the company of friends in whom I can confide.

Force, I think, you would scarcely dare exert, and it would defeat your own purpose."

"Trust not to such fallacious hopes, lady," answered the stranger, fiercely; "you know not to what lengths your coldness will drive one who long has lived but in thinking of your charms! By a fortunate chance you were placed in my power, and, believe me, I value you too much to allow you to escape. You understand not my character when you thus venture to trifle with my feelings, for I am one whom the fear of consequences never daunts in the pursuit of my aims; threats cannot terrify me, and all laws I despise, or can elude. Yes, Donna Clara, I will not deny it is of myself I speak. I would woo you as a humble suitor for your hand; but, if you spurn my love, I have the power, and will exert it, to command you as a master; ay, and I will so tame that proud spirit, that you will crave as a boon what you now so haughtily refuse."

"Never!" exclaimed Clara, with energy; for all the lofty feelings of her noble race were aroused within that bosom, by nature so gentle, and formed for love. "I fear not your unworthy threats. Sooner, far sooner, would I die, than yield to your wishes; for each word you have spoken has but increased the hatred and contempt I have from the first felt for you."

"Ah! is it so, lady?" said the stranger, his voice trembling with rage. "You will find yourself miserably deceived. Hear me for the last time. I have determined to try what leniency will effect in your sentiments; but, if you still refuse to listen to reason, you will lament the consequences of your folly. Do not suppose that you can escape from hence; for you are here as securely guarded as within one of the dungeons of the Jungueira; so build no hopes on that account. But I will not attempt to persuade you further. I now again quit you, to return but once more, when a priest will be in readiness to unite your fate with mine; and be assured that my impatience will brook but short delay. Till then, Donna Clara, farewell!" He bent low, and attempted to take her hand, but she hastily withdrew it. "Well, well, lady," he added, in a scornful tone, "to-morrow, methinks, you will act differently;" and, as on the former occasion, he bowed, and quitted the cottage. When, no sooner had he gone than the fair girl's self-possession gave way, and she burst into a flood of tears.

Volume Two—Chapter Seventeen.

Sad was the change which three days of intense anxiety and suffering had worked on the fair cheek of the still lovely Clara. She might have been compared to the fresh-blown rose, drooping beneath the hot blast of the sirocco, yet still retaining its fragrance and beauty, and which the balmy dews of evening would quickly restore to health and vigour. The old hag had never for an instant quitted her, nor had she been able to extract a single sentence from her, even to learn in what part of the city she was imprisoned. Her thoughts all the time dwelling on the too probable loss of her father, and brother, and of one who she could not help confessing was even dearer than either, yet she did not rely on her informer's declaration of their deaths; and she endeavoured so to nerve her courage, as to resist every attempt he might make to compel her to become his bride. Though he had spoken in a feigned voice, and she had not seen his features, she had no doubt as to the identity of her gaoler; and she felt assured that terror of the law would prevent him from perpetrating any violence,—the abduction only of the daughter of a fidalgo being punishable by death, with confiscation of property; though, had she known the disorganised state of society since the earthquake, her alarm would have been far greater. Since the masked stranger had visited her, no one had appeared, and she was now, with dread and agitation, looking forward to his return. She heard footsteps approaching—her heart beat quick—they stopped at the cottage-door, against which a single blow was struck; but the old woman paid no attention to it. It was again repeated, with the same result. Several louder knocks were then heard, when the hag approached the door, and placed her ear against it, in the act of listening.

"Who is there?" she asked, in a voice like the croaking of a raven. "Go away, and leave an aged lone woman in quiet."

"Open the door first, and we will not harm you," said a voice.

"I cannot open the door, for my son has gone away, and taken the key: you must wait till he returns," answered the hag.

"We should have to wait long enough," muttered some one outside.

Clara's heart throbbed yet quicker; but it was with hopes of liberation; yet she feared to cry out, for the eye of the hag was fixed on her with a malignant glance; and while she held up one finger to impose silence, her other hand clasped the handle of a sharp-pointed knife, with a significant gesture.

"What is that you say about my son?" she asked, with a startling energy, which made Clara's blood thrill with dread.

"We speak not of your son, old woman," said the voice. "Open the door quietly, or we shall be obliged to force it, in the name of the King."

"You had better not attempt it," she croaked forth. "My son is not one who likes to have his house visited in his absence, so go your ways till he returns."

"Delay no longer, but force the door!" said another voice, which caused a tumultuous joy in Clara's bosom, for she knew it to be that of Luis.

"First tell me where my son is?" cried the beldame.

"Your son Rodrigo is in prison, where you will join him, if you do not directly obey our orders," said the former voice.

"Ah! is it so?" she shrieked. "It shall not be without cause, and I will be revenged on you first." Clara uttered a cry of terror,—loud blows resounded against the door,—and the vile hag, with her glittering knife upraised, rushed towards her, her eyes glaring with savage fury; and, with a yell of derisive laughter, she aimed her weapon at the bosom of the fair girl; but her foot slipped, and she fell to the ground. In a moment she rose again, and pursued her victim, who endeavoured to escape her rage.

"Luis, Luis, save me!" cried Clara, in an agony of fear.

The blows against the door were redoubled. The hag, with frantic gestures, followed her. Her last moment seemed come, when the door was burst open; and, while several men seized the wretched woman— yet not before she had plunged the knife into her own heart—Clara, with a cry of joy, fell fainting into her lover's arms.

"Where is my son? you said he was taken," muttered the old woman, as she forced away the hand of Antonio, who was endeavouring to stanch the blood flowing from her wound.

"By this time he is dangling from one of the new gibbets at the gates of the city," answered one of the men.

"Then I will disappoint those of what they would much like to know," she muttered.

She then suddenly endeavoured to tear herself from the grasp of those who held her, uttering shriek upon shriek, mixed with dreadful curses on all around.

"Ay, ay, I see my son in the flames of purgatory, and the devils are dragging me down to him. I will not go yet—I will live to curse those who have slain him. May their end be like his, and may they dwell for ever in the torments of hell!"

She ceased not uttering exclamations like these till her evil spirit fled its vile tenement.

Luis bore Clara from the dreadful scene, accompanied by Captain Pinto, and followed by the rest of the party, till they reached an open space, where a carriage was in waiting; and, as he placed her in it, and took his seat by her side, he caught a glimpse of a tall man, whose features were concealed in a cloak, watching them at some distance. Having received the warm congratulations of his friend, who was obliged to return to his duty, while Pedro and some of the men prepared to accompany him as guards, Luis offered a purse of money to Antonio, as a recompense for his exertions.

"No, senhor," he answered, declining it; "I have but performed the commands of the Minister, and I seek my reward from him alone;" and, bowing profoundly, he took his leave.

We must not attempt to transcribe the conversation of Clara and Luis, as they slowly proceeded by a long and circuitous road towards the residence of the old Marchioness. She first asked eagerly for her father, when Luis assured her that though too unwell to engage personally in the search for her, he was in no danger, and that her presence would soon recover him. Why, we know not, but she did not even mention her brother's name. Luis then told her of his wretchedness, and almost madness, at her loss, and she confessed to have suffered as much, which afforded, doubtless, great consolation to him. Next he told her of all the fruitless endeavours he had made to recover her, which had worn him nearly to a skeleton; and, in answer, she told him of the visits she had received from the masked stranger, and of her suspicions as to who he was; when they both agreed, that, if she was right, the Count had acted so cautious a part, that though he as richly deserved hanging as his assistant Rodrigo, it would be utterly impossible to punish him by any legal means, though Luis vowed internally to take the first opportunity of chastising him. Yet they only slightly touched on these subjects; for there was a far more engrossing one which occupied the greater part of the time, as on it they had very much to say. What it was we leave our readers to guess, it being remembered that they had not met with an opportunity to converse since the evening when they first made their mutual acknowledgments of love; and they agreed that what they then felt was cold and tame, compared to their present feelings, after all the dangers and sufferings they had undergone.

We, however, prefer leaving what are usually called love scenes to be described by our fair sister authoresses; because they can paint the characters of their own sex with far more delicate touches, and, besides, know much more about the subject than we old men possibly can, whose days of tender endearment have so long passed by. We shall, therefore, carry them safely to the gates of the palace, when Luis, lifting Clara from the carriage, supported her to the garden, where, under various tents and sheds, the family were still residing.

The first person they encountered was old Gertrudes, who, the moment she observed them, gazed at them as if they were a couple of spirits from the dead, and then rushing towards them, seized Clara in her arms, with cries and tears of joy, almost smothering her with kisses; and then seizing on Luis, joined him in the embrace, bestowing alternate kisses on him; and if, in returning them, which he was bound to do, he did make some slight mistake in the person, we think he is justly to be excused, considering he had never before ventured on such a liberty. He then resigned Clara into her nurse's care, and was about to withdraw, when, clasping his hand, she raised it to her lips.

"Oh! do not leave me," she exclaimed. "I dread the thoughts of again parting from you: I know not what may occur: I fear some danger may happen to you, or I may again be committed to a convent. Come to my father, and he will thank you for having again saved his child!"

"You had better first go alone and see the senhor your father," interrupted the nurse. "There is a vile story told of Don Luis, which I know is not true, but which makes your father dislike to see him."

"Senhora Gertudes speaks rightly," said Luis. "Go, beloved one, alone to meet your father, and I doubt not he will soon learn to think more justly of me. I will not quit the palace."

Persuaded by this assurance, Clara accompanied the nurse to the shed in which the fidalgo was lying. Gertrudes first prudently entered, to advise the father of his daughter's safety and return, but soon again came out and beckoned her to approach.

No sooner did he behold her, than raising himself from his couch as she stooped to meet him, he pressed her in his arms, sobbing like a child the while. "Thank Heaven that you are restored to me, my

Clara!" he exclaimed; "for I could not bear the double loss I thought I was doomed to suffer,—two children within two days!—it was a heavy blow; but now you are recovered, I must, if so I can, be reconciled to your brother's death."

"My brother dead?" responded Clara, in a tone of sadness. "Alas! I heard, but did not believe, the tale."

"It is but too true, I fear," said the Fidalgo. "He was slain by one you must in future learn to hate,—Don Luis d'Almeida!"

"Oh, do not, do not believe that one so brave, so noble, could be guilty of such a deed! Twice, at the hazard of his life, since we first met, has he saved me from destruction. At that dreadful time, when all others were flying for their lives, forgetful of parents, children, and all the nearest ties of kindred, he rushed among the falling ruins, braving a horrid death to rescue me! In every way has he proved his love,—and he surely could not have slain my brother. Oh, do not, my father, believe that lying tale which says so; for I, whatever befalls, can never cease to love him."

"At the moment you are restored to my heart, I cannot speak a harsh word, my child," said the Fidalgo; "but remember that you are vowed to the service of Heaven; and were you not, you could not wed one whose hands are stained with a brother's blood, although guiltless of the intention of shedding it. That Don Luis has risked his life to save one dear child from destruction, disarms me of my revenge; but from henceforth you must be as strangers to each other."

Poor Clara scarce heard the concluding sentence; the bright hopes which were budding forth with the first gleam of sunshine were suddenly blighted by this confirmation of the masked stranger's report of her brother's death; and instead of feeling joy at her return home, naught but clouds and gloom threatened her future days. She had no arguments to advance against her father's decree; for she felt that what he said was just. Placing her head on his pillow, she burst into an agony of tears.

The fidalgo in vain endeavoured to comfort her; for he had no consolation that could avail to offer her. He assured her that her return had restored him to health and strength, and that he would not willingly contradict her wishes in anything; but that his confessor, Father Alfonzo, had told him that he must determine, if he recovered her, to keep to his original intention of dedicating her to the Church, as the most acceptable way of proving his gratitude to Heaven for the favour vouchsafed to him,—the Father promising not to cease his prayers to the saints to intercede for him, but more especially to the Holy Virgin.

To this the unhappy girl had not a word to answer: it was but, alas! too much in accordance with the creed she had been taught, and she had never even heard that a doubt had been started against its infallibility. Yet her heart rebelled against the decree; but she shuddered at her own feelings, and endeavoured to stifle them; for the lessons inculcated on her mind told her they were sinful.

After some time, in a voice trembling with grief and agitation, she inquired the manner of her brother's death. Her father then told her, that on the morning after the sad occurrence, the one preceding the earthquake, he had become alarmed at Gonçalo's not returning; when the Conde San Vincente called to say, with much friendly concern, that he had been with him on the previous evening, when suddenly they were set upon by several persons, among the foremost of whom he recognised Don Luis d'Almeida, who seemed bent upon engaging with Gonçalo, and that, after exchanging several passes, he saw his friend fall severely wounded; but from having great difficulty in defending his own life, he could not go to his assistance. While thus engaged, several persons who had taken no part in the fray had rushed up, and lifting Gonçalo from the ground, had borne him off he could not tell where, and that, as soon as this was done, Don Luis and his party had drawn off. The Count then said, that he had made every exertion to discover whither Gonçalo had been conveyed; and that he had at length learned from a man who had been engaged in the affair, and whom he could produce, that he had been carried off by order of Don Luis, and that he hoped, in a few days, to discover where.

The fidalgo then said, that the Count had called that very morning on him, having only just learnt where he was to be found; and that his worst fears had been realised. He said that Gonçalo had been conveyed to a house near where the fray took place, and had died of his wound the very morning that the awful catastrophe had occurred; that the house falling, had involved all its inmates in destruction, so that it was utterly impossible to discover any further particulars of the case. The fidalgo finished by lamenting that his own prostration of strength had prevented him from making inquiries, and searching for his children as he earnestly had sought to do.

Clara listened to the account the Conde had given with incredulous ears, and then, in return, narrated the adventures which had befallen herself, and her suspicions that it was from his power Luis had rescued her; but to this her father would not for a moment listen, affirming that he was the soul of honour, and incapable of such an act; nor could anything advanced by Clara convince him to the contrary. We have before remarked, that when once an impression had been made on his mental faculties, it was difficult to remove it. No longer able to bear the conversation, even of his daughter, he sank back exhausted on his couch.

Luis had long been anxiously waiting at the entrance of the garden for the return of Clara, when he saw her approaching with slow and timid steps. He hastened to meet her.

"Oh, Luis, I am very wretched," she said; and she detailed the history she had heard from her father, as the Count had given it, at which the indignation of Luis was excessive; though, as may be supposed, he had no great difficulty in persuading her of its falsehood. Yet her tears flowed fast; for he acknowledged what she hoped to hear him deny, that, though he had striven to avoid it, her brother had been wounded by his hand. "Yet far rather would I myself have been the victim, than have spilt a drop of the blood of one dear to you," he continued. "And believe me, did I deem myself your brother's murderer, I would not have dared to touch you with my polluted hands."

"Oh no, no, I feel that you are not," she answered. "But, Luis, there is a sad foreboding at my heart, which tells me that we must part, and for ever. My father did not forbid me to see you to-day; though, alas! I know full well he will do so to-morrow, and then I dare not disobey his commands. Yet think not, Luis, that I shall forget you; *that* no power can compel me to do; and the remembrance that I was loved by you, will be a soothing balm to my heart for the few remaining years I have to endure my cruel lot. But you must learn to forget me, or to think of me as one already in her grave. You will enter the world, where there is much to drown your thoughts of the past, and where you will meet with one in whose love you may be happy." As she came to the last sentence her voice trembled, and her tears flowed fast.

Luis clasped her in his arms, and she did not attempt to resist. He swore that he could never forget her; and that he could never love or wed another. He entreated her not to despair, or consent to return to a convent, and he promised that he would compel the Count to contradict the vile accusation he had brought against him; and that perhaps then her father might relent. That he could at once prove part of the Count's story false, through his friend, Captain Pinto, who was with him at the time, and engaged in the rencontre. He said, indeed, everything that could possibly be said on the occasion, though he failed of imparting any of his own sanguine hopes to Clara; yet at times she gazed up into his face and smiled, but it was a smile more of sadness than of joy, and her tears again flowed unrestrained. How long the interview would have lasted it is impossible to say, had not Senhora Gertrudes, who had been in attendance at a respectful distance, hastened up to warn her that they must part; and at length Luis, imprinting another kiss on her brow, yielded her half fainting to her nurse's arms, and hurried from the palace.

At the gate he found Captain Pinto waiting for him, who insisted on his accompanying him to his lodgings, and on the following day returned with him to the palace, where he went with the hopes of seeing Clara, or, at all events, having an interview with her father. He had been again unsuccessful in his search for the packet he had received in the hermit's cave, and now all hopes of ever discovering it had vanished with the destruction of his father's house; so he tried to console himself with the hope that it was unimportant; though the contrary would again and again recur to him. As he appeared, a servant handed him a letter, requesting him to read it at once. It was from the fidalgo, expressing his deep obligation to him for rescuing his daughter from destruction, and for having afterwards recovered her from the ruffian who had carried her off; but that these acts could not cancel the feelings he entertained towards the destroyer of his son, even convinced, as he now was, from what his daughter had told him, that he was innocent of any intention to commit the deed. He finished by requesting Captain Pinto would do him the favour of calling, adding, in a postscript, that he had desired his daughter not to see him again, and begging him not to attempt to seek her.

The Captain having but little time to spare, immediately requested to be conducted to the fidalgo, while Luis waited outside. He soon returned, shaking his head.

"The fidalgo is inexorable," he said. "I have convinced him that you neither intended to kill his son, nor had anything to do with concealing him; hinting, that it was our suspicion the Count had done so himself. He seemed struck by the observation; and will make all possible inquiries on the subject; but he insists on your not again seeing his daughter, and he says that when he is perfectly convinced of his son's death he shall return to Oporto, where she is again to enter a convent. It is extraordinary how slow some men are in forming an opinion, and how difficult it is to knock it out of their heads, when once there: now he has taken it into his that the Count is an honourable man, and has much at heart the interests of his family; nor can all Donna Clara and I have said to him persuade him that it was probably he who caused Gonçalo to be concealed after he was wounded, for the sake of making her hate you; and that also it was on his account she was carried away after you had saved her from the ruins. I trust, however, that I have made some impression, though he does not acknowledge it. But come, it is useless remaining here, and I must attend to these disagreeable duties imposed on me."

Luis accompanied his friend, in a state of sad despondency; his hopes again blasted, even on the very threshold, as he had fancied, of happiness.

"Come, rouse thee, my friend," said the Captain. "This is but one of the many trials you must yet undergo in your course through life, to perfect your character as a man; and fortunate are those who are so tried, that when the still greater struggles of life approach, they may not be found wanting. See, it is now my turn to raise, rather than depress your hopes. Look on what has occurred, with the calm eye of philosophy, and you will see that you are not only not in a worse state than you were before the earthquake, but have the additional consolation of feeling that you have saved the life of a very charming lady, I allow. Her father may relent; her brother may not have died from his wound, as we have only the Count's word for it, and he may be proved to be a villain. Here is food enough to supply a lover's hopes for a year at least. However, I not being a lover, must hurry on to take my dinner, so come in, and share it with me."

Volume Two—Chapter Eighteen.

Several days had passed by since the dreadful morning of terror and destruction; and, though slight shocks were occasionally still felt, people had become accustomed to them, and were beginning to arouse themselves from the state of apathy into which fear had thrown them. It was a sad spectacle, to see the forlorn citizens wandering over the yet smoking ruins of their former habitations, seeking, in vain, to find the spots where they had dwelt in peace and happiness; but wheresoever they turned, naught but scenes of destruction and confusion met their view. In vain they endeavoured to recover their property; what the earthquake had spared the devouring flames had consumed. Precious jewels, and rich stores of gold and silver, had been reclaimed by the earth, from whence they were dug; and immense quantities of valuable merchandise had been destroyed; so that the before flourishing merchant or tradesman found himself reduced to bankruptcy and starvation. The historian of the time winds up his description with these words:—"The whole of the centre of Lisbon was reduced to one horrid desert, in which naught was beheld but mountains of stone and ashes; some ruined walls, blackened by the fire, alone rising amid this sea of confusion, sad monuments of those fine streets and spacious squares which, but a few days before, were full of wealth, and crowded with people."

Now was the time that the sagacity, energy, courage, and perseverance, of the Minister were most conspicuous in restoring order, and preventing the site of the city from being deserted altogether. No sooner had the ashes cooled, than, assembling workmen, he caused roads to be cut through the ruins, and immediately commenced rebuilding the city, he himself planning those streets which now form by far the handsomest part of Lisbon.

Since Luis had restored Clara to her father, he had devoted all his thoughts and energies to the task of endeavouring to discover some traces of her brother; but he had as yet been completely unsuccessful. He had applied to Antonio, but he could not, or would not, afford him any assistance; and of the companions of the youth, some had been killed, many had fled, and the rest would not trouble themselves about his fate. Captain Pinto had not even been acquainted with him by sight; and his unhappy father was still too weak to leave his couch, to go in search of him, so that Luis began to fear that he should be for ever unable to prove his own innocence. The Count San Vincente, in the mean time, paid daily visits to the fidalgo, professing to be using his utmost exertions to discover his son, though Clara perseveringly refused to see him nor did he, indeed, appear anxious for an interview.

Luis had one morning wandered, accompanied by Pedro, nearly into the centre of the ruins; for there was something consonant with his own feelings in their desolate aspect, and he loved to be among them; perhaps, that the contemplation of the misery he beheld afforded, in the comparison, some alleviation to his own. The immediate scene we have already described;—beyond, on the hills above, were scattered the tents and huts of the inhabitants; while on every side, in the distance, arose the lofty gibbets, loaded with ghastly corpses,—a warning to the daring banditti who even yet prowled about, thirsting for booty, though their numbers and depredations had greatly been diminished by the summary proceedings against them. As he was returning homeward, he overtook a party of the new guards, dragging a man on among them towards the nearest hall of justice. He was about to pass them, when his steps were arrested by a voice calling to him from the crowd, in accents of entreaty, "Oh, Senhor Don Luis! save me, save me!—You know that I am an honest man and a friar, which I cannot make these gentlemen believe, and I shall be hung, to a certainty, before I can prove my innocence."

On hearing himself addressed, Luis turned round, and beheld his quondam acquaintance, Frè Diogo Lopez, in the hands of the officials of the law.

"Speak a word for me, senhor," he continued. "You know that I saved your life the other day; so, if you have a spark of the noble sentiment of gratitude, you will return me the favour on this occasion, or you will never enjoy another."

"He speaks true," said Luis to the guards; "and if you have no specific charge against him, I will be answerable if you will release him."

"That is utterly impossible, senhor," said the chief of the party. "I have no doubt but that you are a gentleman; but I know that this is a vagabond and a rogue. He is a friar, he says; and see, he is dressed in the gay suit of a dandy; besides, he can give no account of himself."

"Few innocent people can answer, when first accused of some dreadful crime at which their soul revolts," interrupted the Friar; "and then, as in my case, their hesitation is taken as a sign of their guilt. I can clearly account for wearing these clothes; for I had arrived in Lisbon late on the night preceding the earthquake, to be present at the festival of All the Saints; when, weary from my long journey on foot, I overslept myself; so that, when the dreadful event took place, I was fast asleep; and, hastily rising, I rushed out into the street, in a state more easily imagined than described. Now, being a modest man, I was anxious to take the earliest opportunity of supplying myself with garments, and, finding an unfortunate youth, who had been killed by the falling of a beam, with a decent suit on, uninjured, and seeing it could be of no further use to him, I took the liberty of appropriating it."

"That is very likely," said the officer. "But how came you to wear a wig, being a friar, senhor?"

"You would not wish me to wear such clothes as these without a wig, surely?" exclaimed the Friar. "That would have made me look ridiculous, indeed. No, senhores, I knew what was due to my character, and acted accordingly. However, I will not keep you waiting here, away from your duty, and would make you a present for the trouble you have been at to drag me along so far, had you not already eased me of all my spare cash; but I feel confident my friend, Don Luis d'Almeida, who has a sincere regard for me, will be happy, on my account, to make you a present, when you release me; and I shall certainly express to the proper authorities my high opinion of the way you perform your duty, on the very first occasion; whereas, if you blindly persist in your mistake, the Church will pronounce her anathemas on your heads, for having sacrilegiously destroyed one of her servants."

It is difficult to say whether these arguments, which he poured out with a voluble tongue, would have had any effect, had not Luis, anxious to save the man, who, though a most impudent rogue, had preserved his life, pulled out a purse, distributing its contents among the guards. At sight of the money, they immediately began to consider that the Friar had been ill-used and unjustly suspected, though the circumstances under which he was taken warranted what they had done, which, perhaps, accounted for his not threatening them with punishment; and no sooner did they feel the crowns in their hands, than they set him forthwith at liberty. When he found himself free, he rushed up to Don Luis, embracing him cordially, and then made his captors a profound bow, as they moved away.

"Pardon me, senhor, for the liberty I have taken," he said, "in pretending to be your friend; but I had no other chance. You have saved my life, and I shall ever be grateful. Perhaps some day I may have the means of proving it."

"You may, perhaps, at once," said Luis, eagerly. "You aided Antonio, the other day, in discovering where Donna Clara was concealed, and now, perhaps, you may be able to trace where her brother is to be found." And Luis gave him an account of the case.

"I will do my best, senhor," answered the Friar; "but at present I know nothing about the circumstance, though I have no doubt that villain Rodrigo, who was hung the other day, had a hand in it. I wish that I had never known that man: 'evil communication corrupts good manners;' and I confess that I have done some things I had better have left undone; but I made a vow just now, when I was in the power of those myrmidons of the law, that, if I escaped hanging, I would reform; and I intend to keep to my resolution. I will first endeavour to perform the service you require; and, to my shame I confess it, I know most of the rogues and vagabonds yet unhung in and about Lisbon, who are likely to give me information on the subject; and I then purpose to quit this city of sin and temptation, and return to my convent, and lead a pious life."

"I applaud your resolution, my friend," answered Luis; "and I shall, indeed, be grateful if you can afford the assistance I ask; though beware that you are not again captured by the officers of justice: you may not escape so easily."

"Trust to my caution," said the Friar. "A rat once escaped from a trap does not put its head in a second time. Now, adeos, senhor!—By the way, if you could lend me a few crowns, I should find them useful, and shall then be able to purchase another friar's gown, under which I shall be safer than in these gay habiliments. There is nothing like the outward garment of sanctity, when a man's character has been slightly blown upon."

Luis gave him a few crowns, which he could, however, but ill spare, for which the *ci-devant* Friar expressed himself very grateful, and then hurried away as fast as he could.

In the course of his walk, Luis reached a hill, on which had stood the church of Santa Catarina, now a heap of ruins. A crowd of persons, of all ranks and ages, and of each sex, were assembled there, collected round a tall figure, who had mounted to the summit of a heap of stones, and was haranguing them in a stentorian voice, throwing his arms aloft with the wildest gestures, and rolling his eyes around in a delirium of enthusiasm.

Luis inquired of one of the bystanders who the preacher was who was addressing them.

"Know you not," exclaimed the man, with a look of disdain at his culpable ignorance, "that he is one of the greatest prophets that has ever lived,—one to whom the gift of tongues has been vouchsafed, as to the apostles of old,—one in whose presence the kingdom of Portugal has been peculiarly blessed, and who, in these times of horror, pours balm into our hearts from his copious fountain of eloquence?—he is the great and pious Father Malagrida."

When Luis had asked the question, the preacher had just ceased speaking for a moment, coughing, and blowing his nose, in which the greater part of his congregation imitated him.

"Hark!" said the person to whom Luis had spoken; "he again commences."

The congregation now fixed their eyes with an intent gaze on the preacher as he began; and we are fortunate in being able to give an exact translation of his discourse, it having been printed in January, 1756; and a copy having, by a fortunate chance, fallen into our possession; and it serves to prove that some congregations, a hundred years ago, were not much wiser than they are at the present day, and that some preachers were able to convert the Scriptures to their own purposes with equal facility and talent.

See Note.

"Few are there among those who hear me, who do not wish to know the origin of these terrific convulsions of the earth; but this is not the first time that God has confided to the ignorant, and hidden from the wise, a knowledge of his profound secrets. 'Abscondisti haec à sapientibus et prudentibus, et revelati ea parvulis.' (Matt. xi. 25).

"Now, perhaps, some who deem themselves very clever, will endeavour to explain that they arise from natural causes; but yet a man may be very ignorant, and yet be able to convince them that such is not the case. God says it, (and it is enough that He should say it, to be infallible,) that there shall be a great change in our generation. 'Generatio praeterit, et generatio advenit.' (Eccles. i. 4.)

"Moreover, that the machine of the earth will always preserve a perpetual firmness. 'Terra autem in aeternum stat.' (*Ibid.*)

"Hence, it is not necessary to be a sage; it is sufficient to be Catholic, and to believe what God says, to know that the earth is immovable. Thus a believer will declare, although he be an ignorant man, notwithstanding that the Copernicanians say the contrary, who confide more on mathematics than on Christianity: it matters little that they affirm, with sacrilegious zeal against the sacred writings, that the earth moves, and that the sun is fixed; and it is in this way that wise men are deceived, and that the ignorant discover the truth. The earth, then, being immovable, for thus He says, who formed the centre of the world: 'Firmavit orbem terrae, qui non commovebitur,' (Psalm xciii. 2;) and its immovability being sustained by that omnipotent Idea with which the immense spaces of all infinity were built, what madness it is for those who call themselves sages to consider that the convulsions of the earth arise from natural causes. He only knows who made it with a nod, and can move it with a word. To such a height had this delirium, this *inflation of science*, as the Apostle calls it, arrived, that there was a sophist in the days of antiquity, who declared that, had he whereon to place his feet beyond the circumference of the globe, he could lift it with his shoulders; but this science is that folly of which Solomon speaks: 'Stultitia hominis supplantat gressus ejus; et contra Deum servet animo suo.' (Prov. xix. 3.)

"I know not whether this pride, this scientific impertinence to which philosophy always has recourse to banish the fear of strange events, is more presumption than as a punishment for our sins; and it appears fated that this should happen more in earthquakes than in other impulses of the Omnipotent hand."

The preacher then proceeded to show by what sort of fire Sodom and Gomorrah were destroyed, comparing their inhabitants to those of Lisbon, in no flattering terms.

"If you would know the cause of these calamities, listen not to what the mathematicians and philosophers say, but to what God says through the mouth of his prophet Isaias: 'Movebitur terra de loco suo propter indignationem Domini exercituum et propter diem irae furoris ejus.' (Isaiah xiii. 13.)

"Cease to persuade yourselves, then, that the earth is moved, not because the world is living, as some atheists say;—not because it swims on the sea, as Thales says;—not because the subterranean fires and waters meet, as Democrates says;—not because some of its enormous portions are hurled to the centre, as Anaximenes says;—not because the wind confined in the internal caverns of the globe bursts forth, as Aristotle says;—but because thus God shakes it, and because God drives it with an invisible force, proceeding from His sovereign indignation.

"There is no doubt that the prophet foretold the fate of Lisbon under the name of Babylon, when he says: 'Vidi Angelum descendentem de caelo, habentem potestatem magnam; et exclamavit in fortitudine, dicens: Cecidit, cecidit Babylon.'

"Yes, the crimes of the people will ascend to heaven, and remind God of their wickedness, and He will cause their city to become a heap of ruins and ashes, and there shall be death, and mourning, and hunger. Did not all this happen, and did not the King, when he beheld his palace and his city in flames, weep and mourn? 'Et flebunt et plangent super illam Reges terrae cum viderint fumum incendii ejus.'"

He then mentioned the riches that were destroyed exactly as the prophet foretold.

"What further evidence to convince you of the truth would you have? Yet here are others. Did not the pilots and sailors remain at a distance, on the bosom of the Tagus, to behold the miserable destruction? 'Et omnis gubernator, et omnis qui in lacum navigat et qui in mari operantur longe steterunt.'

"Did not also the singers and musicians, who had come from various countries to increase the amusements of the Court, fly away, so that the sounds of their instruments were no more heard? 'Et vox citharaedorum et musicorum et tibia canentium et tuba, non audietur in te amplius.'

"Are not these great and striking evidences that the destruction of Lisbon was foretold? And also all the holy fathers of the Church agree, that when Babylon was spoken of, some other city was meant, supposing it to refer to the destruction and burning of Rome; but now it is confessed by all, that St. John spoke not of Rome, but of Lisbon. Does he not speak of a city built on seven hills, great, flourishing, and powerful, and does not Lisbon stand on seven hills? I ought rather to say, did stand; and was she not one of the first cities in the world? And can there yet be a soul so incredulous, that he should persevere in declaring that this horrible calamity was chance, and not design?—was an impulse of nature, and not a Divine sentence?

"Yes, alas! some are so hardened as still to doubt; for that was also foretold: 'Ingravatum est cor Pharaonis: induratum est cor Pharaonis.' (Exod. vii.)

"Many are the hearts like Pharaoh's, and many are the warnings they have received like him. Say, when the earth shook some years ago, did you then repent?—No. When it shook a second time?—No. And a third time?—No. Will you repent this time?—No. 'Induratum est cor Pharaonis;' for 'Dixit insipiens in corde suo: non est Deus.'"

He then clearly proved that "Mulierem sedentem super bestiam coccineam, habens poculum aureum in manu sua, plenum abominatione," etc, was a description of Lisbon, filled with people of all nations, addicted to all manner of abominations, particularly with Jews and heretics of all sorts. (We have heard rather a different interpretation given elsewhere.)

"And yet some will not believe," he continued. "Well may I say of you, with Jeremiah, 'Ostulti et tarde corde ad credendum!'"

As he proceeded, a bright rainbow was seen hanging over the ruined city.

"See, see! a portend! a portend!" he cried. "If you will repent, if you will no longer live in sin, you will be forgiven. 'Arcum meum ponam in nubibus, et erit signum faederis inter me, et inter terram.'

"The same sign that God gave to Noah has He now given to us, to assure us that the earthquake will cease. 'Et Iris erat in circuitu sedis' (Apocalypse, iv.) But Iris is, it can be clearly shown, as Saint Eupremio and Saint Antonio call her, the holy Mother of God, who has sent the glory which surrounds her head to show us that His anger has ceased; and, as Saint Bernardo says of her, 'Sicut Iris, Virgo scilicet benedicta, in circuitu Ecclesiae constituitur.'

"Oh, pure Virgin! who standest ever before the throne of your Son, with hands uplifted, seeking mercy for our sins, hear our prayers, and speak these words in our favour which Moses spoke for the Israelites. 'Quiescat ira tua, et esto placabilis super nequitia populi tui;' for if the Lord listened to his words, how much more will he to those of the Mother of God! and then let us hear those joyful words; 'Placatus est Dominus ne faceret malam quod locutus fuerat adversus populum suum.'"

As Luis was attentively listening to this discourse, so full of theological erudition and acute reasoning, he felt a hand laid on his shoulder, and turning round, he beheld the holy father, Jacinto da Costa.

"I am glad to see you yet an inhabitant of this world, my good cousin," said the latter, in a reproachful tone; "though, verily, you took but slight pains to discover whether I had escaped this dreadful visitation; however, I have plenty of excuses to offer for you, so do not attempt to make them yourself. Nay, do not answer. I have heard frequently of you. Retire a little from this crowd of fools; for I should be sorry to rank you among them. So, you have recovered from your fit of wretchedness at the loss of our fair cousin, Theresa, and have a second time entangled your feelings in a love affair, which promises to be equally unsuccessful."

"Alas! I fear so," answered Luis; "and that must excuse me for not having visited you."

"I am glad of it. You will have far more opportunities of exerting your energies on the wide field the world offers, than if you wed some weak girl, who would bind you to her apron-strings. Remember what I said to you some months ago; and, instead of repining at your fate, rejoice that the road I then pointed out is still open before you."

"I shall never forget your words, Father," answered Luis; "but were I likely to follow your advice, it would have been then, when I was inclined to despair; now I am buoyed up with the proud consciousness of having my love returned, by a being as lovely, and as perfect in mind and person, as this world can produce."

The Jesuit gazed at his young kinsman with a cold and scornful smile. "So you thought was Donna Theresa," he returned; "so you will think every woman you love, till you awake from your opiate slumber, and find 'twas but a flitting dream. I once thought the same, till the magic key to the human heart was committed into my hands, and in the all-powerful confessional I learned to unlock its secrets. Then I discovered how false had been my early impressions, at the same time that I felt an absorbing interest in the inexhaustible field of study opened to my view. Years have I now spent in tracing the intricate workings of the human heart, and yet, each day am I making new discoveries; but it is with the sex of whom you are most ignorant that I have attained the greatest knowledge, for the reason, that to me they are more ready to communicate their thoughts and feelings, while to you their whole aim is to conceal them,—whereas men rarely allow more to be known than they can avoid. However, I will not now enter into the subject. Accompany me to my convent, which has escaped uninjured, Malagrida and others are convinced, and endeavour to persuade the people, as a peculiar mark of Heaven's favour; and so I might suppose, but that other parts of the city, inhabited by a class to whom the world does not impute much righteousness, have been equally distinguished. We will stay here a little longer, for I wish to know what our celebrated prophet will say to the people. I fear he may commit himself with our arch-enemy Carvalho, who would be delighted to have an excuse to annoy us. Yet, mark how easily the crowd are led, by one little better than a madman, to believe the most absurd nonsense, and to commit follies which make one blush for one's fellow-men."

Luis promised to accompany his cousin, for he had no reason to assign for refusing; yet the sophisms of the latter made but little impression on his understanding, though not a word the Jesuit had uttered was without cause: notwithstanding his extensive knowledge of human nature, he was perhaps deceived in the character of his young relative.

While they were conversing apart from the crowd, Malagrida again mounted the heap of ruins, and commenced speaking, in a voice which was heard for a wide circuit round.

"You have been firmly convinced, O ye people! that the late awful visitation was by the direct command of Heaven; but why did the Lord thus suddenly think fit to manifest his anger? Was it on account of the increased wickedness of the people? No! they had not become worse than they always were since the city was built; but it was because he looked down on the city and beheld his true and faithful servants, whose whole lives have been spent in forwarding his works, thrust out from their offices, and treated by the rulers of the land with scorn and neglect. Could he longer endure such impiety? No! Now mark where the whole fury of his anger fell. See, the once proud palace of the King a heap of stones and ashes! Why was this? Who is the culprit? Who but the King? And why? because he retains in his councils that impious despiser of the commands of the Lord,—that hater of our holy religion,—that persecutor and vile calumniator of the ministers of the faith,—that man in whom none ought to place trust,—whom all must hate,—that man accursed by Heaven, Sebastiaö Jozé de Carvalho! Do any here think I fear him? No, I scorn his hatred—I laugh at his fury. Why should I fear him? I who have stood boldly before the kings of the earth, and have rebuked them for their transgressions; and again do I rebuke the King who now reigns over this unhappy country. Let him beware; for even as the kingdom departed from Nebuchadnezzar, the king of Babylon, so will his kingdom pass away from his hands, and whoso slayeth him shall be accounted blessed in the sight of Heaven."

Malagrida still continued speaking, when Father Jacinto, taking the arm of his young cousin, led him on one side. "I had heard that the horrors of the earthquake had somewhat injured my holy brother's brain, and I came here to endeavour to stop his preaching, fearing that he might commit himself, which he had indeed done; for one might as well expect to stop a winter torrent in its impetuous course as that man, when he has persuaded himself that the Spirit prompts him to speak. My only hope is, that his mad words may not be reported to that enemy of our order, the Minister, or Malagrida will be made to suffer severely for what he has said, and, at all events, banished from hence. I have heard enough to convince me that he is no longer to be trusted, so I shall not remain here. Come with me to my convent; for I can there speak to you on a subject which I have to communicate, but little calculated to raise your spirits; here I will say nothing."

Luis, wondering, yet dreading what the Jesuit had to relate, accepted his invitation; and, as they were passing the crowd, he observed Antonio among them. He longed to speak to him, to ask him if he had gained any information regarding the young Gonçalo; but the crowd was so dense that he could not approach him, nor could he catch his eye, for there was no one more intently listening to every word the preacher uttered than he, nor would any of the bystanders have been supposed more devoutly believing.

"By the God of my fathers, that man strives hard to gain the glorious crown of martyrdom; and, if I mistake not, he will deservedly win it before long," thought Antonio to himself. "He must be got rid of, or, mad as he is, he will find fools enough to follow his counsels, and among them they will commit some mischief before many days are over."

Note. The whole of this Sermon is a literal translation.

Volume Two—Chapter Nineteen.

"Farewell, my kind friend," exclaimed Don Luis, pressing the hand of Captain Pinto, as they stood together in front of their humble lodgings on the outskirts of the ruined city, while Pedro held his master's horse and his own, prepared for a journey.

"Farewell, Luis; we may meet again under happier auspices, when I return from the cruise on which I am now despatched, and you recover from the effects of your disappointment and reverse of fortune."

"The mere loss of fortune I could, as far as I am individually concerned, have borne with fortitude, but that it casts a cloud over the last days of my father's life, and that it deprives me of the last chance of gaining Donna Clara."

"But is your father's property so irretrievably involved, that you may not hope to recover it?" asked the Captain.

"So Father Jacinto, my cousin, informs me, the mercantile house in which the whole of my father's monied property was placed having completely failed, and the estates being mortgaged to their full value.—No, alas! I see no chance of ever being able to recover what we have lost; and with me, I fear, our once high name must end."

"Don't think of such a thing. When you least expect it, Fortune's wheel will turn up a prize, and you will find yourself prosperous and happy. You do not mean to become a friar, I hope? You were fitted for nobler aims than such a life can offer."

"I must visit my father,—I fear it will be but to close his eyes,—before I fix on my future course in life, though surely anything is preferable to hanging about the Court, a poverty-stricken noble, in greedy expectation of some paltry office, cringing meanly to those one despises, to obtain it, as is the fate of many, and would be mine also if I could submit to it; but that I never can. No, I would far rather sink my rank and name, and be forgotten by the world, than lead such a life."

"You are right, Luis, anything is better than that contemptible hunting after place, in which so many men waste their energies; but you need not be reduced to that necessity,—the Minister will gladly give you employment whenever you ask for it, as he has already promised you, and he is not a man to forget his word."

"That was when fortune appeared to smile on me, and I was not a suppliant for charity. You yourself have often told me that people are far more ready to bestow gifts on those who do not ask for them, than on those who are petitioners."

"With people in general, such is the case," replied the Captain; "but the Minister is not to be judged by the same rules as other men: besides, you have other powerful friends, whom you are not aware of, but who would be the last people to wish you to enter the profession of the Church—with due reverence be it spoken. Should you be deprived of your natural counsellor,—your father, do not take any step without consulting one in whose judgment you may place the fullest confidence,—I mean, Senhor Mendez. You will always hear of him at the house where he is now residing, and he will ever be ready to advise you. Do not act like some foolish people, who fancy that it betrays a weakness of judgment to ask advice, whereas another person, of even inferior capacity, may often, from viewing a case calmly and dispassionately, be able to form a better opinion than he who, having to act, is naturally biassed according to his feelings at the time. You will think me an old proser if I continue talking much longer; and, at all events, your servant and horses are impatient to be off, so once again, Luis, farewell."

The friends embracing affectionately, Luis mounted his horse with a sad heart, and turned his back once more on all the horrors and miseries with which for the last few weeks he had been surrounded. He had, in despair, been obliged to give up his search for the younger Gonçalo Christovaö, not being able to discover the slightest trace of him, so that at last he felt convinced that he must have been one of the sufferers in the earthquake.

The fidalgo had recovered his strength, and a few days before had set off on his return to Oporto, accompanied by his daughter, and his confessor, who did not cease to insist on his fulfilling his vow of placing the fair girl in a convent; and it was at last agreed that she should enter the principal one in that city. Clara, broken-hearted and despairing, offered no opposition to the proposed plan, so that it was arranged she should commence her noviciate soon after her return home,—her younger brother, who had been before destined for the Church, being taken from Coimbra, where he was pursuing his studies, little thought of or cared about, to be treated henceforth as the heir of the house.

Luis heard of these arrangements through a message sent him by Senhora Gertrudes, who promised him that, happen what might, her young mistress should never forget his love and devotion; and that to his courage she owed her life and honour. This was the only particle of consolation he received; and, as it was the only food offered to his hopes, it was not surprising that they were left to starve.

He had just passed the last point from which the ruined capital could be seen,—Pedro, observing his master's mood, not attempting to interrupt his meditations,—when a horseman from a cross-road suddenly joined them, and riding up to the side of Luis, accosted him.

"Good morrow, Senhor Fidalgo, you are early on the road," said the stranger, in a clear jovial voice. "By your leave, I will ride on some way with you."

"Many thanks, senhor, for your polite offer," returned Luis, scarcely noticing the speaker; "but I should prefer travelling alone."

"What! Don Luis d'Almeida, the brave, the gallant, and the gay, turned misanthropical?" exclaimed the stranger, laughing. "However, great changes are taking place every day,—honest men turning rogues, and rogues turning honest; one can never tell what will happen next."

As the stranger was speaking, Luis regarded him attentively, nor was he long in discovering, beneath the military curled wig and queue, the fierce moustaches, and heavy travelling dress, the features of the *ci-devant* Frè Lopez.

"I trust that you are one of those making a change for the better, Senhor Padre," said Luis; "but I expected to have met you in a dress more appropriate to your character than the one you wear."

"I am glad to find that you do not forget your old friends, as I was at first afraid you were going to do," returned the Friar. "With regard to my costume, you belie it, to say that it is not suited to the character of an honest man; for let me assure you, that, doubt it as you may, I have turned honest; and where can you find a more honourable dress than that of a soldier?"

"Yet, such is surely not suited to your character as a friar," said Luis.

"Why not? may I not belong to the church militant," returned Frè Lopez. "However, to confess the truth, I have my friar's robes carefully wrapped up in my valise behind me, and I intend before long to don them for ever; for I am growing weary of the fatigues and dangers of the wild life I have led, and pine for the quiet and security of the cloister. Yet, let me assure you that it was for your sake I assumed my present disguise. I heard that you were about to travel this way, and, knowing that the roads were very far from safe, on account of the number of thieves who have been frightened out of Lisbon, I thought it my duty to accompany you, to prevent your suffering from them."

"Many thanks for your attention; but are you not afraid of being apprehended yourself as a suspicious character? You heard that the Minister has issued an order to the corregidors of all the towns in the south, to stop every one who has no pass from him, in case they should be carrying off any property stolen from the city."

"Oh yes, senhor, I heard of the order, and am provided with a pass, if necessary; but I should think it would not be asked for in such worshipful company as yours."

"Then you had some other motive in favouring me with your company?" said Luis, scarcely refraining from laughing at the man's impudence.

"People generally have more than one motive for their good actions," returned the Friar. "Now, if I, being a rogue, preserve you from the rogues, you, in return, being an honest man, are bound to preserve me from the fangs of the law; therefore, the obligation is mutual, and I have the satisfaction of performing a good action, and receiving a service from you besides. Don't think I am the less honest on that account. I tell you my motives, whereas another man would keep them secret, or, at all events, give you only one of them; but I scorn such hypocrisy."

"You are honest," said Luis.

"You flatter me, senhor," interrupted the Friar. "It is the first time, for many a long year past, that I have been told so; and I will endeavour to merit the good opinion you have formed of me."

"I shall be indeed glad to hear that you have foresworn the very suspicious companions with whom I have so frequently met you," said Luis.

"I have already bidden farewell to most of them. There they hang, like fruit on the trees, thanks to the mild clemency of the Minister!" As the Friar spoke, he pointed towards Lisbon. "I am glad enough to get beyond the sight of those ghastly corpses. Ah, senhor! it is a dreadful thing to hang people up in that way; and many an innocent man is among them. Thank Heaven, I have not such deeds on my conscience! That reminds me, senhor, that I have gained some information which may assist you in discovering what you spoke to me about. I was speaking to one of those poor fellows the night before he was caught and hung,—and, by-the-bye, he no more deserved hanging than I do!—he told me that he had been employed, some time ago, in carrying a young fidalgo, who had been wounded in a night-fray, to a house in the outskirts of Lisbon; but that he could not exactly tell where it was, and who was the person. He had been hired by Rodrigo, who did not mention the name of their employer. The poor fellow was to have accompanied me the next day to try and find out the house, but he was hung instead. Ah! I am a great enemy to the system of hanging."

Luis listened with deep interest to this account. Then Gonçalo might have escaped destruction from the earthquake! He might be yet alive! He longed to turn back, and continue his search; but he had slight grounds to go upon; for the Friar could give him no further information, and his father was expecting him at home. With sanguine dispositions, the slightest thing is sufficient to raise hopes which, alas! may never be accomplished, but which it often takes years and years of disappointment to learn to distrust. Now old men, as we have informed our readers we are, even to this day, we find ourselves building castles in the air, of such bright and glowing colours, that our own sight is dazzled by the splendour of the fabric we have raised, when a single word has been sufficient to make it fade away like the morning mist, each brilliant hue growing less and less distinct, till we have wondered that it could ever have existed even in our imaginations; and at other times a rude blow has dashed the lovely edifice to the ground, and as we have flown to the spot, we have not found a fragment remaining.

The words the Friar had spoken had been sufficient to raise just such a fabric in Luis's brain; and, thus occupied, in happier mood he rode on, while the former fell back to converse with Pedro, who was not averse to the company of so amusing a personage, although a rogue. Several very suspicious parties either overtook them, or passed them on the road; but a signal, or a few words, from the Friar, always sent them peaceably away; so that Luis, during the whole journey, met with no adventure worth relating.

"Farewell, Don Luis!" said the *soi-disant* Friar, as they came in sight of the gates of the Count's estate. "I have borne you company thus far, and we must now part. We shall meet again some day, I hope; if not, think of me sometimes, as I would be, and not as I have been; but I fear I shall not be a more honest man as a real Friar than I have been as a pretended one. Adeos, senhor!"

And, without waiting for an answer, he rode back the way he had come; while Luis, followed by Pedro, hastened to embrace his father, although the tidings he had to communicate must, he knew, cause much sorrow to the old Count.

Volume Two—Chapter Twenty.

More than a year had passed since the dreadful earthquake of Lisbon, as the violent convulsion of the globe in 1755 is commonly called, although it was felt over the greater part of Europe, to the north of England, and to the shores of Africa, where many towns were destroyed or severely damaged. Under the energetic superintendence of the Prime Minister, the city was rapidly rising from its ashes; and instead of the dark, narrow, and winding lanes of the old town, fine broad streets were planned by able architects invited by him from England and France.

The tents and wooden huts in which the inhabitants had so long dwelt, were ordered to be destroyed, to prevent the rogues and vagabonds, who it appears had again, notwithstanding the terrors of the hanging system, increased to an alarming degree, from harbouring in them.

The horrors of the previous year began gradually to fade from the recollection of men, and they forgot that beneath the ground on which they dwelt burnt those unquenchable fires which might, at any time, burst forth and again destroy their homes and property.

The King and the royal family had taken up their residence in the Palace of the Necessidades, having dwelt for nearly a year in one built of wood, of one story high, to run less risk of injury in case of a recurrence of the former disastrous visitation.

It was some hours past the time of sunset, when, in a cabinet of the palace, the Minister was seated at a table thickly strewed with papers, deeply immersed in the affairs of the state, it might be presumed, from the lines of thought and care which marked his brow. He wrote on for some time, without stopping or hesitating a moment for want of subject, and then, having concluded the work he was about, he threw himself back in the high leathern armchair in which he was sitting, and resting his brow upon his hand, continued for many minutes wrapped in meditation.

"Men would blame me, did they know the game I played," he thought; "but 'tis the way by which alone I can manage my weak and indolent master:—master!" he muttered, in a scornful tone, "let me say, my slave, my tool! I can brook no master. While he is occupied by some mad folly, or new passion, he will gladly resign all but the empty shadow of power into my hands, and it must be my care to keep him thus employed, while I silence, and for ever, all opposition from without to my aims. His infatuated admiration of this young Marchioness of Tavora may lead to serious results: but no matter; I can easily turn them to my advantage; and, at all events, it keeps him occupied. The pursuit is likely to be a long one, for the lady seems colder and more inaccessible than I had deemed her. Ah! here he comes!"

As he spoke, a door on one side of the room opened, and the King entered. The Minister bowed profoundly as the sovereign threw himself listlessly into a chair, and commenced signing a variety of papers, which the former placed before him, without even glancing at their contents. At last, with an air of disgust, he threw down the pen and rose from his seat, exclaiming, "I can sign no more of your long edicts to-night, my Carvalho. Far more pleasing cares call me elsewhere; and I must snatch a few hours of liberty while my most jealous lady Queen is persuaded I am closeted with my faithful Minister."

"Your Majesty's wishes are ever my laws," returned the Minister; "and I will occupy myself till your return with many important affairs which demand my attention."

"Do so, my good friend," said the King.

"I shall not detain you long. Has Teixeira yet come?"

"I will inquire," answered the complaisant Minister; and quitted the room by an opposite door to that by which the King had entered.

The King walked impatiently about the room till Carvalho returned, accompanied by another person, who bore a large cloak, which he threw over the royal shoulders. The King then wrapping it around himself, so as to conceal his features, left the cabinet, followed by his attendant, while the Minister resumed his previous occupations.

More than two hours thus passed away; not a sound reaching Carvalho's ears, and no one venturing to intrude where his Majesty was supposed to be occupied in framing laws for the welfare of the kingdom committed to his charge.

For the first hour he continued writing without rising from his seat; inditing letters which no eye but his own and the persons to whom they were addressed might see; making notes only of their contents as he folded and sealed them; for it was his principle never to trust any one where it could possibly be avoided: nor did he allow the secretaries and clerks, who were absolutely necessary to carry on the public business, to be acquainted with any affair beyond their immediate office, punishing those severely who betrayed what was committed to them. He then rose and strode up and down the room for some minutes, with knitted brow and compressed lips. "Ah!" he exclaimed, "thus shall all suffer who dare oppose my will. I have given the people of Oporto a lesson they will not easily forget. Their chief magistrate and eighteen of his seditious companions executed; three hundred of the principal people sent to the galleys, and their city given up to the licence of a brutal soldiery. This will, methinks, put a stop to further conspiracies against my authority; and, if not, in every town and village throughout the kingdom I will have gibbets erected, and hang every one who dares to utter a word of complaint. By terror alone can these people be ruled—all mild measures are worse than useless; for, instead of conciliating, they cause the nation to suppose that it is through fear, or want of power, that they are employed. By Heavens! they shall no longer have reason to suppose so. I have begun my reign of terror, and from henceforth I banish all pity or remorse from my bosom; and the abject wretches on whose necks I will trample, shall feel that, at length, they have a man, instead of the drivelling priests or ignorant debauchees who have hitherto attempted to govern them."

Muttering, rather than speaking, his thoughts aloud, he returned to his desk. He was still writing when he felt a hand laid on his shoulder, and, rising from his seat, he bowed to his sovereign, who had entered, if not unperceived, at least unattended to.

"You work hard for our benefit, my faithful Minister," said Joseph, seating himself; "but we wish you would rule a lady's changeful mood as easily as you can govern our kingdom. The lovely Donna Theresa continues cruel as ever: she listens to all my passionate speeches with a smile of satisfaction, and entreats me to return again before long, for that she should die were she deprived of my society; and in the same breath talks of her husband and the honour of her family. Her coldness provokes me, while her fascinations increase my love."

"Your Majesty need not despair," said the sagacious Minister. "A woman who has once consented to admit a lover to an interview without her husband's knowledge will never draw back if he proceeds with caution; and when that lover has the qualifications of your Majesty, her fate is certain. A few weeks' more perseverance and she will yield, or I must renounce all knowledge of the female heart."

"She must, Carvalho, she must!" exclaimed the King, impatiently. "This suspense is dreadful. What advantage is gained by being a King, unless our subjects will dutifully obey us?"

"Your Majesty is perfectly right; and few there are, I trust, of all your Majesty's subjects who would prove thus disloyal, except some of the haughty nobles of the realm, who appear to suppose your kingdom their own; and of one of those families is the lovely Donna Theresa, which will account for her most undutiful hesitation. Yet your Majesty need have no fears of the result."

"I know, I know," said the King, hastily; "I am convinced she loves me; but some foolish prejudice appears to restrain her from her own wishes."

"'Tis the work of those accursed Jesuits," exclaimed Carvalho; "but your Majesty need not fear, and will be able to counteract their aims, if you will follow my advice."

"Your counsel is always that of wisdom," said the King. "Speak, my Carvalho."

"I would, then, advise your Majesty to make a present to Donna Theresa of your favourite dwarf, Donna Florinda. She is acute and observing, and will very soon become mistress of all the young lady's secrets, at the same time that she will counsel her no longer to treat your Majesty with her general cruelty."

"Ah! the idea is indeed worthy of following!" exclaimed the King, enraptured at the bright thought. "Thanks, my Carvalho, thanks. You are truly the most sagacious and first of Ministers. I will persuade our Queen, who will willingly part with her, to send her to-morrow morning; and then, if she succeeds, I shall indeed be thankful to one who has so well aided my wishes."

The King then, holding out his hand, which the zealous and unprejudiced Minister kissed, with every sign of respect, retired to his chamber, and the latter, securing his papers, some in an iron chest, the key of which he kept, and others of more importance about his person, sought his carriage, which was in attendance, and returned to his home.

Volume Two—Chapter Twenty One.

We have, for a considerable time, lost sight of Donna Theresa d'Alorna, now the young Marchioness of Tavora. She was seated in her private apartment, on the morning following the consultation of the King and his Minister, in the palace which had been allotted by his father to the young Marquis, when one of her female attendants entered to inform her that her confessor was in attendance below, and requested to know if she would wish to see him.

"Yes, yes, I will see the holy father; conduct him hither," she exclaimed hastily, and the attendant retired.

"His requests are indeed commands," she whispered to herself. "Alas! I feel a power I cannot see, and know not whence it comes, hurrying me to the edge of a precipice."

Donna Theresa was but little altered since we introduced her to our readers. In beauty she had rather improved; her figure had become more rounded and voluptuous, and the sparkle of her eyes was brighter even than before, with greater expression in her countenance, her polished brow giving more signs of deep thought, and, alas! it might be, of care.

Though she had been expecting her visitor, she started as he entered, and rose to welcome him. Our readers will recognise, by his tall, yet graceful and dignified form, the lofty and marble brow, the piercing cold grey eye, and rich melodious voice, the holy Father Jacinto da Costa, the head of the Jesuits' College.

He took the hand of the young lady, and, with respectful courtesy, led her to a seat, and took one by her side. "I have come, my fair penitent," he said, in a gentle tone, "to hear the result of your conference with the King. He visited you, as you expected, yesterday?"

Donna Theresa cast her eyes to the ground, and then gazing up earnestly at the Jesuit, she exclaimed, with a voice trembling with agitation, "His Majesty did come last night, trusting in my love and faith; but I had not the heart—I wanted the courage—I could not be guilty of the treachery, to ask the questions you dictated. Oh! do not longer impose this odious task on me! If it be necessary for the safety of my family, if it be advantageous to the service of our holy religion, take some other means to attain the same ends, but I can no longer feign love to my confiding sovereign. Every time I meet him, I feel myself lowered and degraded far worse than the guilty thing the world will soon suppose me."

The Jesuit smiled encouragement, as he gently shook his head. "The foolish girl loves this weak puppet already," he thought; but she divined not what was passing in his mind. "No matter, my ends are answered; and if she must be sacrificed, I shall, perhaps, gain the more. Besides, in so holy a cause, I can afford her speedy absolution."

"Theresa," he said aloud, "it pains me to hear one of your soaring and acute mind utter expressions worthy only of a foolish girl. Think of the ends proposed. It is not the King I wish to injure; I alone seek to counteract the machinations of that arch-enemy of your family, and of my order, the Minister Carvalho. Could you once gain that complete ascendency over the King which is within your power, you might not only rule him, but the Minister himself would become powerless to injure any of those connected with you by kindred and by love. Believe me, if you hesitate, that treacherous man has sworn, and will not fail in his oath, to ruin all your race, for their haughty contempt of his plebeian extraction. Choose which course you will; allow your newly-raised scruples to conquer your former resolution, and see all those you love destroyed; or take the means of winning a power far greater than any other female in the land can hold."

"But will the means you advise gain that power?" she asked, with a doubtful tone. "Already have I lost much of my former influence with the King. He begins to doubt the sincerity of my love, and accuses me of coldness and indifference, urging me with prayers and entreaties to give him stronger proofs of my affections, endeavouring to persuade me to sacrifice my honour to his passion."

The priest of God looked steadily at the young girl. "Theresa," he said, "I know that you are superior to the foolish superstitions of mankind; and, being convinced of the fallacy of what many call the moral rules of conduct, you will laugh at the prejudices which now cause you to hesitate in performing a necessary duty. With us, the *only* true priesthood, rests alone the knowledge of what ought or ought not to be performed under certain circumstances. There are rules necessarily promulgated to keep in check the mass of mankind; but they are not without exceptions. What is a crime when performed by one person, becomes a virtue in another. It is the cause and effect of the action which constitutes a crime. When a man in a fit of causeless anger, slays another, he is guilty of murder; or when, to conceal previous guilt, through revenge, or to wrench his gold, one kills another, he is a murderer; but, with the same knife, and in the same way, a man may kill another to attain some good end, or to punish guilt, and he has performed a righteous deed. In the same way, if a woman, through the frailty of her sex, yields to the temptation of passion, she commits what is looked upon as a crime, according to the code at present received as the rule of conduct; but should a woman employ those captivating qualities with which nature has endowed her to attain some desirable object, instead of committing a crime, she has performed a meritorious action; the more so, that she has exposed herself to censure from her fellow-creatures for the purpose."

Theresa answered with energy, "Oh, Father! but it surely cannot be justifiable to deceive my husband, to barter his honour, and to betray the secrets drawn from my confiding sovereign in a moment of affection."

"The honour of a husband you do not love, and whose affection for you you have found but of short endurance, is but of little worth," answered the Father. "Besides, by acting as I would have you do, you perform a far greater service to him and his family than in preserving what he does not value. You treat him far better than he deserves. Let not that thought trouble you. With regard to winning the secrets of your sovereign, you injure him in no possible way; it is through him alone we may hope to arrive at many of the secrets of the Minister; for to no one else are they confided; and against our enemy alone is a blow meditated."

Donna Theresa had no further excuse to make for her refusal; yet her heart (for that was not quite convinced by the cunning arguments of sophistry) told her that she would be acting a treacherous and sinful part in following her confessor's counsels. But then again, her ambition urged her on,—and, more than all, she loved! A moth may not play round the flame without scorching its wings; and a woman can seldom tamper with the affections of another without injuring her own. From the moment that she felt she loved the weak monarch, she was no longer able to act the treacherous part she had before been taught to play. She grew cold and distant, for she could not trust herself; and, while her royal lover fancied himself further from his object, he was on the very verge of attaining it. Now, then, her scruples on one score were banished; for she had no further reason to hesitate, when her only counsellor assured her she was committing no crime; but it was not in her nature to be deceitful, and she began to doubt how far she was justified in gaining the confidence of the King in order to betray it. Before she loved, this thought had never occurred to her. Her aim, from the first, had been to gain power; and vanity had led her on from step to step.

It is extraordinary in what different lights we mortals view the same objects under various circumstances. What at one time appears the thing of all others the most desirable to be gained, and for which we would sacrifice our present happiness, and, perhaps, all those dear to us, we the next instant look upon as worthless. What we once thought a heinous crime, we too soon, alas! learn to consider as a slight failing, though far less often do we shudder at crimes which we before committed with untroubled consciences.

"I do not advise you to yield to the King's passion," continued the Priest; "but as you value all you have loved, at every expense, retain the power you have gained over him. Bind those captivating chains round him, which your charms are so well calculated to forge, and from henceforth it will not be he, but you, who rule these fair realms of Portugal. Promise me you will do this, Theresa, and I will afford such complete absolution for aught which may trouble your conscience, that it shall remain as bright and pure as at present."

"Father, I do promise you," returned Donna Theresa. "You have convinced me both of the necessity of the end, and of the innocence of the means. From henceforth no vain scruples shall deter me!"

There was the slightest possible tone of sarcasm in her voice, for she was not convinced, but she was unable to answer. Such is very frequently the case; and an acute reasoner, who has brought all the arguments of logic and sophistry into play, fancies he has won a victory, because he has silenced a battery, while in reality the fortress remains as impregnable as before. The Jesuit pretended not to notice the irony with which she spoke, as he answered,—"Spoken as I should ever wish my fair pupil to utter her thoughts. By acting as I would desire, you will deserve the warmest gratitude from all you benefit, and the King himself will in time learn to thank you for having rescued him from the thraldom of the tyrant who now holds him in such abject subjection. He is a man who must be governed by some one; and it is far better he should be under the mild sway of a lovely woman, than be the slave of a bloodthirsty monster." He rose as he spoke. "Farewell, Donna Theresa;—a business of importance calls me away; and I trust, when I next call on you, I shall hear you have obtained the valuable information I so much require."

He did not wait to receive an answer, for he felt confident that his object would be attained; and he left his last observations to take their full effect.

As Father Jacinto was leaving the palace, he encountered the little black dwarf, Donna Florinda, just getting out of her chair; but, pretending not to observe her, he passed on, muttering to himself, "Ah! is this the way the royal lover is about to work? Let him beware that the betrayer is not betrayed!"

Donna Florinda was far too much occupied in arranging her own dress, in her eagerness to bustle up stairs to exhibit her credentials to her new mistress, to observe the dark figure of the priest. She had received but one charge, being the very simple one of praising the King, and keeping all other lovers at a distance. The young Marchioness received her with great civility, for she had the capability of making herself very amusing, by detailing all the events and scandal of the Court, there being abundance of material for the latter; and she was, therefore, constantly welcome, wherever she went.

The little sable lady was in no way altered in appearance since the time we first introduced her to our readers, being dressed in the same extravagant and gaudy style of costume, and exhibiting a like perfect unconsciousness of the ridiculous figure she made. This was a failing not at all peculiar to herself in her day, nor do we think any very great change has since taken place in the world. She smirked and curtsied as she entered, and presented a letter to Donna Theresa, who, requesting her to be seated, broke the seal, and scanned it over with eagerness.

"Their Majesties are, indeed, very kind, to make me so valuable a present as yourself, Donna Florinda," said the young Marchioness; "but I fear you will be very unwilling to exchange the splendour and gaiety of the Court for the private residence of one who lives so secluded a life as I do."

"Far from it, my sweet mistress; I am too happy to come and reside with one so charming and gentle as you are, instead of the cross-grained Queen," returned the Dwarf. "You well know how I have always loved you; so I was overjoyed when I heard the King propose sending me to you, and in a fright lest her Majesty should take it into her head to refuse to part with me. As soon, therefore, as the point was settled, I hurried away, after paying my most dutiful respects, lest they should again change their minds. To tell you the truth, the King had some difficulty about the matter, but he knew that it would please you, and that had made him determine to carry his point. Ah, he is, indeed, a King to win the hearts of every one,—so kind, so gentle, so loving! You do not appreciate all his surpassing qualities, Donna Theresa, or you would not be so cruel as I suspect you are to him. The other day, when speaking of the beautiful ladies of his Court, he said there were many bright moons which lighted up the night, but they all faded when the sun rose, by which he meant to hint, where you were present; but you may be assured he did not allow the Queen to hear him."

"His Majesty is very complimentary to my poor qualities," returned Donna Theresa, coldly.

"He does not compliment—he speaks the truth, my sweet lady," said the Dwarf. "He loves you far more than you can tell: if you were aware how much, you would acknowledge his is a heart worth winning."

Donna Theresa answered not, and endeavoured to conceal the pleasure which even this coarse style of flattery gave her. We need not describe it further. Such was the tenor of the words with which the well-trained negress constantly assailed her, and, like water dropping on a rock, they had their effect.

On quitting the young Marchioness, Father Jacinto took his way to Belem, where the old Marquis of Tavora had a Quinta. Here Donna Leonora, his wife, was now residing, since the destruction of their palace in the city; and here she held her coteries of all who were inimical to the King, and haters of his Prime Minister. Of these there were a very large class in the country, some angry at being deprived of the monopoly of legislating, which they had so long enjoyed, without one single qualification for the purpose, except a very common one, the love of place; and others, justly incensed at the cruelty and unwarrantable tyranny of the Minister.

At these meetings the Jesuits were ever the most active members; for to their care had the old Marchioness committed the entire spiritual guidance of her mind, when they, of course, took possession of the direction of every other action of her life.

When the Jesuit reached the gate of the Quinta, he was admitted with welcome, and conducted forthwith to the presence of the lady of the mansion.

His manner was no longer that of the intimate and advising friend, with a slight, though unalarming, tinge of a warmer feeling, doubtful whether that of a parent or a lover, it might have been interpreted either way, as it had been towards Donna Theresa. He had now all the humility and devotion of a subject towards the ex vice-regal lady; piety was his only ostensible motive for action, the thoughts of heaven and religion the only ones which filled his mind, except when occupied in following her wishes. Though humble, he was not cringing; to that his haughty spirit could not bow, even for the sake of deceiving; he behaved more as a minister to his sovereign, offering advice with firm respect, determined to gain his point, yet endeavouring to persuade, rather than to insist on his opinions being followed.

"Do you bring me any news, holy Father?" said the Marchioness, as the Jesuit was ushered into the apartment in which she was seated; and her attendants, at a sign from her, had withdrawn. "Will the King revoke the sentence of banishment pronounced against that pious saint and holy father, Malagrida; or must we still be deprived of his righteous counsels and exhortations?"

"Alas, lady! the heart of the King is still hardened, I fear through the evil advice of that incarnation of the prince of sin," answered the Priest. "He has not only not revoked the sentence, but is planning fresh aggressions against our Church and holy religion. Before long, if such unheard-of wickedness is not put a stop to, we shall become a nation of atheists and heretics."

"The words of the sainted Malagrida will come too true," exclaimed the Marchioness: "our altars will be profaned, and our holy priests driven into exile. His advice must be followed. This wicked King must be removed."

"Heaven forbid that I should say so," said Father Jacinto. "He is the Lord's anointed, and the heritage of this kingdom is his. My brother Malagrida cannot counsel aught that is wrong; but I would first use milder means. I would seek to turn his heart from wickedness, and lead him to the path of righteousness."

"Has not that been tried, Father, and found to fail?" exclaimed the proud Marchioness, impatiently. "Has he not refused to listen to the words of our religion, and banished from his presence those who are alone able to teach them to him? By what other means, then, can you hope to work his conversion?"

"By the gentle influence of your sex, lady, may that happy end be accomplished. The King loves your daughter-in-law, Donna Theresa, with the most ardent passion; but she is cold and indifferent to him, and faithful to her husband. By her means might his heart be turned to religion, if she would exert her power over him. This she will not do while she fears the censure of the world, who, misinterpreting her conduct, will deem her guilty of infidelity to her husband, while she is innocent of any crime."

"What, Father, you would not ask my daughter-in-law to dishonour the proud name she bears!" exclaimed the Marchioness.

"Heaven forbid," interrupted the Jesuit. "I would ask her to do only that which is right. She possesses the means of gaining power to forward a holy cause, and I would counsel her to exert it. But, lady, of her own accord she will not do so; her youth and timidity, her fear of offending you and her husband, prevent her from encouraging the advances of the King. Were you, on the contrary, to sanction her holy efforts to enchain him completely, her scruples would cease; and the censorious world would then be convinced that she was guiltless of dishonouring her noble husband, your son, and that she received the visits of the King through that pure friendship which draws persons of similarity of tastes and disposition together."

"I comprehend your reasons, Father, and pardon me that I should for a moment have misunderstood your expressions. I will see Theresa, and persuade her no longer to treat the King so coldly. I was aware that he had visited her; but my son is still ignorant of the fact, and it will be better not to inform him of it yet; he is young and passionate, and might not understand our motives."

"Your caution is advisable, lady," said the Jesuit. "It is a wise plan never to communicate our intentions to more persons than is necessary; and I would advise you to speak on this subject to no one else."

"I will follow your counsel, Father," answered the Marchioness. "But tell me, should Theresa not succeed in turning the King from his evil course, and, should he still persist in persecuting the servants of the Church, what means must we then pursue?"

"Any will be justifiable," responded the Priest. "Events are in the womb of time, and, according as they appear, so must we guide their course."

The conversation continued for a considerable time longer, chiefly on the same subject; the wily Priest, while pretending to combat, often encouraging the plans of the Marchioness, by advancing arguments against them which he allowed her easily to controvert. At length, having assured himself that his own arrangements were in the proper train, he, with profound respect, took his leave; and, rejoicing at his success, went about many of the minor plots and intrigues in which he was engaged, for the sole purpose of forwarding the great aim of his *Order*.

End of the Second Volume.

Volume Three—Chapter One.

Being very anxious to proceed with our history, we would rather avoid any retrospection; but, that our readers may understand more clearly the occurrences of the times we are now describing, it will be necessary to give a slight sketch of a few events that had already passed. The most important was the revolt of the inhabitants of Oporto, and of the neighbouring provinces, against the authority of the Minister, in consequence of the establishment of a Company, with almost unbounded privileges, to superintend the sale of the wines produced on the banks of the river Douro. The proprietors of the vineyards, who had been accustomed to a free trade, by which they had grown wealthy, were highly exasperated at a monopoly which would so completely curtail their profits, and of course the people whom they employed espoused their cause. They in tumultuous bodies flocked to the city, compelling the chief magistrate, known by the name of the Judge of the People, to espouse their cause, and pillaging the houses of all those they suspected to be favourers of the measure.

No sooner did the Minister receive intelligence of these disturbances, than he despatched three regiments against the city. The inhabitants yielded without striking a blow; but their submission availed them not; their city was given up to the unbounded license of the savage soldiery; and had it been taken by storm, scarcely could more frightful excesses have been committed. The soldiers were then distributed at free quarters on the inhabitants; the unfortunate Judge of the People was dragged through the streets by the common hangman, with a halter round his neck, and then executed with every mark of ignominy. Eighteen of the principal citizens shared his fate, and three hundred persons, who were accused of being concerned in the sedition, were imprisoned, or condemned for life to the galleys.

The obnoxious and tyrannical Company, their charter sealed with blood, was established; for, after the dreadful examples of the Minister's unswerving vengeance, fear prevented the people from making any further attempts to overthrow it. It has since been, if we may be allowed to judge, one of the greatest banes to the country.

Though one of the most determined opponents to Carvalho, our friend Gonçalo Christovaö had, on this occasion, taken no open part in the movement, so that he escaped the punishment which fell on so many others; but he was not the less indignant at the atrocities committed in his native city, and he was, at the time we speak of, on his way to Lisbon, to complain in person to his sovereign, hoping to gain some redress, or, at all events, a mitigation of the grievances under which the people suffered.

We scarcely dare mention the fate of the lovely Donna Clara. For a long period her father had resisted all the persuasions of his confessor to compel her to assume the veil, though she was now almost indifferent on the subject; but he had at length yielded, and she was now performing her year of noviciate at the convent of her patron saint at Oporto, which was considered nearly equal in point of the rank of its inmates to that of Santa Clara at Lisbon. Indeed, since the destruction of the latter, many of the nuns, who were all of noble family, had been conveyed thither. It was a sad *cortège* which had arrived from the ruined city, carefully concealed from the prying eye of curiosity, in closely covered litters, surrounded with a guard of soldiers, who were ordered strictly to keep their eyes turned away from the holy sisterhood. Whether they obeyed the order is a matter of doubt, and whether a delicate hand might not now and then have drawn aside the curtains to admit a breath of fresh air, we cannot aver. This only we know, that the Minister himself had issued an order for their safe conduct; and, as the religious houses on the road were not sufficiently near to admit of their reaching one each day, he commanded that the inns should be prepared for their reception, and that no other travellers should be admitted, which latter order, we suspect, was no slight disappointment to the younger ladies;—but we are growing profane.

To return to the revolt at Oporto. The Jesuits were accused of being the instigators even of this transaction; but we, although no friends of theirs, as may have been guessed, acquit them completely of having had any share in the affair. By an unsuccessful rebellion they could have gained nothing, and must have been aware that such would only strengthen the power of the Minister. We feel assured, therefore, that they were innocent of this charge; nor was it at all in accordance with their usual mode of proceeding: they would have acted far more cautiously and sensibly, so that nothing might be attempted without an almost certain confidence of success. However, the old proverb, "Give a dog a bad name," was fully exemplified in their case, and every disturbance in the country was imputed to them. We think that, in many respects, they were very hardly used; and we might as well suppose that the followers of the new Bible (which a foreigner told us we English heretics had lately published, called the Oxford Tracts,) were guilty of the riots in Wales, as that they would have excited people to open rebellion. The past had, and the present have, a very different aim in view: they seek not to overthrow dynasties, but to establish their power on the weakness and folly of their fellow-men; they wish to hide the gold, that their own base alloy may be taken as genuine ore. While pretending to point out the narrow path to heaven, they, like the cunning fowler, lead their fascinated admirers into their own well-constructed decoys;—more narrow and narrow grows the way, with many a twist and turn, till at length they cast their nets, from whose meshes there is no escape.

Now, it is very far from our wish to speak disrespectfully of the Church of Rome, or in any way to decry it. On the contrary, we cannot conceive an establishment more admirably adapted for every purpose of untrammelled government. It at once puts a stop to all doubts or discussions, pointing out so exactly what people ought to believe, that they have no further trouble on the subject. As when men have learnt to submit in one way, they generally do so in another, were we a sovereign desirous of absolute power, we should prefer it as the religion of the state, and then, keeping its ministers our friends, we should, if we pleased, be able to govern with the most despotic rule.

We esteem many of the ministers of that Church, and if they attempt to convert us to their opinions, we feel that they are but performing their duty: we do not blame them, because they exercise the power which has been confided to them by their superiors; nor do we blame its followers that they practise what they have been taught; but we are called on to exhibit in their true colours those who, urged on by the lust of power, strive to revive a long-disused engine of authority; disused not through forgetfulness of its existence, but from a general conviction of its pernicious effects, from all men being persuaded that it defeated the purposes of true religion.

We, while residing in Portugal, where the Order of Jesus is no longer tolerated, often hear the opinion of those who see clearly what is going forward in our own country. "Ah!" they exclaim, "you will soon become as good Romanists as we are. You have some clever Jesuits among you already,—both open and concealed ones too."

These observations may, perhaps, make some men look into their own hearts, and examine their motives; for the thought of power is very captivating. We would fain save a few birds from the fowlers, and we may trust that some who read this work will be warned in time to avoid those snares, the very first consequence of which is the abject slavery of the mind,—an imprisonment (so cunningly devised, and so strong are the meshes formed) which few are able to break through,—whose captives are ever debarred from the enjoyment of thought, and the light of truth.

From what we have said, we doubt not we shall be accused by one class to which we allude, of being sneerers and revilers at religion; such always is the fate of those who would exhibit existing abuses in their true colours, and who would endeavour to draw out and expose the falsehood from among the truth, in which it may have been shrouded. Let them hurl their anathemas on our heads; they will fall innoxious on our helmet of rectitude. We revere religion, but we detest tyranny and superstition, nor shall we ever cease to strive against both one and the other. But we must not allow ourselves to be carried away by a subject, in which we are so deeply interested, though one scarcely suited to a work of the nature of a romance; we may, however, trust, that while the eye wanders over these pages, in search of amusement, a warning lesson may be received, to beware of concealed Jesuits, who, filling our ears with their sophistries, would persuade us to submit to their power.

We must now return to the current of our story, from which we have so widely wandered. For some time previous to the anniversary of the dreadful catastrophe we have described, various people appeared in and about the neighbourhood of Lisbon, assuming the characters of prophets, and foretelling the final destruction of the city on that day. One of the first who uttered these predictions was the holy Father Malagrida. He probably placed full confidence in them himself; they either being the work of his own distempered brain, or having been put into his head by others for their own purposes.

Whoever was the originator of the deceit, he was the chief promulgator of it, while many others, perfectly aware of its want of foundation, repeated it, in the hopes of driving the frightened citizens from their habitations, while they would be enabled to plunder, without apprehension of any interruption to their proceedings. Such we find the case in the present day: a madman leads fools, and knaves follow, to prey on their folly.

Malagrida had chosen for the scene of his oratory the ruins of a church outside Lisbon, where he had collected a large assemblage of people, women and children predominating, and idle ragamuffins, who were glad of any excuse to escape from toil: there were others also, of all classes of citizens, who were listening to the insane ravings of blasphemy proceeding from his lips.

"Fly from the city of destruction, all ye who would be saved!" he exclaimed. "Escape, ere the crimes of your impious rulers be visited on your heads. Once have ye been warned, and ye would not listen to the warning;—this is the last time that I will speak to ye,—this is the last time that ye shall hear my voice; for the wicked have risen up against the prophets of heaven, their hearts have been hardened, and they have sworn deadly enmity to the true ministers of the Church. Fly, then, from among the despisers of the faith, leave them to the vengeance which shall overtake those whom the Lord has marked for destruction. He who, in self-confidence, vaunts so proudly of his power, shall be brought low; for fire shall rain down on the haughty head of the persecutor of the faithful."

The prophet had for some time run on in this strain, when suddenly a body of guards appeared among the crowd. Two of them advanced, and, placing themselves on each side of him, informed him that his presence was required elsewhere.

"Begone! ye myrmidons of the man of sin, and answer that I come not at his call," he exclaimed in a loud voice. "Begone! I fear ye not."

The men, however, paid no attention to his orders; but, seizing his arms, attempted to drag him forward. Their efforts, however, were vain; for, shaking them off with a powerful exertion, he continued his discourse regardless of their presence. Again they seized him, when a cry arose among the people, who seemed inclined to hasten to his rescue; but the customary obedience to which the Minister had subjected them, checked them, and the remainder of the soldiers advancing, completely surrounded him.

"Down with the tyrant, who would overthrow our religion!" exclaimed a voice from among the crowd at a distance; but no one responded to the cry; and Malagrida, making no further resistance, was conducted before the judge of the district. He protested vehemently against the treatment he was receiving, but to no purpose; he was ordered forthwith to retire to his college, and the next day, he received a command from the government, to proceed to the town of Setubal, and there to remain till desired to quit it. We are not informed why that place was chosen as his abode in banishment; whether it was that the people were so wise, that they would not listen to his mad ravings, or, that they were so foolish, that he could not increase their folly. Thither, however, some of his warmest admirers followed him, to put themselves under his spiritual guidance, and among them, was the devout and intriguing Marchioness of Tavora. For some weeks she resided there, performing what were called exercises, under his directions, during which time, he took the opportunity of instilling into her mind both the necessity of ridding the country of their tyrant, and the lawfulness of doing so, by any means which might offer. Notwithstanding the many disciples he collected round him, his unsettled disposition caused him to pine for more active excitement, and, as we shall see, in despite of the threats of the Minister, he determined to quit the spot assigned to him for his abode.

Though Malagrida was silenced, there were yet a number of prophets, perfectly in their senses, who continued to give utterance to predictions, threatening the utter destruction of Lisbon. The Minister, in consequence, issued a decree, ordering that all such persons should be seized and committed to prison, as rogues and vagabonds. Lest also, the easily beguiled citizens should, trusting to their prophecies, desert their homes on the fatal day, he commanded that no one should quit the city on that or the two previous days; and, to enforce this decree, troops were collected round the barriers, who would allow no one, on any pretext whatever, to pass.

The affrighted people were in despair; but they dared not venture to force the barriers, and the measure proved that a little coercion is, at times, for the benefit of the multitude, notwithstanding what demagogues may say to the contrary; for the day passed, and no convulsion took place. We do not hear if the people accused their prophets of prophesying falsely, though we suspect they probably found some means of excusing them, at least, if we may judge from the credence given to their brethren of the present day, who, let them utter, time after time, the most absurd predictions, always unfulfilled, are not the less believed by their enlightened and educated disciples, they ever discovering some plausible interpretation for their teachers' words.

Volume Three—Chapter Two.

The usual time for paying visits in Portugal is in the evening, when ladies are borne about to the houses of their acquaintances in their carriages or chairs, full dressed, as if for a ball; most families of any pretension to fashion having certain nights fixed for the reception of their guests.

The Marchioness of Tavora, although famed for her devoutness, had become even more particular than before in conforming to all the observances of etiquette, in the hopes thereby of gaining over more partisans in the plots she was forming; and she was on her way to pay several of these politic visits of ceremony, when she alighted at the palace of her daughter-in-law, Donna Theresa. She had gained a considerable influence over the younger Marchioness, more, perhaps, by having inspired awe than love; nor did the latter ever feel perfectly at her ease in her society. Her purpose, at present, was, following the advice given by the Father Jacinto, to persuade Donna Theresa to endeavour to win the confidence of the King at every cost; a task she found no very great difficulty in accomplishing.

"I will assure my son, on the earliest opportunity," she said, "that you have my sanction to receive the visits of the King, which will prevent any jealous doubts arising in his mind, should he discover a circumstance of which he is not now aware. His hot temper, were he to hear of it, before being warned by me, might otherwise take fire, and cause him to commit some mad outrage, which might bring destruction on us all. But be not alarmed; I will arrange affairs so that he shall have no cause to complain of your infidelity; for he will, as I do, put full confidence in your honour; and that your family pride alone will prevent you committing aught derogatory to the dignity of your birth."

Theresa had no words to answer, but she bowed her head in acquiescence of the arrangement; and the elder Marchioness having accomplished her purpose, proceeded on her round of visits.

The young Marchioness, thus urged on by her confessor and her mother-in-law, had no further reason to fly the advances of her royal admirer; yet she trembled for the consequences;—she saw the yawning gulf below her, yet she felt like a person on the summit of a lofty cliff, with an involuntary inclination to leap from the edge, though fully aware that destruction awaited her. How bitterly did she repent that she had sacrificed her love, and stifled all the tender sentiments of her nature, to follow the rugged and dangerous paths of ambition; but there was now no power of receding left: her peace of mind, her consciousness of rectitude, had deserted her; the past was full of useless regrets; and though she felt that they were deceitful and treacherous, the dazzling temptations of the future lured her on.

It was the custom of the King, when driving out at night, to make use of the private carriage of a confidential attendant, who generally accompanied him. This man, of the name of Texeira, was of low birth; but, by various acts of a doubtful nature, had ingratiated himself into his sovereign's favour; presuming on which, he frequently behaved in an impertinent manner towards the nobles of the Court, who, ill-brooking such behaviour, bore a determined hatred towards him. Texeira was waiting in his carriage at the private entrance to the palace for the coming of his sovereign, who proposed paying an earlier visit than usual to the young Marchioness of Tavora. As the King appeared at the door, the attendant stepped out to offer his assistance, and when both were seated, the postillion was ordered to proceed forthwith in the direction Texeira had already indicated to him.

The carriage stopped at the gateway of a palace situated in the western part of the city, when the King, wrapping his cloak closely round his features, descended and entered the building, while his attendant retained his seat. The latter had remained there some time, when he heard a voice, in a tone of authority, ordering his postillion to move onward, and another carriage drew up at the gate of the palace. Senhor Texeira, at first, forgetting himself, felt very much inclined to desire his postillion not to stir from his position, but remembering instantly that it was his duty rather to prevent the King from being discovered, he checked the expressions rising to his tongue, and allowed his carriage to proceed out of the way.

The occupant of the other carriage was the young Marquis of Tavora, who had suddenly returned from some military duty on which he had been despatched from Lisbon. As he alighted and entered his palace, none of his principal servants were in waiting; the porter alone, who, wrapped up in his cloak, had been dozing in a corner, after opening the doors with an amazed and sleepy stare, uttered some incoherent words, to which his master paying no attention, passed onward. A small lamp, suspended at the head of the first flight of steps, afforded the young lord but just sufficient light to see his way as he mounted, summoning his attendants, in an angry tone, to his presence. The porter gazed after him with a doubtful expression of countenance.

"Shall I tell him he had better not go upstairs?" he thought; "but if I do, it will only make him go the faster. It is no affair of mine, and I suppose the King has a right to go where he likes; if not, what is the use of being a King? only I am afraid mischief will come of it."

By the time the porter had got thus far in his soliloquy, his master had gained the summit of the flight of steps which led to the first floor. The young noble was advancing towards the drawing-room, wondering at the unusual silence which reigned through the palace, when suddenly a door opened, and he encountered a figure with a large cloak wrapped closely round him.

"Ah!" he exclaimed, in a voice of suddenly aroused anger, "who does me the honour of paying my palace a visit at this time of the night? Stay, Senhor Cavalhero: I allow no one to pass unquestioned." But the stranger, not heeding his words, endeavoured to pass on his way without answering. "What! you are dumb too! Then this shall compel you to speak." On these words, drawing his sword, he made a pass at the cloaked stranger; the latter, however, stepping back, avoided the thrust; the weapon merely grazing his cloak, and, unsheathing his rapier also, he turned aside, with considerable skill, another lunge made at him.

"Stay, senhor! you know not whom you attack," he exclaimed. "Allow me to pass without further hindrance."

But the passion of the Marquis was aroused to the highest pitch from the very opposition he received, it preventing him from distinguishing the voice of the stranger.

"Daring villain, no!" he answered, "speak your business in this mansion, and let your own words condemn you."

"I allow no one to question me, so stand aside, senhor," said the stranger, endeavouring to put aside his antagonist's sword; but the Marquis, parrying the thrust, attacked him furiously, without deigning a further reply.

The stranger was now obliged to defend himself in earnest, for after several passes given and taken, he discovered that the young noble was the better swordsman.

"Hold!" he cried. "Beware what you do; I am the King!"

"I believe it not!" responded the Marquis, in a loud tone; "and I acknowledge no King who would thus treacherously intrude into the habitation of a subject."

As he uttered these words, he whirled the King's sword from his grasp, and the point of his own weapon was at his sovereign's throat; for, as may be supposed, the stranger was no other than the King.

In a moment the life of Joseph would have been terminated, when the young Marchioness, attracted by the sound of angry voices, and the clash of swords, hastened from her apartment. She uttered a cry of horror, when, at a glance, she discovered by the light which Donna Florinda, who followed, carried, all that had occurred.

"Hold, Luis, hold! 'tis the King, indeed," she exclaimed, throwing herself, without hesitating, before her husband; but, putting her aside—though the action saved him from being guilty of regicide—he exclaimed, "'Tis false! You would, by such a subterfuge, guilty woman, attempt to save the worthless life of your seducer; but it shall not avail you or him: he shall die."

"I am guiltless of any crime towards you," responded Donna Theresa, with energy, again throwing herself before her husband. "It is, it is our sovereign you have so guiltily attacked. Hear me swear to the truth of my assertion."

While this colloquy was going forward the King had recovered his sword, and now stood holding it with the point to the ground, the light falling more strongly on his features than before, as he said, "Hear me, Don Luis de Tavora. Your wife utters naught but the truth. She has in no way betrayed your honour. Had not your first fierce attack prevented me, I would at once have informed you that I was your sovereign; but your anger is excusable, and you are forgiven."

As the King spoke, he held out his hand for the young Marquis to kiss; but the latter, with a glance of proud disdain, pretended not to observe the action.

"Your Majesty must suppose me, forsooth, a most complaisant husband, that I should discover a stranger in my palace at this hour, and not seek to question his purpose; but your Majesty has, doubtless, full power to command all us, your humble servants, and I have now no further right to complain. I retain but the privilege of settling the affair with my lady, and in that point I shall exert a husband's power as I think fit. By your Majesty's leave, I will order your carriage, which waits at a short distance, to the door, and humbly conduct you thither."

"This language sounds somewhat like the insolence of treason, young sir," said Joseph; "though, as you might have cause to be exasperated, I will, for this time, overlook it; but let me hear no more such words."

"Your Majesty shall be humbly obeyed," returned the young husband, in an ironical tone; "and Donna Theresa will, doubtless, explain all matters entirely to my satisfaction. Has your Majesty any further commands?"

"No, sir! no!" said the King, turning to the Marchioness. "Lovely lady, adieu! We trust you will be able fully to pacify your lord's irritated feelings. Now, my lord Marquis, we will beg you to lead the way to the hall; some of your servants can light us thither."

By this time all the household had collected round the spot, eager to see the termination of the affair; the circumstance of the King's visits being known among them all; but, supposing the Marquis was privy to it, they did not venture to speak to him on the subject.

Again bowing to the Marchioness, Joseph was conducted to the door of the palace with every outward ceremony, the Marquis leading the way, and the servants on each side holding waxen flambeaux; but could he have looked deeper into the young noble's heart, he might have learned to tremble for the consequences of his own conduct. As it was, he had been taught to look upon his subjects as his slaves, and was astounded at the idea of their having a will of their own. He felt, however, that he had played but a poor figure in the drama, and had lowered himself materially in the opinion of the spectators, so that he was well contented to find himself once more safe in his carriage with Texeira, to whom he detailed all his adventures.

The young Marchioness stood gazing with looks of despair on her husband and the King, as they descended the stair; but, alas! she trembled more for the safety of the latter than for that of the man she ought to have loved. She knew her husband's fierce and vindictive disposition, and she felt assured that he would hesitate at no means to accomplish his purposes of revenge.

Having escorted the King to his carriage, the Marquis returned; a dark frown on his brow marking his inward feelings. "I have humbly to thank you, madam, for procuring me the honour of a royal visit; though, another time, I beg you will give me due notice, that I may be prepared to receive so exalted a guest as becomes his rank," he began, in a taunting tone, mingled with anger; "yet I ought to be grateful that, since you have thought fit to select a lover, you have not debased yourself with one of low degree. But know, lady, his station shall not shield him against my vengeance."

"Oh! believe me, I am innocent!" exclaimed the Marchioness, in a voice trembling with agitation. "Your own mother is aware of the visits of the King, and she will explain all to you; but do not suspect me wrongfully."

"Oh! doubtless, your conduct has been perfectly irreproachable," responded her lord, in the same strain as before. "All ladies will swear the same, and hope to make their credulous husbands believe them; but, although some choose to be willingly deceived, I do not. I doubt not, Donna Florinda, whom I have the honour of saluting, will confirm all you aver. Pray, madam, is she your guest, or have you added her also to my establishment?"

"She was presented to me by their Majesties," said Donna Theresa, glad of an opportunity of stopping the current of her lord's passionate sarcasm.

"I shall take the liberty, then, of returning her to her royal donors," said the Marquis. "You will take it as no disparagement to your matchless charms, Donna Florinda, that I am anxious so soon to part from one whom all admire; but I prefer that my wife should have no female counsellor who will teach her to consider her husband a tyrant and endowed with qualities inferior to all other men."

"You forget your gallantry, Senhor Marquis, when you talk of sending me out of your house, like a roll of silks returned to the mercer as not required," cried the sable lady, delighted to have an opportunity both of loosing her tongue, and of relieving her young mistress from the wrath of her husband. "Truly, I am surprised to hear *you* speak thus, whom all the Court acknowledge to be the most gallant of knights. What would Senhora Amelia, or the fair Condeça de Campo Bello say, if they heard you give utterance to such expressions? You would never speak thus to them, I feel confident; but then they are not cruel to you, it is whispered. Come, come, senhor, you have no right to complain if your lady thinks fit to receive the visits of our sovereign."

"Silence, wretch!" thundered the Marquis. "Begone to your chamber, and let me not see your hideous countenance while you remain beneath my roof. That you claim to belong to the female sex, alone prevents me from ordering you forthwith to be put outside my doors."

"The man is to a certainty mad, to call me such horrid names," cried the Dwarf, judging it, however, more prudent to obey. "I trust the cool reflection of the morning will make you think better of your present determination, as I should grieve to leave my lovely mistress so soon."

"You need enjoy no such expectations," answered the Marquis, as the little being retired. "And now, madam," he added, turning to his wife, "retire to your apartment, and quit it not without my permission. As it appears that the King has chosen to become the master of my palace, I shall no longer reside here. Farewell, madam, for the present; I have affairs of importance to transact. In the morning I shall return."

"Stay, Luis, stay!" exclaimed the Marchioness; "do not leave me thus in anger. Say you do not believe me really guilty;" and she endeavoured to clasp his arm to detain him, but he tore himself angrily away.

"Oaths and prayers will avail you naught, madam," he answered. "Obey my commands for the present; how I may think fit to act for the future you shall hear:" saying which, he turned aside from his young wife, and descended the stairs, muttering, as he went, between his closed teeth, "I might have better borne a rival with some gallant qualities to boast of; but this wretched King, who gives himself up to the power of a base plebeian,—'tis a double disgrace. My lady mother aware of it! I must see to that! Impossible! It was but a flimsy excuse to avert my anger."

Entering his carriage, he ordered the postillion to proceed to his father's Quinta at Belem. How dreary and long seemed the way as he passed the shapeless masses of ruins which everywhere presented themselves on the road, appearing yet larger and wilder amid the gloom of night; his mind, too, like them, torn and agitated by a thousand conflicting emotions!

When he arrived, he found that his father was from home, and that his mother had retired to her chamber; nor could he venture to disturb her. The only member of his family not yet retired to rest being his younger brother Jozé, to him he poured out his indignant griefs and vows of vengeance against the sovereign, whom he imagined had cast so great a dishonour on their name. Don Jozé, being of a far milder temperament than his brother, endeavoured to calm his anger, by pointing out to him the possibility of his wife's having spoken the truth; that if their mother was aware of the King's visit, at all events there was some excuse for her; but, at the same time, he pledged himself to aid him by every means in his power, if his worst suspicions were confirmed. The greater part of the night had passed in these discussions, before the young Marquis, throwing himself on a couch in his brother's room, endeavoured to find some rest to his troubled thoughts.

Little did the Sovereign of Portugal dream of the plots against his crown and life hatching within the boundaries of his capital; nor was even his sagacious Minister aware they had advanced so far.

Early in the morning, the young Marquis sought Donna Leonora, his mother, eager to learn if she had sanctioned the intimacy between the King and his wife. She confessed that she had done so, and her motives for the act; which, although it satisfied him that his wife was not so much to blame as he had suspected, did not lessen his anger against his sovereign, or cause him to alter any of the plans of revenge he had harboured in his bosom. His conduct towards the King, when told to his mother, caused that ambitious lady to hurry on events which might otherwise have been longer delayed; for feeling that the Monarch would take the earliest opportunity to punish the insolence of his subject, she determined to use her best endeavours to prevent his having the power to do so.

The young Marquis now returned home with rather a lighter heart; for though he had neglected her, he yet loved his beautiful wife, and was unwilling to part with her. He loved her, but his love was not deep; he had soon discovered that the ardent passion he had once felt was not returned; and though a *woman* may yet love on through coldness, neglect, and scorn, a man never can; his love depends on its being returned, and it is the perfect confidence that it is so which will alone cause his to endure beyond the first few months of possession.

When he entered his wife's chamber, he found her seated at the toilet, pale and wan, for sleep had not that night visited her eyes. Too clearly had her fate been revealed to her. The dread future had spoken words of awful warning to her ears, but she, alas! had determined to close her senses to both.

"Theresa!" said her husband, kindly approaching her, "I wronged you; but let this be a warning to you. Whatever others may counsel, remember first to obey your husband's wishes; and I do not choose to be sneered at, even for the sovereign's sake, or to win the worthless state secrets which alone Carvalho is likely to confide to his puppet. From henceforth, therefore, when the King thinks fit to come to my palace, refuse to see him. Say such is your husband's wish; if you obey me not, the consequence be on both your heads. Speak, Theresa, do you hear me?"

At these words of her husband's, the countenance of Donna Theresa grew yet more pallid. Her voice trembled as she answered, "I cannot promise to obey a command which I may not have power to perform; but, my lord, do not give utterance to those dreadful threats, which you cannot—you dare not execute, for destruction would inevitably overwhelm you, and all engaged with you in them."

"Let that care be mine," exclaimed her husband. "The cause is in your hands. Should the King again visit this abode, and you send him not forthwith away, he dies! and his blood be on your head! If I fail, you will have mine to answer for."

These threats increased yet more the agitation of the young Marchioness. She full well knew her husband was not a man to utter empty vows of vengeance; but could she consent to see no more the man she loved? Could she give up all her long-cherished hopes of power? Yet, if she disobeyed, what a dreadful alternative was presented to her—either she must warn the King of his danger, and thus be an accessory to her husband's death, perhaps to the destruction of his family, or she must allow the former to run every risk of destruction! Such thoughts rushed tumultuously through her mind; but, alas! pride, ambition, and a fatal contempt of the warnings of her conscience, prevented her following the only secure, because the only right, course. When her husband quitted her, he had yet failed to draw a satisfactory promise from her that she would obey his orders; but he comforted himself with the idea that his threats would have their due effect. How vain were his hopes! What would have made a weak woman tremble, caused Donna Theresa only to persevere more daringly in her course.

Volume Three—Chapter Three.

In the neighbourhood of Lisbon, the Crown possessed one or two parks, of great extent, which were called Coitadas, stocked with every description of game, both to follow on horseback, or for the exercise of the fowling-piece; that of Alfitte, on the banks of the Tagus, being by far the largest, covering many thousand acres of ground. The King, who was passionately fond of the chase, was in the constant habit of resorting to a country-house he possessed on the borders of the forest, accompanied by some of his favourite courtiers, when, flinging aside all thoughts or cares of government, he gave himself up entirely to his favourite amusement. The kingdom, on these very frequent occasions, would have been allowed to take the best care it could of itself, under a less energetic minister than Carvalho; but that sagacious statesman, encouraging his sovereign in his pursuits, seized with avidity the opportunity of exercising the uncontrolled power thus delegated to him, to the yet further disgust of the haughty nobles of the land. Sometimes, however, he himself, who was a proficient in all manly and athletic exercises, would steal away from the city to join in the sport, though the same evening he might be again found at his post, deeply engaged in the many momentous and difficult affairs which occupied his attention.

It was a bright and glorious morning; the sun had just risen, tinging the topmost boughs of the forest trees, glittering with the clear drops of a gentle shower, which had fallen during the night, giving an additional freshness and lustre to the smiling face of nature. The birds sang their sweetest notes to welcome the morn, as they flew from spray to spray, rejoicing in their unrestrained liberty. The air was soft and balmy, laden with the delicious odours springing from the flowering shrubs and plants which filled the forest glades. Not a human sound was heard to disturb the harmony of nature. It was such a scene as our great poet of rural beauty loves best to describe. Through an opening in the wood, at the end of a long vista, might be seen the shining waters of the broad Tagus, flowing onward in tranquil majesty; and, in every direction, other glades led far away, now lost to view by some gentle elevation, or sinking into some narrow valley.

Suddenly a tall dark figure emerged from the thickest part of the forest, and advancing into the open ground, looked cautiously on every side. Though his step was firm, it possessed none of the elasticity of youth, as he stalked forward, unconsciously lifting his long thin arms aloft, in the energy of his thoughts. His dress, of the coarsest materials, was that of a common labourer; a broad-brimmed hat, from beneath which escaped a few hoary locks, partly concealed his emaciated and parchment-like countenance; yet, though age had there set its furrowing marks, it had not dimmed the wild lustre of his large and rolling eyes. In his right hand he bore a long staff, with an iron point; but he made little use of it to aid his steps, seeming to carry it more as a weapon of defence, than for any other purpose: at his side hung a wallet, such as is used by beggars to contain their food. What was his usual occupation it was impossible to say; for, though his costume betokened the countryman, his manner and words seemed to contradict that idea; and, indeed, from his behaviour, it appeared that he was there for some secret, perhaps no good, purpose.

"Ah!" he exclaimed, as he strode rapidly onward, casting his searching glances around, "the time has arrived when the wicked shall be brought low, and the proud abased; when vengeance is about to fall on the heads of the persecutors of the prophets of Heaven! yet must the task which I am called on to fulfil be accomplished; the words of warning must be spoken ere the blow is struck. Even as the seers of old were sent to those evil kings of Israel who worshipped strange gods, and hearkened to the counsels of their idolatrous followers, so must I utter the messages of Heaven to this hard-hearted Monarch; yet will he not hear, but will continue on still in his wickedness."

Muttering such words as these, the person continued his course, where we must leave him, to turn to a far more exciting scene, which was enacting at no great distance.

The hunting villa attached to the royal chase was a low straggling building, without the slightest attempt at architectural beauty, the lower story being devoted entirely to the use of the horses requisite for the sport, and their attendant grooms; the upper, possessing a row of windows at equal distances from each other on every side, was divided, with the exception of a few large rooms appropriated to the royal owner, into a number of small ones for the numerous guests who attended him. In front was a broad court-yard, now filled with a large assemblage of horses and their grooms, while several men held in leashes a number of dogs, who were barking loudly, in their endeavours to free themselves from thraldom; some of them, indeed, from being more tractable, probably, than their brethren, were allowed to wander loose among the steeds: the latter, too, were neighing, and pawing the ground, eager to rush forward in the exciting course, which they seemed aware was in store for them. The grooms and huntsmen, while waiting for the appearance of their masters, were laughing and hallooing to each other, cracking their jokes with unreserved freedom, none of that strict decorum usually observed in the neighbourhood of royalty being there perceptible. On a sudden, however, the noisy mirth was checked, and all eyes were directed towards the open gateway, through which the majestic person of the Prime Minister was perceived advancing, mounted on a coal-black steed, which he sat with perfect ease and command. The animal's moistened neck and panting breath showed that he had not tarried on the road. As he drew in his rein, twenty servants sprang eagerly forward to aid him in dismounting; but, dispensing with their services, he threw himself off, and, without deigning to turn a glance towards them, entered the building.

A few minutes only elapsed, when the King, who had apparently been awaiting his arrival, issued forth in a hunting costume of green and silver, closely followed by several of his nobles, the one nearest to him being his chief favourite, the Marquis of Marialva, (Note) to whom he was addressing his observations; but there was one among the party who seemed neither to consider it an honour nor a pleasure to be in attendance,—this was the Duke of Aveiro, who had, by the Minister's advice, received a command to accompany his master in the proposed sports of the day. He took but little pains to conceal his dissatisfaction, as he walked on with a haughty air and frowning brow, yet, at the same time, he would not yield the position in the *cortège* which his rank entitled him to hold, though he neither regarded nor addressed any near him.

"A fine morning we are favoured with, Senhor Marquis," cried the King, in a joyous tone, speaking to Marialva. "We shall have some good sport, if I mistake not, and many a long-tusked boar will die to-day. Who will be the happy man to kill the first, I wonder?—'twill be your chance, my friend, I trust."

"Your Majesty is generally the most fortunate hunter," returned the Marquis; "for few can successfully compete with you in the chase."

"That is because others are apt to hold back at times, I suspect," said Joseph, laughing; for the anticipation of his favourite amusement had raised his usually grave spirit. "But to-day, remember, cavaliers, all must endeavour to do their best. We will allow no one to draw rein till they come up with the chase. Listen to my commands, Senhor Duque d'Aveiro. You are but a sluggard sportsman, I fear; but we must imbue you with some of our own fondness for the exciting pastime, and then you will vie with the best."

"When your Majesty commands, your subjects must obey," returned the Duke, in a tone which was far from agreeing with the obedient tenor of his words; for he neither had any predilection for the chase, nor was he famed for his proficiency in equestrian accomplishments.

"We will tarry no longer," exclaimed the King. "To horse, to horse, cavaliers! 'Tis a sin to lose a moment of this tempting weather." As he spoke, he laid his hand on the bridle of a steed which some grooms had been leading backwards and forwards in readiness, but which they had now resigned to several of the nobles, the Marquis of Marialva performing the office of holding the stirrup while he mounted.

No sooner was he in the saddle than the rest of the party followed his example, a fresh horse being brought out for the Minister, who seemed to enjoy the thoughts of the sport as much as the youngest or idlest among them.

The King led the cavalcade, a little in advance, with Carvalho by his side, who seemed to be communicating some matters of importance, at all events not intended for the ears of the rest. Then came the Duke of Aveiro, the Marquis of Marialva, and other of the first nobles, followed by a crowd of attendants and huntsmen, among whom appeared that faithful counsellor of the Duke's, Senhor Policarpio; for without him his master never now went abroad. That discreet personage did not seem to partake at all either in his ill-humour or dislike to the amusement, chatting and laughing familiarly with his fellows, who could not fail to regard him as a most amiable character.

Hunting parties have been before so often and ably described by far greater artists than we can ever hope to be, that it were useless and tiresome to our readers to mention the costumes of the sportsmen, and the trappings of their steeds, the numbers of attendants, with their leashes of hounds, the men with long sticks and clappers to rouse the game from their lairs, the cheering sound of the horns, the neighing of the horses, the barking of the dogs, and the shouts and cries of the human beings joining in one wild and exhilarating chorus. We defy any, except the most apathetic or heart-broken, (including some, perhaps, who experience a considerable share of fear in being obliged to sit on horseback at all,) not to feel their spirits rise, and their hearts throb with eagerness to come up with the chase, when they find themselves in such scenes as we have seen depicted.

We do not, for another reason, mention this more minutely; for we suspect that, were we to paint it exactly as it was, it would be found to fall very far short, in interest and even in magnificence, of an English meet, just as the fox breaks from cover. Boar hunting is a very fine thing, we doubt not; but it cannot *beat that*. The boars in question being detained within the precincts of the park, by sundry tempting baits from time to time held out to them, on condition that they would make no objection to be hunted on occasions, and killed when required, were not quite so fierce as their brethren in the forest of Ardennes, or those which the German barons hunt, as narrated in every romance the scene of which is laid in that picturesque country of rocks, woods, and castles; nevertheless they were formidable adversaries to encounter when their bristles were up, without a long spear and a sharp couteau de chasse in the hand; then an expert butcher could easily cut their throats. They were worth killing, too; for we can vouch for the very excellent hams which their descendants of the present day make, when dried and salted. But we are descending too much into common-day life, so must again mount our Pegasus, and follow the hounds.

The party rode on for some distance into the wood, at that easy pace which enabled the footmen to keep up with them without difficulty, being joined every now and then by some of the nobles who had been more sluggard in their movement.

There was, indeed, a gallant assemblage of cavaliers collected by the time they reached a broad, sylvan glade, in the neighbourhood of which it was expected that a boar, or perhaps a wolf, would be found; for both animals were equally objects of their search. Of the latter there were great numbers in the country, who, descending from their mountain fastnesses during the frosts of winter, took refuge in the forests on the lower lands, where, finding an abundance of provision, they remained till hunted and destroyed, every one waging deadly war against them.

The beaters, with the huntsmen and dogs, now went in front, the first forming a long line; and, with loud shouts and cries, striking every clump of brushwood in their way, advanced slowly forward, the royal party following them closely.

At length, a magnificent boar, of larger size than usual, started from among a mass of tangled shrubs. For a moment, he gazed at his enemies, as if he would have rushed on them, when the footmen retiring behind the cavaliers, the latter galloped their horses towards him. Instinct pointing out to him the hopelessness of contending with so large a force, he turned, and endeavoured to escape by flight. Vain were his efforts: his speed did not equal that of his pursuers; the King, by the tacit consent of his courtiers, being allowed to be the first to come up with him; for, although pretending to urge on their active steeds to the utmost, by swerving more than necessary, as if to avoid the brushwood in their way, they easily effected their purpose. The dogs rushed on him from all sides, compelling him to stand at bay; two he laid, covered with gore, upon the turf; but the others he could not shake off, when the King, plunging his spear into the brawny neck of the now infuriated animal, brought him to the ground. He uttered a loud cry of pain and impotent rage, and the Marquis of Marialva, leaping from his steed, finished the beast's life, with a stroke of his short hunting sword. The footmen then hastened forward to take possession of the carcass, which was to be conveyed to the royal residence.

While this scene was enacting, Captain Policarpio rode up to his master, the Duke of Aveiro, who had loitered at some little distance apart from the other sportsmen.

"It would save much trouble, if one of the brethren of yonder fierce beast, were to plunge his long tusks into the side of this hunting-loving King of ours," observed the former, in a low tone.

"You speak truly, my good Policarpio," replied the Duke; "but such a chance, I fear, is not to be ours. He is too closely surrounded by those sycophantish nobles, who, I verily believe, would risk their own lives to save his, and these brutes have seldom the fortune to kill their hunters. We must wait our time, and trust to our own good arms, and steady aim."

"An opportunity may offer we thought not of before, though one, we should do well not to lose, if I may so advise your Excellency. The forest we shall traverse is thick, and the probability is great that the King will be separated from the rest of the party. Let him be our game, and let our whole care be to closely follow his movements, never, for an instant, allowing him to escape our sight; then should we find him for a moment alone, and no person at hand, one well-aimed stroke would place the crown on your Excellency's head."

"The idea is not bad; but it is utterly hopeless. Even if the King were separated from the others, we should not be able to slay him, without a certainty of discovery," said the Duke.

"Have no fear on that score, your Excellency; such deeds have often before been done. The bough of a tree may have thrown him from his horse; some concealed assassin may have shot him, or the very animal he was in search of may have overpowered him. We ride on, as if nothing had occurred; the hunters will have gained a long distance from the spot, before they perceive that the King is not of the party; then some time will elapse before any go in search of him, and still more before his corpse is discovered. This will fully account for the escape of the assassins: your Excellency, in the mean time, can easily overtake and ride among the foremost of the hunters, so that no one will suspect you, while I will keep among my equals, and shout, and laugh the blithest of any."

"You are truly a valuable counsellor, my friend, and with your aid, Heaven favouring me, I may yet succeed. I will follow your advice; but keep not too much in my company, the so doing may draw suspicion on us."

The weak Duke had just made up his mind to act according to his cunning servant's suggestion, when a she-wolf started from a cover some way beyond where the boar had been finally brought to bay. Fresh dogs were, as soon as possible, let loose on her; but she had, in the mean time, gained a considerable start of them, making the utmost of her advantage; and giving one fierce glare at her pursuers, she directed her course towards the centre of the forest. Every one was in eager pursuit; but the trees, in some places, grew so densely, that it was impossible for the huntsmen to keep together, or in sight of the quarry. The King, the most excited of any, encouraged them with shouts and gestures to the chase, many, indeed, unintentionally having actually passed him; but the Duke and his wily attendant, holding back their steeds, kept a hawk-eyed glance on his every movement. Suddenly, to their great satisfaction, they observed their intended victim take a narrow path to the right, from supposing, probably, that it would afford a shorter road, while the rest of the party followed a broader way straight forward. The King galloped on, when he found that he had made a mistake, the path leading him at each step further from the cries of the dogs, and the shouts of the men: he perceived also, that he was followed by none of his own attendants; two horsemen only being distinguished approaching him at some little distance. He listened attentively for the sounds of the chase, and could yet clearly distinguish them on the left, in which direction he searched eagerly for an opening in the wood, through which he might proceed at a fast pace, without running the risk of being bruised among the trees. At last he arrived at a part of the wood where the trees grew further from each other; and just as the Duke and Senhor Policarpio were about to gallop towards him, the latter, with the intention of plunging his long hunting spear into his back, he disappeared among them. The King, little thinking of the treachery meditated against him, passed through what he found to be merely a narrow belt of trees, closely pursued by his intended murderers, till he found himself in a small amphitheatre; the soil soft and damp, from a bubbling stream, which issued forth from some rugged, dark rocks, which rose on every side, while the most lofty trees of the forest grew around. He had before been led to the spot, in the course of a day's sport, and he knew it to be near the centre of the domain. There was but one path which led from it, in the direction he wished to pursue, between two overhanging rocks, and this he was about to take, when the traitors again overtook him. It was a spot fit for their fell purposes; no prying eye might observe them, nor was any huntsmen likely to be led thither. Another moment, and his life would have been ended; when a tall dark figure rose directly in his path. The woodland apparition, for so seemed the stranger to the guilty consciences of the assassins, caused them to pause in their intention. The King's steed snorted and reared at the sudden interruption to his career, nor was his rider less amazed at beholding the strange figure, who, with wild and frantic gestures, presented itself before him. As our readers may possibly have guessed, he was the same mysterious personage whom we described as wandering about the wood in the early part of the morning.

The Monarch was the first to speak, for he conjectured that some insane peasant, probably, having wandered into the woods, had been startled from his sleep, and was not aware of the impropriety of his actions.

"Who art thou, friend, who thus venturest to intrude into our royal domain? Say, what wantest thou? but, be quick in thy speech, and impede not our progress; for we yet hear the sounds of the chase at a distance."

"I am one whose hands thou hast kissed, and whose feet thou hast washed, proud King, in the days of thy innocence and happiness; but one whom thou hast since despised, and driven from thy presence with ignominy. Will that suffice thee? My message I give not in the presence of the vile panders to thy follies and vices I see approaching."

And he pointed towards the Duke of Aveiro and Senhor Policarpio, when the King, now for the first time, perceived that he was not alone. While the stranger was speaking, they came up, bowing profoundly; but the Monarch had been seized with a strong desire to know what the aged man before him could possibly have to say; and, being well armed, he thought not of personal danger. He therefore desired the Duke and his attendant to ride on, and endeavour to discover the rest of the party, saying he would follow in their track, as soon as he had listened to what the peasant had to communicate. The Duke was obliged to obey, although he regarded the stranger suspiciously; for, at the first glance, he recognised in him the holy Father Malagrida, and it instantly occurred to him, that he was about to betray his own treacherous designs. At first, it flashed across his mind, that his only chance of safety would be to destroy both Joseph and the Priest at once; but his superstitious awe of the Father, prevented him from committing the deed. He rode on, therefore, followed by Policarpio, their former intention yet unaltered.

"Let us draw rein here, if it please your Excellency," said the latter, as soon as they had lost sight of the King; "we shall have now a fairer opportunity than ever. As he passes by, we will rush at him, and strike him dead. Yonder peasant will be accused of the deed, and we shall escape suspicion."

"Know you not who yonder seeming peasant is?" exclaimed the Duke. "He is no peasant, but the holy Jesuit Malagrida, for what purpose come hither, I know not; but I fear me much it cannot be for any good, except he seeks to take the trouble off our hands by despatching the King himself."

"It would be a useful deed, forsooth," said Policarpio. "Yet, no matter, if he slays him not; his very appearance will aid our purpose; for many must have seen a stranger wandering about, who will be the first suspected; and, as he will probably make his escape, he will inform no one that he saw us. Does not your Excellency think so?"

"Your sagacity is above all praise," answered the Duke. "You deserve to be a prime minister, my good Policarpio; and you shall be if my plans are successful. They must be so, or—"

He dared not to utter the alternative.

"Fear not, my noble master; success must attend us," interrupted Policarpio.

Such was the conversation the pair, worthy of each other, held, while concealed among some thick-growing shrubs, in anxious expectation of their victim's arrival.

As soon as the King found himself alone with the aged peasant, he repeated his former question—"Say, what wantest thou, my friend?"

"For myself, I require naught; but I come for thy benefit, O hard-hearted and impious King; for our Lord, in his mercy, remembering the bright promise of thy youth, in the days of thy tainted father, has taken compassion on thee, and will not suffer thee to be destroyed without a given warning. Hear me, O King! while I speak the words of Heaven! If thou turn not from thy evil course; if thou ceasest not to cherish the persecutor of our holy religion, in the persons of her most faithful servants; if thou still wilt refuse to receive the fathers of the Order of Jesus into thy palace, and trustest to the vain words and counsels of the pampered and false sons of our Church, then will a speedy vengeance fall on thy head. Even now is thy name registered among those doomed to die, who will not repent of their sins: even now has the fiat of thy fate gone forth, which naught but the prayers of the faithful can turn aside. Be warned, then, O King! in time. Repent! and be saved from destruction. If not, before many suns have set, thy haughty head shall be brought low, and thou shalt mingle with the dust from whence thou sprangest. Ah! thy dying groans now ring upon mine ear. I see thy blood-stained corpse upon the ground, while the demons of hell rejoice that they have gained another victim. Thy proud race shall cease, and thy name shall be held in abhorrence by all the faithful followers of our holy religion."

"Cease, cease, whoever thou art, mysterious man," exclaimed the King, interrupting him, and trembling with agitation. "We tarried not to hear words like these. We fancied that thou earnest to inform us of some plot against our throne and life. Speak, who art thou? that we may know how much credence to give to thy words."

"I am one whom thou hast persecuted—I am the Father Malagrida!"

"Ah! why, then, this strange garb? and how darest thou to approach our royal person?" cried the King.

"I dare do all that is commanded me; and for this peasant garb, it enabled me, unperceived, to enter this domain, where, living on the berries of the trees, and roots from the earth, have I long waited to meet thee thus. Wilt thou then promise to amend and turn from thy wickedness?"

"Silence! daring Priest!" cried the King. "Begone to the town appointed for thy residence, or I will command my attendants to seize thee, and commit thee to the lowest dungeon in our prisons."

"I fear thee not, and dare thy vengeance! Thou hast set the seal upon thine own fate. From henceforth no warning voice shall meet thine ear; and rapidly shalt thou run thy course unto destruction. I would have saved thee, but thou wouldest not be saved. Wretched Monarch, we meet no more!"

Joseph, who wanted not personal courage, (indeed cowardice has never been a failing of his race,) and was above the vulgar superstitions of his country, enraged more than terrified by these daring threats, made an attempt to seize the mad Jesuit; but Malagrida, perceiving his intention, eluded his grasp, and uttering a loud laugh of derision, plunged among the rocks and brushwood, whither it was impossible for the King to follow on horseback.

In vain the Monarch attempted to cut off his retreat. After searching for him for a considerable time, he was obliged to desist; and then set off at full speed, in the hopes of quickly finding the Minister and his nobles, and despatching people to apprehend the daring Jesuit.

The Duke and his attendant watched eagerly for his approach; every instant they expected to triumph in his destruction; at last they beheld him galloping towards them through the wood, when the loud shouts of men, the sound of horses, and the barking of the hounds, broke on their ears, nearer approaching the spot where they were concealed. Onward came the King, when, as he was within a few yards of them, a wolf, closely pursued by the most active dogs, dashed by, his eyes straining, and his mouth covered with foam from rage and terror. The King, forgetful of the scene in which he had just engaged, and of everything except the excitement of the sport, turned his horse's head, and gave chase after the wolf. The savage animal, already almost spent with fatigue, was quickly overtaken, and ere he could stand at bay, the spear of the King had pinned him to the ground, when the dogs setting on him, had almost torn him to pieces, before a party of the noble hunters, with Carvalho at their head, could come up. What was their surprise on finding their sovereign in at the death, when it was supposed that he had followed another quarry in a different direction. All, of course, were loud in praise of his skill and address; none more so than the Duke of Aveiro, who soon rode up as if he had never harboured a thought of treachery.

At last Joseph recollected Malagrida, and calling the Minister to him, he recounted all that he had said. Carvalho, inwardly cursing his master's supineness, in not having at once informed him of the circumstance, advised him to summon all the party to aid in apprehending him. Leaving, therefore, all thoughts of further sport for wild beasts, they eagerly joined in what was, after all, far more exciting, and suited to their natures—the hunting down a fellow-creature, though none were told who was the person. They searched everywhere; not a bush in the neighbourhood was left unbeaten; but Malagrida had escaped, and, at last, in despair, they were obliged to desist, when fatigue warned the King that it was time to return home, and Carvalho immediately set off on his return to the city.

Note. This is the same worthy noble Mr Beckford so frequently mentions, and with whom he was residing while at Lisbon.

Volume Three—Chapter Four.

We have just discovered that we have written five chapters of our history without once mentioning the name of one who played so conspicuous a part in the commencement: we mean our most particular friend, Don Luis d'Almeida; and, lest any of our readers should begin to suspect that we have laid him on the shelf altogether, and should, in consequence, throw down our book as of no further interest, we will again return to the narration of his fortunes.

He was seated by the bedside of his father, the old Count d'Almeida, in the country-house we have before described, near Coimbra. His eyes were directed towards the invalid, with a glance of filial affection and deep sorrow; for on his countenance too clearly had the stern hand of death set his seal to claim his victim. A great change had come over Luis; disappointment, grief, and illness, had done their cruel work on him; he was no longer the sanguine and gay youth who laughed at misfortunes as things which might strike, but could not injure him; he was now the grave and thoughtful man: he had learned the great lesson—that sorrows must visit all but the few, and those few not to be the most envied, perhaps; but he had also learned to face disappointment with fortitude and resignation. The many months which he had spent in retirement, by the side of his dying parent, he had devoted, when not in actual attendance on him, to severe study. He had discarded all frivolous or light reading, drawing his ideas alone from the pure springs of knowledge and of truth, among the authors of antiquity; and truly did he find his mind strengthened by the invigorating draughts he had imbibed. For several weeks his father had not risen from his sick couch, and both were aware that they must soon part, though the son imagined not how soon.

The old Count had been sorely afflicted at the thoughts of leaving the son in whom all his affections centred, his pride and boast, so ill-provided with a worldly inheritance. He left him his honoured name, and his title; but beyond that, except the small Quinta on which he resided, all the residue of his fortune had been lost by the earthquake. The merchant who managed his affairs, and held possession of all his monied property, had failed, owing to that dreadful event, when several houses, from which he drew a considerable portion of his revenue, were also entirely destroyed; so that Luis would, with the greatest economy, be but barely able to support the character even of a private gentleman. For this he cared but little. Of what use now to him was wealth and rank, since she for whom alone he valued either was lost to him for ever? His ambition lay buried in that living tomb which now enclosed his Clara—now doubly lost; for, had he not been supposed to be the destroyer of her brother, and should he ever find means to clear himself from that imputation, yet would her father never consent to give her to one destitute of fortune. He had long banished from his mind all thoughts of happiness through the tender sympathies of our nature. A wife's sweet smile, issuing from her heart of hearts, he should never know; the name of father, uttered by the lips of his first-born, he should never hear: cold and solitary must be his course—yet both loving and beloved—but apart from his soul's idol—he knew her love would endure, and that consciousness would prevent his from ever changing. Since his return from Lisbon, he had once only quitted his father's house: it was to pay a short visit to Oporto, in the faint hopes of gaining an interview with Donna Clara. He saw her, as we shall hereafter describe; but, alas! little was gained to either, except a confirmation of their mutual constancy.

The old Count had been sleeping. As his eyes languidly opened, they met the earnest gaze of his son. "Luis," he said, in a feeble voice, "I must deceive you no longer. I know that I have not many hours to live. Before the sun again rises, I shall be taken from you; but yet, my boy, I die contented; for, though small is the share you will possess of this world's wealth, I leave you rich in all the endowments which conduce to true happiness. I dreamed, too, just now, that all your wishes were fulfilled—that she on whom you have set your heart was restored to you, and that wealth from an unexpected source flowed in upon you. Such, I know, are vain thoughts for one whose heart ought to be set alone upon the world towards which I am hastening; but Heaven will pardon a father for thinking of his only child."

"My dear father, speak not thus of quitting me!" exclaimed Luis, his voice choking with grief, and with willing blindness deceiving himself; "Heaven will yet spare you to me."

"Do not flatter yourself with false hopes, Luis, which will unfit you for the moment which must so soon come," answered the Count. "Yet, before I go, I would speak to you on a subject which has long oppressed me. Do not judge harshly of any man till you know the motives of his actions, nor bear hostile feelings towards him because he differs from you in his opinions, unless they advocate immorality or irreligion. Alas! I wish that I had always acted as I now counsel you to do. I had a brother, some few years younger than myself, a gay and gallant youth, with impetuous feelings and headstrong passions, but possessed of a noble and generous soul, which despised danger, and could but ill bear restraint. At an early age he became imbued with the heretical doctrines of religion, then first introduced in this country. He was also strongly opposed to the system of government which has for so many years existed, and took no pains to conceal either one or the other. The expression of his religious opinions might have passed unnoticed, as he never attempted to make converts to them; but when he ventured to lift his voice against what he called the vices of the priests, the bigotry of the people, the sycophancy of the nobles, and the tyranny of the sovereign, all joined in condemning him; even I, as his brother, deemed that his presumption ought to be punished. He was persecuted on every side; his life, even, was demanded as the only recompense for his crime, and the Inquisition endeavoured to lay hold of him. He came to me for aid to escape, but I looked upon him as an infidel and a traitor, and refused my assistance, telling him as my reason, that I could not answer to my conscience for my doing so. I remember his last words: 'Brother,' he said, 'I shall not cease to love you; for you act as you think right—I speak according to my judgment; though I should have been *wiser* to have held silence. I will not now ask you to do what you consider wrong. Farewell!' Without uttering another word, he left me, and I saw him no more. My heart smote me for my cruelty and want of brotherly affection; but my confessor, the Father Jacinto, who had urged me so to act, assured me I had done rightly; for that it would have been participating in the sin to have aided so impious an heretic: yet I could not forget his last words, nor have I ever forgiven myself. My brother could not effect his escape: he was seized, imprisoned, tried, and condemned to expiate his crimes on the burning shores of Africa, where death would soon have finished his career, but he never reached his destination. The ship which bore him was never more heard of, and was supposed to have foundered in a violent storm, which was known to have raged in the latitudes where she was. I have never received further tidings of my unfortunate brother. Alas! my conduct towards him is the bitterest draught of death; but we shall yet meet in another world, where he will forgive me my trespass towards him."

Exhausted by the exertion he had made to speak, the Count fell back into his son's arms.

Luis now gazed with alarm at his father's countenance, which had assumed the ghastly hue of death; but, in a few minutes, the Count again revived, and gave his hand a gentle pressure, to assure him of his consciousness, yet some time elapsed ere he again spoke. We need not detail more of the conversation between the father and son, nor are we fond of describing death-bed scenes, where no object is to be gained by the contemplation. We delight not to harrow up the feelings of our readers by descriptions of those mournful and inevitable occurrences with which we must all be more or less familiar, and which cannot fail of bringing back melancholy recollections to our minds, while we have a long catalogue before us of strange and terrible events, their very strangeness interesting, though persuading us that we can never be doomed to witness the like.

The conversation of the Count and his son was interrupted by the arrival of the priest to administer extreme unction to the dying man, the voice of the choristers, chanting the hymn of the dying, being heard without. How mournfully did the notes strike upon the ear of Luis! Often had he heard them before, but then they were sung to the departing soul of some person indifferent to him—now, to the being he revered most on earth.

The Count having confessed his sins, and the last sacrament being administered to him, the priest, in his gilded canonicals, took his departure, bearing in his hands the sacred emblems; his head being protected from the sun's rays by a silken awning, supported on poles by four attendants, when the sick man was left to die in peace.

Ere another sun arose, the old Count's forebodings were fulfilled—he had ceased to breathe, and Luis found himself alone in the world. On the following day, the body of the Count, dressed in full costume, and decorated with the orders he possessed, was laid out in an open coffin, placed on high trestles in the centre of the chapel belonging to the house. Here all the surrounding population attended, with marks of real sorrow, to take a last farewell of one who had ever been an indulgent landlord to his tenants and a friend to all.

In the evening it was carried to the neighbouring church, where was the tomb of his family. The interior of the church was hung with black, and a canopy of black cloth and silver was erected over the spot where the body was deposited during the performance of the service, the tenants, and those friends who had been enabled to arrive in time, lining each side of the building, with thick wax tapers in their hands, upwards of seven feet in length. The service being over, the lid of the coffin was closed, and the key delivered to the care of the person of highest rank present, whose duty it was to present it to the heir of the deceased, the young Count d'Almeida.

The day after the funeral, as Luis was seated in solitude, his mind dwelling with sad satisfaction on the affection and the many virtues of the parent he had lost, Pedro entered the room, and placed a letter in his hands. He examined the seal, which appeared to have been broken and again closed without much care; but he thought not more of the circumstance after he had torn open the envelope. It was from his young friend, Don Jozé de Tavora. His colour went and came, and his eye flashed, as he read on. The words were to this effect:—

"Much esteemed and dear Friend,—Knowing you to be a man of that high honour and integrity, surpassed by none, to you I write freely and openly. I have been very wretched lately, not on my own account, but on that of my brother; he has been insulted, grossly insulted, by one from whom he can gain no satisfaction, who would be above all laws, human and divine, and who would, to gratify his own evil inclinations, trample on our dearest rights and privileges—he hopes with impunity. In that he is mistaken. He forgets that his nobles, at least those who are worthy of the name, cherish their honour before their lives, and that they wear swords to protect both one and the other. His name I will not mention—you know it. You have not forgot, I know, your promise to defend, to the last drop of your blood, the fame of your cousin Theresa, my lovely sister-in-law. The time has now arrived to do so. She has been daily persecuted by the attentions of that high personage during my brother's absence. I believe her innocent of all crime; for surely one so lovely cannot be guilty; but my brother, mad with jealousy, is not so persuaded, and has sworn to be avenged on the disturber of his happiness. No plan is yet arranged, but whatever is done will require the aid of all the high-born and pure nobles of the land to carry into effect. To you, therefore, Luis, I write, to summon you, without delay, both to counsel and to act. More I may not say, but I rely upon your not failing to fulfil your promise. Adeos, dear friend, and fortunate am I to be able so to call you."—The letter was signed, "Jozé Maria de Tavora."

"Theresa in danger!" he exclaimed, "the greatest danger which can befall a woman;—she I once loved so fondly! I must fly to rescue her. But how? Alas, we cannot tear her from the hands of our sovereign without being accused of treason! Even that risk would I brave to secure her innocence. No, Theresa would not, cannot be guilty!"

With a troubled mind, forgetting entirely his own cause for grief, Luis arose, and summoning Pedro, ordered him to prepare for a quick departure for Lisbon. He then set to work to perform the many duties his father's demise had rendered necessary before he could leave his home. Pedro was in high glee at the thoughts of another visit to Lisbon. He had grown heartily weary of the monotonous quiet of his master's home, after the bustle and activity to which he had become accustomed during his travels; and he had managed to quarrel with his country love, so that he had become very anxious to renew his acquaintance with the fair one he admired in the city, should she still remain faithful to him.

Two days necessarily passed before the young Count, for so we may in future call Luis, was prepared to quit his home. The journey was a sad and silent one; for he was far too deeply occupied to listen to the idle prating of Senhor Pedro, who considered it part of his duty to endeavour to amuse his master. Luis, though fully alive to the danger he ran by engaging in any conspiracy against the sovereign, his principles, indeed, determining him not to do so, unless driven to it by the most direful necessity, yet forgot, for the time, all the warnings he had received from his friends Captain Pinto and Senhor Mendez, also from the Minister himself, not to allow any intimacy to spring up between himself and the family of the Tavoras. This advice he had disregarded when he gained the friendship of young Jozé de Tavora, but he could not resist the amiability, candour, and high feelings of the youth, though with no other member of that once proud race had he become intimate. What further befell him we will reserve for a future chapter.

Volume Three—Chapter Five.

When the Father Jacinto da Costa quitted the Quinta of the Marchioness of Tavora, he paid several visits, in different parts of the city, to forward the various plots in which he was engaged, and towards the close of the evening he approached the ruins of the church and convent of San Caetano, where, as we have described, Malagrida had, some time previously, been seized, while preaching against the authority of the King and his Minister. No attempts had yet been made to restore the buildings, so that the spot presented a wild scene of havoc and destruction, increased by the thickening gloom which pervaded the city: here a few blackened and tottering walls, there vast masses of masonry piled one on the other, among which dank plants and shrubs had begun to spring up, already eager to claim the ground so long the abode of man.

The Priest walked round to the back of the ruins, where a wall, in some places thrown down, served to enclose the garden of the convent. He here easily climbed over the fragments, and found himself on comparatively unencumbered ground. He wound his way among the moss-grown paths, impeded by the luxuriant vegetation of the geraniums and rose trees, which, long unpruned, sent their straggling branches in every direction, filling the cool night air with the sweet scents of their flowers. The once trimly-cut box trees had lost all signs of their former shapes; the fountains had ceased to play; the tanks were dry, once stocked with the luscious lamprey, and other rich fish, to feed the holy friars on their days of fasting and penance; indeed, desolation reigned throughout the domain.

The Priest heeded not these things, his eye was familiarised with them; nor did he cast a pitying thought upon the worthy friars who had been driven forth to seek another home;—they were his foes—his rivals on the field he sought to claim as his own. His mind, too, was occupied by matters of vast import to the safety of his order; yet he doubted not that he should ultimately come off victorious.

With some little difficulty he reached the centre of the garden, and, looking carefully around, he seated himself on one of the stone benches by the side of a large circular tank, now empty. He waited for some time till he heard a step approaching, when, starting up, he beheld the figure of a man closely shrouded in a cloak, emerging from among the thick-growing shrubs. He advanced towards him with an eager step, which betrayed his deep anxiety, so unlike his usually cold and calm demeanour.

The stranger threw back his cloak as he approached the Jesuit, so as to exhibit by the uncertain light the features apparently of a young and handsome man. "Father, I have come at your command," he said, "though with great risk of discovery, if I hasten not back to my post."

"It is well, Alfonzo. What news do you bring me?" demanded the Jesuit.

"I have naught but the worst to reveal," answered the young man.

"Speak it without fear: no one can here listen to your words," exclaimed the Father. "Stay, we will examine well the neighbouring bushes, to see that no lurking spy is there concealed."

The Jesuit and his young companion, having concluded their search, seated themselves on the stone from which the first had risen. "Now, speak," said the Father.

"I have long watched for an opportunity to ascertain what you desired," began the stranger. "Yesterday, while the Minister was absent, I opened his bureau with the key you gave me. With trembling hands I searched each paper, and from all of importance I have made notes. At last I came to one roughly drawn out in Carvalho's writing: it was a plan to be submitted to the King for abolishing your whole order throughout the kingdom. He proposes to implicate you in some act of rebellion, or some illegal practice; then to surround your colleges, and to embark all who are professed, on board vessels for the coast of Italy, banishing you for ever from Portugal. He advises the King to allow no delay in executing his plan; for that every day you are increasing in power and malevolence, and that you will in time sap the very foundation of his throne."

"Ah! thinks he so?—he shall find that he is not mistaken!" exclaimed the Jesuit, with greater vehemence than he had ever before given way to. "No time must then be lost in putting our plot into execution, and we will try the success of both. Alfonzo, you have acted well, and will meet with the approbation of our general. You will, when you profess, rise rapidly to the highest rank in our order, and will become one of its brightest ornaments."

"I merit no praise," returned the young neophyte, for such the Father declared him to be. "I have but done my duty."

"You might yet win far greater praise," said the Father, scarce noticing his answer. "It would be a noble thing to destroy the great enemy of our order. It would at once free us from all further fear of danger."

The young aspirant started. "I understand not your words, Father," he said.

"I speak of Carvalho's death," answered the Jesuit, calmly. "It is said that the dagger of the assassin cannot reach him,—that often has his life been attempted, but each attempt has failed. What steel cannot accomplish, the poisoned chalice may."

"What mean you, Father?" gasped forth Alfonzo.

"It is simple to understand, my son: now listen calmly," returned the Jesuit, in a voice calculated to soothe his listener's fears. "It is a law, founded on nature and on justice, that we have a right to defend our lives and properties, at every cost, against those who would deprive us of either. No one would scruple to strike the assassin dead who would take our life, or the robber who would steal our purse: then can it be a sin to destroy the man who would blast our name, who would deprive us of our lawful power, and drive us forth to beggary and to death? Can Heaven blame us that we seek to deprive him of life who would thus treat us? No, my son; be assured that the death of that man of crime would be an acceptable sacrifice to the Ruler of the Universe."

The pupil answered not.

"Listen, Alfonzo," continued the Master. "You have determined to become the follower of the great Loyola: you seek by that means to gain power and influence among the men you have learned to despise. The way is open to you to follow if you will; but while Carvalho lives, our order in Portugal can never flourish. In him we have the most inveterate and deceitful foe we have ever known. He must die, or we shall meet a certain destruction. Hear me, Alfonzo: I speak not to a weak and trembling child, but to a man who has boldly dared, and successfully performed, and who will yet do more!"

The Jesuit took from beneath his robes a small box, and extracted from it a paper closely folded, which he placed in the hands of his companion. "Take this parcel," he continued. "It contains a powder, which, when mixed with a glass of water, will not dim its crystal purity. Its effects are deadly, but slow, and no antidote has power to act against it; nor will the most clever physician be able to detect its workings on the human frame. Watch your opportunity, and mix it with the first beverage you see prepared for him; but beware no one else tastes of it, nor do you lose sight of it till he has drunk it to the dregs. Now then will our mighty tyrant have become a thing to loathe!"

"Father!" exclaimed the young man, in a scarcely articulate voice, "I have ever obeyed your commands to the utmost; I have acted a part from which my heart revolts; I have betrayed the man who has confided in me,—but I cannot become a murderer. I could not live, and see the man who has taught me to admire and love him writhing in agony, and know that it was the effect of my foul act. In mercy take back the deadly powder."

"Alfonzo, I expected not a like answer from you," replied the Priest, quietly taking back the paper. "I trusted that you had been taught to rise above the common and false prejudices of the world,—that you had bravely conquered the weak feelings of human nature, and were each day advancing in qualifying yourself to become a professed member of our order; but I see, alas! that I was mistaken, and that you are still held back by weak bonds, which a bold man would long ere this have broken through."

"Spare me, Father, spare me a task I cannot perform!" cried the young man, clasping his hands convulsively together; but the other gazed on him sternly.

"Alfonzo," he answered, "you have another motive than dread of the deed for your refusal to obey the commands of your superior. I have watched you closely, when you little thought it. I know your inmost feelings. You love! Ah, you start, conscious of your guilt. The fair daughter of the Minister has drawn you from the path of duty. While you betrayed the father, you allowed your heart to be led captive by the daughter's charms. She loves you in return, perchance; but, think you, even were you to desert the colours you have determined to follow, the powerful and haughty Minister would listen to the suit of one without wealth or family? Naught but the infatuation of madness can lead you on; yet, try your fortune, and hear his answer: he will scorn and drive you from him with derision, even if he consign you not rather to one of the lowest dungeons of his prisons; then, in darkness and solitude, except when the executioner is sent to torture you, will you spend your days, till death puts an end to your sufferings. Such will be your fate if you destroy him not."

"Such, then, be my fate; I cannot murder," answered the youth, in a deep tone.

"Have I not told you that self-defence is not murder?" returned the Jesuit. "On my head be the sin, if sin there be. Take your choice. If you still determine to follow our banner, obey my orders; if you seek to continue as a layman, and would gratify your passion by wedding the daughter of Carvalho, take this paper—'tis not you that give its contents, 'tis I—and no crime can be laid to your charge. 'Tis the shedding of blood alone against which the Scripture speaks. While Carvalho lives the fair girl can never be yours; if he dies, you may find means to win her; but if you pertinaciously refuse to follow my counsels, no power can avert your destruction."

"Give me the fatal powder," exclaimed the youth, in a faltering voice. "I will not pledge myself to administer it, but I will act as circumstances demand. You, Father, shall not have cause to taunt me with my faltering purpose."

"Spoken like one worthy to belong to our holy order," said the Jesuit. "Take the paper, and preserve it carefully. Meet me here to-morrow, if possible, at the same hour, and bring me all further information you can collect. Falter not in your purpose, my son, and let the high destiny which awaits you be an encouragement to perseverance in the holy course you have chosen."

The unhappy youth took the packet containing the poison, and the Jesuit, as he delivered it, felt his hand tremble.

"Alfonzo," he continued, "I know full well what is yet passing in your mind. You hope to escape the performance of your promise. Remember, I speak in kindness, but I warn you. An ever watchful eye notes your every action, ay, and reads your inmost heart; and should you harbour, even for a moment, a thought of treachery, an awful doom will be yours, far more terrible than any the Minister, in his most savage mood, can devise."

"I know it, I know it," exclaimed the aspirant, "but my task is a hard one."

"The more glory in the performance, my son," returned the Father. "Now go, I have detained you too long already. Farewell, and the blessing of Heaven attend your enterprise."

The young man, without answering, bowed low before the Superior, and again shrouding his features in his cloak, took his way towards a fallen part of the garden-wall, and walking rapidly onward, found himself on the road towards the residence of Carvalho, before he allowed a definite thought to take possession of his mind. He gained the house, entering by a private door, and, mounting the stairs, eagerly examined the office he had quitted. The Minister had not returned since his departure, and his breathing became more regular—the fear of immediate detection was passed. He endeavoured to apply himself to a task he had left uncompleted, but his hand refused to obey his powerless wishes. One burning thought filled his mind; a weight like molten lead pressed down his soul; he endeavoured to exert his faculties, but the effort was vain. Again and again the one dreadful idea rushed with tenfold vividness before him; he writhed in agony, as the iron entered his soul—he cursed, bitterly cursed, the adamantine fetters with which he lay bound—break loose from them he knew too well he could not. He thought of all he had sacrificed,—youth, talents, happiness, for what? To grasp a shapeless phantom—to serve a lord unseen, unknown, more inexorable than death. Death can but command once, and must be obeyed; the stern dictates of his chief must be followed through a long life, while he must look for death as the only harbinger of freedom. He almost shrieked as he thought of the effects of the act he had undertaken to perform. He beheld the man who had trusted in him, the father of her he had dared to love to desperation, sinking in anguish by the consuming fire he must administer; that manly and majestic form reduced to a mass of inanimate clay; that mighty spirit, which held a whole people in awe, driven forth by his fell deed. He thought, too, that she who had awakened the better spirit within him would recoil with horror as she felt the impious touch of her father's murderer; instead of love, her bosom would become filled with hatred, with loathing and disgust towards him. Remorse, bitter and eternal, must be his lot. As he mechanically bent over his paper, his pen not moving from the spot on which he had first placed it, the ink dry, a noise startled him—he looked up, and beheld the Minister sternly regarding him. In a moment his faculties were restored to wakefulness.

"You have been somewhat dilatory, Senhor Alfonzo," said the Minister. "Are the papers I left you prepared?"

The secretary, with some confusion, acknowledged they were not.

"You have been worked hard lately, my good youth, so I will not blame you," said Carvalho. "This is, however, no time for idleness, and you must persevere, for there are so few I can trust, that I can procure no one to aid you."

Those few kind words saved the life of the Minister, and sealed the doom of many. In the mean time, the Father Jacinto paced the star-lit garden with slow steps. More than an hour passed away as he was thus left to his solitary meditations; what they were we cannot pretend to say, nor whether his calculating reason, or his cold philosophy, whichever it might be called, had managed to stifle all compunction for his acts—all the whisperings of conscience. Could he have been able calmly to contemplate the moment when his deeds must be tried before the awful judgment-seat of Heaven? for, if he could, he had persuaded himself that he was acting a just part. The sounds of life, which had arisen from the city, had long ceased; it was now close upon the hour of midnight, when he heard a slow and firm foot-fall approaching, and, emerging from the gloom, the tall gaunt figure of the Father Malagrida stood before him.

"I have, at your desire, ventured hither, my brother, in spite of all the dangers with which the wicked threaten me," said the latter. "What would you of me?"

"The time has arrived for action, and I would consult with you about the means," returned Father Jacinto. "The Minister has already formed a plan to banish every member of our order from the shores of Portugal. In a few weeks, or perhaps even in a few days, we shall be deprived of our liberty. The King has but to sanction the plan, and it will forthwith be executed."

"Then the impious Monarch must die," exclaimed Malagrida. "His death be upon his own head. I have warned him, and he would not listen. I will warn him no more."

"He deserves no warning voice, holy brother," said the Father Jacinto, not believing that Malagrida had really appeared before the King. "But haste, inform all those who are willing to become the instruments of Heaven's vengeance that they must delay the work no longer. Let them take what means they think fit; it matters little, so that the deed be performed. Urge them to it by that mighty eloquence with which Heaven has endowed you for great purposes. Assure them that they are performing a righteous act, which cannot fail to prosper; and thus many whose fears have restrained them, will gladly join in the enterprise. One steady hand might perform the deed; but, alas! no man can be found alone to do it; they all suppose that security exists in numbers."

"'Tis enough for me to know that it must be done," answered Malagrida. "Fear not, my brother, I will take measures that it shall be done. By to-morrow night, I will assemble all those who are inimical to Joseph, and will so persuade them, that they shall no longer hesitate to execute my commands."

"You will perform good service to our holy order, and to our sacred religion," returned Father Jacinto.

"To that have I ever devoted my life and energies," said Father Malagrida.

"Truly have you ever been the great upholder of the faith, and have gained the esteem of our community, and the admiration of the world," answered Father Jacinto.

"A little flattery will incite this madman to the work," he thought. "If it fails, it will be easy to persuade the world that the idea arose but from the wild workings of his disordered brain. No one will venture to suppose that we could have been the instigators."

"Brother, I must depart to the wilderness, where the wickedness of this second Pharaoh, and his evil counsellor, have compelled me to dwell," said Malagrida. "In three days we shall meet again, I trust triumphant; till then, farewell."

"Farewell, my brother," returned Father Jacinto, and they separated; the latter, after leaving the deserted garden, returning to his convent, while Malagrida sought the river's side. He there found a boat awaiting him, with a single rower. He silently took his seat in the stern, and the man plying his oars with vigour, the small skiff shot rapidly from the shore. The Jesuit, keeping a watchful eye on every side, directed her course so as to avoid any of the boats rowing guard on the river, which might have impeded his progress.

Volume Three—Chapter Six.

On the following morning, the King, accompanied by his Ministers, and the chief officers of his household, held a grand review of all the troops quartered in and about Lisbon, in an open space in the neighbourhood of Belem.

After performing various evolutions, in no very perfect manner, it must be confessed, the troops marched past him in close order. At the head of a regiment of horse, called the Chaves Cavalry, rode the Marquis of Tavora, he being their colonel. He bowed respectfully to his sovereign, and passed on to form his men in line with the other troops, before firing the parting salute.

"That man can be no traitor," said the King, in a low voice, to Carvalho, who was close to him.

"I wish he was the only one in the kingdom," answered the Minister; "but I fear me there are many more."

"I trust you are mistaken, my good friend," replied Joseph. "If there are no worse than the Marquis of Tavora in my kingdom, I shall have little to fear."

"Some day I shall be able to convince your Majesty by clear proofs," said the Minister; "otherwise I would not thus alarm you with reports which may seem idle."

The Portuguese army was at this time the very worst in Europe. Through the supine negligence of former sovereigns, it had been allowed to become completely disorganised. The troops were ill paid, ill clothed, and ill fed. The officers, chiefly of the inferior grades of society, were ignorant of their duty, and illiterate, without a particle of the *esprit de corps* among them; nor did Carvalho, among his other designs at this period, take any measures to improve them.

The review being over, the King returned to his palace at Belem, where he received all those who had the *entrée* at Court. On these occasions, it was the custom for the nobles to assemble first, when the sovereign, entering the rooms, passed among them, addressing each in their turn in a familiar way.

It was the duty of Teixeira, the chief domestic of the King, and the confidant of his amours, to stand at the door of the ante-room, to see that none but the privileged entered. He had, some time before, from some insolent behaviour, seriously offended the Marquis of Tavora, who threatened him with punishment. When the Marquis now approached, Teixeira, who was standing directly in the way, pretended not to observe him. The Marquis, enraged at the premeditated insult, exclaimed, "Stand out of my way, base pander, or I will run my sword through your body."

"If I am a pander, as your Excellency thinks fit to call me," answered Teixeira, turning round, and eyeing him malignantly, "I am one to your wife and daughter, haughty noble."

"Wretched slave, dare you speak thus to me?" returned the Marquis, forgetting, at the moment, that he was within the precincts of the palace; "you shall rue those insolent words;" and half drawing his sword, he made as if he would put his threat into execution.

"Your Excellency forgets where you are," exclaimed the servant, trembling for his life.

"I do not, nor do you, when you venture to speak thus," answered the Marquis; "but remember, insolent wretch, you will not escape punishment as easily as you expect;" and passing on, without speaking another word, he entered the principal apartment.

When the King appeared, he made his complaint of Teixeira's insolence; but the former, assuring him that the insult was not intended, took no further notice of the circumstance.

The Levée, for so it might properly be called, being quickly over, the King retiring to his private apartments, the Marquis returned to his home. As he sat down to dinner with the Marchioness and his family, while the domestics were standing round, he complained bitterly of the manner in which Teixeira had insulted him, and of the King's indifference to his complaints.

"The servant has but learnt to copy his master," said the Marchioness. "Yet he deserves a severe chastisement, though it would disgrace your rank to bestow it. There are, however, many of your followers who will gladly avenge their master's honour."

Several of the attendants, who hated Teixeira for his good fortune, not more than for the insolence with which he had treated them, looked eagerly towards their master, as if they would willingly undertake the office; but he, either not observing them, or pretending not to do so, made no answer, and soon turned the conversation.

When left alone with her lord, the Marchioness used her utmost eloquence to persuade him to take instant vengeance for the insult he had received; for the circumstance alarmed her, lest her own plots might, by some extraordinary means, have been discovered.

"Depend on it," she said, "if the servant dares thus to act, he knows full well that his master will not be displeased."

"I think not thus of the King," answered the Marquis. "He has some faults, but he has too much respect for himself to ill-treat his nobles. On another occasion, I will complain of this villain Teixeira's conduct, and I doubt not he will be dismissed."

"I think far differently from you, my lord," returned the Marchioness. "The King, by the instigation of his upstart Minister, has become jealous of the power and wealth of our Puritano families. In every one of us he has been taught to suspect a foe, and he waits but the first opportunity to crush us."

"Your feelings of indignation have exaggerated the danger, Donna Leonora. The only foe we have to fear is the Minister; and we must endeavour, by exhibiting our love and devotion to our sovereign, to counteract his evil influence."

"It will be the very way to increase the suspicions of the King," returned the Marchioness. "Half measures are of no avail. If we are to retain our wealth and influence, if we are to remain grandees of Portugal, we must either compel the King to dismiss his counsellor, or he himself must suffer the punishment of his obstinacy."

"What mean you?" exclaimed the Marquis, with an alarmed expression of countenance.

"I mean, my lord," returned Donna Leonora, with a firm voice, "that the King who dares insult his nobles, who interferes with our privileges, who is a despiser of religion, and heaps contumely on its ministers, must die."

"Great heavens! utter not such dreadful treason!" cried the Marquis. "The very walls might hear you; and such thoughts alone might bring ruin on yourself and your whole family. From henceforth banish such an idea from your mind."

"Never!" exclaimed the Marchioness. "I have far too great a respect for our family honour, and for our holy religion, to submit tamely to such indignities. If you forget that you are a Tavora and a Catholic, I do not forget that I am your wife."

"I prize the honour of my family as I do my life, but it shall never be said that a Tavora became a traitor to his sovereign," said the Marquis.

"None shall have cause to say it, my lord," answered his wife; "it is unsuccessful treason which is alone so stigmatised, and the noble enterprise in which I would have you engage will, I have been assured by a voice from heaven, succeed."

"Say rather, by the instigations of the evil one," said the Marquis, with agitation.

"It was through the voice of that living saint, the holy Father Malagrida," responded Donna Leonora. "He has ever led me in the right path to holiness, and why should I now doubt his words? Oh, harden not your heart, my lord, but put faith in that holy man, for be assured whatever he utters proceeds alone from the fountain of truth. Of what object would have been all his fastings, his penances, and his prayers, if Heaven had not more particularly selected him among men to utter the words of truth to mankind? I feel assured that those who follow his advice cannot err; then wherefore hesitate in this ease?"

"I doubt not the sanctity of the Father Malagrida, Donna Leonora, but I have reason to doubt his sanity. His enthusiastic mind has been overthrown, and what he now conceives to be the inspirations of Heaven, are but the workings of a disordered imagination."

"Cease, cease, my lord, from giving utterance to such dreadful impiety," exclaimed the Marchioness, interrupting him; "do not peril your immortal soul by speaking blasphemy. The holy Father Malagrida insane? The greatest prophet of modern days, the speaker of unknown tongues, a mere mad enthusiast! Oh, my beloved lord, say not thus, as you value my happiness."

"I will not discuss the character of the Father Malagrida," answered the Marquis. "But tell me how you would wish me to act, for against the sacred life of his Majesty will I not lift up my hand."

"I would wish you to act like a high noble of Portugal, worthy of your Puritano descent," returned Donna Leonora. "I would wish you to protect the high order to which you belong from the encroachments of the King and his Minister, and I would wish you to take fitting vengeance for every insult offered you."

"In overthrowing the Minister, am I ready to hazard all; and never will I act otherwise than as becomes a high noble of the realm; nor will my sword be slow to avenge any insult offered to me or mine; but of the King have I ever been a faithful servant, and faithful will I die. Urge me then no more to engage in conspiracies which can but end in the destruction of all concerned." The Marquis rose as he spoke, and quitted the apartment, as the most easy way of finishing the discussion.

His lady gazed at his retiring form, but attempted not to stop him. "Oh! that I were a man, to lead the faint-hearted beings with whom I am associated!" she exclaimed. "The slightest shadow of danger frightens them from the most noble undertakings; the prophets of Heaven counsel them, but they will not listen to their words; even if the dead were to arise to assure them of it, they would not believe that the deed is a righteous one, and must be successful. Yet have I still some hopes that my lord will not close his ears to the divine words of the holy Malagrida, and that he may be brought round to follow his counsels. I will pray to the Blessed Virgin that she will turn his heart to the right path."

The Marchioness then retired to her own chamber, and, throwing herself on her knees before her private altar, she poured forth her prayers to her patron saint for the success of an enterprise, which was for the destruction of a King, the placing an usurper on his throne, the restoration of a tyrannical order of the priesthood, and the enslaving a whole people with the grossest of superstitions; yet not for a moment did it occur to her that she was performing an act otherwise than grateful to Heaven. No; she fully believed that her motives were pure and holy; and she felt assured that pride, ambition, and hatred formed no part of her incentives to action. Yet were they the chief motives, veiled from her own eyes by a fancied zeal for religion.

In the mean time, Antonio and Manoel Ferreira, two of the principal servants of the Marquis, as soon as they were released from attendance on their master, hurried off to the Quinta of the Duke of Aveiro, which was at no great distance from that of the Tavoras.

"What think you that villain Teixeira deserves for thus daring to insult our lord?" said Manoel to his brother, as they walked along.

"Nothing less than his death would satisfy me, if I were in our master's place," answered Antonio.

"My very thought," said the other.

"But then, you know that it would be beneath the dignity of so great a lord as our master to slay with his own hand a man of such low birth as this upstart Teixeira," observed Antonio.

"The very thing I was going to say; but should we not be doing a service to our lord, think you, and be well paid for it too, if we were to put a piece of lead into this impudent servant of the King's," said Manoel. "For my part, I should have no scruples on the subject, and we should have plenty of opportunities as he drives about at night in his carriage, for no good purpose either—the base villain—I warrant. How proud he has become, too, with his fine clothes and his carriage! Why, I recollect him no better than either of us were at that time, when he was glad enough to call us his friends, and now he would not speak to us if he met us."

"True enough, brother," observed Antonio. "Yet, where is the difference? We are honest men, and serve a Marquis, he is a rogue, and serves a King;—so he rides inside a carriage of his own, while we ride outside our master's."

"The vain upstart! He does serve a King, in more ways than one; but he shall pay dearly for it," exclaimed Manoel. "You heard what our lady said at dinner to-day, and I think it is our duty to take the hint."

"What mean you?" asked Antonio.

"Mean I? it is clear enough—that we are bound to shoot him, of course," returned the other. "You have grown dull, Antonio. You see we shall thus serve ourselves and our master into the bargain."

"I understand you clearly enough now; but should we not to a certainty be discovered?" asked the less daring Antonio.

"It would matter little if we were, after the deed was done. Our master could protect us," returned Manoel.

"We will think about it to-morrow," said Antonio. "I wonder what Senhor Policarpio wanted with us this evening, that he insisted we must visit him."

"We shall soon learn, for here we are at the gate. Now, he is a man I like; though he is chief servant of a duke, there is no pride or vanity about him. He is just as friendly with us as ever."

Manoel having pronounced this eulogium on Senhor Policarpio, they entered the gates of the Quinta, and went in search of their friend. He received them with all imaginable courtesy, and conducted them to his own apartment, where a repast was spread in readiness for them by his own servant.

"Welcome, senhors," said Senhor Policarpio. "I have done my best to entertain you; for, when such friends as you are honour me with their company, I like to be hospitable." The two followers of the Marquis bowed at the compliment. "Ah! it is not every day I have this pleasure," continued the host. "But never mind, we shall soon all see better days, when a certain friend of mine becomes higher than he even now is, and Senhor Don Joseph finishes his life. The sooner he does so the better, as far as I am concerned."

We do not intend to detail the conversation of these worthy personages; indeed, it is so nearly illegible in the manuscript before us, that it would be a work of great labour to decipher it. During the time, Senhor Policarpio went to a closet, from which he produced three guns, or rather blunderbusses, praising their excellent qualities. At first sight of them, his guests seemed much alarmed by the observations he at the same time made; but, quickly recovering, he persuaded them to repair with him to a retired part of the garden, where they might exercise themselves by firing at a mark.

While they were thus occupied, the lovely Duchess of Aveiro was seated in her drawing-room, with her embroidery frame before her, gazing over the orange groves at the lovely scene which the Castle of Belem on one side, and the placid river, now shining in the light of the setting sun, and covered with vessels and boats, presented. A fine boy, of some fifteen years old, was in the room; her only son, the young Marquis of Gouvea. He was leaning against the side of the window opposite to her, regarding her with a look of affection and respect, when the Duke abruptly entered. He threw his hat on the table with an indignant air, as he exclaimed—"By Heavens! I have again been insulted by this King beyond all bearance! He has had the audacity to declare to me that my son, forsooth, cannot marry the daughter of the Duke of Cadaval; and when I demanded his reasons for the refusal, he chose to give none. I told him that they were betrothed, and that I had set my heart on the match, as one in every way suitable to both parties; when he only answered, that he had arranged it differently. What say you, my son? how do you like losing a fair bride through the caprice of a tyrant?"

"That I wish I were a man, to carry her off in spite of him," answered the young Marquis.

"Spoken like my son!" exclaimed the Duke. "But you shall not be disappointed. His days are numbered; and then we shall see who will venture to dispute our authority."

At these words the Duchess looked anxiously up at her husband. "I trust that you allude not to the designs you once spoke to me about," she said. "I had long hoped you had abandoned them."

"Why did you nourish so foolish a hope, lady?" exclaimed the Duke. "I should have thought my wife was equally interested with myself in their success."

"I hoped so because I feel convinced that they cannot fail to bring destruction on yourself, and ruin on all your family; to drag many to the scaffold, if you are unsuccessful; and to introduce the horrors of a civil war into the country should they succeed: but such cannot be; Heaven will not favour so guilty a purpose. Oh! hear me, my lord. Abandon the dark and evil designs you have meditated. If you have any remaining love for your wife, if you regard the interests of your son, think not again of them."

The Duke laughed scornfully, as he asked, "What! would you not wish to be a queen, and see your son a prince?"

"I would far rather be a peasant's wife, than the queen of a bloodstained usurper; for, to become a king, such you must be," answered the Duchess, boldly. "No, my lord, I would not be cheated of my happiness by so deceitful a phantom."

"Silence, madam!" exclaimed the Duke, angrily. "This is but weak folly. Would not you wish to be a prince, my boy?" he said, turning to his son.

"Gladly, if my father becomes a king," answered the young Marquis.

"Fear not, my boy. You shall be so; before long, too; but speak not of it, though I know I can trust you. Such I cannot your cousin, who would turn pale at the very thoughts of the enterprise; so utter not to him a syllable of what I have said."

His wife rose, trembling with agitation, to make a last appeal, and laying her hand upon his arm, she exclaimed, "Let me solemnly implore you to desist from this purpose; it cannot thrive—even should the King fall, you cannot succeed to his throne; the nobles and people would rise up in one body against you, and hurl you, with your few friends, to destruction. Many who now, for their own interests, are cordial, would desert you, and, instead of a throne, you would mount a scaffold."

The Duke turned a scornful smile on her as she spoke, but she continued boldly,—"Last night I dreamed of this, and that I saw you, mangled and bloody, upon the ground, while a rude mob stood around, gazing at you with scoffs and jeers."

"Silence, foolish woman!" suddenly exclaimed the Duke, shaking her off, though turning pale at the thought of what she described. "I remain not to hear such mad nonsense as this. Go, and learn more wisdom;" and, with an angry frown on his brow, he rushed from the room.

The Duchess gave vent to her feelings in a flood of tears, while her son threw himself into her arms with fond solicitude, endeavouring to soothe her agitation, but in vain. She saw too clearly the dreadful future.

Volume Three—Chapter Seven.

If the country inns of Portugal are bad, those of the cities are very little better. So thought Luis d'Almeida, as, towards the evening of a day at the very end of autumn, accompanied by his faithful Pedro, he rode into the capital. So think, also, most travellers of the present time, except when they are fortunate enough to secure rooms at the one or two tolerable hotels which Lisbon now affords.

Luis had never before been compelled to seek lodgings, having always had his father's palace to which to resort; so that now he was at a loss whither to direct his steps; for so unfitted did he feel himself for society, that he was very unwilling to seek for the hospitality of several friends, who he knew, however, would be very willing to afford it.

At last Pedro, who was very anxious to get housed in some place or other, intimated to his master that he had the honour of claiming as a relation an old lady who lived in a small house in the suburbs; that she was of the highest respectability, for her husband had held an office under government; and, indeed, she was apt rather to look down upon the number of poor relations who insisted on her acknowledging them as nephews, nieces, and cousins, to the sixth degree. Pedro, however, felt confident that, notwithstanding her high pretensions, she would be happy to receive, as a lodger in her house, a young nobleman so highly esteemed as his master; and he undertook, if Don Luis would ride as far, to assure him of a cordial reception, provided she had not, by any chance since he heard of her, departed this life, or from any other reason changed her residence. Luis very gladly acceded to Pedro's proposal, for he was fatigued both in body and mind, and he thought that, in so remote a part of the city, he should be better able to avoid the annoyances to which he must be subject in a more public situation.

As they reached the house Pedro had indicated, he looked up, and, to his great delight, beheld an old lady busily employed in knitting at the open window.

"There she is, Senhor Conde," exclaimed Pedro. "That is my good aunt, and as kind an old lady as ever lived, when nothing puts her out of her way."

The old lady, hearing horses stopping at her door, put her head out of the window to see what it could possibly mean, when Pedro, bowing most respectfully, exclaimed, "Ah! my good aunt, my master and I have come a long way to see you; now do not come down, I will run upstairs to explain matters;" and, leaping from his horse, he begged the Count to excuse him, while he performed his promise.

As may be supposed, he had no great difficulty in persuading the old lady to receive a gallant cavalier like Luis for her guest, and she forthwith hurried down to pay him due honour. Pedro, assisting his master to dismount, the hostess conducted him upstairs, when, begging him to be seated, after various little complimentary speeches, she set about preparing a repast for him: with the aid of Pedro, and a little damsel, her maid-servant, a room also was made ready for his reception.

By the time these arrangements were completed, it was too late to think of going out in search of his friends, and he was glad when he was at length able to retire to his room. He threw himself on his bed, but not to sleep; the images of the past haunted him, and sad forebodings for the future. He thought of the danger to which Theresa was exposed, indefinite, and therefore more to be dreaded, and of the aid which he had pledged himself to afford, by means uncertain, perhaps criminal. He knew full well the passionate and fierce disposition of the young Marquis of Tavora, and that no fears for the consequences would make him hesitate in proposing any measures which might rescue his wife, or, at the worst, vindicate his honour.

Early the following morning, Luis despatched Pedro to inform his young friend, Jozé de Tavora, of his arrival; for, remembering the warnings of the Minister and of his mysterious friend, Senhor Mendez, he was unwilling to become more intimate with the rest of the family than was necessary, and therefore refrained from visiting at their house except on occasions when custom required it.

Luis had just taken his morning meal, when the young Tavora rushed into the room, and embracing him with affectionate warmth, exclaimed, "I lost not a moment, my dear Luis, in hastening hither, when I heard of your arrival. Say, you have come to aid us; you have come to join the noble cause of justice and honour, arrayed against the overbearing tyranny of the plebeian Minister, and his profligate tool—the so-called King of Portugal?"

"I came to offer my aid, if necessary, in rescuing my cousin Theresa from the persecutions of the King," answered the young Count; "but in no other scheme ought I to engage, nor will I; for I feel assured, that maintaining the peace and happiness of the people at large is of paramount importance, to avenging any slight, which we nobles, as a body, may conceive ourselves to have suffered. Beforehand, therefore, I warn you not to attempt to induce me to engage in any enterprise which will in any way cause disorder or bloodshed in the country."

"What! can you, one of the purest of our class, speak thus?" exclaimed the young Tavora. "Is not our honour paramount to every other consideration? Surely we ought not for a moment to weigh it with the interests of the base plebeians,—the scum of the earth,—wretches beneath our notice. In that creed have I been educated, and in that will I die."

"'Tis a creed, my young friend, which, put in practice, has already injured us, and will finally drag us all to destruction," answered Luis. "Let us endeavour to maintain our position in the scale of society, as did our noble ancestors, by being the foremost in every danger, the most upright, and the most honourable; then no one will venture to molest or insult us; but, by following any other course, we may, in a moment, find ourselves hurled from our high posts, and trampled on in the dust damp with our gore."

"In Heaven's name, my dear Luis, where did you gain these extraordinary ideas?" cried his visitor. "I did not suppose such could exist in the brain of any fidalgo in Portugal."

"They are taught by the study of every history, from the earliest times to the present day," answered Luis, smiling at his own vehemence. "But we will not now discuss the subject. Tell me, where are Donna Theresa and your brother?"

"She is at their palace; but he,—you know his temper,—is not there. He is offended at her conduct, and vows he will not return to her till she promises never again to exchange a word with the King. This she, being equally firm, will not do; so that they are not exactly on the best terms for husband and wife; but I suppose that they will, before long, get tired of being separated, and so make up their quarrel, as other people do."

"Alas! I regret to hear this," said Luis. "She is thus left exposed to the persecutions of the King."

"So I tell my brother," interrupted the young Tavora; "but do not speak of it—my heart burns when I think on the subject. Will you come with me to-night where you can meet him, and you may be able to persuade him what is right to be done? He knows, perfectly well, since his quarrel with the King, that he hates him; so that he has thought it wiser not to appear anywhere in public, and is, at present, in a place of concealment, whither I will conduct you. Will you go with me this evening?"

Luis, without making further inquiries as to the spot where the young Marquis was concealed, promised to visit him, in company with his brother. After some time more spent in conversation, the younger Tavora agreed to call for Luis, with a horse for his use, desiring that Pedro might be in attendance, to take charge of it, while they approached his brother's abode on foot. These arrangements having been made, his visitor took his departure; leaving Luis, for the rest of the day, to his own solitary meditations; for he felt utterly averse to moving from the house, and mixing with the noisy and careless crowd in the city below. He attempted to read, but in vain, so he threw his book aside, and paced the room for many hours, unable to concentrate his thoughts on one point. He could not divest himself of the feeling, that some indefinite disaster was hanging over him, yet that he wanted the power to avoid it. It is a sensation we have often ourselves experienced, although our forebodings have seldom, if ever, been accomplished; until, at last, we have learned to consider them as arising more from the effects of past sorrows, fears, or annoyances, than from any prescience of forthcoming events. Luis, however, had many reasons for his feelings, both from the past and for the future. His spirits were lowered by many griefs; the loss of her he loved—his father's death—the destruction of his property,—and he was too well aware that many dangers surrounded him; for, from the language his young friend had used, in the course of their conversation, he could not help suspecting that the younger Marquis was meditating some desperate plot against the government, if not against the King himself; nor could he tell how far he might find himself compromised by his connexion with him.

Daylight had nearly departed, when Jozé de Tavora, with a servant on a second horse, rode up to the house.

"Up, mount, my dear Count!" he exclaimed, as soon as Luis appeared at the door. "I have brought you a good steed, and we have no time to lose. Our servants must follow in the best way they can on foot, and keep us in sight. I will tell you whither lies our course as we ride along."

Luis, accordingly, desiring Pedro to follow, mounted a dark stout Spanish horse, provided for him; and at an easy pace, the fastest, however, that the execrable roads would allow of, they wound their way for a considerable distance through the outskirts of the city, to the north of Belem, passing beneath one of the vast arches of the grand aqueduct, which had, fortunately, escaped the devastating effects of the earthquake with but slight injury, and then, turning to the left, they approached the river to the westward of the castle.

"Whither are we going?" asked Luis. "Are we near your brother's abode?"

"We are yet a long way from it," answered his companion, "though we go not much further on horseback. I ought to have told you, that a considerable part of our journey must be by water; yet, as it is a fine night, that will be by far the most agreeable mode of conveyance, if you do not object to it."

Luis assenting to the proposal, they soon after reached a sheltered spot beneath a high wall, where, dismounting, they left their horses in charge of the servants, and proceeded on foot to the river's side.

The bank was in that spot high and steep, so that they were obliged to descend by a narrow and winding path to reach the water, and when there, no boat was to be seen, and not a sound was heard but the gentle ripple of the tide upon the shore, or the sudden splash of some finny inhabitant of the stream, as it leapt up from its limpid home. Jozé de Tavora, after waiting impatiently for some minutes, gave a low whistle; the silence still continued unbroken,—he again gave a second and third signal, when it was answered, at a short distance from where they stood, and a boat shot from behind a little promontory which jutted out into the river. The crew, on seeing two persons, seemed in some doubt whether they ought to approach, but the young Tavora again signalising to them, they pulled in without hesitation.

"Why were you not waiting at this spot, as I ordered you?" he asked.

"We came here first, senhor," answered one of the two men in the boat; "but we saw two or three persons on the shore, who seemed watching us, so we pulled round beneath yonder point, where we could be out of sight."

"You did well, though they were, probably, but chance idlers. Come, Luis, we will embark," he added, stepping into the boat, followed by his companion. "Now, my men, bend to your oars!" he said, taking the helm, and guiding the bark down the stream.

It was a lovely night, though so late in the year: the air was soft and balmy, the water smooth as a polished mirror, reflecting the bright and glittering stars which shone from the deep blue sky. The scene and hour had a soothing effect on the spirits of Luis, as he leaned back in the boat, and gave himself up to their calm influence. Now and then they would pass through a shoal of fish, sporting on the surface, their bright scales shining in the light of some lustrous star. Far off, too, the song of the fisherman would rise in the still air, as he sallied forth to his night of toil; and in the distance might be seen the sails of the larger fishing-boats, as they slowly glided up with the current, or the canvas of some vessel looming large through the obscurity, like some giant phantom of the deep. Not a word was exchanged for some way; and at length, when Jozé de Tavora broke the silence, by addressing his friend, their conversation was carried on in low whispers, which could scarcely have been heard by the men who rowed the boat. After rowing about two miles, at a sufficient distance from the shore to be unnoticed from thence, the boat's head was directed again towards it, at a spot where the shattered remains of some building could be seen rising against the sky. Luis demanded of his companion whither they were now going.

"To yonder ruins," he said, "of a summer residence of the good monks of the convent of San Bento. It was once a lovely spot, but the sea destroyed the grounds, and the earthquake shattered the walls, though there are still some chambers which escaped total destruction."

He had got thus far in his description, when the boat ran alongside the remains of a quay and jetty, from whence the friars used to embark on their fishing expeditions, or when they chose the water as a means of conveyance to the city. Stepping on shore with Luis, he ordered the men to wait their return, and led the way towards the ruins, which were at some little distance from the landing-place. They proceeded among heaps of walls overthrown, shattered pillars, formed to support the graceful vines which overshadowed the long cool walks, and fragments of broken statues, which had ornamented the sides of the tanks, once stocked with fish; but the flood had uprooted the vines, and carried away the aqueducts which supplied the tanks. Passing beneath an archway, once forming the entrance to the convent, and winding through several passages open to the sky above, they arrived at a small door, through the chinks of which a light streamed forth. The young Tavora knocked three times without hesitation, at the same time mentioning his name, and begging to be admitted.

"You will find more persons here than you expect," he said to Luis, during the time which elapsed before the door was opened; "and many whom you will be surprised to meet in this place; but they are all friends of my family, who have come hither to listen to the exhortations of a holy and pious man, who has resided here for some time past, concealed from the persecutions of those who hate him for his virtue and zeal for religion."

"I thought we had come hither to see your brother," answered Luis. "If there are strangers here, whom I may not wish to meet, I will wait outside in the garden till they have departed, or till he can come to meet me."

"There are none you can object to meet," eagerly responded Jozé de Tavora. "See, the door opens. Come, you must enter, or our friends will be disappointed, and look upon you in the light of an enemy." And, taking the arm of Luis, he led him forward a few steps through the portal, when the door was suddenly closed behind them.

"Your blessing, Father," said Jozé de Tavora, to a tall figure, in the black habit of the order of Loyola, who stood before them, holding a lamp in his hand.

"You have it, my son," answered the deep-toned voice of the Jesuit Malagrida. "And blessed are all they who follow my counsels! Who is your companion?" he added, in a different tone. "I recollect not his face among the millions I have known."

Jozé de Tavora explained who Luis was, and that he had brought him to see his brother.

"My blessing on his head, if he joins our righteous cause!" exclaimed Malagrida.

While this conversation was taking place, Luis looked round the chamber in which he so unexpectedly found himself. It was low and vaulted, the roof being supported by rough stone pillars, and had, apparently, formed a capacious cellar to the not over-abstemious brethren of San Bento. Some rude attempts had been made to convert it into both an habitation and a chapel, it would seem; for great was the surprise of Luis to observe, at the further end, a rough altar, on which lights were burning before a figure of the Virgin, and a number of people seated on benches on each side of it; others, standing about in knots, and conversing, their glittering swords and rich dresses forming a strange contrast to the ruined and sombre appearance of the chamber. He had just finished this slight survey, when one of them, rising and advancing towards him, he perceived the young Marquis of Tavora. The latter, giving him an embrace, exclaimed, "I am, indeed, grateful for the favour you do me by coming here, though prepared for it by a message my brother sent me; and I must rejoice that there is another partisan added to the cause of honour and the privileges of the nobles."

"I certainty, when I promised your brother that I would visit you, did not expect to find you in so strange a place as this, and with so many companions," returned Luis.

"As for my abode, it is one selected by the Father Malagrida, where no one has ever thought of coming to search for him; so I was advised to share it with him; and for my companions, they are my nearest relations and friends, so do not be afraid of them," answered the Marquis, in an offended tone.

As he finished speaking, the Father Malagrida addressed them. "Come, my sons," he said, "let us not tarry here, at the portals of my abode, but straightway join the goodly company who are called together to hear my words, and to consult about the welfare of our holy Church."

Having thus delivered himself, he led the way to the further end of the vault, followed by the young men; for, though Luis felt that he had been unfairly seduced into associating with persons whom he more than suspected were met together for some unlawful purpose, it was now, he thought, too late to withdraw. As they approached the party, who were all in earnest conversation together, Luis, to his still greater surprise, perceived a lady among them, in whom he recognised the elder Marchioness of Tavora. She was the only female among the party; but there were present, besides many members of her own family, several nobles of the highest rank, and dignitaries of the Church, with a few of inferior grades in society, attached to the houses of the fidalgos, and whose only rule of action was their masters' will. With many of the persons assembled Luis was already acquainted; and, as he advanced among them, they rose to receive him, and welcome his return to Lisbon. The Marchioness was most particular in her attentions, thanking him for the interest he took in the welfare of her sons, and assuring him that she should be for ever grateful for what he had done.

"Why have you brought me here?" said Luis to Jozé de Tavora, as soon as he could escape from the Marchioness, and had led his young friend on one side of the vault, out of hearing of the rest of the party. "Had you forewarned me of whom I was to meet, I might have acted as I thought right."

"I brought you here to give you an opportunity of listening and judging of the truth," was the answer. "Had I told you that you were to meet some of the first nobles in the land, who were engaged in forming plans to protect their honour, their lives, and fortunes from destruction, you might have answered that you would engage in no conspiracy; and as I was not at liberty to reveal any of their intentions, I could not have reasoned with you. But now you are here, stay and listen to what is proposed; if you like it not, you can depart without hindrance, for I will answer for your honour."

"I will remain, to convince those assembled here that I will not betray their place of meeting; but, except for the purpose of protecting my cousin, will I engage in no scheme whatever. My refusal arises from no fear of danger to myself individually, but from a dread of the consequences to the nation at large. Inform your friends of my opinions, and I will here await the result."

"Such is unnecessary; they will ask none to join them who do not willingly enter into their projects; so come, we will return to our friends; for hark! the prophet is addressing the assembly, and when you have heard him, you will be convinced that his words are those of inspiration."

Although there was, at that time, a more general belief in prophets and saints, than there is, in Portugal at all events, in the present day, Luis was surprised to hear his young friend profess faith in the inspired character of a man whom he had learned to look upon as a madman, if not an hypocritical impostor; but still greater was his astonishment when he discovered that the whole assembly placed the most implicit confidence in his declarations. On one side of the altar a sort of pulpit had been formed of rough boards hastily nailed together, and into it Malagrida now mounted, stretching forth his hands to bless his congregation. A complete silence ensued, and for some minutes he refrained from speaking, to cause a greater effect; at length he commenced, in a slow and impressive tone, to deliver a discourse, of which we shall venture only to give a few sentences.

"You have assembled here, my children, to listen to the words of one who has propagated our holy religion even in the far corners of the world, but who now, through the wickedness and impiety of the rulers of this hapless country, is compelled, like a fox, to burrow beneath the earth, and to hide his head from the bright light of heaven. Will you—can you—allow sin to be thus triumphant? Will you stand calmly by, and see our holy religion trampled in the dust, your altars profaned, your priests degraded?"

"No! no! we will die to protect them," answered several voices.

He continued, without noticing the interruption. "Will you allow all you have considered sacred to be despised, and yourselves to be insulted by the tyrant and his Minister?"

"We will not! we will not!" repeated the voices again.

"Hear me, then. Even now a decree is about to come forth to banish all the true priests of the order of Jesus from the land. A few days, and the impious command will be executed, if our rulers are not stopped in their heaven-accursed career of crime. What say the sacred writings? 'The judges of the earth stand up, and the rulers take counsel together, against the Lord, and against his anointed.' Such do our rulers, and they will not listen to the words of warning. Thrice has the King been warned, and he has turned a deaf ear to our words; still does he persist in his wickedness. We have, then, but one course to pursue—to avenge our wrongs, and right our grievances. Boldly I speak it, for I speak what is just, what Heaven demands at our hands—the King must die! and blessed is the man by whose hands the deed is done!"

The speaker paused, and at these words fear and trembling took possession of his infatuated audience. They doubted not that he spoke the words of inspiration, but each man feared lest he himself should be called upon to perform a deed which he had longed to see executed by the hands of another. At last the young Marquis of Tavora, with much of his mother's boldness, mingled with superstition, arose and exclaimed, "I have been the most grievously wronged, and I will undertake to avenge the cause of all. I will lead a chosen band of followers into the very heart of the palace, while others surround the building; and, while the King deems himself most secure, I will accuse him of the foul injury he has done me, and slay him on the spot. I will teach a lesson to all his successors, and sovereigns shall learn to tremble, who, presuming on their power and station, dare to insult the dearest rights and honour of their subjects."

Some of the younger conspirators applauded the speech of the Marquis, but the older men shook their heads in disapprobation, and were silent, till Malagrida took upon himself to answer. "Alas! my son," he said, "such plans are hopeless! By force alone can force oftentimes be repelled, but never thus openly attack power. To ensure success, commence with secrecy and caution. Let not your enemy suppose that you feel aught but friendship for him, and then strike him unawares, when none can know who did the deed: the poisoned bowl, the dagger, or the pistol, are far more certain means than such as you propose. As the injuries our foe inflicts are silent and secret, so, does Heaven decree, must be the retributive punishment."

To these observations the older men more cordially assented, but no one proposed any definite plan. An air of doubt and uncertainty hung over all who were present, except the Marchioness, her eldest son, and Malagrida. Many whom they expected had not arrived; others had refused to join them till their plans were successful, and all danger was passed; these last were very numerous, and, in this case, the wisest part of the nobility; "others," they reasoned, "will be found to risk the peril, while we shall equally secure the profit, if they succeed."

"Why came not the Marquis of Tavora with his lady?" asked one of his neighbour.

"He knows not of our designs," was the answer. "It is supposed he would not approve of them, and his sons fear to confide them to him."

"The Duke of Aveiro ought to have been here long ago," said another noble. "He told me that he purposed coming, and no common cause would, I am sure, detain him."

"On the former night we met he seemed eager in our enterprise," responded a fourth. "Can he have been suspected and apprehended? I always fear that vigilant-eyed plebeian—nothing escapes him."

"Can the Duke, fearing detection, have repented of his intentions, and, perhaps, informed the Minister of our designs?" observed one who was cynically inclined, and had ever hated the Duke. "It would be a certain way of securing his own pardon, though at the expense of a few of us."

"In mercy, do not put such dreadful thoughts into our heads—you quite unnerve me," said the person he spoke to. "I wish I had refused to join the enterprise."

"That is a pity, seeing you will probably share the fate of all, if it miscarries," answered his friend. "Do, my dear Count, *pretend* to be brave, or you will frighten the rest. You will not feel comfortable, I fear, till it has succeeded."

"You offer rather doubtful consolation. I wish some one would propose himself to kill our tyrant quietly—it would save much discussion."

"Likely enough. What, and if he happens to have a secret enemy among us, who might be tempted to turn traitor, how completely he would be within his power without risking the safety of the rest? No, no; we have, doubtless, a good many fools among us, but not quite so great a one as you suppose."

"You are in a severe humour this evening, my friend."

"Have I not cause for it, when I have heard so much nonsense spoken, and our enterprise not advanced since the first day it was proposed? It provokes me: I shall lose my South American property before anything is accomplished, I very clearly perceive, so I think of embarking for France to await the result."

Such was the style of conversation carried on in all directions round Luis, so that he began to entertain hopes that the conspirators would abandon intentions which he considered, notwithstanding the assurances of the prophet, to be both highly criminal, and dangerous in the extreme.

All were looking for the arrival of the Duke of Aveiro, who, having more to gain by the destruction of the King, was the most active leader in the conspiracy; but, after waiting a considerable time longer, some of the party expressed their impatience to depart, and the Duke came not at all.

The assembly at length broke up, Malagrida first performing a short religious ceremony at the altar, dismissing them with his blessing.

Before Luis took his departure with his young companion, he addressed the Marquis. "Tell me," he said, "how can I aid you in the object for which I came here? How and where is Theresa?"

"Speak not of her, my friend," exclaimed the young husband, with vehemence. "I live but for revenge! Farewell! I ask you not to share our dangers; but you will pardon what you look upon as a crime, when you know the cause which has driven me to desperation."

Jozé de Tavora took Luis's arm. "It is time to go," he said. "Follow me closely, for the night is dark, and you know not the intricacies of the path. We will still trust to the river, though no one else ventures on it. The rest have departed in different ways and directions, and my lady mother passes the night at a house at no great distance, whither my brother will conduct her."

On emerging into the open air, they found the night to have become excessively dark, there being no moon, and a thin mist obscuring the brightness of the stars; but they soon sufficiently recovered the use of their eyes, to be able to find their way among the ruins towards the landing-place, where the boat was waiting. Not a breath of wind stirred the silent night air, their footfalls alone being heard as they proceeded through the ruined garden.

Just as they were about to step into the skiff, not having exchanged a word on their way, for fear any foe might be lurking in the neighbourhood, Jozé de Tavora fancied he heard a shout in the distance: they listened attentively, but it was not repeated; and at length, being persuaded that it was but fancy, they took their seats in the stern of the boat, the crew pulling rapidly up the stream, which was now in their favour. So dark was the night, that they had much difficulty in seeing their way, and had they not kept close in with the banks, they would have found it nearly impossible to steer a direct course.

Luis was silent; for, though unwilling to blame his young companion, he felt that the latter had not acted towards him with openness and honour. Of this Jozé de Tavora seemed aware, as he was the first to speak. "Luis, I must crave pardon for what I have done; for I now see, when too late, that I ought not to have led you blindfold into the society we have just quitted, which seems not to your taste; but say, will you forgive me?"

He spoke in so deprecating a tone, that Luis could not resist his petition; and, giving him his hand, in token of forgiveness, assured him that he believed his motives, at all events, had been good.

After nearly an hour's row, they reached the spot where they embarked, and near which they found Pedro and the other servant waiting with their horses,—Jozé de Tavora insisting on accompanying his friend to his lodgings. Thus so much time passed, that the first streaks of dawn were in the sky before the latter was seen to enter the gates of his father's Quinta at Belem.

Volume Three—Chapter Eight.

We left that very respectable personage, Senhor Policarpio, entertaining two friends in the garden of the Duke of Aveiro's residence. As it grew dark, he invited them again into the house to partake of a supper he had prepared for them. After the repast was finished, and he had plied his guests well with wine, he opened an attack which he had been meditating.

"So the Marquis complains that he has been insulted by that low-born villain Teixeira, and that the King will give him no redress," he began. "Now, that is what I call not acting in a kingly way; and I think your master very ill-treated."

"Your observation is a just one, Senhor Policarpio," answered Manoel. "And this is not the only instance in which he has been ill-treated. He applied to be created a duke the other day, and the King, without any reason, refused his request, to the great indignation of the Marchioness, who had determined to enjoy the title."

"Ah! if the Marquis would but follow the advice of my master, he might easily be made a duke," said Senhor Policarpio; "but that he will not do, talking instead about his loyalty, and all that sort of nonsense. Now listen, my friends. It strikes me that we might arrange these affairs ourselves, without consulting our masters till the work is done, when they will reward us accordingly. We are not likely to be made dukes and counts, but we are certain to get as many purses of gold as we want, which are far better than all the titles in the world without them. As we well know, there are certain plots and conspiracies hatching, which will, if not discovered, all end in smoke. Now, when I have an object in view in which I wish to succeed, I entrust it to no one more than is necessary. You feel assured that your master would reward you, if you were to punish this Teixeira for his insolence; and I am ready to aid you, on condition that you speak to no one on the subject, or it will be certain to fail. This is my plan:—Teixeira drives out every night in his carriage (vain as he is of it) to some place or other. I propose to watch for him, mounted on good horses, when, as he passes by, we will fire into his carriage, and cannot fail to kill or wound him severely. We may then, favoured by the darkness, easily escape before any alarm is given, and you may then claim a reward from your master. For me, it will be sufficient to know that I have served you; besides that, I owe him a debt of vengeance on my own account."

The brains of the two servants being by this time considerably confused by liquor, they willingly assented to Senhor Policarpio's proposal, not having sufficient judgment left to perceive that he had probably other motives for the deed than their interests, or his own wish for revenge.

"Well, then, my friends, there is no moment like the present, when work is to be done," he continued. "I have notice that Teixeira will this night visit a certain house; and I propose to waylay him on his return to the palace, and pay him his deserts. Are you agreed?"

"Agreed! agreed!" exclaimed both the men. "We are ready to do anything so honourable a gentleman as yourself proposes."

"You flatter me, gentlemen, by your good opinion. We will not dream on the work, then—this night it shall be done. I must tell you, another friend of mine will join us; but do not speak to him, as he wishes not to be known. We will divide into two parties. You, Manoel, must accompany my friend; and you, Antonio, keep by my side; then, if the first shots do not take effect, the second ambush will be more fortunate. Come, gentlemen, we will prepare for our expedition. I have horses in readiness at a stable in the neighbourhood; for I fully counted on your assistance. Another glass to our success. Nerve your arms for the deed, and it cannot fail!"

It was an intensely dark night, when three men, with masks on their faces, (for a guilty countenance would fain hide itself even from the sight of Heaven,) sallied forth from the Quinta of the Duke of Aveiro. They walked some way, when, stopping before the door of a low, solitary building, the principal of the party applied a key to the lock, and, all entering, they found three steeds ready saddled. Without uttering a word, they led forth the horses, the last closing the door; and, mounting, they rode back in the direction they had come. They had not proceeded far when they encountered a fourth horseman, dressed completely in black, with a black mask, and a horse of the same hue.

"Who goes there?" said the principal of the three, in a low voice.

"A friend of religion," was the answer, in the same low tone.

"'Tis well," said the first speaker. "This is the friend I expected," he continued, turning to one of his companions. "Do you, Manoel, accompany him. Fire, when he fires, and keep close to his side. We will all again meet at the stables, where we will leave our horses, and return on foot to the Quinta. Onward, my friends, to our work."

The stranger, accompanied by him who was addressed as Manoel, now separated from the other two, both parties, however, proceeding by different routes toward the upper part of Lisbon, to the neighbourhood of a house called the Quinta da Cima, which lay directly in the way between the residence of the young Marchioness of Tavora and the royal palace.

Antonio and his companion, who, as our readers may have suspected, was no other than Senhor Policarpio, rode on in silence whenever they passed any houses, the former, who was of a more timid disposition than his fellow-servant, already repenting of the deed he had undertaken to perform.

"Hist!" he said, drawing in his rein as they were passing between some of the high blank walls with which that part of Lisbon abounds. "Are you certain there is no one following us? Methought I heard a horse's footsteps."

"On, on," muttered his companion with an oath. "The more reason for speed."

They proceeded a few paces further, when the other again stopped.

"I am sure I heard the sounds again," he whispered.

"Cursed fool, his cowardice will spoil all," thought Policarpio. "'Tis but the echo of our own horses' feet, friend," he said aloud. "Fear not; 'tis too late now to draw back, and the work must be done."

They again rode on, encountering no one on their way; for, at that late hour, and in those solitary roads, few ventured out, if they could avoid it, and then only in large parties, with servants and torches, to guard against the daring marauders who infested them, committing every atrocity with impunity. They at length observed a number of people advancing towards them with torches, the flames throwing a lurid glare on their figures and the surrounding walls; but Policarpio, desiring his companion to follow, turned down a lane on one side, till they had passed by. Riding a little further on, Antonio again vowed he heard the sounds of horses' feet. Policarpio listened.

"Yes," he said, "'tis our friends—we are near the spot agreed on."

As he spoke, four horsemen were perceived emerging from the gloom towards them.

"How is this?" exclaimed Antonio in a tone of alarm. "There were but two!"

"They are more of our friends," was the answer.

"What, all enemies of Teixeira?"

"All, and trusty men. Speak not again, friend. We come to act, not to talk," whispered Policarpio.

The six horsemen rode on at a slow pace, so as to allow their horses' hoofs to emit the least possible sound, till they arrived at a deep archway, into the recesses of which not a ray of light penetrated. Here the stranger, in sable garments, with his companion, Manoel, took their posts, their horses' heads turned towards the road, so as to sally forth at a moment's notice. This was the ambush nearest the residence of the young Marchioness of Tavora. A little further on, a lane between high walls turned off to the right, and towards it Policarpio and Antonio directed their course; the two other unknown horsemen passing further on to another place of concealment.

"Halt here, my friend," said Policarpio; "we shall not have long to wait; this is the best place we could have selected. As soon as the deed is done, follow me down the lane, and we will make a circuit to the Quinta."

"How is it there are so many engaged in the work; I thought we three only were to be privy to it?" observed Antonio.

"The man has many foes," was the laconic reply. "Now silence."

Slow seemed the hours of darkness to lag along over the heads of the intended assassins. It was a time of the most harrowing anxiety, of doubts and fears to them all. During the bright glare of day, or when excited by wine and conversation, they had contemplated the deed as a duty they were called on to perform; but now, on the silent watch, when the moment for action was drawing on, they felt that they were about to commit a deed such as would, if discovered, hold them up to the execration of mankind. Darkness, which serves to cloak a crime from the eyes of others, reveals it to the startled conscience of the criminal in its native deformity. In vain each man sought to banish the voice which rung in his ear—Murder! murder!—but that mocking voice would not be silenced; and yet it was a useless warning, for each had resolved to do the deed, and now it was too late to fly; besides, when one would have done so, the thought of the reward to be reaped rose up in his mind, and determined him to persevere in spite of all consequences.

Policarpio listened eagerly for the expected sound of the carriage-wheels. "Ah! he comes," he muttered, as a low rattling noise at a distance was heard; and even he, cool and hardened villain as he was, felt his heart beat quicker, and he drew in his breath at the thought of what he was about to do; he felt almost a relief from suffering as the noise died away in a different direction. The clear ringing sound from the clock of a neighbouring church now struck; he listened attentively to mark the hour—one, two; he counted on—ten, eleven, and no more. He must have been mistaken; he thought it was much later. Another dreadful hour of suspense must elapse, for their intended victim was not expected to pass till nearly twelve o'clock, and he was sometimes much later. His doubts were soon set at rest, for another clock, at a greater distance, now gave forth the hour of eleven. Thus they waited, sometimes supposing that their enemy had not paid his usual visit; that he might have taken another road, or that, by some mysterious chance, he had been forewarned. There was one among those midnight assassins whose fierce and fiery temper could ill brook this delay, and, as he sat on his horse beneath the arch, he gnashed his teeth with impatience, and grasping a pistol in his hand, longed for the moment to use it. Twelve o'clock struck, and scarcely had the sound from the last stroke of the bell died away on the calm midnight air, when a carriage was heard rapidly approaching. Each of the assassins gathered in his rein, and more firmly grasped his weapons to prepare for action. There could be now no further doubt—another minute and their victim would be in their power!

Onward came the carriage. It approached the dark archway; it had scarcely passed it, when the stranger in black, followed by Manoel, dashed forward, discharging his pistol at the head of the postilion; but the piece missed fire, as did that of his companion.

"Curses on the weapon," he cried, raising his carabine, as the carriage dashed by; he fired, but the ball took no effect.

"Forbear! forbear!" shouted the postilion, as he drove on; "'tis the King you are firing at!"

He had just uttered the words, when Policarpio and his companion rode furiously towards him; the former discharging a pistol, but without effect. On their approach, he was seen to turn rapidly round before Policarpio could come up with him, and to drive down a steep and rugged path, towards the river.

"Fire!" shouted Policarpio to his companion, as they galloped after the carriage. "Fire! or they will escape us!" and, at the same moment, both discharged their pieces at the back of the carriage. A loud cry was heard, but they could not further tell the effect of their shots, for the postilion, driving for his own life, as well as that of his master, if he had escaped destruction, urged on his mules at a furious pace beyond their reach, before they had time to reload their fire-arms.

"What shots are those?" cried a voice from a window above them. "Murder! murder!"

The sound struck terror into the bosoms of the guilty assassins; and, turning their horses, they galloped off from the spot, by the roads previously agreed on, fancying that they were closely pursued. Onward they dashed, the dying shriek of their victim ringing in their ears, mixed with unearthly sounds—it seemed like the mocking laughter of demons. But at that time they dreaded not the supernatural powers half so much as the anger of man; him they had made their enemy, and now detection was what they most feared. "Whoso sheddeth man's blood, by man shall his blood be shed," was the rigid law to which they had become amenable. No obstacles stopped them in their course. Their steeds, as if conscious of their masters' haste, leapt fearlessly over the fragments of ruins which, in many places, strewed the road. With bridle and spur their riders kept them up, for a fall would have thrown them into the power of their fancied pursuers. After making a considerable circuit, Policarpio and Antonio approached the stable where they were to leave their horses. Leaping from his horse, Policarpio opened the door of the stable, for they were the first arrived, and entered, ordering his companion to follow, and to take off the saddles from their steeds. Having placed the horses in their stalls, they waited the return of the other two, in anxious expectation. Some minutes elapsed, and yet they arrived not.

"Can they have been seized?" muttered Policarpio to himself; "if so, all is lost, and I must make my escape."

"We have made Teixeira pay dearly for his insolence," said Antonio Ferreira. "Think you he could possibly have escaped? We sent shot enough through the carriage to kill most men."

"Think you we should have run all this risk, and taken so much trouble, merely to kill a vile wretch as he is? But talk not of it again. We aimed at far higher game than he is; he may have been within, for it was his carriage; but it was not his paltry life we aimed at. It is the King we have killed!"

"Heaven pardon me!" exclaimed Antonio, in a trembling voice; "I thought not to have done such a deed!"

"Bah! this is no time for repentance," answered Policarpio. "What is the difference between one man's life and another's. You have done your master a greater service than you thought. But silence; some one may overhear us: the devil has quick ears."

They waited some time longer for their companions.

"I fear me, Manoel and your friend have been captured," whispered Antonio.

"If so, we shall to a certainty be betrayed; and in flight is our only chance of safety. Adeos! friend Antonio. I shall take one course, and you may take another. This country will be no longer a safe abode for either of us."

He went, as he spoke, to the door of the stable, and was about to hasten away, when he heard the sound of horses approaching, and directly after, the masked stranger, with Manoel, rode up. The former leaping to the ground, gave the reins to Policarpio. "I shall return homeward on foot," he said. "Let silence and discretion be your motto, my friends, and you are safe; you shall not be forgotten." And the stranger in black disappeared in the obscurity. Having relieved the horses from their saddles, and well fed them, Policarpio, with his two friends, returned to the Quinta.

As they entered a room, where lights were burning, they gazed at each other's pale and haggard countenances, on which guilt had already stamped its indelible marks. Conscience-struck, they scarce dared to speak of the deed they had done. Policarpio was the first to recover his usual daring.

"Come, my friends," he cried, filling for himself a bumper of wine, "banish these childish fears. Here's to the health of the next King who shall reign over us, and may he prove a better master than the last!" His companions endeavoured in vain to imitate his careless bearing, though, at his desire, they gladly pledged him.

"Ah!" he continued, "to-morrow the whole city will ring with this night's work! but no one will suspect us of the deed; and if they do, it matters little—we shall be above all fear of punishment."

"I wish it were not done," muttered Antonio; "I thought not to kill the King."

"I pray we have not missed doing so," answered Policarpio. "Curses on the weapons that failed when most required."

"Who were those who accompanied us," asked Manoel; "they seemed not of low degree?"

"That matters not, friend," responded Policarpio; "you will gain your reward, and seek not to know more."

Fearful of returning home, the two servants of the Marquis of Tavora threw themselves, overcome with fatigue, on the ground; but sleep visited not the murderers' eyes that night, their victim's shriek still rung in their ears, and their guilty hearts still beat with fears of the future.

Volume Three—Chapter Nine.

In a large saloon, richly furnished with every article of luxury then invented to minister to comfort or to pride, a young lady was seated on a sofa, before a table, on which had been thrown some fancy-work, with which she had been endeavouring to amuse herself. Her face was turned towards the ground, and while, her elbow resting on a cushion, she supported with her hand her small and delicately formed head, her other arm, of beautifully rounded proportions, hung carelessly by her side. A greyhound, of the graceful Italian race, and of pure fawn colour, was leaping up and licking her fingers, in a vain endeavour to attract her attention to himself. A lamp, which hung from the lofty ceiling, (for it was night,) cast a bright light upon her high and polished brow, from which her hair, as was the fashion, was drawn back; and it seemed that those long silken eyelashes of jet, which scarce concealed the lustre of her eyes, cast down though they were, were glistening with tears. One of her small feet, on which she wore a high-heeled satin shoe, resting on a cushion, an ankle of the most slender proportions was revealed. Her gown was of the richest flowered silk; her whole costume, indeed, notwithstanding that she was thus alone and sad, was arranged with the greatest elegance and care.

More than once a deep-drawn sigh escaped her, as her bosom heaved with agitated throbbings, which in vain she endeavoured to calm. Alas! lovely and young as she was, anguish was at her heart; for an accusing conscience was already at work within. Yet were others far more guilty—traitors doubly damned, who walked abroad in the well-sustained characters of honest men; while she, the betrayed, the abandoned wife, was left to mourn alone, or to receive the treacherous consolations of the subtle seducer, a licensed prey to the slanderous tongues of the malignant.

Time passed on, yet she stirred not from her position; nor did any of her domestics enter to interrupt her solitude. Her little dog had desisted from his attempts to gain her notice, and, weary with his gambols, had lain himself down at her feet, yet anxiously watching to win a look of encouragement from her eye. A clock, on a side table, had some time given notice that it wanted but two hours to midnight, when the Italian greyhound lifted his broad falling ears, half rising from his recumbent position. In a few seconds more, the noise which had first aroused him was reiterated, and, leaping up, he ran towards the door, uttering a shrill bark, again running back to his mistress.

"Lie down, my pretty Fiel, lie down," the dog instantly obeying her. "Ah! you will not too desert your mistress," she said, and relapsed into her former thoughtful mood.

The next moment the door opened slowly—so silently, that the lady did not look up; but her four-footed companion bounded forward, and leapt up fawningly on a gentleman who entered, of a dignified figure, dressed in a handsome costume, with a sword with a richly jewelled hilt by his side. He allowed his hand to caress the little dog, as he advanced close to the lady, and pronounced the name of "Theresa!"

The lady starting, with marked confusion, instantly rose, making one step towards him; while he, stooping low, took her unresisting hand with respectful devotion, imprinting on it a kiss: he then led her back to the sofa, and seated himself by her side, gazing with deep admiration on her lovely countenance, now softened by an expression of melancholy which rather increased than dimmed its attractions.

"Theresa, in spite of your commands, your wishes, I could not resist the temptations of my heart again to visit you. I come to entreat you to withdraw your cruel prohibitions, which must reduce me to despair," and the stranger knelt at the feet of Donna Theresa de Tavora.

"Rise, in mercy rise!" she exclaimed, with a trembling voice. "Your Majesty must not thus kneel to a subject."

"I will not rise till I know from those sweet lips that I am forgiven for my fault," answered the King, in a tone of tender passion; for he it was who thus took advantage of the forced absence of her husband to urge his criminal suit.

"Your Majesty has committed no fault which I have power to forgive," returned the Marchioness; "'tis I alone who am to blame for having dared to cherish a sentiment—for having owned that unhappy love which has attracted your Majesty hither.—Rise, Sire, I must not see you thus."

"Your words afford balm to my bruised heart," answered the King, in an enraptured tone, again placing himself by her side; but she gently withdrew her hand from his clasp.

"Your Majesty mistakes my meaning," she said, with a vain attempt at firmness; for her lips quivered as she spoke. "Hear me, my liege: it is not on my own account I speak; for myself, I have no longer the power to retract. You know too well the secret of my heart; from henceforth my lot is one of sorrow and remorse: but it is for your Majesty's sake, I beseech you to come hither no more. There is a danger in it which I may not—I dare not reveal, so terrible that I tremble at the thought alone."

"For your sake, sweet one, I would brave all danger," answered the King, with a gallant bow and a smile of incredulity; then suddenly changing his tone, he added, "Surely no one would venture to lift his arm against our person? Speak lady, does your husband meditate revenge, that we have more highly appreciated those matchless charms than himself?"

"Oh! do not ask me, my liege," exclaimed the unhappy lady. "My husband has always proved himself a loyal subject; and surely naught but the most aggravated offence would drive him to commit treason against your Majesty. I speak not of what I know, but my fears have raised up suspicions, perchance but phantoms of the brain, yet should I be far happier if I knew that you, my sovereign, would avoid the risk you run by pursuing one whose love may bring destruction on your head."

The King seemed dissatisfied with this answer, and the recollection of his Minister's assertions, that plots and conspiracies were constantly brewing, but were discovered and defeated by his sagacity, now recurred to his mind with full force. In his fear, he forgot the character of the lover he was playing. "You hint to me that you have suspicions of danger to my person; but you neglect to tell me how to discover and defeat it," he said, in a far different tone to that in which he had before spoken.

A woman is quick to perceive when the lordly heart of man begins to tremble with fear, and as Donna Theresa's discerning glance fell on the countenance of her royal admirer, for the first time a feeling nearly allied to scorn entered her breast: it was transitory, but it left an impression not easily effaced. She wished to warn, but she loved him the less that he was so easily alarmed. Such is woman. She will fondly cling to man—she will idolise him, in the full majesty of his power, even though he treat her as an inferior being, so that he exert that power to shield her from harm; but let him once show that he is equally alive with herself to the sensations of fear, which is cowardice in him, he at once sinks in her estimation to a level with herself, and she no longer regards him as her lord and protector.

The young Marchioness withdrew her eyes from the King, as she answered, "Pardon me, your Majesty, I spoke but of my own womanly fears, indefinite also, and perhaps groundless they are, yet, when once they had arisen in my bosom, I could not but speak them; then, if I possess your Majesty's love, do not press me further. Mine is a cruel, a hard duty to perform, yet for your sake, my King, I will not shrink from it. We must part now and for ever!"

"This is a tyranny, lovely lady, to which I cannot submit," exclaimed the King, his passion for the moment conquering his fears; "I should pine to death were I to be banished from your sight."

"Your Majesty possesses the hearts of many other ladies, who will console you for my loss," returned Donna Theresa, with a faint smile.

"What! 'tis but a fit of jealousy then!" thought the King. "No, lovely one, believe it not," he exclaimed aloud. "None have enchained my heart as you have done. Tell me that you will receive me to-morrow. Let my unswerving devotion, since you first honoured my Court with your presence, plead for me: let my ardent love be my excuse if I disobey your commands," and he again took her hand, and would have knelt, but rising from her seat, she drew back.

"Let me be the suppliant," she said. "Do not work upon the weakness of my sex, but exert your powerful judgment, my King, and ask yourself whether the pursuit you follow will repay you for risking both life and crown. No, Sire, it cannot; and therefore I once more beseech you to desist. I should indeed be doubly guilty were you to suffer for my sake."

Her voice faltered as she uttered the last words. Never had the young Marchioness looked so lovely as now that she stood with her hands clasped in an attitude of entreaty before the sovereign; the energy of her feelings throwing the rich blood into her hitherto pallid cheeks. It served unhappily to increase the King's admiration.

"It is useless, lovely Theresa, thus endeavouring to dissuade me; crown, life, all, I would risk to retain your love."

How easily are our most firm resolves turned aside,—how wonderfully is our judgment obscured, when passion intervenes! Man, with all his boasted power of intellect, in a moment sinks to the level of the soulless beings, who have but despised instinct for their guide. Let haughty man remember, secure, as he fancies himself in the strong armour of superior wisdom and calculating judgment, that he, too, is but mortal, and liable any instant to fall; and let him learn not to pass too harsh a judgment on those whose reason has been, perchance, but for one fatal moment overcome.

Donna Theresa's rising feelings of disdain, her fears for his safety, all other thoughts were forgotten at the King's last passionate declaration of his love; and, in a fatal moment, she consented no longer to persist in her determination to see him no more.

Having gained his point, the King soon after took his leave, with further protestations of unalterable constancy. On entering his carriage, in which Teixeira was waiting for him at the door, he threw himself back in his seat, exclaiming,—"Truly these women are wonderful creatures; changeable and uncertain in their tempers, as the vane on the topmast head! At one moment, my lovely Marchioness vowed she would enter a convent, or see me no more; and the next she was all love and affection. At one time, overcome by fears that her husband, I suppose, in a fit of jealousy, would attempt my life, and then forgetting all about the matter. The truth is, she loves me to distraction, when a woman is always full of alarms; but methinks none of my nobles are of that jealous disposition, that they would endeavour to revenge themselves for the honour I pay their wives."

"Few, perhaps, would harbour a treacherous thought against your Majesty; but all are not equally loyal," answered Teixeira. "The Tavoras are of a haughty and revengeful disposition, and it would be well to guard against them. I told your Majesty how, the other day, the old Marquis almost struck me in the palace, because, not seeing his Excellency approach, I was by chance standing in his way."

"What, do you truly think there is danger to be apprehended from them?" said the King, in a voice expressive of suspicion.

"I have no doubt of their disloyalty, if such a feeling can possibly be harboured by any against your Majesty," answered Teixeira.

"We must speak to Sebastiaö Jozé about it," said the King. "He will know well how to discover their feelings."

"Senhor de Carvalho is of my opinion, that they are not to be confided in," observed the confidant, who had thus the power, with a few words, to cast the taint of disloyalty on a whole noble race.

"I thought that Donna Theresa's fears arose from idle fancies, though I now suspect she had some foundation for her warnings," observed the King. "Sebastiaö Jozé, however, will discover whatever is wrong."

"The country is truly blessed, which possesses so good a King, and so wise a Minister," said the confidant.

"Which way are we going?" asked the King, looking out of the window, though, from the darkness, it was impossible to distinguish the road.

"I ordered him to drive the usual way, past the Quinta da Cima, and down by the Quinta do Meyo," answered Teixeira. "We are now near approaching the arch of do Meyo."

"'Tis a night, which an assassin would select to commit a deed of blood," said the King; the thought arising probably from his own fears, and from the observations of his servant. He had scarce uttered the words, when both were startled by a loud cry from the postilion, Custodio da Costa, and by seeing the flash of a pistol in front; the next instant two musketoons were discharged, the bright flashes from which lighted up the dark figures of two horsemen, urging their steeds towards the carriage, and several shot rattled past the window.

"Jesu Maria! what means this?" exclaimed the King, in a tone of terror.

"Foul treason! your Majesty," answered Teixeira. "We are betrayed."

"Stop, fool! or you die!" shouted one of the horsemen to the postilion; but he, disregarding the command, boldly galloped on his mules, crying out, "'Tis the King you are firing at!" when two other horsemen rushed out towards him from behind a high wall. With admirable presence of mind, though at great risk, he suddenly wheeled round the carriage.

"Stay, mad fool!" cried the assassins; but he heeded them not, and proceeded down a steep path to the left, nearly in the direction from whence he had come. Just as he had succeeded in turning, the report of two fire-arms was heard.

"Holy Virgin! I am slain!" ejaculated the King, falling backwards.

"My life shall preserve your Majesty's," cried Teixeira; and, with a heroism worthy of a better man, he forced his sovereign down into the bottom of the carriage, covering him to the utmost with his own person.

The urgency of the case added nerve to the postilion's arm, and keenness to his sight; for, avoiding all obstacles, he galloped on through streets where it would seem almost impossible that he could pass; which, as the chronicler observes, "was one of the wonderful and miraculous works performed on the unfortunate night of that most horrid and sacrilegious insult, in order to preserve the inestimable life of his most sacred Majesty, for the common benefit of these realms of Portugal."

The postilion, Custodio da Costa, (for he deserves that his name should be commemorated, on account of his gallantry and presence of mind), as soon as he perceived, after driving some way, that he was not followed, stopped the carriage, when his anxiety for his Majesty's safety was relieved by hearing his voice ordering him to proceed to the palace of the Marquis of Tancos, which was close at hand.

"Say not what has occurred," said the King to the postilion, as, descending from the carriage with Teixeira's aid, a cloak being thrown over his shoulder, he entered the palace of the Marquis.

The noble host, wondering at the cause of his being honoured by a visit from his sovereign at so unusual an hour, hastily rose from his bed, and entered the apartment into which his royal guest had been ushered.

The King, who was seated on a chair, was pale, but perfectly calm. "I have met with an accident, my friend, though I know not its extent," he said. "Send for Senhor Assiz, my chief surgeon, and speak to no one else of the affair."

The Marquis immediately sent to obey the commands of the King, who, on his return desired that his chaplain might forthwith be summoned; when, all retiring except the holy man, he returned thanks to the King of kings for the preservation of his life from so great a danger, and then confessed himself of his sins at the feet of the minister of the gospel.

In the mean time, the honest Custodio could not restrain his tongue from whispering to the servants of the Marquis, under promise of secrecy, an account of the dreadful occurrence; and they, of course, repeated it to their fellows; so that, before the morning dawned, the tale, with wonderful additions and alterations, was spread far and wide.

On the arrival of the surgeon, he and the Marquis, with Teixeira, were again admitted into the presence of the King, who had concluded his religious devotions; and the horror of all may be better conceived than described, when, his cloak being taken off, his breast and right arm were perceived covered with blood, which had trickled down over the rest of his dress. Without having uttered a word of complaint since he was wounded, the King now submitted himself into the hands of his surgeon, who, to the extreme satisfaction of his friends, pronounced the wounds to be unattended with danger, although they were very severe. Several slugs had entered his shoulder and breast, tearing away the flesh from the arm, but no other injury was committed on his person.

"Another mark of the miraculous interference of Divine Omnipotence," as again observes the chronicler, "on that night of horrors; for it cannot be in the common order of events, nor can it be in anywise ascribed to the casualty of accidental occurrences, that two charges of slugs, fired out of such pieces, should make their way through the narrow space of a carriage, without totally and absolutely destroying the persons who were in such a carriage."

The surgical operation having been performed, the King took leave of his host, and, accompanied by Teixeira and the surgeon, returned to the royal palace; the Marquis, however, with two of his servants, riding on each side of the carriage, to protect him from a further attack; nor did he quit his post till he had aided his sovereign to descend at the private door, where he was in the custom of alighting.

Pale and agitated with the alarming occurrences of the night, the King entered his private cabinet, where the sagacious Minister was still seated, deeply immersed in business. Carvalho rose as he entered, but started back with horror as he beheld the countenance of his sovereign. "What has happened to your gracious Majesty?" he exclaimed.

"Foul treason has been at work, Senhor Carvalho; though, through the mercy of Heaven, we have escaped destruction."

"Alas! then, my fears have not been groundless," said Carvalho; "and your Majesty will be convinced that there are men wicked enough to seek your life. Let me now entreat you to retire to your chamber, where, if it pleases your Majesty, you can detail all that has happened."

The King, when placed in bed, no one but the Minister, his surgeon, and Teixeira being admitted, gave an account to the former of what had occurred.

Carvalho listened with breathless anxiety, and well he might; his fame, his life, and power depended on the preservation of the King. A slight frown was on his brow, and a quivering movement might have been perceived on the upper of his closed lips, but he gave no other evidence of the thoughts passing within, till he answered, in a deep voice, "I will discover every one of the instigators and perpetrators of this atrocious outrage; and I ask but one condition of your Majesty:— Let me deal with the vile monsters as I may deem expedient, and all others shall learn such a lesson that, from thenceforth, your Majesty shall have no cause to dread a recurrence of such deeds. Will you, my Liege, grant this promise, which you owe to your own safety, and to the happiness of your people?"

"I give you the power you ask, my friend," said the King.

"Then am I satisfied," said the Minister.

Those words sealed the fate of the nobility of Portugal.

Volume Three—Chapter Ten.

On the morning after the events last described, a rumour was spread over Lisbon that something dreadful had happened; and people met each other in the streets with alarmed and inquiring countenances. Some said the King had been assassinated; others that his carriage had been overturned, and that he had been killed by the shock; others that he had died of apoplexy; while others, again, affirmed that he was still alive. The greater number, however, fully believed that he had been assassinated, several declaring that they had been aroused from their sleep in the dead of night, and looking out of their window's had perceived the dark figures of horsemen galloping along at a furious rate. By degrees, large crowds assembled in the neighbourhood of the palace, all anxious, from many different motives, to learn the truth; but the windows were kept closed, and not a person was seen to issue forth to give the information sought for.

"I wonder who will be king now," said a seller of lemonade, to a fisherman, who stood near him with large baskets of fish balanced at each end of a pole upon his shoulder. "Some say it will be Dom Pedro. I hope so; he encourages religion and processions, and they bring people abroad, and make them thirsty. Who'll buy my cool lemonade?"

"For my part, I care little: one king is as good as another," answered the fisherman. "What difference can it make to us who sits upon the throne? I hear the Duke of Aveiro is a likely man, and he is a friend of the Jesuits, who patronise fasting and fish-eating, which is all I have to look after. Fresh fish! alive and jumping!" he cried in a loud drawling tone, and passed on.

Men now inquired of each other who had committed the deed, if an assassination had been perpetrated; and several persons were seen moving among the crowds, spreading various reports. It was soon loudly declared that the Jesuits were the perpetrators of the outrage; while others whispered that the members of the Tavora family knew more about the affair than anybody else, for that their servants were the first to inform them that the King had been killed. Some, again, contradicted that report, declaring that one or two people had first heard of it when going, in the morning, to the Quinta of the Duke of Aveiro; and that Senhor Policarpio had not only affirmed that the King was dead, but that, if a certain noble Duke came to the throne, he would establish some more saints' days, encourage the ceremonies of the Church, and bull-fights, with unprecedented magnificence; that he would abrogate all taxes, and increase the pomp of their processions.

"The Duke will make an excellent king," whispered many; "he is so religious and so generous."

The friends of the Tavoras, though they credited the report of the King's assassination, stoutly denied that that noble family could be in any way implicated in so atrocious a crime. Unfortunately, however, for their assertions, a little humpbacked water-carrier declared that he knew every member of them perfectly well by sight, for that he had served the palace of the Marquis with water for many years, till it had been destroyed by the earthquake, and, while in the hall, had seen them go in and out a thousand times; and that he was confident he had seen young Jozé de Tavora, at day-break on that very morning, galloping towards Belem, from the upper part of Lisbon. This story gained rapid credence, and, as it spread from mouth to mouth, various additions were, of course, made to it; so that, before many minutes had passed, it was currently believed that the old Marquis of Tavora, with his two sons, had been encountered, with pistols in their hands, rushing from the spot where the King had been assassinated.

On an occasion like the present, our friend Antonio, the *soi-disant* cobbler, was certain not to be absent; and, unnoticed by any, in his working costume, he moved among the crowds, collecting the various reports with indefatigable industry; though, whenever he had an opportunity of putting in a word, he cautioned his hearers not to accuse any without clear evidence of their guilt, but that if the criminals were discovered, they would deserve condign punishment. Great, however, was the surprise of all, both the friends and enemies of the Tavoras, when the Prime Minister himself appeared at a window of the palace, and, lifting up his hand to impose silence, assured the populace that not only was the King alive, but that, as far as he could learn, no attempt whatever had been made against his august life; that the report had arisen, probably, owing to some words uttered by the postilion in his alarm, when the mules of his Majesty's carriage had taken fright; that, owing to the latter circumstance, the carriage had been thrown on one side, by which his gracious Majesty had received a slight injury in the arm.

"Long live the King!—viva, viva!" exclaimed the populace, on hearing this announcement; for they are ever ready to shout, it matters little to them for whom. The cry saluted the ears of the Duke of Aveiro, who, followed by Senhor Policarpio, rode up, with eager haste, the very first of the nobility, to make inquiries for his sovereign's health. His cheek, perchance, turned a shade more pale, as he heard the cry; but, dashing onward, regardless of the collected rabble, he dismounted at the gate of the palace, desiring to be admitted to the presence of the King. The Prime Minister alone received him in the audience-chamber, and, with marked suavity and courtesy, assured him that the King could not then receive him, but would do so on the earliest occasion.

"I came to offer my services to sally forth, with my attendants, in search of the vile perpetrators of the dreadful outrage committed against his Majesty," said the Duke.

"What! my lord Duke, do you give credence to the absurd story which has got about, that our beloved sovereign's life has been attempted?" said the Minister, with a bland smile. "Calm your apprehensions: I trust so black a traitor does not exist in Portugal."

The Duke was completely deceived.

"I indeed rejoice to hear that the report was unfounded, Senhor Carvalho," he answered; "and pray inform me the first moment his Majesty is sufficiently recovered from his indisposition to receive me, for I long to throw myself at his feet, and express my deep loyalty and devotion."

As the Duke took his leave, and was retiring, the Minister muttered, gazing sternly after him, "So humble and loyal already, my lord Duke? Your pride shall yet be brought lower than you think of!"

The nobility now flocked in numbers to the palace, some, perhaps, with a hope that the report might prove true, others with fears for the consequences, and, among them, the Marquis of Tavora drove up in his carriage. Carvalho received him with the most respectful courtesy, assuring him of the King's regard; the frank expression of the Marquis's countenance setting at fault the sagacity of the Minister, if he had entertained any suspicions of his loyalty.

"Ah, my lord Marquis, it would be happy for other countries if they possessed no worse traitors than live in Portugal!" observed the Minister. "By-the-bye, you made an application to his Majesty for a ducal title, not long ago, and I heard the King regretting he had then refused you, but observing, that he now considered your services in India entitled you to the rank. He does not forget his friends."

"I am grateful for his Majesty's recollection of my wishes. I shall esteem the honour greater as a gift from him," answered the Marquis.

"I shall have much pleasure in reporting what your Excellency says," returned the Minister, as the Marquis, pleased with the idea of at length having his request acceded to, took his leave, with a less haughty air than was his custom.

"If the report I have just heard, and my own suspicions, are correct, that man is an admirable hypocrite," thought the Minister. "He will be a difficult person to deal with; but I think I have lulled his fears, if he entertained any."

"I regret that his Majesty cannot see you to-day, but you are one of the first he will receive," said the Minister to the Marquis d'Alorna, who then entered. "I trust your lovely daughter is well, for whom both the King and Queen entertain the most respectful regard?"

His hearer, who could not be otherwise than fully convinced of the truth of his words, answering briefly, retired.

What golden opinions Sebastiaö Jozé de Carvalho that day won from all classes of men! It was one of difficulty, though of triumph, to him; for he felt that he was now fully establishing a power no future events could shake.

He did not, however, use the same style of language towards all. When the King's favourite, Marialva, appeared, he drew him aside.

"I know, my dear Marquis, that you can thoroughly be trusted," he said. "It behoves all true friends of our gracious sovereign's to be prepared for his protection. He would see you, but it would excite jealousy in others. He has been wounded, though, under the grace of Heaven, not severely; and I leave you to judge whether by traitors or not. We must exert ourselves to discover and bring them to punishment, even if they are our brothers or dearest friends. Yet speak not your suspicions to any."

Marialva promised to follow Carvalho's advice, and left him, with a conviction that he was the most sagacious of ministers, and the most attached servant of the King.

At last the young Count d'Almeida appeared, to make the usual inquiries, and to express his sorrow at the King's accident.

"I am glad to see you again at Court, for you have been long a truant," said Carvalho. "Should you wish for employment, I can now better fulfil the promise I made long ago, to give you some post worthy of your talents."

Luis expressed his gratitude and willingness to serve the state in any capacity for which he was fitted.

"I am glad to hear you say so," answered the Minister, adding, with emphasis, "We have need of honest men to guard the country, when treason stalks abroad with daring front. I trust never to have to number the Count d'Almeida among the traitors in Portugal."

Luis started, and his heart beat quick, as if with conscious guilt; for he remembered the scene, in which he had been an unwilling actor on the past night. For an instant it rushed across his mind that the Minister must have been aware of the meeting of the conspirators, and he trembled for the safety of them all. The dangerous position in which he himself also stood occurred to him; for, though feeling himself innocent of any evil intent, he well knew that, in the eye of the law, he was equally amenable to punishment for concealing the conspiracy. When the first reports reached him of the assassination of the King, the dreadful thought occurred to him, had any of those whom he had met in the vault of Malagrida been the perpetrators of the act?—he could not banish the suspicion that such might have been the case. He had quitted the ruin at an early hour, and there was then time for a horseman to reach the city before midnight, when, it was said, the event had taken place. Might not even suspicion alight on him, and on his young friend, of the Tavora family, too, who were already suspected,—at that very hour they were abroad, armed, and on horseback, perhaps passing near the spot? Would not his landlady, when she heard of the outrage, suspect that he was concerned in it? Should he be once apprehended and interrogated, what plausible reason could he possibly give for having made a secret expedition at night? If he said that he had gone at the request merely of his young friend, Jozé de Tavora, he would at once condemn both himself and all he had then met. Whichever way he looked at his case, it appeared desperate; and, for the first time in his life, that sinking, that paralysing sensation of fear, struck his heart,—not the fear of death, but of dishonour and disgrace,—of seeing his hitherto proud name branded as that of a traitor and assassin; and he shuddered as he thought that his life must end on the scaffold, amid the hootings and execrations of the populace, without the slightest means of vindicating his character from opprobrium. He knew Pedro was to be fully trusted, and he wished to beg his hostess not to mention to any one his having quitted home on that fatal night; but the request itself would seem to have been made from a consciousness of guilt, so he resolved not to speak to her on the subject.

At one moment he thought of hastening to the Minister, who, having before expressed an interest in his affairs, would, he trusted, believe him, and of confessing that he had been abroad on that night on horseback, and that he had thought it wiser to say so, lest any unjust suspicions might be raised against him, resolving, at the same time, to endure every torture, and death itself, rather than betray any of those who had confided in his honour. Then it occurred to him, that the very confession itself, notwithstanding all his caution, might throw some suspicion on the young Tavora, and from him on his relations, so he quickly abandoned his purpose. Next he thought of instantly quitting the country, but then he should leave his character open to the mercy of any who might choose to blacken it; or should he not be able to effect his escape, (a difficult undertaking in those days, when every ship was searched before sailing,) the very attempt would offer a presumptive proof of his guilt. At last he came to the determination of braving the worst, and, buoyed up with the consciousness of innocence, trusting in Heaven's protection, to repair at once to the palace, to make his personal inquiries as to the state of the King.

What was his surprise and satisfaction, then, on approaching the neighbourhood, to hear that the reports were false, and that the King had met merely with a slight accident. His confidence being thus perfectly restored, he appeared before the Minister with a calm heart and clear brow; nor had he any cause to dread the consequences of his unfortunate expedition, till he heard the last words the latter uttered.

Carvalho's hawk-eyed glance marked the agitation Luis could not entirely conceal; a dark shade, like a cloud on the summer sky, passing across his brow; but his countenance again shone with deceitful smiles; for it was his purpose to lull in fancied security, not to alarm, the guilty ones. He had, throughout the day, marked, with unerring acuteness, every look, every variation of feature, of those with whom he had made a point of conversing when they visited the palace; and many, who fancied that they had outwitted him, had but the more completely betrayed themselves. He was still more courteous, and full of expressions of regard for Luis than at first; but from that moment he suspected him of being privy to the conspiracy; for that there was one against the King had not escaped his searching vigilance, from many facts which had come to his knowledge.

As he contemplated the dreadful punishment which awaited the young Count, he felt a regret for his fate, slight and transient though it was, and one of the few, perhaps, which ever passed through his stern, unyielding heart; for Luis was akin to a dear friend, early lost, and long mourned; but he banished the weakness, and resolved to perform his duty.

"I shall see you soon again, Count, when his Majesty has recovered, which I trust will be in a few days, when we will arrange about the post you are to fill," he observed, as Luis took his leave, and he, with a bland smile, turned towards some of the other courtiers.

As the Count d'Almeida was quitting the palace, he encountered in the passage his former and hated rival, the Count San Vincente. The two young nobles regarded each other, as they advanced, with fierce glances, when the latter, casting a look of scornful triumph at Luis, passed onward, almost brushing him with his sword. Luis, recollecting that he was within the precincts of the palace, was unable to take any notice of the intended insult, though he longed for a day of retribution, when he might avenge himself for the deep injuries he had received at the hands of the treacherous noble. Brooding over the feelings which the meeting with the Count had raised, he returned homeward, at the same time fully satisfied that he was free from any danger on account of his unfortunate excursion with Jozé de Tavora.

Many days passed away, while many-tongued rumour was busy with spreading tales of various colours in all directions, blasting the characters of some of the highest and noblest in the land. Few, at length, there were who disbelieved that treason was on foot; the names of some were ascertained, it was said, without a doubt, and were whispered abroad in every circle, except where the true conspirators moved; for, as often happens, reports, whether true or scandalous, often reach last the ears of those most concerned. Thus, the Duke of Aveiro, whose wishes had, at all events, instigated the assassins to their deed of blood, appeared everywhere in public with an untroubled brow, and continued to be the most assiduous in his inquiries at the palace after the health of his Majesty.

The King, however, still kept himself closely confined to his chamber, to which even the Queen was not admitted; the Minister, as before, receiving all guests with the most affable courtesy, seeming to take a delight in paying them attentions, and holding them in lengthened conversations. Many an eye sunk beneath his piercing glance, though a smile wreathed itself about his lips, and his voice was softly modulated, and many a heart trembled lest he should read its inmost thoughts. Two or three nobles, from whom, not suspecting them, he had less concealed his thoughts, passed their estates in trust into other hands, being suddenly seized with a strong desire to visit other lands; not even waiting for permission to leave the country. Those who did so, had full reason, shortly afterwards, to congratulate themselves on their caution. The flight of these gave security to others; the young Marquis of Tavora being advised to return to the city, and plead illness as an excuse for his short absence,—while his father rejoiced that he himself had not acted according to the counsels of his wife, lest suspicion might have fallen upon him.

Among the visitors at the palace was our friend Gonçalo Christovaö, who had, a short time before, arrived in Lisbon. Senhor Carvalho welcomed him with even more than his usual courtesy, regretting that the King could not receive the petition, which he understood he had come to present from the city of Oporto; but assuring him, that he would use his utmost endeavours to abolish the grievances of which the inhabitants complained. He then took him aside.

"I have a subject, Senhor Christovaö, which I have long wished to broach to you. It is to make a request, which I trust you will not deny me, for it will conduce to strengthen your family interests, and add honour to mine."

The high-born fidalgo gazed at the Minister with an air of surprise, wondering what he could possibly mean.

"You have a fair daughter, full worthy of her high name," continued the latter, "whom my son beheld when Lisbon was honoured by her presence." The fidalgo started, and a frown gathered on his brow. "He has ever since pined to possess her; and, as I hear she is still not betrothed, I now ask her hand in marriage for him."

If a leper, or one of the vilest of the children of earth, had made the same request, the proud fidalgo could scarce have cast a look more full of indignant scorn towards him than he now threw at the powerful Minister, as, in a tone of mingled anger and disdain, he answered, "You strangely forget our relative positions, Senhor Carvalho; but know, senhor, that in my garden there is no room for oaks." Alluding to his hereditary estate called the "Fair Garden," and the name of Carvalho, which is the Portuguese for an oak.

The Minister bowed, and returned a smile, which could scarce be called treacherous, if the fidalgo had not been too much excited by his indignation to observe the withering gleam which shot from the eyes of the man whose vengeance he had thus provoked, but the latter in no other way committed himself.

"You indulge somewhat in pleasantry this morning, Senhor Christovaö," he said, in a tranquil tone. "However, I conclude that you have good reasons for refusing my son's suit, and I therefore withdraw it."

"You act wisely, senhor," answered the fidalgo, still in an offended tone. "My daughter's hand is not to be bought and sold, and of her own free-will she has dedicated it to the Church."

"The young lady has not professed yet?" asked Carvalho.

"No, senhor; some months must yet elapse before she takes the final vows," said the father.

"It were better she abandoned her project," observed the Minister. "It is one few young ladies so lovely as she is follow willingly; and remember, Senhor Christovaö, the King has determined to allow the inclinations of no lady of this realm to be forced in that respect—I must see to it."

"I require no one to dictate to me how I am to dispose of my daughter," answered the fidalgo, haughtily.

"Your pardon, my dear sir," returned the Minister.

"Present my duty to the King," said the fidalgo, taking his leave.

"I will not forget you, Senhor Christovaö," said the Minister, bowing him out.

"Haughty fool!" he muttered, as he returned to his seat. "Dearly shall you rue your insolence. Sebastiaö Jozé de Carvalho never forgets his friends or his foes."

Several weeks passed tranquilly away, so tranquilly that men began to suppose they had mistaken the character of the Prime Minister, and that, weary of bloodshed and severity, his government was to be henceforth one of mildness and conciliation. The larger number were loud in their praise of the great man; favours which had long been sought for were now granted, promises were made to others, even his former enemies appeared forgiven; the Duke of Aveiro, among others, requested leave to retire to his country seat at Azeitaö, and permission was instantly given him to do so. Some few suspected, it is true, that this mild behaviour was like the treacherous calm before the hurricane; but they were cautious, and uttered not their opinion.

Volume Three—Chapter Eleven.

"O who would wish to be a King?" said the gallant King James of Scotland, when the fantastic, fickle, fierce, and vain herd were shouting the name of Douglas; and we ask, Who would wish to be a Prime Minister? No one, surely, who has any regard for his own tranquillity or happiness; no one who cannot scorn the base revilings of the thankless crowd, in whose service he is exerting all the energies of a noble intellect, and wasting his health; no one who is not prepared to encounter the treachery of friends, and the hatred of enemies; who has not a heart of adamant and nerves of steel; unless he be a true patriot, and *then* the consciousness of rectitude and nobility of purpose will support him through all.

A fair girl was leaning over a balcony in the residence of the Prime Minister of Portugal, inhaling the sweet odours which rose from the garden beneath. Her light hair, not yet brought under the slavish subjection of fashion, fell in long ringlets over her fair neck, while her laughing blue eye, and lips formed to smile, betokened her German extraction, for she was the daughter of Sebastiaö Jozé de Carvalho and the Countess Daun; though neither in her gentle disposition, or her small and beautifully rounded figure, did she partake of her father's qualities. She started, for a sigh was breathed near her, and she beheld a handsome youth by her side, gazing at her with a look of enraptured devotion. A blush mantled on her cheeks as she asked, "What brings you here, Senhor Alfonzo? I thought you were with my father at the palace."

"I am about to go thither, Donna Agnes," answered the youth, "but I sought first to see you."

"Pardon me, senhor, I must not delay you," said the young lady.

"Lady, in mercy save me from destruction!" exclaimed the youth, in a tone which thrilled to her heart.

"What mean you, Senhor Alfonzo? In what way can I aid you?" said the Minister's daughter.

"In your hands is my fate, either to leave me a wretch unworthy of existence, or to raise me from despair, and grant me bliss incomparable."

"I dare not, I must not, understand the meaning of your strange expressions," said Donna Agnes, her hand, which rested on the balustrade, slightly trembling. "Let me entreat you, senhor, to leave me. I would not be the unhappy cause of your ruin."

"You, you alone, can be the cause of my salvation," exclaimed the youth, with enthusiastic passion. "Donna Agnes, I love you."

"In mercy to yourself—to me, do not say so," faltered the young lady.

"My spirit would not rest, when I am in the grave, had I not declared the love I bear you," exclaimed the Secretary.

"Oh no, no; it must not be thus! Say you will not utter those words again, and I will endeavour to forget what you have said. You cannot know my father, if you think that he would let me listen to such declarations," answered Donna Agnes.

"I know him well—he has ever been my benefactor, and I would show my gratitude," responded the youth.

"Then, as you value his favour, do not renew this conversation. It has caused me much pain already," said Donna Agnes.

"I cannot longer conceal the consuming love I feel for you," exclaimed the Secretary. "Can you, in return, hate me for it?"

"Oh no, no," responded Donna Agnes.

"Will you, can you love me, then?" exclaimed the youth. "Will you grant me but one hope to endure existence?"

The colour forsook the fair cheek of the Minister's daughter; her bosom heaved, and her eyes sunk to the ground.

"Oh leave me, leave me, Senhor Alfonzo!" she cried. "These words are cruelty to me and to yourself. It cannot be. My father esteems you, and confides in you; but, did he suspect what you have told me, his anger would be aroused to a pitch you little dream of, and of my hand he has already determined the disposal; but I shall ever regard you as a friend."

"Then were you free, you might, you would love me?" exclaimed the infatuated youth. "Donna Agnes, you do love me?—utter but the word, and no power shall tear you from me."

"This conduct is ungenerous, unworthy of you," responded Donna Agnes. "I would not speak harshly to you; but you drive me to it. From henceforth, I must fly your presence. Again I ask you to leave me. I never can be yours."

"Then you have sealed my doom and your father's,—his death be upon your head, cruel girl!" ejaculated the Secretary, as he rushed from the spot where they stood, and hastened to the royal palace.

"Oh stay, stay!" cried the young lady, alarmed at his agitated look, and extraordinary violence; "what mean you?" but he was gone; and, placing her fair young face in her hands, she wept bitterly.

Poor girl, she had never before been told by any one that she was beloved; and for two years past daily had she seen the young and handsome Secretary, who, grave and reserved as he was towards others, could teach his tongue to utter the softest eloquence to her; and when his eye met hers, his whole countenance would beam with animation,—yet she had performed her duty to her father, and promised to marry whoever he might select. He had made his choice, and she must abide by it.

The Secretary hastened to the cabinet in the palace, where the Minister always employed him; but the latter had not arrived. He first opened some papers on which he was employed, and then examined every corner of the room with the utmost care. His naturally pallid cheek was more bloodless than usual; his hands trembled; his eyes cast furtive glances around, even though he had convinced himself no one was present. Every instant he started,—his knees knocked together; but still he went about the work he had vowed to perform: his determination was strong, though his frame was weak. A small ewer of water, with a tumbler, stood on a table, on one side of the closet. He eyed it for some time, with his hand grasping the back of a chair, to give himself support—his breath came and went quickly. At length he approached it—for an instant he bent over it—he drew from his bosom a small packet—he tore it open, and poured a powder it contained into the ewer, then, securing the empty paper beneath his dress, he waited another minute without moving. So pale was his cheek, so rigid did he stand, that he looked more like some statue of bronze or marble, than a living man. Again he started, and seizing the ewer, he poured some of its contents into the tumbler: the liquid was pure and sparkling as crystal. He heaved a deep, long-drawn sigh, and turned away; but there was a fascination in that fatal goblet! Again and again were his eyes attracted by it, till the orbs almost started from his head—his lips were parched—there was fire in his brain, yet his heart was as ice. The first fatal step was made! the rest was easy. He endeavoured to collect his thoughts—to grow calm, and reason with himself. What had he done? He had committed no crime,—no one had suffered by his hand,—he was not a murderer! Oh no. Then why this abject fear? He attempted to smile at his first sensations,—he recalled all the rules with which he had been taught to reason at college; all the later lessons he had received from the Father Jacinto, and he was successful. He sought to reason against conviction. The struggle was severe,—intellect (he called it) against conscience; and intellect was the victor! Yes, the victor! But how long would it remain so? He knew not what an active, harassing enemy was conscience,—how it seizes on its victim in the dead of night,—how it rushes on him, when laid prostrate by disease and sickness! Then which is the victor? Then does it take ample vengeance on intellect for its former defeat.

The apt pupil of the Father Jacinto da Costa now seated himself calmly, to finish the copy of a despatch on which he had been employed. He then arose, and taking a key, which hung suspended from his neck, beneath his clothes, he approached the Minister's private cabinet. He opened it, and searched carefully among the papers, endeavouring to replace each as he found them. At last he came to one, which he seized eagerly; and running his eye over it, he carried it to his desk, rapidly making extracts from it, and placed the paper which he had written in his bosom. With the one he had taken he returned to the cabinet, kneeling to restore it to the spot it had occupied, and to search for another. Deeply absorbed, his eye running over paper after paper, he heard not the door open. A hand was laid heavily on his shoulder; he started, as if it had been a hand of fire, and, gazing upward, he beheld the stern features of the Minister! The paper he held dropped from his grasp,—despair was marked on every lineament of his countenance, and, trembling and pale, he would have sunk on the ground, but that an arm of iron upheld him.

"Fool!" said the Minister. "Is it thus you return my confidence? Have you before betrayed the secrets of this cabinet? Speak! You answer not,—your silence is a confession of your guilt. Behold yon bright sun—'tis the last time its beams will glad your sight; for know, he who possesses the secrets of Carvalho must be surrounded by stronger walls than his own bosom affords; the deepest dungeon in the Jungueira will henceforward be your abode." The Minister withdrew his hand.

"Stir not," he added, as he walked towards the door, to summon some attendants who were without. At first they did not hear his voice, and he was obliged to go to the end of the passage again to call them. They rushed up hastily, and followed Carvalho to the apartment. On entering, the young Secretary was discovered stretched on the ground in a swoon, it seemed, close to the open cabinet. They raised him up, and endeavoured to restore animation, while the Minister went to his desk, and wrote a few lines.

"When he revives, bear him hence," he said, "and deliver this paper to Senhor Fonseca;" and, without appearing to pay further attention to what was going forward, he continued writing.

The endeavours of the attendants were soon successful, for the unhappy youth opened his eyes, gazing wildly at those surrounding him. "Water! water!" he murmured.

One of the men, observing the ewer on the table, pouring out a tumbler-full, brought it to him, and placed it to his lips—he eagerly drank off the cooling draught. They threw some on his head, to cool his brow, and again gave him to drink. The water completely restored him, and, as they led him away, he ventured not to turn his eye towards the man he had deceived; but, as he passed the door, his glance fell on the fatal ewer. A thought like the vivid lightning, scorching all in its path, crossed his mind. Had he been given to drink of the poisoned water? Impossible! He felt no ill effects from it; but he dared not ask the question.

That night the young Alfonzo, the highly endowed in mind and person, lay on a wretched pallet, chained, like a malefactor, to the humid stone-wall of a low dark dungeon beneath the castle of the Jungueira. Not a gleam of light, not a breath of pure air, entered his abode; *then* it was that conscience triumphed over intellect. He thought of his days of childhood and innocence, before he had learned the rules of sophistry. His mother's face appeared to him, smiling with love, but full of sadness. Suddenly it vanished, and one of dreadful scowling aspect took its place. He thought of the dark lessons he had received from his instructors, and he called on God to curse those who had blasted his heart with scorching words. The Father Jacinto, too, came before him, with a calm and benignant countenance, and voice of mellifluous softness. Suddenly he changed, and, in his stead, arose a vast serpent of glittering scaly sides, moist with slime, which coiled and twisted its enormous folds around him, hissing as it breathed forth a fiery breath upon his face. It seemed to bear him down, when the earth beneath him opened. "Oh, Heaven!" he cried, "I sink, I sink, I sink!"

The next morning the gaoler entered the cell. The prisoner stirred not, nor answered to his call. He took his hand,—it struck a chill to his heart,—he held the lamp over him,—he was dead!

One person only ever knew the cause of his death, and that very day he heard of it. "It were better so, as he had failed in his purpose," he muttered. "He knew too many secrets of our order to be trusted. Had he been tortured, as he most assuredly would have been, he might have betrayed them. Requiescat in pace!"

The master never again thought of the pupil till he lay on his own death-bed, with his flesh lacerated and his limbs broken by the wheel; but he felt not those pains; there was another far more acute within; conscience had re-asserted its sway, he remembered him he had betrayed, and *how* he had died. (Note).

Note. The Father Jacinto was soon afterwards imprisoned and tortured. He died in confinement from the effects of his treatment, say the Jesuits.

Volume Three—Chapter Twelve.

It was the middle of winter, but, notwithstanding the season of the year, the sun shone brightly forth, shedding a genial warmth upon the beggars and dogs who were basking beneath it in the streets of Lisbon. The former were stationed at the posts they had each appropriated, exhibiting every species of loathsome deformity, and imploring the charity of the passers-by in the name of Heaven, warning them of the opportunity afforded of bestowing alms for the benefit of their souls. The dogs were enjoying their time of rest, every now and then uttering a growl of defiance if any stranger encroached on their districts. The Galician water-carriers were filling their barrels at the fountains, laughing and joking among themselves, strangers as they were in the land, happy by nature, and independent of all the plots and conspiracies which agitated the natives. Some women were washing at the tanks, and striking the linen to rags against the stones, while they gaily sang in chorus; while others, sitting at the corners of the streets, were employed in roasting chestnuts in little earthen stoves, and calling on the passers to buy. Fishermen were selling the produce of their nets, or wild-fowl; country-women their poultry. Now a citizen might be seen closely muffled up in his large cloak, more to hide the dress beneath than to keep out the cold; then a gentleman would hasten along in his bag-wig, and sword by his side, long flowered waistcoat, and deep waisted coat, politely returning the salutations of all who bowed; indeed, all the world was abroad, a few in carriages or on horseback, but mostly on foot: it was not yet dinner time.

Among the pedestrians was our old friend Antonio, the cobbler, who had long since given up his former occupation, and by many was supposed to live completely on his wits—not a bad compliment to them, however. His keen eye, as he walked along, observed all that was taking place around him. He saw a beggar walk merrily to his post, kicking a dog out of his way, and then ask alms in the character of a confirmed cripple. He laughed—he was fond of laughing, somewhat bitterly oftentimes.

"There are a good many knaves in the world," he muttered, "of all classes, from the lordly traitor, who would barter his country's honour and safety for gold to supply his extravagance, to this loathsome wretch in rags and tatters."

He next observed a boy stealing a coin from a blind man's hat placed before him, when the seeming blind man, dealing a heavy blow, struck the youthful vagabond to the ground.

"Ay, we can see sharply enough when our own interests are attacked, and fight hard to defend them," said the Cobbler, as he walked on. "That young rogue has learned a useful lesson, he will make sure that a man is blind before he tries to pilfer his property."

Antonio passed through several streets, till he came to an open place. There a crowd was collected round a man perched on a high stool, who was selling nostrums, and making the people laugh by his wit and jokes: a real object of pity lay at a doorway, half dead with starvation and disease. A rich man passed by, looking coldly on the wretched beggar, turning aside, and refused his earnest appeal for a copper to relieve his hunger; but when he came within hearing of the quack, he stopped to listen; when the latter, uttering one of his best jokes, and paying him a well-timed compliment, he threw the knave a crown, and, laughing, passed on.

"Such is the way of the world," thought the Cobbler. "The impudent charlatan succeeds and grows rich, while the honest and humble poor man is left to starve. The foolish rogues are soon hung; 'tis the cunning ones who live and thrive. Bah! it makes me sick to think of it. What fools men are! they will often confide in a plausible knave, when blunt honesty is kicked out of doors."

The Cobbler saw much more in his walk, on which he made his observations. He did not seem to have a very good opinion of the world he lived in. Whether he thought worse of people than they deserved we cannot pretend to say.

He now left the city behind, and, passing through the suburbs of Belem, directed his course to the Quinta of the Marquis of Tavora. He came under a garden-wall, in which was a window, and out of the window a pair of sparkling black eyes were gazing. He kissed his own hand, for he could not reach that of the lady, and she kissed hers in return; so he went and stood as near her as he could get.

"Oh! my pretty Margarida, how I love you!" he began. At which words, the eyes sparkled even more brightly than before. "I have many wishes, and the first is, that I was on the other side of the wall."

"Hush! senhor, you must not say that; at least, not so loudly," softly murmured Margarida; "some one will hear you, for people are passing constantly this way; but the window is not so very high from the ground."

"Ah, dear one! I could leap up in a moment, if you do not run away," said the gallant Cobbler.

"Oh! no, no, senhor! some one would see you to a certainty, while it is light," answered the coy Senhora Margarida.

"I have many things to say to you, pretty one. When will you like to hear them?" asked Antonio.

"Cannot you say them now, senhor?"

"Some one will hear me, you know. Wait till the evening, and then nobody will see me jump in at the window. Remember to leave it open."

"I will forget to shut it," innocently answered Margarida. "But tell me, senhor, are you really a fidalgo?"

"I will tell you all about it, with my other secrets, when I come at night. Remember to forget to shut the window; and do not forget to come yourself, Adeos for the present, my pretty charmer! I see some one coming." And Antonio walked away, humming a tune, while the pair of black eyes disappeared from the garden window.

If the Portuguese are fonder of one employment than of another, it is looking out of window; they all do it, from the highest to the lowest. There is so little mental or bodily exertion required for it; and there is always something moving in the streets, either men, dogs, or rats. Even watching a pig will afford amusement; and anything is preferable to reading, working, or thinking; therefore they always have looked out of windows, and always will, till their taste improves. Antonio proceeded on till he came to the side of the river, where he sat himself down on the bank, to wait till the evening, and to meditate. He thought a great deal, light-hearted and merry as he seemed, often very gravely, sometimes fiercely, as he remembered the foul wrongs and insults the race to which he belonged had for centuries endured, and for which treatment their cruel tyrants had sought every excuse which cunning hypocrisy, or the fiercest bigotry, could invent, claiming ever the authority of God for their cursed deeds. "Miscreants!" he muttered, "where in the Christian's gospel can they find permission for the rapine, murders, and cruelties, with which their souls have been stained since the triumph of their faith? Fools! who practise not what they preach, and yet expect to be believed." He would then think on for some time, and, giving a deep-drawn sigh, would conclude with the oft-repeated apophthegm, "What cannot be cured must be endured;" he then, growing calmer, would turn to other subjects. "Yet," he continued, soliloquising, "it is a hard office to bide this life of concealment, of deceit, and treachery; but it must be endured till my object is accomplished. The time draws near, happily, when my toils may be at an end; and then, if faith can be placed in the word of man, I shall reap the rich reward of all. Can I confide in him? Yes, 'tis his interest to fulfil his promise. There is one thing troubles me more than all the rest; how some men would laugh to hear me, if I confessed it! My pretty Margarida! Now that girl is fully persuaded I love her to desperation; and, assuredly, I have done my utmost to make her believe so, to learn, through her, the secrets of the Tavora family. They little think how closely the meshes of the net are drawn around them, to enclose them ere long, and drag them to shore, as yonder fishermen are now doing with their prey." As he thought this, he was watching a party of fishermen hauling in their seine. "I must try and make amends to Margarida, poor girl! I feel an interest in her. I did not think she would so soon learn to love me. I was not born to be that cursed wretch who would win a maiden's affections for the base, cowardly satisfaction of tampering with them, and then deserting her. I leave such work to the wealthy and high-born. May they reap their reward!"

The sun was now setting over the mouth of the Tagus, casting a broad, glowing line of fire upon the smooth bosom of the stream, and tinging the tower of Belem, the gothic spires of the church, and the hills beyond, with its ruddy hue. Antonio rose, for he calculated that it would be dark by the time he reached the Quinta of the Marquis of Tavora. He met but few people on the way, nor were any near when, without much difficulty, he clambered in at the window in the garden-wall, which Margarida had, according to her promise, left unbolted.

It was now as dark as it was likely to be in a star-light night. Antonio carefully shut to the window, and looked around, but Margarida was nowhere to be seen. He softly called her name, but she did not answer. He then observed a building, which appeared to be a summer-house, at the end of a walk. "Ah! she will probably go there to look for me; and if any one by chance comes into the garden, I shall not be exposed to view as I am here." He accordingly advanced towards it, but when he arrived there, he found the door closed. He tried the handle, but it was locked. He just then heard a step at a distance. He listened attentively; it was too heavy for the elastic little feet of his mistress. It approached nearer, and in the direction of the spot where he stood. "I must find some place to hide in, or I shall be caught," he muttered.

At the back of the summer-house there were some shrubs growing closely together, a window overlooking them, which spot Antonio, as he looked about, selected to conceal himself till the person who was coming near had retired. He shrunk down on the ground, under the walls of the building; and he had scarcely done so, when a person, applying the key to the door, entered. Striking a light, the man lit a lamp on the table, in the centre of the apartment, which, from the noise he made, he appeared to be placing in order. After having performed this office, he again opened the door, when, at that instant, Antonio heard a light step coming along the path, and which he fancied he could recognise as Margarida's. Of this he was soon convinced, by hearing a voice, which he knew to be hers, exclaim—

"Oh! Senhor Ferreira, is that you? You quite frighten me! What are you doing?"

"Let me rather ask you what you are doing here at this hour of the evening, Senhora Margarida," was the answer.

"I came out to pick some flowers for my mistress, which I forgot to do in the day-time, so, if you are gallant, you will come and assist me," said Senhora Margarida.

"An odd time, to pick flowers in the dark," answered the man-servant; "but I cannot assist you now; I must return to the house."

"Many thanks for your gallantry, Senhor Ferreira," she responded, as he turned away; "I dare say I shall find enough myself;" and she stooped over the flower-beds, as if in search of flowers.

Antonio guardedly peeped out of his concealment, and seeing his mistress alone, "Hist, Margarida, hist!" he whispered. "Come beneath the shade of the summer-house; that prying servant will be less likely to observe us."

"Oh, Senhor Antonio, I am so glad to have found you, for when I passed by I found the window closed, and I was afraid you might not have got in," said Margarida.

They sat themselves down on a stone bench placed against the side of the building. Antonio, while declaring his affection for the young lady, some of which he had really begun to feel, at the same time managed to draw from her various pieces of information he was anxious to gain. A few minutes had thus passed rapidly away, when the sound of approaching footsteps was again heard.

"For the love of Heaven, conceal yourself," exclaimed Margarida, jumping up and seizing a bunch of flowers, with which she had wisely provided herself previously to coming into the garden. "They will see you, if you attempt to reach the window. Down behind the summer-house. 'Tis the young Marquis and some visitors. I must away." And she tripped along the walk towards the house. "Who goes there?" exclaimed a stern voice, as she passed the party by a different though parallel pathway.

"I have been gathering flowers, Senhor Duque—see, here they are," answered Margarida, quickly.

"Gathering flowers at this time of night, indeed! Say rather, looking for a lover, senhora," exclaimed the voice; "think you we can distinguish them in this light? Go, Manoel, and watch her safely into the house—we must have no prying eyes and listening ears to what we are about."

Manoel being despatched to follow Margarida until he saw her out of their way, the party advanced and entered the summer-house, where, fresh lamps being lit, they took their seats round the table which the servant had arranged.

Antonio, in the mean time, unable to escape, was obliged to resume his position among the bushes, expecting every instant that the party would search round the building, and feeling confident from what he had learnt from Margarida of their proceedings, that he should fall an instant sacrifice to their fears. He was somewhat relieved when he heard their feet on the floor of the summer-house, and their voices speaking in tones which showed that they had no suspicion of the presence of a spy upon their actions.

After waiting some time, the persons within the summer-house having become highly excited in their discussion, whatever it was, Antonio thought he might venture to move his position, so as to gain a view of what was going forward. The shutters of the window, which looked over the shrubbery in which he was concealed, were left partially open, so that by carefully lifting his head among the branches of the evergreens, he was able to see clearly into the room without incurring any risk of being himself observed.

At one end of the table, sat, or rather now stood, the Duke of Aveiro, who was, with vehement gestures, addressing the party: on each side were various members and connexions of the Tavora family, among them being the young Marquis and his brother, the Conde d'Atouquia, the old Marchioness, and the Jesuit Malagrida.

"Ah! ah! thou old hypocrite," muttered Antonio, as he observed the last-mentioned personage. "Wherever thou art there is sure to be mischief brewing; but I have thee now, if I mistake not;" and, like an Indian warrior approaching his foes, he crept close to the window, placing himself behind the shutter, so that, although he could hear more clearly, he was less able to distinguish what was taking place, till he discovered a broad chink, and, by putting his eye to it, he had complete command of the greater part of the room.

"The very persons who met at the Jesuit's vault down the river," he thought to himself, "when they all fancied themselves so secure and unobserved; as did yon mad priest deem himself hidden from the searching eye of the Minister: yet, forsooth, he made a capital bait to catch others. Ah! I am glad to find my young friend the Conde d'Almeida is not among them, and he has certainly not fled the country, for I saw him this very morning."

We do not intend to give the whole particulars of the conversation which Antonio overheard; suffice it to say, that he heard enough to prove that a dangerous and powerful conspiracy existed to overthrow the power of the Minister; and more, that one had existed to destroy the sovereign, fomented and encouraged by some of those now present, if indeed the actual would-have-been assassins were not among them. Antonio noted well every word they uttered, every gesture they made, words sufficient to bring the speakers, as they themselves well knew, to the scaffold, had they deemed that an ear was listening to them; but, infatuated as they were, they triumphed in fancied security, calling on Heaven to aid them in their wickedness. Now some were seen to draw their swords, and to kiss the blades, as they ratified some dreadful oath; others grasped their fire-arms, and vowed to use them to better effect than before; when Malagrida stood up and blessed the assembled conspirators and their cause.

Some movement now taking place among them, Antonio, fearful lest his face might be perceived through the casement, stole back to his leafy shelter; and fortunate was it for him that he did so, for some one, perceiving that the shutter was unclosed, sent Manoel round to fasten it. Antonio held his breath, hiding his face beneath his cloak, for the man's feet almost touched his as he passed; and had not the eyes of the latter been dazzled by the light within, he could not have avoided perceiving him; as it was, the man performed his orders, and quickly returned to hear what his superiors were saying. Suddenly the lights were extinguished, and Antonio heard the party hurrying from the building towards the house. He waited some further time, with eager anxiety to bear the important information, for which he had so long toiled, to his employer, till the sound of voices and footsteps had died away. He listened attentively—not a sound was heard. He started from his lair towards the garden window, which afforded the easiest means of escape; for, if found in the grounds after what had occurred, he well knew he must expect nothing short of death from the conspirators. As he gained the front of the summer-house, what was his horror to perceive two men standing beneath the porch before it, so earnestly engaged in a whispered conversation, that they did not perceive him! He stepped back cautiously a couple of paces, so as to be out of their sight, but was afraid to retreat further, lest he might attract their notice. The movement was not, however, entirely unremarked.

"Did you not hear a noise, Senhor Policarpio?" said one of the persons.

"Stay! listen, Manoel. I hear nothing. Oh, it was but the wind rustling the leaves," answered Senhor Policarpio, and they continued the subject of their discussion, but in so low a tone that it was impossible to distinguish what they said.

Antonio waited, intending to dodge round to the back of the summer-house as soon as Policarpio and his companion moved, when the sound of their footsteps would conceal his own. He wished they would hasten, for he longed to be off, to give the information he had gained; but minute after minute passed by, and still they continued in the same place. His impatience prompted him to make a bold push for the window, but his prudence withheld him. At last they moved away, taking the walk leading past the window, and he slid behind the summer-house; but what was his vexation to hear them stop at the only outlet for escape that he was aware of, one of the men exclaiming, "Curses on this window, 'tis the second time it has blown open to-night; I will secure the bolts well this time;" then followed a noise as if the bolts were driven down by a stone.

The footsteps of the men receding, he again advanced from his hiding-place, and, seeing no one, hurried to the window. It was securely closed. He tried to force up the bolts, but they resisted his efforts. He then groped about for the stone which had served the purpose of a hammer to the others, and, after some time, having discovered it, he attempted to drive up the bolts. He knocked away till one only remained to set him at liberty, when suddenly a gleam of light fell on the shutter before him, and, turning his head, to his dismay, he beheld the two persons who he thought had entered the house hurrying towards him. Not a moment was to be lost, if he would escape with his life. He knocked away at the bolt, but it had been driven deep down.

"Death to the cursed spy!" shouted the voice of Senhor Policarpio, as he rushed forward, with his sword gleaming in his hand. The threat did not the less cause Antonio to endeavour to loosen the obstinate bolt. The point of the sword was within a few paces of him, when the bolt gave way. He threw open the shutter, and leaped on the window-sill. Policarpio made a thrust with his rapier at him; but, jumping fearlessly down, he alighted safely on the ground. Stopping not to see if any followed, and diving among the narrow lanes in the neighbourhood, he was soon safe from pursuit.

Volume Three—Chapter Thirteen.

The Prime Minister was seated in the private council chamber of the King, to which we have frequently before introduced our readers. A lamp stood on the table, throwing its light on numerous packets of papers strewed around, and on the sheet on which he was earnestly employed in writing.

Who would, we again ask, seek to occupy such a post as he filled? What can make a man sacrifice his health, his strength, peace, happiness, and safety,—to toil for hours while others sleep,—to bear the abuse of his adversaries, the revilings of the mob, the obstinacy of coadjutors, and the caprices of the Monarch,—but ambition? The ambition of some leads them to noble ends; for others, it wins but the hatred of mankind. It is ambition which excites the warrior to deeds of heroism,—the merchant to gain wealth,—the poet, the painter, and the sculptor, to win fame; and it is ambition which causes us to spend day after day, secluded in our study, employed on this work—the ambition of gaining the approbation of our countrymen.

Carvalho wrote on, unmindful of the lateness of the hour, when he heard a knock at the door, and, ordering the person who knocked to enter, a page appeared, informing him that one waited without who sought an audience on some important matter, which would admit of no delay.

"Let him be admitted," said the Minister; and before a minute had elapsed, Antonio stood before him. The attendants who had conducted him thither, to guard against treachery, were ordered forthwith to retire.

"What information do you bring me, my friend?" inquired the Minister.

"That which you have long sought, please your Excellency," answered Antonio.

"Ah! let me hear it without delay," said Carvalho, eagerly.

"I have learned the whole of the plot against the lives of your Excellency and his Majesty, and discovered many of those engaged in it;" and he gave an exact account of all which had taken place in the summer-house, and the names of the persons assembled there, of which the Minister took notes as he proceeded in his description.

"Now, then, ye haughty nobles, I have ye within my power!" exclaimed Carvalho, exultingly. "Sooner will the vulture abandon his prey than I will allow you to escape my grasp! Friend, you have well won any reward you may please to ask,—the treasury shall supply you—"

"Stay, your Excellency," interrupted Antonio. "I before said, I serve you not for money. I am, as you well know, of the race of Abraham; but I am not, therefore, of necessity, mercenary. Think you that any gold you can bestow could repay me for all I have endured to serve you,—for the degradation, the toil, the dangers I have undergone,— the deceit, the disguises, the watchfulness I have practised, for many years past, because you assured me you could find no other to do the work you required, in whom you could confide? Think you that it was for gold I abandoned my home and my kindred, to mingle with the most base and vile on earth, to curb their passions, and to guide them according to your will?—that for this I introduced myself into the palaces of the rich and powerful, to learn their secrets, and to act as a spy on their actions? No! your Excellency has known me long, and knows me better. What I ask, you have power to grant. I demand freedom for my people! We have in all things conformed to the customs of those among whom we dwell; to their religion, in every outward observance, which is all you can require; we pay tithes to your priests; we give alms to the poor; our manners, our language, have become the same; we obey the King and the law; and yet have we not been allowed to enjoy the rights of citizenship in the land which we enrich by our industry and our commerce. A mark has been set upon us; and wherever we move, still is the stigma of being New Christians attached to us. I demand, then, as my reward, that you should abolish that invidious distinction, and that, from henceforth, if we conform to the worship of your Church, we may likewise enjoy all the privileges of the other subjects of his Majesty."

"Your demands, my friend, are somewhat extravagant," returned the Minister, taken rather by surprise by Antonio's unexpected harangue; "but I will consult his Majesty on the subject, and be guided by his decision: if unfavourable to your wishes, you must make some other request. You know well that, of myself, I have no power to grant this one."

"Pardon me, your Excellency, I know well the power, both to will and act, rests with you, and you alone," answered Antonio, vehemently. "And this is the only reward which I seek, or will receive. If you grant it me not, my labour has indeed been labour in vain."

Carvalho was secretly pleased with the disinterested, and, more than that, the dauntless spirit of the speaker, so like his own, and perhaps also with the confidence he placed in his power to fulfil his wishes. The measure was, indeed, one he had before contemplated, and which he was anxious to bring about, though he was too good a diplomatist to acknowledge his intentions, or to commit himself by making any definite promise to perform what he might afterwards have reason to wish left undone; he therefore gave Antonio a vague answer to his petition.

"The matter you propose, my good friend, is one of vast importance, which will require mature deliberation before I can give you any hopes favourable to your wishes; but, believe me, I will do my utmost to gain that justice for your people which has so long been denied them: in the mean time, you may perform for me many more important services; for to crush this vile conspiracy at present demands all my attention."

"I would willingly serve your Excellency and the state yet another year, to gain justice for my people," answered Antonio. "In your word have I trusted, and in that do I still trust. Has your Excellency any further commands?"

"None, my friend; for this night you may retire. Call here to-morrow morning, and I shall claim your services."

As the door closed upon Antonio, the Minister, securing most of his papers in the bureau, took in his hand the notes he had made from Antonio's information, and, late as was the hour, repaired to the chamber of the King.

Joseph was about to retire to his couch when the Minister entered: his cheek was thinner and paler even than usual, from sickness and confinement, though he moved his arms without difficulty, as if perfectly recovered from the wounds he had received. Re-seating himself in a large, high-backed arm-chair, before a table on which his supper had been spread, he desired, in rather a querulous tone, to be informed why business was thus brought before him.

"It is a matter of the utmost importance, which will admit of no delay, Sire," answered Carvalho. "I have, at length, the strongest evidence of who were the perpetrators of the sacrilegious outrage against your Majesty."

The King's tone and manner instantly changed. "Ah! and you can prevent any like attempt for the future, my good friend," he answered eagerly. "Let me hear the particulars."

On this the Minister laid before him several papers, with the notes he had taken of Antonio's account, and a long list of the persons he had cause to suspect; many of whom Antonio had also mentioned. As the King read on, Carvalho leaned over him, making his observations on the different points of the case.

"Holy Virgin!" exclaimed Joseph, his voice trembling with agitation as his eye glanced down the long list of names. "Here are many of the most powerful and wealthy nobles of my land. It is impossible that they can all be traitors. Some of them I have ever deemed the most loyal and obedient of my subjects."

"Still greater, therefore, is their treachery, Sire; and greater must be their punishment," returned Carvalho, firmly.

"But what cause can they have to seek my death?" said the King. "Have they not already all they can desire? Do they not enjoy the highest rank, and fill all the posts of honour I have to give?"

"As their ambition and pride are boundless, they would create yet higher ones," answered Carvalho. "If your Majesty would again enjoy security and repose, these guilty persons, without distinction of their rank or station, must suffer the penalty of their crimes."

"Alas! I fear it must be so," said the King, hesitatingly; "but I had never supposed my nobles could have been guilty of so great a crime. Surely the assassins must have been villains of a lower order. Aveiro, the Tavoras, never could have done the deed."

"There are strong proofs of their guilt; and on their trial there will yet appear stronger," answered the Minister. "On my head be their blood, if they be innocent. I must request your Majesty to sign these warrants for their apprehension, and I will issue them when I see a favourable opportunity. We must proceed with caution, for they have a powerful party in their favour. Unless this is done, I cannot, Sire, answer from day to day for the security of your life or crown."

The King unwillingly took the blank warrants which the Minister had brought, and signing them, returned them to him, as he wrote on each the name of some person from the list before him.

"According to the information I receive, I may have occasion to apprehend some of these criminals before your Majesty rises tomorrow morning; but perhaps it may be advisable to allow some days further to elapse, that any others who are engaged in the conspiracy may further commit themselves," observed Carvalho, collecting the warrants.

"You have on your list the name of the Marquis of Tavora; but he is not mentioned as having been present at any of the meetings with the others," said the King.

"But most of his family were, Sire," returned the Minister. "They must inevitably suffer, as being the most guilty; and he must not be allowed to escape, lest he endeavour to avenge their deaths. He, also, in the eye of the law, is equally criminal, for he might have prevented their guilt; and the safety of the state demands his punishment."

"Be cautious that none but the guilty suffer," said the King.

"That shall be my care, Sire," answered Carvalho. "Your Majesty's sacred life has been, and will be still, in jeopardy, if their punishment is not severe; but I will make their fate such a lesson to others, that, from thenceforth, treason shall be unknown in the land; and these proud fidalgos shall no longer insult your Majesty with their haughty bearing. Have I, Sire, your full authority to act as I deem requisite on this momentous occasion?"

"You have, you have, my friend," answered the King. "Your judgment is always right."

"Then, haughty fidalgos, you are mine own," muttered the Minister, as he retired from the presence of the King.

The meanest subject in those realms slept more calmly that night than did King Joseph and his Prime Minister.

Volume Three—Chapter Fourteen.

The young Count d'Almeida had, since his arrival in Lisbon, been leading a life of complete retirement, at the quiet abode Pedro had selected for him. He had withdrawn himself from the society of the Tavoras, even from that of young Jozé de Tavora, whom he could not entirely forgive for the deceit he had practised on him, in leading him into the meeting of the conspirators on the fatal night of the attempted assassination of the King. He could not banish from his mind the suspicion that some of the persons he had there met were, in some way or other, connected with that diabolical outrage; and he felt assured, from knowing the character of the Minister, that it would not, as people supposed, be overlooked; so that, notwithstanding the apparent tranquillity which reigned in the city, the culprits would, sooner or later, be discovered. Of his own safety, though innocent of any criminal design, he was not at all satisfied; and each day that he rose he felt might be the last without the walls of a prison.

His friend, Captain Pinto, was at sea in the frigate he now commanded; and she was not, it was said, expected in the Tagus for some time.

When he inquired for Senhor Mendez, he was informed that, as soon as his health had been restored, he had sailed for England, nor did any one know when he was likely to return; so that Luis found himself deprived of the advice of the two persons in whom he could most confide. For his cousin, the Father Jacinto, he had long conceived the most complete distrust; and had not, therefore, even informed him of his return to Lisbon, nor did he believe the holy Jesuit was aware of the circumstance.

Our fair readers will naturally inquire if he had forgotten Donna Clara. He would have been unworthy of the pen of an historian if such could have been possible. He loved her as devotedly as before their separation, even though the last glow of hope was almost extinguished in his heart; but the spark still existed, for the fatal vow had not yet been pronounced, which, like death, must tear her from him for ever, and, till then, he would hope on: his love, he felt, could end but in his grave.

After some months of quietude, Lisbon was aroused from a lethargy (into which she was, in those days, rather more apt to fall than at present, when, every six months or so, she undergoes the excitement of a revolution) by the marriage of the eldest daughter of the Prime Minister with the Count Sampayo, to celebrate which important event preparations on a grand scale were made throughout the city. The King, who had not yet appeared in public, would, it was said, give a grand ball at the palace, to which all the first fidalgos were invited; and the foreigners had also issued invitations for a magnificent fête, which they purposed giving on the occasion, at their own ballroom, which might vie with any other in the kingdom.

The fidalgos, unsuspicious of danger, flocked into Lisbon from all parts of the country; some really anxious to pay their respects to their sovereign, and perhaps their court to his Minister; others, from very different motives, afraid of absenting themselves.

The Count d'Almeida had determined, on this occasion, to enter for the first time into society, since the death of his father. Late in the day, he rode out into the country, as was his usual custom; and, after proceeding some distance, he observed a large body of cavalry advancing rapidly towards the city. To avoid them, he turned his horse into a cross road, which led him into another highway, when he found himself in the rear of a regiment of infantry. By making a still larger circuit he hoped to escape the annoyance of having to pass them; but, to his surprise, he again encountered another body of troops.

At last, he determined to return homeward, wondering for what purpose the garrison of Lisbon was thus so suddenly increased; and, as he approached the barriers, he found each avenue to the city strongly guarded; he being allowed to enter, but several persons, who seemed anxious to go out, were detained without receiving any explanation.

We often blame ourselves that ideas should not have occurred to us, when after circumstances have proved the great advantage we might have derived from them; and so Luis had cause to think before he closed his eyes in sleep on that eventful night. He arrived at his solitary home without meeting any one from whom to inquire the cause of the sudden movement of the troops. While dressing for the fête, he inquired of Pedro if he had heard anything on the subject; but the latter, whose mind was full of the magnificence of the preparations, could only inform him that it was reported, a few more military had marched into the city to attend a review which the King was to hold on the following day.

Satisfied with this answer, Luis drove down to the palace, in front of which a large body of guards were drawn up, while carriages in great numbers were thronging to the spot. As he entered the hall of the palace, his eyes were dazzled by the brilliant illumination which met his view from hundreds of lights suspended from the roof, and above the broad staircase in front, glancing on the polished arms of the guards, who filled every part except a narrow passage for the guests between them. A military band, stationed on each side, was playing some loud and martial airs, which drowned the voices of any who attempted to speak. Luis passed on, and had reached the foot of the stairs, when two officers stepped forward.

"The Senhor Conde d'Almeida," said one, politely bowing.

"The same," answered Luis.

"You will please step this way, senhor, by the order of the King," returned the officer, opening a door on one side, through which Luis was obliged to pass, and which was closed directly after them. His attendants then conducted him down a long passage, which appeared truly gloomy after the blaze of light he had quitted, and to his inquiries as to where they were going, they held an ominous silence. He could not but feel alarmed at the extraordinary circumstance, though he had but short time for reflection, before he reached the opposite side of the palace, when his former conductors delivered him into the custody of two others, who seemed prepared to expect him.

"What is the meaning of this, senhores?" he asked.

"You are our prisoner, Senhor Conde, by order of the King," answered one of his new guards. "Please to accompany us, a carriage awaits you."

The men placing themselves one on each side of him, so that escape was impossible, led him down a flight of steps to a small door, on the outside of which more soldiers were stationed, and where a coach was in waiting. The soldiers then formed round the coach, keeping all spectators at a distance, while his guards desired him to enter it, seating themselves, with drawn weapons, opposite to him. The coach then drove quickly away, while another appeared to take its place.

"Ah!" thought Luis, "I am, alas! not the only wretch who will this night be deprived of liberty."

He was anxious to learn of his attendants whither they were conducting him, but the only answer he could draw from them was far from satisfactory.

"Silence, senhor," said one. "Our orders are to treat you with every respect but, if you attempt to speak, or to cry out for assistance, we are to run our swords into your body."

After this, he deemed it the more prudent plan to keep silence, lest they might think it necessary to obey their orders to the letter.

As he was driven along through the dark and narrow streets, he knew not whither, without the remotest chance of escape, his meditations were melancholy in the extreme. He could not doubt that he was going to that dismal bourne from which so many travellers never return—a dungeon, or from which, too probably, he might be led forth but to the scaffold. After driving for a considerable distance, he again ventured to ask his destination, but a gruff "Silence, senhor! remember!" was the only answer he received. At length the carriage stopped. He heard the heavy sound of bolts being withdrawn, and chains dropped, when the mules again moved onwards a few paces. He could hear the gates, through which he had passed, again close with a loud grating and clanging noise, which struck a chill to his heart, and he was presently afterwards desired to alight. As he stepped from the vehicle, he looked round him, to endeavour to discover to what place he had been conveyed, and, by the glare of a torch which one of the under-gaolers held, it seemed to him that he was in a small court-yard, surrounded by lofty walls, and in front of a small door thickly studded with iron bolts. His attention was, however, quickly directed to other subjects, by the door opening, and the appearance of a personage who announced himself as the Governor of the prison, and to whom, with the most polite bows, his former attendants now delivered him. He was a small man, habited in a complete costume of black, with a placid expression of countenance, and a mild, conciliating tone of voice, more suited to a physician than the keeper of a prison, it appeared, on the first glance, as many of those unfortunate persons who came under his government supposed; but, on a further acquaintance, a most ominous gleam was observed to shoot from his cold grey eye, when the smile which usually played round his lips would vanish, and a frown, in spite of himself, would gather on his brow, betokening too clearly his real character.

The Governor's first address was cordial in the extreme, though Luis would willingly have dispensed with his hospitality.

"You are welcome, Senhor d'Almeida, to my abode, and all which it contains is at your service," he began. "I see you still wear your sword. I beg your pardon, but I must request you to deliver it up to me.

None here wear arms but the guards, nor will you need it for your protection. We take very good care of our guests."

Luis, as he was desired, unbuckled his sword, and, without speaking, delivered it into the hands of the Governor.

"Thank you, Senhor Conde," continued the latter personage. "It is a pretty weapon, and I will take the greatest care of it for you. I will now, by your leave, conduct you to your apartment. It is rather small, and somewhat damp; but, to say the truth, we have but little room to spare, for we are likely to be crowded soon, and you will have plenty of companions. However, I am of a hospitable disposition, and I like to see my mansion full; yet I know not if you will be able to enjoy much of each other's society, for our rules are rather severe in that respect."

While the Governor was thus running on, he was conducting Luis through several arched passages, a man preceding them with a lantern, while four others followed close after, armed with drawn swords, as a slight hint to the prisoner that his only course must be obedience to orders. They then descended a flight of stone steps to regions where, it seemed, the light of day could never penetrate, so damp and chill struck the air they breathed.

"We lodge you on the ground-floor, Senhor Conde," observed the facetious Governor. "It has its advantages and disadvantages. You will find some amusement in hunting the rats and toads, which are said to be rather numerous, though I confess that, in winter, the climate does not agree with some constitutions—perhaps it may with yours. Oh, here we are."

Producing a large bunch of keys, he ordered one of the men to unlock a door, before which they stood.

"Enter, Senhor Conde. You will not find many luxuries, and, as for conveniences, I must supply those you require."

Luis felt it was useless striving against fate, so he unresistingly walked into what was, in truth, a wretched dungeon, with little more than sufficient height to stand upright, and about eight feet square. It contained a pallet, destitute of any bedding, a single chair, and a rough deal table, with a pitcher to hold water. The only means of ventilation was through a narrow aperture, sloping upward, far too small to allow a human body to pass, even had it not been closely barred both inside and out.

"I have other guests to attend on, Senhor Conde, so I must beg you to excuse my rudeness in quitting you so soon," said the Governor, as one of the under-gaolers lighted a small lamp which stood on the table, while the others withdrew. "I will send you such bedding as I can procure. However, for your consolation, I can assure you that some of your friends will be worse lodged to-night than you are. I wish you farewell, senhor!"

And, before Luis had time to make any answer to these rather doubtful expressions, the polite Governor had disappeared, and, the door being closed, barred, and bolted, he found himself alone, and a state prisoner. We need not describe how he felt. Most people, in a like situation, would have felt the same—deprived of liberty, which, with the greater number of men, next to life, is dearer than all else. To some, life, without it, is valueless, and eagerly do they look forward to the moment when, released from all mortal bonds, their fetterless souls may range through the boundless regions of a happier world, in wondering admiration of the mighty works of their Creator. Such has been the dream of many a hapless prisoner, for many years doomed to pine on in gloom and wretchedness, waiting, in anxious expectation, for the time of his emancipation, which, day after day, has been cruelly deferred, till hope and consciousness have together fled.

As the sound of the falling bolts struck his ear, Luis stood for some minutes gazing at the iron door, like one transfixed. He then took several rapid steps the length of his narrow prison, and, at last, throwing himself on the chair, and drawing his cloak, which he had fortunately retained, around him—for his gala costume was but ill-suited to protect him against the cold and dampness of the season—he gave way to bitter and hopeless thought.

The predictions of the Governor were but too correct. During the greater part of the night, Luis could plainly hear the arrival of carriage after carriage. Then came the sound of many feet, the barring and bolting of doors, the fall of chains, and all the accompanying noises to be expected in a prison. After about an hour, his own door opened, when he observed a guard of soldiers drawn up in front, and two attendants entered, with a mattress and coverlids, which they threw on the bedstead, placing some coarse bread and fish before him on the table; and then, without uttering a syllable, they again withdrew.

In the mean time, the gaieties in the city continued unabated, though all people felt a more than usual degree of restraint on their spirits in the palace. To the great displeasure of many, the King did not make his appearance. Indeed, some suspected he had never intended to do so, though his Minister took upon himself to perform the necessary honours, and, moving among the crowd, he allowed no one of importance to pass without a word or so of compliment. One witty nobleman, indeed, whispered to another,—"If King Joseph is dead, King Sebastian has come to life again!" Before many days were over, he had cause to repent his words. Several persons who were expected by their friends did not make their appearance, though it was affirmed some were even seen on their way thither.

"Where is the Conde d'Atouquia?" asked the young Count Villela. "He owes me two hundred crowns; the dice were unfortunate to him, but I wish to give him his revenge, or I may, perhaps, double the sum."

"He followed me through the hall of the passage, but I saw no more of him," was the answer.

It was an admirable device of the Minister's to prevent a disturbance, had he dreaded one; for all those whom he had reason to suspect were, like Luis, requested to walk on one side, when they were quietly apprehended, and driven off to prison, without any of their friends suspecting what had become of them.

The residences of the various members of the Tavora family were surrounded by troops, so that none could escape. The old Marchioness was one of the first seized. She had retired to her chamber, where her attendants were unrobing her, when a party of men burst into the palace and, without ceremony, entering her room, the chief of the police commanded her to accompany them without delay. Allowing her scarcely time to resume her gown, she was hurried to a carriage in waiting for her, and, without permitting her to communicate with any one, was driven to the Convent of Grillos, at some little distance from Lisbon. This convent was one belonging to the most rigid of all the monastic orders in Portugal; and tales were told of the deeds done within its walls, which make one shudder at their bare recital. It possessed damp and gloomy passages, and subterraneous chambers, into which the light of day never penetrated. The only garment which the hapless recluses wore was one of the coarsest cloth; their food, which they ate off plates of rough earthenware, was vegetables, without salt; and the singing of hymns, and the monotonous service of the Church, was their only employment. In this lugubrious retreat every warm affection of the heart was chilled—the thoughts of all its inmates were sad and mournful; for no one would have willingly entered it, unless impelled by the remorse of conscience, for some heavy crime, in hopes of gaining forgiveness from Heaven, by penance and fasting. The unfortunate Donna Leonora was committed to the charge of the Lady Abbess of this establishment, with strict orders to allow her no possible chance of escape, to ensure which a guard was also stationed outside the building. Here she was left, after being informed that every member of her family was likewise imprisoned.

When the officers sent to apprehend the Marquis arrived at his palace, they found that he had quitted home, and was supposed to be at the house of his sister, the Countess of —, whither they immediately proceeded. He was engaged in conversation with that lady, when a servant entered, with alarm on his countenance, to inform him that some persons were inquiring for him below, who were evidently emissaries of the Minister.

"Oh! do not venture down, then," exclaimed the Countess. "Conceal yourself here till you can fly elsewhere for safety; for, depend on it, the Minister contemplates some injury to you."

"I feel myself guiltless of any crime against the state, and fear not his malice," replied the Marquis. "I will see what the persons require, and return to you directly."

"Oh, in mercy, do not go, my brother," reiterated the Countess, endeavouring to detain him. "I have lately had sad forebodings that some danger was impending over you, and now, alas! they are about to be fulfilled."

The Marquis having with difficulty, for the moment, calmed his sister's fears, proceeded down stairs, when, no sooner had he reached the hall, than he was surrounded by armed men, the leader of whom peremptorily demanded his sword.

"I shall give that to no one but my sovereign, to whom I shall this instant go, to learn the cause of this insolent outrage," answered the Marquis, endeavouring to pass on. "Let my carriage be brought to the door this instant."

"My orders are peremptory," returned the officer. "I must conduct you forthwith to prison."

"To prison!" said the Marquis, starting, "of what crime am I accused?"

"Of high treason," answered the officer. "Thus much I am permitted to inform you; the other members of your family are already in custody, and I am ordered to conduct your Excellency to the same prison—this is my warrant;" and he presented a paper, which the Marquis took, glancing his eye over it.

"I see it possesses his Majesty's signature, and that I never disobey," he answered. "Do your duty, senhor; I am ready to accompany you; but I should first wish to change my dress at my own palace."

"I have no power to permit it: your Excellency must repair forthwith to the prison."

The Marquis, without deigning further reply, stepped at once into his carriage, which, surrounded by a body of cavalry, drove quickly away. It stopped at length before a building lately repaired by orders of the Minister,—no one had been able to understand for what purpose; where, before the earthquake, wild beasts had been confined, as objects of curiosity; but at the time of that event it had been thought necessary to destroy them, for fear of their getting loose. He was here unceremoniously ordered to alight, and conducted, between guards, into the interior, where a person who acted as governor of the new prison—a creature of the Minister—led the way, without speaking, to a cell, the last occupant of which had been an untamed lion. It contained no other furniture than such as had served the wild beast of the forest, a bundle of straw scattered on one side forming the only couch. Into this place the unhappy nobleman was thrust, the door was closed upon him, and he was left to ruminate on the cause of his apprehension, and the probable fate he might expect, judging from the barbarous treatment he now experienced.

Volume Three—Chapter Fifteen.

Our history carries us once more to the country-house of the Duke of Aveiro at Azeitaö, where the noble owner had arrived the morning after the family meeting at the Quinta of the Marquis of Tavora, of which Antonio had so unexpectedly become a witness. The Duke, who was supposed to be still in the country at that time, had secretly visited Lisbon for the occasion, where he had now left his confidant, Senhor Policarpio, to watch the progress of events, and to give him timely notice of what was taking place. So confident was he of the success of their plans, and of the Minister's entire want of suspicion that he was in any way connected with the attempt on the life of the King, that he would listen to none of the warnings which some of his more sagacious friends had lately sent him. One contained but the following lines:—"Beware of the tiger and the lion!—if, perchance, you fall into their den, they will devour you." Another letter was rather more explicit:—"I fear that our meeting will be rather more numerous than it ought to be. A secret is out when many people know it, and on these occasions a man requires three heads under his cap."

These letters arrived by the post, and had the infatuated Duke examined them well, he would have discovered that the seals had been previously broken. After reading them, he threw them aside, with an exclamation of disdain. "My worthy friend truly seems to have a mighty fear of this Sebastiaö Jozé; but we will soon show him which is the tiger to be dreaded," he observed.

The very day previous to the apprehension of the Marquis of Tavora and his family, the Duke received notice from a friend that a vessel was prepared, and would sail that evening, recommending him to escape in time from the storm which was then brewing; but, with the most extraordinary infatuation, he refused to take advantage of the offer, declaring his conviction that no injury could possibly be done him. His Duchess, in whom he had not ventured to confide, and who had long suffered from dreadful suspicions that he was implicated in the conspiracy, in vain also urged him to fly the country.

"What! fair lady, and quit these realms which may soon be my own?" he answered. "No!—I put more confidence in the prophecies of the holy Father Malagrida than to do so—his promises will not fail me."

His friend set sail without him, and escaped. We shall see how far Malagrida's words were made good. Yet, reader, condemn not the mad Jesuit alone; there are many of his class, in the present day, who would equally lead their deluded followers to destruction, did they not, fortunately for themselves, live in happier times, and under a more enlightened government, without having their own wisdom, we suspect, to thank for their safety.

The Duke had just risen, and was seated, in his morning-gown, in the room he usually inhabited, when his son, the young Marquis of Gouvea, entered, with a gun in his hand, equipped for a shooting expedition. The youth was in high spirits at the thoughts of his day's sport; and the father, with his many faults, was proud of his noble boy, and blessed him as he parted from him.

Scarcely had the young Marquis quitted the house, when Senhor Policarpio, with disordered dress, and covered with dust, rushed into the presence of his master. "Fly, my lord!" he exclaimed,—"we are betrayed, and all is discovered! There is not a moment to lose: the Marquis of Tavora and all his family were apprehended last night, and the moment I heard of it I hurried off here to warn you of your danger."

"Whither can I fly?" exclaimed the Duke. "It is useless; besides, no one will dare to injure me. Even that bold plebeian, Sebastiaö Jozé, would not venture so far."

"Pardon me, your Excellency, then," answered Policarpio; "I feel very certain that he will venture to hang me, if he can catch me, so I must take care of my own life." And, without waiting to hear anything his master might wish to say further, he hurried from the apartment.

His first care was to go to his own room, and to collect in a bag all the money he had hoarded up. He then threw off the garments he wore, and dressed himself in some ragged ones, which he had brought under his cloak. The latter garment served to conceal his new costume, as, seizing his bag of coin, he hastened from the house, unnoticed by any one. He took the least frequented way across the estate, stopping every now and then to listen and to look around, lest any guards might be approaching. He then, after quitting his master's property, hurried across the country, and halted not for many miles, till he arrived in the centre of a pine-forest, through which ran a clear and tranquil brook. Having looked carefully around, he sat himself down on the bank, and, drawing a knife from his pocket, he deliberately cut off every particle of his hair, throwing it, as he did so, into the water. His next operation was to scratch the entire surface of his face and neck, and the greater part of his legs and hands, with his knife, rubbing them over at the same time with an ointment he had provided. With this application the skin became swollen and discoloured to a frightful degree, so that, after a few minutes had passed, it would have been utterly impossible, even for the most intimate acquaintance, to have recognised him. He next tore and dirtied still more the garments he wore, and, cutting a rough staff from a branch of a fallen tree, he left the spot with the exact appearance of a loathsome and wandering beggar. For many years was that wretched figure seen roaming from spot to spot, expecting every instant to be recognised, daring to confide in no one, without a friend in the world, conscience-stricken and miserable, yet clinging to life—no one suspecting that beneath those rags was hidden the atrocious criminal, Joseph Policarpio.

We must now return to the Duke of Aveiro. For some time he would not believe the account Policarpio had given him; but sat waiting, every instant expecting his return, to give him further information, when his servant, Manoel Ferreira (who, at the particular desire of Policarpio, had, for obvious reasons, transferred his services from the Marquis to him), rushed into the room with the information, that an officer of justice, and a considerable body of armed men, were approaching the house.

He now, for the first time, showed some symptoms of comprehending his danger; and, when his Duchess, entering the apartment, and throwing herself at his feet, entreated him to fly, he no longer hesitated to comply with her urgent prayer. He hastened to the window, which commanded a view of the entrance to the grounds, and there, at a few paces off only, he beheld a body of cavalry, advancing rapidly up the avenue. He stood for a moment, irresolute what course to pursue.

"Come, my lord, we must not stay here to be taken like rats in a trap," exclaimed Manoel, whose impatience had become excessive. "We have yet time to escape into the woods, where we may remain concealed till we learn the worst that is likely to happen to us."

"Oh! follow Manoel's advice," added the Duchess. "I will stay, and endeavour to delay the police."

"Close every door and window in the house," she cried to the other servants, who crowded in to learn what was the matter. "Haste, haste! not a moment is to be lost—your master's life depends on your alacrity. We may hold out for some time, before they suspect we are deceiving them."

While the servants hurried off to obey her orders, she took her husband's hand, and led him to a small door, at the back of the building, whence he might escape across a field, into the woods which surrounded the Quinta. She here resigned him to Manoel; for so completely had terror now mastered him, that he seemed incapable of guiding his own steps, while she retired to an upper window to watch his progress.

The Duchess gazed anxiously from the window. She saw her husband pass through the garden, without being observed; and he had already crossed more than half way the field which separated it from the wood, when the tramp of horses sounded in the paved court, in front of the building. No one yet followed him. A loud knocking was now heard at the hall-door, and a voice, in an authoritative tone, demanded admittance in the King's name. She longed to watch, until he was in comparative safety; yet she feared, lest the servants, becoming alarmed, might open the door to his pursuers, when his capture must be inevitable; for, exposed to view, as he now was, from every upper window at the back of the house, they could scarcely avoid seeing him, as they hurried through the rooms in search of him. Casting a last glance in the direction he was pursuing, she hastened down stairs, where she found most of the servants collected in the hall, consulting as to the prudence of admitting the emissaries of justice. The blows on the door were repeated with greater violence; the old major-domo, trembling with alarm, had his hand on a bolt, about to withdraw it.

"Would you murder your master?" she exclaimed, seizing the old man's arm. "If you are men, protect him to the last; I will be answerable to these people for all that may happen."

With prayers and commands, she then persuaded the domestics to retire to the upper part of the house, whither she followed them; and, throwing open a window, she inquired, in a calm voice, the object of the visit of the military.

"We come to demand the body of Don Jozé de Mascarenhas, Duke of Aveiro," answered the Desembargador, the officer of justice, who had charge of the party. "If he does not forthwith deliver himself up to our lawful authority, we shall instantly proceed to force open the door."

"Let me first see the warrant for his apprehension, and I will then obey your commands, if I find you speak the truth," returned the Duchess, anxious by any excuse to gain time.

"That cannot be," answered the officer. "Either at once open the door, or we must find some other means to make an entrance."

"Do so at your peril," said the Duchess, firmly. "The Duke does not feel disposed to allow any stranger to enter his house; but, if you will wait, I will go and consult his wishes with regard to our proceedings;" and, closing the window, she hurried away to the back of the house, leaving her enemies under the belief that the Duke was still within.

The servants were running backwards and forwards, wringing their hands, and sobbing with alarm, as they entreated her to allow them to throw open the door. Again insisting on their obeying her orders, she looked forth towards the wood.

"Oh! Heaven protect him!" she exclaimed, as she saw the Duke and his attendant, still at some short distance from the wood. "In two minutes more he will be hidden from their view."

Scarcely had the Duchess uttered these words, when again the loud blows on the door resounded through the house. Again they were repeated; a crashing noise, as of wood rent asunder, was heard. The women shrieked, and fled in all directions to hide themselves, followed by the men-servants, except a page of the Duke's, who, seizing a sword, seemed determined to defend his mistress from insult. The door was thrown down, the tramp of feet echoed through the hall, heavy steps were heard ascending the stairs, but the Duchess heeded them not; her gaze was fixed on her lord. A few paces more and the trees would have concealed him, when the door of the apartment was thrown open, and several men rushed in. She could endure no longer, and uttering a cry of despair, she sank, fainting, on the ground. The page in vain attempted to prevent the soldiers from approaching the window; he was soon disarmed and bound, when, at that moment, the officer of justice entering, his keen eye caught sight of the persons of the fugitives in the distance. He at once guessing who they were, and the reason of the Duchess's refusal to admit the party, despatched some of his followers in pursuit.

The Duke's courage had revived on finding that no one followed, and he was congratulating himself on his chance of escape, when, as he and Manoel had just entered the wood, the latter, turning a glance towards the house, beheld, to his dismay, several persons emerging from the garden.

"On, on, my lord! we are pursued!" he exclaimed.

"Then all is lost!" cried the Duke, abandoning himself to despair.

"Not so, your Excellency. By plunging deeper into the wood, we may find some spot where, throwing ourselves on the ground, we may remain concealed till the soldiers have passed by," the servant answered.

The Duke caught at the idea as a drowning man will at a straw; and, his courage once more reviving, they ran forward among the trees, completely screened from the view of those who were on the other side of the field. They ran for life and liberty, straining every nerve, and exerting every faculty, to escape, while their pursuers were urged on in the chase by the hopes of the reward they expected to receive, and the excitement of hunting a fellow-creature. We leave the case to moral philosophers to determine which have the most powerful incentive, the hunted, or the blood-hounds thirsting for their blood; though we should be inclined to award it to the latter. The first can but, at the worst, be captured and slain, while the hunters may gloat over their prey, and talk in after times of the deeds they have done.

The Duke and his servant now reached a deep dell, to cross which was absolutely necessary; yet, on mounting on the opposite side, they must be exposed to observation.

"We are lost!" cried the Duke again.

"No, no, your Excellency," returned Manoel. "Quick! quick! it may prove our salvation. See those piles of wood heaped up at the bottom, which the wood-cutters have left, we may crawl beneath some of them, and the soldiers will, probably, in their haste, not think of stopping to search for us."

This being the only feasible plan, they hurried down the bank towards the piles of wood. They could hear the shouts of their pursuers, just entering the forest, as they reached their place of refuge. A quantity of branches and brushwood had been cut down, and lay scattered about. These they hastily collected together against the piles of newly-cut wood, when, an instant before the foremost pursuer had reached the summit of the bank, they crept beneath the heap. Onward came the hunters in full cry. They rushed down the glen.

"He has gained the opposite bank," cried one.

"Yes, I just now caught sight of his dress among the trees," shouted another.

"Hurra for the reward of the lucky one who captures him!" echoed several.

"Courage, comrades! Onward, on!"

The Duke trembled with alarm, as these sounds reached his ear. The tramp of feet was heard hurrying close by the place of their concealment—they passed—they mounted the bank,—their voices grew less distinct, and at greater distances from each other, as if they had extended their line. Gradually the noises altogether ceased, and the Duke and his companion breathed more freely. Manoel ventured to look out, and, as far as he could see, no one appeared.

"What shall we now do, my good Manoel?" asked his master.

"We must remain quietly here till the night," was the answer; "we may then with some degree of safety be able to reach the interior of the country before the morning breaks; but never must we allow ourselves to be discovered by daylight on the road."

"This is a very uneasy posture I am in," observed the Duke.

"It is better than your Excellency would enjoy on the scaffold," pithily answered the servant; and the master made no further complaints. "Hark! what sound is that? Footsteps approach—silence, for our lives!" whispered Manoel.

When the Desembargador had despatched the soldiers in pursuit of the fugitives, he had also ordered the Notary, Senhor de Leiro, to accompany them, an office that respectable personage was not very well qualified to perform, seeing that, although his fingers, from constant practice, were active and pliant, his legs, as for many years they had never moved faster than a sedate walk, were very far from being so. He had also read that the van of an advancing army was a far more dangerous post than the rear; and, as it was said that the terrible Duke had fired at the King, he felt that he would make very little ceremony in shooting him outright; he therefore allowed the fighting party to precede him, while he advanced in a more dignified way in the same direction. By the time, however, that he reached the side of the dell, the soldiers had already run completely out of sight. He sighed as he thought of the toil before him; but his duty peremptorily called on him to proceed; or it might have been that he dreaded the loss of his situation if he neglected it; so he managed to reach the bottom of the glen, and to scramble again up the opposite side. Here, however, fatigue overpowered him, and he was obliged to seat himself down on the bank to rest. While there, hoping that the soldiers would quickly return with the prisoners, and thus save him further exertion, and, bemoaning his hard fate, he observed a heap of dried boughs at the bottom of the glen begin to move, and a man's head protrude beyond it.

"Ah!" he thought, "that head belongs to one of the criminals, to a certainty. Now, if I were a strong man, I would capture him myself; but as I am not, I had better not attempt it, for he may think fit to give me a quietus instead."

The Notary having come to this judicious resolution, kept a vigilant watch on the heap of branches, in the hopes that some one would pass that way to afford him assistance in capturing the prey; nor had he long to wait before chance led a farmer and his servant to cross the wood at no great distance from where he sat. On his beckoning to them, they immediately came up to him; when, in a few words, he explained that he was on the watch for an atrocious criminal, and promised them a reward if they would assist in capturing him. They immediately assented, when they all three set forward towards the spot where the wretched Duke was concealed.

"Seize the traitor, alive or dead!" exclaimed Senhor de Leiro, in a loud voice, as he pointed to the underwood.

On hearing these words, Manoel, finding further concealment was hopeless, sprang up, determined to make one struggle for life, the Duke following his example, with the intention of flying. The appearance of two desperate men somewhat staggered the valour of the Notary, particularly when Manoel, rushing towards him, seized the sword from his side, and would have run him through with his own weapon, when a cry from the Duke drew off his attention for the moment. On turning round, he beheld his master dragged away by the farmer and his servant.

"Release him, villains!" he cried; "he is the Duke of Aveiro!"

"We know that well enough," answered the farmer. "He shot at our gracious King!"

Manoel was about to avenge his master, or endeavour to release him, when the shouts of the soldiers, returning through the wood, struck his ear. He now saw that all further attempts to save the Duke would be hopeless; so, abandoning him to his fate, he rushed past the Notary, who tried to impede him, and sought his own safety in flight. He was still in sight when the soldiers appeared on the top of the bank, and the Notary, pointing in the direction of the fugitive, some set off in pursuit, while others hastened forward to secure the greater prize.

The unfortunate Duke was dragged back to his mansion, and, without being allowed even to alter his dress, or to see his Duchess, he was hurried into a carriage, waiting ready in the court-yard to receive him.

Just as he was driven off, he saw his young son brought in, vainly struggling in the grasp of the rude soldiers who held him.

No sooner had the Duke disappeared, than the Duchess was led down stairs, and desired to enter her own carriage, which was now brought round to the door. Almost fainting with grief and terror—for she had beheld her husband a prisoner, and her fears pictured his too probable fate—she requested that her son might accompany her; but this was peremptorily refused. She then entreated that she might be allowed to see him.

"Such cannot be, madam," answered the Desembargador. "My orders are explicit to allow no communication between the prisoners. Your destination is the Convent of the Grillos; the young Marquis must accompany me." Without waiting to hear the answer of the unhappy lady, he ordered the driver to proceed.

A third carriage was in attendance to convey the young Marquis to the prison intended for him. He was now brought out of the house in the custody of some soldiers. The news of his parent's apprehension had come on him like a thunderbolt; but he neither shed a tear, nor uttered a complaint. On being informed that he must quit his home, he insisted on being allowed to prepare for his journey: this was refused him. He then desired to return to his room, to procure some money and necessaries.

"No, senhor," answered the Desembargador, "you will require no money where you are going, and all necessaries will be supplied you. Come, quick, young sir; I am hurried."

"You seem to have the power to enforce your commands, so I must obey," said the young noble, haughtily, as he stepped into the carriage. Looking from the window, to take a last farewell of the house, destined, poor youth, never to be his own, he saw, to his sorrow, the servant Manoel dragged forward bleeding, with his hands bound, and, with his father's page, thrown into a cart, which had been provided for the occasion. All the other men-servants were, likewise, carried as prisoners to Lisbon, while the officers of the crown took possession of the house.

The Desembargador then took his seat by the side of the young Marquis, and, as they drove towards Lisbon, he endeavoured, by a variety of questions, to gain as much information from him as possible respecting the Duke's movements; but the son was on his guard, and refused firmly to answer a word. He was then offered his liberty, if he would agree to assume the cowl of a monk.

"No," he answered, boldly, "I was born to be a noble of Portugal; and never will I consent to become a lazy monk. Lead me to prison: I am innocent, and fear you not."

"We shall see, young sir, if in a few days you do not change your tone," said the Desembargador, as the carriage stopped before the gloomy walls of the Jungueira.

"Never!" answered the young Marquis, firmly: nor could the dungeon into which he was thrown, and the barbarous treatment he received, compel him to change his determination.

Much of the above description we have extracted from a manuscript work written by the unfortunate Marquis d'Alorna, who was confined for many years in the Jungueira.

Volume Three—Chapter Sixteen.

Luis d'Almeida had already spent some time in prison, each successive day expecting to be informed of the cause of his detention, and to be brought to trial; but nothing of the sort occurred. He received, it is true, several visits from the polite and complaisant Governor, who appeared to take great pleasure in his conversation, and who was most liberal in his promises of a more airy and commodious lodging, and of every luxury which he had the power to bestow; but his memory appeared to be very bad, for the prisoner found no improvement in any way in his treatment. It is true that, on the night of his incarceration, he had been supplied with bedding, which the Governor, on his first visit, assured him was procured with considerable difficulty and expense, hinting that his most advisable plan would be to pay for it at once, lest it might be required for some other person, who might possess sufficient means to purchase it. Luis at once paid the exorbitant demand, requesting, at the same time, to be furnished with writing materials, which, though they were at once promised him, never made their appearance. He begged also to be allowed to send to his lodgings for a change of linen and clothes; but this was at once refused, he being informed that his friends must not learn even the place of his imprisonment.

On the first night after his incarceration, when the outer world was hushed in silence, as he lay awake on his wretched pallet, he fancied that he heard suppressed groans, as if proceeding from the ground beneath his cell. He listened attentively, and became certain that his senses had not deceived him. "Alas!" he thought, "can a human being be confined in a yet more wretched abode than I inhabit?" The groans were continued at intervals, and proceeded, apparently, from some unfortunate prisoner suffering from pain and sickness. Day after day they continued, but Luis was left in vain conjecture as to their origin.

One day, at about the usual hour, the Governor, with a complaisant smile on his countenance, made his appearance, and bowing politely to his prisoner, he seated himself on the bed, begging him to occupy the chair near the table.

"You must excuse ceremony, Senhor Conde," he began; "but though, to say the truth, I am rather hurried, I wished to enjoy the pleasure of a little conversation with you. I fear you must find it very solitary here, and must be getting heartily tired of your present life."

"Indeed I am, senhor," answered Luis; "and I shall much rejoice to find myself at liberty."

"Very naturally. Most prisoners think the same; but do not despair; you will, in the course of time, get perfectly accustomed to it. I have heard of people living twenty years in prison very happily, so that, at last, when they were allowed to quit it, they preferred remaining where they were."

"I trust that will not be my case," observed Luis.

"That depends on circumstances," said the Governor. "I might, indeed, point out a way by which you might instantly gain your freedom."

"Pray then inform me what it is, for I would do much to be set at liberty," said the prisoner.

"I am glad, at length, to hear you talk so reasonably," said the Governor. "I need not tell you an execrable conspiracy has been discovered against the life of his Majesty, in which several known friends of yours are implicated; now, if you will give information on the subject to the Minister, he will not only overlook any share you have taken in it, but will reward you in any way you may wish."

"As I have entered into no conspiracy against his Majesty, it is impossible that I should give information, which, in fact, I do not possess," answered Luis; "but assure the Minister, that my very soul revolts against the foul crime which was almost perpetrated, and that I would gladly assist in bringing the criminals to punishment."

"All prisoners speak much in the same strain, my dear sir; but, when once at liberty, they are very apt to forget their former promises," returned the Governor. "Though you may, for many reasons, not like to give any information direct to the Minister, if you will confide it to my ear, you may depend on my making a favourable report of your case to him; if not—I speak as a sincere friend—I fear that you will be deprived for ever of your liberty, if a worse fate does not await you."

Luis at once saw completely the object of the Governor's observations, and was ready to answer them. "I must prepare, then, to meet my fate to the best of my power, for information of any sort I am unable to give," he said.

"That is the answer many gentlemen similarly situated make at first," observed the Governor, smiling; "we find, however, that when put to the question, their powers of recollection are wonderfully stimulated. Of course it will not be necessary with you, Senhor Conde. Heaven forbid it, for the agony few people can support. To be sure, there are occasions when but little respect is paid to persons; indeed, to tell you the truth, such is the case at present; for the Minister has determined to sift this mysterious affair to the bottom, and he is not, you know, very scrupulous about the means he employs. It is whispered about in the prison circles, that the Duke of Aveiro, the Marquis of Tavora, with his sons and sons-in-law, and a few other individuals, underwent the question yesterday. The Duke suffered the most severely, and made extensive confessions; in consequence, several other persons were apprehended during the night. Oh, there is nothing to be compared to the question, for extracting the truth!" and the Governor fixed his keen grey eye upon his prisoner's countenance; but Luis retained his composure, as he answered calmly,—

"I cannot doubt, senhor, your wisdom and experience; but I do the efficacy of the measure you propose for learning the truth. Some men will endure the most excruciating tortures rather than reveal what they have vowed to keep secret; and others, again, who are unable to bear pain, will, in the hopes of avoiding further suffering, even invent a story, and accuse others falsely to save themselves."

"Silence! silence! Senhor Conde, this is blasphemy and treason you are talking," interrupted the Governor. "What! dare to doubt the efficacy of the rack and the thumb-screw? Horrible sacrilege! How could a good wholesome despotism exist without them, I should like to know? Take care,—such expressions are strongly confirmatory of your own guilt. Beware!"

A cold shudder passed through Luis's frame as his eye met the threatening glance of the Governor fixed on him, but he winced not under it, and, folding his arms on his breast, he prepared to listen in silence to whatever observations his unwelcome visitor might think proper to make.

The Governor, however, appeared satisfied that he could gain nothing from him by ordinary conversation, and therefore rose to take his leave, with his usual mock civility, after looking at him with the same sort of eye with which an experienced butcher regards the calf he has just bought, and is leading home to slaughter. "He is a tough subject, and will endure much before he utters a syllable," he muttered loud enough to be heard, as he left the cell, though Luis fortunately did not understand the tenor of his words.

The next day passed, much to his satisfaction, without a visit from the Governor, though an under-gaoler brought him his food, and cleaned his cell, as usual. This man, whose manner and words showed him not to have been completely-hardened by the sufferings he had witnessed, would generally stop a few minutes more than his strict duty required, to offer a few expressions of comfort to the prisoner, for whom he had conceived a compassionate feeling.

Luis now took the opportunity to inquire from whence and from what unhappy prisoner the groans he had heard for several days past proceeded.

"Ah, senhor, I, am sorry they disturb you," answered the gaoler. "There is a poor gentleman confined in the very next cell to yours, who is continually groaning with pain, and bemoaning his hard fate, at being shut up for no crime at all; but the walls are so thick, that I should have thought you could not have heard the sounds."

"Know you his name?" asked Luis.

"I have never heard it, senhor, and never thought of asking him, but I will do so, and tell you. Poor young gentleman, I fear he will not last long."

"Do you think, my friend, that you could manage to let me see my fellow-prisoner?" asked Luis, who felt that it was his duty to offer every consolation in his power to the sick man, besides a natural curiosity to learn more of one whose voice had sounded in his ear for so many days past; "you may trust to my discretion, and that I will not betray your kindness."

"I am not afraid of you, senhor; but if it was by any means discovered that I allowed such a thing, I should not only lose my situation, but be imprisoned in one of the darkest cells, as a warning to my brother gaolers, though I wish that I could do as you desire, for I do not see that any harm can come of it."

Luis was, however, determined not to be defeated in his project; and taking the opportunity to make a present, which he had before intended, to the kind-hearted gaoler, he at length induced him to promise that he would allow him to pay a visit to the neighbouring cell on the first safe opportunity; probably directly after the Governor had gone his rounds,—the time which, in all prisons, gaolers seize to afford similar favours to their captives, as our readers have no doubt observed while perusing every history or romance on the subject.

To a prisoner, the slightest variation in the monotonous routine of his life affords subject of interest; and thus Luis looked forward with anxiety to the time when he was to be allowed to pay a visit to his companion in captivity, though he was aware that but little benefit could be expected to result to either of them from the interview. The Governor at last came his rounds; Luis heard the bolts of his cell door withdrawn, but that worthy personage, merely putting his head in to see that his prisoner was safe, wished him good night, and again retired.

After he had been gone about half an hour, the under-gaoler, faithful to his promise, made his appearance, having carefully opened the door, which, by long practice, he was able to do without any noise, and telling Luis to follow, he gently opened the door of the cell in which the sick man was confined, when, desiring him to enter, he closed and bolted it as before.

The sick man scarcely noticed the entrance of a stranger, as Luis placed himself by the side of the rude couch whereon he lay; but continued his groaning and piteous cries for fresh air and liberty. A lamp, burning on the table, shed its feeble rays around the cell. Luis rose to trim it, and again seated himself, the sick man continuing with his face averted towards the wall. Luis spoke to draw his attention.

"I have come, as a brother in affliction, to offer every assistance in my power to a fellow-prisoner," he said.

Suddenly the sick man turned round, when the light falling on his thin and emaciated countenance, Luis started with amazement, a thrill of joy shooting through his frame; for in those features, though sadly altered by disease and confinement, he beheld the long-lost brother of his beloved Clara, of whose death he had been accused,—the younger Gonçalo Christovaö. He pronounced his name.

"Who is it that calls on one long-lost to the joyous world?" exclaimed the young Fidalgo, in a feeble voice, raising himself on his arm, and gazing wildly at his visitor.

"One you have seen but seldom, who has been vilely traduced, and accused of your death—Luis d'Almeida."

"You have been amply avenged, then, senhor, for the evil thoughts I entertained of you," answered the young Gonçalo. "This is true charity—thus to visit, in a loathsome dungeon, one who has so wronged and injured you. Ah! It is too late now—I have but short time to survive." And he again sunk down exhausted.

"I have never for a moment had a hostile feeling towards you," said Luis, offering his hand, which the other took, with a grateful expression on his countenance.

"Thanks, thanks! it is a consolation to know that a friend of those dear to me will receive my dying breath, and convey my last wishes to my father and sweet sister,—or do I see in you the husband of Clara?"

"Alas! no, my friend," replied Luis, deeply affected. "I am a prisoner like yourself, and, perchance, shall be released but by death."

"What! have you also fallen a victim to the wiles of that vile miscreant, San Vincente?"

"I know not even of what crime I am accused," answered Luis; and he explained, in a few words, the supposed conspiracy, and its fatal consequences. "But tell me by what extraordinary circumstances I see you here?" he continued.

"By the machinations of a villain!" returned the young Fidalgo. "But I am faint, and can scarce tell my tale. A few drops from yonder flask of wine, supplied me by the charity of my kind gaoler, will give me strength to proceed, if you will hand it to me."

Luis brought the flask, when Gonçalo, somewhat revived by a draught of the light refreshing wine of Lisbon, commenced an account of his adventures since the fatal night when Luis had so unintentionally wounded him. His sentences were short and broken, he frequently being obliged to stop, in order to recover strength to proceed.

"I was half mad with intoxication and the excitement of revelry, when, urged on by my evil counsellor, San Vincente, I made that wanton assault upon you, for which I have been so severely punished; but I must confess, that when your sword entered my side, I felt that I deserved my fate. When I returned to consciousness,—for in my fall I must have struck my head, which, aided by the effects of wine, had rendered me insensible—I found myself borne rapidly along the streets by several men. I inquired where they were carrying me; but, though I repeated the question several times, I received no answer; and at length, from the copious effusion of blood, I again fainted. When I once more recovered my senses, I found myself in a low vaulted chamber, on a mean pallet, with the rest of the scanty furniture of the commonest description, and a wrinkled old hag, of the most sinister expression of countenance, sitting in one corner, occupied in spinning. I anxiously inquired where I was; but, putting her finger to her mouth, she pretended to be dumb, to prevent my asking further questions; nor had I the slightest means of conjecturing to what part of the city I had been conveyed. When I endeavoured to rise, I found myself too weak to stand, and was obliged to give up the attempt in despair. It now occurred to me that I had been brought to this place for some sinister motive, and, though I acquitted you of having any share in my detention, I began strongly to suspect that San Vincente was the author of the outrage. I had for some days previously entertained uneasy doubts as to his character, which, in my more serious moments, made me regret that I had favoured his suit to my sister. I recollected, also, that I had lately won from him, at the gambling-table, some large sums of money; and now, incensed against him, I deemed him capable of the darkest acts. It struck me that he supposed, if he married my sister, I should release him from his debt, or, if he could get me out of the way, he should be equally free. Subsequent events proved the correctness of my supposition. Why he did not murder me at once, when I was so entirely in his power, I have never been able, to this day, to determine. Either he is not so bad as I suspected, and felt some compunction at killing an old friend, and the brother of his intended wife, or the fear of discovery and punishment deterred him. I remained thus for two days, without seeing anybody but the old woman, who still retained her taciturnity, and even when she brought me a scanty allowance of food, did so with a morose and unwilling air.

"Never could I forget, if life were prolonged, the awful sensations I experienced when the first shock of the earthquake was felt. I was alone, unable to move,—the terrific sound rang in my ears,—the groans of the dying, the shrieks of despair, reached even that remote spot,—the walls and roof trembled and cracked,—pieces fell around and on me,—I was almost stifled by the dust; yet, utterly helpless, I resigned myself to my fate. Shock after shock occurred, yet still, to my surprise, the walls stood uninjured. I was reserved for more severe suffering."

He ceased speaking, from exhaustion.

"Ah!" thought Luis, as this account brought back the recollection of that dire event, "at that time was I rescuing your sweet sister from destruction. Both our fates have been cruel; yet yours, poor youth, even worse than mine."

Gonçalo, now recovering, continued. "For the whole of that day of horrors, and the following one, I continued without food, becoming each moment more weak, till I thought death must put an end to my suffering, when a tall masked figure entered the vault, a few streams of light, entering from a barred window near the roof, enabling me to distinguish him. At a glance, notwithstanding his disguise, I recognised the Count San Vincente. He looked eagerly towards the spot where I lay, and Heaven forgive me, if I wrong him in believing that he felt disappointed on discovering I was still in existence. Without uttering a word, he directly quitted the vault, and soon afterwards returned with a basket of provisions, which he placed within my reach. He remained not a moment longer than was necessary, nor did I venture to trust myself in speaking to him. I heard him lock and bolt the door after him, as he retired. The old woman never returned; and for the two following days I was left entirely alone.

"During the third night, I was aroused from slumber by a noise near me, and, looking up, by the light of a lantern I beheld several men standing round my bed; a cloth was then thrown over my head, my arms were bound, and I felt myself lifted up, and placed upon a sort of litter, as I concluded, for immediately I perceived that I was being borne along at a rapid rate, and in the open air. I was too feeble to raise my voice; but once, when I attempted to cry out, a person whispered in my ear a warning to be silent, or that death would be my fate. The motion continued for some time, till at last it stopped, and I found myself again placed upon a bed. My arms were then released, but, before I could remove the cloth from my head, my bearers had disappeared, and I found myself in total darkness and silence. Here was new matter for speculation, but I was still utterly at a loss to comprehend the reasons for my removal, or whither I had been conveyed; indeed, I have never learnt to a certainty, though I suspect it was to some house belonging to my persecutor, San Vincente. When the morning dawned, I found that I was in an apartment rather better furnished than my last place of imprisonment, but with only one small window, high up in the wall, and that closely barred with iron. A surly-looking ruffian made his appearance twice a day to bring me food and make my bed, but, like the old woman, he never uttered a word. He, however, brought me a collection of books, which solaced my captivity, and I verily believe prevented me from losing my senses altogether. Several months thus passed away, and I was at length able to rise and walk about my room. The first use I made of my renewed strength was to try the door, but I found it secured by bolts, and plated with iron. I then climbed up to the window, but the walls were thick, and a board sloping upwards from the lower part prevented me seeing aught but a broad expanse of sky. This was a grievous disappointment; indeed, my spirits sank under it, though my strength continued to improve. When my surly attendant perceived that I was strong enough to attempt to, escape, I observed that he invariably came into my room armed with a pistol and dagger, keeping a wary eye, during the time he remained, on every movement I made. This dreadful life of solitude I could no longer endure; my health gave way under it, and I again took to my bed. I entreated the ruffian to send a physician to me, or a priest, to give me the consolations of religion, but he looked at me with a grim smile, without answering, and no one appeared. Gradually I became worse and worse, till I fully believed myself to be dying, so thought also my attendant. One night I awoke from my sleep to find my eyes blinded, and my hands bound as before, when I was brought thither. I was then gagged, while a voice whispered in my ear, 'If one sound escapes you, this dagger shall silence you for ever!' and, at the same time, I felt its sharp point at my breast. I was now lifted up, and found myself suddenly placed in a carriage, which immediately drove on for a considerable time; when it stopped, I was once more lifted from it, and borne along till I heard the sound of bolts and bars withdrawn, when I was placed on the bed where I now lie, and from which I never more expect to rise. Here I have for months been confined, and it seems a miracle to myself that I have existed so long. Except the compassionate gaoler's, yours is the first friendly face I have seen since you last beheld me with my sword raised against your life. Pardon me, my friend, for that deed, for I have bitterly expiated it."

Luis assured the unfortunate youth not only of his forgiveness, but of his sincere commiseration for his sufferings.

"Soon after my arrival here, I gained a clue to ascertain the reason of my last removal," continued Gonçalo. "The Governor of the prison came one evening into my cell, and no sooner did my eye fall upon him, than I recognised a person on whom I had once inflicted chastisement for an insult he had offered me, and whom I well knew to have been at one time an intimate acquaintance of San Vincente's, though he had latterly pretended to have discarded him. I knew why he came—it was to gloat over my sufferings—to reap his revenge. He is a wretch capable of any atrocity—base, mercenary, and avaricious. He told me that I was a prisoner for life, accused of treason; that my name was Diogo Lopez, and that I was spared under the plea of insanity. He then quitted me with a grin of gratified malice on his countenance. I feel confident that the plot was concerted between the two. San Vincente has easily bribed him to engage in it, and gratify his own revenge at the same time; he probably feared that I should die in his custody, when he might have some difficulty in disposing of my body; or, perhaps, he was anxious to destroy me sooner, which he knew sending me here would do. Once incarcerated under a false name, as a condemned criminal, I should here remain without a hope of release, all responsibility being removed from him; and dying, as he knew I soon must, I shall be buried with the other wretches who end their lives here. This is my allotted fate, and, had you not discovered me, it would never have been known. You will, I know, inform my father, and aid him to bring the miscreant San Vincente to the punishment he deserves."

Luis promised to obey his wishes, if he himself ever escaped from prison.

"I have one more request to make," said Gonçalo: "I long, ere I die, to perform the last duties of religion, but I have, in vain, asked for a confessor. The Governor knows I have nothing to reveal. You may in this assist me, by desiring to see one yourself, and you may then, in the same way that you have come, conduct him hither."

"I will use my utmost endeavours to do so," answered Luis, "though I fear much I shall be unsuccessful."

Gonçalo now made many inquiries about his family, to which Luis answered to the best of his knowledge; and when he told him that Clara was about to take the veil, his self-reproach knew no bounds.

"Alas, alas!" he exclaimed, "this has happened through my own mad obstinacy: had I not praised San Vincente to my father, she might even now have been your bride, and both might have been happy."

"Heaven willed it otherwise," said Luis, checking his rising emotion, when he endeavoured to console his unhappy friend; and so far succeeded, that he already appeared to have recovered strength—his spirits, more than his body, had suffered. The gaoler, now softly opening the door, beckoned away Luis, who, pressing Gonçalo's hand, returned to his own cell, reflecting, that if he himself had suffered much, others had yet more to endure.

The following day the Governor thought fit to honour the Count d'Almeida with a visit. He entered, bowing and flourishing his little three-cornered hat, as usual, smirking as he seated himself on the bed. "I fear that you find your life in prison a very dull one, my young friend," he began; "most people do, yet such is the fate of those who will disobey the laws. In the course of a year or two you will become more habituated to it, and then you will learn to like it, if—for I am sorry to say there is an alternative—you are not proved guilty of a crime of the first magnitude;—but, in the latter case, you must prepare for death! Ah, you start;—it is very sad to die, but, I wished to spare your feelings, and therefore concealed your fate from you till now; however, feeling a sincere friendship for you, I would point out the only means you have of escaping. Make a complete confession of all you know, and then, probably, a short imprisonment will be your only punishment."

Luis watched the Governor's eye while he spoke, and although he did not believe his assertions, he felt that they might too probably be founded on truth. Not disconcerted, however, by unmanly fears, he, recollecting his promise to Gonçalo, pretended to credit them; and, on the plea that, perhaps, his death was near, he petitioned to have the consolation of religion afforded him.

"I rejoice, my young friend, to hear you speak in so proper a frame of mind," said the Governor, sententiously. "Even to the prisoner's cell the Church extends her benign influence, and Heaven will be pleased if you confess your sins to the holy man I will send you. He shall visit you this very day, and, putting full confidence in him, let me advise you, as a sincere friend, to follow implicitly his counsels." The Governor, flattering himself that he had gained the very point at which he was aiming, bidding his prisoner be of good cheer, withdrew.

The Governor was in this case true to his word; late in the evening the friendly gaoler entering Luis's cell to inform him that a Friar waited without to see him.

"Beg him to enter," said Luis.

The gaoler retired, and directly after returned, ushering in a cowled and bare-footed Friar.

"Pax vobiscum," said the holy man, as he entered. "I come, my son, to bring food and comfort to your soul. Leave us," he added, turning to the gaoler, "I would be alone with the prisoner."

No sooner had the gaoler withdrawn, than the Friar, throwing back his hood, exhibited to the astonished gaze of his intended penitent, the rotund and ruddy countenance of the holy Frè Diogo Lopez.

"Hush!" said that worthy person, putting his finger to his lips. "I am sorry to find you a prisoner here, though I am glad that it is I who have been sent to you. Come, give me an embrace, to convince me that you retain a kindly recollection of me."

Luis, scarcely able to speak with surprise, performed the ceremony; indeed, the face of one who, though he considered him a rogue, had always shown a friendly disposition towards himself, could not but afford him pleasure.

"Now, we will make ourselves as happy as circumstances will permit," continued the Friar, at the same time producing from beneath his gown a good sized flask, and a couple of glasses, which he placed on the table, a smile curling his lips, and his eyes glistening the while. "Stand there, my friends, till you are wanted," he added, as he seated himself on the bed. "Now, Don Luis, I wish to convince you that, although you once thought me a rogue, I can, at all events, be honest towards you. I am sent here to pump you, to discover all your secrets, and to betray them to the Governor. Now, take my advice; do not tell them to me, or any other confessor; and as there are no proofs against you, as far as I can learn, you have a chance of escaping the punishment many others are about to suffer. This plan will prevent either of us incurring any risk, and I shall feel a wonderful satisfaction in deceiving that cunning devil of a Governor. Ha, ha! the very thought amuses me. I little thought that you were among the unfortunate prisoners shut up in this horrid place, till the Governor sent for me to-day, and informed me that one of his pets desired to see a priest, in order to make confession, desiring me to learn all I could, and let him know without delay. I have done so often before, without feeling any compunction on the subject; for there are so many knaves in the world, that I considered it as merely telling one rogue's secrets to another rogue, besides being well paid into the bargain. I do not wish to know yours, in case I might be tempted to betray them. With me the old weakness is as strong as ever. I cannot resist temptation, though I bitterly repent it afterwards. I, by chance, inquired the name of my penitent, when, to my surprise and sorrow, I learnt it was you. However, I soon made up my mind how to act, and, providing myself with that flask of good wine, I determined to make a jovial evening of it with a clear conscience, instead of hypocritically drawing the secrets from some poor wretch, to betray him afterwards. So now, my dear Don Luis, or rather I ought to say Count, let us to business. I can give you a short shrift afterwards, if you require it, when we have finished the bottle."

So saying, the Friar drew the table between himself and Luis, and filling both glasses with wine, he nodded familiarly to his penitent, draining his off, and smacking his lips, to set him an example. He then indulged in a low quiet chuckle at the young Count's astonishment.

Luis first felt inclined to be disgusted with the Friar's open acknowledgment of his contempt for the sacred office he performed; but the imperturbable coolness and thorough good nature of the latter, at last conquered that feeling, and, forgetting that he had come to perform a religious rite, he could no longer refrain from pledging him in return.

"Well, my dear Count, I am glad to find that you have at length conquered your scruples," said Frè Diogo, laughing. "I have always said it is impossible to know what a man really is till you learn his works. Now, if I had put on a sanctimonious face, played shriver, and betrayed you, you would have considered me a very pious man; and now, because I tell you the truth, and kick hypocrisy to the devil who invented it, you, in your heart of hearts, believe me a knave. Well, it cannot be helped, such is the way of the world. Come, Count, don't be cast down, you have many years to enjoy life yet before you, if I mistake not. Fill your glass, and drive away care. I wish I could venture to sing a stave, it would wonderfully rouse your spirits, but it would not do to be heard—even I could not pass it off as a hymn." And the Friar hummed a few lines of a song in a low tone. "Bah! the effect is spoilt; you ought to hear it trolled forth by a jovial set of us, the roof of the old hall of our convent rings again. Oh, that would do your heart good!"

Luis, in spite of himself, could not help joining in the Friar's merriment, which seemed to give the latter much satisfaction. "That is as it should be, my friend; I wish the gaolers were deaf, and that the rascally Governor was not likely to be prowling this way, for we might drink and sing away to our heart's content. Come, help me to finish the bottle, or I shall not be quite in a clerical state to make a clear report to the Governor of your confession."

There was such a laughing devil in the Friar's eye all the time, that it struck Luis he might even then be playing off some trick upon him.

"How comes it, Frè Diogo, that I see you here in Lisbon as a professed Friar, when, the last time we met, you acknowledged you had never taken the vows?" he asked.

"Don't you remember, that I told you, at the same time, I intended to repent of my sins, to return to the convent in which I once served, and to take the vows? I did so, and have ever since been a most exemplary Friar; so much so, that I soon rose to a responsible situation in my convent, and was sent up to Lisbon on a mission, when I was selected for my peculiar qualifications and knowledge of mankind, as confessor to the inmates of this and some other prisons in the metropolis. I was obliged to accept the office, though I cannot say I like it; for I miss my jovial brothers, and hate the hypocrisy and treachery I am obliged to be guilty of, though, to say the truth, I have saved many a poor wretch from committing himself, which is some consolation to my conscience."

Luis had not forgotten poor Gonçalo's request; but he was considering in his mind whether the priest in question was a person qualified to administer the consolations of religion to a dying man; but there was a sincerity in the eccentric Friar's manner, which at last determined him, for want of a better, to confide in him. At all events, he felt that it might afford satisfaction to the dying youth. He, therefore, told the Friar of his interview with his fellow-prisoner, the young Gonçalo Christovaö, whom he had been accused of killing, recalling to his mind their fruitless search, and finished, by begging him to administer, with the utmost decorum he could assume, the rites of the Church appointed for the sick or dying.

"You seem by your words, to suppose that I am not as capable as the most rigid and sanctimonious confessor, who ever shrived a fair penitent, to put on a serious air when necessary," said the Friar, laughing. "There you are wrong again; and I will show you that I can equal the best of them. By the way, now you mention the name of Gonçalo Christovaö, it reminds me that, in a most wonderful way, I came into possession of the very letter I gave you with the jewels in the cave, and which you lost before you could deliver it to the person to whom it was directed,—the father of this same hapless youth. You will not press me to explain exactly how I got it—suffice it to say, I found it in the pocket of a coat which, doubtless, had been yours, and which I strongly suspect had been stolen."

"Have you the letter still?" inquired Luis, eagerly. "I have ever since had cause to regret its loss; for, though I know its contents, I have had a feeling that it might have saved much wretchedness to one I love dearer than life itself."

"It struck me, also, at the time I found it, that it might be of some consequence, so I preserved it carefully for several months in my breviary, intending to restore it to you or Senhor Christovaö, should I meet either of you, though I had long forgot all about it; whether or no it is still there, I cannot say," said the Friar. "I fortunately brought the book to Lisbon with me, so if the letter is in it, I will bring it to you on my next visit. I shall take care, by my account to the Governor of your confession, to be sent to you again."

"Thanks, my kind friend," answered Luis. "You may thus render me a great service, though, could you send it to Gonçalo Christovaö yourself, it would sooner reach him. I know not when my term of captivity may end."

"I will endeavour to do as you wish," answered the Friar. "Now, my dear Count, I am speaking more seriously to you than I ever did to any one in my life. I have a true regard for you, and sincerely wish to rise in your opinion. Do not think me a scoundrel, for I am better than I have too often appeared. Will you promise me this?" The Friar spoke with energy, and a tear stood in his eye, as he took Luis's hand, and pressed it to his heart.

"I firmly trust in you," answered Luis, "and know you to be my kind and generous friend,—one of the few I now possess on earth."

"Thanks, Count, thanks! your words have made me a happier and better man," said the Friar, much moved. "The knowledge that I am esteemed by one honest person, who knows me as I am, will prevent me from ever again acting the part of a knave." He drew a deep sigh. "Ha! ha! we must not let care oppress us, so we will finish our bottle before the turnkey comes to summon me away. I will then visit your sick friend, and do what I can to comfort him. Remember, whatever happens, confide in me. If I find that your life is in the slightest danger, it shall not be my fault that you do not escape from hence."

Luis warmly expressed his thanks to Frè Diogo, for he now felt convinced that he had gained an invaluable friend, and the dull leaden sensation he had experienced at the thoughts of his speedy execution, gave way to a renewed hope of life.

"Ah! here comes the gaoler," exclaimed the Friar, as steps were heard in the passage; "he is a worthy fellow, and the only honest man employed in the prison. I now and then crack a bottle with him for society's sake;—thinking of that, I must hide my friend and the glasses under my robe; so fare you well, Count, till to-morrow." As he spoke the turnkey opened the door, when Luis, entreating him to introduce the Friar to the sick man in the next cell, he promised to comply, and the Count was left alone to meditate on his own fortunes.

Volume Three—Chapter Seventeen.

Words are insufficient to describe the sufferings of the high-born captives who lay in those wretched cells, formed to contain wild beasts instead of human beings, whither the stern policy of the Minister had condemned them to be conveyed. Kept apart from each other, in darkness and solitude, though near enough to hear each other's groans and cries, they were allowed no change of garments from those in which they were first apprehended; straw heaped in a corner on the floor, unswept since the removal of its former savage inhabitants, formed their places of rest; the coarsest food, sufficient to sustain nature, was alone supplied them, and no one but the officers of justice was allowed to visit them.

Day after day they remained thus, in anticipation of their dreadful fate; then came ferocious looking men, callous to the sufferings of their fellow-beings, whose appearance bespoke them to be the detested executioners of the law; even the guards and gaolers shuddered as they beheld them entering the prison, bearing their implements of torture. Two Desembargadors, a notary, and a surgeon followed, repairing to a large hall, round which the cells occupied by the prisoners were ranged, their fronts being now blocked up with masonry. The executioners had here erected their instruments of torture, chairs being prepared for the judges and notary, with a table for the latter to take minutes of the examination.

The first prisoner led forward was the Duke of Aveiro, but he refused to answer any of the questions put to him.

"Since you refuse to speak in any other way, we must try what effect the rack will cause," said one of the judges. "Let the question be administered to him."

The Duke turned pale, but answered not a word till the dislocation of his limbs commenced, when he gave way to shrieks and cries for mercy, which rang through the hall, piercing to the cells of his fellow-prisoners, and giving dreadful warning of the fate awaiting them.

"I will confess! I will confess!" at last he cried, unable longer to endure the agony; but when, on being cast loose, he again denied any knowledge of the occurrences the Desembargadors mentioned, he was once more placed upon the engine of torture, nor would they listen to his entreaties to be released till he had further felt its power.

"Mercy, mercy, mercy!" he cried, when the surgeon approached him, and his cries ceased. He had fainted. He was lifted off the machine, and carried back to his cell, where restoratives were administered, and he was left till sufficiently recovered to bear further questioning.

The Marquis of Tavora was then brought forward, and subjected to the same system of examination; but not a word, to criminate either himself or others, could be elicited from him. His sons, the Conde d'Atouquia, and the servants of both houses, followed in succession; the agony of their sufferings drawing statements from some of them which the others denied. Young Jozé de Tavora was the only one, who, like his father, boldly and firmly persisted in the declaration of his innocence of the crime laid to his charge.

"Were I guilty of the deed of which you accuse me, I would acknowledge it," he exclaimed; "but no tortures the cruelty of Sebastiaö Jozé can invent have power to make me speak a falsehood."

"Take him to his cell," thundered the Magistrate; "he is obdurate. Bring back the Duke."

The same scene of horror was again enacted, when the wretched noble, overcome by terror, made a long statement, which was eagerly committed to paper by the Notary, accusing himself, his fellow-prisoners, and numerous others of the highest nobility in the land, of conspiring against the life of the King. Whether his account was true, or whether it was the invention of his brain wrought into madness by agony, has never yet been satisfactorily determined. We leave our readers to form their own conclusions.

We do not venture to describe more minutely the dreadful scene of tyranny, injustice, and human suffering; for we have yet in store horrors sufficient to make the heart of the strongest sicken at the recital; and we would advise those who would avoid having their feelings harrowed with the tale which truth compels us to narrate, to pass over the chapter succeeding this.

At last, all the evidence which could be wrung by torture from the prisoners, or obtained from other witnesses, being collected, their trial formally took place. On the first day, the judges appointed by the Minister to preside could not come to an agreement; two of them firmly refusing to sign the process. Carvalho, probably, firmly believed most, if not all, of the prisoners guilty; and, after the violent steps he had taken, his own existence depended on their condemnation; but, owing to the absence of clear and satisfactory evidence, this was difficult to be obtained. He therefore instituted another court, taking care that the presidents should be creatures entirely devoted to his service, and the result of the trial may be anticipated.

The weak and timid Monarch yet remained a close prisoner in his palace, suspecting a traitor in each noble of his court, and starting at every sound, fancying it a signal of rebellion. His physician had just quitted him, Teixeira was absent, and the Minister had himself gone to watch the proceedings at the trial of the conspirators. He was alone—his feelings were oppressed, his thoughts gloomy; for his disposition was naturally mild, and indisposed to bloodshed; and he now knew that the blood of his first nobles was about to flow like water for his safety. Yet what injustice will not fear make a man commit! He wept.

"Alas!" he cried, "they must die. The trial must, ere this, have been concluded, and I shall then know the punishment awarded them. It must be so; I cannot feel security till they are no more."

The King heard a suppressed sob near him, and looking round, he beheld a young page kneeling at a short distance from where he sat. He started, and rising, retired a few paces, for in every human being he had been taught to suspect an agent of treason.

"What brings you here, boy? How could you have entered unperceived?" he exclaimed rapidly, as a strange thrill shot across his bosom. "Speak! who are you?"

"A wretched suppliant for your Majesty's clemency," answered the Page, in a low and broken voice.

"What mean you, boy? There are too many such in our dominions," exclaimed the Monarch, bitterly. "But rise, boy, and retire: this intrusion ought to have been prevented. Whatever petition you have to make, present it to our Minister, Sebastiaõ Jozé, two or three days hence, when he will have time to attend to you. We would be alone."

"Alas! two days hence will be too late," responded the Page, in the same low tone as before. "It is not to that cruel unbending man I would make my prayer. It is to your Majesty's compassionate heart alone, a miserable guilty creature would appeal. Hear me, my liege; hear me. By my guilty conduct, many of those I was bound to love and honour—my kindred and connexions—have been, like the vilest felons, imprisoned and tortured, and some have, within this hour, been condemned to an agonising death and everlasting disgrace. For them I come to plead—their lives, their honour, are in your power. Spare them, my liege, and let me be the victim; for I, and I alone, have been the cause of all their sufferings."

"Great Heavens! Whose voice is that?" exclaimed the King, more agitated than his suppliant, towards whom he hurriedly advanced, and whom he raised from the ground. "Donna Theresa!"

"Would to God you had never known that name, my liege. I am that wretched woman," ejaculated the seeming page, still keeping her hands in a suppliant attitude before her, while the King gazed fondly at her care-worn, though yet lovely, countenance. "I have braved all dangers and difficulties,—I have deceived your guards,—I have penetrated to your Majesty's retirement, to throw myself at your feet, and plead for my kindred's lives. They cannot be guilty of the foul deed for which they are condemned;—they never could have sought to injure your Majesty, though even I have been accused by some (to heap greater wretchedness on my head) of having falsely accused them of the crime. Your Majesty knows I am thus far guiltless; and, if my injured husband, incited by jealousy and indignation of his wrongs, should have harboured a thought of malice, oh! show your magnanimity, by pardoning him and his family. Disarmed by your clemency, they could not then further injure you; or let them retire to some other land, where they may repent of ever having given cause of suspicion to so good and kind a master. This act of mercy alone would put down sedition, and bind more firmly all the nobles of the land to your service, and, revered while you live, your name would descend to posterity as a magnanimous and generous prince, who feared not to pardon those who had offended him. But, if your cruel Minister requires some one on whom to vent his hatred, of the aristocracy of the land, the legitimate and noble guardians of your person, whose jealousy he well knows has been aroused at his persevering interference, let me be delivered up as the victim of his vengeance. My fatal love for my sovereign first kindled the spark which has never yet burnt into a flame, and I alone ought to be sacrificed for my crime, if so your Majesty deems it."

The King was deeply moved at the energy of her passion, her tears, and prayers. He led her gently to a chair, and insisted on her being seated, while he stood before her with his arms folded on his bosom; but, as soon as she perceived it, she rose, and threw herself kneeling on the ground.

"This must not be, Donna Theresa," said the agitated Monarch, again attempting to raise her, but she would not quit her suppliant posture.

"Rise, madam, rise. I have no enmity against your relations. It is not I who accuse them. They have been tried by the laws of the country, and, if guilty, I have resigned all power over them. My crown, my life, the happiness of my people, and the tranquillity of the land, require their punishment. It is by my Minister's advice I act thus, and to him you must plead their cause."

"Oh, say not so, your Majesty. Do not thus yield to the grasping ambition of that enemy of our race, who seeks to rise by their destruction," exclaimed Donna Theresa. "Exert your own royal authority, and act according to the generous dictates of your heart. You have the power—exert it, and be merciful; if not, before two suns have set, such deeds of cruelty will have been perpetrated as will cause the nations of Europe to execrate the very name of a Portuguese."

The King's firmness was fast yielding to the entreaties of his lovely petitioner. "I will endeavour to mitigate the rigour of their sentence for your sake, fair lady," he answered. "If clearly proved, for the sake of my successors, I have no right to overlook their crime."

"Rather let it be supposed by posterity that such a crime was impossible in Portugal," interrupted Donna Theresa; "or teach your successors the virtue of clemency."

"You plead most powerfully to my heart, Donna Theresa, nor can I longer withstand the energy of your prayers," said the King. "Rise, then, and let me rather ask pardon for the anguish I have caused you. I it was who ought to have knelt to you."

"I cannot rise till I hear their pardon pronounced by your gracious lips," returned Donna Theresa. "Let me, to prove my innocence of betraying them, be the bearer of your forgiveness."

"I do forgive them," answered the King; "yet, in so important a matter, I may not act further without consulting my Minister."

"Then their doom is sealed!" cried the unhappy lady. "Sebastiaö Jozé has moved heaven and earth to destroy them; and unless your Majesty rescues them by a determined act, they can in no way escape death."

The King still looked as if he was about to deny her.

"Oh! hear me, your Majesty,—by the devoted love you so lately professed to bear me, by all your tender endearments, by your vows of constancy, by the sacrifice of my name and reputation to your passion, pardon those innocent ones—at all events, comparatively innocent—and let the punishment fall upon my guilty head!"

Where is the man who can withstand a lovely woman's prayers, when, weeping, she pleads, and pleads for justice? The King could no longer resist her entreaties; he gently raised her, and, pressing his lips to her hands, he was about to pledge his kingly promise that none should suffer—the words faltered on his tongue—the door opened, he looked up, and beheld the commanding figure of the Prime Minister! The latter stopped, gazing with amazement. Donna Theresa saw not, heard not aught but her sovereign, as she waited eagerly for the words he was about to pronounce.

"You promise, then—you promise they shall be pardoned?" she ejaculated.

The King's eye sank before the searching glance of his potent Minister.

"Pardon me, your Majesty, for my intrusion, and will you graciously deign to explain the meaning of this lady's presence?" exclaimed the latter, advancing rapidly, for he had heard Donna Theresa's last words, and in a moment clearly comprehended the cause of her visit. He felt that his own power hung upon a thread, and he foresaw that, if she gained her cause, he must inevitably be the sacrifice.

In an instant he had arranged his plan. "I need no explanation,— Donna Theresa de Tavora has ventured hither against your Majesty's commands, to impose, with a false tale of her relatives' innocence, on your gracious clemency, and, for the sake of saving the guilty, would sacrifice your life and crown to their implacable hatred. Be not deceived, Sire, by the treacherous tongue of an artful woman. I come now from the trial of the once so-called Duke of Aveiro, the Marquis of Tavora, and their associates: the judges have found them guilty of the most atrocious of conspiracies, and have condemned them accordingly. Your Majesty's sacred life had nearly fallen a sacrifice to some unknown traitors. For months have I incessantly toiled, day and night, to discover the miscreants, and at length I have been successful, and they are about to receive the punishment of their deeds. Let not, then, all my exertions prove vain; and, above all, Sire, do not jeopard your own precious life by mistaken leniency."

The Minister watched the King's countenance, and saw that he had won his cause. He advanced to Donna Theresa, and grasped her arm: "Come, madam, you must no longer intrude upon his Majesty!" he exclaimed.

She started at his touch, and turned an entreating look towards the King. The Monarch's eye was averted. "All, all is lost!" she cried, and, uttering a piercing shriek, sank senseless upon the ground.

"Pardon this seeming harshness, Sire," said Carvalho, deprecatingly, as he raised Donna Theresa in his arms. "It is necessary for your safety."

"You are always right, my friend," said the King. "Let every care and attention be paid her; and let some one be with her to console her for her disappointment;" and he turned away to hide his own emotion: he longed to hide his feelings from himself.

"'Tis another step gained towards supreme power," thought the Minister, as he bore his unconscious burden from the apartment, and committed her to the charge of his guards, with strict orders not to allow her to depart. He then returned to the King, with the fatal document in his hand,—the condemnation of the noble prisoners. His Majesty's signature was required; nor had he now much difficulty in obtaining it.

When nearly all of the most influential in the country were interested in the preservation of the accused, and all feeling that Donna Theresa was the most calculated to persuade the Monarch to pardon them, she had experienced but little difficulty, aided by high bribes, in penetrating to the apartments of the King; though, on Carvalho's endeavouring to discover the delinquents, every one solemnly averred that they had never seen her enter,—though, in her page's suit, she might have passed them unobserved.

Let her fate be a warning to others. Let those consider, whom passion would lead from the strict path of duty, that not themselves alone, but many others also, whom they once loved, and by whom they were beloved, they may drag down to perdition.

When Donna Theresa returned to consciousness, she found herself surrounded by her own attendants, and when she was pronounced in a fit state to be removed, she was conveyed to the Convent of Santos, where a large income was settled on her, and a retinue appointed to attend her. Though nominally a prisoner, she had perfect liberty. She did not die:—such was too happy a lot for her. For many, many years she lived on, a prey to remorse, hated and scorned by her few surviving relatives, till age had wrinkled her brow, and no trace of her former enchanting loveliness remained. Guilty of one crime she was, but not that of which she was accused; yet none would believe her assertions, when she had failed to procure the pardon of her husband. Such was her punishment!

For eighteen years did her father, the Marquis d'Alorna, his wife, and children, languish in separate dungeons, and scarcely one of his kindred escaped the like fate.

She became deaf and blind, and at length she died. On her tomb was found inscribed, "The Murderess of her Family."

Volume Three—Chapter Eighteen.

We would gladly avoid detailing the following narrative, but no one who is writing the life of the great Prime Minister of Portugal can pass it over in silence; and while his name is mentioned in history, so will be the dreadful tragedy in which he was the principal actor, with the execrations of all who have a sentiment of pity for human suffering in their bosoms; even had the sufferers been proved guilty, which we, as Britons, and lovers of our own just laws affirm they were not. Guilty in the sight of Heaven, some of the accused too probably were, but by no law founded on common equity or humanity were they proved so.

The morning of the 13th of January broke dark and gloomy on the heads of a vast concourse of people, already assembled in a large open space on the borders of the Tagus, near the Castle of Belem.

In the background was the Quinta of Bichos, the entrance-door of which opened towards the river, and round it was now stationed a strong body of troops under arms. Here the noble prisoners since their condemnation had been confined, and thither also, during the dark hours of night, the Marchioness of Tavora had been removed from the Convent of Grillos. In front of the gateway, and close to the water, appeared a scaffold, which, since the setting of the sun, workmen had been incessantly employed in erecting, and on which the sound of their hammers was still heard. It was fourteen feet high by thirty long, and twenty broad, covered with black, without ornament of any sort; a wide flight of steps with balustrades leading up to it, on the side towards the Quinta. On the scaffold were seen two posts painted black, a chair, and a bench, on which were placed heavy iron mallets, and an instrument with a long handle, and an immense iron weight shaped like a quoit at the end of it; there were, besides, several large St. Andrew's crosses of wood, and the same number of wheels, and many other instruments of torture. Two regiments of infantry and two of cavalry were drawn up from the gate of the Quinta to the steps of the scaffold, extending their lines also on each side of the square; the embouchure of every street leading to the spot was also occupied by troops, companies of cavalry moving up and down them continually, and allowing no one to pass who wore a cloak, or could in any way have concealed arms about his person, without examining him. Notwithstanding, however, every impediment, thousands of persons pressed eagerly forward to the scene of execution, of every rank, age, and sex, mostly excited by that vulgar curiosity which has, among all nations, and in all times, drawn people together, however revolting the spectacle might be, one would suppose, to human nature.

Here were collected, mothers with children in their arms, whom they held up to behold the black scaffold, and the glittering arms, and gaudy uniforms of the soldiers, the little wretches cooing with delight, unconscious of the meaning of the scene: here were old men leaning on their staves, and discussing the late events with stoical indifference; sturdy ruffians, who longed eagerly for the commencement of the horrid drama; boys, youths with the down still on their lips,—ay, and young maidens too, listening to their tones of courtship, and smiling as they listened; many sat in groups discussing their morning meal, regardless of which they had hurried from their homes;—yes, there was love-making, laughter, and feasting; but dark Death, with his most terrific horrors, was the great actor they came to behold—all else, like a dull interlude, was insipid and tame.

The water also was covered with boats crowded with people, many too, of the higher ranks, anxious to behold the scene, yet unwilling to be observed by the common people, as they sat shrouded in their cloaks, waiting in silence for the commencement.

There was one boat which attracted great attention; it was a barge, moored to the quay, and loaded with faggots, wood, torches, and barrels of pitch.

"What, is all that firewood for?" asked a nursing mother of her husband; "there is enough there to supply us to the end of our lives."

"What, in that boat? Oh! that is doubtless the wood to burn the criminals."

"Jesu Maria!" exclaimed the woman, "they are not going to burn them alive?"

"Why not?" answered the man, "the holy office does so, and what they do must be right."

"Ay, yes, I forgot; of course, they are right," muttered the woman.

"Burn them, to be sure they will," chimed in a neighbour; "and will serve the regicides right. Do you know what they did? They tried to kill the King, the Queen, the Minister, and all the royal family, the wretches!"

"What! did they? Then they deserve to be burnt, doubtless," cried the woman.

"Ay, that did they, the haughty fidalgos!" exclaimed the neighbour; "we shall, now we have got rid of them, have some chance of becoming fidalgos ourselves."

"Oh! it will be a glorious sight!" cried another of the crowd, "full fifty fidalgos all burning and shrieking together; far better than any Auto-da-fé—the holy office never burns more than eight or ten at a time."

"Full fifty! gracious Virgin!" cried a girl. "Who are they?"

"Ay, and more than fifty. Let me see; there are the Duke and Duchess of Aveiro, and all their household and children, the Marquis and Marchioness of Tavora, the younger Marquis, his brother and their sisters, the Marquis of Alorna, and his family; the Conde de Atouquia, and Captain Romeiro. Let me see, there are many more—oh! there are Gonçalo Christovaö, who excited the rebellion at Oporto, and the young Count of Almeida, the Count of—"

"Who did you say?" exclaimed a young man, a stranger to the party, who was standing near. "Who was the last person you mentioned to be executed?"

"The Count of Almeida," answered the oracle of the party, coolly. "He came to Lisbon the very morning of the outrage, and has, it is said, the very look of an assassin."

"It is a vile falsehood, and anybody who says he is guilty, is a villain," exclaimed the young man, vehemently. "My master would never hurt a lamb, much more fire at a king."

"Your master? then you ought to be in his company, my fine fellow," answered the man, who was in a most loyal mood. "The masters and servants are all to be burnt together."

"Burnt! my dear master burnt alive!" ejaculated Pedro, almost unconsciously; for it was he, having wandered about the city, daily, unable to gain any tidings of the Count, till he, at last, heard his name mentioned among the captives, and had now, with sorrow and fear, come to the place of execution, expecting to see his beloved master among the sufferers. Not knowing the precautions taken to prevent a chance of escape, he watched, with feverish anxiety, the appearance of the prisoners, in the hopes of finding some means of rescuing him. Not liking the proposal of the people, near whom he was standing, and being unable to gain any further information from them, he moved away to another group, one of whom appeared to know a great deal about the matter.

"Can you tell me, Senhor, the names of the conspirators who are to suffer?" asked Pedro, with tears in his eyes, and a faltering voice.

"Of course, my friend, I shall be happy to enlighten you to the utmost of my power," answered the person he addressed, enumerating the same names as the former one, with a few additions.

Poor Pedro wrung his hands with agony.

"Alas, alas! are they to be burnt alive?" he asked.

"Oh, no, not all of them," said his informant. "Some of them are, for which purpose you see those black posts erected, to fasten them to. The ladies are to lose their heads, the leaders are to be beaten to death, and the others are to be strangled. A few only are to be burnt alive, to please the people; and then the scaffold, and all the bodies, will be consumed together and thrown into the river."

Pedro could listen to no more of the dreadful details, but, hurrying away to a distance, he sat himself down on a stone, and hiding his face in his hands, he gave way to the anguish of his feelings, in tears. Suddenly, however, recovering his presence of mind, he considered how he might yet afford some aid to the hapless young Count.

While the scene we have described was proceeding, one of violence and destruction was enacting in another part of the city. A vast mob were collected in and around the palaces of the Marquis of Tavora and the Duke of Aveiro; some employed in dragging forth the rich and valuable furniture, breaking it in pieces, and piling it in heaps to burn; some endeavouring to conceal the smaller articles about their persons; and others fighting and wrangling about the booty. A few minutes sufficed to accomplish the act of destruction, when workmen instantly commenced demolishing the entire edifices, and ere their once proud owners had ceased to breathe, already were they in ruins. When the palaces were completely razed to the ground, salt was sprinkled over their sites; and on that of the Duke of Aveiro a column was erected, on which was inscribed his crime and punishment.

To return to the former scene. At length, at seven o'clock, the gates of the Quinta were thrown open. "They come! they come!" murmured the crowd, as a body of horsemen were seen to issue forth, some in uniforms, being the chief military commanders of the kingdom, others in dark cloaks, who were the principal officers of the crown, the ministers of justice, the criminal judges, and others. The Prime Minister was not among them. He, it was said, contemplated at a distance the work he had ordered.

Forming in two lines, between them appeared a sedan-chair, painted black, the bearers dressed in the same hue, and on each side walked a friar of the Capuchin order. As they advanced towards the scaffold, the dragoons formed round them, and, at the same time, the chief executioner, with three assistants, mounted the fatal platform to receive the wretched occupant.

When the party arrived at the foot of the flight of steps, every voice was hushed, and every eye was strained to see the first victim. The door of the sedan-chair was opened, and a female form was led forward. "The Marchioness of Tavora!" ejaculated the crowd.

It was, indeed, that unhappy lady. Firm and composed, she advanced to the first step of the scaffold, where, kneeling down between her ghostly comforters, she performed the last duties of religion, employing thus upwards of half an hour, during which time some further arrangements on the dreadful theatre were being made. At the end of that time, the executioners gave a signal that all was in readiness for the first scene of the tragedy, and, rising from her knees, she mounted, without faltering, the fatal steps, appearing in the same robes of dark blue satin, her hair dressed with white ribands, and a circlet of diamonds, as when she had been apprehended. On the summit, the friars delivered her into the hands of the executioners, who first led her round to each side of the platform, to show her to the people, and then, with a refinement of cruelty worthy of the brain of an Eastern barbarian to conceive, they, according to their orders, exhibited to her the knife by which she was herself to suffer, at which she merely smiled. But when she beheld the rack, the crosses, the mallets, and other instruments of torture prepared for her husband, children, and the other partners of her fate, while the chief executioner explained their object, the intrepid spirit which had hitherto sustained her in that hour of bitter anguish, at length gave way in a gush of tears.

"As you hope for Heaven's mercy, oh! hasten with your work," she exclaimed.

Even the executioner was moved. "I perform but my orders, lady, and pray your forgiveness," he answered, as he hurriedly performed the hell-invented task, and led her to the chair in the centre of the platform.

Throwing off his cloak, he appeared in a close-fitting black vest. As he stooped down to fasten her feet, he raised her clothes slightly.

"Remember who I am, and respect me even in death!" she exclaimed, proudly; but the moment after, seeing the man had done so unintentionally, as he released her hand, she took the circlet of diamonds from her head, and presenting them to him, "Take this as a token of my forgiveness," she said, clearly. "Now Heaven receive my soul, and forgive my murderers!" These were her last words. The executioner, now securing her arms to the chair, took the handkerchief from her neck, and bound her eyes, the friars repeating the prayers of a parting sinner; he then, seizing a large knife, shaped like an eastern scimitar, took her long hair in his left hand, and lifting high the blade, gave one stroke on the back of the neck, for the sake of greater ignominy, the head falling on the bosom, a second being required to sever it from the body. The butchery being finished, he exhibited the head to the people, while his assistants untied the body, both being thrown on one side, and covered with a black cloth, from beneath which the blood flowed, trickling down the outside stage.

Thus died Donna Leonora de Tavora, once Vice-Queen of India, one of the most lovely, high-spirited, and most noble ladies of Portugal; the favourite of the former Queen, and the most admired dame of the Court! Either her own fatal ambition, or the envy and revenge of another, was the cause of her untimely end, which, no one can now determine.

During this time, the day still remained obscure, some thought, as a signal of Heaven's disapprobation at the bloody scene which was enacting. Alas! if the sun shone but when the land was free from crime, when should we enjoy a clear day? It was at last discovered that an eclipse was taking place.

This execution being concluded at half-past eight, the ministers of justice still remaining in their places, the sedan-chair, escorted by the dragoons, proceeded to the Quinta; from whence it again returned, a friar, as before, walking on each side. From it was led forth, trembling with agitation, the young Jozé de Tavora, dressed in a suit of black; and supported by the friars, he mounted the scaffold. As he was led round to be exhibited to the people, wearing his long, light hair in curls, his youth, his graceful figure, and the sweet engaging expression of his countenance, gained him universal commiseration. He regained his courage, and spoke a few inaudible words; then petitioning pardon for his own sins, and for those of his enemies, he resigned himself into the hands of the executioners. His eyes being bound, he was fastened by the wrists and ankles to a cross, brought forward to the centre, and elevated nearly upright, the whole weight of the body hanging by the arms, increasing the agony of the sufferer, while the chief executioner passed the cord, to strangle him, round his neck, and the assistants with their iron clubs broke the eight bones of his arms and legs. His shrieks resounded through the assembly, drawing tears of pity from the eyes, and cries of sympathy from the breasts of many, even of the most hardened. The mangled corpse, being exhibited to the people, was placed on one of the wheels, and covered with a black cloth.

Poor Pedro watched this execution with the most dreadful anxiety; for in the young Don Jozé he had recognised the companion of his master during the excursion on the fatal night of the attempt against the King's life. He turned his straining eye-balls towards the gate of the Quinta, as the third sad *cortège* issued forth in the same manner as the first towards the scaffold; but instead of the Count the young Marquis of Tavora appeared.

With an impatient step he mounted the stage, dressed in full court costume though bare-headed; and, walking round, he attempted, in a loud voice, to address the populace with a declaration of his innocence.

"Hear me, Portuguese!" he cried. "My kindred and I have been sacrificed to the lust of a weak King, and the ambition and hatred of a tyrant Minister; but our blood will not cry in vain for vengeance; and for centuries, war, disorder, and wretchedness are in store for our hapless country. A dying man speaks."

"Silence, base traitor!" thundered forth the chief criminal magistrate. "Commend your soul to God, or you shall be stopped by a gag!" at the same time giving the signal to the executioner.

To spare him the agony his brother had suffered, he was seated on a chair, made fast to the cross, with his hands fastened above him, and being then strangled, and his legs and arms broken, the body was shown to the people, and placed on another wheel, likewise covered with a black cloth.

"Ah! my poor master will be the next," cried Pedro. "I will die with him; for I shall never be able to rescue him from their clutches, the barbarians!"

The next sufferer who appeared from the sedan-chair was the Count of Atouquia. He mounted the steps with a furious and indignant air, and when he attempted to speak, he was compelled to hold silence. He was executed with the same ceremonies as his brother-in-law.

Manoel Ferreira, the Duke's servant, Captain Braz Romeiro, of the Marquis of Tavora's late regiment, and Joaö Miguel, the Duke's page, then followed in the order named, dressed in ragged and scanty garments, and were executed like the previous victims.

Carpenters were now employed to make several alterations in the scaffold, and two large crosses, without a centre-post, were brought to the front.

The body of Donna Leonora, with the head, were placed on a bench in the centre, so as to meet the view of her husband, who was destined to be the next victim.

As the unhappy Marquis appeared, the muffled drums of the military bands gave forth irregular sounds, the troops whom he had once commanded with distinction and honour, and through whose lines he was now led, turning their left shoulders as he passed. He mounted the steps with a quick and firm pace; but started with horror, a death-like pallor overspreading his countenance, as he beheld the mangled, body of his wife, whom he had last seen in all her pride and beauty before their apprehension. The lacerated bodies of his sons and servants were then exhibited to him, as well as the instruments of torture with which he was to suffer death. He was next led round to be shown to the populace, whom he did not attempt to address, and returning, as soon as he was permitted, he knelt down by the side of the cross. He then humbly confessed himself to his ghostly attendants, and, when they retired, boldly extended himself upon the cross laid flat on the ground, to which he was then bound; the executioner next lifting a vast iron mallet, with a long handle, struck him three blows on the chest, the stomach, and the face, besides breaking his arms and legs,—his sobs and pitiable groans of agony being heard for some minutes ere he expired.

It was past two o'clock when the Duke of Aveiro mounted the scaffold, dressed in the morning-gown in which he had been taken, bare-headed, and holding a crucifix in his manacled hand. The anticipation of an agonising death had somewhat humbled his once presumptuous pride, though, perhaps, even at that moment, indignation at the ignominy with which he was treated was his predominant feeling, as he gazed around with looks of rage and despair. He underwent precisely the same ceremony as the Marquis; but the executioner, through nervousness, struck the first blow on his stomach, causing him the most excruciating tortures, as was known by his heart-piercing shrieks, and it was some minutes ere, by this most barbarous method, life became extinct.

Next was brought forward Manoel Ferreira, and with him an effigy of Joseph Policarpio, who had escaped,—the former habited merely in a shirt and drawers. The unfortunate wretch was bound to one of the posts, seated on an iron chair, with the effigy opposite to him, two friars administering to him the consolations of religion. The boat was then unloaded of its cargo of wood and barrels of tar, which were placed under and upon the scaffold, he being surrounded by faggots, and a pan of sulphur placed beneath him. The executioners and workmen now descended from the scaffold; a friar, prompted by zeal for the welfare of the criminal's soul, and feeling he might afford him comfort in his moments of agony, with noble intrepidity remained to the last moment, while the former, lighting their torches, set fire to the fabric in every direction. The wind having blown till now across the scaffold, it was expected that the flames would soon put an end to the wretch's sufferings; but, suddenly changing, it blew them directly away from him; his shrieks and groans, while he thus slowly roasted, being dreadful to hear, the good friar remaining near him till he was himself scorched, and compelled to fly for his life, hitherto regardless of the shouts of the people to call him away.

The greater proportion of the populace were horrified at this dreadful event; but some were not yet satiated with blood. "What!" cried one ruffian, "are these all? I thought we were to have many more."

"Stay patiently, my friend, till to-morrow," answered another; "we shall have a fresh batch then. This is far better worth seeing than a bull-fight, or an Auto-da-fé. Our Prime Minister is a fine fellow; he does not do things by halves."

"Thank Heaven, my dear master is still alive!" exclaimed Pedro, with a deep-drawn breath, as he hastened, sick with horror, to make further inquiries for the Count.

The flames burnt brightly up, and, after twenty minutes, the shrieks of the burning wretch ceased,—death had put an end to his sufferings.

At length, by four o'clock, the bodies of the ten human beings, who had that morning breathed with life, the scaffold, and all the instruments of torture, were reduced to one small heap of black ashes. One ceremony remained to be performed. The ashes were swept together by the executioners, and scattered upon the bosom of the Tagus, so that not a vestige remained on the face of the earth of those who had once been. People gazed upon the spot of the tragedy: one blackened circle alone marked it. All that had passed seemed like some dreadful dream of a disordered brain. People rubbed their eyes, and looked again and again, to persuade themselves of the reality.

When the account was brought to the Minister—"Tremble, haughty Puritanos!" he exclaimed. "Now I have ye in my power."

The military band now struck up a martial air, the troops moving off the ground to their quarters, and the officers of justice to their homes.

That very evening, the King, for the first time since the attack, appeared in public, holding a Court for all his nobility. None dared absent themselves; but all wore an air of gloom and fear; for, feeling as they did, it was impossible to say who might be the next victims to the Minister's policy.

The account of the above-mentioned dreadful execution we have translated from a very valuable manuscript work in our possession, written by one who was, we conceive, an eye-witness of the scene he describes, though we have rather softened and curtailed, than enlarged upon, its horrors. He was certainly no friend of the Prime Minister's; but there is a minute exactness in his descriptions, and an upright honesty in his observations, which gives us no reason to doubt their correctness.

The fidalgos of Portugal have never forgotten the lesson they that day learned. Alarm and mistrust entered into every social circle; no one dared write, or scarce speak, to another, for fear of treachery; and day after day the prisons were filled with fresh victims of the Minister's despotism. The most trivial expressions were remarked and punished with rigour. One day, a nobleman, a licensed favourite at Court, was conversing with the Queen and a party of ladies, when the subject of the lost King Sebastian was introduced, one asserting that the common people firmly expected his return. "Oh, they are perfectly right," exclaimed the Count: "King Sebastian reigns at present in Portugal."

A few days after this speech he found himself an inhabitant of a prison, in which he lived for many years.

The King now bestowed on his Minister the title of the Count of Oyeras, nor was he made Marquis of Pombal for many years afterwards.

Though the King still drove about as usual unattended, Carvalho never appeared abroad without a body-guard to attend him, so fearful had he become of the revenge of the friends of those he had slaughtered or imprisoned. The most beneficial act of his life to Portugal was the expulsion of the Jesuits, nearly all of whom he transported to Italy, the rest he imprisoned; among the latter was the Father Jacinto da Costa, who never more appeared in the world. He was too subtle a foe to be allowed to wander loose. He is supposed to have died in one of the solitary dungeons built by Carvalho's command.

Malagrida was also imprisoned; but three years passed before he was brought to trial. He was delivered up into the hands of the spiritual court of the Inquisition of Portugal, who found him guilty of heresy, hypocrisy, false prophecies, impostures, and various other heinous crimes, for which they condemned him to be burnt alive, having first undergone the effectual public and legal degradation from his orders. He obtained, by way of mitigation, that he should be strangled before the faggots were kindled around him. The whole ceremonial was adjusted according to the fashion of the most barbarous times. A lofty scaffold, in the square of the Rociò, was erected in the form of an amphitheatre, and richly decorated, convenient seats being provided for the most distinguished nobility, and the members of the administration, who were formally invited as to a spectacle of festivity. Fifty-two persons were condemned to appear in the procession of this Auto-da-fé, clothed in red garments and high conical caps, with representations of devils, in all attitudes and occupations, worked on them; but Malagrida, who walked at their head, was alone to furnish the horrible amusement of the day. Crowds assembled from all parts to witness the spectacle, and shouted with savage glee as the flames consumed the remains of the insane old man. Hypocrite and knave though he had been, he was then more fit for commiseration than punishment.

As his ashes were scattered to the wind—"Now!" exclaimed the Prime Minister, "I have no other foes to fear!"

Volume Three—Chapter Nineteen.

Ours is a tale of human woe and human suffering; of blighted hopes, of disappointed ambition, of noble promise, and of bright aspirations doomed never to be realised; of crime, of repentance, of despair a description of a dark and gloomy picture, with but a few green spots to enliven it—a picture of the world!

We have long lost sight of the beloved of the Count d'Almeida, the fair Donna Clara Christovaö, and we now return to her with delight, for we love to gaze upon a being young, innocent, and lovely as she was. On her return from Lisbon, her father had allowed her to remain at home for some months, to recruit her strength and spirits among the scenes of her childhood, after all the terror and danger she had undergone; nor did he, during that time, once refer to the monastic life to which he had dedicated her; indeed, he tried to forget it himself; and would, perhaps, though not addicted to changing his purpose, have deferred the fatal time from year to year till death had removed him from the world, had he not his father confessor by his side, who at length thought fit to remind him of his vow. It is needless to say, he had repented of it, though he would not acknowledge it to himself, and he strenuously endeavoured to persuade the father that he could in no way compromise his soul by deferring the commencement of the year of probation to a future period; but the latter was firm, painting the enormity of such conduct in colours so glowing, so that the unhappy father was obliged to yield, and promised to make no further delay.

For reasons known only to herself, Donna Clara had firmly refused to perform her confession before Father Alfonzo, and taking advantage of the privilege allowed to every member of a family, she had selected a venerable and worthy priest as her confessor, whose best qualification was his kind and simple heart, and his innocent and credulous belief in all the miracles, the relics, and the infallibility of his Church.

Father Alfonzo, who well knew his character, lost no opportunity of winning his regard, and thus making a tool of him in his plans on Clara, which, though delayed, he had not abandoned. No; the devil, in whatever shape he appear is ever treacherous, watchful, and persevering, and naught but the armour of innocence can turn aside his deadly shafts.

Clara had learnt to confide in the good priest, and flew to him on all occasions for consolation and advice; and now, when the fidalgo, urged on by his confessor, again proposed to her to fulfil her mother's vow by entering a convent, she requested permission, before determining, to consult her ghostly adviser on the subject.

She hastened to the aged priest, telling him her unwillingness to give up the world, and her feeling of unfitness for a life devoted wholly to the services of the Church.

"Alas! my daughter, it is hard for an old man, broken by infirmities, with one foot in the grave, to advise a young and joyous being to abandon all her hopes of domestic felicity, and the pleasures which the world affords, for a life of ascetic seclusion," he answered; and Clara felt her heart lighter at his words. "But," he continued, "as a minister of religion, it behoves me to advise you to obey your father's wishes, and to fulfil your mother's vow. There is but one course, my daughter, marked out for you to follow—the stern one of duty; and your duty demands the sacrifice of yourself; yet weep not, my child, a few years will quickly pass away, and you will no longer regret the world you have left, with all its vanities, while an immortal crown of glory will assuredly await you, the blessed reward of your virtue and resignation. Think of this world as it truly is, a vale of tears, and place your hopes of happiness in a heavenly future.—My fair daughter, you must become a nun."

Pale and trembling, Clara listened, and bent her head in meek resignation, while the tears stole down her fair cheeks. The advice, though good and pious, doubtless, was not such as to afford consolation to a lovely girl of nineteen, who might naturally and innocently hope to find some enjoyment in the world her aged confessor likened to a vale of tears; yet she had determined to abide by his counsel, and her fate was sealed.

She made no further resistance to the fidalgo's commands, consenting to recommence her noviciate whenever he should think fit. A day at a short distance was fixed, and Father Alfonzo saw with malignant satisfaction the commencement of his long sought for triumph.

The Convent of Santa Clara, at Oporto, is situated on the brow of a steep hill to the east of the city, overlooking the rapid Douro. It is a lofty and handsome building of carved stone, the windows looking towards the outer side being strongly barred; the church stands on one side of the entrance, which is through a court-yard with wide oaken gates. A long and steep flight of steps leads up to it from the river, but on the other side it is approachable by a broad though winding road, with the backs chiefly of some large houses and dead walls on each side, making it altogether a most secluded situation. The garden is surrounded by a high dark wall, with pointed battlements, exactly similar to the walls of the city; indeed, one side of it is enclosed by them, and at the end furthest removed from the convent is a summer-house, likewise, alas! securely grated, from whence a beautiful view is obtained both up and down the river. On the opposite side, on the summit of a precipitous cliff, at whose foot the river rushes with impetuous force, stands the Serra Convent, with its high cupola-roofed church, then surrounded by groves of fine trees and lovely gardens, and inhabited by the most wealthy and high-born monks of Oporto, that of Santa Clara receiving none but the daughters of fidalgos. On the right is a view of the city, and the town of Villa Nova, with the heights beyond, between which the river winds its way towards the sea; while on the left, a soft and smiling scene, with rich green banks rising from the water, is beheld, beyond a narrow gorge of dark rocks.

To this convent Clara was now conveyed, and, torn from the embrace of the good Senhora Gertrudes, notwithstanding all the old nurse's entreaties that her darling might be allowed to remain at home with her.

It must be confessed that Clara had but little to complain of during her noviciate in this lovely spot, and she had much to make her contented. She had many companions of her own age; merry, light-hearted girls, who laughed and talked all day long, hurrying over the daily ceremonials of their religion to laugh and talk again. Then their confessors would come, who never troubled them with too severe penances, entertaining them instead with many laughable stories. They would no more have thought of imposing any disagreeable task on the fair young fidalgas, than would a fashionable preacher in London of annoying the consciences of his hearers. Then the doctor would come and feel their pulses, while he detailed all the anecdotes he had collected during his professional visits, and indeed everything that was going forward in the world.

All, however, were not thus happy; the young love of some had been blighted in the bud, and they had retired thither in the expectation of finding peace and a solace for their woe in the duties of religion; others had been compelled by cajolery or threats to embrace a life they detested and despised, these invariably recompensing themselves by indulging in every license within their power, for they soon discovered "that where there's a will there's a way." We well recollect the Convent of Santa Clara, the most fashionable of our day, so we must not be scandalous.

The fair flower of his garden, as her father used to delight to call Clara, found naught congenial to her feelings and thoughts in this new life, and with fear and sad forebodings she looked forward to the time when it must irrevocably become hers for ever. She pined for freedom, and she thought of the love and devotion of her poor, though high-born, lover, Don Luis. In vain she tried, for she thought it her duty to banish his image from her mind, but she had engraven it too deeply to eradicate it. Each time it returned with greater beauty than before, till at last she gave up the attempt as hopeless; so she cherished it with greater fondness than ever.

About two months of her noviciate had passed, when one evening, as she was seated in the summer-house, inhaling the fresh breeze, and gazing on the lovely view, her companions having all quitted her, she heard a low strain of music, sounding as if it came from far down the cliff below her. She listened attentively for some minutes—it ceased—when it again sounded as if from directly beneath the wall. At one of the windows a bar had been loosened, so that it could be easily removed, as the fair birds were, it must be confessed, rather frequently in the habit of doing. She soon discovered the necessary way to do it, and, looking out, she beheld a graceful figure, with a cloak over his arm and a guitar in his hand. As he gazed up towards the window of the high tower, he struck a few low notes on his guitar, as if to draw the attention of any fair captive within. The eye of love was not slow in piercing the thickening shades of evening, and her heart beat with tender emotion as she distinguished Don Luis d'Almeida. He stood evidently uncertain whether he was known, or whether it was Donna Clara herself towards whom he was looking; he feared, she thought, to pronounce her name, lest it might in any way betray her, and she equally trembled to speak his. She held in her hand a handkerchief marked with her name, "Would it be wrong?" she let it drop, and had just time to see him spring forward, seize it, and press it rapturously to his lips, when the bell for vespers rang, and she was obliged to hasten into the convent.

The following evening she anxiously watched, from the window of the tower, the return of Luis. He at length appeared, having climbed, with great difficulty and danger, the steep heights from the river; but this time he had not encumbered himself with a guitar. Clara looked hastily into the garden below her—no one was within hearing.

"Oh, Luis," she cried, "your presence gives me both joy and pain; joy to know that you are near me, and pain that I feel it will soon be sin even to think of you."

"Say not so, my beloved Clara; I come to tell you to hope," answered Luis. "Resist to the utmost taking the fatal vows. Defer it in every possible way, and something may yet occur to favour our wishes."

"Heaven grant there may!" exclaimed Clara; "but, much as I delight in seeing you, for my sake, do not venture here. Ten months must elapse before the dreaded time arrives; ere that time, return again here, and believe me, I will trust in your constancy. I have seen and heard such things within these walls as make me almost doubt whether I am bound to obey my father's commands by remaining in them till released by death. It is treason to speak this; but thus much I must tell you, Luis. Hark! some one approaches. Farewell!"

"I will rescue you or die," whispered Luis, yet loud enough to reach her ears; and while she watched him, as he disappeared over the brow of the cliff, a young novice entered the tower.

"What! sister Clara, ever meditating in our bower?" exclaimed the girl, laughing, "I shall begin to suspect you have some lover among the gallant friars opposite, or perhaps some one has managed to fly to the foot of the tower; for Love, we are told, has wings, though he generally uses them rather to fly away; but in no other way could a human being contrive to get there, I am sure. I quite forgot—I came to bring you a message from the Lady Abbess, to say that your father and a certain Padre Alfonzo are waiting to see you."

"I will accompany you," answered Clara, taking the arm of Sister Amalia; and the two young ladies entered the convent together.

More trials awaited Clara. Her father received her with an angry brow, unusual to him, and chiding her, gravely informed her that he had received intimation that Don Luis had been seen at Oporto, whither he had doubtless been attracted for her sake, insisting on her promising never, without his leave, to see him. He little suspected that she had, within the last few minutes, both seen and heard him.

"Remember, too," concluded the Fidalgo, "that although he has not been convicted as the murderer of your brother, he has not proved his innocence, and he is without either fortune or influence; were it not so also, you are dedicated to the Church, and can never be his. Pass your word to me, therefore, that you will not see him; if not, you must, by the advice of the Lady Abbess and the good Father Alfonzo, be subjected to such a confinement as will preclude the possibility of seeing him, or receiving any account of him."

"I trust, my father, that the love and respect I hear you, and my own honour, are a sufficient guarantee of my not disobeying your commands when they are just and right; but no further promise will I make," answered Clara, firmly. "Pardon me, my beloved father, that I should ever have spoken thus to you; but I will not be unjust to myself, or to one whom I know truly as innocent of any crime except that of loving me."

Clara continued firm in her determination, notwithstanding all the Lady Abbess, her father, or the priest, could say to her; and at last, wearied out, they were obliged to desist from all further attempts to make her alter it. Their system of tactics then changed. She was from henceforth never allowed to leave her chamber, or to walk in the garden without an attendant; and though at first she bore up with spirit against this irksome species of petty tyranny, at last her health gave way, and it was not till she was allowed, as before, to wander alone in the garden that she at all recovered. It certainly did not increase her taste for a monastic life. Her father at length departed for Lisbon. Three months of her noviciate only remained to be accomplished, and she had not heard from Luis. Week after week passed by, yet he came not. With all a woman's trusting love, she felt confident he would come to see her, and bid her farewell, if not to bring proofs that her brother fell by another's hand, and to rescue her.

At last the alarming accounts reached her of the apprehension of the conspirators, among whom the name of the Count d'Almeida was mentioned. She believed him innocent; but he was in prison, and escape was hopeless. Then arrived the dreadful description of the cruel execution. She trembled as she listened, but his name was not among the sufferers. She thanked Heaven that he was preserved, though for herself she had ceased to hope.

At last came the stunning intelligence that her father also was a prisoner on the charge of high treason. It was the very day before she was to pronounce the final vows. She longed to fly to him, to comfort him in prison, but she was told such was impossible. With tears and entreaties she petitioned the Lady Abbess to allow her to depart, yet in vain. The fidalgo had committed his daughter to her charge, and by his permission alone could she allow her to quit the convent under any pretext. His confessor, in whom he placed implicit confidence, assured her such was his wish, and by him was she guided.

Despairing, therefore, of all human aid, Clara yielded to her fate, trusting, as she did so, that Heaven would afford her peace of mind, and reward her for obeying her father's commands and her mother's wish.

It was a bright and lovely morning, although in winter, when she rose from her couch, whereon she had spent a sleepless night; several attendants being in readiness to robe her for the last time in the garments of the vain world. Bright flowers were braided in her fair hair, glittering jewels decked her neck, and a robe of white satin, richly ornamented with lace, clothed her graceful form. She appeared as a bride about to be led to the altar—a lovely sacrifice to Heaven; say rather to bigoted superstition and priestcraft, the worst remnant of heathen idolatry and imposture: and let us bless the era, and the true patriot, who, with one daring stroke, banished for ever those vile institutions from his country. (Note.)

Before Clara left her chamber for the last time, her future abode being a narrow cell without ornament, and with but scanty furniture, old Gertrudes was permitted to visit her. Tears and sobs almost choked the poor nurse's utterance, as she embraced and kissed, over and over again, her young charge.

"Oh! and you look so lovely in that beautiful dress!" she exclaimed; "and they are going to cut off all that fair hair, and put you on a dull, ugly habit, which you must wear all the rest of your days—Oh dear! oh dear!" and she burst into a fresh shower of tears.

"Do not thus mourn for me, my good nurse; I care not for my change of habit," answered Clara, smiling mournfully; "and I trust I shall be happy in the consciousness of performing my duty."

A sister now entered to inform Clara that the procession was nearly ready to enter the church, so Senhora Gertrudes was obliged to tear herself away to witness the sad ceremony, while Clara accompanied the sister to the hall, where the whole community were assembled previous to entering the church by their private door.

Two other novices were that day to be professed, and a large assemblage of their friends, kindred, and acquaintances, besides many strangers, had collected in the church to witness the ceremony.

Preceded by the cross-bearer, with slow and measured steps, and singing the hymn, "O Gloriosa Virginum," the procession of nuns entered the sacred edifice, and took their allotted places. The holy Father Alfonzo, also the professor extraordinary to the convent, first preached a sermon from the altar, with the postulants seated before him, giving the most glowing picture of the religious life they were about to enter, so that not one of the audience could doubt they were peculiarly blest in their choice.

The Bishop of Oporto, in his full canonicals, standing before the altar, with his chaplains on either side, the postulants were next led up the steps to him, when he severally interrogated them, first addressing Clara.

"My child, what do you demand?" he said.

"The mercy of God, and the holy habit of religion," answered Clara.

"Is it with your own free-will that you demand the holy habit of religion?"

"Yes, my lord," faltered forth Clara.

"Reverend Mother," said the Bishop, turning to the Lady Abbess, "have you made the necessary inquiries, and are you satisfied?"

The Lady Abbess signified her assent.

Several other questions were asked, to which the young postulants responded satisfactorily, and they were then led forth to put off the garments of the world, and assume that of religion.

During their absence, the assembled monks and nuns broke forth in a solemn harmonious chant: "Who is she who cometh up from the desert, flowing with delights, leaning on her beloved?"

They soon returned, clothed in the habit of the order, yet wearing their long hair covered by their white veils, and again knelt before the altar, holding lighted tapers in their hands.

On one side was a bier, as if prepared for the dead, on the other a table, with the act of profession and implements for writing placed on it, while the black veil, which, once assumed, would separate them for ever from the world, lay upon the altar.

Clara trembled violently—a faintness came over her—she saw not the assembled crowd;—she heard not the rich melody, and scarcely the voice of the officiating minister. A dull, stunning feeling oppressed her—she was scarcely aware of the answers she made; but the Bishop appeared satisfied. He then, with a solemn prayer, blessed the black veils, and sprinkled them with holy water. A rich melody pealed through the church, while sweet scented incense ascended to heaven.

The eldest postulant then, led forward by the Lady Abbess, after further questions from the Bishop, pronounced her vows, while he held upraised the holy sacrament, and the organ sent forth its most solemn tones. With a trembling hand the young girl signed her renunciation of the world, and a tear-drop blotted out the mark of the cross she made.

The Bishop then severing a lock from her hair, the professed sisters advanced, and placed her on the bier, and while the black veil was thrown over her, the organ now sent forth a mournful dirge for the dead. For three minutes did she thus remain, all standing round as if mourning her dead, and when the veil was again raised, the sisters, lifting her hand to aid her to rise, it fell powerless by her side. A thrill of horror crept over them—for they thought her dead indeed; yet it was not so; the solemn mummery had overcome her—she had fainted; but the organ ceasing, and then changing to a triumphant air, she gave signs of returning animation. She was lifted from the bier, and borne from the church.

It was now Clara's turn. The Lady Abbess, taking the lighted taper from her hand, led her forward, giving her the act of confession. Almost fainting, she then knelt, the richest tones of human voices floating round the building, while the Bishop bore towards her the adorable sacrament. A dimness came over her sight—her voice faltered as the moment to pronounce her final vow had arrived. Scarce had she uttered the first word, when a voice—it sounded like that of human agony—rung through the church. "Stay, in mercy stay!" it cried; and at those tones Clara sunk senseless to the ground.

Note. Dom Pedro, the father of her present Majesty of Portugal.

Volume Three—Chapter Twenty.

We left the Count d'Almeida an inmate of the Jungueira prison, from whence the stern policy of the Prime Minister allowed few captives to depart, except to the scaffold and to death. Many an unfortunate victim of this iron despotism remained there year after year, demanding to be brought to trial,—to be told of his crime,—to have the witness of his guilt produced, but his petitions were unheard or disregarded; he might, if free, become dangerous, so he was allowed to pine on in chains, till death, more kind than man, released him.

Luis sat disconsolate and sad in his narrow cell, with few happy remembrances of his past life to dwell on, and without a book to withdraw his mind from the melancholy present. For his own fate, come what might, he was prepared; but he thought of Clara, and there was bitter anguish. He could now prove himself innocent of her brother's death, but he was a prisoner, without a hope of escape, and within a week, at furthest, perhaps at that very time she might be pronouncing the fatal vow which would tear her from him for ever! The thought almost drove him to madness—his feelings may be more easily pictured than described. He felt that he was shrieking, but his voice gave forth no sound,—that he could dash himself against the door, but yet he sat, his hands clasped before him, without moving,— a statue of manly grief.

His meditations were interrupted by the opening of his prison door, and his worthy friend, Frè Diogo Lopez, stood before him.

"Ah! my dear Count, you see I have not delayed long in fulfilling my promise," began the Friar.

"I saw your young friend, and offered him such consolation as was in my power, and now I have brought you a fresh bottle of wine, to keep up your spirits. I offered him a little, but he could scarcely drink a drop. I fear he is going, poor youth."

"I much fear so too," answered Luis. "But tell me, have you found the letter to his father, you spoke of? It has been so wonderfully preserved, that I fain would think it of importance."

"I have it here. Is not this it?" answered the Friar, producing a much soiled packet. "Read the superscription, for my eyes are dim, and cannot well decipher it."

"The same. Now will you undertake to forward this to Senhor Gonçalo Christovaö," said the Count.

"It will not have far to go, then, for he is a prisoner within these walls," answered the Friar.

"Merciful Heaven!" exclaimed Luis. "Then I may prove to him that I am not the murderer of his son. Does he know that the poor youth is here?"

"I have not myself spoken to him, though it is almost impossible he should discover it," replied the Friar.

"Then, in pity to all, contrive to let him see his dying son, and I, too, long to converse with him. It is the greatest favour you can afford me, next to one which I scarce dare hope for, to aid me in my escape."

The Friar shook his head—"Your last wish is impossible; the first I will endeavour to accomplish. You know not all the precautions taken to prevent escape. Were your life in danger, it might, perhaps, be done at the risk of both our lives, or of perpetual imprisonment in some loathsome dungeon, to which, in comparison, this is a palace."

"For the purpose I have in view, I would risk death, torments, and imprisonment!" exclaimed Luis, vehemently. "Unless I succeed, all I value in life is worthless. Within a few days from hence, Donna Clara de Christovaö will be compelled to assume the veil, if I do not contrive to rescue her from the convent at Oporto, where she is confined. I vowed to her to attempt it, and if she hears not of me, she will deem me faithless, and yield without a struggle to her fate."

Frè Diogo smiled, as he shook his head. "You might as well attempt to rescue the lamb from the talons of the eagle, as to carry off a fair girl from the clutches of those who have her in their power," he answered. "In any possible plan I would, if in my power, aid you gladly. But consider a moment. If you could escape from hence, which is next to impossible, you manage to reach Oporto, though the chances are, that you are recaptured before you arrive there;—you demand the young lady;—you are refused even an interview. You then contrive to let her know you are in the neighbourhood;—she sends you word she is shut up, and cannot get out. Or suppose you have surmounted all difficulties, and you have managed to carry her off; whither would you fly? In each direction the Minister has his spies, who would soon restore you to your present abode, if not to a worse, and the lady to her convent. No, my dear Count, be advised by me, do not attempt an impossibility. You have but one course to pursue; practise your patience: when a man is at the bottom of a well, he cannot go lower."

"No, but he may be drowned, though, when the water flows in," said Luis, despondingly.

"Not if he knows how to swim," answered the Friar; "and then the water, which would destroy another, will be his preservation. Let that be your consolation."

"Alas! I fear your observations are too correct, and I must submit to my fate," said Luis. "Can you, however, contrive to let me see Gonçalo Christovaö?"

"There will be no great difficulty, for since the execution, in some parts of the prison, the captives are allowed to communicate with each other."

"Of what do you speak?" inquired Luis; and the Friar recounted to him the dreadful tragedy which had taken place. "Alas!" he exclaimed, "and has that gay and bold youth been a victim?" and while he shuddered, as he recollected the risk he had run of sharing their fate, he thought how nobly young Jozé de Tavora had behaved in not betraying him; for, as he heard, torture had been administered to extract confession.

"Come now with me," said the Friar, interrupting his thoughts. "The turnkey waits without, and will, under my responsibility, allow you to visit this old fidalgo, for his cell is close to this, I heard as I came hither."

"Then no delay!" exclaimed Luis, starting up; "I will this instant accompany you."

The turnkey, on the representations of the Friar, was easily persuaded to allow them to pass, and enter the fidalgo's cell.

The old man started with terror, as he beheld them, fancying that they were officers come to lead him to trial, or to death.

"Lead on, ye myrmidons of tyranny! I am prepared!" he exclaimed, rising.

"You are mistaken, senhor," said Luis. "I come as an old friend, a fellow-prisoner, to offer such consolation as is in my power."

"Thanks, senhor, for your courtesy, but your name has escaped my memory," said the Fidalgo, scanning him closely.

"Luis d'Almeida."

"What! the murderer of my son?—the destroyer of my daughter's peace?"

"Certainly not the murderer of your son, for he yet lives; and rather would I die a hundred deaths than cause one pang of grief to your fair daughter."

"My son lives, say you?" exclaimed the Fidalgo. "Bring him hither, then, that I may embrace him before I am led forth to death."

"He lies himself upon a bed of sickness; but I trust, Senhor, to be able to conduct you to him," answered Luis.

"In mercy then, without delay, let me hasten to my long-lost boy," exclaimed the Fidalgo. "Is he within these cruel walls—a prisoner like ourselves?"—"He is, senhor, alas! and this good Friar will arrange an interview, which will require some precaution," answered Luis; and turning to Frè Diogo, he requested him to learn from the gaoler, when they might visit the cell of the unfortunate youth.

"Pardon me, for the want of courtesy with which I received you, Senhor Conde," said the Fidalgo, as soon as they were left alone. "I owe you much for the news you bring me; and my poor boy, does he know I am near him? and what crime has he committed to be confined within these walls?"

Luis described, in as few words as possible, the dreadful treatment his son had suffered, and the fatal results he apprehended. We need not describe the father's grief, or his regrets for the manner in which he had treated his guest; but his emotion was far greater, when, on Luis presenting the long-lost packet, he tore it open, and his eye hurried over the contents.

"Great God! how have I been deceived in that man!" he cried, in a tone of agony. "My child, my sweet child! and thou hast been the sacrifice! Oh, for freedom, that I might hasten to rescue her from the bondage she detests! A week hence, and her fate will have been sealed, when I, alas! shall have no power to release her. And I—oh, how cruelly have I treated her! Curses on the stern tyrant who thus detains me. He is a father, and did he know the cause, he would release me. No, the base upstart would but smile the more to see the high-born fidalgo's agony. May Heaven's anger blast all the works in which he prides himself! May—ah! I am raving—oh! God, support me!"

Luis stood amazed at this sudden outbreak of the usually sedate and dignified fidalgo, though scarcely himself less agitated in his eagerness to learn the contents of the letter, the purport of which the fidalgo's words appeared to intimate. The old man saw his inquiring gaze. "See," he continued, extending his hand with the paper. "Read that, and see how I have been deceived; and alas! my poor child has been sacrificed;" and he sunk into his chair, covering his eyes with his hands, while Luis read the letter. It was to the following effect:—

"Heaven has thought fit to summon me from this world, during your absence, my beloved husband, and already do I feel the near approach of death. Alas! I have no one to whom I can confide my dying wishes, and a secret which I would entrust but to your ears alone. I therefore write with faltering hand this paper, which I trust may be seen by our sweet Clara, and given to you. It is for her sake I am anxious; for I see perils surrounding her course through life, which will require all a mother's care to guard against.

"Do not, as you value her happiness or your own, confide in the Father Alfonzo. He is a wretched hypocrite; yet till lately I discovered it not. For many days past has he been endeavouring to persuade me to devote our Clara to the service of the Church; but I know too well the misery and wretchedness it will entail on her, and firmly have I refused to sanction his plan. While I spoke, he smiled scornfully in return, nor do I doubt his purpose. He has long hated me, for he knew I was not deceived in him. As you love me, as you prize our child's happiness, let her select her own lot in life; but warn her against the dangers of a convent. She will never insist on wedding one beneath her in family; but never insist on her marrying one she cannot learn to love. My eyes grow dim, my hand weak, yet do I exert myself, during the absence of Frè Alfonzo, to finish this, lest he should return before I have concealed it. Adieu! my beloved husband! ere you can reach your home, I shall have ceased to breathe; and, as you have loved me in life, forget not my dying prayer."

The last lines were faint and almost illegible. Luis returned the paper with a look of despair, and, for a minute, the father and the lover stood gazing at each other, without uttering a word.

"What hope is there?" at last exclaimed the Fidalgo.

"Alas, none!" was the dejected reply of Luis; then, suddenly rousing himself, he exclaimed, "Yes, there is hope! I will escape from hence, and save her, or die in the attempt! Give me but your written order to the Lady Abbess, to prevent your daughter's taking the veil, and I will bear it to her, and also a note to Donna Clara, to assure her of her mother's real prayer, and of your consent to her following her own inclinations."

"Alas, I fear such is but a hopeless chance," said the Fidalgo. "We must confide the order to some one who is at freedom."

"No one can be found who would hasten as I will; for no one has the same excitement," answered Luis.

"Remember you are still a captive," said the Fidalgo, mournfully.

"Alas! too true," ejaculated Luis.

Just as he spoke the door opened, and the gaoler, whispering to them to walk carefully, beckoned them to follow him, while he led the way to the cell of the young Gonçalo. The son uttered a cry of joy, as he rose to embrace his father, and then sunk down languidly on his couch. For many minutes they remained in earnest conversation; the fidalgo seeming to forget his daughter in the joy of recovering his son, while Luis, in the mean time, explained to Frè Diogo the importance of the paper he had preserved, beseeching him to lend his assistance, either in aiding his escape, or in forwarding the fidalgo's despatch to Oporto.

"I am happy to do all I can to mitigate the irksomeness of your imprisonment, my friend; but it is more than I can do to risk my neck in aiding your escape, or carrying any communication beyond the walls of the prison, which would, most certainly, be discovered, and punished with almost equal severity. Think better of it, Count; there is no use running so much risk for the sake of any girl under the sun. Let her take the veil, she will be happy enough; and, when you get out of this place, you can easily find another to make amends for her loss."

"You have never been in love, to speak thus," exclaimed Luis.

"No, thank Heaven, I never have," answered the Friar. "I never saw any good come of such folly."

"Then, have I no hopes of your assistance?" asked Luis.

The Friar shook his head.

Meantime the fidalgo rose from his son's couch, over which he had been leaning, and took the Count's hand—"Pardon me, for all the wrong I have done you!" he exclaimed; "but you see how severely I have been punished. My poor boy!" and he pointed to young Gonçalo, and his voice faltered—"and my fair daughter. Have you persuaded the good Friar to forward the letter I will write to the Lady Abbess?"

"He refuses to aid me," answered Luis, again appealing, in vain, to the Friar.

"Then I have no hope!" exclaimed the unhappy father, sinking into a chair.

The bolts, as he spoke, were heard to be withdrawn, and a stranger entered the cell.

Volume Three—Chapter Twenty One.

The day following the execution of the Duke of Aveiro and his unhappy companions, a fine merchant ship was seen to glide slowly up the broad Tagus, dropping her anchor within a short distance of a frigate, which lay off Lisbon. A person of some consequence seemed to be on board the former, for a boat quickly pushed off from the sides of the frigate, bearing her Captain; and approached the merchantman. He eagerly stepped on board, and hastened towards a venerable and dignified-looking man, who was pacing the deck, with short and hurried steps, casting anxious glances towards the city, while several attendants stood round, and various chests and packages lay about, as if ready for speedy disembarkation.

No sooner did the stranger see the Captain of the frigate, than he advanced to embrace him, with an expression of satisfaction, "Ah! my kind friend, Captain Pinto," he exclaimed, "this is kind indeed! The last to see me off, and the first to welcome my return to Portugal, no longer a wanderer and an outcast, but at length with my toils at an end, and my property secured."

"I rejoice to hear it," answered our old friend, Captain Pinto, "though I have some sad news to give in return, which I will communicate as we pull on shore, if you are now prepared to accompany me."

"Gladly! I long once more to tread my native land," returned the stranger, as he descended with the Captain into the boat. The distance to the landing-place was not great; but, during the short time occupied in reaching it, many important matters were discussed; and, for the first time, the stranger learned of the conspiracy, and the dreadful punishment of those supposed to be the chief leaders, and the imprisonment of many hundreds of others implicated in it.

"Poor boy! it wrings my heart with grief to hear it!" exclaimed the stranger, as they neared the shore: "I cannot believe him guilty."

"Nor I neither," said the Captain. "I have in vain endeavoured to discover the place of his imprisonment, and would risk all to save him. It is reported that the Minister has determined to punish many more, either by banishment to the coast of Africa, or by death; but, without interest, as I am, I could do nothing till your arrival, for which I have anxiously waited. Our only chance of success is by an appeal to the Minister himself."

"To the Minister we will appeal, then," said the stranger; "I have some hope through him. He will scarcely refuse the first petition of an old and long-lost friend."

"We have not a moment to lose; for Sebastiaö Jozé is a man both quick to think and to execute, and even now my young friend may be embarking for Angola," said the Captain, as the boat touched the shore.

A smile of satisfaction passed over the stranger's features, as he once more landed in his native country, but it quickly vanished as he thought of all the miseries that country was suffering; and, accompanied by Captain Pinto, whose well-known person enabled him to pass without the interference of the police, he hurried towards the residence of the Minister. As they arrived in sight of the house, they observed a strong body of cavalry dashing down the street at full speed, who halted in front of it, and, from among them, the commanding figure of Carvalho was seen to dismount from his horse, and enter the building.

"What means this?" asked the stranger. "Does the preserver of his country require a body-guard?"

"The corrector of abuses, we should say, or the despotic tyrant, as his enemies call him, does," observed the Captain, cautiously. "Alas! by such means only can our countrymen be governed."

When they arrived, they found a guard drawn up in the entrance-hall; and after Captain Pinto had sent up his name, requesting an audience, they were compelled to wait a considerable time in an ante-room, before they were admitted.

The stranger smiled,—"Times have changed since we parted," he said.

The great Minister rose to receive them, with his usual courtesy, as they entered, desiring them to be seated, while his piercing eye glanced sternly at the stranger with an inquiring look, as he demanded of the Captain the cause of his visit.

"I came, your Excellency, to introduce one, whom, with your permission, I will now leave to plead his cause with you," and, bowing profoundly, he withdrew.

The Minister rose, as did the stranger.

"I cannot be surprised that you should not recognise in these furrowed and care-worn features the countenance of him who was the friend of your youth," said the latter.

"My recollection is not liable to be deceived," said the Minister, scanning the stranger still more earnestly. "They recall the likeness of one long since dead, and truly mourned—one to whom I owed a debt of gratitude never to be repaid—the preserver of my life!"

A gleam of satisfaction passed over the stranger's features. "I am not forgotten, then!" he exclaimed. "You see before you one long supposed dead—him, I trust, of whom you speak."

"What!" cried the Minister, grasping the stranger's hand. "Speak! are you the friend of my days of neglect and poverty,—does the Luis d'Almeida I loved so well still live?"

"The same, my friend," cried the stranger, as they warmly embraced; "and great is my satisfaction to find that I am not forgotten."

"'Tis a happiness I can seldom, if ever, enjoy, to call any one my friend," said the proud Minister; and a shade passed across his brow, as he thought how completely he had isolated himself from his fellow-men. He had chosen his station—it was one of power and grandeur, but of danger and remorse. In each statesman of the country he saw a foe eager to hurl him from his post; and in no one who exhibited talent would he place confidence; he perceived treachery and hatred in the glance of every courtier around him, though he felt he could rule them but with a rod of iron.

The two friends talked long and earnestly together, forgetful of the flight of time.

"I have one petition to make to you," said Senhor d'Almeida, for so we may call the stranger; "it is my first, and it shall be my last."

"What! cannot I see my only friend without hearing that hateful word?" interrupted Carvalho, and a frown darkened his brow. "Yet let me hear it, for I would not willingly refuse you."

"I would ask for the pardon of one in whom all my affections are centred—the young Count d'Almeida, my nephew."

"Ah! I have been deceived in that youth! He is accused of the darkest treason," exclaimed the Minister.

"I will answer for his innocence—he is incapable of a dishonourable deed," answered the uncle, warmly.

"He is in prison with others equally culpable, and I have vowed to show no mercy to any," returned the Minister. "If I waver, they deem mercy arises from weakness, and my power is at an end."

"Then have I lived and toiled in vain," said the stranger. "Pardon me, I ask but this grace, and I find that I have presumed too far on the love you bore me."

"Stay, my friend!" exclaimed the Minister. "You wrong me and yourself: I will not refuse your request, but on one condition: your nephew must forthwith quit the country, and till he embarks, appear to no one. He is not proved innocent, and the guilty must not escape punishment. I will send some one who will, this night, set him at liberty, and conduct him to the house where you reside: from thenceforward he is under your charge; and remember, he must run no risk of being retaken."

The stranger expressed his sincere thanks to his powerful friend; and at length rose to depart. Carvalho accompanied him to the ante-room, and as he saw the worthy Captain Pinto still waiting—"Senhor Pinto," he said, "prepare to sail, to-morrow morning, for England; I have despatches to send by you."

The Captain intimated the readiness of his ship for sea; and, accompanied by the stranger, whom the Minister again affectionately embraced, he withdrew.

Volume Three—Chapter Twenty Two.

We must once more return to the cell of the younger Gonçalo Christovaö, in the Jungueira prison. The person who entered, narrowly scrutinised the features of all the occupants; the only one of whom that seemed rather uneasy under his glance being the good Frè Diogo.

"What! you here, and in this disguise, my old friend," he said, laughing. "Are you caught at last, then?"

"I am in no disguise, but in the habit of the order to which I belong, Senhor Antonio," said the Friar.

"It matters not—my business is not with you, but with the Senhor Conde d'Almeida, if he will favour me with his company," said the stranger.

Luis started as he spoke, for he recognised the officer of police who had assisted him in his search for Clara; and he fully believed that he had now come to conduct him to some other prison.

"I shall be ready to follow you when I have taken farewell of my friends," he answered.

Antonio approached him, and whispered in his ear, "Fear not, I come to set you at liberty."

Delightful words to a prisoner! A thrill of joy shot through the Count's heart—he might yet be able to rescue Clara! "Stay," he answered; "a few minutes are precious. Senhor Gonçalo, I have the means of conveying the order to the Lady Abbess to set your fair daughter at freedom."

Writing materials were soon procured by the kind-hearted gaoler, and the important document being written, and signed by the fidalgo, he committed it to the care of Luis, saying, as he did so, "Should better times come round, and should you regain your liberty, and your fortune, to no one would I more gladly consign my child's happiness."

"My liberty I trust to regain, but my fortune, alas! is irretrievably gone," answered the Count, despondingly.

Taking leave of Clara's father and brother, the latter of whom appeared revived by the sight of his parent, Luis signified to Antonio that he was in readiness to accompany him. Frè Diogo followed them from the cell, the door of which the gaoler locked behind them, and then bringing the Count's cloak, and throwing it over his head, carefully led them along the low, dark passages which Luis had traversed on his entrance, and now sincerely hoped never to see again.

"Farewell, my dear Count," whispered the Friar, as they were about to enter into a more public part of the prison; "I may as well not be seen with you, for I must take care of my character, you know. May Heaven bless you!" and he gave Luis a hug which almost took the breath out of his body; then, putting his mouth to Antonio's ear, he whispered, "Have more regard to a holy friar's cowl and gown, than to allude to days when I was sowing my wild oats: I am a reformed character, now. Adeos!" and, with a low laugh, he glided away.

At a signal from Antonio, the guards at each post allowed him and his charge to pass without question; and soon, to Luis's delight, he once more found himself breathing the free air. A carriage was in waiting, which quickly conveyed them to the other side of Lisbon, where, stopping at the door of a house, Antonio begged Luis to descend. "Adeos, senhor, we may not perhaps, meet again," he said; "'tis my last day of service, and an agreeable duty I have performed. You will find friends awaiting your arrival."

Luis sprung eagerly up stairs, and, entering a room, found himself in the warm-hearted embrace of his kind friend, Captain Pinto. "Ah!" he exclaimed, as soon as he was released, "I am rejoiced to see Senhor Mendez also."

"No longer Senhor Mendez, but your lost uncle, Luis d'Almeida," exclaimed the Captain.

Luis threw himself at the feet of his uncle, who, raising him, pressed him affectionately to his heart. "This is, indeed, a happy moment to me, my nephew, after all my sufferings, to find one of my family who learned to love me as an outcast and a beggar!" he exclaimed.

The young Count was soon informed of the means taken to procure his liberation, and of the banishment to which he was doomed; his uncle, however, assuring him, that it should not be passed in poverty.

"Alas!" he answered, after expressing his gratitude, "liberty and fortune are of no value, except I can share them with one to whom my heart has long been engaged;" and he hurriedly described his love for Donna Clara, the position in which she was placed, and her father's authority delegated to him to rescue her.

His uncle and the Captain looked at each other disappointed. "It cannot be helped, Luis," said the latter; "you must be on board my ship to-morrow morning, when I sail for England; and all I can promise is, to land you for an hour or so at Oporto, if the sea is smooth; when you can deliver her father's despatches to the young lady, and pay a farewell visit."

"That plan will never do," exclaimed Luis: "contrary winds might delay us, or a rough sea might prevent my landing, and Clara would be lost to me for ever. I will trust only in my own exertions; and I purpose this very hour to start on my journey, for I cannot rest till I know that she is free."

"I see how it is," said the Captain; "there is but one way for it. What hour is it? Not ten: then the Minister will yet see me. He is a stern ruler when political necessity demands it, but he has yet a kind heart. Let me see, I know all the story." Without waiting to hear what anybody might say, the Captain hurried away.

Scarcely had he gone, when Pedro rushed into the room, embracing his master's knees, in his joy at seeing him alive, and at liberty; but Luis was obliged to hurry him away, to bring a change of raiment from his lodgings, and to procure horses, and make other preparations for his journey.

We need not give the interesting conversation which ensued between the uncle and nephew; one important part of it was, that the former informed the latter that he would find five hundred pounds at his immediate disposal on his arrival in England; and that he had already settled the bulk of a far larger fortune than his family had ever possessed upon him, nor did he doubt, if he was in time to prevent Donna Clara from taking the veil, that her father would longer hesitate to bestow her upon him.

The Captain now returned in high spirits. "I told him the whole story, how the fidalgo had shut up his daughter in a convent, and how you wished to release her: so, as he hates the system of convents, and, I verily believe, would like to thwart what he imagines the fidalgo's wishes, he has given you a passport, and an order for horses wherever you may require them, besides an order to the Lady Abbess to deliver Donna Clara de Christovaö into the charge of Don Luis d'Almeida: so now, the sooner you are off, after taking a little rest, the better. I sail to-morrow by day-break; and shall land at Oporto, while my ship cruises outside. I will wait for you, and take you on board after you have seen the lady, and restored her to her home."

This plan being arranged, and Pedro having returned, and reported that he had selected a couple of strong horses for the journey, the Captain repaired on board his ship; and Luis endeavoured to snatch an hour's sleep before the horses were in readiness. Long before daylight he was in the saddle, after taking an affectionate farewell of his newly-found uncle. He had a journey of full one hundred and fifty miles before him, over rough roads, with dangers of all sorts; but he thought not of them, his only consideration being how he could most quickly perform the distance. The time of year was in his favour, but three days was the very least he could hope to do it in, and all depended on finding fresh horses on the road.

"Pedro!" he exclaimed; "we ride for life and death! You will not desert me? We must place Leiria to the south of us before we rest."

"Fear me not, my dear master, I will follow wherever you lead," answered Pedro, with enthusiasm; and away the two horsemen galloped; and before the sun rose, Lisbon was many leagues behind them. So well did the horses perform their work, that it was still daylight when they reached the gates of Leiria. The Count, with the magic order from the Minister, instantly went in search of fresh steeds. Of course, no one had them, till he fortunately encountered an old acquaintance, who indicated to him where they were to be found; and, with delight, he soon discovered two, fresh and strong for the road. The surprise of the inhabitants was great indeed to see the travellers again in their saddles, and galloping out of the town. Night overtook them just as they reached the little inn, where, two years before, their adventure with the banditti had occurred; but they thought not of danger, as they threw themselves from their saddles, and, seeing their horses carefully attended to, were, it must be confessed, after a hasty supper, soon fast asleep. The buxom maiden of former years had now become the landlady, nor did Pedro forget to whisper Frè Diogo's name in her ear, for which he got a good box on his own. Again they were on the road, and "Onward, onward!" was Luis's cry. Coimbra was reached safely, and once more they were fortunate in finding even better steeds than before. Pedro was already almost knocked up with the fatigue, but the lover felt it not, as he galloped onward. He thought but of one thing the whole time, the quickest way to reach the end of his journey.

Alas! the end was not to be so prosperous. Within five leagues of Oporto both the horses began to stumble through fatigue, and at last that of Luis came to the ground. He was himself, fortunately, uninjured, but for some minutes the horse refused to move, and at last they found it utterly impossible to proceed further. A small inn was at hand, where they took shelter, and from whence, the next morning, they again set out.

The sun was already high in the heavens when they came in sight of Oporto, rising on its cluster of hills directly opposite to them. The sight of a goal, where his hopes were to be blest or blasted for ever, inspired Luis with renewed ardour. He dashed down the steep hill, through the town of Villa Nova, and reached a pontoon bridge which connects it with Oporto. He crossed without an accident, and the first person he encountered on the opposite side was Captain Pinto.

"Not a moment is to be lost, Luis," he exclaimed, pointing to his boat, a fast pulling, six-oared gig. "Up that way, and then up a flight of steep steps, you will reach the church—the ceremony has begun, but cannot have concluded."

Luis waited not to answer him, but, throwing his horse's bridle to a bystander, as did Pedro, he sprung up the steps near him. He flew like lightning: breathless he rushed into the church. He gazed wildly around—Clara was at the altar. Had she pronounced the fatal oath? He stopped not to inquire; but, thrusting the spectators aside, he uttered the cry which caused her to faint. He sprung forward, he lifted her in his arms, and exhibiting to the astonished eyes of the assembled monks and nuns the orders both of her father and the Minister, he bore her to the open air.

"She is mine!" he exclaimed, "and I confide her to no one else."

"They are base forgeries," he heard the voice of Frè Alfonzo exclaim, as he stood in advance of the rest. "Seize the sacrilegious wretch! The holy Inquisition must be his judge."

Luis waited not to hear more; but, pressing the yet unconscious girl to his heart, he leaped down the steep steps, while Pedro closely followed, keeping any one from attempting to seize him. Captain Pinto caught a glimpse of him as he neared the place of embarkation, and, shouting to his crew to be prepared, he hastened to assist him in lifting the lady into the boat. Pedro jumped in after them, and the boat had just gained the centre of the stream as a group of monks and priests, with Frè Alfonzo, had collected on the quay, uttering their anathemas against the daring marauder, who had robbed the Church of their prey. The young Count, his heart throbbing with joy and fear, heard them not, as he bent over the yet senseless form of the lovely Clara. There was but one course now to pursue. He well knew the dreadful deeds which had been done by the ministers of religion and he could never venture to entrust the rescued girl within the powers of the infuriated monks. He must bear her on board the frigate.

"The only safe plan," said the Captain. "You have the Minister's authority, her's you will soon get, and her father can give his when you return; if not, you must do without it. Give way, my men!"

The boat shot rapidly down the stream, and ere long was breasting the rolling billows of the Atlantic. The frigate stood towards her, the lady was carefully lifted on deck, the boat was hoisted in, and when Clara came to herself she found herself in the cabin, her head supported by the young Count, who was kneeling by her side. She pronounced his name. "Where am I?" she exclaimed, gazing wildly around.

"In safety, and borne onward, I trust, to happiness," answered her lover; and a very few sentences sufficed to explain all that had occurred.

"Thank Heaven," she whispered, "I am not shrouded, as I fancied, in that dreadful black veil."

Favourable breezes carried them to the free and happy shores of England, where, a few days after their landing, they were married, with due pomp, at the Portuguese Embassy, a measure Gonçalo Christovaö highly approved of, when he discovered that the Senhor d'Almeida had settled a handsome fortune on his nephew.

For many years they resided in England, where their generous relative joined them; for his principles but ill agreed with the bigotry and ignorant superstition which he encountered on every side. Clara had the happiness of hearing of her brother's recovery and escape from prison; but the Conde San Vincente, by high bribes, avoided punishment.

The only person of whose fate we are not quite certain was Frè Diogo, though we have our fears that he figured in an Auto-da-fé in 1765; his crimes being, speaking ill of the holy office, not paying due reverence to the holy sacrament, and entertaining scandalous and heretical opinions.

The fate of the Prime Minister is well known. On the death of Joseph, he was deprived, by Donna Maria the First, of his offices, and banished to his native town, where, at an advanced age, he died, his sons inheriting his titles and property, of which his enemies could not deprive him.

Finis.